Inspirational
Romance
Reader

A Collection of Four Complete, Unabridged
Inspirational Romances
in One Volume

• Contemporary Collection No. 2 •

Design for Love
Janet Gortsema

Fields of Sweet Content
Norma Jean Lutz

From the Heart
Sara Mitchell

Llama Lady
VeraLee Wiggins

BARBOUR
PUBLISHING, INC.
Uhrichsville, Ohio

Published by Barbour Publishing, Inc., P. O. Box 719, Uhrichsville, Ohio 44683
http://www.barbourbooks.com

 Member of the
Evangelical Christian
Publishers Association

Printed in the United States of America.

Design for Love

Janet Gortsema

Chapter One

From her perch on the edge of the loading platform, Tam could get a breath of air, eat a quick supper, and relax for a few minutes with Vickie and Barbara. And Hope, of course.

Here at the Food Mart they all did the same kind of work and Hope did her share, but Hope was different. She had "college" written all over her. In just a few years she'd be on her way to the beautiful life Tam used to dream of.

When Tam was sixteen, her mother was alive and her father was still top salesman for Archetype Office Supplies. Tam planned to study art in college, maybe finish in Paris. Then she'd be a commercial artist or, probably, an interior decorator. She loved to work with beautiful things.

She'd always had a way with color and design and could draw well enough to put her ideas on paper. She could see, in her mind, exactly how a room would look, even before the decorating was started. She thought she could have been a good decorator.

Now, at twenty-seven, the only artwork Tam did was painting occasional sale signs or setting up a fancy display of catfood.

Barb and Vickie teased her about being arty, but they teased gently. Tam was as stuck in Food Mart as they were, so they forgave her for dreaming.

They didn't forgive Hope for being lovely and for coasting through their lives on her way to easy living. They teased Hope too, but not gently.

"What do you suppose Hopeless is looking for in the garbage?" snickered Barbara. The acid in Barb's voice said Barb wasn't really asking what Hope was doing, but was inviting Tam and Vickie to join in her favorite game of badgering Hope.

Just off the far end of the platform, the target of Barb's game was tossing aside citrus wrappers and pushing away boxes, her slim young figure and satiny blond hair as foreign in the rubbish pile as caviar in oatmeal.

Tam sighed. She disliked this game and tried to avoid it whenever possible, but she knew she had to play along if she wanted to keep peace with Barb and Vickie. She needed these friends who worked cash registers next to her.

"She's probably hunting for a little snack," Vickie sniped. "Maybe a not-too-rotten orange to take home."

"No," said Barb. "She's looking for more honey to put on her super-sweet personality."

Hope heard, as they intended, but she didn't respond. She kept searching.

Answer them, thought Tam. *Just once, answer the way they deserve so they let you alone.* But Tam knew Hope couldn't. Or wouldn't. Tam said, "What are you looking for?"

Hope straightened. "I thought I heard a noise, a soft cry, like a kitten. I don't hear it now. It must be gone."

"Careful, Hope," warned Tam. "It might be a rat."

Hope jerked her hands back.

"Maybe not," Tam went on, "but. . . ."

Hope reluctantly backed out of the trash pile.

"Maybe you just thought you heard something," said Vickie.

"Yeah, Hope," Barb said. "Maybe you imagined it, like you imagine that stuff about heaven and angels. With your connections in heaven, you should be able to imagine a kittycat into existence out of nowhere if you want to. Or a tiger. Yeah. If you imagine a cat, make it a big one. A full-sized tiger shouldn't be hard for someone with your connections."

Hope didn't answer. Tam wished Barb would stop, but once Barb started on Hope about religion, she wouldn't stop until she had worn the subject out. For Tam it was worn out already.

Enough, thought Tam. She stood, saying, "I think I hear something too— Mack yelling for us to get back to work."

"Mack can wait till I'm good and ready to come in," grouched Barb. "It's not 7:30 yet and I'm not ready."

"It's 7:30 by my watch," said Tam. "I'm going in. I need this job. You know Mack gets angry when we're late. Maybe Mack is sweet on you, so you can get by with it, but he's not in love with me. I'm going." She started toward the heavy fire door to the back storeroom.

Being teased about Mack was like candy to Barb, who reacted as Tam hoped she would. Barb would let Hope alone if she could have more teasing about Mack. She followed Tam through the door. Neither mentioned that the time clock showed only 7:27.

Talk about Mack's being sweet on Barb was only talk, of course. No one even remembered how it got started, certainly not from anything Mack said or did. As far as Tam knew, the only thing Mack cared about was his grocery. Employees were workers, nothing more. Besides, only a brave man would stand up to Barbara's dangerous comments. Tam couldn't think of a man who dared try.

Barbara wasn't so bad. Now and then something brought out that little mean streak, but mostly she was pretty good company. She could even be kind and steady, as she was when Tam's mother died. Inside, far inside, Barb was a softy.

If anyone had told Tam when she first took the grocery job that Vickie and Barb would be almost her only friends, she would have laughed. She had laughed more readily then and had had many friends. Most had gone through school together in the smallish Indiana "city" of Empton. Most went to the same church, where they learned to sing "Jesus Loves the Little Children" in Sunday school and sat on the same hard benches to listen to their pastor, Mr. Simms, on Sunday mornings and evenings. In high school they all belonged to youth group and grew even closer.

Tam cherished these memories, but at twenty-seven they seemed like some-one else's life. High school was finished and most of the old gang had married, or moved away, or both. Even Robert was gone.

"Rabbit" they called him, the first kid in his class with big front teeth replac-ing his baby teeth. "Rabbit," until they fell in love in high school. Then he was Robert, and she was Tamara, not the "Tam" she was to everyone else.

Well, Rabbit or Robert—what difference? He was gone. He went to college; she stayed to finish her senior year, to graduate and join him at Indiana State, as planned.

Then Dad's stroke ended the plans. He never worked again. His mind tangled his speech. The clinic called it "sensory aphasia." Words no longer came out right. He might be thinking "pocket," for example, but say "shoe" or some other word that made no sense. No one knew what he would say next. Sometimes he said appalling things. If it weren't so awful, Tam thought, it might be funny.

A salesman without words is lost. He had covered most of Illinois and Indiana, his territory. Now he went nowhere but to the clinic once a week, and to the library after that.

Tam didn't go to college, not with an out-of-work father and an overworked mother. Tam and her mother had done their best to hold things together. Tam had already been working part-time at Food Mart. When she graduated, she moved to full time, working days and asking for overtime.

Her mother worked nights at Lincoln Elementary as custodial matron, scrub-bing bathrooms, cleaning the main office. That and taking care of her husband had worn her out. When flu caught her two years ago, she had no strength to fight off the pneumonia that followed it.

Nothing much changed after that. Tam still cared for her father and the house. She forgot about art and decorating and a social life—all those non-essentials. She forgot about Robert, almost, which was lucky, because Robert definitely had for-gotten about her.

She worked, slept, cared for her father, worked, slept—round the circle of her days, day after day, night-shift after night-shift. (Nights pay a little more.)

She wasn't unhappy. Or happy. She was numb, going through the motions of living without having a life.

If she had looked, she might have found more friends, perhaps even a new man. He wouldn't have replaced Robert, but he'd have been someone to share with, maybe even to love.

She didn't look.

The only men she knew well were the ones at work—gangling teens and men not interested in a drab leftover in her late twenties. (Well, middle twenties, but it felt late.) She didn't blame them.

At work she wore the company smock over old cotton skirts and blouses, summer or winter, glad to save clothing money for things needed at home. She told herself she had better things to do than keep her hair curly and her clothes smooth.

She'd changed since she was a black-haired, blue-eyed, willowy teenager. Her eyes were still deep blue, but they no longer sparkled. Her hair was still black, most of it, but she could see traces of white. She solved that problem by not looking. When she didn't tie it up out of the way, her hair still hung long, but it had no more life than her laughter. She had almost stopped laughing.

Almost. Sometimes at work things were so crazy she just had to laugh. Vickie and Barb joked through the hours at the registers, making the night short and light.

Barbara survives by laughing, Tam thought. Barb was about Tam's age, but had a little daughter. Barb had never been married and her life was not easy, even with her sister's help.

Vickie was different. Younger, she still lived at home and probably always would. Learning was difficult and she felt lucky to have a job she could handle. She knew she still would have been sweeping up if Barb and Tam hadn't spent hours teaching her to operate the register. Luckily the machine figured correct change, so Vickie could manage.

Vickie was first to punch in every day, glad to be there, anxious to put her fingers to the numbered keys, to call out the prices proudly.

Vickie followed Barb and Tam back to those registers from the supper break. That's the way it was. Barb was the leader, Vickie the follower, and Tam neither.

They still had a minute left when Tam replaced Mack at the register. He looked at the clock and then at her, puzzled, but she merely shrugged. He didn't need to hear why she had hurried to end the dinner entertainment.

Next in line was Mr. Brill. He came in often, usually for one or two items. The "girls" always asked if he had forgotten anything. Mr. Brill always said, "Whatever it is, I'll get it next time." It was ritual. Next time would be tomorrow, or the next day, at the latest.

"Only bread tonight, Mr. Brill?" Tam asked. "What did you forget?"

"Whatever it is, I'll get it next time," he said. "I only come in here to see you good-looking girls."

He said things like that and they played along. "Sure," Tam answered. "You come in here to see our beautiful smiling faces. Right?"

"Right. Where else can I talk to such girls?"

Barbara called from her register one, "Come through my line next time, Mr. Brill. You always get in Tam's line. You never talk to me any more."

"Tam's my favorite," he called back, winking broadly at Tam.

Barb knew it was only talk and called, "All right for you, Mr. Brill. If you don't love me anymore, I'll get a new boyfriend."

He laughed, lapping up the attention. "Don't I get carry-out service?"

"For one little loaf of bread? With all your muscles, you should be able to manage with no trouble at all," teased Tam, bagging his rye with caraway seeds. "Shall I call Al to carry it out for you?"

"Never mind; I'll struggle along by myself." He picked up the bag with one hand. "See you next time." He winked again and was gone.

"Tam's got an admirer," laughed Barb.

"You're just jealous," answered Tam, because she knew it was nonsense. "Besides, a girl could do worse. He can't be much over fifty, not bad looking, and still has his own teeth. Must have, if he buys bread with seeds in it."

"Listen to her, Vickie. She's inspecting his teeth now. This girl gets right to the important stuff."

They passed the hours talking of one thing and another. Some regular customers came in and there were the usual quiet spots between rushes. When not up front, they helped with pricing and shelving or with returning "orphans," items shoppers abandoned in the wrong places: a tomato in the soap section, milk with the frozen juice, bread perched on the eggs. Keeping busy made the time go faster and kept Mack happy. The stock boys appreciated the help too, and returned the favor by bagging at checkout.

Quitting time came fast enough. At eleven the girls went back to hang up their smocks and punch out.

They had worked there so long that each had several smocks. Some were badly worn, kept only for emergencies like the time a big bottle of grape of soda exploded all over Vickie.

As Tam reached up to hang her smock on the hook, Barb said, "Better take yours home tonight, Tam. Looks like it needs washing."

"I just washed—"

Barb cut off Tam's words with a sharp elbow to her ribs. Looking quickly about, Barb pushed a large package of gum into Tam's and showed her the pocket of her own smock. It held more gum packages. "Better take your smock home tonight," she said. "Vickie and I are."

Tam put the gum back in Barb's hand. "Not tonight. It's clean enough."

Barb shrugged and dropped the gum into her pocket, folding the smock over her arm to hide the bulge. "Watch it," she warned, not quite in fun; "You'll get as pure as Hopeless over there." She jerked her head toward the corner where Hope was hanging up her smock.

"No chance," said Tam.

Barb grinned and nodded, friendly again. "See ya."

"See ya, Barb. See ya, Vickie." Tam loitered a bit on fake business to avoid walking out with Barb and that pocketful of gum. Barb took things now and then, little things. Tam objected, but Barb always argued that the store wouldn't miss a few inexpensive items and that the little bit Mack paid wasn't enough. She felt he owed her a candy bar or a package of gum if she wanted it. It wasn't as if she stole cash from the register, was it?

Tam felt oddly guilty, though she hadn't accepted the gum. Telling Mack would cause trouble and it didn't seem worth taking a chance on getting fired over a silly package of gum or two. Still, Tam was uncomfortable with it.

"I'll walk out with you," Hope offered. They took their time cards from the rack and, Tam first, pushed them into the slot of the time clock far enough to trigger the old-fashioned stamping mechanism. Seven minutes after eleven. They went through the swinging door next to produce and walked past packaged meats and down frozens to checkout and then out the front door.

After eight, Mack wanted those back doors locked and bolted and no one was allowed to go out that way. Tam was glad to comply. At night the loading platform was much less friendly looking than it was in the daylight, even with two big spotlights on. She felt better going out the front door into a parking lot with cars and people in it.

At the edge of the lot, where their pathways divided, Hope said, "You were right."

"About what?" Tam asked.

"About the gum," Hope said. "You were right about not taking it. She's going to get herself fired one of these times."

Tam snapped to attention. "How did you know?"

Hope said, "Everybody knows."

"Are you going to tell Mack?" asked Tam.

Hope considered. "I don't think so. No. Anyway, I think he already knows. He just hasn't said anything yet. If she stops now, maybe he never will say anything. I'd try to get her to stop before she gets fired, but she wouldn't listen to me. She'll listen to you, though."

Tam shook her head. "I don't know about that. Barbara does what she wants to do. If I tell her not to take things, she might take something bigger just to show me she can do as she pleases. Besides, why should you care what happens to her? She's not exactly gentle with you. How do I know you're not trying to break up our friendship to get even with her for all the hard times she gives you?"

Hope smiled. "You don't know. You'll simply have to make up your own mind whether or not you can trust me. Think about it. Think about your friend Barbara too, and what will happen to her if Mack fires her. Then do what you think is right."

"You have more confidence in me than I have," Tam mumbled.

"Yes, I do," said Hope. "I have a lot of confidence in you. See you tomorrow."

"Yeah," Tam said, and turned to the left without looking back.

Strange girl, that Hope, she thought. Tam's steps lengthened as she swung into the rhythm of the long walk home. She headed toward the center of town where the streets were lighter than they were on the shortcut through the side streets.

On the way to work in daylight, Tam usually took the shortcut. She'd walked the side streets so often that she had come to know some of the people along the way; not by name, of course, but well enough to nod to and exchange greetings. In the dark, though, she went out of her way to take the brighter streets across one end of the main part of town.

At sixteen she had been afraid on the dark streets alone at night. At first, Robert had taken care of her, meeting her after work and riding her home on his motorcycle. Once or twice, after he had gone, she had tried waiting for the bus. It was a long, dark wait at eleven o'clock. Better to keep moving if she had to be out there alone. It might not be safer, but it felt safer.

Two short blocks led to the bright lights, then eight long blocks through town before the five unavoidable dark blocks through neighborhood streets. She knew it by heart and strode home night after night without thinking where to turn. Her father used to say that his car knew the way home by itself, like an old horse. So did Tam's feet.

Sometime she ought to add up all the blocks she had walked in the last eleven years. It must be hundreds, maybe thousands. While she walked, she thought, doing most of her private thinking in the night streets.

That night she thought about Hope. Strange girl. Hope must be so tired of Barb's unending sarcasm that she would be glad of a chance to get even, to give Barb a little slap, kind of. Maybe that's what Hope wanted. Maybe she thought she could use Tam to get at Barbara. Maybe Hope thought she could break up the three friends.

She ought to know better. They'd been friends too long for that.

Hope sounded concerned over Barb's losing her job. What would Hope know about that? To Barb and Tam that job was food on the table. Without it they'd be in big trouble. But Hope didn't have to support anybody else. If the job blew up she could go back to her books. In another year or so she wouldn't need Food Mart. She'd be living one of those lives Tam used to dream about. What difference did it make to Hope what happened to Barbara?

On the other hand, in the whole year and a half that Tam had known her, Hope had never given any reason not to trust her. In fact, only yesterday she could have blamed the broken bottle of ammonia in aisle four on Tam, but she hadn't. Hope was out of aisle four before the ammonia smell got to the front where Mack noticed it. When the fumes hit his nose, Tam was right there at the end of that aisle. Hope didn't have to tell him she knocked it off the shelf. When she did tell him, she could have pointed out that she knocked it off because Al had shelved it too close to the front edge. She didn't say that. She said she knocked it off and was sorry and would clean it up right away. That's all. Al helped her, which was only fair.

If she really wanted to get even with Barb, she had had plenty of chances. Yet she never answered Barbara the way Barbara spoke to her. Never. Even when Barb sneered about her religion.

Hope was too smart to think she could get at Barb through Tam, and Tam couldn't imagine her doing something just for spite. There was no spite in her.

Maybe, thought Tam, *Hope really cares what happens to Barbara. She might be right about Mack's knowing what was going on.* Hope said she wouldn't tell and Tam believed her.

Hope could be right about the rest of it too. If Barb would listen to anyone, that person would be Tam.

I'd rather stay out of it, Tam thought. But as Barb's friend she was already involved. Tam might be able to convince her. After all, Hope said she had confidence in Tam. Tam was surprised how good that made her feel. She would try.

Five blocks from the parking lot, a long green car pulled up to the curb next to her. She saw it out of the corner of her eye, but she didn't turn. She had read somewhere that women walking alone at night should look as if they knew where they were going and should move purposefully ahead, not making eye contact with strangers. She hurried purposefully ahead.

"Tam? Is that you, Tam?"

At the sound of the familiar voice she turned to look at the car cruising slowly along the edge of the road, staying even with her. She stopped.

"Mr. Brill?" She peered at the face behind the passenger's window. She could see him stretching across as far as he could to speak to her through the open window. "Is that you, Mr. Brill?"

"It's me all right, Tam. Want a ride?"

"No, thanks. I like to walk."

"Are you sure? It's no trouble. I'm going this direction anyway."

"No thanks. I need the exercise." She started walking again.

He waved and she waved back. Then he drove on down the street, gave the horn a little beep at next corner, and turned left.

She felt silly then. It was a long walk home and she was tired. She wished she'd taken the ride. He'd caught her offguard and she wasn't thinking fast. After all those nights of walking in the scary dark and hoping no one would notice her, she was simply not ready to hop in the car with the first person who offered a lift, even though she knew him.

Silly, she thought. *I wish I'd taken the ride.*

Chapter Two

At almost midnight Tam opened the side door of her house on Terhune Street. It was dark, with no light at all except the light in the attic next door.

Tam gazed up at the light. Mrs. Warren was usually asleep by this time, worn out from cleaning. She was the cleanest person in the neighborhood, maybe the whole town. If it stood still, she cleaned it. She even took those little plastic plates off the wall, the ones behind the light switches, and cleaned behind them. Tam decided she must still be up hunting for dust.

Nevertheless, midnight was way past Mrs. Warren's usual bedtime. She might have gotten into one of her famous disasters, like the time she tried to wash the ceiling over the basement stairs and fell off the wobbly board she was balancing on. She'd broken an arm and was lucky, at that. Tam had heard the crash and had come running to rescue her.

Mrs. Warren, Tam's mother's best friend, had lived next door since before Tam was born. Her children were older than Tam, big kids when Tam was little, and had homes of their own now. Mrs. Warren was left alone in her spotless, empty house.

I'd better check, thought Tam.

She crunched onto the gravel driveway between the two houses, around the back of a beat-up, no-color van parked there. Van? Mrs. Warren didn't have a van. Her little sky-blue sedan was doubtless tucked neatly away in her spotless garage. Company? No. The kitchen would be lit, and probably the living room. Tam had to know if Mrs. Warren was all right.

From the middle of the drive, behind that strange van, Tam whispered loudly up to the open attic window, "Mrs. Warren?" Silence. She called again, more loudly. Silence.

She found a piece of gravel and threw it lightly against the screen. "Mrs. Warren?" As her second stone hit the screen dead center, a face appeared in the window. A man's face.

"What do you want?" the stranger growled.

"Where's Mrs. Warren?"

"In bed, of course," the man answered. "Why?"

Tam ignored his question, demanding, "Who are you? Why are you in Mrs. Warren's attic?"

"I'm Luke and I live here. Okay?"

It was definitely not okay. Tam yelled, "Mrs. Warren?"

"Here I am, dear," said Mrs. Warren's voice from close by. The kitchen light came on, illuminating her neighbor's face at the kitchen window. "I'm all right, dear. Just fine. You go in now."

"But. . . ."

"It's all right, Tam. Really. I'll explain tomorrow. Now stop upsetting the neighborhood. Good night." She left the window and the kitchen was dark again.

Tam looked up at the silhouette in the attic window. He didn't speak, didn't move.

Weird, she thought, waiting another second or two before turning away. She let herself in her own side door and from behind the curtain watched the face watch her door. The face vanished. *Weird. What had Mrs. Warren gotten into this time?*

By the glow of the kitchen nightlight, Tam put the tea kettle on as she did every night and went to see if her father was awake. She knew he would be; he always was. As usual she pretended to think he was asleep alone in the house.

"Dad," she whispered at the door of his room, "Are you awake?"

"No," he said. He wasn't trying to be funny. "No" was one of those favorite words he said whenever he couldn't say the word he wanted.

"Good," said Tam, knowing exactly what he meant. "I'm having a cup of tea. Would you like one?"

"No," he said. "I'll get the cups."

Every night they sat together at the kitchen table, sharing tea and the news of the day. Mostly, Tam talked and he listened, but sometimes in the relaxed quiet of the night he tried to say things.

She listened for the meaning behind his words and didn't correct him when he said something silly or empty. She might repeat what she thought he meant and ask if that was right, but she was careful not to sound critical.

That half hour in the middle of the night was important to both of them. They savored the closeness before she tucked him in for the night. When Tam was little, she never felt officially in bed until she'd been tucked in by her mother. Now she tucked her father in.

As she turned off the kitchen light, a car pulled into Mrs. Warren's driveway. From the window she could see the zippy little sports car park behind the van. A man got out and went into the side door directly across from Tam.

She followed his progress through the house by the lights he turned on and off. He went to Billy's room and stayed there. *Now what?* She could hardly wait to see Mrs. Warren in the morning.

She locked up and went to bed in the little room between the kitchen and Dad's room, the room she'd slept in all her life. Breezes from the open window were cool across the foot of the bed, so she put her pillow at that end and lay wrong way, enjoying the air.

Billy's room was still bright. So was the attic.

~

When she woke, both cars were gone and laundry was already hanging in the backyard. Clattering dishes told her Dad was in the kitchen. The therapist insisted Dad wasn't to be babied; he was to carry whatever part of the work he could manage. Dad could manage breakfast, so it was his job to make tea and toast for Tam and orange juice and hot cereal for himself.

Occasionally Tam thought she might prefer a little variety, but changes were upsetting to him and therefore to her so she resigned herself to finding exactly the same breakfast ready every day when she came into the kitchen, dressed for the day.

Eight was about as early as she ever woke up, so nine was her usual breakfast hour. Even then she was not wide awake and cheery like those peculiar people on television commercials whose chief joy in life is cereal.

Dad, however, woke with the birds. He loved the birds. First thing every morning, winter or summer, he went to the back window to see which of "his" birds were out there. He knew them all by name and habit because he'd looked them up in the bird book he kept handy on the table. He'd borrowed it from the library so often that Tam had given him a copy for his birthday.

This interest was an outgrowth of the therapy sessions, "lessons" that had been regular practice with Tam and her dad ever since his release from the hospital. He'd flatly refused to work with her mother, perhaps out of pride, so Tam had tried. In the beginning, it was difficult for both of them. She didn't know what to do and he didn't want to cooperate. Gradually it got easier. He grew accustomed to learning from his own child and she grew more confident. They settled into a prolonged experiment in communication.

The clinic's speech therapist told Tam what to do and let her watch Dad's Tuesday morning therapy sessions. At home Tam tried to copy what the therapist had done, with minor variations to keep Dad interested. That's how they got involved with birds.

Tuesdays, Mrs. Warren lent them her car to go to the clinic. To prolong the luxury of having their own transportation, they had developed the habit of stopping at the library on their way home. It made the morning fuller, richer, and Mrs. Warren didn't mind.

Dad would browse, sometimes in the reference section, randomly opening dusty atlases or encyclopedias, turning pages until he found an item that caught his interest. Then he'd take his volume and settle in the large window seat until time to go.

Meanwhile, Tam looked for something interesting to take home for those lessons. First she tried sports books, especially baseball. After months of batting statistics and World Series records, they switched to travel. She'd name a place and he would try to tell her what country or state it was in. Sometimes he couldn't say it but could point to it. Other times he rattled off names of places like nothing was wrong with him. When they found places neither of them had heard of, he looked them up in the index—valuable practice in alphabetical organization, very important, according to the therapist.

After sports and geography came math, at which he was very clever. She couldn't predict what he would or wouldn't be able to do. Both were surprised that, after wrestling with the alphabet, numbers were a snap.

Tam read to him often, usually from westerns. Then she discovered he could read perfectly well by himself. She still read to him occasionally, to keep him company and break the television monotony.

He could also write, which seemed odd to her, considering the difficulty he had with talking. Writing helped when he had something to say and the words wouldn't come out.

After baseball and travel and math came birds. One day he picked up *The Audubon Society Field Guide To North American Birds, Eastern Region,* and fell in love with birds.

It took much patience on his part to pull from his memory things that any child knows and that he knew too, if only he could remember them. With frustration always just beneath the surface, he had only tenuous control of his temper.

When he shouted and stamped off to turn on the television in the middle of a lesson, Tam wished he were more easygoing. Then she reminded herself that this stubbornness kept him trying day after day, kept him getting up in the morning, when there was nothing to look forward to but another "lesson" and afternoon television.

After two years of lessons, the therapist took Tam aside and explained that Dad wasn't going to get better. Two years was the general rule, she said. He had improved as much as he was going to. Tam should quit trying so hard. Progress from then on would be slow indeed and probably not worth the time and effort.

Tam still got angry when she thought of the therapist telling her to quit, but now she realized that the therapist was just trying to spare Tam some heartache. Too late. Tam already had the heartache and she had no intention of giving up on her father. If he was stubborn, so was she.

Improvement came slowly now. Each rare, tiny gain was a triumph.

He was sly though. If the right word took too much effort, he took another word. Once he had a word that sounded good to him, he stayed with it until it was the easiest word, almost the only word he could think of. That June, his best word was "no."

That's what he said when Mrs. Warren stuck her head in the back door that morning. "No," he said, in greeting.

"Yes," said Mrs. Warren, and came right in with some lettuce from her garden. "You'll have to wash this. I just picked it fresh."

"Thank you," said Tam, thinking that in Mrs. Warren's garden the vegetables probably wouldn't dare get dirty. "We'll enjoy it, won't we, Dad?"

"No."

"Knew you would," said Mrs. Warren, pulling a chair out and settling herself at the table. "Thought you might like to know who that man was you yelled at in the middle of the night. Can't have you calling the police on me."

Tam started to object that she was just worried, but Mrs. Warren raised a hand to silence Tam and went on with her explanation.

"Oh, I know you were just worried, and I appreciate it. Nothing like having good neighbors to watch over you. Makes me feel real safe over there alone just knowing you folks are watching out for me. It's good to know you're here, but it's not enough. With the children married and William gone, there's nobody for me to look after.

"Too quiet too," she went on. "I miss the noise the kids made. The radio's no good to talk to or cook for. Got to have more than that."

Tam said, "You have more than that. You're always helping somebody out. Dad and I wouldn't know what to do without you. And you teach Sunday school and belong to—"

"Bible Study and Missionary Circle," she finished for Tam. "And of course there's ceramics class on Tuesday nights. I'm busy enough. It's not that. I need somebody to care for. You understand, don't you, John?"

Tam's father nodded.

"I need somebody in the house, somebody to make noise and eat my cooking and stir up some dust. That's why I asked Stewart and Luke to live with me. Don't scowl, Tam; they're perfectly nice boys. Stewart's from Rev. Moore's old church in Ohio and Luke's his army buddy. Reverend Moore told me about them. He brought them over yesterday and they liked the house so much they checked right out of that motel.

"Moved in yesterday, if that's what you call it. Everything they had was in that old van of Luke's. They were real glad to get out of that motel, practically jumped at Billy's and Lucy's rooms. The clincher, though was my attic. Luke needs a place to work and the attic's the very thing.

"Nice to have a little activity in the house again." Mrs. Warren looked pleased with herself.

Dad cleared his throat and looked at Tam, who said what they both were thinking. "Just how old are these 'boys'?"

"A little older than you, I'd guess, Tam. About the age of my children."

Dad spoke. "Do they. . ."

They waited while he groped for the rest of the words.

". . .work?" he finished triumphantly. "Do they work?"

"Oh, yes," Mrs. Warren bubbled. "At least, Stewart does. That's why they're here. He's overseeing the opening of the new Haberson's store in the mall, the new one they're building out on the bypass. I don't know how long he'll stay, but he'll be here till it opens at least, and maybe a while after."

"What about the other one?" asked Tam. "The one who wants to work in your attic."

"Luke. He's an artist. Isn't that wonderful?" said Mrs. Warren. "Imagine being able to paint pictures right from your imagination. You would understand that, Tam. Luke has the whole attic, except for the end where I store my Christmas decorations and off-season clothes. He can paint up there as long as he likes and nobody will bother him."

Tam speculated, "He must be a very successful artist to be able to live on the income from his paintings. If he's that good, why doesn't he have a studio somewhere?"

"Well, he doesn't actually support himself with his pictures yet." Mrs. Warren said this uncertainly, as if she'd rather not say it at all. "He's out looking for a job to live on so he can devote his time to his real work. I'm sure he'll find one soon."

Mrs. Warren had made up her mind about these "boys." That was evident by the way she defended them to her friends. It was useless to try to change her mind, whatever misgivings they might have.

"I hope it turns out the way you want it to," offered Tam.

Dad said, "Hope it turns out."

"It will; don't you worry. It's going to be fine. Got to go get that cobbler baked and the mess in the driveway cleaned up in time to make those boys a decent supper. So much to do. Isn't it lovely?"

"No," said Dad, and Tam knew he meant it that time, but Mrs. Warren didn't hear him because she was gone before she had finished talking.

Tam watched her prance across the driveway and wondered vaguely where the mess was. She didn't see one. What she saw was a very happy neighbor lady who looked years younger than she had last week.

Amazing, thought Tam. *Who would believe that having someone to take care of would make her so young? It doesn't have that effect on me. What makes her so happy?*

She sighed and turned back to her father. "Just one more time through the exercise and we'll quit. Repeat: 'Breakfast is ready.' "

" 'Breakfast is ready,' " he repeated, and smiled.

"Good, Dad," she said. "Did you fix the lawn mower?"

"Did you fix the lawn mower?" he echoed.

"No, Dad, I'm asking. I want to know if you fixed the mower."

"No," he said.

She looked at the knee-high weeds in the backyard, a shabby tangle next to Mrs. Warren's manicured green. It would take more than a mower to cut through that. It would take a haying machine.

"We could get a goat," she said, looking him straight in the eye. There was absolutely no trace of a smile on her face. "Mrs. Warren would love living next door to a goat."

He looked away. He could easily have fixed the mower and they both knew it. In a slump, feeling that he was good for nothing but watching television, he did little else.

Tam was tempted to hug him and tell him not to worry about the mower, that it didn't matter, that she would take care of it.

This was exactly what she could not do. He had to be responsible for doing his own jobs. He needed to work, to have the self-respect that comes from doing a job. It was, however, difficult to get him going now and then.

She said, "You'll have to fix it, Dad. It's embarrassing borrowing Mrs. Warren's mower all the time, getting it dirty when I use it. Promise me you'll fix ours today."

"No."

He neither nodded nor shook his head so she didn't know what he meant. She could push him only so far, though, so she let it go. She didn't have time to argue. She had to do laundry and find something easy for Dad to fix for supper, pack her own supper, get ready for work, and be out the door by two o'clock for the other half of her life.

These halves seemed entirely unconnected, as if she were two separate people living two separate lives. That's what she liked best about her job. It gave her a world away from her worries at home and kept her too busy to think much.

At two, when she left for work, the driveway was empty. Too bad. She was curious about "the boys" and wanted to get a look at them in the daylight, especially the one with the little sports car—Stewart, the manager. She wondered if he looked like Mack, the manager of Food Mart. Do all managers look alike?

She'd seen enough of the other one, the artist, to know she didn't like him.

Artist. Big deal.

But it was a big deal. That's what hurt her. Bad enough to give up her own dream of studying art without having to live next to a real artist. Painter, Mrs. Warren had said.

Artist, painter—either way he's unemployed. He'll never find a job. Probably doesn't intend to.

She could imagine him applying for a job. "Do you have a job for an artist? Something not too strenuous or time consuming so I don't have to waste my creativity on ordinary triviality?"

He'll never find a job, she thought. *He'll sit up there in that attic and paint and let his friend support him. When Stewart leaves, he'll have Mrs. Warren to mother him. He'll never have to come down to the real world at all.*

Easy life, she thought, *having a friend support you. He must be a nice person, that friend. Not like the painter.*

Tam puzzled over it on the way to work, along with ways to interest Dad into trying harder. On this warm, sunny afternoon people out in their yards nodded or waved as she passed. The walk to work always seemed faster than the walk home. Actually it took longer because, although it was a shortcut, she took her time and enjoyed the walk, even in rain.

Going home in darkness was a different matter. Going home, she hurried.

Work went all right. She was uneasy about the gum incident, but nobody mentioned it and Mack seemed unaware.

Mr. Brill came in and joked around as usual, but he didn't mention stopping for Tam. She was glad. It was bad enough that Barb and Vickie asked her about his teeth as soon as he was out of the store. If they'd known about the ride offer, they'd have teased her all night.

They were always busy on Friday nights. People got paid at the end of the week and seemed to take their money directly to the grocery. Activity made the time go fast; it was eleven before she knew it.

She hurried through the dark streets, wishing she had a ride. Once she thought she saw Mr. Brill's car cross the intersection ahead, but she must have been mistaken.

Lights were on in the attic next door when she got home, and both cars were in the driveway. No other lights were on. She stood in the shadows, listening. The street was silent, as it was every night. Except for the attic light and the two cars, nothing was different. Looking from her side door, she saw no silhouette darkening the window.

What was it like to be up there all alone in the still night, painting? With hours to spend and no one to make him feel guilty about spending them on art. Such luxury. Did he have any idea how lucky he was? Probably not, she thought.

She sniffed the air for traces of turpentine and linseed oil, but smelled none. *Too bad.* She liked the smells of painting. Perhaps he used watercolors, which don't have much smell. *If it were me,* she thought, *I'd use oils.*

She thought she might still have some oil paints someplace. It had been a long time since she'd used them.

She and Dad had their tea and went to bed. She turned her pillow to the breeze again and lay staring up at the attic window, wondering. Once she thought she saw his shadow, but maybe not. She promised herself she'd get a good look tomorrow and slept.

ه‌

She did get a good look the next day, when she went over to borrow Mrs. Warren's lawn mower. She didn't really go over to see "the boys," but she was curious, so when Mrs. Warren asked her in to meet Stewart, she went.

He was tall, tan, blond, lean, and athletic looking, the owner of an intimidating, dazzling smile—a marvel of a man, absolutely everything the driver of that little yellow sports car should be and then some.

He rose from his chair to press Tam's hand and smile into her eyes. He remained standing while she shifted from one foot to the other in embarrassment, wishing for all she was worth that she looked better. If she had known. . . .

"Hi,"she said, in not quite a squeak.

"How do you do, Tam," he said, in smooth rich baritone.

"I. . .uh. . .just came over to borrow the lawn mower again," she stammered. *Nobody,* she thought, *could accuse her of charming him with brilliant conversation.*

Mrs. Warren didn't seem to notice Tam's sudden loss of intelligence. She said, "Your dad didn't fix it yet, huh?"

"Not yet," Tam answered, relieved to have something sensible to say. "He will, I think, if I can just get him past this little slump." Tam knew this made no sense to the mass of tan sophistication standing next to her, but it would have to do. "If I could just borrow your mower to do the front yard. . . ."

"Sure, Tam. You know where I keep it. Help yourself."

"Let me get it for you," said Tan-with-Teeth.

"No! I mean, no thanks. Thanks anyway." Tam hurried awkwardly out and down the steps, glad to escape.

Stewart was more than she was ready for. She wished she didn't have to cut the grass. Not out in the yard where Stewart could see her and watch her get sweaty. If she had to cut the grass, she wished she could do it inside the house.

She'd start on the other side of the house, where Stewart couldn't see her. By the time she finished the hidden part, Stewart might be gone. Then she could sweat all over the front yard without his seeing.

Don't be silly, she told herself. *Everybody sweats.*

Not Stewart, she thought.

He won't look at you, she told herself. *You could push that mower round and round, wearing your best bikini, if you had one, and he wouldn't notice. Grow up. Get out there and cut that grass. Now. Before you lose your nerve.*

She started on the far side. Sure enough the little butter-yellow car hummed out of the driveway just as she finished. With Stewart gone, she zoomed through the front at top speed, anxious to finish and disappear before he came back and caught her sweating in her old cotton skirt and worn blouse.

She didn't need to rush. He wasn't back when she wiped the last blade of grass off the mower and returned it. He wasn't back when she left for work either. Good!

And where was the artist all this time? She wondered. She saw him go out to the van, which in daylight was nondescript blue-black with rust spots. She was cutting back and forth across the front lawn at that time and when she cut back to that side, he and the van were gone.

His attic light was on again when she came home from work that night, and both cars were back. Everything was quiet.

She stopped to gaze up at the light before going in for tea with Dad and wondered if the artist up there was aware of neighbors with concerns that kept them as busy as his painting kept him. She wondered if he cared.

That was Saturday. Sunday was like any other day, a work day. She could do as she pleased in the morning though, if she stayed where Dad could find her.

She thought about going to church. Occasionally she went. Church was only two blocks down the street and one block over, not too far to walk. Dad could do it if they walked slowly. He seemed to enjoy going, but getting him up and ready was not easy.

If he decided he wanted to go to church, he was up and dressed and sitting in the kitchen, tapping his foot for her to hurry. But if he decided he wasn't going, every sock, every button, every little move was a fight and not worth the struggle.

That Sunday morning was a struggle, so she quickly gave up. She slid into another old skirt and went to enjoy a leisurely breakfast with the Sunday paper. Pages were already spread out all over the kitchen by her father, who always picked it up from the driveway and read it before Tam woke.

It was raining lightly, and the gravel in the driveway was the dark gray it turned when it got wet, instead of its usual chalky near-white. Mrs. Warren would be getting ready to go teach her primary class and, sipping tea, Tam absently watched for her.

At nine, on the button, Mrs. Warren stepped off the back porch, Sunday school materials and Bible tucked under her arm. With her, resplendent in navy blue blazer and gray flannel trousers, like a fashion ad in the Sunday paper, was Stewart.

He hesitated by the little yellow car. Mrs. Warren shook her head and walked on toward church with her umbrella still furled and swinging by her side.

Tam chuckled. Mrs. Warren was treating her "boys" exactly as she had her own children. No doubt they would learn to love her too.

What's-his-name-the-artist didn't appear. Tam wondered how he managed to stay home, but was willing to guarantee his exemption from church attendance wouldn't last long. Anyone living in the Warren house went to church. It was that simple. When her children used to complain, she always said, "Other people's children may do as they like, '. . .but as for me and my house, we will serve the Lord.' "

It's hard to argue against a mother who quotes Scripture and lives by it, so soon they gave up and began to finish the verse before she did. Later, when they were teenagers, they would say, "We know. . .Joshua 24:15," and would go ahead and get ready for church.

Wait until what's-his-name-the-artist runs up against that, thought Tam.

When Stewart and Mrs. Warren strolled home in the pale sunlight between drizzles, Tam was still in the kitchen with tea and Sunday papers. She spent most of the morning there.

On Sundays Tam cooked with more regard for Dad's taste preferences than during the week, when he adhered strictly to his diet. Sunday was treat time.

She and Dad had their usual weekend tournament of games, mostly Parcheesi this weekend, because he was feeling less confident than he had last week when he had trounced her soundly at checkers. "Children's games" had been part of his therapy long ago and had become one of their rituals. He wanted to play more often, but there was less time for games during the week than there was on weekends.

His heart wasn't really in the games that Sunday, nor in taking a walk or in sitting on the porch. She tried reading to him about whales. He had liked it at the library, but now it didn't appeal to him.

When Tam left for work, Dad was staring at a *National Geographic* special on gorillas. When Tam returned, they had tea and went to bed. . .a typical Sunday.

The attic was lit when Tam went to bed, again.

She thought she might stay up some night and see what time he turned the light off, if he ever did. *Maybe he just left it on all the time and wasn't there at all.*

Or maybe he never left the attic. Never. Stayed there, day and night, morning and evening, painting, painting.

No wonder he was a grouch. He never slept.

Maybe. Or maybe sleep was all he did. Maybe the story about being an artist was a cover for his abnormal desire to sleep all the time. After all, Tam had only Mrs. Warren's word that he was an artist, and she had only Mr. Moore's word, and

Mr. Moore had been their pastor for such a short time, a few years. . . .

Okay, so he was an artist.

What did he do up there?

Chapter Three

Monday morning's steady gray drizzle lacquered leaves and roofs, bringing out dark tones which sunshine usually glared into hiding. It also lacquered the beat-up van but failed to enhance its miserable looks. *The little yellow car looks sunny in any weather,* thought Tam; but by breakfast time, the little car was gone. The attic light was still on.

Dad's dreary mood persisted. Although he'd rehearsed it for days, he refused to announce "Breakfast is ready," either when breakfast really was ready or later, at his lesson time, but Tam gave him no peace about it.

Slogging through the exercises frustrated both of them. They quit early, with considerable relief.

Few birds appeared, so television began early. Tam forced herself to make the best of a dull day by doing dull jobs. While she worked, she tried to think of a fresh idea to spark Dad's interest. She was still thinking as she left for work in the drizzle.

Tam liked walking in the rain, if the rain was a light rain and the air was warm on her face. Drizzly days sound different, softer, more private. They changed the face of the familiar to something a little mystical, but friendly and cozy.

Walking silently in her hooded slicker, she stopped thinking and let the softness of the rain soothe her. By the time she got to work, she was ready to meet the world again.

All evening the few people who came in complained about the weather. About eight it rained harder and the customers were scarce, even for a Monday.

With no customers watching, Barb offered Tam some pretzels from a bag she had "borrowed" from the hang-ups near the soft drinks.

"My treat," Tam said.

Barb said, "Don't be stupid. Nobody pays. Pretzels come with the job."

"I can't do that," Tam said, "I feel like a thief."

Barb was insulted. "Is that what you think of me?" Barb demanded. "You're calling me a thief."

"I. . ."

"Listen, Tam; everybody takes. Ask Vickie why she never has to buy toothpaste. Ask Al, who opens sweet pickles, eats one and puts the lid back on so no one can tell. Ask anybody."

Tam said, "If it's okay to take them, why not walk out with them in your hand, instead of hiding them from Mack?"

"Mack!" Barb sneered. "He's a manager. Managers aren't regular people like you and me. Managers just care about getting their money's worth out of us.

They don't care what we do as long as they make money. What's the matter with you, anyway? I thought we were friends."

Tam said, "We are friends. That's why I don't want you getting in trouble over a couple of packs of gum. You could get fired for that."

Barb laughed. "It won't happen. Trust me. Old Barbara won't get caught, unless you decide to tell on me." She narrowed her eyes in sudden suspicion. "You gonna tell Mack?"

"No," Tam said firmly. "You know I won't."

"Then what's the matter with you, Tam? You been talking to that crazy Hope? You getting religious on us?"

She hit too close to truth and Tam winced, saying innocently, "What do you mean?"

Back on her favorite subject, Barb sneered, "You know. All that stuff about sin and wickedness—all that Bible stuff. Next thing I know you'll be a Christian."

"I am a Christian," Tam said. "Aren't you?"

"You mean like not Jewish or Arab or something? Yeah, I guess I'm Christian. I just don't let it get in my way. What difference does it make, anyway, unless you're getting married or buried or something like that? Even then, marriages don't last, no matter how fancy the ceremony is." Tam's dismayed look stopped Barb.

More quietly, to excuse her outburst, Barb said, "If you want to call yourself Christian, Tam, go ahead. Just don't get crazy with it, like Hope does. I think she actually believes that stuff."

"She does," Tam said. "Lots of people do. I go to church myself, sometimes."

"Well, that's different," declared Barb. "You have enough sense not to act like it. Nobody would ever mistake you for a Christian."

"That's funny," Tam said, thinking it was not funny at all. "I always assumed they would."

"Oh, Tam, you say the silliest things."

"That's the artist in me," Tam said, trying to brush off the subject. "I'm serious about the pretzels, though. I worry about you. I'd feel a lot better if you wouldn't do it anymore."

Barb patted Tam on the head, mother to child, "Okay, I won't do it again. And when I do, I won't tell you about it. How's that?"

Pulling out from under the patting hand, Tam said, "I'd rather you just never did it again. Period."

"Sure, honey, whatever you say. You can even pay for these if it will make you feel better. Now have some."

Tam took some pretzels and went to the office to get change from her purse to pay. Talking with Barb had been every bit as difficult and useless as she'd thought it would be. From now on, Barb would just not tell her.

Okay, thought Tam, *at least I tried.*

Hope came by a couple of times while Tam was on checkout. Tam understood Hope wanted to talk, but Tam didn't—not to Hope. So Tam ignored her and soon Hope went away.

Tam's mind stuck on what Barb had said about Hope's being serious about her Christianity. Hope really believed and that made her different. Barbara wouldn't understand why Hope wanted to be different and what Barbara didn't understand, she didn't like. She didn't like Hope.

Tam realized with a jolt that Barb wouldn't like her either if she were like Hope.

No problem there. No one would ever suspect Tam of being a Christian. Barb said so. No one would suspect Tam of actually believing the Bible.

Tam tried to erase that thought but it remained, like a thorn, pricking and itching. She thought everyone knew she was a Christian. She'd gone to Sunday school when she was a child. She still went to church now and then. Her mother and father had always gone to church too. Even her neighbors went. What else would she be, if not a Christian?

Having argued the question to this point, she tried again to erase it, but it wouldn't go. As soon as she concluded that of course she must be automatically Christian, the thorn pricked again and she was back to Barbara's statement that no one would suspect it.

So be it, she thought. *My friends like me the way I am; I'm not so bad. I'm religious enough for practical purposes. I don't have time or energy for more than that. Somebody else will have to teach Sunday school and sew for the missionaries. I've got my hands full right here at the checkout counter.*

Tam rang up prices and still the thorn stuck, along with another thought: *If it doesn't matter, why is it bothering me?*

She counted out change and pushed the bag over to the customer, then stepped on the conveyor belt pedal to move the next customer's groceries up.

A box of soap and a can of beans. Into the bag.

"Aren't you going to ask if I've forgotten anything?" asked a familiar voice.

Tam looked up to see Mr. Brill smiling at her. "Sure," she said. "Did you forget anything?"

"If I did, I'll get it next time," he said. "Why so serious?"

"Just the rain, I guess," she said, passing it off lightly. "It's coming down hard now. Drive carefully. The roads might be slippery."

"I'll be careful. See you." He took his little bag and nodded. At the electric eye he called a good night and pulled up his collar against the rain before hurrying into the night.

At least Mr. Brill is unchanging, Tam thought. _Dad has moods and Barbara gets mad and I spend too much time worrying about what other people think, but good old Mr. Brill never changes._

She yawned and stretched and went to look for something to do. Vickie could manage the front alone. The dairy case stank from leaky milk cartons, so Tam went to clean it. Since no one would come around to talk until they were sure they wouldn't get stuck helping, the unpopular job suited Tam fine. It provided time to think without having to make small talk.

By eleven the milk was neatly arranged in a sparkling clean case. Tam was tired but satisfied with the way it looked. _Mrs. Warren must feel this way when she finishes one of her cleaning jobs,_ Tam thought. Mrs. Warren would love to clean the milk case, where she could really see a difference.

Barb and Vickie and Tam punched out together. Tam hadn't talked to Barb since their meeting over the pretzels, and she wanted to make sure they were on friendly terms. If Barb and Vickie were going to stay for a cup of coffee before braving the rain, she'd stay and chat for a bit to kind of ease any leftover bad feeling.

"What's happening?" Tam asked, to open communications. Barb looked at her with a sly smile. "You sure you want to know? You'll be happier if I don't tell you."

"You're right," Tam said. "Don't tell me." She put on her slicker and pulled up the hood. Hope, watching from her corner, said nothing and looked away quickly.

"See you tomorrow," Tam said to no one in particular. She pushed through the swinging door and stamped past the frozens to the front door.

What is the matter with me, she wondered. _I'm stamping around like a two-year-old. Why snap at Barb over an answer no different from dozens of other answers I've gotten from her?_

She felt awkward and foolish and wondered if she should go back and apologize.

What a day! First Dad and his moods, then a fight with Barbara, and now Tam had made a fool of herself. _I should go back and straighten things out before I leave,_ she thought.

As she started back through the frozens, she heard Vickie say, "What's wrong with Tam?"

Barb's voice was closer. "Oh, nothing. She's probably just worried about her Dad. You know how she. . . ."

At the end of the aisle the three girls met and for an awkward moment stared at each other. Barb spoke, "Walking out with us, Tam?"

The three walked to the front together, as usual, and stopped at the door. "See ya," they all said. Taking huge breaths in unison, they plunged into the cold, heavy curtain of rain, half-running their separate directions.

To see where she was going, Tam had to look up. To keep dry, she had to keep her head down. She compromised by peering out from her hood, and it wasn't bad until the blackness at the end of the lighted lot.

She thought quickly of those extra blocks through town, balancing them against the darkness of the shorter way through neighborhood streets. She feared those dark side streets, but the main streets would be dark in the rain too. It was about even.

She went left, away from the lighted streets of town, moving faster down the black tunnel under the trees.

It was inky black, scary. With no one out, not even the neighborhood dogs, the night was deserted, silent except for her breathing and the hollow echo of her footsteps. The only signs of human existence were eerie green-blue glows from television screens and an occasional yellowish light from a lamp.

If anyone is out here, hiding, waiting...

Don't be silly, she told herself. *No one with any sense would be out here in this wet.*

She began to jog.

Behind her, car tires sizzled on the street and came to a stop next to her at the curb. She kept on running, catching a quick look over shoulder, hoping a local resident was coming home, parking in front of his, her, own house.

The car did not stop. It crept along next to her, keeping up with her. She ran faster.

"Tam? Tam! It's me, Mr. Brill. Get in and I'll take you home."

"Mr. Brill? Is that really you?" She stood there, dripping, uncertain.

"It's really me. Get in." He reached across and opened the door.

She saw the light on his face and recognized him. She got in.

"You're all wet," he said, setting the car in motion before she shut the door. "Put your seat belt on. Now that I've got you in here, I don't want to take a chance on losing you." He laughed a little as she pulled hard against the door to shut it and began to fumble with the unfamiliar seat belt.

"Pull the buckle over to the middle and snap it in that slot," he instructed.

The belt wouldn't pull longer. She tugged again and again and each time she heard it click solidly to a stop. He reached across her and drew the buckle slowly to the middle and locked it firmly into the slot. "There," he said. "You just have to know how it works."

He drove slowly, his headlights making a path through the blackness that enveloped them in the capsule of his car. Dim illumination from the dash lit his face from below, giving him a ghostly appearance.

He snapped the radio on and romantic music filled the capsule. He smiled and she smiled back, tightly, not quite comfortable. Nothing was wrong exactly, nothing specific, but. . .

He turned left at the next corner, and right at the next one, the way she usually walked home.

"How did you know where to turn?" she asked.

He smiled smugly. "I know the way you walk to work and the way you walk home. I know where you live. I've known for some time now."

Tam shivered. "You've been watching me."

"Are you cold?" he asked. "Let me turn on some heat."

He fiddled with some knobs and hot dry air blasted her ankles. She winced. He turned the heat down.

She slid her left hand slowly down to feel for the seat belt slot. "How long?" she asked. Her fingers followed the belt to its release button. She held the belt away from her with her right hand and pressed the button, shuffling her feet to cover its noise. The belt jumped and she stiffened so she didn't jump too. She held it fast and eased her left hand up to grip the edge of the seat. "How long have you been following me?"

"A long time now, Tam. I like to know where my friends go."

"Why didn't you ever tell me?"

"You weren't ready," he said. "I couldn't tell you till you were ready."

She shivered harder, her teeth starting to chatter. "I'm still not ready. I don't like this."

He reached over to stroke her hand where it curled in a fist on the edge of the seat. "Don't be afraid," he said, in a chillingly caressing tone. "I'm your friend. You know I won't hurt you." He stroked her hand as he talked.

For a moment she froze, her breath sticking in her throat. Then she pulled her hand away from his and gathered her purse from her lap. "Let me out. I'll walk the rest of the way."

He kept driving. "I can't let you do that."

"Yes, you can," she pleaded. "I'm only a few blocks from home now."

"No," he said, shaking his head quickly. "No. Why don't you want to ride with me? I thought you were my friend."

"I am. I just want to walk." The seat belt zipped away as she let go to pull at the door handle. "I want to get out of here."

"No!" He stepped on the accelerator and the car leaped forward, throwing her back against the seat.

She had to get out.

At the corner he slammed on the brakes for the stop sign and she would have been thrown against the dash, but she was ready this time. When he squealed to a stop, she flung open the door and jumped out, landing on her hands and knees in the wet street. She scrambled to her feet and began to run.

Behind her a car door opened and she heard him shout, "Stop! Come back!"

She didn't stop, didn't look back. She ran through the deep puddle by the curb and up onto the grass, where he could not drive to follow. She dodged into some tall bushes between two houses and stopped still, listening for his step.

Nothing.

Cautiously, she pulled aside the branch in front of her face and looked for him, expecting him to be looking back at her from the other side of the bushes. She saw nothing on the lawn.

The car sat at the corner. She couldn't see it, but she could tell where it was by the illumination from the headlights and the faint sound of the radio. She stood absolutely still, not breathing more than she absolutely had to. Listening. Watching.

All was quiet but the rain and the sounds of the car.

Slam! A pause and then Slam! again as the two car doors shut. The engine raced and tires squealed as Mr. Brill tore off.

Tam's chest hurt from holding her breath and her heart pounded loudly in her ears. She gasped, drawing in great ragged breaths, then scraped through the bushes to the open lawn.

Without the car lights, the street was totally dark and for the first time she was grateful for the cover of the night. If Mr. Brill came back, he would have a hard time seeing her.

A dog barked inside the nearest house, the bark bringing sharper awareness of her isolation. If she hadn't just escaped from a "friend," she might have asked for help. She considered it, but she didn't know these people.

They might let her use the phone, but she had no one to call. Dad couldn't come get her; he no longer dared drive and had no car. The police? Mr. Brill was gone and she was unhurt. The police would think she was imagining things, afraid of shadows. A taxi? Only four blocks from home?

She might as well walk. Or run.

Experimentally moving her legs, she discovered that she had difficulty moving them in smooth coordination. She was shaking, wobbly. Her knees hurt. She peered at them in the dark, but couldn't see them. She must have scraped them when she fell, scraped her hands too, judging by the way they stung.

Wobbly or not, she had to get home before Mr. Brill came back looking for her. He knew where she lived. He might be along the way, waiting, even in front of her house. There was no way to know what he would do.

Before tonight, Tam would never have believed that this little man with thin gray hair and the beginnings of a pot belly would be dangerous. Fifteen minutes in his car had changed her mind.

She tested her legs again, bending her knees a little more than necessary for walking. They seemed all right. She sloshed across the lawn, water squishing loudly in her shoes.

The sidewalk was easier going, but her regular determined stride was too much for her damaged, unreliable knees. She wobbled along, heedless of puddles and careful of curbs and rough places, keeping to the darker side of the street. The last block, her own, she greeted with a smothered cry of relief and broke into a hobbling kind of run.

Mr. Brill was nowhere to be seen. Reaching Mrs. Warren's driveway she whooped aloud with joy at being home and safe. The crunch of gravel beneath her feet was the sound of home.

Then she fell, tripping over some invisible bump and landing smash on the driveway, parked like a very small third car behind that dismal-looking van.

Somewhere a door opened and a screen door slammed, but she didn't care. She was home and in a minute she would get up and go in and have tea, just as she always did. Everything would be all right.

She propped herself up on one hand and pulled her legs under herself to get up. Footsteps crunched gravel to her right. She jerked around to see blue jeans approaching. She looked up past jeans and T-shirt to an unfamiliar face. She held up her free arm to protect herself and tried to crawl across the gravel toward her own door. "No," she whispered hoarsely. "No."

"Be still! It's only me. . .Luke."

"Luke?"

"Your neighbor. I moved into Mrs. Warren's house last week," he said. "Come on. Let's get you inside."

Huge, warm hands under her arms lifted her as if she were weightless and stood her on her feet, where she swayed dizzily. A familiar pungent odor tickled her nose. Turpentine. "Luke?" she puzzled aloud. "What's-his-name-the-painter?"

"That's me: What's-his-name-the-painter. Easy does it. I'd better carry you. Hold on."

With that he picked her up and held her against his chest, bumping along with her face against the T-shirt, to a door. He pulled at the knob with the hand nearest it and caught the door open with his foot. Then they were inside Mrs. Warren's kitchen.

He set her on the kitchen counter like a small child and backed away to get a good look at her. "You're a mess," he said. "You're soaking wet."

She blinked in the bright fluorescent light, looking away quickly from those too perceptive brown eyes.

"Are you hurt?"

She shook her head, looking at the floor.

"Let me see those hands," he said, taking one of her fists and opening it in the light. "You've scraped this one. Let's see the other. This one's worse. Sit right here while I get something to clean that up with." He reached to the sink to put some warm water and soap on a paper towel.

While he was turned partly away from her, not looking through her with those eyes of his, she took a long, direct look.

He was huge. Perhaps it was only because at that moment she felt so small and helpless, but she thought she had never seen anyone that big before. She was positive she had never been this close to anyone that big.

He was tall, 6′2″ or more, and his T-shirt-covered shoulders were massive. They tapered to a trim, unbelted waist in a smooth line unbroken by bulges or ripples of flab. He looked like the result of hundreds of hours of lifting weights. No wonder he had carried her so easily. Her 115 pounds must have felt like nothing in his arms.

In his arms, she thought, and her stomach felt the way it did in a fast elevator descent—as if the bottom had dropped out of it.

As he turned back to her, she looked away. The nearness of this huge man in Mrs. Warren's kitchen confused her. She was embarrassed, sitting there making puddles on the countertop and floor with the run-off from her dripping clothes, and she was confused. She was not frightened.

How odd, she thought, *to feel safe with this huge stranger after being frightened by little Mr. Brill.*

She held out her hand for the towel to clean the scrapes, but Luke took her hand in his great paw and gently dabbed at the raw flesh with the towel.

She sat perfectly still while he did first one hand and then the other. The memory of Mr. Brill's touch on her hand made her stomach turn over. She shuddered.

Luke stopped immediately and looked sharply at her. "Hurt?"

She shook her head.

"You're shaking," he said. "You're cold sitting there in those wet things. We'll get you home as soon as we can." He paused. "You must have fallen harder than I thought."

He looked at her again, more closely. "That's not it, is it." His statement required no answer. She gave none. "What's happened to you?" he asked.

She tried to avoid his steady, searching look by twisting away, but he took her trembling chin in his warm hand and turned her face up so she had to meet his gaze directly.

"What happened?" he repeated.

Her face grew hot in his hand and she knew she was blushing. That knowledge made her blush more. She shut her eyes against his closeness, but the tangy smell of turpentine and oil paint, and the firm hand on her chin, made it impossible to shut him out. She tried to shake her head but it was too firmly held. When she opened her eyes, he was still waiting for an explanation.

"What happened?" he persisted. His voice was not as gruff as she remembered it from the night he shouted at her from the attic window, but it was every bit as deep and commanding. This was a man accustomed to giving orders.

She jerked her head up and free and pulled away. "I was hurrying and I tripped," she answered.

"Yes? And more than once, I think," he said. "Your hands and knees have black marks on them, like you've scraped them on blacktop. The gravel isn't black."

"My knees. Oh." Tam had forgotten them, but now she saw that they, too, were scraped and bleeding. "I jumped out of the car."

"Now we come to the real problem," he said, beginning to dab carefully at her blackened knees. She reached again for the paper towel and pulled away from his touch, but he brushed away her hands and continued dabbing. "Go on. Let's hear it."

So she told him the whole miserable thing—about nice little Mr. Brill who wasn't nice after all, and about jumping out at the stop sign, and about the bushes and running home and all of it—nonstop, talking without interruption while he cleaned her scrapes and treated them with something from Mrs. Warren's perfectly ordered first aid kit.

When her story was finished, she was trembling and close to tears. Tam was long past the stage where she cried easily, but she felt the tears in the back of her tight throat, could hear them in her voice. They didn't come to her eyes.

"Didn't anyone ever tell you not to accept rides from strangers?" Luke scolded angrily.

Tam's anger rose in defense. "He wasn't a stranger. I thought he was a friend. I saw him many times and he was always nice. I've seen you only once. I know him better than I know you. How do I know what you're really like? For all I know you're as bad as he is. Worse, maybe."

He studied her in silence and she glared back at him, taking in his shaggy chestnut hair and straight brows and paint-splotched shirt. It was difficult to focus directly on those wise brown eyes.

When she did, she saw his anger give way to a flicker of amusement. She thought it was amusement. His expression hadn't really altered, but he seemed less stern somehow. When he spoke the gruffness was there, but not as fierce as his scolding had been.

"You're right. You don't know me," he said. "And I don't know you. You might be making all this up just to get in here to rob Mrs. Warren."

"I wouldn't do that. That's ridiculous," she scoffed.

He shrugged those giant shoulders. "How do I know?"

"Ask Mrs. Warren," she said.

"Good idea," he said, moving toward the stairs. "I'll wake her up and ask her."

"No, don't wake her up. You can ask her in the morning. I'll just go home and leave you alone and you won't have to worry about being robbed." Tam wriggled toward the edge of the counter to hop down.

He caught her mid-hop and eased her to her feet. "Independent, aren't you?" he said.

"I have to be," she answered. "And I have to get home. Dad will be worried about me."

He nodded. "He should be. What you need is dry clothes and some hot coffee. Can you walk, or should I carry you?"

"I'll walk," she said, remembering the strength of those arms and the feel of his shirt against her cheek.

"Of course," he said, sounding amused.

Tam looked at the puddles she had made. What a mess. She reached for the roll of paper towels to mop it up. He put them out of her reach on the counter. "Later," he said. "Let's get you home."

It was still pouring outside. She said, "I'll go; you stay here. No point in both of us getting wet."

"Too late. I'm already wet," he pointed out.

He was, especially where he had held her against his shirt. Looking more closely, she realized that some of the paint on his shirt was blood. Hers. Not thinking about what she was doing, she reached out to brush at the spot on his sleeve. His arm was warm beneath her touch. She stopped.

She could feel the blush begin and ducked to hide it, pulling back from him. He caught her hand as she pulled away and held it for a long second. Neither spoke. Then he released her hand. He pushed her toward the door and opened it, ushering her out into the rain with one arm loosely around her shoulders.

Across the gravel they went, Tam hopping while Luke held her more or less off the ground so her hops were moonwalk long. At her door he let her go and waited for her to open it with the key she kept in her purse.

Purse. She didn't have her purse. She felt for it frantically, but there was no place for it to be.

"My purse," she said. "I must have dropped it."

Luke was out in the driveway and back with the dripping purse before she had moved more than two feet from the door.

"Good thing it's plastic," he said, handing it to her.

She groped around in the soggy bag for the key. "Here it is," she said, and opened the door to the dimly lit kitchen.

"I don't keep coffee in the house," she said, "but I have tea. Would you like a cup of tea?"

"No, thanks. What I want is for you to get out of those wet things as soon as possible, before you get pneumonia and blame it on me."

"I. . .Thanks," she began. "Thanks for. . ."

"Nothing," he finished. "I couldn't leave you lying in the driveway, could I? I'm just glad I heard you cry out."

She mumbled, "I'm so embarrassed."

He looked at her and through her with those serious eyes, and said softly, "Don't ever be embarrassed with me. Or afraid. Ever." He touched her bedraggled hair tentatively with two fingertips. "Get into dry clothes. Now." And he was gone.

For a moment she stood in the silence of the empty kitchen, half expecting him to materialize out of the dark again, but he didn't. She touched her hair where he had touched it, and felt it wet and stringy against her raw palm.

She sighed. Relief, of course, she told herself. Why else would she sigh?

Suddenly conscious of the cold wetness of her clothes against her shivering goose-flesh, she moved to follow Luke's orders, to get out of those wet clothes and into something dry.

Dad wasn't worried about her at all. In dry robe and slippers, she sat with him in the quiet kitchen and he filled her in on the day's quiz shows. She didn't tell Dad about Luke-the-painter or Mr. Brill. He didn't ask about her scrapes. He seemed to notice neither them nor the fact that she said almost nothing.

Chapter Four

In the morning, nothing was left of Tam's adventures but raw hands and knees and some sore muscles. Both car and van were gone. The attic light was out. The rain had stopped and, except for puddles and general wetness, there was no trace of yesterday on the face of her world. It might never have happened.

Twenty-seven-years-old and already senile, she thought. *You really have some imagination. You probably thought poor old Mr. Brill had wicked plans for you. You must have scared him as badly as he scared you.* She pictured him standing in the rain next to his car, calling for her, wondering where she'd gone, finally giving up and going home. She supposed he went home, unless he had followed another girl and offered a ride to her.

She laughed aloud over her toast, startling both herself and Dad. She looked up to find him watching her, puzzled. She laughed again, this time at herself. She was middle-aged and definitely showing it, dirty and tired from work last night, smelling of the milk case and dripping wet. And she imagined herself attractive to that little man. She must have looked a sight.

She laughed again. This time Dad laughed cautiously with her, keeping a wary eye on this peculiar daughter who laughed over toast.

He picked up the other piece of her toast and inspected it, both sides, and put it back. Nothing funny about the toast. He waited.

I really have to stop being so silly, she thought. *This isn't senility. It's delayed adolescence. Only a teenager would leap from a car at a stop sign. Or lurk about in bushes. Or fall down and scrape hands and knees. An eight-year-old might, but an eight-year-old wouldn't just lie there in the driveway looking like a refugee from a war-torn country. An eight-year-old or a teenager would have enough sense to get up and go into the house before a neighbor had to come out and get her.*

What do I mean, "had to"? she thought. *Nobody asked him to come out there in the wet and pick me up. . .and hold me. . .next to his chest. . .and carry me in.*

His arms were strong, she remembered. *He hardly felt her weight. He was gruff, not smiling, but he wasn't as terrible as I expected. He was. . .nice.*

I must have looked awful, she thought.

It was dark. Maybe he didn't see her.

Of course he did. It was plenty bright in Mrs. Warren's kitchen. When he first saw her, he said, "You're a mess."

Oh, she thought, *I wish it hadn't been Luke-the-painter who found me.* In the same second she was glad it was Luke instead of Stewart, smooth, blond, handsome Stewart. She'd have died of humiliation if it had been Stewart.

Too bad it wasn't Mrs. Warren. She was used to mishaps and would have known exactly what to do. It wouldn't have upset Mrs. Warren at all. Actually Luke hadn't seemed upset either, except for being a little angry. He behaved as if rescuing people were natural. He was kind too. Even Mrs. Warren couldn't have been kinder.

Still, she wished he hadn't seen her bedraggled and battered. She blushed. She could never look him in the face again. She hadn't been able to look him in the face last night, either.

That little speech she had made about having to be independent didn't help, especially when she followed it by telling him she'd lost her purse. So much for independence. At least she'd had the presence of mind to thank him, although he'd brushed it off as nothing. She thought of him standing there, telling her not to be embarrassed, not ever, with him. She sighed.

He was nice to me, she thought. *Oh well, he probably would have done the same for a dog. He probably thought I was a dog.*

She hoped, she really hoped, she wouldn't see him again. Ever.

She almost got her wish.

Dad wasn't doing much talking that day and Tam didn't want to talk either. They meandered through the lesson, both preoccupied with private thoughts. Dad wasn't putting much effort into the lessons and she had no idea how to pull him back to caring.

She was dragging him along, doing all the work while he resisted. They were both glad when the lesson was finished and he could go out on the back porch to check the bird population.

Mrs. Warren didn't come over, so Tam supposed Luke hadn't told her Tam was the one who had messed up her kitchen. Either that or she was too busy cleaning up the mess and restoring the glow to the kitchen floor to discuss the condition of Tam's knees.

When Tam went over to borrow the car for the regular visit to the clinic and the library, Mrs. Warren was indeed busy with the kitchen floor. She didn't mention the puddle, though, or Tam's scrapes.

The next day Tam had to go back to work. The day off helped her get some distance from her scare, but even in daylight, Tam dreaded the walk to work. Dread it or not, she had to go, and the short way was the best way for her knees. She left a little early so she could walk slowly.

Would Mr. Brill come in? She wondered if he would have the nerve. Or did he think she was the one who should apologize? He might think that she had insulted him.

I'm never going to get in that car of his again, she thought. *Never. Even if he follows me home every step of the way.* She shuddered. He might, but not through that neighborhood. She wouldn't go that way in the dark any more, even in a hail storm. He mightn't be so bold on brighter streets. Of course, he had stopped her on the main street once before. Perhaps the lights wouldn't help at all.

Later, she thought. *I'll worry about it later. One thing at a time. First I go to work and do my job, then I worry about getting home.*

Punching keys on the register wasn't bad, but bagging and lifting the groceries hurt her hands. She was glad it was a slow night and she could spend most of it stamping prices on cans. Of course Barb and Vickie had to know what had happened to her hands and then so did everybody else. Tam told them. She thought it best they know about Mr. Brill in case he ever tried anything again. She thought Barb would joke about it, but she didn't, and so neither did Vickie. Tam didn't tell about the driveway part, though, or about Luke. She wanted to keep that event to herself a while and savor it. She hadn't told anybody.

Mr. Brill didn't show up and it was just as well. Barb was in a crazy mood and when she got in that mood, she would do anything. She might threaten to beat him up or call the police or even dare him to try anything funny with her.

By break time Barb was winding up to something, anything, casting about for mischief to get into. She found it when Al put money into the coffee machine and pushed selection buttons to get himself a cup of coffee. Out came the coffee, straight out—a horizontal shower of hot coffee that sprayed most of the front of his smock. His smock was always messy, so it was no big loss. Nobody was hurt. After the initial shock, it was funny.

Al looked so surprised standing there with the empty cup in his hand and a whole smockful of coffee all over him. He laughed too. What else was there to do?

He took a lot of kidding about whether or not he got the cream and sugar and about wringing the coffee out of his smock. Comments like that, all in fun. By the time he went back to the produce, Barb and Vickie and Tam ached from laughing.

That's when Hope came in. She almost asked what was funny, but she caught herself. She should have been even more cautions. Barb's unusually friendly tone should have warned her.

Barb said, sweetly, "Hello, Hope. How's the meat section doing tonight?"

Vickie and Tam exchanged glances. Barb was up to something. Hope didn't suspect a thing.

"Not too busy," said Hope. "How's the front?" She looked mystified by this sudden friendliness, but her pleasure was evident.

"Can't complain," said Barb, still sweet. "How about some coffee?"

Hope obviously couldn't believe her luck. In all the time she'd worked there, neither Barb nor Vickie had shown any interest in her except as an object of insult and scorn. Now they seemed friendly. She smiled, warming to Barb's sweet tone and kind words. "Thanks. I'd like some coffee," she answered. "How about you? I'm buying."

"Sure," said Barb. "I take just sugar."

Hope dug in her pocket for change and came up with some coins, which she began inserting in the slots. Barb watched, grinning. Tam looked at Vickie, who began to grin too. Hope's hand was on the red rectangular button.

"No," Tam began, reaching out to stop Hope. "Don't . . ."

"Hmmm?" said Hope, turning around, her hand still on the button that would trigger the fountain of hot coffee.

"Don't. . .Ow!" Barb's foot crunched down on Tam's, cutting off Tam's warning.

"Oh," said Hope, pushing the button, and then "OH!" as the hot coffee hit her, catching her higher than it had caught Al, because she was smaller. Coffee spat all over her smock, her neck, her arm, the side of her face, and her hair. It hurt. Tam saw the pain in her face and jumped to help, grabbing for the rag they had used to mop up Al's coffee bath.

Barb beat Tam to it, patting and mopping with the cloth, slathering Hope with unctuous sympathy. "Oh, Hope," Barb gushed, "What happened? Oh, how awful. Let me help you. Oh, how did this happen?"

Vickie was a step behind, but only a step. She didn't have a cloth, but she had honeyed words to pour on Hope's discomfort.

Tam was sickened by the cruelty of Barb's act and the charade of kindness. Hope was helpless in their hands. Tam's stomach twisted and she reacted with sudden anger.

Grasping Hope's arm, she jerked her out of their reach, shoving Hope into the tiny bathroom and locking the door. Tam leaned on the door, staring at Hope, who stared back, confused and hurt.

"What. . .?"

With a shake of her head Tam turned Hope to the sink. Hot water for coffee stains? Cold water? Tam couldn't remember. But cold water for burns. It made no difference; the water from both faucets was room temperature.

"Here, give me your smock." Tam said. "You can wear my clean one. I'll wash this one and bring it back. Some of those splashes burned your cheek, I think, and your neck too. I'll get the first aid kit from the office." Tam caught Hope's eye in the mirror. "Sorry I was so rough with you."

"It's all right, Tam. Thanks."

"Don't thank me. This wouldn't have happened if I'd stopped you instead of just standing there. I. . ." She shrugged in apology.

Hope smiled gently. "Thanks."

Hurrying for the first aid kit, Tam pushed through the sympathy squad, Barbara and Vickie. Their kindness had given way to hilarity and they leaned against the wall laughing, repeating fragments of the incident to each other.

"Hey," gloated Barb, catching Tam's arm. "What do you think? Wasn't that the funniest thing you ever saw? Did you see her face when the coffee hit her?"

Vickie added, "The best part was the way we gave her all that help and she just stood there looking stupid."

Barbara said, "I loved it when you grabbed her and shoved her into the bathroom without a word. You really did a job on her. Good going, Tam."

Tam shook herself free.

Barb stopped laughing. "Hey, what's the matter?"

Tam wanted to say how ashamed she felt, wanted to shout at them. She couldn't think of anything to say. She walked off.

After that Tam avoided all of them, even Mack and Al, who had nothing to do with it. Eventually she would have to talk to them. First she needed time to think through, to make sense of her feelings before she tried to defend them. There was no question that she would have some defending to do, to herself and to others.

Defending her own actions was the hard part. Impossible. Sure Tam wanted to protect her friendships by going along with a joke. Yes, she tried to tell Hope not to push the button, and no, she didn't realize the coffee would burn her skin. Not enough. Tam could have stopped her if she had risked the anger of her friends.

Since when am I so afraid of losing my friends that I do things I'm ashamed of? Tam wondered. *What's happened to me?*

She had changed. These were her only friends and it was extremely unlikely that her world would provide others. She was trying to make the best of what she had. That's all. She didn't have much, but she wanted to keep it.

Even if she was ashamed? She was—for herself and for Barbara and Vickie, although they seemed to have no sense of having done wrong by causing pain.

That was the heart of the problem. They didn't feel the way Tam did and wouldn't understand her explanation. They would see her as snobby and unfriendly and would never forgive her.

Tam wouldn't tell them how she felt. No one would ever know she felt different than they felt.

No one would ever suspect, just like no one would ever suspect she was a Christian. Barb had said that. It was supposed to be a compliment but it was a thorn, because it was true.

Tam thought of Mrs. Warren and they way she lived, and of Hope. They weren't like Barbara, not like Tam. They were different.

Their lives are easier, Tam thought. *They aren't shut into their own little corners with family to care for and almost no friends to make the caring easier.*

Nonsense, Tam thought. *That's self-pity, not good sense. Mrs. Warren is more alone than I am, or she was until "the boys" moved in. Her caring has made my life easier for years. It's simply the way Mrs. Warren is. Hope too. Different.*

Perhaps going to church all the time did that, kept you more aware of other people's needs and weaknesses. It probably helped to have the church behind you when things got tough too.

Sunday maybe I'll go, thought Tam. *Church didn't do much for me before, but if I had a different church. . .I'll ask Hope where she goes and try that church, if it isn't too far to walk.*

Meanwhile, she had Barbara and Vickie to deal with. She couldn't hide behind the corn flakes forever. Barbara was coming down the aisle with a basket of orphans. If Mack asked what she was doing, Barb would say she was returning misplaced items. Tam would have said Barb was looking for her.

"What's wrong with you?" Barb demanded, stopping almost nose to nose with Tam.

Now or never, Tam thought, and plunged in. "I don't like what we did to Hope. I feel mean and ashamed of myself. We shouldn't have done it."

Barb said, "You're talking about me, aren't you? I'm the one you think is mean."

Tam said, "I'm talking about me, and you, and Vickie. All three of us. We shouldn't have done it. It might be all right if you did it to me; I know we're friends and it's okay if we pull tricks on each other. Hope didn't know it was a trick. She really believed you were being nice to her. It wasn't funny. I felt sorry for her."

She paused to let her words sink in and then went on. "She got burned," Tam said. "Did you know that? In red patches on her face and neck."

"Yeah," sneered Barb, "and I bet she whimpered around plenty about it too. Probably filled your ears with stories about how mean I am to her."

"She didn't say a word," Tam said. "We shouldn't have done it."

Barb wasn't going to admit she was wrong without an argument. "Hmph! She's been asking for it for a long time with that sweet little girl act of hers. I finally got her. That's the truth and you know it."

"Why?" Tam asked.

"Why?" echoed Barb. "She's so. . .You know."

Tam persisted. "No, I don't know. What did she ever do to you?"

"It isn't what she did. It's what she is."

"Nice?" Tam suggested.

"Yeah, sticky sweet, nicey nice. Yecchh."

"Happy?"

"Yeah, that too. Always humming those little tunes under her breath. And smiling. Normal people don't smile that much. All those sparkling teeth make me nervous."

"How about young? And pretty?" Tam said.

"She's not so pretty," Barb said. "And as for being young, she can have it. It wasn't all that great being y. . . . Wait a minute. What are you trying to say?"

Tam said, "I'm saying that you don't like her because she's young and pretty and nice and happy and all the other things that we're not and wish we were. That's it, isn't it? You hate her for having all the things you'd give your right arm to have."

"Me!" Barb exploded. "Me! What about you? Don't stand there and tell me how I think. You're no better than I am."

"You're right, Barb," Tam agreed. "I'm not one bit better. I'd change places with Hope right now if I could. I hate being like this. Only it's not her fault that she has everything and we don't. She probably doesn't even know how well off she is. It's no use hating her for what she can't help being."

Barb regarded Tam as if she were a stranger. At last Barb said, "She's poisoned your mind against me. I thought you were my friend."

"I am."

"No, you're not, or you wouldn't take her side against me. I thought you were my friend."

"That's what Mr. Brill said," Tam mumbled.

"Yeah? Well, I know how he feels." Another glare and Barb flounced off down the aisle, ditching her orphans into a bin of pudding mixes.

Tam shook her head, wondering why she hadn't kept her mouth shut. Life was so much easier when she went along with people and didn't try to go her own direction.

Tam had been going along with her mouth shut for so long that it was almost second nature with her. Almost. She didn't know what had happened to make her speak up this time unless it was the craziness with Mr. Brill. Or being lifted from the gravel by Luke.

She sighed. *That must be it,* she thought. *That would unsettle anyone, especially a person whose life is the same day after day, year after year.*

Suddenly her whole life was changing. She didn't know if she liked that. Handsome, blond, sophisticated Stewart next door, and Luke-the-painter, and Barb's temper, and Hope. . .Tam wasn't sure she was ready for that much change. Things were beginning to get too complicated for comfort.

Business picked up around 9:30 and Mack opened up all three registers. For more than an hour they kept busy. Ordinarily they found time to exchange comments and laugh back and forth, but that night they were all business. Even Al, who always had something to say, packed for Tam without a word.

Mack was around, close. Tam saw him out of the corner of her eye now and then as he lingered in the front of the store. He knows something's wrong, she thought. Tam had gone to the office for the first aid kit, so he knew somebody had been hurt. Those searching eyes of his ought to have seen the red spots on Hope's face by now, although if he didn't know what to look for, he might not notice them.

Nobody would tip him off.

As he passed close to Barb, Tam caught her glance. Barb's look asked if Tam had told him about the hot coffee incident. Tam shook her head and Barb looked away.

Mack lingered, straightening magazines, rearranging candy bars, keeping ears and eyes open, especially near Barb.

He didn't hear much. He must have been as sharply aware of the absence of play as everyone else was, but that was the only clue anyone gave. He didn't see much either. The checkers worked together as usual, checking prices, sharing bags or pencils.

They were terribly helpful and polite, all four of them in the front—Barb, Vickie, Al, and Tam. Hope was back in the meat section, so they didn't have a chance to see if Mack took a good look at those red spots.

When things eased up a bit, Mack sent Al back to help clean out the meat cases and took Al's place as packer. He packed only when the front was desperate for help and they weren't, so Tam knew he was hanging around for some reason other than packing.

"How are your hands?" Mack asked, trying to sound casual.

Tam held up her palms for him to see.

"Show him your knees, Tam," called Barbara.

"Never mind," said Mack, and left for the office, where he stayed till almost eleven. Then he reappeared next to the time clock. He fiddled with the time cards, watching each punch out, returning their goodnights in a preoccupied manner.

Hope left first, obviously glad to be out of there. Tam was a close second. Tam wanted Barb to know that if there was trouble, Tam didn't cause it, so she made sure not to speak separately with Mack. Tam and Hope walked through the frozens together, talking of meat, the 9:30 rush—unimportant things. Nearing the ice cream, Tam said, very casually, as if she said things like that all the time, "Say, Hope, you go to church, don't you?"

Hope smiled. "I do. It makes my whole week so right."

"You're not doing so well this week," Tam pointed out.

Hope laughed. "I know what you mean. It's not all bad, though, and the week's not over."

Tam said, "You must go to a pretty good church if you like it that much. Where do you go?"

"Same place you go. Didn't you know?" said Hope. "Mr. Moore asked if I knew you when he found out I work here. I haven't seen you there, though. You must sit in the back."

Tam nodded. In the back. Whenever she went she sat where Dad could be near the door. He liked to be first out.

"I'll look for you next Sunday," said Hope. "Maybe we can sit together. I'll sit in the back if you like." She smiled another of her guileless smiles.

Tam seriously considered it. She was curious about what Hope got out of going to church that she hadn't gotten. *Maybe this Sunday,* Tam thought, as Hope went through the automatic door.

Tam hesitated, nervously rubbing her scraped palms on her skirt and shifting uneasily from one foot to the other. She had put Mr. Brill from her thoughts, pushing to the back corner of her mind her fears of seeing him pull up alongside the curb next to her. Since the coffee "accident" Tam had been so distracted by other problems that she had forgotten until now that she was going to walk home in the night again. Now she was going to have to do exactly that. She was more afraid than she had expected she would be.

"Scared?"

Tam jumped at Barb's gibe.

"Scared big bad Mr. Brill will get you?" jeered Barb.

"Yes," Tam said.

Barb looked at Tam uncertainly. The jeer faded to concern. Barb said, more softly, "I'd be scared too. Be careful."

Tam began, "Barb, I want. . . ."

"Don't tell me about it," Barb said. "I'm not in a mood for any more talk. And don't start thinking we're still friends just because I don't want you to get hurt on the way home. Come on, Vickie."

Vickie was right behind her. "Coming. 'Nite, Tam." She slid past, looking uncomfortable, then came to a complete halt with the automatic door stuck wide open. "Wow," she said. "It's Prince Charming."

Tam looked in the direction of Vickie's stare to see what it was that had stopped her. So did Barbara, who said, probably loud enough for Prince Charming to hear, "Wow is the right word, all right. Definitely wow. Who is he?"

Tam knew. She recognized the little yellow car from Mrs. Warren's driveway, the blond wavy hair, the perfect good looks of the driver who lounged in careless elegance against the passenger door. Stewart.

Of all people to see me like this, she thought. She took a deep breath and said to herself: *Try to act like a grown-up this time.* She tentatively waggled her hand in feeble greeting through the window. He waved back and in one fluid motion opened the car door. He didn't actually bow, but the effect was the same.

As Tam came cautiously through the door, he asked, "May I offer you a ride home?"

"Yes," said Barbara and Vickie in unison. Tam discovered she had no voice. She nodded.

Tam floated. . .well, all right, she walked carefully. . .past Barb, who murmured as Tam passed, "And to think I was worried about how you would get home."

Tam didn't answer. She was concentrating on floating gracefully to the car. It wasn't easy to float without falling over her own feet. She hadn't had much practice recently.

"*T.T.I.*" Her high school gym teacher's old admonition to "Tuck Tummy In" popped into her head from nowhere, along with her mother's lesson that a lady always walks with her back straight, and somebody-or-other's instruction to keep her head up. Tam tried to do everything at once and still look calm. Floating.

Walking is a difficult exercise, once the walker begins thinking about how to do it. Tam frowned with the effort and found herself standing, at last, next to the car, frowning down at the pavement.

"May I offer you a ride home?" he repeated, indicating by moving the door a little that Tam should get into the car.

She got in.

The door shut solidly and she heard him go around the back of the car to the other side and get in. She tried not to look at the hands that started the car. She tried not to look at the hand that shifted gears.

Automatically, expectantly, accustomed to hearing Barb's judgments, Tam listened for her voice as the car rolled quietly out of the parking lot. She didn't hear it.

Chapter Five

Tam barely managed to sit still. She knew the enchantment would end soon, so she inhaled the magic, saving it for later, when she was alone again.

"A longer way home," he answered to the question she hadn't asked. "The night's too beautiful to waste." Stewart sounded reasonable—just a normal, handsome, elegant, sophisticated man who was driving her home in his little yellow convertible, the long way, because the night was too beautiful to waste.

Of course.

They cruised through the business district and round again. Gradually relaxing, she settled into the leather bucket seat, and lifted one hand to play with the air currents.

"You're smiling," he said at a light.

She nodded, "It's beautiful."

"Yes," he said.

She stole a glance at him. *Was he real? Impossible.*

As they pulled into Mrs. Warren's driveway, Tam said, "Thank you for bringing me home. But how did you know, I mean. . . Why did you offer me a ride?"

"You needed one."

"Yes, but why. . .?"

"Luke sent me."

"That's all? You came because Luke sent you?"

"Yes."

She shut her eyes. To be picked up like a pound of liver—how humiliating! "Sorry," she said.

"Don't be," Stewart answered. "I enjoyed it. I'll be there tomorrow night."

She stared at him. "Tomorrow?"

"If you don't mind," he said.

He saw her fumble for the door handle and was out of the car and opening her door before she could connect with either handle or words. She struggled out of the car, too dazed to try floating.

"One thing, though," he said, holding her arm to steady her, "I open the doors. You just ride."

"Yes," she said obediently.

At her door he held out his hand. She looked at it.

"Key," he prompted.

"Yes," she said, forgetting "Thank you" and "Good night."

"Yes," she repeated later, alone.

Tomorrow. Maybe Luke had sent him this time, but Stewart had volunteered for tomorrow.

Why hadn't Luke come?

Strange. Everything about Luke was strange. An unpredictable presence, appearing and disappearing. Rescuing her in the night. Sending a ride. Almost as if he cared.

No. If he cared he'd have come himself. Never mind. Thanks to him, Stewart had come and this time she'd managed quite well. *Except for my looks,* she thought, remembering her droopy hair and worn cotton skirt. *He must think I'm a charity case. And my life is as drab my looks.*

Even a tiny sprinkling of stardust would help, she thought, *and Stewart has enough glamour to share.*

She looked up at the attic window, thinking: *I know you're up there, Luke, painting in that turpentine T-shirt. With those giant hands. You sent your friend because you didn't want to take time to drive me home. Stay up there. I don't need you. You won't have to miss a single brush stroke.*

Suddenly she was angry—angry that he had sent Stewart, that Luke had seen her in the driveway and had taken her in his arms. Angry that he was there at all.

Next morning the van was gone; so was Stewart's convertible. Mrs. Warren was in her garden; Tam's tea and toast were on the table. Dad was on the porch, probably watching birds. She took her breakfast out to join him. He was sitting on the steps with small pieces of wood scattered about him, engrossed in sanding one edge. He didn't notice Tam until she spoke to him.

"Good morning, Dad. What're you doing?"

He looked more alive than he'd looked for a long time. His eyes lit up as he answered, "Making a bird feeder. We'll have more birds if we feed them regularly all seasons." His words flowed, enthusiastically, if not smoothly.

He showed her the floor, the three sides and the roof, which would be slanted when fastened to the walls. It would go on a pile among the backyard weeds.

She thought it was a terrific idea. Once he saw his creation surrounded by weeds, he might fix the mower. She didn't mention it.

He said, "I have to finish sanding before Luke gets home."

"What does Luke have to do with this?"

"It was his idea. . .his and mine," he said. "Luke says he'll come over after work. He's picking up paint on the way home. Red. House paint, not picture paint. Luke says. . ."

She listened to an hour of "Luke says. . .Luke says." She learned that Luke was working for Hoosier Tree Service, using skills he'd developed working in his uncle's landscaping business. The job provided enough to live on but left him free to do his real work, his painting. Because he wouldn't be climbing trees in bad weather, he could spend those days painting too.

Luke said he liked to work outdoors. That was funny, Tam said, considering that he spent every free second in the attic. Perhaps that was the reason, her father suggested. Perhaps his job was the only chance he had to see the outside. It made sense.

Luke said birds had to be fed all year round or they'd become accustomed to your feeder and then go hungry if you forgot them. Luke knew those things. He knew as many of the birds by name as Dad did and he knew more about their habits.

Luke said sunflower seeds were best for the birds in that area, especially for jays and chickadees.

Luke said. . .Luke said. . .Luke said. . .

Her father was full of what Luke said, full of the project and full of life. Two days ago she had despaired of a way to interest him. Luke had solved that problem.

She watched him on the porch, enjoying his enthusiasm, until she felt she had to get some work done. Inside the house, however, she was restless and kept returning to the porch. At last she brought the ironing board out on the porch so she could watch him while he worked. This gave her a kind of contentment.

By the time Tam went to work, the bird feeder was nearly put together. He'd have time to finish it and have his nap before Luke came. She hoped Luke remembered the paint. Maybe she could stop on the way to work somewhere. No. If she bought paint that would spoil the whole thing. She would leave that to Luke and her father.

Besides, she had other things to think about, like what to wear to work that would still look reasonably good after a night at Food Mart—good enough for the ride home with Stewart.

Nothing she owned looked good enough in the first place, much less after eight hours at work. It had been a long, long time since she'd worried about her looks.

Briefly, she considered taking along extra clothes to change into after work, but decided she couldn't appear in the parking lot with her Sunday dress on, carrying work clothes. He'd think she dressed up just for him. It would be true, but there was no point in advertising it.

Besides, he'd already seen her when she wasn't expecting him. She hadn't combed her hair or anything.

Remember, she cautioned herself, *this is nothing to Stewart. He's only a neighbor with a generous disposition, a neighbor who is doing his good deed for the day, or night. . . A neighbor who has a perfect smile, who. . .*

She had to do something with her hair.

She lifted one limp lock and let it drop. Hair spray wouldn't help. *A hat,* she thought. *A wig?* She pulled her hair back at the nape of her neck. *Better.* She'd wash and dry it before she left. *It's the best she could do,* she thought, and shrugged at her image in the mirror.

Later, clean and neat in starched blue blouse and dark blue skirt, with sun-fluffed hair tied back with blue ribbon, she was as ready for work as she could get.

She planned to walk slowly, but once on the way, her feet moved faster and faster, hurrying to meet the evening. In spite of all her "slow walking," she was early to work. She knew her friends would put her starched, shiny look together with the handsome stranger in the parking lot. Wait till they saw him again tonight!

Be careful, she thought. *False hopes are a trap. Cinderella is for children. Convertibles and college and happily-ever-afters are for other people. When the fancy ride is over, I'll still be punching that time clock at three and eleven.* She'd enjoy this while it lasted and not hope for more.

I can do that, she thought, and wondered if she could.

Hope punched in, looked Tam over approvingly and said, "You look nice. I didn't know you knew the newcomer at church."

"Who?" Tam asked.

"Stewart. He was in church Sunday and Mr. Moore introduced him. I. . . didn't realize you knew him." Hope faltered on these last words, blushing.

"He's my new neighbor."

"Not bad, not bad," crowed Barbara, punching in. "Where did you find Prince Charming with the classy wheels?"

"Next door," Tam ventured cautiously.

"Next door! Then why haven't we seen him before?"

"He just moved in," Tam explained, keeping her answers minimal. Part of her wanted to bubble over with excitement and part of her wanted to keep it secret from Barbara so she wouldn't have to hear it every night for the next ten years. She'd tell the minimum and hope they wouldn't exaggerate simple kindness into a passionate love affair. Dealing with Barbara was never easy.

Barb was beginning already. "So this gorgeous hunk of man moved in and you never breathed a word about him to us. Some friend you are! The least you could do is let us know before he shows up so we could comb our hair. It's not every night we have a chance to watch you drive off with a movie star. I mean, there he was, smack in front of us, and you never breathed a word, not a word."

"I didn't know he was coming," Tam said. "It was a surprise."

"It sure was," Barb said. "And who's coming tonight?"

"He is."

"You're kidding," said Vickie. "He's coming here again tonight and you can stand there that cool? Aren't you even excited?"

Barb said, "She's excited, all right. Look how shiny bright she looks with her hair pulled back and her clothes all done up perfect. She's definitely excited. Come on, Tam; what's the story?"

"No story. Honest. Of course I dressed up the best I could. Wouldn't you? But to Stewart I'm just a neighbor who needs a ride. That's all."

"That's his name? Stewart?" asked Vickie.

"Stewart," said Barb, considering it.

"Stewie," simpered Vickie.

"Don't," Tam said. "Just don't. Nothing like this has happened to me for years. Please. Be my friends. Don't spoil it for me."

Vickie looked to Barb for direction. At Tam's back she could feel Hope watching. At last Barb said, "Okay, if that's the way you want it."

Tam nodded.

They were busy that night, but not too busy to joke back and forth. Hope, working in back, wasn't included, but the tension of the coffee incident was over, set aside to maintain good working relationships.

At break they sat on the edge of the loading platform as always—Vickie, Barb, and Tam, with Hope several feet to Tam's left. It might have been any other night in the last few weeks except that things lay between them now that made them uneasy with each other.

Neither Barb nor Vickie would mention those items that went home in the pockets of their smocks, not in front of Hope. Tam didn't think Barb had told Vickie they'd quarreled. Vickie was no good at keeping secrets; she'd have said something if she'd known.

Hope hadn't confronted Barb about the coffee machine, and Barb hadn't apologized. They went on, pretending nothing had happened. The one change was that Barb was letting Hope alone. She wasn't exactly pleasant to her, but she wasn't badgering her either. Tam wondered if this would be the new pattern of their relationship or whether Barb would return to annoying Hope after the caution wore off. Either way it was an improvement.

"You look nice," Barb ventured. "Blue is good on you."

"Thanks," Tam said, grateful for easy conversation. "I had trouble finding something that looks good."

"Your hair is better that way too," Barb said.

"I can't do anything with it. It just hangs there like ears on a hound."

Barb suggested, "You'd look cute with short hair. Why don't I cut it? I cut my daughter's hair all the time, and my sister's too. I can do it."

"I don't think so."

"Why not?"

"Vickie, don't you think Tam would look cute with short hair?" Barb leaned back so Vickie could study Tam's hair and come up with the opinion Barb had already given her.

"You'd look good with short hair," said Vickie.

"See?" said Barb.

With Barb's talk of the best style and when and where to cut, Tam felt she barely managed to escape the break with hair still on her head. She promised to think it over, which was as far as she was willing to go with the idea.

It was nice of Barb to want to help, though, thought Tam. Barb could be a good friend when she wanted to be.

On their way back to checkout, Mack stopped to ask if Mr. Brill had been in since Tam had jumped out of his car. He hadn't. Barb said she didn't think he'd have the nerve to show up after that, but Mack didn't agree.

"He'll be back," he said, "and when he comes in, I want to speak to him. I can't have him scaring my help like that. You let me know right away when he comes in."

They promised. *Another friend,* Tam thought. *He may be primarily concerned about his groceries, but he's trying to protect me.* She wondered what Mack would say to Mr. Brill if he ever did come in, which he wouldn't.

Because they were busy after break, Tam didn't start watching the clock until almost nine. Once she did start, the time crawled by. She checked the clock after each customer. At ten she began keeping one eye on the entrance, just in case Mrs. Warren wanted Stewart to pick up some cereal or something, since he was going to the grocery anyway.

At ten thirty she began watching the cars in the parking lot.

Her unreliable stomach was beginning to twist and her hands were cold. The register keys played tricks on her; she made mistakes she'd never made before, not even when she was first learning how to use the register. Her knees felt watery and she grew clumsy. If eleven did not come soon, she would break a bottle or drop eggs or squash grapes or bounce a bag of flour off her foot.

It was a very long half hour. At the end of it, at eleven, no little yellow car sat outside the door.

Tam tried to tell herself she was glad. She was a nervous wreck and was relieved no handsome Stewart was there to see her disintegrate behind the counter. She was also disappointed.

She told herself it was all right that he had forgotten to appear, that it wasn't really important, that she could get home alone. She told herself that, but she didn't believe it.

Barb and Vickie dawdled with their cash drawers, hanging around in front so they could see Stewart drive up. In the back room Tam freshened up the best she could, combing her hair and brushing her teeth with the toothbrush she had brought in her purse.

He's not there, she thought, *but I might as well do the best I can, just in case.* She tried to look nonchalant as she hung up her smock, but her eyes met Hope's and they both knew Tam was not calm at all.

"He's here!" croaked Barb in a hoarse whisper. She and Vickie dashed into the back room. "He's here! Let's see how you look." She straightened Tam's collar in the back. "Not bad, kid." She gave Tam's hair a quick pat and pushed her toward the door.

"Wait! I forgot to punch out," Tam cried.

"I'll do it," said Barb. "Get going."

Tam went.

Chapter Six

In the softness of the lovely evening. Tam's head and heart betrayed her. She no longer had to concentrate to seem to float on air. She floated without aid or effort, lighter than the evening air that whispered through her idle fingers.

This second of many rides home was the beginning of a dream life. At first she felt like a stranger in this magical world of romance, but she soon adapted. Before too many rides she began to feel a part of it, as unreal as the rest of the setting. Each night at eleven she stepped from paper bags and potatoes into stardust and sophistication. By twelve she stepped out of the dream and into the dim kitchen.

She agreed to the haircut on the condition that Barb forget movie stars and keep the cut simple. Barb agreed, so early Saturday morning Barb came to cut, shampoo, and set.

. . .And to catch a close-up, "accidental" look at Stewart. Barb was disappointed. Stewart and Luke were gone.

Barb was drying Tam's hair in the sun, coaxing it into waves, when Mrs. Warren came to inspect the little red-roofed bird feeder high on its metal pipe pole in the weeds. She pronounced it just the thing. Luke said she would like it and she did. Luke also said Dad might make her one.

Luke said. Luke said.

Mrs. Warren asked, as usual, if Tam intended to attend church the next day. She was used to evasive answers, but Tam's determined "Yes" surprised and pleased her.

"Just church, Mrs. Warren, not Sunday school."

"Whatever you say, dear."

Tam didn't admit that she was motivated primarily by curiosity about what Hope drew from church. If Tam had, Mrs. Warren would have discussed it, which Tam didn't want. She wanted to see for herself.

Mrs. Warren didn't mention Stewart. Tam thought that, for a woman who loved to talk, Mrs. Warren had been exceptionally closed-mouthed recently. Mrs. Warren might think Stewart was the reason Tam was going, but she didn't say so. *Good,* thought Tam. *Maybe Mrs. Warren won't send Stewart over for me on Sunday morning.*

Telling Mrs. Warren she wasn't going to Sunday school should stop that. Mrs. Warren always went to Sunday school and surely would take "the boys" with her.

❧

"Who's Luke?" asked Barb, when Mrs. Warren had gone.

"The other neighbor," Tam said. "Nobody special."

"That's what you said about Stewart," said Barb.

Tam shrugged.

In less than an hour, Tam's hair was dry, Barb was gone, and Mrs. Warren was inspecting the results, claiming the hair was "a picture, an absolute picture."

Mrs. Warren stood watching Dad mark out the bird feeder pattern on the scraps of wood and then announced—too casually—that she and "the boys" would like Tam and her father to join them for Sunday dinner.

"No," said Dad.

"Fine," said Mrs. Warren. "Come over right after you get home from church."

Dad blinked at Tam in surprise, wondering when he had decided to go to church. Tam smiled as if to say there was nothing she could do about it now that Mrs. Warren had made up her mind. He raised his eyebrows but didn't argue. Tam hoped he'd be as cooperative in the morning.

At noon Mrs. Warren was back, this time with a dress, still in its plastic cleaner's bag. "Would you do me a favor, dear?" she asked.

She'd found this old dress when she cleaned out the attic for Luke. Well, actually it was almost new. Anyway, it didn't fit her and there was no use pretending she'd lose enough weight to wear it, especially since it was too tight when she bought it. But it was too good to waste—real silk—no good to anybody in the attic. All it did was take up room. A real shame, considering how much she had paid for it.

"Would you mind trying it on to see if you could get a little use out of it? As a favor?"

Tam knew Mrs. Warren was only slightly larger than she, but arguing was impossible, especially since Tam didn't try very hard.

The dress was the most beautiful garment she'd touched in years, possibly in her whole life. It slid on smoothly and hung evenly at exactly the right length, as if made for Tam. The soft rose-pink added color to her face and softened the shadows around her eyes. When she moved, it moved with her, whispering lightly as a sigh as she turned this way and that in front of her mirror.

Silk.

Tam wriggled her shoulders against the downy fabric. "Are you sure?" she asked.

"Sure as sure, honey," Mrs. Warren said. "It was your dress all along. I just didn't know it till now."

"I'll wear it to church," promised Tam.

"Yes, and to my house for dinner." Mrs. Warren kissed Tam lightly on the cheek and left her admiring herself in the mirror.

The day had flown by and so did the night. The haircut was a great success. Everybody at work liked it, even Mack. She loved the approval in Stewart's eyes as he said, "Nice haircut."

Sunday morning, with her new haircut and rose-petal dress, Tamara looked younger and softer than she had dared to hope. She was up and dressed early, and Dad was in a good mood. He wore his blue blazer and his white shoes, matching her with a snappy look of his own.

They were early enough to secure a back seat. She knew her father would go home rather than sit up front.

The organist was playing something subdued in what the bulletin said was "time to sit quietly in our pews and prepare our hearts for worship." Tam found this difficult. People kept stopping to speak to her or to Dad.

You'd think we haven't been here for years, Tam thought. *We were here just. . . Easter. Oh.*

The big welcome was embarrassing but warming. Dad's first responses were stand-offish and brusque, but he rapidly relaxed.

Hope came in, looked around for Tam, smiled delightedly, and came directly over. Tam introduced Hope to Dad, who offered to move over so she could join them.

Tam said quickly, "Hope always sits in the front. She says she likes to be surrounded by the singing."

"That's all right," Hope said. "I'd rather sit with you."

Dad urged Tam to sit with her up front, but Tam was not persuaded until Mrs. Warren appeared, followed by Stewart, smiling in Sunday perfection, and Luke. Tam waited to greet them before going to sit up front, watching and pretending not to watch for Stewart's reaction. She needn't have worried.

His smile radiated over all three of them. He lingered briefly over Hope's hand when he shook it and seemed to have difficulty breaking eye contact with Hope. *His natural charm,* Tam thought, noting that his impact on Hope was as forceful as it had been on her. Hope was blushing, visibly flustered by his touch.

He must be used to that, she thought. *My own awkwardness must have seemed quite normal to him. He might even miss it if it were not there.* She repressed a giggle and looked away to hide it. . .

Right into the knowing brown eyes of Luke.

Waiting to be introduced, he observed Stewart's charm and Hope's confusion, then focused on Tam. She knew she might have hidden her laughter from the others, but not from him.

His slightly puzzled frown pleased Tam, who liked knowing he couldn't read every wrinkle in her brain.

Perhaps he was puzzled that she hadn't seemed jealous or possessive when Stewart charmed Hope. If so, Luke was forgetting two things: Stewart wasn't seriously interested in her, and Stewart couldn't help being charming.

He is what he is, thought Tam. *Surely Luke knows that.*

Mrs. Warren introduced Luke to Hope and it was Tam's turn to observe reactions. Too well she knew the strength of Luke's hand, the power it had to melt her bones. As Hope's meeting with Stewart had echoed Tam's own, so Hope's meeting with Luke would confirm Tam's response to his strength. Tam waited for the fluttering that would give Hope away.

She didn't flutter. They shook hands and exchanged How-do-you-do's and smiled. Tam saw nothing of that weakness that had washed over her when. . . .

It wasn't the same. Shaking hands in the aisle of the church wasn't the same as being swept up in his arms in the rainy night shadows. If Hope had been there, thought Tam, she'd have felt it too.

Hope's gaze remained on Stewart and his on her. Tam shifted uncomfortably from one foot to the other, knowing Luke was studying her again, this time with a trace of anger in his face—anger mixed with something unidentifiable. Concern?

Perhaps.

"Let's sit," Luke said gruffly, pushing Stewart into the pew across from Dad and sliding in after him, leaving Mrs. Warren to sit with Dad. Hope and Tam settled in the fifth row, far in front, just in time for the Call to Worship.

Tam's mind was miles away from hymns and prayers. No, not miles. A few rows. She scarcely heard the opening of the service or the first hymn.

Next to her, Hope's voice—sweet, clear, young—rose in light soprano with the worshipers, and Tam wondered again what Hope found here.

Tam listened for it, watched for it, but didn't find it. Church was like it always was—pleasant, but not the answer to her question.

For Tam the best part was the stained glass window which filled the entire right wall of the sanctuary. In high school, she had asked Mr. Simms, their pastor then, about the window and learned it was called "The Road to Emmaus" and that it was about a place where Jesus had walked with two of His followers after He had risen from the grave.

Jesus' friends hadn't recognized Him, Mr. Simms had explained. They walked and talked with Him, but didn't know Him. Not until later, when Jesus had opened their eyes to Him, did they know Him.

As it had a hundred times before, Tam's imagination wandered down the Road to Emmaus on the caramel glass between leaded trees and the milky blue of the stream.

She wondered what it was like to meet Him on the road and whether she'd have recognized Him. When she was younger she was sure she'd have known Him instantly. Now she thought not. If His close friends failed to know Him, why would she?

Would Jesus have walked with me? she wondered. He had walked with two who were His followers, two Christians. Tam was Christian. She'd always considered herself Christian, anyway, even though Barb said no one would ever guess it.

With Hope it was no secret. Her faith was one of the first things people noticed about her. They might not always like it, but they noticed. It was so much a part of her that it was impossible to imagine her any other way. It just sort of radiated from her.

Am I a Christian? She knew the answer was no. Not like that.

Hope pulled at Tam's elbow for her to rise and Tam realized that the congregation was singing. She followed the words in the book Hope held, but did not sing.

She bowed her head for the closing prayer and the benediction, but she did not pray. She was on the Road to Emmaus.

Slowly becoming aware that people were filing out, Tam edged into the aisle, followed by Hope, who breathed, "Wasn't it wonderful?"

"I. . ." Tam struggled for words, but none came.

"What is it?" Hope asked.

Above her head "The Road to Emmaus" glowed rich with sunlight. Tam shook her head. *She might understand,* Tam thought, *if I could explain. Then she might answer my question.*

Some other time, Tam thought, *when I have the words.*

Then Tam felt sudden empathy for Dad, a glimmer of understanding of his inability to find words, of being able to feel but not able to express the feeling.

She looked for him where she had left him, but he was gone. Slipped out a little early, as usual, she guessed. Crowds frightened him since the stroke. He worried about being able to get out fast if he felt ill. He probably was already outside.

Tam glanced at the back aisle to be certain, and found her eyes locked again with Luke's.

Stunned momentarily by the contact, she didn't notice that Stewart had pushed through the crowd and was almost next to her. His voice close to her ear startled her and she jumped guiltily, breaking the link with Luke.

"You're dreaming, Tam," Stewart joked. "You're not used to getting up so early." She had no clever answer, so she just shrugged.

Stewart moved between Hope and Tam, steering them up the aisle with a hand on the shoulder of each. Tam banged against a pew, driven into it by Stewart, who was trying to crowd three across a two-person aisle. Absently she shook his hand from her shoulder and moved a little ahead, leaving him to steer Hope.

Hope apparently liked the arrangement and would have continued that way if Luke hadn't pushed into the aisle next to her. His huge shoulders were too much for Stewart, whose hand was jostled off Hope's shoulder as Luke forced him ahead of Hope and next to Tam. It looked like natural casual jostling, the way Luke intended it to look.

Hope was still with Luke when they gathered outside to walk home together, so naturally Mrs. Warren asked her to join them for dinner. Hope accepted eagerly and chatted easily with Mrs. Warren as the group paraded two by two to Mrs. Warren's house. Next to Tam, Dad was quiet but in good spirits. "The boys", last, were silent, but Tam felt their presence and was glad to be wearing the lovely silk dress.

Mrs. Warren had gone all out to produce one of her famous dinners. Not one of those chilly affairs with finger bowls and place cards, it was a dinner like the ones she had prepared for her husband and children.

In spite of the heat, she served roast beef, dark brown and fork-tender, with mashed potatoes and gravy, green beans from her garden, biscuits with her own peach jam, and an extravagant gelatin salad with whipped cream and fruit and baby marshmallows. At the foot of the table she smoothed her hands over her apron and beamed at them over her grandmother's cut-glass pitcher.

At the head of the table, across shared joys and sorrows, Tam's father smiled back. Mrs. Warren nodded to him, but he shook his head almost imperceptibly, so she asked Luke to say grace. She knew, of course, that Dad wouldn't risk praying aloud in front of the group, but asking him told him the choice was his.

Luke's voice was deep and rich as he gave thanks for God's blessing. His prayer was simple, not elaborate, the prayer of a man with a close relationship with God. What was it that marked these people, made them special?

Dinner was a clatter of forks, chatter, and laughter—Thanksgiving Day in midsummer, without the stress of the holiday season. They set in with good appetite, especially "the boys", and did justice to the feast.

When all declared they couldn't eat another bite, not another bite, Mrs. Warren brought the blackberry cobbler, still warm from the oven, and vanilla ice cream to go on top. They found that they could, after all, eat just a little more.

After that they groaned and moaned and held their stomachs, declaring they were too full to move and wouldn't have to eat again for a month.

Satisfied, Mrs. Warren passed the great old family Bible over to Luke, who read a chapter from Romans before closing with prayer, officially ending dinner.

When Mrs. Warren rose to begin clearing the table, the younger guests insisted that she and Dad rest while they did dishes. Mrs. Warren and Dad retired to the front porch swing, where the regular squeak of the swinging chains against their ceiling hooks announced that all was well.

The dishes dirtied by only six eaters were enough to have fed Tam and Dad for a week. Tam washed. The others took turns drying and putting away.

They were all the way down to the roaster and the cobbler dish when Mrs. Warren reminded Tam that it was time to go to work.

Tam had forgotten.

"Oh dear," she said, snatching up the cobbler dish. "I've got to hurry. What about you, Hope?"

"I don't work Sundays," Hope said.

"Oh, yes, that's right. Well, I do, and I have only thirty-five minutes to get there," Tam said.

Luke pushed her away from the sink, taking the cobbler dish from her hands. "I'll finish this," he said. "You get ready. Stewart will take you to work. Right, Stew?"

"Right."

Tam dried her hands and ran. At home she pulled the silken dress over her head and laid it carefully on the bed. She popped on the first clean skirt she found and topped it with a crisp white blouse, then turned to the mirror to run a comb through her short hair. Ready.

Outside, Stewart was holding the car door open. Even in a rush, he did things gracefully. As he shut the door, Tam said, "You don't have to do this, but I'm glad you are. I don't want to be late. I need that job."

"It's a pleasure," Stewart responded. "For a girl who looked as lovely as you did in that pink dress, I'd drive across town anytime."

"Thank you," she said.

"You don't really need that job, you know," he said. "You could get another one that isn't so exhausting, one with better hours. Why do you stay there?"

Tam never had given it much thought. Whenever she thought of the job, she was glad to have it. She hadn't wanted to spend her life in the grocery, but an art career was impossible. Without that, one job was as good as another.

She didn't explain that, saying honestly that it was the only job she knew how to do, that she had no other skills.

"Learn to type," he said, "or to do computer programming."

"That costs money," she answered, "and I'd have to go to school at night to learn. I work at night."

He nodded. "I see what you mean. We'll have to think this over."

"We?"

"You and I," he explained, "and Luke, of course."

"What does Luke have to do with me and my job?"

"Nothing. It's just that Luke always knows what to do. If it hadn't been for Luke I'd have been lying dead in the middle of nowhere and no one the wiser. He pulled me out of there and saved my life. He's the one who knew I would do well in business administration and helped me get started. He was right too.

I'm happy with my job and my employers are happy with me. Luke says. . . ."

"Luke says, Luke says," Tam objected impatiently. "That's all I hear. What's so wonderful about Luke that every word he says has to be quoted?"

Stewart turned to her with raised eyebrows and an astonishment that almost immediately gave way to amusement. He chuckled softly. "Luke said you had a temper."

"Aarrrgh!!!" Her growl drew Stewart's laughter. Scootching low in the seat, she barricaded herself with folded arms and glowered at the dashboard.

These arrogant men with their lives grasped firmly in their hands were beginning to annoy her. They imagined that all she had to do was decide to have a new life and a new life would happen.

They didn't know about giving up dreams. They hadn't sat for hours with a father who was clinging to remnants of his self-respect. They didn't know how quickly the little security she had managed could evaporate in sudden illness or a lost job.

Tam knew. She knew the job market was almost zero for people with limited experience and no skills. She also knew that she couldn't afford to be unemployed while she sought a new career.

Stewart with his fine job and Luke with his eternal painting had no one but themselves to spend their money on. *I will have to be careful,* she thought. *These people could put grand ideas in my head, make me long for things I could never have, make me lose what little I have. Glamour and romance were fine, but they weren't enough to live on.*

What I should do, if I have any sense at all, she thought, *is stay away from Stewart. One day he'll find a new neighbor to feel sorry for and I'll be left with nothing but a broken heart and a set of overgrown expectations.*

She didn't want to stay away from Stewart. That was the problem. If this was all her future held, she wanted it. When he left, she would still have memories. It was better than nothing.

The trick was to let her head float above the clouds, but keep her feet firmly on earth. Not so easy. She wasn't sure she could do it.

"We're here." Stewart's voice broke through to her and she raised her head to see the orange and blue Food Mart sign directly in front of the car. She turned to thank him, but he was already out and standing by her open door, waiting.

She wondered how long she had sat engrossed in her own thoughts. She thought she saw amusement in his eyes, but when she looked more sharply, it was gone.

Thanking him quickly, she dashed in the front entrance, entirely forgetting that Mack wanted them to use the back one during daylight hours. She never did that, never did the unusual. Day after day, night after night, Tam's comings and goings were regulated by the clock, steady, dependable. Dull. Not the way she'd been acting lately.

Once she punched in, the rudeness of her behavior in the car hit her. What had she done? Stewart was interested, trying to help. She should have been grateful, or at least civil. Instead she had snapped at him and quarreled. She had been rude without excuse. Why was she being so disagreeable?

It was that "Luke said" business that set me off, she thought. *Every time I turn around it's "Luke said." He is definitely getting on my nerves.*

Why? He hadn't done anything to her. She had barely spoken with him since that first night.

Dad saw him, often, when she was not home. They worked on bird feeders and discussed sunflower seeds and all kinds of things.

Mrs. Warren saw him enough to begin to depend on him. She had asked Luke, not Stewart, to ask the blessing at dinner.

Stewart saw him. Everybody saw him but Tam.

You would think, wouldn't you, she fumed, *that after he carried me from the driveway and patched up my hands. . .and knees. . .and saw me safely home. . . .*

You would think that the next time I saw him he would at least be friendly instead of acting like we've never met. He scarcely spoke to me, never once mentioned that night.

At dinner he had been quieter than the others except where Hope was involved. He was always quick to sit next to her, walk next to her, talk with her. You would think the only person in the place was Hope, that I didn't exist.

Except that now and then, when Tam wasn't expecting it, she had met his eyes by accident. It was unnerving, that steady look of his. It confused her. It almost frightened her, but not really. It wasn't that kind of look. It was a kind of concerned interest, guarded, but knowing.

She couldn't decide what to make of it. She did know, however, that Luke was an infuriating, frustrating, annoying man. A mere mention of his name set her teeth on edge.

Nonsense, she thought. *Luke is a man who lives next door. Our meeting was accidental and unimportant to him, except as an embarrassment he preferred not to mention.*

Tam could understand that. She felt the same way here at work sometimes. Moreover, from what he had seen of her, she was sure he found her childish and tiresome.

More childish than Hope? Evidently. Absolutely. She guessed she couldn't blame him.

Nevertheless, Luke was Stewart's friend. To get along with Stewart she would have to get along with Luke. She also was reluctant to cause any trouble between

Dad and his new friend. That would be cruel.

She would get along with him, that's all, and be nice about it. It wouldn't be difficult, considering how rarely she saw him. And she would have to apologize to Stewart.

With all this on her mind, she was in no mood to joke and play or be around others who were lively. She felt itchy, wriggly, snappish. To Barb's hints about her ill-tempered distance, she was unresponsive and even more distant.

Nothing went right. They were busy, but she wanted to be alone. She found conversation an irritation, but every customer was chatty. Barb was in one of her easy-going, funny moods; Tam had no patience.

The conveyer belt had a nasty habit of moving when she pressed the foot control, even though she didn't intend to press the control. The lights all worked for a change, so the light seemed glaring. Mack was nosy, hanging around, keeping an eye on everything. Nothing went right.

At six Mack pulled her off checkout and put her to sorting good strawberries from bad and she retired to the relative seclusion of the produce department. Relieved, she set in with a will, applying stifled energies to the simple task of creating clean, attractive baskets full of good berries.

That's where Mr. Brill found her.

He crept up behind her from the other side of the potatoes before she realized anyone was there. He took the plastic basket from her hands and clasped them in his, looking soulfully into her eyes.

"Tam," he whispered, "why did you leave me like that?"

"Let me go," Tam demanded, pulling back.

He was stronger than he looked. Holding her hands firmly, he whispered, "I can't let you go. I've searched for you all my life. You belong to me."

"I'll scream."

"No, you won't scream. You know that I'm your friend." He smiled sweetly, close to her face.

"Mack!" The cry came from inside her before she realized it existed. "Mack!" she shouted again.

"Why did you do that?" whimpered Mr. Brill, squeezing her hands tightly. "Why did you do that?"

Then Mack was there and so was Al, and between them they opened Mr. Brill's grasp and released her. Mack led Mr. Brill away to the office, talking quietly to him. Al held onto his other arm, his height ensuring that Mr. Brill cooperated. Mr. Brill looked small between them, and helpless. Poor little man. Tam felt sorry for him.

Far away, at the other end of the aisle, Tam saw Mack pick up the telephone, tap the number buttons, and talk briefly into the receiver. Interesting, but not important. She was calm, glassy calm. She stood absolutely still next to the mound of strawberries, calm. Mack cast a worried glance in her direction and shouted for Barbara.

Tam smiled vaguely. *Mack must think I need help or comfort, but I don't. He must expect me to be upset, to break into tears or have hysterics or something, but I won't. None of this is important.*

She was absolutely calm.

When the police arrived to question her about the incident, she patiently told them what had happened. They and Mr. Brill seemed to know each other. They left with poor little Mr. Brill in the back of their squad car. He looked lost, alone.

"Are you all right?" Barb asked.

"Fine."

"Why don't you take a break? Mack will let you go home early. Let me call you a cab."

"I'm fine," Tam repeated.

"Don't you want to rest a while?"

"I'm fine," Tam said, and mechanically picked up the basket Mr. Brill had taken from her. She saw the worried looks Barb and Mack exchanged, but the looks meant nothing.

Mack said something about calling Tam's father, but it was not important. It didn't penetrate her perfect calm. She went back to her sorting: good berry in the basket, rotten berry in the box, good berry, rotten berry. . . .

Luke?

Luke was there. How odd. And he was very angry. Scowling. He brushed the berries away like sand from a child's hands. She regarded him placidly. His scowl deepened.

Grasping her firmly with one arm round her shoulders and taking her purse from Barbara, he maneuvered Tam through the store and out the front. She went passively along, although she knew Mack would want her to use the back door.

In the parking lot Luke stuffed her unceremoniously into his van and jerked into gear. He drove home in angry silence and Tam had nothing to say either.

Dad was in the driveway and so was Mrs. Warren, who hustled Tam into her own room and into nightgown and robe. A rattle of dishes from the kitchen told Tam Dad was making tea. Tam observed this from another dimension. It was not important.

On the bed where she had laid it after the dinner was the glorious pink silk dress. Tam drifted over to it and ran her hand across its softness. Holding it up to her robe, she swayed a little, feeling the silk follow her movement. *Lovely,* she crooned to herself. *Lovely.* She turned to the mirror to dream in the reflection. She spread the skirt, holding one fold so that the fullness of the fabric floated when she moved.

Lovely.

Something was on it, some bit of fluff or thread. She brushed at it with the back of her hand but it remained. She leaned closer to the light and held up the offending spot for closer inspection. The dark gray-blue smear would not brush off. She rubbed but it remained. *Stubborn,* she thought. *What was it?* She held it closer to the light and rubbed again.

Blackberry.

Please, not blackberry. It would never come out.

"No," she wailed, "not my new dress. Please not my new dress."

She sank to the bed, pressing her delicate pink silk to her heart and sobbing for all she was worth.

"Now, now," soothed Mrs. Warren, hurrying in from the kitchen to cradle Tam in her arms, but it did no good. Tam's tears, once started, would not stop, until she cried herself to sleep.

Chapter Seven

Dark. Tam squinted at the luminous dial of her clock radio. Three o'clock. Groan. Her head hurt as she sat up and threw off the clinging sheet. She rolled forward to lie with her head in the cool breeze at the foot of the bed and gazed out at the night.

Luke's attic light was on. She pictured him up there, painting, scowling. With sudden pain she remembered the evening and sat up again, abruptly, then sank back to the pillow. *Poor Mr. Brill,* she thought. *And poor Luke—always having to rescue me from one scrape or another. No wonder he avoids me.*

He'd seen her looking normal only one day—at church and at the dinner, in that lovely silk. . . .

Blackberry stain. She remembered that now too, and the flood of tears that followed the discovery. *Strange,* she thought, *I was calm with Mr. Brill but not with the stain. I must have upset Dad.*

She went to see if he was all right, gliding along in the unlit house with ease born of a lifetime of familiarity.

He was awake. Over tea in the kitchen, she told him about Mr. Brill and that eerie calm she had felt. Shock, he decided, which explained her over-reaction to the stain. That was a shame, they agreed, but it wasn't worth tears.

Tam nodded, thinking, *It's the way I am—calm in disaster. Later, I fall apart.*

The night Dad had had his stroke she had sat waiting calmly in the hospital. Later, at home, alone, tears came.

Jumping out of Mr. Brill's car was less serious, but it was the same pattern. She was scared out there in the bushes, but she kept her wits all the way home. Then, when she knew she was safe, she fell.

It's a good way to be, she supposed, except since no one saw the lonely tears, no one suspected how dearly she paid for the calm. Other girls cried or fainted; Tam coped. She saw no choice, no one to lean on.

Except Dad, of course, but she was careful not to upset him. Mrs. Warren was always willing to help, but she was a neighbor and friend, not family, not someone whose love made him part of her.

Sometimes Tam had lain awake at night, imagining that Robert still cared and had returned to hold her close and protect her, folding his arms around her, saying, "Lean on me." Robert couldn't have prevented the trouble, but his understanding would have helped.

Seeing that other people's lives were easier and that public weepers got more sympathy had made her resent the injustice. Then, realizing that "unfair" is for children, she began to suspect that she wasn't the only person carrying a burden in silence. Others around her must also be struggling alone. She grew more sensitive to others' pain, finding it in Barb, in Mrs. Warren, in Dad, and took comfort from knowing that if they were managing, she could.

How silly to cry over a dress, Tam thought. *I can cope with that. Tomorrow. And Dad? Luke had told him not to worry.*

Luke said. . . .

His light still burned when Tam finally returned to bed. She found that curiously comforting. She would thank Luke when she saw him, if she ever saw him.

For a second or two she considered throwing pebbles at his window again to speak to him. She couldn't run out in the driveway at four o'clock in the morning in her nightgown and throw pebbles at the neighbor's window! What was she thinking of?

She shut her mind and went to sleep, waking to a normal Monday morning.

Mr. Brill lurked in the fringes of Tam's mind, as frightening in daylight as he was that night in the car. Tam pitied him, but he scared her. He was stronger than he looked, and more determined. Worse, there was no telling what he would do next. She tried not to think about him.

While Dad counted birds, Tam inspected the ruined silk dress, hooking the hanger over the top of the open kitchen door where the light was best. Could it be washed?

She thought so, but would the stain get better? Or worse? She tried washing just the stained section of the skirt with mild soap, then stronger soap. No good. The stain lightened a smidgen and changed from blue-gray to gray and the pink was fading too.

She quit. She toweled it dryish and rehung it in the doorway, a sad, limp little dress.

Ruined, she thought. *Give up.* But she couldn't. Even ruined it was the loveliest thing she owned. She would hang it in her closet, royalty among the cottons, to look at and caress occasionally. As it moved in the breeze she remembered how it had felt—like a flower petal.

Mrs. Warren brushed past it when she came in. How was Tam today, she wanted to know, and how was Dad, and what could she do to help, and here was a little salad for lunch. When Mrs. Warren thought of comfort and support, she thought of food.

Mrs. Warren turned to the miserable-looking silk. "What are you going to do with it?"

"Hang it in the closet," said Tam, "unless you have a better idea."

"Well," said Mrs. Warren, "once we covered a hole in my Sally's dress with a big flower—sewed it on like a patch. Looked liked it belonged there."

"Not in the middle of the skirt, though," Tam pointed out. "And not that big."

"No. You can't go around with a bouquet stuck on the front of your skirt. Too heavy. Must be something you could put there to cover it up. A little ruffled apron, maybe. A pocket?"

"A coat?" Tam suggested.

"Don't be fresh, Tamara," Mrs. Warren said, laughing. "Too bad it's plain pink. If the fabric had flowers all over it, the spot wouldn't show so bad."

"Flowers all over. That's it!" Tam cried.

"Too heavy."

"Not if they're painted on."

Mrs. Warren spread the skirt, trying to picture flowers. Her slow tentative nod grew into enthusiasm. It was exactly her kind of crazy idea.

They needed paints. Tam had some, someplace, but where?

In the last place she looked, of course—on the top shelf of the coat closet, under postcards her mother had saved. The brushes were stiff, but could be softened with turpentine, if it hadn't evaporated. The paints were hard in tubes that cracked when Tam squeezed them. The linseed oil was yellow and sticky. The palette was still good, though, and clean. She'd use Dad's turpentine and make do with the rest.

Mrs. Warren washed the dress free of dry cleaning chemicals and ironed it dry in little more than an hour. She arranged it on the super-clean kitchen table, putting newspaper inside to separate front from back so paint wouldn't soak through to the back.

With mounting excitement, Tam mixed the paints on the palette. *Flowers, she thought, soft and floating colors for a soft and floating dress. Rose and greens. A touch of lavender for balance. Gray to blend into the gray stain.*

Humming, she blended the colors in different strengths and combinations, adding a little white here, a little cadmium red there. When she was satisfied, she thinned them with turpentine so they would flow on easily. Turpentine would make it dry faster too.

Filling her widest brush with the lightest of the colors and taking a deep breath, echoed by Mrs. Warren, Tam touched the brush to the edge of the stain and stroked it lightly across the silk. The color stayed where she put it, almost transparent in its thin solution, but firm enough to cover the color of the skirt.

The first stroke was the hardest. After that she relaxed, humming as she worked.

Loose, soft-edged flowers appeared under her hand and spread themselves across the skirt diagonally up to the waist. From there they flourished across the bodice and up to the left shoulder. It was tempting to go on making flowers up the other side and down the back and on the sleeves, but Tam stopped.

"What do you think?" she asked Mrs. Warren.

"Lovely," Mrs. Warren breathed softly. "No one would ever know. It's better than it was before."

"It needs a sprinkle of white for contrast, and maybe a line or two of black," Tam mused, and picked up a finer brush, to add the delicate touches. "There."

"Lovely," repeated Mrs. Warren. "I have a white silk blouse. Do you think you could. . ."

"Of course. Right now, before I put the paint away."

Tam used Mrs. Warren's kitchen table for the blouse, so both blouse and dress could lie undisturbed to dry. When it was done, they surveyed the morning's work with satisfaction, pleased with themselves and the results.

"You were humming while you worked," said Mrs. Warren. "You did that when you were little, but I haven't heard you do it lately."

"I haven't been this happy for a long time," Tam said. "I forgot how much I enjoy painting."

"You ought to take it up again."

"I don't have much time for things like this."

"No, I suppose you don't. It's a shame to waste all that talent." Mrs. Warren shook her head.

Tam and Dad ate on the back porch because the kitchen table was covered by the dress.

"Those weeds are getting pretty high," Tam said.

Dad shook his head. "No. Butterfly garden." He pointed to a flash of yellow fluttering near the pole. "Luke says. . ."

Luke again. He had convinced Dad not to cut the weeds, explaining that butterflies thrive on weeds and need them for home and food. They like variety and depend most heavily on the very weeds Tam was trying to eliminate—goldenrod, clover, thistles, ragweed, dandelion. They are especially fond of small, simple flowers like the daisies, phlox, petunias, and alyssum in Mrs. Warren's garden.

Furthermore, butterflies need nearby bushes, like the hedge across the back of the yard, and trees. They would love the willow behind the garage. The back yard was a perfect butterfly garden, Luke said.

"There's no such thing," Tam argued.

"No," Dad argued back, nodding his head yes.

Luke said Winston Churchill had had one at his estate to show off to visitors. Churchill had even stocked it with more impressive specimens when he was expecting more impressive guests.

Churchill and Luke were too much for Tam. She might as well accept the butterfly garden and forget about cutting weeds.

Tam hoped Luke had told Mrs. Warren about the butterflies. Tam was sure Mrs. Warren didn't consider the weeds beautiful and didn't view her flowers as dessert. If Luke said it, though, Mrs. Warren would approve.

Two young squirrels chased and wrestled, and Tam laughed to see them scramble up and down the pole, stumbling onto the birds' sunflower seeds. A bonanza! They stuffed their cheeks, reaching with clever hands into the feeder for more, depleting the seed supply.

Dad refilled the feeder right after lunch. Tam heard him telling someone about the squirrels and looked out to see Luke with Dad by the garage. She saw him rarely, so she seized the opportunity to thank him for bringing her home and to apologize for being a nuisance.

He virtually dwarfed her father. Before her courage could falter, she marched right up to Luke and spoke directly to the fourth button of his blue denim work shirt.

She met his eyes, which was difficult because his face was so far up and because he looked through her. She also knew that he had seen her looking terrible too many times. One time was too many.

"I want to thank you. . ." she began, looking at the button.

Luke said, "Stewart would have come if he could. He won't be back until tomorrow. He must have told you."

He hadn't. Tam said nothing.

Luke said, "I know he'll feel terrible about being gone when you—

"Don't remind me," Tam said. "I'm sorry to be such a n—"

"You're not. You have no reason to be embarrassed," said Luke. "Not with me, not ever. I thought you knew that." His eyes held hers, until she forced herself to look away.

"I'm not embarrassed," she lied.

"Yes, you are. Don't be."

She said nothing.

Luke said, "Don't worry about getting home tonight. Mack says to tell you to take today off instead of tomorrow."

"Mack said that?"

"On the phone this morning," said Luke, as if it were reasonable.

"Oh. Thank you," she said quietly.

"You're welcome." After a long silence, Luke said, "You need a baffle."

"Baffle?" echoed Tam, startled into looking up. Luke was talking to Dad, seeming to have forgotten her.

"Baffle?" she repeated.

Luke looked down at her. "For the squirrels," he explained, and, to Dad, "You need some obstacle that squirrels can't get past, like a barrier on the post. You can buy one but an old pie tin will do. Do you have one?"

For a moment she didn't realize the question was directed at her. Luke smiled. "Do you have a pie plate you don't need?" he repeated.

"Pie plate," said Tam. Luke nodded. She went to look and returned holding one out to him, "Will this do?"

"Thanks," said Luke, holding out his hand for the tin without glancing at her.

That man! She turned on her heel and huffed into the house. He was absolutely infuriating.

Except when I was in trouble, she thought, *like the night before at the Food Mart. When I saw him there, I knew everything would be all right. Luke could handle it. I felt safe.*

It must be his size, she thought, *and his strength. If he weren't so enormous, he would be an ordinary person like everyone else. What else but his size made people put up with his directness and made them quote him incessantly?*

They also know he means every word he says and every word is true.

Stop defending him, she told herself. *He's doing very well on his own. Better than I am.*

That man!

Dad came in pleased with himself and anxious for the squirrels to test the baffle. He sat by the window, but it was too dark to see the feeder, so he reluctantly turned on television for the first time that busy day.

Suddenly aware of the change in him, Tam saw his shoulders were straighter, his movements quicker and more certain, his general appearance more alert. It wasn't just an increased interest in feeding birds. It was an attitude of belonging to the active world.

Had Luke done this? Had those visits in the evenings while Tam was at work brought back her father's confidence? If so, she owed Luke thanks for this too.

She seldom saw him. He sort of came and went at the edges of her days, visiting with Dad when she was at work, working when she was at home, appearing only in disasters. Since the next week was peaceful, she didn't see him at all.

She went to work the next afternoon, Tuesday, embarrassed about being sent home like a child whose mother had sent big brother to collect her. Mack immediately let her know that Mr. Brill would never bother her again if Mack had anything to say about it. Then, satisfied that she had returned to normal, he put her up front on the cash register again.

Barb must have been satisfied with Tam's recovery. She resumed teasing where she had left off, joking about all the men coming to take Tam home. (Stewart and Luke, that is—Barb didn't mention Mr. Brill.)

"All kinds of handsome men are waiting in line to take me home," Tam told her.

"Of course," laughed Barb. "Don't they always? Which one can I have?"

"Take your choice," Tam told her. "If you take the one I want, I'll get another one."

"Which one do you want?" asked Barb.

"Be serious," said Tam, dismissing the joke, and the possibility, with a wave of her hand.

Catching Tam alone at break, Hope talked of church and Mrs. Warren's dinner before getting to what was on her mind. "You and Stewart kind of go together, huh?"

Tam said, "Not really. We haven't known each other very long. He just takes me home from work. What about you and Luke? You spent all afternoon together."

"Luke's nice," Hope said.

"Nice? That's all? After he followed you around all afternoon watching like diamonds would fall from your mouth? I bet he took you home." Tam was guessing correctly.

"Well," Hope said, "Stewart offered, but Luke said he was going that direction anyway, so Luke drove me." Hope didn't look as pleased about that as Tam thought she would.

Tam said, "I think Luke's interested in you. He certainly hung on your every word. Every time you started to talk to Stewart, Luke was right there between you. If he drove you home, that proves it. He doesn't give up precious painting time for just anybody."

"He did for you," Hope said.

"That was an emergency. He'd do the same for a lost dog," Tam said.

"Maybe," Hope said, "but I think he likes you, not me. Don't you notice the way he watches every little thing you do?"

"He's an artist," Tam said. "Artists watch everybody and everything. Besides, if he likes me so much, why does he send Stewart to get me instead of coming himself? And why does he avoid me? I think he wants Stewart to keep me out of his hair."

"Maybe, but Luke says—"

Tam groaned. "Oh, no. Not you too. Does everybody I know have to go around quoting that man?"

"I thought you'd like to know," Hope said. "Luke says you're perfect for Stewart and Luke says if Stewart's got any sense at all he'll hang on to you."

"Luke said that?"

Hope nodded. "So I thought I would ask. . . ."

"You know more about this than I do," said Tam. "Luke didn't tell me and I sincerely hope nobody tells Stewart. I don't like being pushed at him like a vitamin pill. Promise you won't say a word."

Hope promised. Quickly.

On the ride home, Tam tried to find out if Stewart knew Luke's opinion, but Stewart mostly seemed glad to be back and apologetic for not being there when Mr. Brill appeared. He'd gone to Ohio unexpectedly on family business, he said, and stayed through Monday to report to the Haberson's Company headquarters. He said they liked to know how things were progressing at the mall.

Stewart looked almost as angry about Mr. Brill as Luke had. "Call me immediately," he said, "if you ever need help."

Tam promised.

"Too bad about your dress," he said. "Mrs. Warren said you fixed it up better than new and she showed me the blouse you painted. Mrs. Warren told me you had talent, but I didn't realize you could do things like that. I'm impressed. You'll have to show me the dress."

Tam glowed under his praise. He liked her work and wanted to see the dress. If Tam were a large cat, she would have purred loudly with pleasure.

The talk turned to Mrs. Warren's dinner and Tam assured him, when he asked, that both Dad and Hope had enjoyed themselves.

"Nice girl, Hope," Stewart said.

"Yes," said Tam.

After breakfast the next morning, Tam took the dress next door so Mrs. Warren could show it to Stewart when he came home from work. Let Mrs. Warren show him, Tam thought, so I won't feel like a kindergarten child showing my finger-painting.

Mrs. Warren must have told him quite a lot. Stewart was all admiration and enthusiasm that night when he picked her up. He wanted to know where she got the pattern, how she knew what colors to use, the whole story.

"I just know," she said. "I've always liked designing things. Once I thought about studying interior decorating, but it didn't work out."

"Are you serious about wanting to design?"

"As serious as I can be, under the circumstances. Food Mart doesn't have much designing to do, besides displays and signs. Painting the dress was like breathing—that easy and much more fun. I really enjoyed it. I wish I could do more."

"Then why don't you?" he urged. "Get some silk blouses—three or four different ones. Paint them like you did Mrs. Warren's. You don't need many. Just a few samples. Then I'll take them around to two or three shops I know. I think when they see what you can do, they'll order some to sell."

"I can't," Tam said.

"Why not?"

"Nobody would buy them," she said, thinking it over.

"Leave that to me," said Stewart. "I'm a pretty good salesman when I've got something people want to buy."

Tam considered. "I can't. I don't have money to buy silk blouses. Mrs. Warren already had that white shirt and she gave me the dress. There's no way I can buy three or four silk blouses. It sounds terrific, but if I can't buy the blouses, I can't paint on them."

Stewart said, "I'll lend you the money."

"I couldn't take your money."

"Strictly business," he said. "Consider it a business investment. We'll draw it up nice and legal. You can pay me back when you sell your first order."

Tam was beginning to think this insane scheme might possibly work, but she was cautious. She said, "What happens if I don't sell any?"

"Then you'll pay me off in merchandise and I'll have Christmas presents for four lucky ladies," he said, laughing. "Don't worry about it. They will sell. Your biggest problem will be producing them fast enough to fill the orders. I'll take them around to a couple of friends of mine in the business, and you'll have more orders than you know what to do with. Luke says. . ."

Not Luke again, Tam thought, but she didn't say it. She said, "You and Luke have already talked this over?"

"It was his idea," Stewart said. "Mrs. Warren thought it was a good idea too. She says she'll go with you to buy the blouses, if you want her to. Your dad should be able to handle the bookkeeping. Luke says your dad knows all about that sort of thing. Mrs. Warren will help you shop, your dad can keep the books, and I'll do the selling. All you have to do is create beautiful clothes. Yes?"

"I don't know," Tam said slowly.

"Luke says he's never seen anything like them. He says you can't miss."

"All right. I'll do it," she decided, right there in the driveway, and suddenly she was determined to make it work. *Crazy. Impossible,* she thought. *I might regret it, but I'll do it. We'll do it.*

Chapter Eight

The business of painting silk blouses moved rapidly. They all caught the success bug.

Stewart sent them to a wholesale contact of his in Indianapolis, because they needed to get many of the same kind of blouse and only a wholesaler or manufacturer could offer that at reasonable cost.

Mrs. Warren consulted Tam about color and style, then took Tam's opinion about color and chose the style herself.

"We carry three qualities," said the short, round-faced wholesaler, "and seconds. If you want seconds, I'll make you a special price."

"How much?" asked Tam.

"No, thank you," said Mrs. Warren.

"But I might make a mistake. I can't paint on something perfect," argued Tam.

Mrs. Warren said, "Of course you can, dear," and bought six beautiful silk blouses in five luscious pastels and one in white. "If you want to do business with fine shops, you have to provide fine merchandise. Our clientele will be expecting luxury. Luke says. . ."

"Never mind."

Mrs. Warren brought paints and brushes over, explaining, "Luke says you should use acrylic paint, not oil, because acrylic dries faster and is more flexible on fabric. He says you can manage it if you work fast. He says he isn't going to use these and you might like to have them."

"Luke says. Luke says," muttered Tam under her breath.

"What, dear?"

Tam said, "Please tell Luke I said thank you." She knew better than to argue. She also had sense enough to do it his way.

Soon she was painting expertly, creating beautiful designs, and humming as she worked. *I never had so much fun,* she thought. *I told Stewart painting those clothes was like breathing, but it's better.*

She studied each blouse, then mixed the colors she felt, put a brush to them, and out came the flowers, flowing through her fingers like water through a pipe. Each blouse was a little different, but they all bore the distinct mark of her hand, identifiable immediately as hers.

In a week they were finished and hanging in the cleared hall closet. They looked so pretty there that Tam couldn't shut the closet door on the little cluster of flowers.

Stewart looked them over and nodded enthusiastically. "You need a name for this line," he said, "a label. Something like 'Fashions by Tam.'"

"Or 'Tamara's Silks'," suggested Mrs. Warren.

"It sounds like race horses," said Stewart. How about 'Floating Flowers'?"

"Water ballet," objected Mrs. Warren.

Dad said, on paper, that the poet Robert Frost had referred to butterflies as "flowers that fly." So how about "Tamara's Butterflies"? or just "Butterflies"?

" 'Butterflies?' Perfect!" pronounced Mrs. Warren.

"I like it," said Stewart.

"Me too," echoed Tam. "I didn't know you read Robert Frost, Dad."

"No," said Dad and wrote, "Luke."

"Of course. I should have known," said Tam.

Tam painted labels on silk ribbon and Mrs. Warren sewed them in. They could order professional labels later.

Dad was in his element, delighted to prove himself valuable. Using his book-keeping, he established a tentative wholesale price, which he doubled to a suggested retail price.

Tam gasped at the retail price. "I could buy a whole outfit for that."

"Not a designer original," Mrs. Warren said. "I think it's quite reasonable."

"We'll know soon enough when I take these samples around to a few buyers," said Stewart, taking her Butterflies, each meticulously ironed and encased in its own cleaner's bag from Mrs. Warren's collection. "Don't worry," he said, several times. "And don't ask. I'll let you know when I have orders. Don't worry."

That week Barb caught Tam humming at work, several times. "You're in love," Barb said.

"I am," Tam agreed. "I'm in love with painting silk blouses."

Barb shook her head. "You're in love with Stewart."

Tam laughed at that. "Be serious, Barb. Stewart's a friend."

"Friend!" Barb snorted. "Stewart's not a friend. He's a dream. Listen to Barbara. Grab him before some other girl gets him."

"That's a little cold-blooded," Tam said.

Barb said, "Not if he loves you."

"He doesn't," Tam said.

"Of course he does. And you love him. Look at you. You're a different person. I tell you that man is good for you."

She had a point. Tam was happier. Painting blouses was a joy. Dad was alert and more confident. Tam felt better and she knew she looked better.

Maybe Barb is right, Tam reflected. *Maybe I'm in love and don't know it.*

Stewart certainly had all the right ingredients for a dream come true. Did he love her? That didn't seem likely. But he did appear every night and always seemed glad to be with her. Perhaps he did love her, a little.

"I don't know, Barb," Tam said. "I thought if you were in love you'd know it. Bells ring or something."

"Don't believe that stuff," Barb said. "That's only in books."

Tam said, "I was in love once. In high school. I knew that time, no question. Fireworks went off every time we got near each other."

"You were a kid. Now you're a grown-up," Barb said. "It's different."

"I don't know," Tam said. To Barb she might be a different person, but parts of her were unchanged.

One part of me is caution, she thought. *I don't jump into things. The last thing I jumped into was Mr. Brill's car, and that had been a mistake. I wouldn't have jumped into the blouse business, but I was pushed. Besides, I had already tried painting and knew she could do it.*

Another part of her was stubbornness that made her keep going when anyone else would say she had already been beaten.

Practicality was another part, useful when her pride wouldn't let her quit.

The odd part, the part that didn't belong with the rest, the part Barb refused to recognize, was romance. Barb said to forget romance, but she didn't want to. She needed to believe that love is possible—if not for her, then for other people.

Barb would say that was dumb, that Tam should grab what she could, but Barb's love had gone bitter. If Tam couldn't find real love for herself, she was sure she would know it. She told Barb that then, and the next night, and the night after that.

Barb kept telling Tam how handsome and successful Stewart was, how smooth his manners were, how good they looked together. She said Tam would be a fine wife for a rising executive.

That last point was debatable, Tam thought. Stewart was too classy for her, too sophisticated. Still, with more time and more money she might look classy too.

Maybe not, she thought. *I'd spend that time and money doing something I really want to do. Other girls can paint their toenails and embroider rosebuds on their underwear. If I had the time and money, I'd study art. I'd paint or design or. . . .*

Hope never stayed around to listen when Barb started teasing Tam. To Tam it seemed reasonable that Hope wanted to avoid such scenes. Some other things seemed less reasonable.

For example, some nights Stewart would ask Hope if he and Tam could drop her off on the way home, although Hope lived in the opposite direction.

Irrelevant. Stewart was generous with his car.

Hope always said she'd rather walk, that she needed the exercise. She'd walk past the car and out of the lot, Stewart watching her go. Something about this felt wrong, but Tam couldn't put her finger on it, so she tried to shrug it off.

Sunday morning Mrs. Warren assumed Dad and Tam would go to church with them. Dad didn't put up a fuss. He preened himself in the blue blazer and Tam wafted around in her designer silk dress. . .an original Butterfly. The original Butterfly.

At church, Mrs. Warren left them to go down to her primary class, and they went upstairs to join Hope in Adult Bible Study Class. Dad liked to sit on the aisle, any aisle, so Tam hung back to sit with him. Luke shuffled in first, next to Hope, followed by Stewart and Tam, and then Dad. It crossed Tam's mind that Luke had arranged again to keep Hope to himself and away from Stewart. Possible? Definitely!

Tam hadn't attended Sunday school in years, since youth group had met in this room on Sunday nights before adjourning to the basement for games and ham salad sandwiches over those years, and an unknown number of chocolate cupcakes.

This adult class was following Paul's journeys, which Tam found fascinating. Dad seemed interested too. Perhaps he would come again.

After class they meandered into the sanctuary, stopping every few feet to talk to acquaintances. Dad and Mrs. Warren sat in back and Hope led the rest to the front. This time Tam watched and, sure enough, Luke arranged things so they sat in the same order until Hope traded Luke places to sit by Tam. Tam wondered if Hope realized how efficiently Luke was keeping her to himself.

Let him sit by her, Tam thought wryly. *Let him see what good it does him. When church starts, she won't even know he's there.*

At the Call to Worship, Tam saw that Hope had begun to close out distractions. A penny hit the floor nearby and a fan buzzed faintly, but Hope was oblivious to those noises.

Stewart seemed as absorbed as Hope. Was Luke? Tam leaned a bit forward and stretched to see his face, half expecting to meet his eyes. They were closed. His face was softer than usual, more peaceful. Seeing him this way, Tam realized how stern and intense he often was.

One of Tam's old friends with whom she had lost touch, Marg, sang a solo, like she often had when they were in school together. Her voice was rich and full, improved with time, and as Tam listened, time ran backward. Marg and Tam were kids again, with Ben in the pew watching Marg, and Robert next to Tam. Marg poured her feelings into the air. The music stopped in the hushed sanctuary and a man across the aisle breathed a soft amen. Tam turned to share with Robert. But it wasn't Robert. It was Stewart, and she covered her face with her hands.

If I had known, she thought, *I would not have come.*

Squaring her shoulders, she pulled her hands down, away from her face and folded them tightly in her lap. She hoped Stewart hadn't noticed.

She would be more wary. She would protect herself by keeping joy at a distance so joy would not open the gates to old sorrow. *Tougher is better. Use your mind,* she said to herself. *Keep your heart out of this. Concentrate.*

She concentrated on the Road to Emmaus in the stained glass window, glowing in the sunlight above Luke's head and lost herself in the vibrant colors again.

They were walking, she and another traveler, and a Stranger joined them. They told Him about Jesus. He told them more than they knew about God, more than the rabbis in the temple knew. Tam wondered at His wisdom, but she did not guess who He was.

That's where her imagination always ended. She never got to the village, never reached the part where her eyes were opened and she suddenly knew Him. Would she have recognized Him, if she had been on that ordinary dusty road from one town to the next?

People's heads were bowed and she realized that Mr. Moore was closing his sermon with prayer. *Another Sunday,* she thought, *without finding the key to understanding.*

Another hymn and the benediction, and they filed out. In the aisle and at the door, on the outside steps and on the sidewalk in front of the church, people greeted each other and chatted. Tam wanted out. She needed time to think.

Dad and Mrs. Warren met friends. Hope dashed away to catch a girl she knew from college. Stewart stood involved in conversation about building supplies with Ben, Marg's husband.

Tam found a place apart from smiles and handshakes, under the little maple between the sidewalk and the curb. She waited there silently.

"You've had a long morning." Luke's deep voice startled her. She hadn't seen him approach.

"What?" she said.

"I was saying that you've had a long morning. A difficult morning."

Tam studied her shoes. "Yes," she murmured. "I was thinking of other things."

"Like the stained glass window?" he asked.

Tam had thought no one saw.

"And the solo?" he went on.

Tam abruptly turned her back to him and his words. She shut him out to protect herself. Luke had a way of going directly to her hidden hurts and uncovering them. He knew too much.

"Tell me," he ordered, gently.

She shook her head, standing with her back to him until Stewart returned with Hope. She wanted to walk home alone. Luke was right; she'd had a long morning.

That was the trouble with Luke, she decided. He was always right. He'd be easier to like if he weren't so nosy, so perceptive.

Hope walked next to Tam, keeping the silence.

Hope? Was Hope going to Mrs. Warren's again? Luke was determined to be with her!

Fine, thought Tam. *Let Hope spend the afternoon being the object of Luke's attention. She can have my share. I just want to go home.*

"Only a light lunch," Mrs. Warren was saying. "I know you like to eat conservatively."

"No," smiled Dad, accepting for himself and Tam. He did things like that, forgot she was a grown-up person who might have ideas of her own, instead of just a daughter.

"Okay, Tam?" asked Mrs. Warren.

Tam smiled and nodded. What else could she do?

Mrs. Warren's light buffet lunch was light only in color: pale pink cold cuts, salads of pastel greens and yellows, pink gelatin, beige breads, and homemade bread-and-butter pickles in a color-coordinated pale grayed-green dish. It looked cool and inviting. If Tam could have eaten alone, if she were hungry, she would have enjoyed it.

She wasn't hungry but couldn't say so. Instead she chose foods which took lots of plate space, but little stomach space.

One thin slice of ham covered half her plate. If she did it right, using her fork to cut it into meticulously measured little bites, she could make a slice of ham last for at least ten minutes, maybe more. Carrot sticks and celery stuffed with cream cheese were good time wasters and, artistically arranged on her plate, they took up lots of space. The rest of the plate was covered by lettuce, a wonderful space waster.

Selecting took a long time. That was the point. Time spent selecting was time she didn't have to spend sitting, arranging and rearranging carrot sticks. It was also easier to avoid talking to people at the buffet table than at her place. Then she sat.

Suddenly Stewart said, "What about you, Tam?"

Everybody waited for her answer, but she didn't know the question. She blinked.

"Of course she does," said Mrs. Warren.

Tam nodded. It must be the right answer. Conversation resumed and Tam returned to her lettuce.

Of course I do what? She wished she had been listening. She peeked at her watch. One thirty. At two she could excuse herself to go get ready for work. She could go now. She rose to carry her plate into the kitchen.

Mrs. Warren took it. "You go on upstairs, dear. I'll take care of the dishes."

"I have to go to work," Tam said vaguely.

"I know. You'd better look right away if you want to see them, and I know you do. Luke?" Mrs. Warren handed Tam over to Luke, who said, "Stewart?" and handed Tam over to Stewart. She felt like one of the plates.

Mrs. Warren said, "Come on, Hope, if you want to see Luke's paintings," and Hope rose also.

Stewart followed Tam to the foot of the attic steps, where they filed behind Luke up to the studio.

Ironic, Tam thought. *If they had asked me yesterday, I'd have jumped at the chance to see his paintings. I'd like to know if he's any good and what kinds of subjects attract this man who sees through people and knows too much.*

Today though, she didn't want to be within fifty feet of Luke. Bad enough to have him watching her in church and prying into her thoughts afterward without having to look at his pictures and make polite compliments. *Suppose he is awful,* she thought. *What will I say?*

She checked her watch again.

Luke opened the attic door and flipped the light switch. He waited there to catch their initial reactions. Tam knew that trick. She'd done it herself to see people's true feelings in that split second before they drop polite masks over their faces. He wouldn't catch her off guard. Not again.

But he did.

The power of his work sprang out at her as she came through the door. Canvas after canvas spoke of passion and pain as clearly as if they had shouted. More clearly. They lined the walls and leaned in groups against the upright beams—dozens of them, dozens of shouts of pain and cries of sorrow, condensed emotion, solid, almost tangible.

Tam raised her hand to ward it off. Her eyes stung with it and her throat ached. It pulled her closer, to stand before one after another of the paintings. Absorbed, she forgot Luke and Stewart and Hope. She moved slowly down the rows, studying each piece.

As she moved, she felt the sorrow in the paintings gradually give way to anger. An undercurrent in some of the paintings, anger surged to dominance in others. A few were pure rage made graphic in brush strokes. These frightened her. She backed away.

Luke's hand on her arm stopped her before she backed into an easel. His eyes were anxious. She searched them for the fury she saw in his work, but there was none. What she saw there was something she couldn't read. Sorrow? Not quite. What?

Luke led her to the other side of the attic where more canvasses crowded floor and walls. These were different. By another artist, she guessed at first, until closer inspection showed the swift power of Luke's hand. Here was no anger. Sorrow still, and pain, but the shout had become only a murmur. Here was calm.

Smoother brush strokes, gentler shapes, and a softer palette with subtler transitions between colors made peace with the power behind the hand. There were faces here, as there were on the other side of the attic, but these were not twisted. There were landscapes here, with trees and streams instead of the torn and blackened ruins in the other pictures. It was relief from the anger and pain. Here was peace and comfort, and she stood before them, opening her heart to them, feeling them spread comfort on her own spirit.

"Tam?" Mrs. Warren called from the bottom of the stairs. "Tam, you have to go. It's after two."

Already? She had just come up the stairs. "Coming," Tam called.

She looked around for Stewart and Hope, but they had gone. She'd been so engrossed in Luke's work that she was unaware of anything else.

And she hadn't seen all the paintings. Under the dormer window was another stack. She couldn't resist a fast look before she left. She put her hand on the corner of the first one in the stack to turn it so she could see it.

"No!" barked Luke.

Tam froze, her hand still on the canvas.

"No," he said, in apologetic gentleness, "Not those."

She took her hand away. "Sorry," she said.

"No, don't be."

"They're wonderful. Thank you." She reached out to touch the hand that created those paintings. He closed her small hand in his two large ones.

"Tam," called Mrs. Warren again.

He opened his hands as if releasing a butterfly and Tam pulled her hand away, unable to break the gaze that bound her to him. Then she shut her eyes and turned abruptly, hurrying down the stairs and out, calling her thanks to Mrs. Warren as she ran.

Stewart was waiting with the engine running when she had rushed into work clothes and out to the car. She hopped in and slid low in the seat to catch her breath. Luke's paintings had taken her by surprise and she was profoundly moved by the depth of them.

Stewart said, "Luke's a pretty good artist."

She said, "He's wonderful."

Stewart laughed. "I told you he was," he said. "Why are you surprised?"

"I guess I didn't expect quite that much. I had no idea he felt so much sorrow and anger."

Stewart said, "It's the war, partly, I guess. None of us are the same after we see buddies blown to bits and innocent people destroyed. He never talks about it, but I know he hasn't forgotten. And of course, his wife is part of it."

"His wife?" Something lurched in Tam's chest. She swallowed and said, "I didn't know he was married."

"No, you wouldn't," Stewart said. "He never mentions her. She died in a car accident while he was overseas. By the time the news reached him, she'd been dead and buried more than a week. He never shed a tear, not then. Just went out and killed as many soldiers as he could for the next three days. Dived into them like he didn't care if he lived or died. That's how we got trapped and knocked out of action for a while.

"He carried me out of there. I never could have made it if he hadn't. By the time they decided we were well enough to send back to the front lines, the fighting had stopped and they didn't need us anymore."

"So you came home together," Tam prompted.

"Yes."

"What about his family?" Tam asked.

"Dead."

"Oh."

They rode in silence for a while, each deep in private thoughts. Tam's went back to the paintings. She understood now. The anger must have come before the sorrow, not the other way, as she had first thought. She was misled by the order in which she'd seen them. The peaceful ones must have been painted first, before the troubles, although the technique in those was so far advanced from the others and the touch so much surer that Tam had felt certain they were painted afterward.

Stewart said, "The angry paintings, then the sad ones, were done in the hospital and when he came home to his wife's grave. The other ones, the quiet ones, were painted after he met Jesus."

After he met Jesus. Did Jesus do that—change ferocious violence and unbearable pain to peace? He must have. Tam had seen the evidence. All her life she had heard of the power of God to change men's lives, but this was the first time she had actually seen it for herself.

Luke's paintings told their story. The fury gave way to grief and then to misery. She had seen the transitions. The other paintings were entirely different, with no transition. Changed totally.

Traces of sorrow remained. She'd seen that. But the sorrow was no longer dominant. It was present, but it was subdued. Not tightly controlled like the tears of a man refusing to cry. Eased. Acknowledged and eased.

"Is that what Luke says? That it changed after he met Jesus?" she asked.

Stewart nodded. "That's what Luke says."

Chapter Nine

Barb was wild that night, heckling co-workers and customers alike. Tam recognized this mood and knew Barb was working off tension.

"What's wrong?" asked Tam.

"Nothing," Barb snapped.

"None of your business," she said when Tam asked again.

"Nothing I can't handle," she said the third time, but this time she answered more gently. Tam asked again.

"My daughter," Barb said. "Sara wouldn't eat supper and cried when I left for work. That's not like her." Barb's sister thought it was just a mood, but Barb didn't agree and said she'd feel better if she were home, but she couldn't afford to lose the work hours.

"Your sister will know what to do," Tam said. "Phone home at the break. If you want to go home then, go. It's a slow night. Vickie and I can manage."

Barb was calmer after that, but tighter. She had started out laughing, letting off steam in play. Now her play got rougher. If Hope had been there, Hope would have been miserable.

At break, Barb learned Sara had a fever, but her sister said children often have light fevers that disappear as mysteriously as they begin. If the fever went up, she'd call the doctor. Barb might as well stay at work.

Barb stopped playing.

At 10:58 Barb left the register for the back room, pulling off her smock as she went through beauty and hygiene. Going to punch out, Tam met Barb hurrying to the front door.

"Let us take you home," Tam offered. "Stewart won't mind. Wait for me out front. I'll hurry." Without waiting for an answer, Tam dashed to punch out.

On her way up front, Tam saw Barbara and Mack near the office arguing angrily. Mack was pulling at Barb's smock, trying to snatch it from her hands. Barb clutched it tightly, pulling toward the exit. She jerked the smock. Tam heard the rip of fabric and the thunk of plastic hitting the floor. A bottle of aspirin lay there between them. Mack bent down and picked it up. He held it close to Barbara's face and leaned his own face closer.

His voice was angry, but too low for Tam to understand the words. She could guess. Barb had hidden the aspirin in the pocket of the smock, like the gum, and Mack had caught her, tonight of all nights.

Barb argued, red-faced, but Mack turned his back and left her standing with the torn smock dangling from her fingers. She turned abruptly, stamped to the door, and was outside before Tam caught her.

"What happened?" Tam asked.

Barb jerked out of Tam's grasp. "He fired me."

"Are you sure?" Tam said. "Maybe he's just mad."

Barb said, "I'm sure. He doesn't want me back, not even to pick up my pay. Would you. . ."

"Sure. I'll pick it up and bring it to you," said Tam, "but did you apologize? Did you tell him you're upset about your daughter? Did you offer to pay for the aspirin? Did you. . ."

Tam knew by the set of Barb's jaw that arguing was useless. Barb wanted to go home.

In Stewart's car Barb bumped along in the cramped back seat in tight-lipped silence. Her face was ashen. She did not cry.

At her apartment she squeezed out before Tam could lean the seat forward. "Thanks," she said, rushing off.

"I'll call you," Tam shouted after her.

Barb waved her hand to signify that she had heard, and disappeared into the dark building.

"Thanks for taking her home," Tam said to Stewart, and explained what had happened. Together they sorted through the few possibilities, trying to find a way to help. Tam could try to get Mack to let her come back. Stewart could see if he could find her a job. They'd offer to help, especially if Sara was worse in the morning.

That's all they could think of, except, Stewart said, to pray. Sitting in the driveway, Stewart held Tam's hand and they bowed their heads together asking God's help for Barbara and her daughter.

Tam wondered what good her little prayer would do, since she was not on close terms with God. But Stewart was. God would listen to him, she thought, and she felt better.

"Thanks for listening," she said. She gave his hand a little squeeze and let go. "And thanks for caring about Barbara. You're a good friend."

Stewart looked at Tam oddly and took her hand again. "Is that what I am? A good friend? I thought I was more than that."

She stared at him, slowly comprehending.

He saw her confusion and chuckled.

"Don't laugh at me," she said.

"I can't help it," he said. "You're funny. You really never believed I might be interested in you, did you? I drive you home every night and spend my free time helping you get started in business so you can do something you enjoy for a change. I sit next to you in church and walk you home and you think I am nothing more than a friend. Do you think I do this for every pretty girl I meet?"

Tam said nothing, confused.

Stewart went on, "You do, don't you! Only, you don't think you're pretty. Luke said that but I didn't believe it. I've seen so many girls who pretended they were modest that I didn't recognize the real thing when I saw it. You don't realize how attractive you are." With his free hand he traced the side of her cheek. "For your information, Miss Tamara, you're a very attractive young lady and I have been more than interested in you for a long time. Come here, pretty girl."

He leaned closer. His lips brushed her forehead and then, tilting her face up to meet his, he kissed her lightly on the lips. He leaned back a little to study her face. Then he opened the door and came around the car to let her out.

Somehow she got into the house without letting him see her face again. Before she let him see her turmoil, she had to understand it herself. She shut the door tightly behind her and leaned on it, letting out a long, slow breath.

She had never imagined. Barb had been teasing her for weeks and she never seriously thought it was possible that Barb could be right. It still didn't make sense. Why would Stewart—polished, gorgeous, successful Stewart—be attracted to Tam?

A thousand girls would jump at the chance to go out with him. Look at the way they all reacted when they met him. She herself had stammered and stumbled like a child. Barbara and Vickie had stopped in their tracks. Even Hope, with her silky hair and college freshness, had been fascinated. The man had everything.

Tam had nothing to offer him. She took quick inventory: Grace? Wit? Style? Don't be silly, she said to herself. Education? Social connection? Zero. Personality? She wasn't sure she still had one. Good looks? Definitely not, no matter what he said.

How about modesty? *No,* she thought, *just honesty.*

On the other hand, she thought, *I'm not a total waste of protoplasm. I'm a hard worker. I have some art talent. I can make a small income go a long way. And I don't cry easily, although sometimes I'm not as tough as I'd like to believe.*

I like dogs and children. And birds. What more could a handsome man like Stewart want?

Be serious.

Tam had tea with Dad and told him about Barb and tucked him in for the night. He was in a strange mood, she thought—very mysterious. He seemed to know something she didn't and he wasn't telling. She asked if anything was wrong, but he passed it off with a funny grin. She shrugged and let it go. If it was important, it would come out soon. For a man with speech problems, he had a hard time keeping secrets. Besides, she had her own secrets.

When he was in bed, she returned for another cup of tea, and turning the ceiling light out, sat in the dim kitchen, listening to the refrigerator hum and letting her tangled feelings unravel.

Stewart seemed sincere when he said she was pretty, but she knew she wasn't. Perhaps pretty to him meant something other than it meant to Tam. Perhaps to him all girls were pretty.

Luke had said she didn't think she was pretty and he was right. He knew because he saw her the way she saw herself. He would. He had an artist's eye. He wouldn't miss the sprinkling of gray in her dark hair nor the purple ink stains on her hands. He wouldn't dismiss her thinness as ethereal nor her short stature as cute. He would register the worn sneakers and the dismal cottons she wore day after day, except on Sundays, when she blossomed in silk.

Still, Stewart had said she was pretty, and he'd kissed her. Not a passionate embrace, it's true, but a kiss. Two.

What would Luke say about that?

Tam knew what Barbara would say. She'd already heard it.

And what did Tam say? That sitting in the open car with a picture-book hero holding her hand and kissing her lightly on the forehead and lips was romantic. She'd do it again, if she could. She would definitely do it again.

Why not?

If Stewart wanted to kiss her and drive her around, who was she to question it? *Enjoy it,* she told herself. *Don't question a gift like this. Accept it.*

When she went to bed, she didn't look to see if the light was on in the attic next door. She almost did, out of habit, but she caught herself. She didn't want to think about Luke up there anymore. She wanted to think about Stewart and the kiss in the car.

She closed her eyes and tried to feel the kiss again. Nothing. She tried again, this time going back to the prayer and reliving the conversation, working up to the kiss.

No use. Images of Luke's canvasses crowded into her mind. She shut her eyes tighter to erase them. Behind her lids, Luke's rage and grief cried out in passionate colors. Very well then, if she could not shut out his paintings, she would select a particular one to remember. A peaceful one.

In her mind she ranged through the collection of peaceful canvasses, settling on one that had particularly attracted her—a landscape, with a country road next to a meandering stream. The scene was familiar. Oh, of course. It was like the stained glass window in church—the "Road to Emmaus."

The road beckoned and she wandered down it. A Stranger met her and walked with her and they talked. She didn't recognize Him, even in the dream.

❧

Monday she spent the morning catching up on the work she hadn't done the week before. It busied her and that was good, because if she stopped to think, she might have frightened herself out of her resolve to enjoy Stewart's company. This was one of the days he planned to contact a potential buyer for her Butterflies. Between hoping for a sale and trying not to think about Stewart, she was torn in two directions. She needed to keep busy.

She called Barb, who was feeling both better and worse. Sara had chicken pox, which was unpleasant but not terrible. The doctor said it was good thing she hadn't given Sara aspirin, since that might have caused serious complications.

Tam didn't point out that of all nights for her to be caught stealing, that was the right night because it kept her from accidentally harming Sara. She did ask if Barb had reconsidered apologizing.

She had. She had telephoned but Mack wouldn't listen. Tam had no more ideas. All she could give was sympathy and encouragement. Tomorrow she'd do what Mrs. Warren would have done—take Barb a casserole. It couldn't hurt.

Stewart asked about Barb when he picked Tam up from work. He also wanted to know if Tam would enjoy dinner in a restaurant with him at, say, seven the next evening. Tam would, but checked with Dad to see if he objected to eating alone. He didn't seem pleased, but he didn't object.

When Stewart came for her, Dad was waiting in the kitchen for Luke, who had promised him a game of chess. Dad hardly looked up as they left, not even to tell them to have a good time.

They went to Chez Raoul, the poshest place within twenty miles. Stewart said it was the only place stylish enough for Tam's silk dress. It was so stylish that Tam couldn't read the menu. It was in French, six pages of it. Tam didn't recognize, and couldn't find, chicken. She also couldn't order by picking the cheapest thing on the menu because her copy had no prices. She let Stewart order.

"Have you been here before?" he asked, when he and the waiter had decided what Tam would eat.

"Not since it was Napoli's Pizza Palace," she said. "It looks different with tablecloths."

Napoli wouldn't have recognized the old place. Chez Raoul was dark, lit by candles. As her eyes adjusted to the dimness, she squinted at the pictures on the walls. She couldn't see them. From the darkest corner, behind what seemed to be an enormous blue chicken, came piano music. The player must be blind, she thought. Who else would be able to find the keys?

"What do you think of the place?" Stewart asked.

"Very romantic," she said, twisting her napkin.

"That's the idea." He pried one of her hands away from the napkin and spread the hand, palm down, on the corner of the table. In the darkness the purple ink on her fingers was barely visible. He traced each finger with his own, slowly, and then covered her hand with his hand. She watched.

When dinner arrived, she slid her hand off the table and picked up her fork. In the dark, she could distinguish lighter and darker lumps, largish ones, in some kind of sauce.

"What is it?" she asked.

"Poulet en Cocotte a la Paysanne," said Stewart.

She stirred it about, cautiously, and took a very tiny taste, then a bigger taste. "Mmmm," she said. "Delicious. I'm so glad you did the ordering. I'd probably have gotten something ordinary, like chicken."

"It is chicken. Poulet is French for chicken."

"Oh. It's delicious."

They ate slowly. Stewart talked of many things: his family in Ohio, the job, his plans, many things. She listened, thinking he was easy to listen to.

They selected desserts from the dessert cart—a napoleon for Tam, because she especially like them, and a strawberry tart for Stewart. Then she had tea; he had coffee. They dawdled over the drinks, making playful conversation. She forgot her nerves and had a wonderful time. Robert had never taken her to a place like this.

We were too young then to appreciate it, she thought. *Now I am exactly the right age for Chez Raoul.*

She was exactly the right age to be kissed in the moonlight too. When he leaned toward her and slid his arm around her shoulders she was nervous, but she lifted her lips to meet his in a long, lingering gentle kiss. And another. She sighed and leaned against his shoulder, filling her nose with the scent of his shaving lotion.

"Thank you," she whispered. "It was wonderful."

"Yes, it was," he whispered, lowering his lips for another kiss.

"The dinner, I mean," she said, pulling back.

"That too," he said, and kissed her again.

He would have kissed her at the door too if she'd stood still long enough, or if Dad hadn't been sitting at the kitchen table waiting, with all the lights on, including the one over the door. Instead she said a quick good night and watched him go off to his own door.

At that moment she thought she saw a shadow move at the attic window, just flicker across it and vanish. She peered more closely, but saw nothing in the attic light.

Did she have a nice time, Dad asked her, and where's the tea? She might have been coming home from work, no more, instead of returning from the first real date she'd had in years. Here she was with news to share, and no listener. *Wait,* she thought. *Just wait until he wants to show me some new bird!*

In the morning Dad was indifferent to her adventure and Mrs. Warren was entirely absent. The excitement cooled and she was left with doubts to mull over alone.

Halfway to work she remembered the casserole she had meant to make for Barbara and was immediately stricken with remorse. She'd better phone at break.

Hope worked Wednesday, which was unusual. Mack was filling in Barb's hours with part-timers. Hope was glad to have the extra time so when Mack called her she jumped at the chance for more pay. College is expensive.

"I wish I didn't feel like I was taking food from Barbara's mouth," Hope said, punching in.

"You are," said Vickie, who was not in a forgiving mood. "You got her fired. If you hadn't told Mack on her, she'd be at that register tonight, instead of you."

Hope's mouth dropped open. "I didn't. I wouldn't do that."

"Not much you wouldn't," said Vickie.

Hope looked for help to Tam, who shook her head slightly to indicate the futility of arguing. It would only make things worse.

The three worked next to each other in strained silence for almost an hour before Hope dropped a closed sign onto her conveyor counter. She said, "That's all. I can't stand it anymore."

"What are you going to do?" asked Vickie.

"Quit," said Hope. "Then Mack will have to call Barbara back."

"Good idea," said Vickie.

Tam said, "Don't do it. It won't work. He'll hire somebody new and you'll be out of a job."

"Good," said Vickie.

"I have to do something," Hope said.

"I'll talk to Mack," said Tam. "Maybe he'll change his mind." She didn't intend to say that. The words flew out of her mouth before her brain could stop them. She had no idea how to get Mack to listen, but she had said too much to back out.

Hope went with her to the office, and then Vickie dropped a closed sign on her aisle and followed.

The first thing Mack said when he saw all three at the office was, "No registers are open."

"We'll open as soon as you talk with us," Tam said.

He said, "If it's about Barbara, I don't want to hear it. You three knew she was stealing and covered up for her. Now you come around wanting favors. Forget it."

"We do want a favor," Tam said. "We want you to give her another chance."

Mack snorted. "Why? So she can steal more? That stuff costs money. Little by little she costs this store a fortune."

"How much?" asked Tam.

"Huh? Oh, I don't know exactly. I'd have to figure it out. It's not just one bottle of aspirin, you know." Mack's crossed arms and stubborn jaw indicated little mercy.

"I know. You figure it out and tell me how much. I'll pay for it," Tam said, setting her jaw as stubbornly as Mack's.

"You can't," said Hope.

"I will. Mack, you figure it out and take it out of my pay every week, ten dollars, until it's all paid. How's that?" Tam folded her arms to match Mack's folded arms.

"It's no good," said Mack. "She'll run you into the poor house."

"Not if you tell her I have to pay for whatever she takes," Tam argued. "She knows I can't afford it."

Mack thought it over. "It might work at that. Barb's a good checker and it's worth a try. I'll tell you what. We'll try it for a month and see how it goes. If she doesn't rack up more debt, she can stay. I hate to do this to you though, Tam."

"You're not. It's my own choice." Tam was firm in that.

"I hope she appreciates it," he said.

Tam smiled and put her hand out to shake on the deal. Barb wouldn't have to appreciate it to make Tam happy. All she had to do was get her job back and hang onto it. That was worth ten dollars a week to Tam.

Hope offered to help pay, but Tam didn't want her to. Tam had made the deal, so she intended to be the one to stick to it.

"You were terrific," said Hope, out of Mack's hearing.

Tam said, "Not really. I didn't know I was going to say that."

Vickie turned on Hope with scathing sarcasm. "You weren't so terrific, Hope. If you and your God are as close as you claim, why didn't you ask Him to do something about Barb's job?'

Hope smiled. "I did."

"So?" said Vickie.

"So He sent Tam," she said, and smiled at Tam's blank look.

Crazy, Tam thought. *I went to the office because I decided to, not because I was sent. But where did I get the words that made Mack take Barb back? Not from me. I was as surprised to hear it as anybody. Could Hope be right?*

Vickie had the last word. She said, "Barb's not going to like this." Tam hoped she was wrong.

She was. The next night Barb was early. She was huffy and stand-offish, letting on that she was doing Mack a favor by coming back, but they all knew she was glad to be there. Mack ignored her and after a while she stopped trying to cover her feelings.

At break Barb wanted to thank Tam, saying, "I never thought a friend would do that for me. I'll pay back every penny. Honest."

Tam laughed, "You'd better. I'm only doing this because I can't work here without you to pester me."

Barb put out her hand to Hope in apology. She was sorry, she said, about the way she had acted in the past. She had accused Hope of getting her fired, but now she knew that wasn't true and wanted to apologize. "Friends?" she asked.

"Friends," said Hope.

"I might even go to that church of yours some time," Barb ventured, and laughed in embarrassment, then scooted out the door before she exposed more softness.

"Look what you did," said Hope to Tam.

"I can't claim credit for that. I just did what came to mind," Tam said. "Ten dollars isn't such a big deal, if you think about it."

"If you can see that, you should be able to understand why God gave His Son for us," Hope said. "He's the best Friend we have."

"Then why don't I feel what you feel in church?" Tam asked. "You get more out of it than I do. You seem to soak that stuff up. My mind wanders. I think about all kinds of things. I hear the songs and the prayers, but they're not inside me. Not the way they are with you."

"That's because Jesus isn't in your heart yet. Once you let Him in, your whole life is different."

Tam said, "I don't think I really know Him. I can't seem to find Him."

Hope said, "Just ask. That's all. He's right there waiting for you. Would you like to pray together?"

"No," Tam said, feeling awkward.

"Then I'll pray for you," Hope said. "I'll keep on praying till I know you've found Him."

Tam didn't answer. She didn't like the idea of being prayed for. It made her uncomfortable. The conversation had gone too far.

After that she tended to avoid Hope. Too many feelings were out in the open and Tam needed space to think in. The others felt that way too. They were much less social than usual. Even Mack kept his distance, sensitive to feelings unexpressed, although his employees would never believe he cared about anything but groceries.

Around eight Stewart came in. He had never come early before, so immediately Tam knew something was wrong.

"Get your things," he said. "I'll tell Mack you're leaving."

In the car, Tam said, "What's the matter?"

"Your dad's had another stroke," Stewart said. "He'll be all right, we think, although it's too soon to tell. We knew you'd want to be with him."

Tam wanted to scream and cry and kick. Instead she sat calmly listening to the details and asking sensible questions. She might have been discussing a register error for all the emotion she showed on the surface.

Stewart talked quietly as he drove to the hospital, explaining the details and re-explaining when she asked him the same questions again and again.

Dad had been watching the bird feeder when the squirrels came after the sunflower seeds. Mrs. Warren saw him charge off the porch with a broom, flailing at the squirrels and shouting. Then he dropped the broom and clutched at the arm which had held it and which now hung lifeless by his side. He leaned against the pole.

Mrs. Warren ran to catch him, shouting for Luke as she ran. Luke carried him into the house and made him comfortable while Mrs. Warren called the ambulance and sent Stewart to Food Mart. They would stay with him, Stewart reassured Tam, all the way to the hospital, and were probably there already.

Luke, Tam thought, and was grateful. Luke could take care of things. He and Mrs. Warren were as good as you could get in emergencies.

At the end of the third telling, Stewart pulled up to the emergency entrance. Tam jumped out, leaving him to park the car.

I know this place, she thought, hesitating at the uninhabited information desk. *This is the place that took my mother and the place where my father left his career.* She shuddered involuntarily. She looked anxiously around the empty area and wondered where everyone was.

Looking for somebody, anybody, who knew where her father was, Tam dashed past the desk to the waiting room and into Mrs. Warren's arms.

"It's all right," Mrs. Warren crooned. "It's all right. He's in there and the doctor is with him."

"How is he?" Tam asked.

"We don't know yet. We'll have to wait for the doctor's report. Luke's with him. They wanted him to wait out here but he insisted on seeing that they took your dad immediately."

Luke could do that, Tam thought. *If I tried it they would flick me away like a gnat, but it's hard to flick him away.*

A nurse came to get Tam then, to ask questions for those papers they always fill out. By the time the blanks were filled in, Stewart was there, and Luke, and there was nothing at all to do.

Except pray, Mrs. Warren reminded Tam. As the four linked hands in the waiting room, Tam felt the strength of their faith stand strong around her.

Tam's own faith was a blade of grass in high wind, but these friends had firmness of faith that shielded that little blade of grass so it stood in the storm.

They settled in to wait. How long was it before the doctor came out? Tam couldn't guess. It might have been an hour and a half, which is what the chrome-rimmed clock above the door said, or it might have been ten hours, which is what her heart said. She and Luke rose to meet the doctor.

Doctor Thomas said, "He's had another stroke, but it's too early to assess the damage with any degree of accuracy. That will take several days. It would be my guess that the damage is less severe than the damage he suffered from the last stroke."

They would have to keep him under observation until they were reasonably certain there would be no immediate recurrence and his condition was stable. Then it was vital that therapy begin as soon as possible to help him regain use of his right side.

He was conscious, but extremely tired. Tam might see him before they took him up to Intensive Care, but only for a few minutes and only if she took care not to worry him.

She promised.

Lying on the gurney, hair and skin gray against the white sheet, he looked smaller than Tam remembered. More fragile.

She took his "good" hand and held it with steady pressure. "Doc Thomas says you're going to be okay," she said. "You caused a fuss, but it's all right now. I'll stay with you tonight. I won't go home until the sun comes up. I'll be right here. Okay?"

He tried to smile again and nodded and she knew it mattered to him that she would be there. He waved a wobbly good-bye as the orderlies wheeled him off to the intensive care unit.

"I'm going to stay," she told her friends. "He'll feel better knowing I'm here with him. You go on home."

They offered to stay, to sit with her, to bring supper, to get coffee. At last they agreed to go, leaving Tam in the glass-fronted ICU lounge, waiting alone for the sun to rise.

Chapter Ten

At two A.M. the ICU lounge of Graham Memorial Hospital was hollow-quiet. Aside from the occasional squeak of foam rubber soles passing by on polished floors and the regular click of the wall clock hand pouncing on the next minute, her own breathing was the only sound Tam heard.

The ancient magazines couldn't interest her in making Christmas wreaths of bread wrappers and Easter baskets of empty bleach bottles, not in August. The drinking fountain down the hall produced warm, iron-flavored fountain water, but she made several trips to taste it, not because she was thirsty, but because there was nothing else to do. When Dad was here last time, Tam's mother had knitted a whole sweater while she waited. *I should have learned how to knit,* Tam thought.

Tam's feet were cold in their sneakers. She pulled them up under her on the green plastic sofa. Air conditioning set for many visitors overcooled the deserted room. She curled into a ball, conserving the little warmth her lean body produced, and tried to go to sleep.

She wished she were not alone.

At six-thirty, visitors would be allowed to enter to sit with patients as they breakfasted. The sign on the door said so, but it didn't say that breakfast would probably be intravenous. Four and a half hours wasn't so long, Tam thought.

But she wished she were not alone.

She twisted into another position, laying her cheek against the back of the sofa. Maybe this way she would sleep.

She couldn't.

Dad was all right. He had to be. She refused to think of any other possibility. Concentrate on something else. Painted silk. She wondered if anybody would buy. Luke said they would. . .Luke said. . .

Think about work. Mack had let her go when Stewart came. That was nice of him. Tam would thank him tomorrow. . .today. . .when she went to work. Mack was nice about Barbara too. He told Barb straight what the deal was and why he was angry, and he did it without meanness. Some people can't do that. Everything's personal with them. Not Mack. He was willing to give Barb another chance. Barb couldn't ask more than that.

Of course, he wouldn't have been so generous if I hadn't promised to pay, thought Tam, *and I wouldn't have thought of it if Hope hadn't made me feel I should do something. Hope's as beautiful inside as she is outside,* she thought. *Like Stewart.*

Barb had apologized and had even hinted she might go to church. That was a change.

Luke should paint that, Tam thought. He painted his own change so clearly that she could feel it. *He should paint a change for Barb. Or for me.*

Tam longed for the peace reflected in Luke's work. She wanted what he had found and what Hope and Stewart and Mrs. Warren had.

Just ask, Hope had said, But. . .

"I thought you might want some company," said a deep voice from the doorway.

"Luke!"

"I can't work tonight anyway. Might as well come sit with you a while. Brought you a hamburger and a chocolate shake." He held out a little white bag.

"Thanks," Tam said. "I didn't know I was so hungry." She took a long drink of the shake and shivered. "Delicious," she said.

"Cold," he said, and left the room.

In a few minutes he was back with a blanket and a pillow, both welcome.

"Thank you," she said again, wondering where he had gotten them. "I say that to you pretty often. You always seem to be there when I need you."

"Yes," he said, simply. "Any news?"

"No."

He strode directly to and through the extra wide doors labeled "Authorized Personnel Only." Soon he was back with the news that Dad was sleeping and was no worse. Knowing this was a great relief, and Tam wondered why she hadn't thought of opening those doors to ask.

"How did you know to do that?" she asked.

"Do what?"

"Go in there and find out how Dad is," she said.

He shrugged. "One hospital is pretty much like another. If you want something, you have to ask for it."

"You should like Hope," she said.

"I don't understand," Luke said.

"Never mind," she mumbled. "It's hard to explain."

Without another word he sat next to her, filling the entire middle of the sofa and adding a turpentine tang to the air. He pulled off her sneakers, tucked the blanket around and under her cold feet, then pulled the wrapped feet onto his lap, where he massaged them firmly, warmly with one hand, as if he massaged her feet every night.

"Now explain," he said. "And take your time. We have all night."

So she told him about wanting to study art, about giving up that dream and settling for Food Mart. She told him about losing Robert and Mother, about fears of losing Dad, about being alone, and about trying to be tough when she wasn't tough at all.

He listened.

She poured out her whole heart to him, telling secrets she had hidden in her heart for years.

She hesitated.

He waited.

Then she told him about the "Road to Emmaus" and how she wanted whatever it was he and Stewart and Mrs. Warren and Hope had. "You know how to find it," she said, sitting straight up, dropping feet and blanket to the floor. "I saw it in your paintings. Hope said to just ask, but it isn't so easy."

"No," he said, almost smiling, "not for someone as stubborn as you are. It's hard to ask and you have to do it yourself, but you only have to ask once."

Luke prayed with her, supporting her with his strong faith as he had supported her with his strong arms another night when she was lost, until Tam could ask for the peace she wanted.

Then Luke talked quietly of the changes in his own life, letting Tam hear the hurt under his gruffness. As he spoke, she relaxed, safe with him, and when he lapsed into silence, she fell asleep against his shoulder.

He pulled her awake when the pink-smocked volunteer arrived at six-fifteen to make coffee and sit at the desk for visiting hour. Other visitors came in and Tam had barely enough time to splash water on her face and comb her hair before time to go in.

"Thank you, Luke," Tam said, again, and he nodded.

Dad looked better, but was docile, a sure sign he was not feeling well.

Luke took Tam home by way of the diner on the bypass, where he fed her pancakes and sausage. She said she wasn't hungry at all but she ate the whole stack.

"You need some sleep in your own bed," he said.

He pulled the beat-up van behind Stewart's car quietly, letting the neighborhood sleep, and eased out of his door, not quite shutting it. Tam eased out on her side, opening her own door. This was not Stewart.

"Wait," he whispered.

He let himself in Mrs. Warren's kitchen door and in a moment or two he returned with one of his canvasses, the one that reminded Tam of the "Road to Emmaus."

"Thank y—"

He put his fingers over her lips before she could finish it. He shook his head. She nodded and he smiled.

In the deserted house she put Luke's painting on the bookcase, where she could see it from her pillow. She lay there looking at the picture, allowing herself to wander down that road again. She heard the stream and felt the dust beneath her feet. Tall cedars swayed on the other side. She was alone on the

Road to Emmaus.

The Stranger waited ahead. She didn't recognized Him, but she welcomed His company. They talked and she understood things she had never understood before and felt a peace she had not known. At the bend in the road He turned toward her and she suddenly knew Him. Jesus.

In peace and safety she slept soundly through the morning.

The phone woke her, cutting through her sleep. The hospital? She jumped up and ran to answer.

"Hello? Tam?" Mack said.

Tam exhaled in relief. She hadn't given Food Mart a thought. Now she did. She had to get to work.

"Tam? Are you there?"

"I'm here," she said. "It's a good thing you called. I might have slept through my shift."

"That's why I'm calling. Would you like to change to days until your father gets out of the hospital? Then you could see him at visiting hours."

Tam hadn't thought of that. Unless she missed work, she could see Dad only at breakfast. Changing shifts would solve that problem.

Mack assured her she could change back to evenings as soon as Dad was better. "Come in at seven tomorrow morning. You can make this day up next week."

Tam said, "Thanks, Mack. I appreciate it. It's kind of you to offer."

Mack laughed. "I don't know how kind it is. Luke says if I want to keep you, it's the only sensible thing to do."

"Luke says?" Tam echoed.

"Yeah, Luke," said Mack. "He stopped by a few minutes ago. Nice guy."

"Yes." What else could she say about a man who was everywhere in her life?

She went back to bed, closed her eyes, and the phone rang again. Stewart. Luke said her schedule was changed and she shouldn't worry about getting to the hospital for evening visiting hours. Stewart would take her.

It was useless to try to get more sleep. She might as well get dressed.

Before she was finished with her hair, Barb called to find out how Dad was and to offer to work her Wednesday shift if Tam needed to take the time off. Tam was explaining the shift change when Mrs. Warren knocked at the back door with two plates of lunch.

Mrs. Warren listened to the conversation while she set the table. She wouldn't have considered eavesdropping, but if someone carried on a conversation where she could hear easily, she naturally assumed it was for her ears too.

When Tam hung up, Mrs. Warren said that since Tam's schedule was changed, they could go to the hospital together at three. Mrs. Warren stayed to eat and to chat a while before she left. That's when Tam noticed how quiet the house was.

She turned the radio on. It helped.

To get away from the strangeness of the house, she went outside to the backyard. Butterflies flickered about in the sunlight above the weeds, the butterfly garden. She hadn't taken time to watch them before, but now she saw that they truly were as lovely as flowers. "Flowers that fly," Luke had called them, quoting some poet.

One squirrel scrabbled in the bird feeder for seeds that weren't there. *I'd better fill that thing for Dad,* she thought. *I know he'll ask.*

She wondered if he could ask, could say those words, or if they were back to the beginning of those speech exercises again. Poor Dad. How much had he lost this time?

The squirrel scurried down the pole. *He's lucky I'm not chasing him with the broom the way Dad did,* Tam thought. *It would be funny if it weren't so sad,* she thought. She'd never known Dad to do such a thing before the first stroke.

In the living room, she put Dad's corner to rights, setting his chess board, ready for him to come home to.

Alone in the house.

Luke had said she would never be alone again. She looked at Luke's painting, "The Road to Emmaus," and knew as she had known the night before that when she traveled that road, Jesus would talk with her. She was not alone.

With Mrs. Warren she visited Dad, who was in good spirits. His language seemed no more scrambled than it had been before. His right arm didn't work yet, but the therapist already had been there and Dad seemed hopeful. His right leg was affected too, but it seemed improved already. Tam could see for herself that his face was more mobile.

Tam knew that most recovery takes place very soon. If damage is not reversed within the first few days after what doctors insist on referring to as a "neurological accident," the damage may be permanent.

"Neurological accident"—the term made a stroke sound like some little error to avoid by being careful. It didn't seem that minor when the accident happened to a real person.

"He looks pretty good," said Mrs. Warren on the way home, and Tam agreed.

That night Dad was tired so Tam didn't stay long. Stewart stopped in for a few minutes and said Luke would be in at breakfast. Dad was pleased with that. He and Luke had grown close.

Dad liked Stewart, too, but it wasn't the same relationship. With Stewart he talked business and joked around. With Luke he played chess and talked of birds. Tam wondered what else they discussed.

After the visit Tam was too tired to accept Stewart's offer of supper. Besides, she had to get up early for work. She was also too tired to make polite objections when Stewart announced that he would drive her for visiting hours every night and that she should plan on supper with him the next night.

She went to bed just after dark and fell asleep watching Luke's attic light.

The next day went fine after she pulled herself out of bed at six. She had forgotten how early six was. She didn't know the day crew, but they were friendly and easy to work with.

When she punched out at three, she halfway expected Stewart to be waiting. Of course he wasn't. He was at work. Besides, there was no reason to drive her home in the daylight. Instead, she went to the hospital on the bus and would ride home with Mrs. Warren.

That routine lasted for the first week. After that, Dad was moved out of ICU and into a regular room with one o'clock visiting hours, and that was hopeless for Tam. She went at seven with Stewart and left the early afternoon to Mrs. Warren, who usually brought one of Dad's friends, like Mrs. Ellis from the library.

Stewart said Luke had breakfast with Dad every morning, helped Dad eat, and kept him company. Tam didn't see Luke at all. She left the house in the morning after Luke had gone and was at the hospital when he came home. She knew he was working in the attic; she saw his light. Otherwise, he might have vanished, as far as she was concerned.

When did he sleep?

She missed working with Hope and Vickie and Barbara, but they checked in when she checked out, so they stayed in contact. The only person she spent time with was Stewart. They spent hours together in those two weeks. Once she stopped fearing Dad would die and saw he would regain most of the use of his stricken right side, she settled comfortably into a new pattern.

In many ways it was the most normal life she'd had since school. She rose in the morning with the rest of the world and went to work when they did. She came home in daylight and went to bed at ten. It was so wonderfully, blessedly normal.

Stewart was always there. She never quite got used to his dash and glamour. She had difficulty believing he chose her to spend his evenings with, but he did.

They ate out, everywhere. She never knew what she was going to eat when she ate with him. She tried Ravioli con Pesto, which turned out to be fried ravioli in a green, creamy sauce. It tasted pretty good, once she got past the color.

Sauerbraten mit Spaetzle at the Alpine Inn wasn't bad. She could have eaten twice as much spaetzle and half as much sauerbraten, but she didn't know that when he ordered it.

The Acropolis had both best and worst. Moussaka, with eggplant and olive oil, was the worst, but Baklava had to be the world's best dessert.

At Szechuan Blossom, Tam thought she'd have Chicken Chow Mein or Chop Suey, the only things she recognized. Stewart ordered Sesame Chicken instead, and Beef with Orange Sauce. At his insistence, she tried both. The beef set her mouth afire. Stewart said, too late, that she wasn't supposed to eat the black bean things. She had most of the chicken.

Tandoori Chicken from India Palace was great, and of course she liked the Chimichangas at El Rancho, though she preferred tacos.

Empton didn't offer these foreign foods. Empton had hamburgers and fried chicken. Stewart found these strange foods by driving all over Indianapolis. Her mother had always said Tam left enough food on her plate to feed the starving children of China, so Tam pictured the children of other countries eating the same things she did, like peanut butter. Stewart fed Tam foods she never knew existed.

Mrs. Warren was shocked when she discovered that Tam was wearing her same old cotton skirts to all these places and insisted Tam borrow two of her summer dresses. Not silk, these were fresh cottons which were newer and finer than Tam's old clothes. Mrs. Warren didn't like the looks of Tam's shoes either, but Tam promised to invest in some new ones soon. Until then the old ones would be fine. Tam was glad Mrs. Warren hadn't seen her underwear. It was spotless, clean, of course, but worn-out.

Stewart was too gentlemanly to complain about her clothes. He just complimented her extravagantly when she wore something different. Tam got the idea.

It was a busy two weeks. Every night they took their stomachs to another country, another adventure. For Tam, who hadn't been anywhere for years, each night was a party.

Several times she tried to tell Dad what fun they had and where they had been and how nice Stewart was to her, but it seemed to irritate him. She knew she wasn't doing anything he could disapprove of, but because he seemed upset by it, she stopped telling him unless he asked.

Stewart was the most exciting date a girl could have—considerate, kind, and lots of fun. He probably knew that; Tam didn't see how he could miss it.

He also knew she was nervous. He didn't rush her into passionate embraces. He kissed her once or twice every night, carefully and gently, with enormous tenderness. That was all, except that now and then he took her hand and turned on charm so thick she couldn't look at him. Or he slid his arm around her shoulders and ruffled her hair at the back of her neck while they waited in a booth for their orders.

Initially these touches intimidated her and she had to steel herself against pulling away. Gradually she became accustomed to it, more or less. This was Stewart, after all; kind, good Stewart.

The one place she didn't go with Stewart, although she wanted to, was church. With her new schedule, she missed church entirely. She wanted to worship with others and lose herself in the service as Hope did. She understood why some people refused to work on Sundays, but she needed the work. For now, she had to rely on her own prayer.

Stewart brought messages from people at church who asked how Dad was, and he repeated as much of the services as he could remember, so Tam didn't lose out entirely. Hope said she and Stewart particularly enjoyed the choir that first Sunday and that she was sorry there wasn't a recording of it so Tam could hear it.

Other than missing church and running back and forth to Graham Memorial, the days were pleasant. Occasionally Tam would catch herself wishing they would go on forever, but she dared not get accustomed to this life as she had gotten accustomed to those rides home from work. One day it would stop. She must be ready to accept that.

By the middle of the second week, however, she was deep into the routine and enjoying every second of it. It was fun and she welcomed fun and laughter. She reveled in the admiring glances Stewart drew from other girls and smiled to think that he was with her. If things had gone on that way, exactly that way, she would have been content.

Perhaps she should have seen what would happen, but she didn't. She wouldn't have believed it if she had. She hadn't believed Barb either, when she said Stewart was interested in her. So, for Tam, what happened was a surprise.

The Madrid, a Spanish restaurant where they had gone for Paella, was on the far side of Indianapolis, and the cook had given extra time to preparing their dinner, so they came in later than usual that next Saturday night.

Stewart turned off the engine and Tam waited for him to kiss her two or three times and take her to her door, as he always did.

He didn't.

He sat for a long moment and then, without speaking, reached for her hand. He held it against the cool leather of the seat, absently stroking the back of her hand with his thumb.

What's wrong? she wondered. Then she knew this was the night the party would end. He was trying to find a kind way to tell her he was not going to take her out any more, that the romance was over but that they could remain friends. He was trying not to hurt her feelings.

Well, all right, she could cope with that. She'd been expecting it. She'd make it easy for both of them. She'd thank him for all the fun and they would part friends.

"Tam," he began, and she braced herself as he looked straight at her, "Tam, I . . .Oh, I'm not very good at this."

Releasing her hand, he dug in his blazer pocket and fumbled out a little square box. "Open it," he said.

Inside, glittering against blue velvet, was a breathtaking diamond ring.

"Will you marry me, Tam?" He took the ring from the box and slipped it on her finger, where it glittered in the moonlight.

"It's beautiful," she breathed.

"So are you," he whispered. "You and I can have a good life together."

She fluttered her fingers slowly, watching the moonlight play on the diamond. It dazzled her. Moonlight, handsome man, diamond—a dream, perfect. Almost. She said, carefully, "You haven't said you love me."

He looked away and then back. "If you want me to say it I will, but. . . Look. I like you better than any other girl I've known, and I think you like me. That's enough for now. Love will come, in time. Until then, let me share my life with you. Let me give you things, beautiful things. We can go places, do things. You can study interior decorating, if you like. You can fill my life with home and children and laughter. You can make me very happy, and I promise to try to make you happy too. Please say yes."

Slowly, very slowly, still watching it sparkle, she drew the ring from her finger and held it out to him. He didn't take it. She opened his hand, laid it on his palm, and closed his hand over it.

"I can't," she said. "I know this has to be the dumbest thing I ever did in my life, but I can't. You're a wonderful man and you'd be a wonderful husband, but I can't marry you."

"Think it over," he said, trying to give back the ring.

She said, "I don't have to. I know I can't. I'm sorry."

"If you change your mind, the ring will still be here," he said. "I can wait. I know we're right for each other. Luke says you're one girl in a million and that if I know what's good for me, I'll marry you fast. Luke says you—"

"Luke says?" Tam's eyes opened wide and she sat straight up. "Luke says?" she repeated. "What does Luke have to say about whether or not you should marry me?"

Stewart swallowed. "Nothing. . .not exactly. He just said he thought you were the girl I needed. That's all."

"So, you're proposing to me because Luke told you to," she said, in dangerous, measured tones.

"It isn't like that," Stewart protested. "Not exactly. I wanted to ask you. I did. I do. Luke says—"

"Luke says!" she fumed. "Always 'Luke says.' All I ever hear is 'Luke says.'" Her voice was gaining volume as her temper rose. "Can't anybody make a move unless Luke says? Can't you even marry without his permission? Do you let him tell you what to think and who to love? That's crazy! It's disgusting!"

Her anger mounted and she gave words to it. "You tell Luke to mind his own business. You tell him I don't want to hear another thing he says. I don't care what he says. You tell him the next time he wants to arrange my life he needs to ask me first. You tell him—"

"I won't have to tell him if you shout any louder," said Stewart.

"Good! Then I'll shout!"

She climbed out of the car and stood beneath the attic window. "Luke? Luke!" she shouted. "Do you hear me?"

"I hear you," he growled from the window. "Everybody in the neighborhood hears you."

"Fine," she called. "That's just fine. Let them all hear that I am sick and tired of your meddling in my life. Who do you think you are to decide who I should marry? Who asked you? How dare you! Mind your own business. Leave me alone!"

No answer. Her words died on the night air. He stood looking down at her, silent. She glared up at him. Silence.

She huffed back to the car.

"I'm sorry," she said to Stewart. "It's not your fault. You should be glad you're not marrying me."

She slammed the car door, leaving him sitting stunned behind the wheel. She slammed the kitchen door behind her. When she looked back, Luke was still standing at the attic window.

"How dare he," she muttered under her breath. "How dare Luke try to push his friend into marrying me. Who does he think he is?"

She stamped through the dark house to her bedroom and glared at the angry reflection in the mirror. *How humiliating,* she thought. How perfectly wretched to be pushed at some nice guy like Stewart. Stewart probably would have done it, too, married her—just because Luke said he should. How awful. How depressing.

I'll never be able to face Stewart again, she thought. *Not now. Not after I sat there and let him propose to me like that. He and I both know he doesn't love me. And I don't love him either.*

He probably thought I'd jump at the chance to get married, especially to him. Me, the girl with nobody and nothing, and I turned him down. He must have been surprised. He should have been stunned, she thought, and humphed a little sound of disgust.

Well, I told him. . .him and his friend Luke. I really told them.

Her stomach turned over. She had refused a diamond ring and a storybook future from the nicest man she had ever gone out with. She had stood out there in the driveway and shouted angry words at his friend Luke, who had been there every time she needed a friend, who had done nothing but good for her.

Luke! Unless he was meddling in her life, she never saw him. He never visited unless she was away. He avoided her and devoted his attention to Hope. He grouched at Tam, looked through her, looked into her heart. He popped in and out of her life, understanding and ignoring her in turns, lifting her up, and dropping her into Stewart's hands.

Luke, she cried inside. *How could you do this to me?*

"Luke. . ." she cried aloud.

Then the anger and dismay welled up and overflowed, falling in tears and shaking her in great gulping sobs that she buried in her pillow.

Chapter Eleven

"Stupid," said Barb.

Tam hadn't intended to tell her, but every time they met Barb asked when Stewart was going to propose. Tam always laughed it off. The day after the driveway disaster, Tam didn't laugh. At first she didn't answer at all, and then the whole story was out.

"Stupid," repeated Barb. "You should have grabbed that diamond quick. I would have. If Stewart needs a wife, send him to me. I'll marry him."

"But we're not in love," Tam protested.

"Listen," Barb said. "Do you know how many married couples don't even like each other? Stewart likes you and you like him. That's more than most people get. He didn't lie, either. He could have lied and said he loved you and you wouldn't have known different until after you were man and wife. Maybe not even then."

"I don't want like," Tam said. "I want love."

"So maybe you'll learn to love each other," Barb said. "It happens."

"No."

Barb persisted. "You'll never have another chance like this. Think it over."

"No."

But she did think it over, walking home in the afternoon sun. *Maybe Barb was right,* she thought. *Only a fool would refuse to marry Stewart.*

Then she was a fool, that's all. In the brightness of day she examined the choice she had made in moonlight and knew it was right. She wished. . . What difference did it make what she wished? With Tam it must be love or nothing.

That was no excuse for her exhibition of bad temper, however. Shouting. Childish. She cringed at the memory of it.

She hoped she didn't run into any neighbors. They were bound to have heard, especially Mrs. Warren.

Childish. Embarrassing.

Tam owed Stewart an apology. She had apologized last night, but she did it in anger. He deserved better.

And Luke. . .She didn't know about Luke. She was angry with him last night and angry today. Thinking about him standing silent made her furious all over again. Surely she was right to tell him to mind his own business. Surely she was entitled to be angry.

Of course I was, she thought, but did I have to tell the entire world? At the time it felt very satisfying. Now it seemed a bad-tempered over-reaction to Luke's meddling.

So who gave him the right to meddle? Tam did. She welcomed his meddling when he came out in the rain to lift her from the gravel and she was grateful when he roused her father's interest with the bird feeder. She was in the blouse painting business because Luke made Stewart believe she could do it. She'd welcomed Luke at the hospital that night too. She could never forget that.

What should she do about Luke?

About three minutes after Tam got home, Mrs. Warren tapped on the door and stuck her head in. "I brought some zucchini bread," she said, sitting down at the table. She went directly to the point. "I heard you last night."

"You and the rest of the neighbors," Tam said. "I'm sorry. I behaved like a child having a tantrum. I had no business yelling like that."

"You can yell if you want to," Mrs. Warren said. "You can even keep me awake with your crying. You can not expect me to ignore it."

"I didn't realize I was crying so loudly. I should have shut the window."

Mrs. Warren said, "Our houses are very close together. I couldn't help hearing anymore than you could help crying. You might as well tell me about it. I'll find out anyway."

"Stewart asked me to marry him last night," Tam said.

"I know," Mrs. Warren said. "He told me. He also said you turned him down."

"I had to."

"I know," Mrs. Warren said. "Your father and I told Luke it wouldn't work. He didn't ask our opinion, you understand. We just guessed what he was up to. First, Luke insisted that Stewart pick you up after work, which was funny because Luke was the one who worried about your getting home all right.

"Then he wanted me to invite you over after church. That was fine. I love having you and I would have asked you even if he hadn't asked me to. It was his wanting me to that caught my attention. That and the way he made sure Stewart spent every second of the afternoon with you."

"Poor Stewart," Tam put in.

Mrs. Warren was indignant. "Forget that 'Poor Stewart' nonsense. Stewart's a big boy, and a stubborn big boy at that. If he didn't want to drive you around in that little car of his, he wouldn't. Taking you out to eat at those fancy places was his idea. He wanted to take you out and he enjoyed it. He likes you."

"He told me," Tam said. "But why me? I should think he'd go out with girls more like he is. He could have his choice of pretty girls with college educations and rich clothes and time to spend enjoying themselves."

Mrs. Warren laughed. "He does, honey. Haven't you seen the way Hope looks at him? She'd go out with him in a minute if he'd just say the word, but not as long as she thinks you're in love with him."

"Where did she get the idea I was in love with Stewart?"

"From Luke," Mrs. Warren said. "You must have noticed the way he cuts in when those two get close together. He keeps Hope away from Stewart."

"I thought Luke wanted Hope for himself," Tam said. "He sure spends time looking into those blue eyes of hers."

Mrs. Warren said, "That's not the way it is, believe me. Luke says he doesn't want to get involved with anyone, ever. He must have been terribly hurt when his wife died."

Mrs. Warren paused, then said, "Now tell me why you were crying up a flood."

Tam thought it over. "I'm not sure I understand it myself. I just got so angry all of a sudden."

Tam tried to explain how angry she was with Luke for pushing Stewart at her, and how tired she was of hearing what Luke said, and how humiliated she felt, and how ashamed.

"I'm still angry," she said. "I know I shouldn't be, but I am."

"So that's how it is," Mrs. Warren said. "I thought so."

"Now what?"

Mrs. Warren shook her head. "You've got a problem, all right. If I were you, I'd pray about it."

Munching warm zucchini bread after Mrs. Warren had gone, Tam knew she was right. She would have to pray for help. For a new Christian with a temper, it would be a real test, but she would do it. She wondered where Jesus would lead.

Good thing I have the zucchini bread, she thought. *After last night I won't be seeing Stewart again. I'll have to make this my supper and get to the bus stop if I want to see Dad.*

⁊⁊

A familiar slam of a car door caught her attention. Looking out the window, she saw Stewart. *A time to apologize,* she thought, and ran out the door.

Stewart came warily toward her. Suddenly she felt foolish and schoolgirlish standing on the steps with half a slice of zucchini bread in her hand. He didn't seem to notice.

"Stewart," she began, "About last night. . ."

"Later," he said. "I want to change out of this hot suit if I'm going to drive you to the hospital."

"You don't have to do that."

He said, "I know." He reached out and took the bread and stuffed it into his mouth. "Thanks," he said with his mouth full, and walked off, leaving her with butter on her fingers.

He's not angry, she thought, in amazement and relief.

In the car she tried to tell him how sorry she was about the way she acted. "I'll stand out in the driveway and shout that I'm sorry, if it will help," she offered.

He said, "Forget it. I'm sorry about the way I proposed. I'm not very good at asking girls to marry me. I've never done it before."

"It was beautiful," she said. "Saying no was probably the dumbest thing I've ever done."

"Right! I think you should reconsider," he said.

"No, I have and the answer is still no. You're a fine man and I'd be proud to be your wife, but we don't love each other. With me it's all or nothing. Sorry."

"Me too," he said.

They didn't tell Dad. Tam thought he looked surprised to see Stewart with her, and wondered who had told him. Maybe Luke or Mrs. Warren had told him in the afternoon. Or perhaps she was reading more into his look than was there.

The good news was that Dr. Thomas said Dad could go home in two or three days—Monday maybe, or Tuesday.

Monday afternoon would be terrific, Tam said. She'd work day shift on Monday and ask Mack to put her back on evenings for Wednesday. Since Tuesday was her regular day off, that would work out fine.

She left the hospital in better spirits. Dad was coming home. Stewart was still her friend. She had a few problems, mainly Luke, to solve, but she would trust Jesus to show the way.

"I'm glad you're not angry, Stewart," she said, as they drove home.

He laughed. "I can't fight with you. We're business partners. You owe me money and I intend to see that you pay it back."

"I will. I promised," she said. "I shouldn't have tried to start that business."

"Too late," he said. "You have orders to fill." He had orders for a dozen blouses at one store and six at each of two other stores—two dozen blouses—for immediate delivery.

"I don't know where to start," she said, panicking.

"Order blouses from the Indianapolis supplier, get those labels run off, set up a work area. . . ." He reeled off instructions.

"Right," she said, biting her thumbnail.

That was Saturday. Tam couldn't do business with suppliers until Monday. At Food Mart she checked out groceries and thought of painting blouses. She punched the time clock and calculated costs of labels and two dozen plain silk blouses. She spoke to customers and pictured them wearing her Butterflies.

Walking home, Tam realized she had completely forgotten to be angry with

Luke. Creative work, right when she needed it. *Lucky timing,* she thought. *No, a gift from God. Thank You, Jesus,* she breathed as she walked. *Thank You.*

When Tam said that Dad had been managing her little blouse business and asked if it would be too taxing for him, Dr. Thomas said it was exactly what he needed. Dad was delighted when Tam and Stewart told him about the blouses that night and glowed when they told him they needed his business skills. *Another gift,* Tam thought, and breathed another *Thank You.*

There was to be a special song service after church that night, Stewart said, beginning whenever church let out. They had time to make it if she wanted to go.

Of course she did. She used to go to those song services when she was in the youth group. The whole gang went to church and always, every Sunday night, met afterward downstairs or in someone's home. When there was a special service, they were automatically part of it. It would be like old times.

Hope sat alone in the fifth row. Tam had seen her outside and had nodded, but Hope looked quickly at Stewart and then away. *Staying away from him,* Tam thought. *I'll fix that.* She led Stewart to Hope's row and slid in next to her. Stewart followed. Then Tam said to Stewart, "Do you mind if I sit on the aisle?" Tam rose and slid past him. Now he was between Hope and her. *Take that, Luke,* she thought, pleased with herself.

Hope was blushing. *She likes him,* Tam thought, startled. Luke must have known. How dare Luke meddle in other people's lives! Stewart and Hope were perfect together.

Mr. Moore announced the first hymn and they sang without a leader, harmonizing, moving easily from one favorite melody to another and then another. Sometimes the transition was without break. Other times, a song would end and then, after a moment's quiet, a new song would begin quietly with one person. Those who heard picked up the melody until all joined.

They sang enthusiastically, raising their voices in praise. Then, by unspoken agreement, their selections grew more introspective, until the voices were a prayerful whisper.

Mr. Moore asked if there were requests for prayer. Mrs. Warren, in the back, asked for prayer for Tam and her father. Ben mentioned an unfamiliar name. Other names were mentioned, and then unnamed requests were made by uplifted hands. Tam lifted her hand. She had much to ask. She felt Stewart's arm move as she raised her hand. She would pray for him and for Hope.

After prayer, old Mr. Chartwell rose to thank God for his eighty years and to declare that he would spend his remaining time praising and thanking God. A woman across from Tam rose to say that she was new to the community and had been drawn to the church by the welcoming friendliness of its members. She thanked God for leading her to this place of fellowship.

Amens followed, and then a long silence. "Alleluia" they sang then, and Tam's heart was full. They sang more joyously with each song, and it was time to close. They held hands, all up and down the rows and across the aisles for the final prayer and through the last song, the same song they had sung years ago when Tam was in the youth group: "God Be with You Till We Meet Again," and then they released hands and filed out quietly.

In the aisles some reached out to touch others, to hug, to share, but they didn't speak.

Outside Tam said, "I think I want to walk. I need to keep the silence a while longer." She noticed Hope walking the other direction and said, "Hope has a long walk home, though. She might appreciate a ride."

Stewart looked long at Tam, then nodded and leaned down to kiss her lightly on the forehead before hurrying to catch up with Hope.

She didn't plan to send Stewart after Hope, but when it happened it felt right. She pictured them together—a handsome pair.

Shadows played on the sidewalk beneath the trees on the familiar, friendly street. She strolled slowly, enjoying the soft quiet of the evening. Home was a short walk away. She wanted to make the most of it.

Dad would come home tomorrow; she would no longer have to return to an empty house. They'd begin again. He'd make tea and toast and watch for birds. He'd have a lesson in the morning and no doubt be as difficult as he was before. His temper was part of her life by now and was almost lovable. Her own temper needed work.

In the afternoons he'd watch television and Tam would go to work. At night she'd make tea and tuck him in. They'd go on as they had before, endless days stretching before her in accustomed sameness.

Fine, she thought, _just fine._ Where once she had wriggled and itched under the drabness of her life, she now accepted the routine, but with some important differences.

No longer would she mourn her lost art studies. She would plant lovely gardens on silk and know that her work brought pleasure to the wearers. She'd hum as flowers flowed from her brush, content with creating beauty.

She was finished wishing for Robert. She was glad to have loved him, but she'd no longer resent his leaving.

Life had not passed her by after all. Stewart had shown her kindness and pleasure and had thought highly enough of her to ask her to share his life. She had the consolation of knowing that and of knowing she had made the right decision.

Most of all Tam had found peace. She knew now that she belonged to Jesus and that he would keep her in His care. It made all the difference.

Footsteps and voices sounded behind her. Mrs. Warren was in earnest discussion. The volume seemed to drop as the footsteps grew closer, but it didn't matter. Tam wasn't listening.

Mrs. Warren must have seen Tam, but she did not call out to her. That was good. Tam wanted to be alone and she supposed Mrs. Warren and her companion wanted to continue their private talk, so Tam crossed the street and walked faster, glancing over her shoulder. Mrs. Warren's friend was Luke.

I didn't see Luke in church, Tam thought. *He must have sat in back. As big as he is, it seems impossible that I overlooked him outside. But then, I wasn't looking. He would never bother to avoid me by blending into the background and out of my sight.*

No? Then why don't I ever see him? For a man who lives next door, a huge man, he's nearly invisible.

She'd have to see him one of these days to apologize, but she dreaded it. She was afraid of what he would read in her eyes.

Not tonight, she decided, and locked her kitchen door behind her. The solid knock at her door startled her.

"Who is it?" she called.

"Luke."

She unlocked the door and opened it, but left the screen shut.

He said, "We have some talking to do."

She opened the screen and stepped out on the back porch with him. She was glad it was too dark for him to see her face clearly. They stood next to each other at the railing, staring into the night toward the butterfly garden.

She cleared her throat experimentally. "I have to apologize," she said. "I shouldn't have shouted at you like that. I'm terribly ashamed of myself and I don't blame you if you're angry. I'm sorry, really sorry."

No response came from the tall shadow looming next to her in the shadows.

"Did you hear me?" she said. "I'm trying to apologize."

"I heard you," he growled.

"Then say something," she snapped.

No answer. She went to the door and opened the screen.

"Wait," said the shadow. "Please."

She waited.

His voice was husky and low. "I'm sorry I interfered between you and Stewart. I thought it would work out. I'm sorry I messed it up for you."

Tam said, "You didn't. We're still friends, no thanks to you. How could you dump me in his lap like that? How could you do that to him?"

"I thought you were the best thing that could happen to him," he said. "It wasn't dumping. You have so much to offer and you've had such a hard time. I wanted you to have what you deserve. I thought—"

"You thought I'd jump at the chance to marry him," she flared. "You thought

I'd be grateful to marry anybody, even a man you pushed into proposing. Well, I'm not desperate enough to marry without love, not even such a fine man as Stewart."

"It wasn't like that," Luke said.

"Sure it was, only your plans didn't work." She was getting angrier.

"You're shouting," he said.

"I don't care," she shouted. Then she said, very quietly, "Yes I do. Sorry. You make me angry."

"I see that," he said. "What you said, about my meddling in your life. Did you mean it? Do you want me to go away?"

"Yes! No. I don't know," she stumbled. "I mean, you've done so much to help me. I don't even know where to begin to thank you. You're there when I need you and I feel safe when you're near, like nothing can hurt me. You understand when I talk to you and sometimes when I don't. I feel. . .close to you. But. . ."

"But?"

"But then, just when I think you're my friend, you vanish. It's like you're ashamed to have anything to do with me," she said. "Or like you hate me."

"I don't hate you. You can't believe I hate you," he said.

She said, "Why not? One minute you're looking at me like you see into my soul and the next minute you act like we're strangers. When I just about get used to the idea that you don't care what happens to me, you show up again and do something so wonderful that it takes my breath away. Then you're gone again. Friends don't act like that."

"I'm sorry," he whispered. "I don't mean to hurt you."

"Well, you did," she said, feeling more miserable now with anger giving way to confusion.

"I know," he said.

They stood in silence, staring. At last she moved to the door. "Luke?"

"Yes?"

"Luke, I. . ."

"I know," he said. "I'm sorry."

He went into the night. She heard his feet on the gravel and then heard Mrs. Warren's door shut. He would be going up to paint, she thought, gone again from her life. This time he wouldn't be back. Their special link was broken.

She entered the dark house, locking the door behind her.

Special link. She hadn't put it into words before, but it had been there. She'd lost it before she knew it existed. Now it was gone and the loss was painful. Painful.

She slipped through the hall to her room and looked up at the attic window. It was dark.

"What's-his-name-the-painter" she had called him before she knew him. She'd thought him gruff and heartless. Now she knew better.

He was solid and strong. He'd been gentle and kind and caring—almost as if he loved her. With him she found understanding that needed no words. She knew him in the furious brush strokes on his canvasses and felt his strength in the way his hands held her. Strong hands. . .huge arms. . .massive chest with his heart beating against her ear.

She shivered with the memory of that night in the rain.

Stop it, she told herself. *You're making a dream of something that means nothing to him. It's not his fault you love him.*

I love him! she thought with astonishment. *I love him. If I had known. . .*

But she hadn't, and now it was too late.

Oh, Luke!

She sank to the bed in tears. "Luke," she cried. "Luke. I didn't know." And she sobbed.

The pounding on the back door didn't stop. Wiping her tears, she went to answer it.

"Open the door, Tam," ordered Luke. "Open the door right now!"

She opened the door.

He pulled open the screen door and grasped her firmly by the wrist. "Come," he ordered, pulling her out and across the driveway. Mrs. Warren's door was still ajar and he pulled her into the house, through the kitchen, past Mrs. Warren, and up the stairs, across the second floor landing, and up into the attic.

"Stand there," he ordered, "Don't move."

She stood. He flicked the light switch and around her blazed reds and oranges and yellow greens shouting at her in jagged lines of anger. Sorrow spoke in murky amorphous darknesses. Light blues, soft neutrals, and gentle earth tones soothed and softened in peaceful scenes.

He dragged an easel around so she could see what he was working on. "Look," he commanded.

On the easel was a new color, a soft rose-pink, exactly the color of her silk dress. She wiped her eyes to see more clearly. On the canvas, in a rose-pink dress that floated on a light summer breeze, a lovely young woman smiled gently.

Her hair was dark rich brown, almost black, with little traces of white in the front, like Tam's hair, except that in the picture the gray was a sparkle of silver, a diadem. Beneath the graceful hand the lovely young woman had lifted to shade them, her eyes were soft and warm, dreamy.

She looked like someone Tam should know. She looked like. . .

"Me!" Tam gasped.

"Yes," Luke said angrily. "You."

Tam couldn't take her eyes from the girl in the picture. "It can't be me. She's beautiful."

"It's you," he said, "the night Stewart took you to Chez Raoul. I saw you on the step in your pink silk. The breeze caught the edge of your skirt exactly so."

"But her hair—" Tam began.

"Your hair," he corrected. "It's a problem, your hair. I had to do it and redo it to get the silver to sparkle in it the way yours does. But your eyes were easy. They simply appeared there under my hand. . ." His voice trailed off.

They stood silently regarding the picture. Then abruptly he said, "Here. You might as well see the rest of them." In two giant steps he reached the small stack he had kept away from her the last time she was here. Now he set them in the light.

They were Tam. All of them. One was almost a sketch, a face in the dark with a wispy look about it. The next was wildness and hurt, a waif fallen on a background of gravel. In the third she stared with empty eyes that followed the viewer, haunting. In the fourth, a laughing Tam sat at a dinner table. In another, a shabby Tam sat dejected on a step. In one more, the "Road to Emmaus" loomed above her as she searched it, lost.

Canvas after canvas of Tam, recognizable in both look and spirit. She felt again all the emotions in turn as she moved slowly, deliberately from one to the next and the next. At the end of the row she surveyed the whole group. Together they said more than they did individually.

He had placed them in order. She saw that now. Pretty in the first painting, she was lovely in the third and beautiful in the last several. The colors changed too. Early ones were neutrals with a dash of strong color, like emotions breaking through distance. The last one, on the easel, was in rich, warm, vibrant color, with no neutrality about it. Every brush stroke of cherished love.

Love!

"So now you know," he said at last. "I didn't want you to see them because you understand too much when you look at my work. You see into me. I. . .I didn't want you to."

"But why?" Tam said to the girl in the portrait.

"Because you deserve better," Luke said behind her. "You should have an easy life with a handsome husband who is steady and solid."

"So you gave me Stewart," she said.

"I tried to, but you wouldn't have him."

"I don't love him."

"I know," he said, and then there was a long silence.

Luke broke it, saying, "I can't love anybody. I can't. I paint pictures by night and cut trees by day. I have nothing to offer—not much money and very little hope of ever having any—no silk dresses and fancy restaurants. I can't even buy you a house."

"I don't need a house," she said.

"If I gave up painting and took a regular job, I could. . ." Luke began.

She turned to face him and saw his torn look. "No. You couldn't give up painting and still be Luke."

"I tried not to love you," he said.

"I'm glad you failed."

His eyes searched hers and she opened her heart to let him see inside it. She floated in his deep eyes, drowning.

"Tamara," he whispered hoarsely, and then his huge strong arms folded around her, lifting her until she was almost chin level. "I love you, Tamara."

"I love you, Luke," she whispered, sliding her arms around his neck.

He lowered his lips to hers and kissed her, gently at first, and then with a power born of the love he offered, kissed her until she grew dizzy and pulled back from him. He kissed her again, lightly, and slowly lowered her until she could stand. "Marry me," he said.

"Whatever you say, Luke," she answered, and he bent to kiss her again.

Fields of Sweet Content

Norma Jean Lutz

Chapter One

The time-worn hardwood floor came alive with creaks and moans as Alecia Winland moved toward the tall windows of the rural stone schoolhouse. Mellow beams of morning sun intensified the bronze highlights of her thick chestnut hair. Moodily, she lifted her hair off her neck and gazed out at the playground where the laughter and shrieks of the students floated back to her on alfalfa-scented breezes.

Beyond the school yard, on the silver ribbon of highway that split the spring green pastureland, a local farmer was perched on his slow-chugging John Deere tractor. The tractor was in turn slowing the frustrated driver of a semitrailer rig impatiently locked in behind him.

Alecia identified with the rig driver's being forced to slow down to the tractor's pace. This rural Oklahoma ranch land had compelled her to slow her pace as well and like the trucker, she was searching for a quick escape.

A sigh slipped through her unsmiling lips as the rig, glinting in the sun, found its break and surged ahead to freedom, sending excited puffs of black exhaust against the cloudless sky. Regretfully, Alecia was still locked in.

"For I have learned," she had read in chapter four of Philippians just this morning, "in whatsoever state I am, therewith to be content." Why then was she chafing at having to be here? Silently, she prayed for the verse to be fulfilled in her life during these days.

Shading her eyes against the morning sun, she watched the children riding the swings as high as they would go. In the inner city school where she had taught in Minneapolis, the swings weren't so high, and the children were never allowed to "pump" one another. Here at Charlesy School, five miles from the nearest town, situated on the edges of nowhere, the children were allowed to soar in keeping with the free creatures they were bred to be, on this wind-swept land.

In her own childhood days, spent in a relatively small Nebraska town, quiet games such as ball and jacks or sidewalk skating were her pastimes. And never with boys. Her older sister, Nancy, and her mother had strictly warned her about the dangers of becoming a tomboy. Quite different from these children out on the playground.

Lyle Jenkins, the multipurpose principal, teacher, and bus driver had playground duty that morning. For that, Alecia was grateful. She disliked the job because she couldn't bear to watch the children swing so dangerously high.

The paunchy, graying Mr. Jenkins was hunched over, carefully explaining the handholds on the baseball bat to a chubby third-grader. This man who was infinitely patient and easygoing with the children was a marvel to Alecia who had observed the gamut of educators from the best to the worst.

Suddenly her attention shifted as a late model, royal blue pickup turned into the gravel drive at the front of the school. J.D., the curly-haired student who hopped out, could easily have been mistaken for a boy had Alecia not known otherwise. Curious, Alecia stepped nearer the window, reaching up to hold the shade cords and entwining them around her fingers as she craned to see. On the door of the pickup were the white words "El Crosse Ranch." Below that was a scrolled L with a tiny cross in the bottom loop.

Alecia barely caught a glimpse of the driver before he backed out of the drive onto the highway in a frenzy of dust and raced away. She had seen that he was fairly tall and under the typical cowboy hat was a very straight roman nose and a nice mustache. She could tell little else.

J.D., clad in her usual western shirt, Levis, and boots joined the boys in their baseball game without a backward glance. *Why,* Alecia wondered, *was J.D. the only student at Charlesy School who didn't ride the bus?*

The boys seemed content to have her in their midst and Mr. Jenkins instructed her in methods to improve her pitch. From her window vantage point, Alecia could see J.D.'s brown eyes growing wide with appreciation at the instructions.

Alecia glanced at the white-face pendulum clock above the chalkboard. Flossie Cramer, the teacher of the first and second grades, would soon be ringing the bell. Alecia drew herself away from the window and returned to her desk to review the day's lesson plans.

Charlesy School, the last of its kind in the area, couldn't be considered a full elementary school, for it accommodated first through sixth grades only. Two classes were housed in each classroom. The huge stone edifice, which overlooked the pasturelands, also held a small library, a school office, a spacious lunchroom, and a gymnasium with a stage at one end.

Flossie, the paradox of a teacher dressed in a slogan T-shirt and Levis, and no more than two years out of college, stuck her head in Alecia's classroom doorway. "Brace yourself, Babe. It's time." The brass bell was cupped over her hand as she held the clapper in silence.

"I'm ready." Alecia's response was cool. Her years of training in the Minneapolis school system made her recoil at Flossie's unprofessional approach to teaching.

With great clompings, clatterings, and chatterings, the third and fourth-graders converged on Alecia's classroom. During her years in and out of classroom situations, she had never taught two grade levels simultaneously. It was proving to be a greater challenge than she had ever imagined.

In the midst of the noise, she looked up to see J.D. standing before her desk holding out a fistful of wildflowers. The girl's brown eyes were wide and expectant.

"Why, thank you, J.D. These are lovely." Alecia motioned for her to come nearer and gave her a brief hug.

"I knew you'd like them," the girl announced. "Miss Cramer would have called them old weeds."

Yes, that sounded like Flossie, Alecia thought as she instructed J.D. to fetch a vase of water for the blossoms. During the course of the day, Alecia found herself, as usual, involuntarily observing J.D. at her work. The girl's careful habits belied the tomboy exterior. Generally, girls with tomboy tendencies were prone to be lax in neatness, but such wasn't the case with J.D. All her lessons were completed with precision.

Mrs. Dominique, the Charlesy School cook of twenty years, teased students and staff alike during the morning hours with fragrant aromas of baking lasagna. At noon Alecia remained in her room for a few moments of work after dismissing her students for their lunch hour. By the time she entered the lunch room, Flossie and Mrs. Turner, the school secretary, were leaving. Alecia filled her tray and seated herself beside Lyle Jenkins, thankful to find him alone.

"Hello, Miss Winland," he greeted her, assisting with her full tray. "I must say, you're looking very nice today." With an unconcealed chuckle, he added, "A refreshing respite from Flossie's faded blue jeans."

Alecia smiled her thanks, remembering what her sister Nancy had said to her that morning about being "overdressed" for Charlesy School. Actually, the tailored suit was on a par with everything else in her closet. She hadn't much choice.

She let a few meaningless generalities sift back and forth before asking the question foremost on her mind—that of J.D. and her background.

"I don't know all that much about the Lassiters," Lyle admitted. "Rayne, J.D.'s father, is a successful rancher. . .a widower I believe. As you have no doubt surmised, there's not much feminine influence for J.D."

"That's what concerns me."

"Isn't she doing well in class?"

"Academically, I see no problems," Alecia explained. "But socially I can detect problems. She's developing very few relationships with the girls her age."

Lyle smiled. "J.D.'s just her daddy's little ranch hand."

Alecia bristled at his nonchalance. "How unfair. It may interest you to know that a few days ago, I found J.D. sketching pictures during free time. Pictures of elegant ladies in long flowing dresses. Is she being a little ranch hand against her will?"

Lyle cleared his throat. "Now Miss Winland, these people out here are very set in their ways. I'm sure J.D.'s as happy as she can be. If she were disturbed about something, it would show up in her school work."

"Not necessarily," Alecia countered.

"Excuse me. I keep forgetting your background in child psychology and counseling."

Alecia detected his condescending tone was to humor her, but she let it pass. "I think she's unhappy inside, and I'd go so far as to say she's under duress at having to conform to a mold that someone else is forming for her." *Someone such as a stern rancher-father who drives a blue pickup,* she silently surmised, *who won't allow his daughter to ride the bus.* Although the lasagna was delicious, Alecia found she couldn't finish eating.

Lyle thoughtfully rolled his water glass between his palms. "I admire your sensitivity and your concern," he said slowly, "but you'll learn these ranchers are different from people you and I have known."

This was the first hint she had received that someone here was as urban as she was. He continued, "There's an element of underlying pride and individuality that is an unwritten law. It's the code by which Rayne Lassiter and his daughter live. We can be appreciative and sympathetic, but I've found there's nothing you or I can do to change their ways."

Alecia didn't answer, but she had witnessed that individuality he referred to in Nancy. Almost twenty years Alecia's senior, Nancy, during her widowhood, and now during her recovery from major surgery, was indomitable in her determination to hold on to her small ranch.

The sisters had not been reared with such fortitude and love of land. Their lives had been very urban, even though it was small town urban. They were more familiar with sidewalks, storefronts, and shade trees than with open spaces and cattle branding. Alecia could only surmise that Nancy had acquired her stamina and persistence during her years of marriage to rancher Ted Whitlow.

But Alecia didn't voice these thoughts. *People aren't that different, really, no matter where they live,* she told herself. And it still remained that a little girl like J.D. needed a helping hand.

When she looked up to speak again, Lyle was standing to leave. "I'll have to ask you to confine your interests to the classroom, Miss Winland," he told her. This was her superior speaking now. "I appreciate your expertise in other areas of education, but it won't pay for you to use those talents here."

Thoroughly miffed, Alecia dumped her remaining lunch in the garbage can. Too late, she saw Mrs. Dominique peering over her glasses at her with a disgusted gaze that should have been reserved for the students.

That afternoon, J.D.'s usual animation became subdued, and her face was pale. Her brown eyes beneath closely cropped curls appeared larger and wider than ever. Presently, she approached Alecia's desk. Clutching her stomach, she said, "Take me home, Miss Winland. I don't feel so good."

"I'm sorry you don't feel well, J.D. Is your father home? We can call him."

"He might be home, but he's never at the house," she answered, wincing.

"But J.D., I can't leave the classroom."

She brightened. "Mrs. Turner can substitute. She's used to it."

"Very well. Return to your desk. I'll talk to Mr. Jenkins about it. Are you sure you can't make it till school is out?"

Clutching at her stomach again, J.D. shook her head.

A few minutes later, Alecia was standing at the door of Lyle's classroom, feeling a bit foolish for asking for permission to take J.D. home.

"The school policy," Lyle explained, not unkindly, "is for Mrs. Turner to take students home when necessary."

"I know the policy," she replied. She could scarcely believe her own words. She was never one to break policies of any kind. "But J.D. seems to have attached herself to me and has asked me to take her." Blindly, she let emotions plunge on, ignoring the bite of conscience. "Surely it couldn't hurt anything. I believe the child needs an ally."

"Obviously your mind is set, thinking you can do something positive in J.D.'s life. I don't fault you for that, Miss Winland. I just don't want to see you get hurt."

"Are you letting me go?"

Lyle nodded. "Against my better judgment."

"Thank you," she answered, then left before he could change his mind.

Although J.D. was cheered to know her teacher would be driving her home, it was clear the girl was genuinely sick. Mrs. Turner came in to take Alecia's place, as the two of them left before the afternoon recess. J.D. climbed into Alecia's car, running her small hands over the creamy upholstery and admiring the dashboard. Alecia smiled. What a captivating little personality she was.

Nothing could have prepared Alecia for the El Crosse Ranch. For several miles along the narrow road, J. D. was pointing to the rolling hills dotted with passive grazing cattle saying, "That's our land there." Finally, there was an open gate of sturdy white wood with a massive sign above announcing: El Crosse Ranch, with the running L brand burned into each corner. A meandering drive flanked by trim white rail fences and gracefully arched mimosa trees beckoned to them. The mimosas sported fresh pink feather blossoms that waved softly in the breeze.

"Go on, Miss Winland," J.D. urged, bouncing in the seat. "Go on in. This is where I live."

The drive took them up a long steady incline. At the break of the hill, Alecia was stunned to survey the scene below. Spread out across a broad, shallow valley were more than a half-dozen outbuildings, barns, stables, and tall silos crowned with silver domes reflecting the azure sky. The area was cross-fenced with the same neat white fences as those that lined the drive.

The sprawling white Spanish-styled home lay at the forefront of the panoramic view. The lawn was graced by large, shady oaks, and rainbow flower beds.

From J.D.'s few comments about having to help her daddy on the ranch, Alecia had assumed it was the two of them struggling alone. However, there were several men working down by the corral as she pulled to a stop in front of the house.

A measure of J.D.'s animation was coming back to life.

"There he is, Miss Winland. There's my daddy. Down by the corral, working the cattle."

"Shall I drive down?"

"No, ma'am," she said, jumping out. "I'll call him."

When she gave her whoop, all the men looked in their direction but only one, taller than the rest, climbed down from the white fence and moved toward them with purposeful strides. Alecia lifted her sunglasses from her eyes and perched them atop her windblown hair as she stood beside the car. Suddenly she felt very ill at ease.

It was with great delight that J.D. introduced her teacher to her father. Alecia found herself looking up into a handsome bronzed face set with J.D.'s expressive brown eyes. There was the straight nose and trim mustache she had observed from the school window. He took off his hat and reached for her hand. "Rayne Lassiter, ma'am. Pleased to meet you. You're Nancy Whitlow's sister. How's she doing?"

"Nancy's doing better now, thank you." Alecia's hand, strengthened by numerous racquetball and tennis games, felt a strength in his grasp far surpassing hers. "J.D. wasn't feeling well. She, uh, she said you couldn't be reached by phone."

Rayne gave his daughter a stern look as he released Alecia's hand. "I can see you're feeling bad, J.D.," he said softly, "but is that an excuse to story?"

"No, sir."

"You knew Josie would be in the house, didn't you?"

"Yes, sir," came the meek reply.

"And that she could have reached me on the barn phone or the two-way units?"

"Yes." J.D. hung her head, but Alecia could see a slight smile at the corners of her mouth.

Barn phones? Two-way units? Was someone pulling her leg? And who was

Josie? Suddenly, Alecia found herself wishing Mrs. Turner had brought J.D. home.

At that moment the front door of the house opened and a gray-haired woman clad in blue jeans stepped briskly toward them. "My lands, little gal. What're you doing home?"

"Sick, Josie," J.D. replied—the validity of which Alecia now began to doubt. "Meet my teacher, Miss Winland."

Josie's manner was a good deal softer than her leathery old face indicated. Following the introductions, she whisked J.D. into the house.

Rayne, meanwhile, was apologetic. Unhooking a thumb from his belt loop, he jabbed it toward the corral. "Excuse me, Miss Winland, but I've got to get back to work. Sorry J.D. told you that fib about phoning. Guess she was impressed by your pretty little sports car there. Just wanted a ride."

The grandeur of the ranch had almost rendered Alecia speechless, but now she was regaining her professional composure. She had come all this way and didn't intend to be dismissed so quickly. J.D. was more important than cows.

"Rayne, you have a lovely daughter," she said with more boldness than she was feeling under the gaze of the intense brown eyes. "I've been watching her, and though it's none of my business, I thought you should know some of the kids tease her because of the way she dresses."

The tall cowboy straightened himself and said nothing. Alecia swallowed and continued. "When I stopped in Kalado the other day, I saw a dress in Archer's window I'm sure J.D. would adore. With your permission, I'd like to get it for her as a gift. Even if she only wore a dress once in a while."

All the words she had prepared suddenly sounded empty in view of the Lassiters' lifestyle. Her eyes strayed to several large horse trailers in front of the stables with the running L brand, and the words "El Crosse Ranch" in elegant white swirls against the deep blue.

When she glanced back, Rayne's face had gone cold and distant. "If you'd been observing more closely," he remarked, "you'd see that J.D. is the happiest girl in Denlin County. Standing up for what she believes will make her stronger. Now, if you'll excuse me."

Alecia never intended to press him, but why couldn't he see what he was doing to this sensitive child? Short hair, no name, boys' clothes. Ridiculous! "I've seen her sketching pictures of ladies in dresses, Mr. Lassiter," she said, "so they are on her mind. Feminine things are a valid necessity in her life."

Rayne replaced his Stetson, casting a shadow across his somber face. "Miss Teacher Lady, how about if you quietly finish out the school year, then go back and use your high class psychology on those poor city folk who live so close together their brains are tied in knots. We manage to do fine without it, thank you."

She was surprised he knew her background, and yet she shouldn't have been. News spread like a pasture fire in Denlin County. "It's not psychology," she retorted, barely able to cap her indignation. "I'm talking about plain old common sense. Surely you can see that."

But the resistance she had encountered was hard as an Oklahoma dirt clod in August. Mr. Rayne Lassiter tipped his hat and slowly walked away with an easy loose-jointed gait, leaving her fuming.

She slipped behind the wheel and slammed the door of her car with more force than intended. In all her years in the field of education—teaching, administrating, counseling, working with gifted students—never had she made a scene with the parent of a student. What had gotten into her?

She turned the key in the ignition. There was a whining noise, a groan, then nothing. She tried again. Nothing. She was desperate for a quick exit. She felt the heat of her flushed cheeks. How could she let him unnerve her so? Rayne was nearly down to the corral. Surely he could hear the car failing to start, but he kept walking.

She would have to phone Lyle at the school. How humiliating, after she had gone against school policy to come here. "This is what I get, isn't it, Lord?" she muttered, "for asserting myself with this father with no preliminary planning." One last time, she turned the key and accelerated ruthlessly. The engine repeated its pathetic groan.

Down at the white-fenced corral, Alecia watched as Rayne motioned to one of his men to follow him. As he neared her car again, she could see his half-smile that irritated her.

"Pull the hood latch," Rayne instructed her.

Alecia reached down and jerked at a handle, then paused to listen for the click of the hood latch. Looking down, she realized she had pulled the emergency brake handle that wasn't even engaged. She glanced up. Rayne stood there waiting. The other cowboy, who was thinner and more grizzled, grinned at her as he chewed on a match stick. His greasy cowboy hat was curled up on the edges like a dried leaf in autumn.

"The hood?" Rayne repeated.

"Just a minute. I'm getting it." She grabbed the correct handle and the hood gave its releasing pop. She replaced her sunglasses on her nose to hide her embarrassment.

"Sammy," Rayne instructed his worker, "get in and give it a turn."

Doesn't even trust me to start my own car, she thought with disgust, as she slipped over to the rider's side. He must think her a total dunce. She should have protested, but she didn't have the strength. All she wanted now was to get the car started and leave.

Sammy grinned again as he folded his rangy legs into her small car. Alecia cringed as the muddy boots touched the eggshell carpeting.

"Hey, boss," Sammy said, "if this is the new shape of Charlesy's faculty, we'd better get up to some of them PTA meetings."

Ignoring his obvious flirt, Alecia managed to retort calmly, "We'd be pleased to have you at the PTA meetings, Sammy. The school certainly needs more community involvement."

"It's the choke, Sammy," Rayne called from beneath the hood. "Didn't kick in. Try it now."

Deftly Sammy turned the key and effortlessly the engine sprang to life and purred like one of Nancy's barn cats.

"Traitor," Alecia accused it under her breath.

Sammy crawled back out, leaving the remains of various-sized dirt clods around the gas pedal. At least she hoped it was dirt. Now that she had spent time in the feed lots and corrals, she knew what boots could carry.

Disguising her exasperation beneath a thin veil of calm, she scooted behind the wheel and declared a partially sane "Thank you" to the two men.

She expected a cynical accusation to be flung back at her, and was relieved when Rayne simply touched his hat and nodded. "Think nothing of it," he said.

Beside him, Sammy grinned silly and spat out match stick splinters. Rayne turned to his ranch hand and shook his head before the two of them ambled back down toward the corral.

Gone was Alecia's heated desire to spin tires and spit fine white gravel into the air. Cautiously she guided her car down the long drive and waited until she had passed the white gate of the El Crosse entrance before pouring it on. She put quick miles between her and that humiliating experience.

Even though she knew it was her own disobedience that put her there, Alecia hoped she would never have occasion to visit El Crosse again. Why was it that anytime she became uncomfortable here, it caused her to miss Minneapolis more than ever?

"For I have learned, in whatsoever state I am, therewith to be content," she repeated to the wind whipping in the window. "I have learned. I have learned." She shook her head and moaned. "No, I haven't, Lord. I haven't learned at all. And I want to go home in the worst way."

Chapter Two

Thankfully the bus was gone when Alecia returned to the school to pick up a stack of papers to grade that evening. Tomorrow would be soon enough to answer Lyle's inevitable question of, "How did it go?"

Surely by morning she would think up a sensible answer to give him. Sensible. That was a word she often chose when describing her own personality traits. And never before had she acted more irrationally. As she headed out the door with a stuffed folder, she was startled to hear sounds in the next room. Peeking around the door frame, she was surprised to see Flossie still in her classroom. Usually the childlike woman was the first to vacate the premises.

"Hello, Flossie," she said, wishing she had kept walking right out the front door. "Working on lesson plans?"

"Oh no! I'm waiting for Lonnie Wayne to come and get me." She nibbled at the edge of a candy bar. "We're driving into Kalado for something to eat, then to a movie. He said he might even take me dancing at Tiggles afterwards. Lonnie Wayne's quite a spender." Flossie gave a vague smile and hooked her straight hair over an ear. "How'd you make out at the Lassiters'? That Rayne's a real hunk, isn't he?"

The question caught Alecia off guard. "Hunk?"

"He's a lot of man, honey. Three-fourths of Denlin County's female population would give a right arm to talk to him, but Rayne keeps mostly to himself. Smart move for you to get Lyle to let you take the kid home so you could meet him. Wish I'd thought of it."

"Flossie, really. Keep your imagination under control." Alecia couldn't deny her curiosity that morning as Rayne drove up to let J.D. out at school, but it was by no means a romantic curiosity. She wanted to see the kind of man who would dress such a precious little girl in boys' clothes and call her by ambiguous initials.

"I underestimated you," Flossie went on. "Beneath that high-sheen surface beats the heart of your everyday man-chaser. Welcome to the club."

"I'm late," Alecia said, not wanting to be put on the defensive any further. "Nancy will be wondering where I am. See you in the morning."

"Sure thing, Alecia." Flossie took another bite of the candy bar, letting bits of chocolate and peanuts fall to the cluttered desk. "Don't work too hard." Her wave indicated the folder. "Nobody here will be impressed if you do."

Alecia left in silence. No reply was needed. *Why,* she wondered as she turned the car out of the school parking lot, *was that girl even allowed to teach?* Flossie's lackadaisical attitude toward her work grated on Alecia's nerves. Apparently there were no constructive solutions she could propose to Lyle or the school board in the few remaining weeks of the school term. But she was concerned for the first- and second-graders who daily sat under Flossie's teaching.

The tension in Alecia's neck and shoulders did not begin to ebb until she turned off the highway onto the section line road leading to Nancy's ranch. The hay meadows were greening and the cottonwoods were decked out in delicate fringes and miniature leaves. The willows, draping over their farm pond reflections, had been the very first to leaf out and were in full dress. For all the blessings of an early spring, Alecia still longed for the familiar surroundings of downtown Minneapolis.

Delia, her roommate back home, had laughed out loud over the phone when Alecia told her about hiring on at Charlesy School a week ago.

"A country school? Wait'll Superintendent Harwood hears about this," she said. Delia, a marketing analyst, was such a realist. "I didn't know such things still existed."

"There're a few around still gasping for breath. The job was all Nancy's idea," she defended herself. "She was afraid I might pace a hole in the living room carpet. When the opening became available, she practically threw me into it. She called the school and told the principal I could fill in till the end of the term."

Delia laughed again in her deep throaty laugh. "What happened to the other teacher? Catch her hair in the threshing machine?"

"Delia, be nice! Actually she eloped and ran off to Louisiana." But Alecia could hardly find fault with Delia's "country" jokes when she stood guilty of making a few private ones herself.

Before reaching the Whitlow Ranch, the country road dipped down around a series of curves, where a small mobile home was situated in a shaded glen. Alecia could see Jake Shanks sitting outside, with his straight-back chair tilted back against the side of the trailer. She slowed her car to a stop at the side of the road. The old man's felt hat, more battered even than Sammy's, was slouched down over his face.

"Jake!" she called out, rousing him from his nap. The chair dropped to the ground with a thud, and he pushed his hat to the back of his head.

"Hey there, Miss Winland." He waved a half-full whiskey bottle in the air at her. He seemed to keep a solid grip on it even while napping. His wrinkled face spread into a wide smile.

"Nancy asked me to stop and ask if you can come by and fix the south fence sometime soon. She says it's too weak to hold back Roscoe if he starts eyeing the Domiers' heifers."

"Be pleased to assist two such lovely ladies, Miss Winland." Jake rose on unsteady, bowed legs. "Tell her I'll be by soon. We'll keep that old bull where he belongs. Say, how're you doing with the feeding now?"

"Better. Thanks to your effective teaching." Alecia smiled as she remembered how Jake patiently took her through each step of feeding Nancy's livestock at the various feeding stations when she arrived in mid-February. Nancy was still in the hospital then.

"For a city gal, you're turning out to be a good hand. As soon as you get the hang of it, you'll go and leave us." Jake pulled off the companionable hat and smoothed down his scraggly gray hair.

Alecia stepped from her car and crossed the road to where Jake was standing. She caught the sweet fragrance of the black locust trees in bloom. "Looks that way," she said. "Nancy's stronger each day. I'm sure she won't need me much longer. But I'll stay till the end of the school term."

Suddenly the blast of a horn caught Alecia off balance. A beige double-cab pickup with bright red pinstriping and matching horse trailer in tow came barreling through the curves. She immediately recognized Corrine Domier, Nancy's neighbor to the south. The blast sounded again and instinctively Alecia stepped toward the ditch and felt her good suede pumps sink into the soft spring mud.

Corrine sped by with not so much as a nod in their direction. Her brilliant red hair was fastened at the nape of her neck beneath a pale blue western hat.

As the pickup whizzed past, Jake loped over to give her a hand. "You all right, Miss Winland?" he asked as he grabbed for her arm. "No need to dive for the ditch. Them trees woulda protected you." Shaking his head, he muttered, "Them two Lamison sisters used to be the sweetest girls in the county."

Gratefully Alecia let Jake assist her back to her car. "Thanks, Jake. Has that woman got a problem?"

"Not that I know of. Plenty of money and plenty of good looks. She's just one of them determined women."

Of all the friendly ranchers Alecia had met in the area, the Domiers alone had chosen to remain aloof. Alecia was introduced to the couple once, and once was enough. The beautiful Corrine was cool and distant. Her husband, Lavren, had seemed almost frightening to Alecia as he looked at her with steel gray eyes that seemed to want to possess all they surveyed.

Gingerly she removed her muddy shoes and placed them bottom-side-up on the floor before getting in her car. "Thanks again," she told him, "for everything."

"T'weren't nothing." He closed the door after she was settled. "Give Mrs. Whitlow my respects."

How gentle he was. How sad that he should waste his life away, living alone and nursing bottle after bottle of booze.

Arriving at Nancy's house, Alecia was struck with how differently the Whitlow Ranch appeared after seeing the immensity of El Crosse. Nancy's spacious brick ranch-styled home, edged with trim shrubs, seemed miniature in comparison to the rambling stucco home of Rayne Lassiter. And she was certain she had seen only a portion of El Crosse.

The early spring air was cooling as she turned into the drive and that convinced her to roll up the car windows before going in. From one day to the next, one could never predict the Oklahoma weather.

Aromas that greeted her in the front hall told her Nancy had chicken cooking. No yogurt and salad suppers here.

"You're late," Nancy called to her from the den at the back of the house.

"Had errands to run." She slipped out of her muddy shoes at the door and strode stocking-footed out to the den.

Nancy had a small fire going in the glass-fronted woodburning stove. She was settled in the wing-backed chair with a book and a cup of coffee. "Come on in," she said cheerily, "get comfy and tell me about your day. Cup of coffee?"

"Thanks, Sis, but I'd better change and get the chores done first." Alecia stopped a moment and studied her sister's tired face. "Nancy, you look beat. What's the matter?"

Nancy failed to mask her sheepish smile.

"Okay. Out with it. What major task did our recuperating patient undertake today?" It had been close to impossible to keep Nancy down and resting according to doctor's orders. Her determination to keep the ranch in tiptop condition was a driving force.

"It was such a lovely day and I can't be expected to just sit around."

"Come on. Quit stalling."

"The tomato plants. I set them out."

"All fifteen of them?"

Nancy's smile broadened with satisfaction. "All fifteen!" Though her usually ruddy cheeks were lacking their normal color, the sense of accomplishment gave her an inner glow.

"I could have helped you on Saturday," Alecia chided. She lay the folder down on the card table they had set up as her work area. "You should have waited."

"You've done so much already. You dropped everything to come and be with me. I suppose I'll never fully appreciate the magnitude of the project you were working on with Galen. It overwhelms me to think you released it all to come and be an underpaid ranch hand." Her eyes twinkled. "The least I can do is care for a small garden."

Alecia chafed at Nancy's words, for not a day passed that she didn't struggle with those very thoughts. It had been a sacrifice to leave it all—her cozy apartment, the project with gifted students, the city she knew and loved, Delia, Galen. . . . And yet she loved her older sister with an unspeakable love.

Nancy's mention of the gifted children's program stirred her ever present heart's cry to get on with that vital work rather than sitting here in rural America growing stagnant. Stagnant! That was it! She felt stifled and useless here. She longed to be back where she was needed the most. Alecia knelt down and opened the doors of the stove and shook down the charring logs with a poker. She hoped her sister couldn't read her thoughts by her expression.

"And by the way," Nancy said, seemingly oblivious, "don't forget, on Saturday we're attending the Field Day at the Research Station."

"Wow! A step up the social ladder in Denlin County. Gracious, is my feathered Stetson back from the cleaners?" She rose and swung the poker around. "Let me see, do I carry my branding iron in the left or right hand?" She pranced across the den as Nancy chuckled at her antics.

"Joke if you will, but there's an element of social life in this county that would surprise you. Anyway, this is just a Field Day that will end up with a barbecue at one of the area's ranches. The agents will be showing several pasture grasses under experimentation. I'm anxious to learn how to get my northeast pasture in full production next summer. It was nowhere near as lush as it could have been last year."

"By all means then, to the Field Day it is. And now I've got to get out there and take care of all those things that feed on that lush pasture."

Nancy stood up. "I'll get the pickup around."

Alecia stepped quickly and put a firm hand on her sister's shoulder. "You'll do no such thing. Digging in the garden was enough for you today. We'll never get you well if you don't slow down."

Nancy's clear laugh rang out as she sank back down. "Okay, okay. I declare, if you keep worrying about me, you'll have an ulcer. Get on out there, and I'll get supper on."

In her room Alecia quickly changed into blue jeans, a shirt, and boots. Wouldn't Delia have a convulsion if she ever saw this outfit? But Alecia learned quickly that close-fitting western shirts were less binding beneath a jacket while riding. And to round up calves in anything but boots was ludicrous. Especially after Jake told her that rattlers go for the ankle!

Sparkie, Nancy's sheltie collie, met Alecia at the back door, ready and anxious for work. Alecia rubbed the ruff of copper-colored fur around the dog's neck. "Good girl. Let's get these chores done." Sparkie happily trotted ahead of her toward the barns.

New tomato plants peeked bright green fingers through the dark soil of the garden. Alecia remembered Nancy's sadness as she lay in the hospital, unable to get her seed potatoes planted. Alecia shook her head in bewilderment at her sister's motivation in the mundane.

She checked the automatic feeders and waterers, then tended to three orphaned calves who had to be fed from the buckets with nipples fastened to the bottom. She hurried through the series of chores to get to her favorite—caring for the horses.

Before Ted Whitlow died, the stables were stocked with several high quality quarter horses. Nancy was forced to sell most of them, but had kept the exquisite stallion, Raisin Kane, and the mare, Kane Brake. Then there was old Peppy, the solid cow pony who was a worker deluxe. Peppy had been a Godsend when Alecia first helped Jake bring up steers for sale.

There was a sense of peace and order in the stable. The fragrances of hay, leather, and horses were strangely comforting. Over the stalls Alecia spoke to each horse and stroked velvety muzzles. Kane Brake was a brilliant mare and already Alecia adored her. Peppy was accommodating, but Kane Brake was regal.

"Good girl," Alecia cooed to her. "Back up there a minute. Let me get this feed in here. What you need is a good workout, don't you? You and I'll have to start taking long evening rides."

Kane Brake pushed against her shoulder as she worked. For a moment, Alecia stopped and lay her head against the long gentle face as though to soak up the peace and patience dwelling there.

How much longer? she wondered. So much work to be done back home. Galen needed her. Why all the stopping and waiting? "Sure, Lord," she whispered, "if I had nothing else in the world to do, I couldn't think of a place I'd rather be, but—"

Abruptly Kane Brake pulled back from her grasp and shook her head, nickering a scolding for the pity party Alecia was having. She laughed. "Okay, okay, I know. Be thankful for everything. Right? Funny, but I'm usually the one telling that to other people." Stepping out of the stall, she gave the gracious mare one more pat. "Thanks for the consultation, Kane Brake. Have the bill sent to my address. Come on, Sparkie," she called. "We'd better take a look at the south fence for Nancy."

The sheltie raced her to the pickup. As they bounced along across the pasture, she wondered if she would recognize a fence in need of repair when she saw it. Actually she wasn't sure what she was looking for. Later she realized she needn't have worried. The fence along the gully was loose and drooping. And this was the pasture where Roscoe, the bull, was spending his time. Either the fence would have to be repaired soon or all the cows and heifers would have to be moved to another pasture.

Jake had explained to Alecia that the Domiers raised Brangus cattle, a cross breed of Angus and Brahman. Should Roscoe, a polled Hereford, break through that fence, it would spell big trouble for the Domier herd.

She brought the pickup to a halt and stepped out to gaze across the vast expanse of land before her. The stout prairie wind whipped around her. Scissor-tailed flycatchers played tag in the air and the killdeer gave their little screeches as they scurried through the grass near their ill-concealed nests.

The grass was a dull gray-brown when Alecia first arrived in Oklahoma. Now a new birth of green life was coming forth. The land was so different from the Minnesota countryside. What was it that had compelled early day settlers to remain here? They must have had eyes of faith to envision putting roots down in the sunbaked, wind-swept prairie.

The sound of horse's hooves behind her startled her. She turned to see a rider approaching from the Domier Ranch. Presently she recognized Lavren himself astride his silver gelding. Alecia had often seen the rancher from a distance working with his men. Premature graying hair gave him a distinguished look, but his gray eyes were ice cold.

A soft growl came from where Sparkie lay beneath the truck. "Quiet, girl," Alecia ordered.

Lavren's gelding was reined to a halt at the fence. He surprised her by moving the mount close to the fence and dismounting on the Whitlow side. "Fence inspecting, Miss Winland?" He stepped purposefully toward her. As before the harsh gray eyes looked her over.

A shiver ran from Alecia's arm to her neck. Sparkie growled again. "Nancy mentioned it might be weak here. She's having it fixed in a few days."

"In a few days? That might be too late." The voice was as cold as the eyes. "Better advise your sister of that fact. She seems to be growing forgetful of late. She knows this stretch of fence is Whitlow responsibility and I expect it to be fixed before that renegade bull of hers gets over into my brangus heifers." Intermittently he flicked the riding quirt in his hand against his leg.

Alecia knew for a fact that since Ted died, the Atwoods, whose land butted the Whitlow Ranch to the east and north, willingly helped Nancy keep fences in repair. But Lavren Domier obviously never considered extending such favors.

"My sister, Mr. Domier, is recuperating from major surgery. She's regaining her strength and is attempting to keep everything under control. She's aware of the fence and is seeing to its repair." Alecia felt the strain to keep the tremor from her voice. "That should be sufficient."

"Mrs. Whitlow's physical condition is none of my concern. My cattle are. If I find that bull in my pasture, your sister could own a dead bull."

A swell of anger rose in Alecia's midsection. "I hardly call that fair," she snapped. "The fence will be fixed. What more do you want?"

"Assurance," he moved nearer, "that my herd won't be ruined by an infirmed widow running a ranch from her sickbed. And if she's hired that soakhead Shanks to do it, I have no assurance."

Alecia could never remember feeling rage like that which was now rising to a frenzied peak. She wanted to grab his quirt and slap him across his proud face. Nancy was anything but an infirmed widow. This man had to be demented. "Mr. Domier, you happen to be on Whitlow land at this moment. I'll thank you to take your crude expressions and degrading remarks and get out of here!"

The rancher's face relaxed into a sardonic smile. "You're very attractive, Miss Winland. This ranch life is certainly no place for someone like you." He reached out and placed one lone finger on her cheek and let it trail slowly under her chin to lift it slightly.

Disgusted, Alecia raised her hand to land one solid slap, but Lavren was quicker and caught her wrist, squeezing it hard. At the sound of her sharp cry, Sparkie sprang from beneath the pickup and sank bared teeth into Lavren's soft leg, just above the boot top. The expensive pants gave way with a rip as Lavren jumped back while trying to strike at Sparkie with the quirt. "Get away from me, you mutt. Call off this dog! Call him off!" Struggling, he tried to get to the fence, dragging the tenacious animal with him.

"Sparkie!" Alecia commanded. "Stay, Sparkie."

The cool Mr. Domier was now extremely heated up. Alecia could see the jaws set in anger. Free from the dog, he jumped the drooping fence and mounted the waiting gelding. Momentarily he glanced back. "Tell your sister what I said. And I'll send a bill for the pants."

When he was gone, Alecia knelt down and hugged Sparkie in sheer relief. "Really sent him sailing, didn't you, girl? Thanks."

Suddenly Alecia felt a gnawing concern for Nancy's safety. Her sister who had practically reared her—the one so solid in faith and strong in all circumstances—now seemed pitifully vulnerable.

Later that evening when she related the incident to Nancy, her sister was quite cool about it.

"That Lavren," she scoffed. "He's more bark than bite. Don't give it another thought, Alecia. I'm sorry if he disturbed you."

Alecia didn't argue, nor did she explain that he had touched her. Nancy had lived here for many years. She ought to know if the man was harmless or not. But inwardly Alecia still maintained that those steel gray eyes indicated more than a biteless bark.

Another one of Nancy's marvelous suppers nearly erased from Alecia's mind the encounters with the two very different men that day. After the dishwasher was loaded, she took her papers into the den in front of the crackling fire where Nancy was fussing over financial records.

The fire whispered as they worked, wrapped in their individual blankets of thought. Alecia knew she would miss the fire when the days grew warmer. It had, at first, been such a bother to carry in wood and tote out ashes that flew everywhere before she could get the ash pan out the door. But when Nancy was still in the hospital, Alecia chose to sleep on the den sofa because of the warmth and company of the fire.

On top of the stack of school papers on the table was J.D.'s math assignment. Alecia smiled. Each problem was evenly spaced and neatly written. It struck her afresh that this was not the work of a carefree tomboy type. She had done enough counseling to recognize that.

"Alecia." Nancy's voice cut into the quiet. "You never told me why you were late this afternoon. Some errand you said."

Alecia looked up from J.D.'s paper feeling as though Nancy were reading her thoughts. "One of my students became ill and I took her home."

"Anyone I know?"

"I thought you knew everyone," Alecia joked. "It was the Lassiters at the El Crosse Ranch. They call the little girl J.D."

"J.D.? She's in third grade already?" Nancy took a sip from her coffee mug. "I can hardly believe it. Seems like she was a toddler just yesterday. What did you think of their ranch? Something isn't it? Second biggest in the county."

"Unbelievable." Cautiously she asked, "Are you very well acquainted with the family?"

"As well as anyone in a small community. You know about people, but do any of us really know one another? What did you want to know?"

Alecia paused. She wanted to know so much. Everything. "How did J.D.'s mother die?" That would do for starters.

"It was a fire. Five years ago."

"Burned to death? How awful. Where? How?"

"I don't know all the details." Nancy returned her attention to the calculator in her hand. "It's one of those things people want to forget."

It sounded to Alecia like one of those things people would always remember. "Mr. Lassiter asked about you. Do you know him well?"

"Rayne? Through business is all." She poked figures into the calculator. "He taught me a few things about breeding the heifers after Ted died. Ted knew him better than I did." She looked up. "The El Crosse belonged to Rayne's father, Roland, and I imagine it belonged to his father before him. When Rayne married, his father gave him the ranch house, and he moved into a smaller one there on the ranch."

"The name El Crosse, does that mean. . . ."

"That they're Christians? No, Honey, I don't think so. Seems to me the story goes that the ranch was situated at the crossroads of two cattle drive trails, so they simply put the cross in the loop of the L and made the name El Crosse."

Alecia felt a twinge of disappointment. Had Rayne Lassiter been a Christian, perhaps there would have been an avenue of communication there. Oh well. "I'm a little concerned about J.D.," she said aloud after a moment.

"In what way?"

"Her father seems to be rearing her like one of the ranch hands. Short hair, work clothes. He doesn't let her ride the bus. He doesn't even use her name. It disturbs me."

Nancy continued entering figures into the calculator. "She's in good hands. Her daddy's crazy about her."

"Let's not be naive. Surely you're aware of what overprotection can do to the normal development of a child."

"Ranchers are different from people you're accustomed to, Alecia. There's an intrinsic pride—a vein of survival instinct—that has been ingrained through the years," Nancy pointed out. "I'm sure Rayne feels he's doing every possible good thing for his daughter."

There it was again. The excuse that ranchers are somehow different from the rest of society. Alecia shuffled papers and made a few red pencil jots. "Pride can easily disguise selfishness," she intoned flatly.

Nancy smiled her heartwarming smile. "But we can't really be the judge, now can we?"

Alecia knew from experience that the case was closed as far as Nancy was concerned. As usual, her sister's sweet disposition put her to shame.

Later in the evening, they brought out their Bibles and shared their usual devotion and prayer time together. The logs made a soft shuffling sound as they settled down in the ashes, as Nancy read the Scriptures. Though cultures and miles had separated the two sisters for years, their corporate love of God drew them together in an inseparable bond.

Later, alone in her room, Alecia once again thought about her confrontation with Rayne that afternoon. If only she had used wisdom and patience. Why was she so overly concerned about a child she might never see again after two months? Perhaps it was an outgrowth of the restlessness she was experiencing at having to stay here.

Thoughtfully she sat on the edge of the bed brushing her hair. She wanted to have a peaceable spirit. She wanted to be able to look at people and circumstances through eyes of patient love. And yet she had been guilty of letting her emotions rule. She wanted to apologize to Rayne and begin again. But how? She was sure he had given her no more thought than to a pesky horsefly.

"Give it up," she scolded herself as she changed into her gown and slipped between the cool sheets. "Teach the children at Charlesy School, finish the term quietly, and get back to Minneapolis where you belong."

She fell asleep by turning her thoughts to Galen Rustin, their work together, and his dependable tenderness toward her.

Chapter Three

The next morning when Alecia arrived at Charlesy, Flossie was seated on the broad concrete ledge beside the school steps, swinging her legs and chewing gum. Alecia made a determined effort to be friendly, smiling as she approached. "Good morning, Flossie. Have a good time last night?"

Flossie took a lingering look at Alecia's burgundy suit and gave a silly grin. "Lonnie Wayne is a lot of fun. He's one mean cowboy."

Not wanting to take the time to talk, Alecia went on to her room. As she stepped inside, a small figure jumped out from behind the door and yelled, "Boo!"

"J.D.! What're you doing back there? And you're at school early. Feeling better?"

"Lots better. Daddy had to go to a sale so he brought me early. I'm here to help you work. What can I do?"

Alecia looked into the soft brown eyes. "That's sweet of you and I appreciate the offer, but you need to be out playing with the other kids. It's a beautiful morning and the ball team needs you."

J.D. was disappointed, but undaunted. "I can help you quick, then go play." Her eyes darted about the room. "The erasers," she said, "I'll dust the erasers." Hurrying before Alecia could protest, she took the chalkboard erasers outside to slap them together, raising a white cloud in the fresh morning air.

Alecia set about readying her room when Lyle passed her door. "Everything go all right at the Lassiters' yesterday?" he asked casually.

Alecia looked up from her work. "Yesterday? Oh, you mean taking J.D. home. No problem." She swallowed. Not much of a problem anyway.

"Good." He walked on.

J.D. returned the erasers and waited for a hug and a thank you before bounding out to play.

Alecia was the bell ringer today, since Flossie had playground duty. She watched the clock until it said exactly eighty-thirty, then stepped to the window to ring the old brass hand bell. She had the sensation of being caught in a time warp, as though her hair should be skewered in a high bun and her skirts sweeping the floor. Would it be so expensive to install an automatic bell system in the building? Before she could return to her desk, a commotion in the hall caused her to rush in that direction.

There in the foyer was J.D. sitting on top of a screaming, kicking Lanette, who was dressed in a ruffled blue sundress.

"Get off! Get off!" Lanette yelled in protest.

"Take it back!" J.D. answered with equal velocity. "Take back what you said, or I'll cream your ugly face."

"But you do," squealed Lanette. "You look like old Jake Shanks. You dress like him and his initials are J.D. Shanks. J.D.—just like yours!"

"J.D.!" Alecia spoke to her sternly. "Get off Lanette right now."

The child never budged. "Not till she takes it back. She's mean. I don't look like Jake."

"You do. You do." Lanette struggled to get loose of her opponent. "You never wear nice dresses."

"See Miss Winland?" J.D.'s eyes were dulled by the inner hurt. "I'm gonna have to teach her a lesson."

"Not by fighting." Alecia stepped forward to physically lift her off Lanette's stomach. "Differences are never settled by fighting."

Noises from her classroom let her know the other children were taking advantage of her absence. Holding each girl by the shoulder, she steered them into the classroom and was surprised to see Lyle down the hall observing.

She swallowed the temptation to mouth an "I told you so." In her estimation the trouble J.D. had experienced with Lanette was only the beginning. During recess Alecia took the two girls aside and directed them to apologize to one another. But she couldn't shake the disturbed feeling she had about the matter. If only she were convinced that Rayne Lassiter's little girl really enjoyed dressing like a ranch hand.

Throughout the remainder of the week, Alecia kept close watch on the children to see if there were other underlying pressures against J.D. Nothing developed that she could actually put her finger on.

It wasn't until Friday that she remembered she and Nancy had plans for Saturday. She began to wonder what she would wear to a Field Day at an Agricultural Research Station. A stroll in Nicolett Mall it was not.

Nancy had said they would be outdoors most of the day, and yet she dreaded the thought of wearing the one pair of blue jeans she had purchased upon her arrival. It was Saturday morning before she finally decided on her wool slacks, a blouse, and a blazer for a jacket. *Warm, comfortable, and sensible,* she commended herself.

She was dressed and ready when Nancy knocked at her door. "Alecia, a letter from Mom and Dad," she exclaimed, obviously just back from the mailbox.

When Alecia opened the door, Nancy stopped and looked at her. "Are you sure you'll be comfortable in that all day today?"

"What do you mean? All my clothes are comfortable!" She turned and looked over her shoulder at her reflection in the mirror. "The cut disguises the bow in the legs quite well, don't you think?"

Nancy chuckled. "Well, at least wear low-heeled shoes. Heels will never do."

"Hey, what do you think I am—a dude? I'll wear my boots!" In mock disdain, she snatched the letter from Nancy's fingers.

"Breakfast is almost ready." Nancy walked away shaking her head.

The tissuelike letter, postmarked Santiago, Chile, was light as a feather. Alecia marveled at her own parents, called out late in life like Abraham and Sarah, to the mission field.

Both Alecia and Nancy had been shocked when their parents announced they were selling the family furniture store in Nebraska to attend a two-year Bible college. Soon after graduation they were applying for mission work.

Walt and Mattie Winland had been in Santiago barely three months when Nancy's surgery took place. Mattie flew home for a time and had offered to stay and help Nancy. But Alecia refused to allow it. "Mother, no," she said. "You go back to be with Daddy. I'll stay with Nancy."

"But you have your work, too, dear," her precious mother said, her eyes lined with tears. "It will be a sacrifice either way."

In the end it was Alecia who flew back home, packed her bags, and drove back to Oklahoma, and Mattie flew back to Santiago to work beside her husband.

Alecia sat in a chair by the window to scan the letter full of news of the exciting, though tedious, work, and the difficulties they were having learning the language. "The children of our partners here," Mattie's neat handwriting read, "pick up the language so fast. It's not as easy for us old-timers."

Alecia smiled to herself. Before boarding the plane to leave the U.S. for the second time, Mattie told her daughter, "No sacrifice is without reward, Alecia. By releasing me to return to your father and the work there, you've opened the door for the Lord to work His perfect will in your life."

Perfect will? She stared out the window. There was no doubt in her mind God would work His perfect will. But when was she to know what that "will" was?

"Alecia," Nancy called from the kitchen. "This food is getting cold. Come on or we'll be late."

෨

The Agricultural Research Station was larger and more complex than Alecia had imagined it to be. Hundreds of acres were under cultivation here, Nancy explained, with the sole objective of helping ranchers increase agricultural production.

When they arrived at the series of large stone buildings, the parking lot was already filled with pickups, jeeps, suburban vans, and a few cars. Instantly Alecia recognized the Domiers' beige pickup and dreaded the thought that Lavren might be in the crowd.

The ranchers and their families had gathered in an area behind the station where a wide assortment of new farm machinery was assembled. Alecia wondered how much shin-deep grass she would have to drag her wool slacks through. As she and Nancy left the parking area, a familiar voice sounded behind them.

"Miss Winland!" J.D. came running toward her from where she had been playing with a group of other children and flung herself into Alecia's arms.

"J.D.! What are you doing here?" She returned her student's warm hug. She had seen the beige pickup, but had missed the royal blue one.

"Nancy, do you know J.D. Lassiter? J.D., this is my sister, Nancy Whitlow."

Nancy took the girl's extended hand and smiled. "I knew you when you were just tiny, but I've not seen you for a long time. You've grown up."

J.D. looked at her with smiling eyes. "Pleased to meet you." Turning her attention to Alecia, she explained, "Me and Daddy came to learn about the best pasture grass. We want to know how to make our steers really fat!" Her cheeks puffed out as she imitated the fat steer, then she giggled. She seemed pleased to be able to make both adults chuckle. Without warning, she called out to a group of ranchers standing near the building. "Daddy, my teacher's here!"

Alecia could feel her face growing warm as several people looked in their direction. Rayne emerged from the group and strode toward them. The contoured lines of his western shirt made his shoulders seem more broad. At his waist was an ornate leatherwork belt with a gleaming silver buckle engraved with the ranch brand. Alecia was pleased to see his eyes were smiling again. "Howdy, Miss Winland. Nancy."

Alecia wondered if Nancy detected her discomfort. Could he still be upset with her? He had used Nancy's first name, but she was, "Miss Winland."

"Good morning, Rayne," Nancy greeted him. "Perfect weather for the Field Day."

"Perfect." To Alecia, he said, "How's your car been running?"

To her relief he was looking at her with the same openness she had seen when they first met. Even though she remained concerned for J.D.'s welfare, and more so since the fight with Lanette, it was clear she took the wrong approach. "The name's Alecia, remember? And the contrary car, it seems, acts up only when its owner takes a wild notion to step out of line."

"That a fact?" He beamed a smile at her. "Interesting car. If all the vehicles at El Crosse behaved like that, we might never get anywhere."

Alecia felt relief at his joke and felt he understood. She had been privately forgiven, even though Nancy stood nearby and J.D. bounced around them with boundless energies.

Rayne took J.D.'s hand. "See you ladies later," he said, touching his hat.

"What was that all about?" Nancy wanted to know as they strolled toward the demonstration area.

"Inside joke," Alecia said softly.

Grace and Neil Atwood greeted Alecia warmly, as did other neighboring ranchers who now recognized her, not as an outsider, but as one pitching in to help her ailing sister.

Nancy introduced Alecia to the Research Agronomist and the Plant Physiologist who were the Field Day Directors. Both men, two of five research scientists employed at the station, were personable and looked to be near Nancy's age. Alecia wondered how long they had toiled at the job of divulging their scientific knowledge to these strong-willed, hard-working ranchers.

Once the directors began demonstrating the farm machinery, Alecia forgot she planned to be bored. Newer items were demonstrated and explained in detail, as the men answered questions and comments from the crowd. The children played noisily on the fringes and teenaged boys stood with arms akimbo and in the same loose stance as their elders, watching with unconcealed interest. Directly across the way she saw Lavren Domier who stiffly nodded and smiled at her. Beside him stood his lovely wife in a stunning turquoise western suit with matching Stetson. Flaming curls lay carelessly about her shoulders. Corrine appeared restless, causing Alecia to presume she attended at the request of her husband—or orders, which might be more accurate. There appeared to be a sizable age difference between the two. Corrine couldn't be much older than Flossie, although a good deal more polished.

Alecia looked away from Lavren's glances, but she uneasily sensed them coming her way. Feigning indifference she walked nearer a mammoth combine to be shielded from the stares. Within minutes she again felt the glances and looked up to see that he also had moved. This was crazy. With a ravishing wife like Corrine, why should he be staring at her? Still puzzled she strained to give her attention to what Nancy was saying about a lift she needed for the larger-sized hay bales.

Following the machinery demonstrations, the crowd was directed to the field plots where the experimental pasture grasses were under cultivation.

J.D. stayed near her father, but at times turned to shoot Alecia a wide grin.

They were moving from the test strands of Weeping Lovegrass when suddenly Alecia felt Nancy clutch for her arm as she started to fall.

"Nancy. You okay?"

"I don't know. I feel lightheaded."

"We'd better get you home." Alecia was filled with relief for an excuse to get away from Lavren's gray eyes.

"No, no. I'll be all right. Help me get back to the main building. I'll sit down until we're ready for lunch and the ranch tour." She took a few unsteady steps. "I know I'll feel better after I rest. I always do."

Together they moved away from the test plots, with Alecia allowing Nancy to put her weight on her supportive arm.

It was cool and quiet in the deserted lobby of the Research Station. Alecia gently assisted Nancy to a comfortable overstuffed chair.

"Guess I still need to take it easy. Right?" There was exasperation in Nancy's voice.

"Right," Alecia agreed. "Sure you don't want to go home?"

"No, please. I'll be fine. I'm learning I need to rest periodically. Will you be a dear and run back out and take notes for me? They're going to be outlining the new fertilizer programs and if you take notes, I won't have to bother asking questions later."

Truthfully Alecia wanted nothing more than to sit in the other chair opposite her sister and wait it out, but she couldn't refuse. "Got paper and pen?"

"In the glove compartment of the pickup."

Alecia stepped toward the door nearest the parking lot.

"Alecia?" Nancy called after her.

"Yes?"

"Thanks. You're such a blessing."

Alecia smiled. "Anytime."

Opening the pickup door, Alecia leaned in and rummaged through the glove compartment under wire cutters, pliers, and other tools, and found a small notepad and a pen. As she turned to go, she gasped as she found herself face to face with Lavren Domier.

"I didn't mean to startle you, Alecia," he said in a low honey-coated voice.

He had come up behind her like a preying animal. "You followed me! What do you want?"

The steely eyes held a glint of amusement. "Defensive, aren't you? What makes you think I want something? Is it wrong to be neighborly?" Two more purposeful steps brought him even closer. He held the edge of the door with one hand, and rested the other against the side of the cab, fencing her into a corner.

"Your sister doesn't seem to be feeling too well. She's not the tough old rancher she puts on to be, is she? You can see it's not healthy for her to be taking on such hard work. You need to encourage her to sell out and quit, Alecia."

Prickles of fear crawled up her back. "My sister makes her own decisions, Mr. Domier. I've never run her affairs and don't intend to begin now. Please step aside and let me get back. I've promised to take notes."

"Notes aren't going to do her any good if she's too weak to work. Like buying shoes for a man with no feet—senseless." His hand moved to her shoulder. Alecia cringed and her mind raced. Was it better to kick and slap, or scream and run? His hand slipped under her long hair and rubbed across her neck.

Without thinking, her hand flew up to knock his away. As she did, she heard Rayne's voice from the back of the pickup.

"Domier," he commanded. "Leave her alone!"

Anger boiled red in Lavren's face as he drew back. Alecia rubbed her neck to erase the awful sensation of his touch.

"You okay?" Rayne asked.

Now that the incident was over, her knees turned to water. She nodded as she leaned against the pickup.

Though Rayne was taller, Lavren's stocky muscular form would have made it a close match if they went to blows. Alecia held her breath, praying it wouldn't come to that.

Presently Lavren's anger gave way to a sinister smirk.

"Well, well. My apologies, Lassiter. I had no idea the young lady was taken."

Alecia blushed at the connotation. Rayne, however, was unaffected. "Whether or not she's taken is none of your business. The point is, you seem to forget you are."

Lavren scowled. "Don't play nursemaid to me, Lassiter. Sticking your nose where it don't belong could get you in a whole bunch of trouble."

Rayne stepped closer, his voice low and easy. "Domier, you ought to know by now I don't scare easily."

"Some locos don't have sense enough to have a healthy fear," the older man countered.

Rayne had now positioned himself by Alecia's side. She felt him gently take her arm. "Then this loco is telling you to do your business dealings with other people. Leave Alecia alone."

A few moments of silence hung heavy as it became apparent Lavren was relenting—at least for the present. He glanced about as though it suddenly occurred to him their scene might have been witnessed.

The gray eyes came back to Alecia. "I'll be going, but I'd advise you to think about what I told you."

They watched as Lavren returned to his pickup rather than to the demonstrations. He honked the horn twice. When Corrine joined him, they left.

"Are you okay now?" Rayne asked again.

"Really, I'm fine." She shook her hair back and took a deep breath. "Thanks for the rescue. You and Sparkie make a great team."

"Nancy's sheltie?"

Alecia nodded as she moved to close the pickup door.

"Sparkie was the one who chased Lavren off the last time."

"When was that?"

"One evening when I was checking fences in the south pasture. He came to tell me if Nancy's bull got into his heifers he'd kill it."

Rayne turned to face her. "The man's got a legitimate complaint. I'd be angry, too, if a polled Hereford bull got into my Santa Gertrudis heifers. It's just that Domier goes about things in the wrong way. Is Nancy planning to fix the fence or move that herd?"

"Jake Shanks is coming to fix it," she assured him, sensing the return of his show of cowboy arrogance. She stepped away from him. "We'd better get back. I promised to take notes for Nancy." Glancing at her watch she noticed she had been away for only a few minutes. The frightening incident had seemed to last for hours.

Nancy fared well with the afternoon tour. The ride in the tour bus from one ranch to the next gave her time to rest. Determinedly Alecia put Lavren out of her mind as she surveyed the layout of the ranches. The individuality and complexity of each ranch fascinated her. Ranchers, by necessity, must be adept at several occupations, ranging from marketing and finance, to mechanics and construction, as well as the science of agriculture.

At the Atwood Ranch, Neil proudly stood by as his fourteen-year-old son Kramer explained how he had written from scratch a computer program of break-even cost analysis for his thirty-head feeder calf operation.

Alecia's heart was pricked as she thought of the program she and Galen were developing in Minneapolis for gifted children to explore their talents as this young man had. What if Kramer lived in an inner city setting and had never touched a computer? He never would have known he could write a complete program. The Minneapolis project was vital, she told herself with new resolve. These and other opportunities must be made available to as many young people as possible.

Nancy must have been reading her thoughts. She leaned over and whispered, "Brainy, isn't he?"

Alecia smiled. "Sure is. Whoever said country kids were supposed to be klutzes?"

"Who, indeed?" Nancy said with a smile. And Alecia realized she had held that misconception as much as anyone. They laughed together at the unspoken joke.

Nancy failed to mention that the barbecue supper was to be held at the El Crosse Ranch. By six o'clock, participants were back at the Research Station and from there drove their own vehicles to El Crosse for the evening. Alecia's assumption that she had seen only a fraction of the ranch was indeed correct.

The rambling U-shaped home curved around a spacious courtyard that was covered with latticed beams interlaced with leafy ivy. Small trees grew luxuri-ously in open spaces of the courtyard floor, and trailing foliage from hanging planters gave the area a tropical atmosphere.

Josie barked orders in marine sergeant fashion to white-coated workers who were filling the long serving tables with delectable foods. Several men arrived early to help with the barbecue and the aroma filled the warm evening air. Josie recognized Alecia and greeted her with a modicum of friendliness. On the other hand J.D. was ecstatic to have her teacher at her house again.

Alecia settled Nancy in a comfortable chaise, then strolled out away from the courtyard. She followed a series of stone steps down a small grade to where a swimming pool lay, still sporting its winter cover. Adjacent to the pool were lighted tennis courts that looked more inviting to Alecia than the pool. How many weeks had it been since she had played a rousing game with Galen? Much too long!

Rayne kept busy moving through the crowd, having switched his role from that of an observer to that of host for the evening. His fellow ranchers obvi-ously respected Rayne and seemed to value his opinion in ranching matters. Alecia recalled Flossie's remark about Rayne keeping to himself. Quite the opposite appeared to be the case.

Presently J.D. appeared through the shrubs at the edge of the pool. "Howdy, Miss Winland," she said. "You want to come see my room?" She pointed to a wing of the house with patio doors that opened onto the courtyard. "It's right up there."

"But J.D., the party's outside. It wouldn't be right for us to leave right in the middle of everything."

"It wouldn't?" she asked, brown eyes widening.

Alecia glanced back toward the courtyard and saw Rayne watching the two of them. She wondered what this father thought of J.D.'s attraction toward her teacher. Did he still think of her as meddling in his affairs? Actually she was curious to see the girl's room.

J.D.'s mind was never quiet. She tugged at Alecia's hand. "Let's go ask Daddy if it's all right." Alecia could only follow.

The absence of Rayne's ever-present hat revealed softly styled dark hair. As they walked toward him, she marveled at the picture of confidence he present-ed. How could such an intelligent man be so mistaken about the one issue in his life that was nearest his heart—his own daughter?

"J.D.," he said to her gently as they approached, "all the other kids are playing hide-and-seek in the main barn."

Alecia caught the remark as a subtle hint for J.D. to stay away from this teacher.

"I know, Daddy," J.D. answered, bobbing on tiptoes in her excitement. "But can Miss Winland come see my room? Please? It'll only take a minute."

Rayne folded his long legs beneath him and sat back on his custom-made boots, to where J.D. could put her small arms around his neck. "That would be fine, sweetie, but Miss Winland's had a long day. She may just want to find a place to sit down and rest."

Now both sets of brown eyes were studying her. So he had lobbed the ball into her court, had he? Did he think she would just let it drop? "I am rather tired, J.D., but I'd like to see your room too. So let's take a quick look, then I'll rest."

The girl released her daddy's neck and hopped up and down. "Goody, goody. See Daddy, she really wants to."

Rayne's reaction couldn't be measured since Josie came to him at that moment with questions about serving lines. Alecia did hope he wasn't angry with her again.

J.D. pulled at her hand, taking her to the main door at the center of the back of the house. They stepped into a paneled living room with an open-beam cathedral ceiling and a massive native-stone fireplace against the far wall. Above the fireplace hung a painting of cowhands clustered around an orange glowing campfire in snowy winter twilight. There was scant time to study the tasteful furniture arrangements as J.D. hurried her down the hall.

Alecia hoped against hope that she would walk into a room full of ruffles and lace, with stuffed animals and dolls galore. She wanted so much to be wrong about this whole thing. But her heart was crushed anew as they stepped into the room that was extremely neat and attractive, yet gave no hint that an eight-year-old girl lived there.

The furniture was dark walnut, firm and solid. The plaid bedspread and drapes were a mix of chocolate and pale blue. Fluffy rugs lay about on the russet carpeting and the desk and dresser were neat and orderly. Nothing was really wrong with the room. Except for the obvious absence of cute and cuddly little-girl possessions. Not even a jewelry box on the low dresser.

"Do you like it?" J.D. asked insistently.

Alecia wanted to ask J.D. if she liked it. Perhaps she did.

Perhaps she had chosen the colors. Perhaps she had no interest in dolls, doll clothes, doll houses, play dishes, and the like. Inwardly Alecia once again asked the Lord to keep her from making hasty presumptions.

She looked down at J.D.'s expectant face. "This is a nice cozy room, J.D.," she said in carefully chosen words. "You're such a blessed little girl to live here."

The small face lit up in a smile. She turned to the dresser and brought a framed photo to where Alecia had seated herself on the bed. "Want to see a picture of my mommy?"

The photo showed two women standing in front of a two-story house graced in the entrance by large white columns. Alecia recognized one to be a younger Corrine Domier. The other woman, the deceased Mrs. Lassiter, was a bit more petite with darker hair.

"Your mother was very attractive. No wonder you're so pretty," Alecia told her.

"Aw," she scoffed. "I'm not pretty. You heard what Lanette and the other kids say. I look like old Jake."

"No, J.D. You look like your mother and you're very pretty." Alecia looked back at the photo. "Was your mother a close friend of Mrs. Domier?"

J.D. giggled. "I don't know about friends. . .they're sisters. That there's my Aunt Corrine."

Alecia let this morsel of information sink in. Jake's under-the-breath comment came back to her: "Those Lamison sisters used to be the nicest girls in the county." What did it mean? And the lovely Corrine, so feminine and talented. Why didn't she take an interest in her niece, the only child of her dead sister? Surely, she could add a mother's touch in this girl's life.

So Rayne Lassiter and Lavren Domier married sisters, which more or less explained the interrelationship she had sensed as they bantered back and forth that afternoon. It was a tangled, sticky web of circumstances of which she didn't care to be a part.

"Come on, J.D. That hungry mob will get in those lines and not leave us a crumb. We'd better get back."

J.D. replaced the photo on the dresser, pulled open the drapes, and let Alecia through the sliding glass doors that led back to the milling, laughing group of hungry ranchers.

Silently Alecia made a vow that from now on until she left to go back to Minneapolis, she would strictly mind her own business. Nancy may think Lavren was only a blowhard, but personally, she didn't want to take any chances with either Lavren Domier or Rayne Lassiter.

Chapter Four

Kane Brake stepped gingerly but proudly among the scrub oaks, making generous allowances for Alecia's novice riding abilities. The three of them— exuberant Sparkie included—searched out ravines and gullies, through heavy brush, for calving heifers or deserted calves that might starve to death without help.

The work was so appreciated by Nancy who was also delighted that her favorite horse was getting back into shape. Nancy's growing strength was allowing her to take on more housework and even the evening chores, but the doctor insisted she not be in the saddle too much or take bone-jarring cross-country trips in the pickup.

When Alecia volunteered to forego the pickup and use Kane Brake to scout the pastures, Nancy expressed surprise. Ironically Alecia was as surprised as anyone. Never did she think she would volunteer to sit astride a mammoth animal and go gallivanting over the prairie.

Riding stable horses at summer camp was the extent of her equine expertise— and that dated back many years. But Kane Brake was a far cry from those old stable horses. This mare was highly sensitive with a distinctive personality all her own. Although her stance showed pride, her true nature was that of giving . . .humbling herself as she allowed this greenhorn to bounce awkwardly astride her back.

The month of April brushed the prairie with a palette of pastel wildflowers in lavenders and yellows. There was as much color now as there had been lack of it back in February.

A warm, flirtatious breeze ruffled Alecia's hair as she paused for a moment to watch a lingering sunset play a symphony of blazing pink and scarlet across the expanse of sky. Kane Brake waited patiently as Sparkie continued to sniff out every clump of tall grass about them.

Not since her childhood days at church camp could she remember seeing such full, vivid sunsets. She recalled her favorite counselor, a girl of the ancient age of eighteen named Ruth. . .Ruth, like in the Old Testament.

Those lazy summer camp days drew her near to the Lord as she basked daily in the display of His handiwork. It was there in the woods near an open meadow, under Ruth's patient leading, that she made the decision to commit her life to God.

And even here, where the horizon stretched for miles, straight as the ocean's, with nothing but a few trees to block the majestic view, God seemed incredibly near. She enjoyed a ringside seat, with not one skyscraper to blot the brilliance of each new sunset.

Back at the stable, Kane Brake received a well-deserved brushing and grooming before Alecia finally returned to the house. Nancy called out from the den where she was resting. "Find anything?"

"I'm not as thorough as you or Jake," Alecia confessed. "I didn't ride down into those rough places in the northeast pasture, but in all other areas I found no bovines to rescue today." She placed her hat against her chest and bowed her head.

Nancy chuckled and waved her to a chair. "Good. We can relax then. Since gardening began and you decided to take Kane Brake out, I've missed our long evenings together."

"If I sat down for even a moment in that soft chair, I'd never get up. Let me shower, then I'll bring out my papers to grade. I wouldn't dare get the nods with a lapful of work."

In the shower she purposely let the water run cool over her body to provide stimulation for another session of grading papers. In her heart she only wanted to work on the latest material Galen had sent down from her office. She was beginning to doubt the wisdom of taking the position at Charlesy.

Stepping from the shower, she dried briskly, put on her nightgown, wrapped herself in a velvety robe, and scooped up the armload of papers. The ringing phone at her bedside pulled her back into the bedroom. "I got it," she called to Nancy before picking up.

"Hey there, prodigal child. Elusive runaway!" Alecia's heart tripped lightly at the sound of Galen's teasing voice on the other end. "If I'd known when I took this job that you were going to throw me to the lions and then skip the country, I'd have stayed back in Folwell Junior High trying to outguess the troublemakers."

Alecia giggled. "Galen, please. Have mercy. You're making me feel terrible." She propped herself up in the bed against the huge feather pillows.

"You noticed! Doesn't it make you want to rush back to Minneapolis right away?"

If he only knew, she thought. "What? And leave the lonesome little doggies to cry all alone in the canyons? You heartless cad. I knew when I met you there was something sinister in your bones and now I see what it is. Cruelty to dumb animals."

"You're the one who's cruel to a dumb animal—me! This dumb animal was thrown into the midst of a press conference today without the known authority on the stepped-up Gifts and Talents Program that is due to be launched next fall."

"Oh, Galen," she sobered suddenly. "I didn't know Mr. Harwood was going to call one this early. How did it go?" Alecia knew Galen's heart was definitely in this project but he seemed to lack the ease and diplomacy that she commanded when working with the press and public. And he was the first to admit it.

"Those hard-nosed reporters bother me. I wish you had been here to melt their cold hearts and to act as my buffer." Tenderly he added, "And I miss your warmth in my life as well. When are you coming back? Can't we hire your sister a herd of cowboys to get that work done so you can leave?"

Alecia missed Galen as well, but somehow she knew it wasn't quite the same with her. Just prior to Nancy's surgery, their relationship had taken a turn as Galen became increasingly serious.

"Good idea, Mr. Smartie," she bantered back at him, "but a herd of cowboys costs more than you or I could afford on our meager salaries. Besides, they're terrible at keeping up the laundry and dishes and such. And don't forget, I'm committed to the little school until May."

Galen groaned. "Alecia, how could you let yourself get into that bind?"

She chuckled. "I've been wondering the same thing. I guess it was mostly because of Nancy."

"I thought Nancy needed you there."

"She does, but she felt that I wasn't being stimulated intellectually and, when the opening came up, the school was desperate for a short-term fill-in. I was the logical candidate."

"So now you're stimulated intellectually by a room full of third- and fourth-graders, right?"

Alecia fanned through the stack of papers on the bed beside her. "How explicitly you word it, sir. But now, back to the press conference. What questions were asked? Were they fair?"

"Assistant Superintendent Harwood briefed me well. He and I went over all the possible questions early this morning and he had practically all my answers written out on cue cards. Embarrassing, but effective."

His humor buoyed her sagging spirits. "Galen, be serious."

"Well, well!" His voice lowered a pitch. "Just how serious do you want me to be?"

"Galen!" she spouted. He could be so exasperating and so loveable.

"Okay, okay. For the most part, the natives were friendly. There were no surprises anyway. I'll send you the news clips as soon as they come out. You would have been proud of me."

Alecia smiled. She was more than proud of her working companion who had filled in for her and yet hadn't taken over her pet project. Consistently and continually, he forwarded memos and reports to her by the dozens. There was no way she could ever express how much she appreciated him.

She changed the subject then and told him about riding Kane Brake out over the rough terrain to search for new calves.

"You talk like you enjoy that kind of thing," he quipped.

"It's different."

"Well, my advice is don't get too attached to that cowboy lifestyle." He paused and added, "Guess I should be thankful I don't have any competition other than a horse."

Cautiously she avoided the seriousness of his comments and lamely joked her way into a goodbye. As she replaced the receiver, she wondered about their relationship. Had she not been in Oklahoma the past few weeks, would Galen have proposed to her by now? The thought frightened her. She was still unsure of her feelings. Galen's sensitivity was profound and he amazed her with the depth of his faith in God. But did that appreciation of him constitute love? A lasting love?

"Let me know for sure, Lord," she muttered as she headed for the den.

᠅

The next morning she awakened to a radiant spring day. The birds in the hackberry trees outside her window were running the scales in efforts to touch the most exquisite notes. Her heart matched their songs. In less than a month and a half she would be home again. Humming to herself, she pulled the jonquil yellow dress from the closet. This was her happy dress.

At school she once again allowed J.D. to perform a small task in the classroom before scooting her out to be with the others. This had become a daily habit and she feared the other children would add "teacher's pet" to their list of teasing names for J.D.

The day was uneventful. At lunch she had a reasonable conversation with Flossie that caused her to wonder if the girl had more intelligence than she let on. Perhaps her dumb female act was for the benefit of the men in her life.

Nancy had related to Alecia that Flossie had gone to college but instead of leaving home, she drove a distance of fifty miles each day for four years. Hardly the means of widening one's horizons in life, Alecia mused to herself.

At the sound of the bell that afternoon, students scurried out to pile on the bus but, within minutes, J.D. came running back in. "Daddy's not out there," she said. It was a declaration that didn't seem to disturb her.

"Just a minute, J.D.," Alecia told her. "We'll stop the bus and Mr. Jenkins can take you home."

"Oh no! Daddy'll be here in a minute, and if I'm on the bus, he'll miss me," she explained, eyes wide.

There were cleanup chores to be done in the room, then Alecia planned to drive to Kalado to pick up a few things at the store for Nancy before going home. She hoped they wouldn't have to wait long.

"That'll be fine, J.D. You can help by picking scraps of paper up off the floor while I separate these work sheets."

As they worked, Alecia found herself glancing at her watch every few minutes. What should she do if he didn't come?

She picked up scattered storybooks from the reading table and knelt down to slide them into the bottom shelf of the bookcase. As she did, she felt J.D. come from behind her to stroke her hair.

"Your long hair is so pretty, Miss Winland. Especially on your yellow dress."

"Thank you, J.D. I call this my happy dress because of the bright yellow color."

She felt small fingers go all the way down to the ends of the curls. Did this girl wish her hair were not cropped so ridiculously short? Whose idea was the haircut anyway? Could Rayne be so heartless? "Your hair is pretty, too, you know." Alecia turned around and ruffled the ringlets. "Just look at all those curls God gave you. You're blessed."

Alecia started to rise, but J.D. just stood there close. "You're awful pretty too," she said quietly. "I like you." Alecia looked at the intense pixie face. How this child must hunger for a mother's love. Josie was a loving soul, but Alecia couldn't picture the hard-working woman gathering J.D. in her arms and reading her a bedtime story.

"I like you too, honey. You're a special girl. Now," she said, clearing her throat and rising from her knees, "we need to make a decision. I need to drive to Kalado before going home. Can I take you out to the ranch?"

"I know Daddy will come by here." J.D. chewed her lower lip a minute as she thought. "How about if we leave him a note on the outside door? He can wait for us here and I can ride along with you." Her face brightened. "I love shopping."

Alecia nodded her agreement. "I'll be coming back by here on my way home so I guess it'll work. It's better than sitting here. Let's go."

The two of them talked and laughed all the way into town. At the grocery store, J.D. ran about, fetching items from Nancy's list and placing them in the basket. She was sure to bring only the sizes and brands that Alecia had named. Her unassuming attitude was endearing.

Alecia saw her eyeing the candy bars, but she asked for nothing. Before checking out, Alecia asked her if she would like one. She nodded and smiled her thanks.

As they walked to the car, Alecia once more remembered the dress in Archer's window. It wouldn't hurt to walk by and see if J.D. noticed it.

"Let's go window shopping for a minute, J.D. Sound good?"

"Sounds great!"

J.D.'s boots clomped along on the old brick sidewalk as they passed the donut shop and the insurance office on their way toward Archer's. It happened exactly as Alecia hoped it would. J.D. was pulling at her hand. "Look, Miss Winland. There's a happy yellow dress for little girls."

"So there is, J.D. Shall we go take a look?"

J.D. did a little skip, hop. "Oh could we?"

"Sure. Why not?"

She stopped. "Daddy may be waiting."

"You gave so much help in the store, we finished quickly," Alecia said. "And it'll only take a minute to look."

Convinced, J.D. led the way inside. Together they examined the rack of dresses in J.D.'s size. The girl oohed and aahed over each one, but kept going back to the yellow one like the one in the window. She touched the ruffled skirt and puffy sleeves as though it were fragile.

To think Rayne could afford to buy nice things for his daughter but refused to do so. It was cruelty at its worst. Alecia pulled the yellow one from the rack and put it up against J.D.'s slender body. "Want to try it on?"

"Really? Could I?" Her cheeks were aflame with excitement.

"I'd like to see you in it. The color would highlight the color of your hair."

In a few minutes a transformed cowgirl burst out of the dressing room with a squeal of delight. Although it looked a bit strange with boots, the dress was otherwise lovely. J.D. twirled on her heel to make the skirt sweep out.

The salesladies smiled as they looked on. Impulsively Alecia turned to one of them. "We'll take this one, please."

J.D. looked at her in disbelief. "But my birthday's not until summertime when it's hot, and Christmas is even farther away than that."

Alecia put her arm around the child. "Hasn't anyone ever given you a gift just because they cared about you?"

J.D. pondered the question. "Daddy used to. . .a long time ago. Grandpa does, sometimes. He's neat." Then she thought of something else. "This dress is too pretty to wear to school. Where would I wear it?"

"Maybe you could go to church with Nancy and me some Sunday. Now, go change. We'd better hurry."

At the cash register, the saleslady boxed the dress. Looking over the counter at J.D., she said, "Aren't you Rayne Lassiter's little girl?"

"Uh huh," J.D. answered.

Alecia saw the woman shoot a strange sideways glance at the clerk beside her. "And this," J.D. added, "is my teacher from Charlesy."

The lady handed Alecia her change and said, "You must be real new around here."

"I've been here since February."

The ladies exchanged glances once more. Alecia suddenly felt uncomfortable. "Hope you get a lot of wear out of this, little Miss Lassiter," the clerk said, handing J.D. the large box.

Alecia hurried J.D. out the door. *Small towns,* she fumed. *Like living in a fish bowl.* All she had done was buy the girl a gift.

As they approached the school, Alecia could see the blue pickup parked in front. Of course, Rayne might not understand at first, she assured herself. But once he saw how excited his daughter was and how cute she looked, there would be no way he could protest her having the dress.

She was wrong. Dead wrong.

J.D., box in arms, jumped from the car the moment it stopped. "Look, Daddy!" she called out. "Miss Winland bought me a happy yellow dress. Wait till you see it."

Rayne stepped out of the pickup and approached them. The brown eyes were hard and resolute. "A dress, J.D.? What made Miss Winland think you needed any clothes?"

"We were waiting for you, Daddy. Miss Winland had to get groceries, so I went with her and we window shopped and I saw the dress and liked it and she let me try it on. Then she bought it for me because she loves me. Isn't that right, Miss Winland?"

In her very innocence, J.D. made the whole thing sound very contrived. Alecia felt her cheeks reddening.

"Where were you, Daddy? We waited a long, long time."

"Had a flat tire on the way back from a sale." His words came with no change in tone. "Give the dress back to Miss Winland, J.D. I'll buy your clothes for you. Go get in the pickup."

Taught to obey, J.D. looked at her father with an expression of stricken disappointment. Yet, without protest, she handed the box to her teacher with a, "Thank you anyway, Miss Winland," and walked slowly to the royal blue pickup and crawled up into it.

At the click of the door, Rayne spoke. "Archer's! Now all of Denlin County will be buzzing about the latest. Tell me, what gave you cause to think I can't buy anything and everything my daughter might need?"

"It wasn't because I didn't think you could."

"You didn't think I would. Is that it?"

"Rayne, please. It's just a gift. I'm fond of J.D. She's a precious child. I wanted to show her my love with a gift."

"How about a coloring book and a large box of crayons?" His voice was laced with anger, his eyes flashing. "You don't want to give her a gift, Miss Winland. You want to crawl into her mind and rearrange her modes of thinking."

"There's no need to change a girl's way of thinking about a dress she loves." Her words came fast now, like bullets to the mark. "All little girls love dresses, Mr. Lassiter. Or haven't you noticed?"

"All I notice is a meddling, citified schoolteacher messing with my daughter's mind. Can't you people be satisfied with reading and writing? Think you got to psychoanalyze everybody? Let me tell you J.D. is a happy child. And if you keep meddling, I'll pull her out of Charlesy and drive her to Kalado to school."

Alecia shook her head in disbelief. If only he had seen his daughter dancing around the store in the frilly dress. But even then, he might not have accepted it. What had happened in his life to have blinded him so?

"It doesn't take psychoanalyzing a puppy to know it likes to be scratched behind the ears. Only a simple observation." The scalding accusation hung between them. "Very well," she said with sharp resignation. "I'll take back the dress. But I'll never be sorry I bought it." She whirled about and tossed the box in the back seat and jumped into her car.

This time, the car started immediately and provided the perfect opportunity to peel out and send a spray of gravel flying. Just in time, she remembered J.D. She couldn't make a scene in front of her.

She was far down the road before her ragged breathing began to even out. It had happened again. She had let her professionalism fall by the wayside and had allowed herself to be melted like warm butter by this precocious child— then ridiculed by her father. "Lord, what's happening to me?" she moaned as the wind whipped her hair and cleared her mind. Of all the children she had ever met, none had affected her like J.D.

What would have happened, she chided herself, if she had taken even one underprivileged inner city child to a dress shop for a new dress? If word ever got back to her superior, Mr. Harwood, he would have been extremely unhappy with her.

Oh why couldn't Rayne see the negative seeds he was planting in J.D. By the time she turned thirteen, the girl would be in rebellion for sure. Alecia turned the car sharply and the sacks slid across the back seat in protest. That would serve him right, she thought. Then he would see she had been right all along.

But was that really true? She recalled how J.D. respectfully handed over the box and obediently retreated to the pickup. It was the type of obedience Alecia had seen only in children with loving parental authority in the home. What a paradox.

Once before she had made a promise to the Lord—to hold both Lassiters at arm's length. Perhaps the only answer would be to resign her position at Charlesy before the year was completed. But the very thought that she would quit anything was repulsive to her.

Lost in her thoughts, Alecia drove past Jake's mobile home before she noticed him standing outside waving and grinning at her. Absently she thrust an arm up to wave back as she rounded the bend.

She struggled to get her mind back into a semblance of order before talking with Nancy. Her sister had an uncanny way of sensing if anything was amiss.

Chapter Five

"You sound just like Mother," Alecia told Nancy defensively. Her elder sister finally asked Alecia what was wrong. They were clearing away the dishes from supper. Alecia was struggling to mask her distraught emotions and, in doing so, had obviously become all the more transparent.

"I take that as a compliment," Nancy retorted good naturedly. "As Mother always quoted from chapter eight of Nehemiah, 'The joy of the Lord is your strength.' If so, you must be feeling pretty weak right now. You've uttered hardly two words since you came home."

Alecia thought back to her exuberance that morning as she donned the jonquil-colored dress. How foolish it was to let her joy ride on such an unpredictable yo-yo string.

"Oh, Nancy," she blurted out, thankful to be able to unload her misery, "it's the Lassiters."

"The Lassiters?" Nancy looked around from wiping down the cabinets. "What's the problem?"

"Come to my room. I have something to show you." In the bedroom she retrieved Archer's dress box from her closet, opened it, and lay the dress across the bed. Against the flowered spread, the dress looked even more lovely.

Nancy sat down beside the dress, gently fingering a ruffle. "You bought this for J.D.?" Alecia listened for incrimination in the question, but detected none.

"I hadn't planned to. It just seemed to happen." How could she explain? "Rayne was late, so I took J.D. shopping with me. We went by Archer's and she was crazy about this dress. I let her try it on, and she looked so darling and was so excited. . . ."

"And you just couldn't resist?"

"I know it sounds crazy."

"Does Rayne know?"

Alecia could only nod, remembering his anger afresh.

"What did he say?" Nancy's voice took on the sternness Alecia remembered from her childhood.

"He was terribly angry. He made J.D. give it back to me. Can you imagine? Poor child. She needs fussy things. You should have seen her in that dress, whirling and dancing."

Alecia sat down on the chintz chair by the window. "Why can't he see? He's hurting her unmercifully."

"You may be one hundred percent correct in your assumptions, Alecia. . .and

I agree that you may be. But you're going about this all wrong. You're backing a wounded bull into a corner. No matter what you say or do, he's going to come out fighting. And this is a corner Rayne's never been in before."

Nancy folded the dress and placed it back into the box, tucking the rustling tissues around it. "Knowing Rayne," she went on, "I imagine it's a hard lump for him to swallow just to think J.D. has attached herself to an outsider. But for you to move in on his territory like this. Well, stop and think how you would feel if someone came into your office in the education center and began telling you how to run your business. Would you receive it, or resent it?"

Alecia leaned back in the chair, pondering Nancy's words. As usual, her sister was right. "I guess I owe him an apology, don't I?" A real one this time, she told herself. Not a subtle one.

Nancy smiled her approval. "Ever since Rayne's wife died, he's tried to shut out the world. But he loves J.D. deeply. Most of us who know him are trusting that in time he'll see clearly what his daughter needs most in her life. But he'll have to come to grips with it in his own way. That's just the way these people are."

Alecia puttered through the remainder of the evening, trying to keep her mind on her work. How would she ever find the opportunity to apologize to Rayne? And what good would it do anyway? He would certainly rebuff any attempts she made. Never would he believe she truly wanted to apologize with no strings attached.

By the time they settled down to their devotion time together, Alecia asked Nancy to pray that she would have the wisdom to handle the matter. However even after Nancy's prayer, Alecia's frustrations were not eased.

By the time she readied herself for bed, she decided phoning was the only way. She lacked the courage to drive to the ranch and face him. But it had to be settled now. She paced the carpeted room for a few minutes, hands thrust deep into the pockets of her robe. Finally she picked up the thin county phone book and ran her finger down the page listing to the El Crosse Ranch. Ever so slowly, she punched in the numbers.

"Come on, Alecia," she taunted herself beneath her breath. "You were brash enough spit at him like an old hen this afternoon; you can be bold enough to apologize like a woman now."

She dared not take a breath as the phone rang on the other end. A deep resonant voice answered. "El Crosse Ranch. Rayne speaking."

She froze.

"Hello? Who's there?"

"Rayne? It's Alecia."

A stretch of silence weighed heavily. "Yes," he said finally, not unkindly.

"I called to apologize. Sincerely apologize."

"I see." Noncommittal.

"I guess I got carried away. J.D. looked so cute in that dress and kids always . . . ." She stopped. "Oh Rayne, the truth is, I don't know what got into me. I've been in the field of education for many years, and I've never been so drawn to a student before. It's crazy and I'm sorry. I'm not usually so impetuous. From now on, I promise to step back and become more objective about J.D."

Her heart pounded through another silence. Would he believe her? It mattered to her that he did, because now she was being totally honest. At least as honest as she could be. She really didn't know why she felt so strongly about the child.

"I'll give you credit," she heard him saying in his slow way. "It took courage for you to call."

"It was positively terrifying," she admitted.

"You didn't have to call."

"Yes, I did. We need to clear the air for J.D.'s sake. Believe me, I don't want to cause any anxiety for your daughter." She waited through another meaningful pause, only now the pounding of her heart had subsided somewhat.

"She's taken a real liking to you, Alecia," he said. "She doesn't usually buddy up to someone that fast."

Ah, good. Back to first names.

"And," he added with a touch of humor in his voice, "she's even giving the old multiplication tables a second glance now."

"That's music to a teacher's ears. To hear that a child has become motivated to study."

"It's a real switch. Josie and I were having a rough time with her there for a while."

Alecia tried to envision Rayne sitting at the kitchen table like a normal parent, helping J.D. with her math. Somehow it just didn't fit. Absently she wondered if he had his boots pulled off now, with his feet propped up on a footstool in the magnificent oak-paneled living room.

"Well?" she asked.

"What?"

"You haven't told me if you accept my apology after I've come forth in fear and trepidation to call."

"I do accept. And I appreciate the call."

She let these mellow words sink in, hoping he was sincere. It occurred to her that he might apologize to her for his anger as well. But after all, she hadn't called to bait him.

"Say," he added almost as an afterthought. "I've been wanting to ask. Have you heard from Lavren since the Field Day?"

"No. Why?"

"Just curious. Alecia?"

"Yes."

"If you do, you let me know. Y'hear?"

What is this? she wondered. They were talking about J.D. and homework, and all of a sudden Domier enters the conversation. She wanted to forget him forever. "For what it's worth, okay, I promise to let you know."

"Good. Thanks again for the call. You take it easy now. Bye."

Alecia felt strangely light and airy as she hung up the phone. Nancy was surely asleep by now, or she would be tempted to run in there and tell her sister how much better she felt about the entire situation. He had accepted her apology. As livid as he had been that afternoon, she never would have thought it possible. And if she hadn't talked it out with Nancy, the whole nasty incident might have continued to fester inside her for who knows how long. Sweet, kind Nancy. Now that Alecia thought about it, her sister had seemed overly tired this evening and was showing signs of coming down with a cold. She made a mental note to call the doctor as soon as she got home the next day. No sense in taking chances.

❧

It rained for the next three days. . .dreary, sodden, gray rain that lets not a pinch of sunshine squeeze through. The children were restless and Alecia reached deep into her storehouse of memories to come up with ideas to keep them busy during recesses. No sophisticated gymnasium equipment was available as there had been in Minneapolis where schools were prepared for weeks of bad weather.

One afternoon Alecia was down on the floor helping the girls cut out paper dolls during the late recess. J.D. was sitting close to her and when they were alone for a moment, J.D. leaned over with scissors snipping and said in a low whisper, "Do you know what my real name is?"

"No, J.D., I don't. No one ever told me." It was true.

Even on her school record there appeared only the vague initials.

"Want to know?" she asked.

"Oh, yes. Very much." She had often wondered what the initials stood for and why the name wasn't used, even at school.

"Joanna Darlene," she whispered with all the graveness of revealing a deep treasured secret. "J.D.'s just my nickname."

"I had a hunch it was," Alecia told her. "Would you believe when I was in third grade, the kids called me Allie for a nickname? I didn't like it because where I lived, the alleys were narrow streets behind the houses where everyone kept their garbage cans."

"Yuck." J.D. wrinkled up her nose. "Did you wish they would call you Alecia?"

"Many times."

"When we're alone," J.D. said, her face solemn, "without other kids around, would you sometimes use my real name?"

Alecia gazed at the gentle, trusting small face. She forced her mind to recall her most recent resolve—to back off and be objective with her. But how could she? And what would it hurt to promise this? There wouldn't be many more opportunities for them to be alone anyway.

"Okay, Joanna Darlene," she said, pronouncing each syllable quietly and with great care. "When we're alone, I'll use your real name."

Quickly, J.D. looked around, but no one had heard. She looked back at her teacher and smiled a thank you.

Alecia felt a rush of warm contentment flow through her.

ॐ

Saturday was still gray and soggy. Nancy's cold had grown progressively worse. Since it had moved into her chest, the doctor suggested bed rest.

Alecia went out to check on the horses and the feeder calves, stacked wood on the back patio, and then went back inside. It was a perfect day to laze about and get caught up on back work.

Days like this made her miss her metropolitan lifestyle more than ever. If she were home, she would be at the spa today, swimming or playing a game of racquetball with Galen.

The rain chilled the spring air, so a fire in the woodburning stove was the answer to chase away the dampness. Soon the fire was crackling and the coffee perking. On the card table in the den, she spread out the work Galen had sent her.

Carefully she studied the charts telling which schools would be involved in the stepped-up program and the personnel involved. Her pen scratched out meticulous notes in a spiral notebook to share the next time Galen called.

Her longing to see Galen and her desire to return to her work seemed to bleed together in a vague blur. She was unable to fit her feelings in the proper cubbyholes of her mind.

Grabbing her coffee mug, she rose restlessly from her work to the bookshelves by the glass-fronted stove. From the shelf, she took down Galen's photo and studied the generous smiling lips that had touched hers so gently before she left him last winter. The squinting blue eyes that scolded her when she worked too hard and laughed at her when she lost a game of tennis to him. His fair blond hair was full, brushed back casually from his young, almost boyish face. She wondered if he had any such trouble sorting out his feelings for her. From the way he talked to her during their most recent phone conversation, she decided he did not.

When the phone rang, it startled her, nearly causing her to spill the hot coffee. She was thankful she had disconnected the extension in Nancy's room. She replaced Galen's photo and grabbed the phone. She was both surprised and disturbed to hear Lavren Domier's voice.

"Mrs. Whitlow?" he asked.

"This is her sister. Nancy's resting right now. What can I do for you?"

"Alecia!" he said dramatically. "So good to talk with you again, Alecia. I'm sure you won't mind giving Mrs. Whitlow my message. Please tell her for me that I have the bull. And that I meant just what I said."

Alecia bristled. "You're lying. Jake fixed that fence. He told me so. The bull couldn't get through."

"Alecia, dear. You women need to learn you can't trust a drunk. Maybe you'd better drive over here and see if I'm lying. I'd love to have you come and see me."

"If I come to your ranch, Mr. Domier, I'll have the sheriff with me. That bull belongs to Nancy. You can't kill him just because he broke through the fence."

"Bring the sheriff and his two deputies with him. We'll have a party," he said in his churlish manner. "But I must warn you, the law in Denlin County is more afraid of me than I am of them."

This man was talking crazy. Alecia had no idea how much to believe. "Exactly what is it you're wanting? You don't need Nancy's bull and I don't think you'd shoot him."

The calculating voice became even more so. "Don't kid yourself. I'd as soon shoot that bull as look at him."

"That's ridiculous. What would it gain you?"

"Well now, you're beginning to sound more interested. Drive over and we'll discuss the matter. You'll find me extremely businesslike in my dealings. After all, it wasn't my fault the bull came into my pasture."

His smugness was becoming more repulsive. "You seem to be forgetting, Mr. Domier, that bull is of no interest to me anyway."

"Please, not so formal. Call me Lavren. The bull, of course, may not interest you, but without that expensive bull, your sister's ranch would be in dire straits. I happen to know she's come on some hard times. And with your tender heart, you wouldn't want to see her lose the place. Right?"

He was right and he knew it. Ever since the evening he had approached her in the pasture, Alecia had been more concerned for Nancy's welfare. The simple solution seemed to be to sell and get out from under the pressures and hard work. But Alecia knew the love of this land was deeply ingrained in her sister's heart as much at it was in any rancher's in the county.

"What do you want me to do, Mr. Domier?" Never would she give him the satisfaction of addressing him on a first name basis.

"I told you. Come on over and let's sit down and have a long talk together. There are some things I feel you should be made aware of."

Alecia rubbed the back of her neck, remembering the sickening sensation of his touch. Perhaps he didn't have the bull at all and was playing cat-and-mouse with her. But for Nancy's sake, she felt she had to take the risk. "I'll be there in an hour," she told him.

He gave a low-throated chuckle. "Now you're talking. I'll be waiting."

Disgusted, she hung up without another word. Thoughtfully, she went to her bedroom and changed into her boots, blue jeans, and a warm shirt and jacket. As she sat on the edge of the bed to pull on her boots, she happened to notice the note pad where she had sketched as she talked to Rayne a few nights ago. Why hadn't she remembered sooner? He made her promise to call if she heard from Domier again. *Oh, praise God,* she sighed. Rayne would help her.

Her fingers trembled slightly as she dialed and prayed that he would be there. She released her bottom lip from between her teeth when his voice came over the line. Briefly she explained to him the gist of Lavren's call and his threats about the bull.

"And you told him you'd come over?" Rayne asked in a tone of disbelief.

She shrugged. "I didn't know what else to do."

"Stay put," he told her. "I'll be right over."

When she heard his pickup pull into the driveway a short time later, she met him out front to prevent waking Nancy. She felt it was wise to let her sister rest. Rayne would get this mess straightened out quickly.

Alecia wasn't certain if her heart sped up because of the circumstances surrounding the call or because of the way Rayne looked at her as he walked toward her. He touched his hat and gave a nod. His eyes were shining as they glanced over her outfit and returned to linger on her face. "A real dyed-in-the-wool cowgirl." His trim moustache outlined his smile. "You sure look different in that getup."

His attention was totally unexpected. Alecia firmed her hat on her head and returned his smile. "I'm ready to round up them mean cattle rustlers," she joked to alleviate her discomfort. She was delighted, however, that he seemed so relaxed. He had sounded concerned over the phone. Perhaps the situation wasn't so grave as she thought.

"Can you ride?" he asked.

She laughed lightly. "Due in part to Kane Brake's benevolent attitude toward me, I manage. Why?"

"It's too muddy to take the pickup, and I'd like to ride down and take a look at the south fence before talking to Domier. You game?"

"Why didn't I think of that?" she said. "I could have ridden down the fence line to see if he was lying or not. Roscoe could be calmly chewing his cud in his own pasture right now." As Rayne walked toward the stables, she fell into step beside him.

"Better you didn't," he told her. "Domier could have been down there waiting for you."

It upset Alecia to think Lavren could have set a trap for her, but more upsetting was the fact that Rayne should suspect him of doing so. And, she surmised, Rayne of all people should know.

They saddled the horses while making minimal conversation. Rayne allowed Alecia to take Kane Brake and he kindly accepted Peppy, muttering to the horse softly as he worked with her. Intermittently he leaned down to pet Sparkie as the sheltie trotted in among them, appearing impatient to be off on this unknown mission.

The rain had subsided and a light mist veiled the air. Alecia appreciated the brim of her cowboy hat acting as a small umbrella to keep the moisture from her eyes.

They were several feet from it when they saw the break in the fence where Roscoe had plunged through. Rayne pointed it out silently.

"But I was so sure Jake had fixed it," Alecia protested. "He told me—"

"No doubt about Jake," Rayne assured her. "He wouldn't lie. He's a good old boy. Either he didn't fix it good enough, or somebody's been tampering."

Alecia's mind was unwilling to comprehend Rayne's innuendo. "I thought Lavren was leading me on. I was hoping he didn't have Roscoe at all."

Rayne turned in the saddle to look at her, his face soft through the opaque mist. "If Lavren Domier says he has something, he has it. And he's determined to use the incident to his fullest advantage."

"What are you going to do now?" she wanted to know.

His face lit up with a mischievous smile. "You mean, what're we going to do. You and I are going to get the bull back for Nancy."

"How?"

"Simple. We ride over and bring him home."

Everything in her wanted to protest, but he made it sound like they were stopping by the convenience store for a carton of milk.

"You've driven cattle, haven't you?" he asked, straightening in the saddle, sitting high and tall.

"Cows and calves. Not a bull." She remembered Roscoe's mammoth size. He was a giant.

"No different." As though that settled the issue, he urged Peppy down to the fence and let her step neatly over the limp strands. Kane Brake followed as though Rayne were in control rather than Alecia. "Sparkie and the horses will do all the work," he said over his shoulder. "Come on."

He put the cow pony into a smooth canter and again, Kane Brake did the same. Alecia decided to relax and enjoy the loping ride. It seemed strange to think of the two of them coming across the back part of Domier Ranch and Alecia had no idea what they would do when they arrived at the feed lots.

But Rayne had everything all figured out. Since it was a rainy Saturday, he told her, most of the ranch hands would be inside the bunkhouses.

Cresting a small rise, they reined in their mounts to look for a moment across the Domier spread. The expanse of the ranch was larger and more complex than that of El Crosse. Alecia scanned the multiple pens of feeder cattle, the large silos, and myriads of smaller buildings set about. The stately two-story white home of Lavren and Corrine Domier was on the far side, facing the road, graced about by towering shade trees, all gleaming fresh and clean after the rain bath.

At rare intervals, the sun found peepholes in the slate gray skies, forcing bright beams to lay golden patterns on the washed earth. The damp pasture gave off sweet fragrances. Appreciatively, Alecia sucked in the delicious aroma with a deep breath.

She turned to catch Rayne studying her. Embarrassed, she turned her eyes back to the pens below them. Her face felt warm beneath his gaze. "We'll never find him in all those feed lots," she said absently. Was he still trying to figure her out? Is that why he was watching her? Still not trusting her?

Rayne dismounted and called Sparkie to him. "We have our bloodhound with us," he explained. The sheltie's alert black eyes glowed in readiness. Rayne rubbed the thick fur. "Roscoe, Sparkie. Find Roscoe for us. And no barking either. You hear me?"

Alecia was surprised that Sparkie was so quick to obey Rayne. But the tall rancher seemed to have a way with all animals. She wanted to laugh at the thought of Lavren Domier sitting in his big white house, waiting for her to arrive, while she and Rayne were taking the bull out the back way. Sparkie sniffed out the bull in short order, locating him alone in a catch pen near where they rode in. It was a simple matter to open the gate and let Sparkie deftly run him out.

The mammoth bull seemed relieved to be released from captivity and was more than happy to comply. In a matter of minutes, Roscoe had lumbered over the break in the fence and was safe again on Whitlow land.

The gray clouds above them were beginning to thicken again and move in low. Rayne pulled Peppy to a halt. "We should put Roscoe in another pasture, just for good measure," he told her. "I'll send Sammy and a couple of the boys over to fix the fence later. We'll leave it up to Nancy whether to leave Roscoe there and run the cows in there with him, or put him back here and trust it won't happen again."

"I thought," Alecia said, as they rode across the muddy pasture with Roscoe and Sparkie in the lead, "it might be best that Nancy didn't know about all this."

"I understand you're wanting to protect her, but she'll have to know. She has to be on top of all that goes on here. It's the only way to run a ranch—recuperating from surgery or not." He glanced at the clouds that were churning with mounting fury. "We'd better hurry before the bottom falls out of that."

The convulsing, yellowish clouds brought to Alecia's mind all of the Oklahoma tornado stories she had heard. The first of the fat drops struck them as Rayne closed the gate after the bull. Vicious stabs of yellow lightning ripped through the clouds and explosions of thunder shook the ground. Both horses nickered nervously.

Rayne came up behind her, talking softly to Peppy, calming the old cow pony. "Mind getting wet?" His expression was almost like an apology.

She laughed, pulling her hat down more snugly over her eyes. "Wouldn't matter much if I did. I never learned to stay between the drops."

His laughter joined with her. "Lets head for the house then." The horses galloped neck-and-neck out across the great expanses of openness. They were nearly to the gate that led to the stables. The horses were clamoring up out of a steep draw. The rain was pelting them unmercifully. Alecia remembered thinking what a shame it was that Rayne's leather coat should be getting wet. At that moment, Peppy—surefooted Peppy—stepped into wet clay and went down.

Rayne's lean muscular body was at once alert and, like a graceful agile cat, leaped out of the way before being pinned beneath the horse.

Alecia stifled the scream in her throat.

Chapter Six

To see Peppy go down, to hear her cry of fright also terrified the normally placid Kane Brake. Alecia fought to hold her in rein.

"Whoa, girl. Settle down. Easy now." She kept her voice steady, speaking between throbs of furious thunder.

Peppy jumped to her feet quickly, seemingly unharmed, but with a wild glare in her eyes. One more clap of thunder could send the frightened animal off on a dead run, only to be hurt worse.

Rayne stepped toward the pony to grab hold of the dragging leather straps but Peppy backed up, whinnying in fear. As Peppy moved backward in her direction, Alecia gently urged her mount forward.

Kane Brake was unsure, hesitant. Using all her strength, Alecia held tight, urging, encouraging. "Come on, girl. Move up there. Don't be afraid. That's a good girl," she cooed repeatedly.

Peppy regarded them with wide eyes as they approached and was somewhat calmed to see that Kane Brake was still there. Gradually, Alecia moved Kane Brake close enough so she could reach for Peppy's bridle. As she did, Rayne ran to them, retrieving the reins and quickly checking the horse's legs for possible injuries.

"Looks okay," he called out over the noise of the storm. "But no sense in taking any chances. I'd better ride back with you."

She held Kane Brake in check as he swung up behind her. Immediately, she was aware of him as he reached around her to take the reins, his arms pressing against her shoulders. Rayne emitted an essence of tender strength that was measured not simply in physique, but in the very core of his personality.

Together they rode, leading Peppy back to warmth and safety. The dampness of the spring storm hung heavy in the stables, intensifying the aromas of leather, wet horses, and sweet hay. It was a relief to leave behind the blustery elements, which continued to beat against the metal building as though in a vain, but persistent, effort to get at them.

"Good piece of riding there, Calamity Jane," Rayne said as he dismounted.

"You didn't give too bad a performance yourself, Mr. Hickok," she countered. Outwardly, she threw off the compliment, but inwardly she savored it. She swung her leg over to slide down. Rayne reached up to assist her. "What say we take the act cross-country? A world wide event," she said.

She landed on the ground before him, but his hands stayed about her waist. He laughed aloud. "Training for that performance would be sheer agony."

She enjoyed the sound of his deep laughter. Laughter that played its own gay melody inside her.

"There's more power in your small arms than a fellow would guess," he said, still not releasing her.

"Tennis arms," she retorted. There were flecks of mud splatters on his cheek. Instinctively she reached up to wipe them away.

"I play tennis too," he said, his tone going soft. His hands slipped from her waist around to her back, enfolding her to him.

Her heart beat against her chest as she looked up into his searching eyes that were nearly black in the dim, storm-darkened stable.

He lowered his face to hers. "We'll have to play sometime." The very breath of his words lay on her lips.

It was so natural, so easy to rise on tiptoe to meet the warm lips and return his embrace. Her hat fell silently to the stable floor. Her hands moved up his wet jacket to cling to his broad shoulders.

His kisses moved to her rain-streaked face, to her eyelids, and back to her mouth where she felt an inner explosion that equaled the rolling thunder shaking the vast prairies about them.

Already breathless from the ride, they were now weak and breathless from the storm of emotions rising between them.

She moved to touch his face. When she did, he took her hand firmly, then the other one, and stepped back. The brown eyes were smoky, troubled.

"Go on in and change, Alecia," he said evenly. "Before you catch cold. I'll tend to the horses."

Her mind and senses were reeling. She feared if he released her hands, she would surely fall. She nodded her mute agreement, struggling to control her thoughts. She pulled her hands from his and shivered. She was chilled.

Rayne watched as her lithe form bent down to retrieve her hat and place it firmly on her head before going out the door to return to the house.

Whirling around, he blindly slammed his fist into the support post of the stable, shaking it from top to bottom. Then his towering body sagged against it, as he leaned there, letting his anguish consume him.

Never, he vowed to himself, would he be so foolish as to let uncurbed emotions deceive him again.

∂❧

For the next few days in the classroom, Alecia could not bear to look into Joanna's eyes because of the disturbance within her of seeing Rayne's eyes reflected there. They were so similar in expression and beauty. Ironically the more she tried to evade the child, the more Joanna clung to her.

Endlessly Alecia's mind replayed the moment when she slid off Kane Brake into Rayne's arms and into a bottomless abyss of stirred feelings.

And why? Why had he kissed her? She thought he detested her. Confused, she grappled with elusive questions. If he cared for her at all, why wouldn't he listen to her suggestions regarding Joanna? Perhaps there was no caring at all . . .just a lonely widower starved for affection. Had the embrace been an impulse at a weak moment? She threw out that possibility. One thing was certain, Rayne Lassiter was not impulsive.

Nancy had graciously thanked both of them for their help in bringing Roscoe home and eagerly accepted Rayne's offer to send men to repair the fence. Like the coward she was, Alecia chose to stay in her room while Rayne came in to call Lavren. Nancy told her later that the two men exchanged heated words over the phone. But Alecia made a pretense of taking more time than was needed to change, timing it to finish just as he left. There was no way she could face him at that moment—in front of Nancy.

Lavren's actions had not upset Nancy in the least. "Lavren's not actually ruthless," she explained to Alecia. "But he's had his eyes on my ponds for quite some time. He figures he can needle me into selling now that I'm having a rough go of it. Plus there are other problems he's struggling with."

Alecia was indignant. "Ponds? He has ponds. I saw them."

"The Whitlow land has two spring-fed ponds, Alecia. A lovely miracle of God. No pumping water ever. That's why Ted purchased this land in the first place." Then Nancy added with the old fire returning to her tired eyes, "And when I do let this land go, it won't go to Lavren Domier! I can tell you that for sure!"

Alecia moved slowly about her classroom as she remembered their conversation. No matter what Nancy said about Lavren not being ruthless, Alecia wasn't totally convinced. And she didn't see how Nancy would have the strength to go on fighting against him.

The schoolroom windows were open wide, letting long-awaited April sunshine splash into the room. It beckoned to the children to come outside, making them restless at their work.

When Alecia first arrived to teach at Charlesy, her students roamed about the room at will and talked continually without permission. But through perseverance and by using a rewards system, she soon had them striving to earn credit points by obeying the rules she established. When there were enough overall points between the two grade levels, she rewarded them with Friday afternoon parties. This promoted team efforts and encouraged all students, rather than just a few, to participate in the system.

At first they groaned and complained under her leadership, but gradually their allegiance came around. She rejoiced to see them begin to strive for academic excellence.

Although the days were warmer and sunnier than ever, Joanna dallied behind in the classroom at every recess—except when Alecia had playground duty. It became a source of worry for Alecia. Now, more than ever, she realized she should never have purchased the little yellow dress. In doing so she had unwittingly cemented their relationship.

By the time the afternoon recess rolled around, Alecia made up her mind about something. Asking Flossie to take over for her on the playground, she hurried to Lyle's office and knocked lightly at his door. His small office was situated just off the fifth and sixth-grade classroom.

He invited her in without getting up from his ancient wooden swivel chair situated behind the desk. She stepped in and he gestured toward the only other chair, which had a torn vinyl seat.

"What's on your mind, Miss Winland?" he asked, smoothing his hands across his thinning hair.

"It's J.D.," she said, scooting the chair closer to his desk. She had to be careful not to use the lovely name of Joanna.

Lyle raised craggy eyebrows, but said nothing.

"She's become very attached to me and I want to resign now before further damage is done in her life."

There. It was finished. She let out a sigh. If all went well, she could be back at her desk in the Minneapolis Educational Service Center Office within two weeks. She was sure Nancy could get along fine now. Suddenly she felt exhilarated.

Lyle studied objects on his desk for a few moments, then leaned back, folding his hands behind his head. "I'd sure hate to see you quit now, Miss Winland. For several reasons."

"I realize it could leave you in a bind, but surely you can get a good substitute for the few remaining weeks." She took a long breath. "I was wrong to try to become involved in J.D.'s personal life. I can see that now." In her mind's eye, she was already packing.

Lyle's hands came back down and were folded on the desk top before him. The old chair creaked in protest. "Miss Winland," he said, "I've observed with mounting interest the transformation in your students since you've come here. And I want you to know it's a joy to me."

She started to speak, but he raised a hand to stop her. "Flossie also watches you like a hawk. She's young and impressionable." Lyle's eyes, which Alecia normally thought to be a bit dull, held a new spark. "In times past," he continued in his quiet manner, "I have approached our school board with new ideas, and have been repeatedly rebuffed because of lack of understanding on their part. But you've sort of slipped in the back door, so to speak, and introduced innovations, simply by your presence, that I couldn't have done in my position."

Alecia shifted in the uncomfortable chair and fingered the fringed belt of her dress. This conversation was taking an unexpected turn, throwing her off track.

"On our small operating budget, there's no way Charlesy School could afford someone with your caliber of expertise, but here you are right in our midst. I've looked upon your being here as sort of a little miracle." Embarrassed by his own admission, he scooted back the chair with a clatter and rose to fetch a cup of coffee from the pot on the filing cabinet, which Mrs. Turner perpetually kept perked for him. He filled his mug and waved the pot at her, raising his brows in question.

"Yes. Black, please." Where was this strange conversation leading?

He brought the steaming cups and reseated himself. "It has been," he went on with fresh composure, "a continual challenge here to discover methods to interest children in academics. To see your students' enthusiasm with their science projects and their spelling contests was a surprise to Flossie." He gave a wide smile. "And I'd almost forgotten how much fun kids could have in the process of learning."

"I appreciate the kind remarks," she said feebly. She never thought that by doing the things that were natural for her, she was making a contribution. On the contrary, she felt like she was rubbing against the grain.

"Because of your being here, I had planned to undertake an all-school drama," he continued. "This would be an effort to initiate more parental involvement. I was going to present it to you and Flossie today after school." He rummaged in his desk drawer and pulled out a play script copy and handed it across the desk to her. "This is a patriotic analogy, which is both educational and entertaining."

Alecia flipped through the pages with growing interest. She could envision the sixth-grade boys excitedly building stage sets and painting scenery. "Looks like an excellent story line," she commented, scanning the pages. "It's a good script. If they've not been involved in much drama, they'll love doing this."

"Until now," he confessed, "I haven't had anyone who could take the ball and run with it. I know you can. You can arrange for tryouts and plan a fair way of casting, plus choose teams for the supportive work so every student is involved."

She nodded. She could at that. And interestingly enough, she felt a genuine desire to try.

Lyle's eyes narrowed as he watched her. "Just a few more weeks? Charlesy needs what you have to offer."

Alecia thought about Davey, the boy who had been tough and swaggering when she arrived. At his young age, he already had the idea that enjoying school work was beneath his macho image. But he launched into a science project in entomology that astounded his classmates. But still, there remained the problem of Joanna Darlene Lassiter.

As though perceiving her thoughts, Lyle added, "I know I initially objected to your involvement in J.D.'s life, but I've also seen changes for the good in her. I know you feel she is dangerously close to you, but is any relationship without risk?"

This was a new side of this man she was now observing. It shamed her that she had underestimated his depth of perception.

"Even if J.D. never saw you again, you've taught her to be aware of new concepts and feelings she never knew existed."

As indeed, her father has done to me, Alecia thought ruefully. Was it really because of Joanna, or was it because of Rayne that she had suddenly decided to break and run? Discernment eluded her at this point. It was just too painful to sort out.

"The younger Lassiter," Lyle continued, oblivious of her thoughts, "is now aware there is more to this old world than branding cattle. What do you think? Will you stay?"

Well, she thought with a long sigh, *so much for being back home in two weeks.* She took the script. "When do you want to hold tryouts and when is the drama scheduled?"

Lyle drained the last of his coffee that was much too strong for Alecia's taste. "Tryouts, in three days; presentation, the night before the last day of school."

"Sounds fine." She stood to her feet. "I'd better go. Recess is nearly over."

Her boss pushed back the creaking chair and came around the desk to extend his large hand. "I don't think you'll be sorry for staying. And I'm very grateful. Really."

Before the day was out, Alecia had outlined plans to incite the interest of every student and devised costumes that would be quick and simple to make.

She wondered how Flossie would accept her as the director of the show and was pleasantly surprised to note that her coworker's enthusiasm was as high as that of the children's.

When the two of them met together before and after school to line out details, it opened a new door of acquaintance. Alecia discovered a not-so-dumb girl dwelling behind a barrier of low self-esteem. Cautiously, kindly, Alecia searched for ways to draw out Flossie's talents and abilities.

She invited Mrs. Turner and Mrs. Dominique to assist in voting for those who tried out for parts. She wanted to make it as fair as possible. Also she realized that those who were voting were aware of Joanna's background and would refrain from giving her a part.

"If you don't get a part," Alecia explained to Joanna in an attempt to prepare her for the inevitable, "I want you to use your artistic talents to be costume designer with me."

"Thanks, Miss Winland," she said, "but I'm going to be Betsy Ross. I'm going to be the best one in the play. Then they won't say I look like Jake Shanks."

Alecia was sure that after Joanna became involved with the costumes, she would be just as contented as if she had a play part.

Noisy and excited, the children gathered in the gymnasium the afternoon of the tryouts. Flossie was seated beside Alecia on the front row of folding chairs that had been set up in the gym. She tucked a strand of hair behind her ear. "This is the most fun I've had since I started teaching," she quipped.

Alecia studied the face that could have been more attractive if the hair were shorter and softly fluffed to minimize the sharp angular lines. "I'm so glad," she answered. And she meant it.

"Hey, you know what?"

"What?" Alecia shuffled through the sheaf of papers in her clipboard.

"I've accepted a job in Ponca City for next fall. I'm renting an apartment up there and everything."

Alecia was astonished. "You're leaving Charlesy?" The girl who hadn't even left home to go to college?

"Lonnie Wayne isn't too happy about it, but I don't care. Mama says he's not very good for me and I guess she's pretty much right." She flipped through the script book on her lap. "You know," she said slowly, "I didn't much like you when you first came here."

And how I knew it, Alecia thought. But she appreciated the honesty.

"But now I think you're okay. All the kids like you and you make me want to be a better teacher." Flossie blinked her pale eyes that were dabbed with a hasty touch of eye shadow. "I want to learn to motivate kids like you do. I want to do more with my life and I don't think I can do that here." The last comment hung in the air like a question.

"Go for it, Flossie. You can be anything you set your mind to be. Your only limitations are in your own mind." She patted the girl's thin shoulder covered by another wild T-shirt. "I'll be praying for you to make the right decisions in your life. Now," she said, rising to address the Charlesy student body, "we'd better get this show on the road."

❧

At home that evening, Alecia reviewed the results of the tryouts and was mortified to see that all the staff, except her, had voted for Joanna to play the part of Betsy Ross. She wrestled with the predicament. What would Rayne say if his daughter were dressed in a costume for a play? Would that be different than a yellow dress from Archer's?

At least Alecia would stand guiltless since this was none of her doing. The child had received the part, fair and square.

When Joanna stepped on that stage during the tryouts, she displayed none of the giggly nervousness of the other students. Her voice was clear and unwavering: "You're asking me to sew the first flag for our infant nation, General Washington? Oh that I had a thousand hands to set to the task of such a noble purpose." Dramatically she clasped her hands over her heart. "I am indeed humbly grateful to be chosen."

As indeed little Joanna would be humbly grateful when she learned she snagged the part.

Before Alecia was able to sit down to her school work that evening, it was quite late. The warmer the weather grew, the more work there was to do around the ranch. The pace that once seemed painstakingly slow was now accelerated. Never was there lack of something to do.

And Jake was there nearly every day, often sitting down to supper with them, always entertaining them with stories of happier times in his life.

Once, Alecia asked Nancy why she kept him on since he had such a drinking problem. "He's all I can afford," her sister answered with a shrug. But Alecia felt it was because Nancy was the only person who would extend to the man the gesture of trust and acceptance.

On this particular evening, Nancy had offered to clean up after supper so Alecia could get to grading her papers. But learning the results of the tryouts troubled and distracted her. She was curious what Nancy might have to say about it. Her sensible sister might tell her to pull the child out of the whole mess immediately.

To her surprise, Nancy seemed quite pleased with the idea. "A play part, you say? Betsy Ross?" She wrung out the dishcloth and spread it on the towel rack by the sink. "Sounds charming."

"But what about Rayne?"

Nancy grabbed a jar of hand cream and smoothed fragrant cream into her chapped, work-worn hands. "What about him?"

Alecia felt miffed. "Have you forgotten all of what you said to me about intrinsic pride, ingrained sense of survival, and all that propaganda?"

Nancy chuckled gaily. "I told you those things when you were on the man's case with all the stops pulled out. This is different. If, as you say, she was chosen by several voting adults, then I hardly think Rayne would object. This could be a foretaste for him of things to come. Oh, and by the way," she went on, totally changing the subject, "Corrine called me today."

"Domier?" Alecia couldn't imagine Corrine picking up the phone to call Nancy. They were total opposites. Corrine spent all her time training her prize horses and traveling from show to show, dressed to the hilt in western suits of every hue of the rainbow.

"Of course, Domier. She calls me every once in a while when she has exciting news. She's back from Texas where she won first place in one of her more important shows in the Western Pleasure Futurity Division. She called to invite me to the party Lavren is letting her give next Saturday night to celebrate."

Alecia's ears caught the word "letting." Obviously the mistress of Domier Ranch could do little without Lavren's permission. It was a wonder he let her show the horses at all, strange fellow that he was. Alecia had not seen him since his anger simmered at her and Rayne for getting Roscoe back. When Rayne's men repaired the fence, it must have knocked some of the wind out of his sails. Alecia was thankful the invitation was for Nancy. She had no intention of going near the man ever again.

But just as though it were all settled, Nancy added, "The invitation was extended to both of us, and Corrine will be sending an escort for us."

"That's nice of her, but I can't possibly go," Alecia protested a little too quickly. "With the play and all, there's already too much to do."

"Nonsense!" Nancy waved her hand, still shiny from the cream coated on it. "Too much work and no play, you know. Besides, I've not been able to entertain you at all since you've been here." Alecia noted a hint of disappointment in her voice. "Had you come under better circumstances, we would have had so many opportunities for good times."

In her haste Alecia had failed to consider Nancy's feelings in the matter. Of course she would have to go. If she refused, in all probability, Nancy would refuse as well. She shivered as she thought of Lavren. Surely the sour man would keep his distance at a celebration party.

Alecia wondered how Nancy could hobnob with the Domiers on a social level after Lavren had been so cruel to her. And from what Jake had confided to her, there were other instances in the past when Mr. Domier made life difficult for Nancy.

But Nancy remained undaunted. Whenever the subject of Lavren came up, she would say, "I just pray for him. He has no defense against my prayers."

Alecia knew she, too, needed to pray, not only for Lavren, but for herself—that she might forgive him for his advances toward her. She knew it was dangerous to let bitterness fester.

❧

Since it was Alecia's first opportunity in months to attend a dress-up event, by the time Saturday arrived, she was determined she would make the most of it. She treated herself to a luxurious soaking in the tub amidst mountains of fragrant bubbles. She hadn't realized just how much she missed dressing up for evenings out with Galen to the theatre, a concert, or one of their special downtown midnight suppers together.

Deciding what to wear wasn't difficult as she had brought only one formal dress—and marveled that she even thought to pack it. She took ample time with her makeup, applying dark mascara to the very tips of her long lashes and color to her lips and cheeks. Not because of the occasion, but for the sheer joy of fussing with her appearance once again. Never had her complexion appeared so radiant and alive. Surely there was something to be said for fresh air and sunshine.

Her chestnut curls, she decided, would be piled casually atop her head. Smiling at her reflection, she wondered if Lavren Domier would send one of his cowhands in a muddied ranch truck to fetch them.

Nancy interpreted Alecia's fussing to mean she was excited to attend the party, and Alecia hadn't the heart to tell her otherwise. Actually she would rather be going anywhere than to the Domier home.

Nancy was attractive in her floor-length jade dress, but it concerned Alecia that not even the dress and makeup could mask the tiredness in Nancy's eyes. She wished she could convince the determined ranch lady not to work so hard.

The door chimes sent Alecia hurrying through the front hall, brimming with curiosity to see their escort.

Her very heart melted to see Rayne standing there.

Chapter Seven

Rayne's presence filled the doorway. He was taller, more handsome than ever in his gun-metal blue suit. "Hello," he said casually, as though he dropped by every day of the week. "Corrine told me you all were coming to her little shindig, so I offered to come by. Hope you don't mind."

Other than fleeting glimpses of Rayne in his pickup at the school, she had not seen him since the rainy day in the stables. Now as she looked up at the wide gentle eyes, the square jaw line, the full lips, her memories of that day grew warm and glowed inside her like hidden coals in the gray ashes of a woodburning stove.

Instantly she caught herself, for fear he could read it in her eyes. "Mind? Heavens, no." She stepped back from the doorway. "Come in. Nancy's nearly ready."

It never occurred to her that Rayne might attend this affair. Especially after the strong words he had had with Lavren at the Research Center and the even stronger words on the phone following Roscoe's rescue. But, after all, Corrine was his sister-in-law. Perhaps that had some bearing on the situation.

She led him into Nancy's formal living room. "Been catching any cattle rustlers lately?" she asked glibly, waving him to the flowered love seat. It made her almost angry to think he could now fraternize with Domier after the awful things the man had done. And to think he could just walk in here like nothing had happened between her and him that rainy day. Did this man have ice water in his veins?

"No time," came the succinct reply as he sat down. "Too busy with calving and spring roundup."

"Catch 'em red-handed, then hobnob with 'em at the area's social gatherings," she remarked. "Is this some unwritten 'live and let live' code of the old West with which I'm unfamiliar?" She turned to study a watercolor hanging on the wall.

Immediately Alecia wondered what her mother would say if she ever heard one of her daughters suggesting that a grudge should be held. Forgive, forgive, was all Alecia had heard from her childhood up. Yet the more she thought of it, the more ludicrous it was that they should be going to the Domier Ranch as though they were all long lost friends. She felt anger that she had been duped into this whole affair. She winced at the pricks of conscience from the resentment rising within her. But in spite of the painful pricks, she could not, and would not ever like Mr. Lavren Domier.

"An unwritten code? I guess you could call it that," he replied. After a moment he asked, "You been working up any new riding acts?"

Her throat went dry. "No, Rayne, I haven't." The words were cold, empty. "I found the last act too distressful to consider."

The moment the words were out, she regretted them. She was ashamed to admit she had returned his kisses freely. She turned to see the hurt in his eyes, just as Nancy walked in.

"Time to go?" she asked as she entered. "Why, Rayne Lassiter! What a wonderful surprise. What a treat to be escorted to the celebration by such a handsome guy."

Rayne stood to greet Nancy and to receive her motherly hug. Alecia busied herself getting their wraps.

She had never seen Rayne drive anything other than the ranch trucks and was unprepared for the Mercedes coupe parked in Nancy's drive. Nancy urged her in first while Rayne held the door, and thereby, still suffering from her own mortification, she found herself shoulder-to-shoulder with him.

He visited amiably with them as he sped down the section line road leading to the Domier Ranch. Alecia was quiet as she watched his broad hands maneuvering the wheel. If Nancy wondered what was wrong between them, she was sweet enough not to say so.

The words "Domier Ranch" were formed in tall wrought iron letters suspended over the drive entrance between two massive stone pillars. The majestic house that Alecia surveyed that day with Rayne was even more elegant from the front entrance. The sloping manicured lawns were edged with well-tended flower beds and shrubbery. Not until Rayne led the two of them up the broad front steps did Alecia recognize where she had seen this portico before—in the photo in Joanna's bedroom. She experienced a strange sensation, wondering what memories this place held for Rayne.

A thin dark-suited gentleman at the door gave them a colorless greeting, invited them in, and took their wraps. The entry hall was graced by a sweeping curved stairway and glittering crystal chandelier. Although Alecia did not remember seeing pumps on the Domier land, she now presumed his money came more from oil than from cattle.

Before the wispy man could show them to where the festivities were taking place, Lavren descended the carpeted steps on cat feet, head held high and a humorless smile pasted on his face. His ebony suit highlighted his iron gray hair, and if his manner were not so obnoxious, Alecia reasoned that he could be almost handsome.

"What an interesting group we have here," he said as he approached them. "I'll have to begin checking Corrine's invitation lists for these events a bit more closely. Never mind, Boyce," he waved the man back to his post at the door. "I'll show these fine people back to the party."

"Well, well, Lassiter," he rambled on, failing to greet any of them personally. "What could this party possibly offer to bring you out, fit to kill, during branding time?" As he spoke, he let his gaze fall upon Alecia, so that all concerned would know what he was implying.

Rayne and Nancy ignored Lavren's remark, but Alecia's face was ablaze with indignation. Whatever possessed Nancy to want to come here and endure this sarcasm?

Stepping through wide double doors to the spacious room filled with party-goers, Alecia tried to imagine Lavren and Corrine at home alone in this large house. Tall stately windows were dressed in crimson velvet-corded drapes. Ornately carved recessed ceilings glowed with muted indirect lighting. Smaller white colonnades repeated the theme of the portico, both in this room, and in the adjoining one from which were floating melodic strains of a dance number executed by a live orchestra.

In vain Alecia searched the opulent furnishings for signs of Corrine's personal touch. In fact had there been no warm sounds of romantic music or laughter and easy conversation, the house would have resembled a cold museum.

Being her usual gracious self, Nancy socialized among the guests for a time, with Rayne and Alecia in tow. Later she found a comfortable settee and, after seating herself, said with a smile, "I'd better be wise and rest if I want to make it through this evening. Rayne, would you be a dear and finish introducing Alecia around?"

Instantly Rayne took Alecia's hand and was assuring Nancy he would take care of her "baby sister." Alecia was relieved that even after her harsh comment to him, Rayne was still in high spirits.

As the two of them moved through the twittering crowd, it struck Alecia how hurt Galen would be if he saw her coupled up, however inadvertently, with Rayne. She sensed by the turning of heads among the guests, that they were causing a stir. What was it Galen had said about having no competition other than a horse?

Rayne was cordial as he steered her by her elbow through clumps of people, politely introducing her and drawing her into the thin conversations, which ranged anywhere from race horses to ranch irrigation to politics. Alecia mentally checked off the personalities she had met: a Dallas newspaper columnist, two attorneys, a state senator, and several high ranking officials from the national horse show association of which Corrine was an active member. It was a far cry from the barbecue at Rayne's house. Now she realized what Nancy meant by a level of social life here she hadn't known existed.

Strangely enough, the hostess of this whole affair was nowhere to be seen. "Wasn't this supposed to be Corrine's party?" Alecia asked Rayne as they plucked hors d'oeuvres from a tray. "Where is she?"

"Probably down at the stables talking horses with anyone who will listen," he commented dryly. "It's all the girl can think about."

If Rayne were dissatisfied with his role of keeping company with Nancy's younger sister, he made no signs of showing it. At one point he surprised her by ushering her onto the golden hardwood dance floor and leading her in a flawless waltz. Her fingertips spread over the tweedy texture of his suit, sensing the muscular shoulder beneath it. The refreshing smell of his aftershave drifted over her as the gentle refrains of the music wove the two of them together. She smiled her amusement as she relaxed in his arms.

"Share the secret?" he asked.

She hesitated, unsure if she should tell what she was thinking. "I never imagined," she ventured cautiously, "when I first met you that you would be an accomplished dancer."

He looked at her in mock seriousness. "Really? Then it's very lucky you're here tonight."

"And please tell me, sir, why is that?" She knew he was teasing and leading her on, but she didn't care.

He glanced about as if to detect eavesdroppers. "Promise you won't tell the boys from Big D?"

"Scout's honor."

"This whole thing is staged."

"You don't say!"

"I do say. Usually there's just some bluegrass tunes, a few fiddlers, maybe a banjo or two, some tobacco spittin' and a little hoedown. But, out of sheer self-defense, we decided to stage a little spoof to dispel all the Yankee myths about us hicks."

Involuntarily her laughter spilled out, mingling with and then rising above the overture that was playing. She hadn't planned to draw attention. It just happened that way. "And the dancing? What about your fine dancing?"

"Oh, yes. Well, luckily one Saturday morning at the feed store, I had the winning number on my bag of Calf-Gro, and won two lessons at Bertie Mae's Dance Parlor."

By now Alecia feared the tears from her laughter would streak her mascara. "And?" She pressed her lips together to suppress her mirth.

"Can't you guess? I've already had one of the two lessons!"

"Rayne, please," she tried to protest.

"What can I say? I humbly give all the praise to Bertie Mae," he added with a deep bow as the music ceased. He led her laughing from the dance floor. By the time they had danced several numbers, Rayne had drawn her close, laying his cheek against her hair. From deep within her blossomed the same dizzying excitement that surfaced the day he kissed her.

Later in the evening, Alecia saw Corrine unobtrusively enter a side door. The girl was dressed in an off-the-shoulder moss green gown that complimented her cascade of red hair perfectly. The martini glass could have been part of her ensemble as it never left her hand. In spite of her beauty, Corrine lacked the warmth of a hostess. She chose to ignore most of her guests, moving among them speaking to a select few.

Alecia was greatly surprised when the youthful redhead approached her and Rayne with a hand extended and her face wreathed in a bright smile. "Rayne, you came after all!" she exclaimed. "Thank you. And Miss Winland. Welcome."

Remembering the day she had nearly been run off the road by this headstrong girl, Alecia was now puzzled by her overt friendliness. "Since I'm out of the classroom now," Alecia said to her, "let's dispense with the 'Miss Winland' bit. I hear it in excess of a trillion times a day. Just 'Alecia,' please."

"Alecia it is then. And you've been filling in at Charlesy, haven't you? You're J.D.'s teacher now."

As Alecia answered in the affirmative, she could sense the child's name rising up like a needle to a balloon, obliterating the enchanted spell that had held her and Rayne together on the dance floor.

Rayne glanced across the room. "Looks like someone wants to talk business with me," he said brusquely. "If you'll excuse me. I wouldn't want to bore you, Alecia. I'll be back shortly."

Corrine downed her drink and caught a passing waiter to take another. "Want one?" she offered Alecia.

"I'd love a ginger ale."

Corrine gazed at her a moment. "Bring this lady a ginger ale," she instructed the waiter, then to Alecia, "You're something like your sis, aren't you? She won't touch the stuff either. Not a drop." She shook her mane of red hair. "Wish I could say the same thing."

Alecia changed the subject. "I want to congratulate you on your win. Nancy told me that's what this party's all about."

"Thanks." She sighed and seemed to relax some. "It's been a tough battle. Uphill all the way, but I'm finally getting there. I'm showing all of them. They didn't think I could do it. Didn't think I had it in me. But I'm showing them."

Alecia wondered if "them" was Lavren alone. It crossed her mind that she had not seen him since they first arrived. Odd host and hostess—throw a party then disappear. The waiter handed her the ginger ale and she sipped at its tanginess.

Corrine's hand was touching her arm. "Want to see her?" she asked.

Alecia failed to catch the meaning. "Her?"

"Twilight Song. My winning filly."

"Now?" *To the stables in my heels?* her mind asked incredulously.

"Sure, why not?"

Sensing the sincerity and intensity of Corrine's request, she relented. "Why not, indeed? Lead the way."

They set their drinks on a nearby table and slipped out the side door like children sneaking out of church. Corrine led her through a walnut-paneled study, down several halls, and down a flight of stairs before coming out onto a back patio at the lowest level.

Alecia stepped carefully over the rough gravel of the drive that led to the stables. In the moonlight she could make out an enclosed pool and pool house far to their left across the sweeping lawn. Thankfully the stable was not far. Alecia didn't think she could maneuver much farther in her heels.

Corrine stepped through a door and flung on a flood of lights that illuminated a stable nearly three times the size of Nancy's—all immaculately clean. And Corrine was probably spared the backbreaking job of mucking out stalls.

"Wait here," Corrine told her.

Alecia could hear nickering as Corrine spoke in quiet tones to the horse she brought out of a stall and led down the center area.

Twilight Song was a glossy sorrel filly, brushed and groomed to a high sheen. Alecia's freshly born appreciation of fine horses sensed immediately that this was a winner. She reached out her hand to the lovely animal and Twilight Song never flinched at her touch. Like Kane Brake, she was gentle, yet regal.

"She's the most exquisite horse I've ever seen," Alecia whispered in awe.

Corrine's expression glowed at the high praise. "Thanks. I trained her from a colt. She's sired by a national futurity winner and her dam is a race winner. She's an exceptional filly." She led the horse around in a few tight circles and Twilight Song seemed to sense she was on display, lifting her feet lightly and arching her neck proudly. "Some owners hire trainers," Corrine explained, "but I'm owner and trainer."

Alecia stroked the filly's glossy coat. "What a privilege to handle a horse of this caliber."

"Ted and Nancy's line was this good," Corrine confided. "They taught me a lot, and I appreciated all their help. I used to go over there after school when I was a teenager." She paused. "I still miss Ted. He was sort of the father image I never had. I cried when Nancy had to sell the horses, but of course she had no choice. The cattle provided a more settled income for her."

Alecia chided herself for thinking Nancy and Corrine had nothing in common. She had no idea they had been close in years past. Could it be because of Corrine that Nancy fought back against Lavren no more than she did?

Corrine deftly led Twilight Song back to her stall, picking up her long skirt as she went. Her red hair shone in the lights of the stable and Alecia thought it a pity that Lavren could not see and appreciate his wife's beauty and talents.

"I'm glad you came this evening," Corrine said, returning to where Alecia waited at the door. "I've been looking for an opportunity to thank you. To be truthful, it was my ulterior motive in bringing you out here."

Alecia's mind went blank. "Thank me? For what?"

"For touching Joanna in such a special way. She's my niece, you know."

"So I've learned."

"Did you also learn that Rayne will hardly let me near her? But she and I, we sort of find ways. She told me about the dress and about her play part. She's very excited."

Alecia faltered. "I'm sorry about the dress. That was a mistake, I'm afraid. I should have—"

"No, you were right about the dress." Corrine's green eyes glowed with pleasure. "Rayne's wrong in keeping such a tight hold on Joanna, but he won't listen. Just like I wouldn't listen when people warned me not to marry Lavren."

She stepped outside and held the door for Alecia. "See out there?" Corrine pointed to a rubble of foundation laid over with charred planks of wood strewn about. "That's where Darlene died."

"Darlene?" Alecia was shocked. "Joanna's mother?"

Corrine nodded, her lips going tight and pale. "My own sister. She was a wild one. I don't know why Rayne loved her so. She was wild and carefree. A lousy mother and rotten wife." She flipped her red curls back over shoulder as she spoke. "Seemed like a raw deal to me, for her to have such a wonderful family and treat them like dirt. And me. . . ." The words were left hanging in the still night air. Her young shoulders rose and fell in a deep sigh. "Rayne tried his best, but he couldn't tame her. They found her charred body in the bed there in the cabin along with Lavren's top foreman. Reedy, they called him. . .very handsome." She shook her head. "There was some kind of gas explosion and fire. Horrible, just horrible."

Alecia stared in unbelief at the rubble, awash in pale moonlight, and wondered why it hadn't been cleared away and built upon to remove the awful memories. So even Nancy had known the ugly truth, but was unwilling to share it with her.

"It nearly destroyed Rayne when he found out." Corrine's voice was controlled, steady. "He was crushed. We saw him gradually change, retreating into his work and losing himself in the ranch. He's kept Joanna close to him, putting her in a cocoon for safekeeping, insuring he won't get hurt again. He's frightened she'll become like her mother if he releases her." She gave a wry smile. "But of course he refuses to admit that. I used to try to tell him, and now he hardly talks to me at all."

Alecia nodded mutely, thinking how she had ignorantly tread upon his open wound in her brashness. "Why are you telling me this?"

"Rayne hasn't been in our house since the fire." Corrine switched off the lights and closed the stable door behind them. "But he called me this week to find out if you were coming. It appears you may be the one he will listen to."

These truths were hitting Alecia's mind like live electric volts. If Rayne hadn't been in the Domier home for five years that explained the turning of heads at the party. But why with her?

"I thought perhaps if Rayne heard truth coming from a new voice," Corrine went on, "he might see his mistakes. Joanna's going to be beautiful like Darlene. But she's nothing like her mother. There's none of that rebellion in her."

"No," Alecia agreed. "There's a sweet tenderness there."

"You see it too?" There was a short laugh edged with relief. "Sometimes I get to thinking it's my imagination since she's my niece."

Alecia smiled softly, thinking of Joanna. "I see it too."

Corrine moved toward the rubble of the ranch foreman's cabin, still talking. Alecia wondered how long these tormenting thoughts had been tamped down in Corrine's mind with no one to talk to.

"Not only did Darlene wreak havoc during her lifetime, she's continued to do so every day since her death."

"In what way?"

"Because of her miserable reputation, I've been accused of being just like her. Not an easy stigma to live down. And my own husband is the worst of them all. We'd been married only a few months when he learned the truth about Darlene. From then until now, he's never given me a chance to be myself. I have to fight for everything I do here. He treats me like a child."

That was as Alecia had suspected from her brief observations.

"He uses whatever methods he can to hurt me. He attacks Nancy and harasses her because she's my friend. He uses other women to try to make me jealous. It's never ending."

"Why do you stay?" Alecia wanted to know.

Corrine thought a while. "Look at that house," she pointed to where the mansion stood basking in the moonlight. "It's not a bad place to live. And where else would I get to work with such prime horses?" She stopped again. Alecia waited. "Besides all that, I love the guy." She gave a shaky laugh. "Silly, isn't it? I've loved him ever since I was a little girl. And I believe, deep down, if he would stop all his agitating and fighting, he would learn he loves me too. Maybe he's afraid to trust himself to love me for fear he would lose me like Rayne lost

Darlene." She gave a little shrug. "Who knows what twisted things get inside of a person's head?"

The ringing of a phone in the stable froze her question in midair. Corrine lifted her skirt and hurried inside to answer the call. When she returned she said, "More reporters have arrived. They want to ask questions and take photos of the party. I've got to get back. Coming?"

"If you don't mind," Alecia said, "I think I'll stay out a few more minutes. The cigarette smoke was getting to me anyway."

"Sure thing." She turned to go, then over her shoulder added, "Thanks for listening."

Conflicting thoughts plagued Alecia as she strolled back toward the rubble to stare at the remains of the devastation. Some of what Corrine told her confirmed assumptions she had made previously. Other things were totally baffling. Some of Rayne's actions were more understandable now, but she puzzled why he stopped by to get her and Nancy. She didn't dare think it was only because of her. That was too amazing. Too confusing.

"Fitting burial monument, wouldn't you agree?" A low, raspy voice spoke behind her, startling and alarming her. She gasped aloud, whirling around to see Lavren Domier standing in the shadows of the stable.

Chapter Eight

Fear and anger formed an acid taste in Alecia's mouth. It was exactly as Lavren had done at the Research Center—slithering quiet as a snake. Only this time there were even fewer people around.

"I've left this as a fitting monument to the wickedness of hard women." His formidable presence moved close beside her and she felt the flesh of her arms crawl. His voice was hard, bitter. The stench of liquor was heavy. "She was a hard woman." He stared glassy-eyed at the wreckage. "So beautiful. So wicked. So hard." His voice wavered as one who had drunk too much. "I loved her first. Little Corrine didn't say that did she? She still doesn't know. Yeah, I loved her first. But Darlene enjoyed playing both ends against the middle, so she went to Rayne. But she didn't love him either. Made fools of both of us."

Alecia sensed his proud shoulders slumping under the weight of the ugly memories. First Corrine, and now Lavren opening up. What a bizarre evening!

"She dumped us both and took dumb old Reedy." Lavren's hollow laugh echoed into the night air. "But that did her in. Died right here on my land. And she deserved to die," he added sharply.

Alecia's frantic mind sought for an easy way to escape while he was deep in his melancholy musings. Gently, quietly, she took one step back from him, then another.

"So I took second best," he mumbled on. "Took little sister. Another wild one who thinks of nothing but horses. They're none of them like you, Alecia. You're so. . . ." He turned, and abruptly the slurred speech was accelerated as he grabbed for her arm. "Don't go!" he pleaded. "Please, don't leave me. I need you. You're not hard or rough. You're soft. . .tender. . .caring. . . ." His fingers sank cruelly into the flesh of her arm.

"Lavren, let me go! You're hurting me!" No one would hear her cries over the sounds of the music and the party. She had to get away. Her mind was wild with panic. She had no idea what he might do in this state.

"Please, Alecia," he begged, pulling her forcibly to him. She felt the heat of his breath on her neck, her face, repeating her name over and over as he held her in his strong grasp. Frantically she jerked her head from side to side to get away from the fetid breath, the hard lips bruising hers.

"You blind, wretched ogre. Let me go. You don't deserve Corrine's love. You're consumed with hate and bitterness."

Unhearing, he began to pull her toward the stables. As he moved his hand-holds to lift her bodily into his arms, she kicked at his shin with all her might and broke from his grasp. She heard him yell as she pulled away and ran toward the house, kicking out of her shoes as she ran. *Dear God, help me,* her mind screamed silently.

Her sides heaved with sharp stabs of pain. Where was the entry where she had come out? She remembered the patio. If only she had gone back with Corrine. She heard no footsteps behind her, but was too filled with fear to slow down and look back. The house cast a looming shadow over the patio and she cautiously moved into its darkness, feeling for the doorway. When she slammed into a soft form, she screamed uncontrollably.

"Alecia! It's Rayne! What's happened to you? Who did this?"

"Lavren," was all she could say before collapsing into racking sobs released into his chest with his arms tenderly about her. Gently he lifted her into his arms and took her around the house to his car. "I'll take you home," he told her, "then come back for Nancy. I'll take care of Domier later."

The promise made little difference to her. She was safe now and that was all that mattered. In the car he held her to him until her tremors ceased to convulse her body. Once again he transmitted to her his tender strength.

❧

Everyone was embarrassingly apologetic. Rayne. Corrine. Nancy. Nancy, especially, was distraught about the entire mess.

"I had no idea," she told Alecia later, "that Lavren would ever harm anyone. I suppose I underestimated the poison that has festered inside him. From the beginning I should have told you about Darlene's death, but I despise gossip, and have always tried to protect Corrine."

When Corrine learned of her husband's violence, she phoned to personally apologize. Rayne, of course, went back to the Domiers' that night to settle matters, but Lavren was nowhere to be found. By the time he reappeared, Rayne's anger had cooled, and Lavren conveniently remembered nothing of the incident.

Alecia wanted only to let it drop and hear no more of it. She was grateful that she had not been hurt. Grateful it was all over. And even grateful that her best shoes had been returned.

In her free time she began to gather her possessions together in preparation to leave. In time all of this would be a blurred memory. There had been several happenings recently that she had been unable to tell Galen about over the phone. At times long lapses of silence took over the conversation. Uncomfortable lapses. It bothered her.

On the night of the play Mrs. Dominique baked her famous cinnamon rolls—high, light, and shiny with sticky white glaze. She served them with coffee to the parents who had brought their children early for costuming.

Alecia was busy in the girls' dressing room, flitting from one young actress to the other, touching up hair and makeup, and failed to see Rayne when he arrived to see the play.

She had been thankful for her heavy schedule leading up to the play and the last day of school. That way she could somehow function in the midst of a fog of uncertainty and vacillating feelings warring in her heart and mind.

Try as she might, she couldn't shake free of the thoughts of Rayne's alluring low voice near her ear, his sweet touch, his captivating manner. Guiltily she found herself humming the melodies to which they had so effortlessly danced together.

"Miss Winland," a small voice demanded. "Aren't you going to help me?" Joanna was looking up at her with questioning eyes. She had changed from her blue jeans into her calico dress with the flowing skirt, flounced front, and puffed sleeves. She was ready for her hairpiece and her makeup. Flossie had purchased darling hairpieces consisting of long curls that the girls could tuck into their lace caps.

The dressing room was noisier now, and she and Flossie were having difficulty keeping the girls quiet. Lyle was in the other room, taking care of the boys. She could hear the commotion of the sixth-grade boys on the stage preparing the sets. The air was static with the kind of excitement that only children can create.

"What do you think Daddy will say when he sees me?" Joanna asked as Alecia applied the finishing touches of color to the girl's cheeks to prevent a washed-out appearance under the stage lights.

"He may not come right out and say so, Joanna," she said, using a whisper so the other kids couldn't hear her use the name. It was still their secret. "But he can't deny that you look perfectly lovely. Have you told him about your play part?"

"No," she answered with a mischievous grin. "I just told him there was a special program. He doesn't even know it's a play."

Alecia trembled as she adjusted the lace cap over the curls. The child looked incredibly like her mother. *Perhaps,* she thought, *when Rayne sees her looking this lovely, really sees her, this night could be a turning point.* How wonderful for her to go back to Minneapolis knowing everything was all right in Joanna's life.

Once the curtains were opened and the play commenced, Alecia was kept busy backstage with costume changes and set adjustments. Flossie, who loyally sat behind the curtains and prompted the cast, said the entire play was flawless. Alecia knew only that the gymnasium was packed, with standing room only, and that she heard much laughter and applause.

It seemed only a few minutes before she was again assisting the girls out of costumes and back into their regular clothes. Parents were hugging her and commenting how wonderful the show had been and that they never realized such a production could be done with so small a space and so few supplies.

It was some time before it dawned on Alecia that Joanna's clothes were still lying across a folding chair in the dressing room. Nancy was at the door, her expression troubled. "He's taking her out, Alecia. He's leaving."

He couldn't. He wouldn't. Not after—not now! Wild thoughts rolled about in her head in a silent tumult. She grabbed up the clothes and ran out into the parking lot. The other parents were noisily enjoying Mrs. Dominique's rolls in the cafeteria.

There he was at the door of the pickup. Bewildered Joanna was already seated on the rider's side.

"Rayne!" she called out boldly.

He stopped and stared at her. His face was drawn and pale.

"Joanna's clothes," she said, using the given name in her haste and in her hurt.

He moved toward her as though in a trance. "I thought I could trust you," he said, his voice distant and detached as she pushed the clothes into his arms. "I thought I could trust you," he repeated the awful words. "But I should have known."

"Rayne, I didn't—"

"Don't bother to explain. Directly or indirectly, you were at the bottom of all this. This is what you've worked for all this time, isn't it? This was the final touch. The crowning glory. The final encore before you leave this forsaken little place where you've had to work out your psychological experiments on the local folks." The dark eyes were now glaring. "Have a fast trip back to the north country. Don't let anything slow you down."

The pickup door slammed on her pitiful protests to his accusations. Now it was his turn to spit gravel as he gunned the truck from the parking lot.

She stood there, paralyzed in a broken dejection that deadened all her senses. In a grief-filled haze, she forced her feet to move back to the jubilant crowd in the cafeteria.

She remembered what Corrine had said about how desperately Rayne loved Darlene. Alecia tried to imagine what it was like for him to see her almost resurrected in Joanna's face and appearance tonight.

"Don't punish yourself," Nancy begged her as they drove home from the play. "You couldn't help what happened."

Alecia was physically and mentally exhausted. "But he was right this time, Nancy. I did want to knock the prideful chip off his shoulder and I did want him to see things my way. I could have prevented Joanna from getting the part." Nancy had kindly offered to drive home and, as she did, Alecia stared at shadowy objects passing in the darkness. "How I wish I had. Not getting the part would have been far less painful for the child than to see her father in a rage. I'm to blame. I wanted him to see what was right, and succeeded only in being self-righteous."

After a night of fitful sleep, she dreaded facing her last day at Charlesy, which was to be a half-day session. As she had expected, Joanna was not present. Still she was more grieved than she thought possible at being unable to say good-bye to her. They had talked about exchanging letters, but she had never given Joanna her address. No doubt Rayne would forbid such goings on.

Joanna. Precious Joanna Darlene. Why had she loved her so deeply?

Alecia had one last party with her students, laughing and telling jokes together. Several of the girls cried and begged Alecia to please come back to Oklahoma next fall to be their teacher.

She explained to them once again that she had a home and a job far, far away from Charlesy School, Denlin County, Oklahoma. And that she was homesick and anxious to get back. They couldn't understand. All they knew was that they wanted her to stay.

Mrs. Dominique prepared cold cuts for the staff who would be spending the afternoon cleaning and sorting. The elderly cook was also cleaning out her kitchen in preparation for its summer repose.

Alecia was working at a hurried pace when Lyle came into her classroom after having returned from the bus route. Again he thanked her and assured her that she had opened many doors for future activities in the school by her endeavors. "All the parents were ecstatic about the play. It was an overwhelming success."

She pulled another pushpin from the bulletin board, releasing a bright posterboard flower. "All but one," she remarked dryly.

"I'm very sorry about Lassiter." His understanding was soothing.

"So am I," she countered.

"You even had me thinking we could make him see things differently. That's why I voted for J.D. to get the part. I guess it was too much to hope for after all these years. That man is dead set in his ways."

Dead set in his ways? That was exactly what she thought at first. In the beginning, when she was unaware of the pain and suffering. . .the deep inner wounds. Alecia pointed to a large box on the floor. "Want to help carry these to my car?" She put the last of the bulletin board decorations in the storage closet.

"Sure."

Together, they loaded the car with her belongings. In the May sunshine the aged stones of the schoolhouse seemed to glow. She looked at it as though she had never seen it before, pondering its long history and rich heritage. How many other such schools across this nation helped to form the country into what it is today? Funny she should think of that now, after she had disdained it so. Lyle extended his hand. She took it. "Good-bye, Miss Winland," he said warmly. "If you're ever down on a visit, you know you're always welcome here."

She was unprepared for the misting in his eyes. Had she actually made that much of a contribution? It was all such a burden. She came so near to quitting . . .to throwing in the towel. "I don't feel I did all that much. As I look back, I only wish my heart had been more willing. I was struggling, you know."

He smiled. "I know."

"I think, perhaps," she slipped her sunglasses on her nose, "that I should be thanking you."

He stepped back as she put the small car in reverse and turned to drive out of the Charlesy school yard one last time.

Galen. She would call Galen as soon as she got to the house. She needed to hear his voice. That would stabilize her growing perplexities. When she got to Minneapolis, there would still be a week left of their school's session. That meant she would have opportunities to get caught up on details before the teachers scattered for the summer. Perfect. She would be busy, and Charlesy School, sitting like a golden island in the sea of emerald pastures, would be a mere memory.

🙶

The next morning Nancy helped her pack. "Want to take your blue jeans?" she asked with a wide grin. "Or are you going to leave them here for your next visit?"

Alecia was struggling with a box of old books that Mrs. Turner had given her after learning of Alecia's love for old readers. She seemed to be leaving with much more than she came with—in more ways than one. "Leave them," she said. "I can't jog or play tennis in them."

Alecia was scooting the box out the door of her room when the phone rang. It was probably Galen asking when she would be leaving. She had been unable to get hold of him earlier and she was excited when she picked up the receiver. "Hello there," she said lightly.

"Alecia?" It was Rayne. His voice was odd. . .strained. A piercing fear stabbed her stomach.

"Rayne? What's the matter?"

"It's Joanna." His voice caught. Never had she heard him say his daughter's given name.

Chapter Nine

Alecia's knees went limp. She sat down in the chintz chair, nervously fingering the phone cord. "Rayne, what about Joanna? Where are you?"

"Denlin County Hospital in Kalado. Joanna's here. She was in the corral on her horse helping me cut out calves." He was able to say a few words, then faltered again. "The horse twisted somehow. . . ." His voice was trembling. "I don't know how it happened. She's an expert. The horse threw her and a horned steer gored her. . .threw her."

Alecia's heart pounded in her throat, strangling her. "What do the doctors say? What have they told you?" *Little Joanna,* her heart cried. *Precious Joanna.*

"She's in a semi-coma now. "They've said. . .Alecia?"

"Yes."

"Could you come? She. . .when she rouses, she asks for you."

Asks for me, Alecia thought. *How wretched that must be for him on top of everything else.*

"I'll be there soon as I can."

Alecia told Nancy bits and pieces of Rayne's report as she slipped into a clean dress, fluffed her hair, and threw a few things into her purse. "That's all I know," she said. "I'll call you later."

She paused at the front door thinking what else she might need. Then she ran back to her room and grabbed her small Bible from out of her suitcase and tucked it into her purse.

When she stepped off the hospital elevator on the second floor, the acrid antiseptic odors sent her stomach churning. A nurse at the desk directed her to the hall where the room was located. Her heels beat a staccato rhythm as she scanned the doors for number 226. When she saw it, unconsciously, she began to tiptoe. She paused, then pushed at the heavy door that swung open noiselessly, revealing a bent-over Rayne sitting in a chair with his face buried in his hands. The bed was empty.

She studied him a few moments, then he glanced up and stood to his feet. He was still dressed in his work clothes: soiled blue jeans and faded shirt with the sleeves rolled up, exposing the sinewy tanned forearms with a tangle of masculine hair.

"Thanks for coming," he said. "I was afraid you'd left the country."

"I was just ready to leave."

"Will you stay?" he asked unapologetically. "For a while?"

She nodded, unable to speak, feeling totally incapable of helping him at this point. Silently, she prayed.

"They have her in emergency surgery. They told me I could wait in here." Reseating himself, he motioned for her to take the other chair. His voice was steadier now. "It was one of my longhorns. I have only a few. Something spooked them. They were acting nasty. All riled up." He leaned back in the chair and hooked a dirty boot over his other knee. "That crazy kid took off in there to settle them down, but. . . ."

Alecia's mind repulsed at hearing the details. She couldn't bear to think of that vulnerable little body at the mercy of horns and hooves. It wasn't fair. Couldn't he see how unfair it was? She wanted to scream at him of the unfairness of it all. Her nails bit sharply into her palms.

"I didn't see her fall. Don't know how she lost her balance. Sammy and I, we heard her scream and saw the steer get her and fling. . . ."

Alecia's breath caught as her stomach wrenched.

"Mr. Lassiter?" A uniformed nurse appeared at the door.

Rayne rose quickly. "Yes?"

"Your daughter is in the recovery room now. The doctor said to tell you the laceration was not serious. No vital organs were seriously injured."

Rayne nodded, his expression grim.

"However she's not completely out of danger. The doctor will explain everything when he comes. She's had quite a blow to the head and has a badly broken ankle."

The nurse turned to Alecia. "Are you Mrs. Lassiter?"

"No," Rayne answered for her. "She's a friend. Joanna's teacher, actually."

Alecia was amazed to hear him use his daughter's name for the second time. The straight-faced nurse raised her eyebrows. "I see. Well, the two of you might just as well get something to eat. She'll be in recovery for a time. We can call you as soon as she's returned to the room." She left the room, closing the door behind her.

Rayne looked at Alecia. "Want to get something?"

"It's up to you. Think you can?" Actually it was her own stomach she was thinking of.

"Beats waiting in this place." He took her arm and, through the myriad of halls, they found their way to the cafeteria on the first floor. The food aromas reminded Alecia that in her rush to get packed, she had not eaten for several hours.

Over the cafeteria vegetable soup, which they agreed wasn't too bad, they talked of mundane things that painlessly skirted issues that were too touchy to approach.

As they were finishing a call came over the intercom for Rayne. He took it at the counter where he was informed that Joanna was being taken to her room.

Mentally, Alecia attempted to bolster herself as they returned to the room. She must not collapse or give way to emotions. Rayne would need her to be calm.

Joanna's surgeon met them in the hall as they approached the room. He was a young man with wire-rimmed glasses and kind eyes. "Mr. Lassiter, I'd like to talk with you for a moment."

Alecia felt Rayne grope for her hand and clasp it tight. "Yes, sir," he answered.

"Your daughter came through the surgery nicely. The wound was not so bad as we originally thought. Miraculously the horn did not puncture any vital organs. However the next few days will be touch and go. We'll be keeping close watch on her."

The grip on Alecia's hand tightened. "Are you saying we could still lose her?" The words were soft.

The doctor place a gentle hand on Rayne's massive shoulder. "That's exactly what I'm saying, Mr. Lassiter. It was a powerful impact to her head."

"Has she regained consciousness?"

"Not yet, but we feel she will soon."

"Can I see her now?"

The young doctor nodded and stepped aside.

Rayne released Alecia's hand at the door. She saw him stagger as if from a blow when he saw his daughter lying there. Her tiny ashen face was crowned in a swath of pure white bandage, thin arms penetrated by needles and tubes, an exposed leg encased in a cast from the shin down. But he righted himself and moved toward the bed.

"Joanna. Hey, sugar." The voice was full of tender love. "You're gonna be all right. Daddy's here. I'll be right here whenever you need me."

Alecia watched, scarcely able to contain the surging emotions within her at the sight of his broad, calloused hands touching the child's pale cheek. There was no response.

Nurses came in at intervals to take her vital signs. Rayne walked about the room, sat down for moments, then moved back to Joanna's side to touch her, speak to her, check her breathing.

Throughout the afternoon and evening, there were many calls. "No," Rayne told them patiently. "No change. There's nothing you can do now. No, don't bother to come. We just have to wait."

When Josie called, Alecia could hear the woman's strong voice from where she was sitting across the room. The hearty old queen of El Crosse was distraught that her little charge was in danger. It occurred to Alecia that Josie might have taken care of Rayne when he was Joanna's age. No telling how long she had been with the family.

"Get those men fed tonight, Josie," Rayne told her. "Keep them in line and tell Sammy to get them all on the job in the morning. Then you and Sammy come up here tomorrow. Nothing you can do now."

As Rayne was talking, there came a soft knock on the open door. Alecia looked up to see Nancy's pastor, Joe Bob, standing there. She rose to greet him, thankful for a familiar face.

Presently Rayne hung up the phone and came to the door with an extended hand. "Joe Bob Tygert. Haven't seen you in a long while."

"How've you been, Rayne?" The two exchanged a firm handshake.

"You know Alecia Winland," Rayne said. "She's Joanna's teacher at Charlesy School."

"Sure do," Joe Bob said. "She's been one of my parishioners ever since she arrived in Denlin County."

A brief expression of surprise registered on Rayne's face. "Oh yeah, sure," he said quickly.

"How is Joanna?" the pastor wanted to know.

Rayne parroted what the doctor had told him earlier. His voice was hollow as he spoke.

Joe Bob ran his fingers through his curly hair. "Mind if we pray about it?"

Immediately Alecia sensed Rayne's discomfort. Before he could speak, she said, "It couldn't hurt."

Rayne then nodded, his lips pressed tightly together.

Joe Bob's affable manner took no offense. He stepped to Joanna's bedside and placed his hands on her tiny arm and softly spoke to the Father God in her behalf. He included Joanna's father as well, praying for the "peace that passes understanding" to cover him during this time.

As Joe Bob prepared to leave, Rayne asked, "How'd you happen to stop by?"

The good-natured fellow smiled. "I could say that I was on my rounds and happened to see the name Lassiter on the New Patient list. The name does kind of jump out at people around here." He gave a friendly grin. "But truthfully, Nancy called the house after Alecia left, to ask church members to be praying. I thought I would come by to see if you needed anything. Haven't seen much of you for the past few years."

Rayne hooked a thumb in the pocket of his blue jeans. "Our paths split. . . once you chose preaching over ranching."

"My daddy says the very same thing," Joe Bob countered.

They were standing in the hall now and Alecia was surprised to hear Rayne release a light chuckle. Joe Bob had his ways.

"You know," the pastor drawled, "I once thought you and I were gonna get real close. Remember when you were madly in love with my kid sister in sixth grade?"

Alecia smiled, trying to imagine Rayne as a sixth-grader.

"She jilted me," Rayne quipped.

"She told me it was because of them ugly bowed legs of yours," Joe Bob teased.

Rayne shook his head. "Could have been. Or else the fact that I ate the chocolate chip cookies out of her lunch pail every noon hour."

"Mama did make scrumptious chocolate chip cookies. Say, why don't you come on over to church some Sunday? We'd love to have you."

"Church?" Rayne studied the geometric floor tiles, then looked up at Joe Bob. "No. No church. Not for a while yet. Maybe someday. Maybe."

Joe Bob reached out for Rayne's hand. "Alecia has our number if you need us. We're as near as the phone."

Rayne, suddenly mute again, only nodded. He and Alecia returned to the room as the pastor's footsteps echoed down the hall.

Later that evening the calls ceased, and it grew hushed and still in the room. Somewhere in the ward a baby cried and a child called for his mother. But Joanna lay in deathlike silence.

Minutes crept by endlessly. The nurses' bantering out in the hall extended to them a comforting effect, assuring them that there was yet a measure of normality in the universe.

The two of them took turns milking coffee from the impersonal canteen machine down the hall in the waiting room. It tasted terrible, but it kept them awake.

Once, the voices and noises faded far into a vague, muffled distance. Alecia started, realizing she had dozed off. She awakened to see Rayne staring out the window at a sky ablaze with spangles of stars. His expression was strained, almost colorless. When would he break and release the awful torment that was fermenting within him? Was she to press in and assist, or simply wait?

She wanted to tell him how wrong she had been. She wanted to confess to him her horrid self-righteousness. But was this the right time? She remembered what Nancy said about letting him come to grips with things in his own way. . .his own time. This time she wanted it to be God's move, not hers.

At length, he turned and looked at her. "My turn to get coffee," he said. Before leaving he stepped into the restroom and splashed cold water on his face.

He had been gone only a moment when she heard it. A faint, feeble sound. "Miss Winland." The brown eyes were fluttering open, struggling to focus. "Miss Winland?" she murmured weakly.

"Yes, Joanna. I'm here. Your Daddy's here too. Down the hall."

"I was good. Good. . .Betsy Ross." The words came slowly, spaced apart, weak. Oh, so weak. Like a silver thread that would snap at the mere touch.

"You were marvelous, Joanna." Hot tears momentarily blinded Alecia. "I was so very proud of you."

The lashes fluttered again. Her eyes met Alecia's for a fraction of a moment and a slight smile glimmered. "Good Betsy," she repeated. "The. . .best."

That was all. Silence pulled its blanket back over her. The breathing fell back to its slow, steady rhythm.

Was it for this moment she had been prevented from quitting Charlesy and returning home early? Thanks be to God for His dear guiding hand.

When Rayne returned and looked at Alecia's face, he knew immediately. "What is it?" he asked anxiously, placing the steaming cups on the dresser.

"She spoke."

He stepped over to the bed, looking, hoping. Not touching, just looking. "She ask for you?"

Alecia couldn't speak over the knot in her throat. "Uh huh," she whispered.

"What did she say?"

Alecia knew she could easily lie and he would never know the difference. Why heap fresh new pain upon the old?

"I can take it," he said grimly, not taking his eyes off the child. "What did she say?"

Alecia drew a breath. "She said she was a good Betsy Ross." Her voice cracked. "The best."

Rayne's eyes closed and for a moment, Alecia thought he was going to fall over in a faint.

The "if onlys" must be screaming their relentless indictments at him now. *Oh Lord,* she prayed silently, *let the dam within him give way and spill out the ugly contents.*

❧

Dawn streamed in the tall windows, contradictively joyous and golden. It awakened Alecia who had, once again, dozed. She excused herself to the ladies' room down the hall to freshen up her makeup and hair. When she returned to the room, Josie and Sammy were there. Josie was leaning over Joanna, crying softly. "Sweet baby. My sweet, sweet baby," she repeated over and over, stroking Joanna's face.

Alecia sensed that her release of emotions was making it extremely difficult for Rayne. She grabbed up the satchel of clean clothes Josie had brought and handed it to him. "Here," she said. "Josie brought this for you. Why don't you go change and freshen up?"

The soft brown eyes thanked her. He took the satchel and left without speaking.

Sammy stood uncomfortably, twisting his hat in his hands. He wiped a tear off his sandpapery cheek with the sleeve of his worn cotton shirt. Kindly, Alecia urged him to sit down and he perched his lanky body on the edge of the orange vinyl hospital chair as though it were a rattlesnake's den.

Rayne returned looking somewhat collected. He managed to give Alecia a weak smile.

Josie and Sammy left, but others began dropping by. Lyle and Flossie. Rancher neighbors, some she knew, others she had never met. At first Alecia excused herself when people came, but Rayne asked her to please stay. She wondered if they thought it strange that she should be there in the room with them.

She was delighted to meet Rayne's father who greeted her with open warmth. "I've heard J.D. make mention of you on several occasions," he commented after Rayne introduced them. "All good," he added.

Roland Lassiter, impervious to age, stood straight and tall as Rayne. His dark eyes, not wide and expressive like Rayne's, were nonetheless kind and shed open, unchecked tears at his granddaughter's bedside. The silver-haired Lassiter appeared to be so independent. Alecia marveled that he had so completely given over the reins of El Crosse to his son.

Watching him, Alecia for the first time became curious about Rayne's mother. . .her personality and how she had fit into the meshwork of the story of the ranch. It certainly wasn't the proper time to ask. She was sorry she had not asked sooner.

Nancy came by and brought the jonquil yellow dress for Alecia to change into. "Seems I remembered you said J.D. liked this one."

"Joanna," Alecia corrected her.

"Joanna?" There were raised eyebrows, but an excited smile on Nancy's face.

Alecia felt a surge of renewed vigor after changing, but by late afternoon the toll of the previous night began to tell on her. Weariness bound up in her bones, her body screamed for a bed.

She and Rayne were sparked to life by Corrine's arrival. She was dressed as usual in one of her striking western suits and matching hat. Her hair was fastened severely at the nape of her neck. Though concerned for her niece, she seemed to be in good spirits. She talked extensively with Rayne, wanting to know every detail. It seemed to Alecia that she asked more pertinent questions about Joanna's condition than any visitor so far.

As she was preparing to leave, Corrine asked Alecia to walk with her to the gift shop to pick out something for Joanna. Alecia looked at Rayne and he nodded.

True to Corrine's style, she purchased the fluffiest, most feminine looking stuffed kitten in the gift shop and wrote an endearing note on a card. "When she wakes up, tell her this is from her Aunt Corrine," she instructed.

"My pleasure," Alecia assured her. How comforting to hear her say "When she wakes up."

As they approached the elevator, Corrine drew her into an empty waiting room. "Before I go," she said, lowering her voice mysteriously, "there's something I must tell you. It may only be a case of overblown imagination but there seems to be a change in Lavren."

"In what way?" Alecia attempted to be polite, but hated to even discuss the situation.

"First I must explain that Lavren did say he didn't remember all that happened that night out at the stables. As stoned as he was, I don't doubt it. But he did mention one thing you said."

Alecia frowned, remembering the horrible moment when she was so frightened. "What was that?" she asked with some apprehension. Perhaps he had made up something to alleviate his guilt.

Corrine's pretty lips held a vague smile. "He said he remembered your yelling at him that he didn't deserve my love and my affection. Strange as this may sound, I don't think it ever occurred to him that I might love him." She firmed the hat on her head. "And now. . .well, now he seems a little different somehow. We'll see."

Alecia took a breath. "Corrine, I must confess to you that I've not prayed for Lavren as I should have. I let my anger against him take precedence over my need to pray for him. But I want you to know, from this moment on, I'll be praying for the two of you. You deserve to be happy. God meant for life to be enjoyed, not simply endured."

Corrine shrugged. "If you say so. All I've ever known was fight and struggle for everything. But thanks for the good word anyway. Oh, and just for the record," she grasped Alecia's arm, "Joanna will pull through this. I know what kind of stuff she's made of. She's a fighter."

Remembering Joanna's first words when she awakened in the night, Alecia had to agree. "She certainly is."

૨ન

The sky outside the hospital window was pulling a curtain of lavender twilight when the phone rang in Joanna's room. Since Alecia was nearest, she took it.

"Alecia? Is that you? Nancy said you might be there." Galen's tone was harsh. "What is going on down there?"

"Galen. Oh, Galen. I'm so sorry. I completely forgot to call you." How could she have forgotten that she was supposed to be on her way back to Minneapolis this minute?

"Sorry? Sorry?" He was incredulous. "Alecia, I've been more than patient and understanding in this whole matter, but this beats all. What are you doing?"

Alecia could feel Rayne's curious stare on her back. "There's this little girl . . .one of my students. She was badly hurt. I'll be here a few days yet."

"A few days?" His voice rose in volume and pitch. She hoped Rayne couldn't hear him as plainly as she had heard Josie. "What is this child to you? Is she more important than the job that's been held for you these past months?" he demanded with indignation. "You were to be here for an important staff meeting on Friday. I had it all set up. Doesn't this child have any family? Where are they?"

Behind her, she heard Rayne step out of the room. What a gentleman. "Here. They're here."

"Then why, pray tell, are you needed? You can keep in touch with them by phone—like you've been doing with me," he added bitterly.

Alecia strained to collect her thoughts. To make herself clear. To be understood. "I promised to stay."

"It isn't just the job, Alecia." His voice softened somewhat. "You should know that. I miss you so much I can hardly stand it. If the pressures were off here, I would have caught a flight out of here by now."

"I know. This little girl. . .she's special. I can't explain it. She's just very special. I'll leave soon. I'll contact you when I know for sure. I promise." But in truth, at this point, she had no idea when she would be leaving.

She heard him release a sigh. "I can't run your life. However, neither can I guarantee anything in the office from now on. I'll have to tell Harwood you won't be here for the Friday meeting and that you don't know when you'll be coming. It won't sound very good."

"It's the best I can do, Galen. And thank you." With trembling hand, she replaced the receiver in its cradle. "And the rest is up to you, Lord," she whispered.

Rayne asked nothing about the phone conversation and she offered nothing. Things were difficult enough for him without his knowing that her job was on the line because of the extended stay.

The sky outside the window was dark again and clouds covered the stars. The lights of the town of Kalado twinkled in scattered profusion like so many lost fireflies. Nothing like the intensity of the Minneapolis skyline at night.

Rayne was restless. *Such a small space for a cowboy to be cramped into,* she thought. She had been reading the Psalms from her small Bible.

Abruptly he turned to her. "You trust God, don't you?"

His words startled her. She closed the small leather-bound book and let it lay in her lap. "Yes, Rayne, I do."

"I mean trust. . .not just believe. Most everybody I know believes there is a

God. But you trust Him, don't you?"

She nodded. How could she explain to him that her Creator was her best Friend?

He paced to Joanna's bedside and back to the window. "Joanna's no better. And I think I need to pray. But I don't. . .I'm not sure He'll hear. I need your help."

"Of course. Whatever it is you need, I'll try to help."

He stepped over and drew the other chair close to her. "I know you've been praying all along. I can tell. I'm her father. I should be praying too. But I can't." He shook his head. "I just can't."

She reached out to give his arm a reassuring touch.

"I'd like to go to the chapel," he said.

"Upstairs?" She couldn't imagine him wanting to leave the room. He had hardly left, other than a few minutes at a time, since Joanna came out of surgery.

"Will you come with me? It's important."

She slipped the Bible into the pocket of the yellow dress and stood. Possibly, the dam was cracking.

They informed the nurses at the desk where they were going. "We'll keep a close eye on her," one of them said with a kind smile.

Some benevolent person had left a full bouquet of pink carnations and laven-der iris laced with baby's breath, on the chapel's entry table. The fragrance waft-ed gently over them as they entered the small room. Brass wall lamps on each side lent a soft glow. The small pews, altar, and pulpit were in rich hues of mahogany. Cushiony carpet beneath their feet was in stark contrast to the cold hospital room floor.

"It's almost spooky in here," Rayne said, closing the door behind them.

Alecia sat down on the front pew, thankful for the soft comfort. Rayne remained standing, looking ill at ease and staring at the gold cross on the altar. Finally he spoke, his tremulous voice betraying the strain. "What if. . .what if Joanna dies, never having worn the pretty dresses she needed to have?"

"Rayne, don't."

"And the baby dolls, the stuffed animals, hair ribbons, lockets. . . ." His voice broke off in a half-sob. "You were right and I couldn't bear to hear the truth. Corrine was right and I ordered her never to see Joanna again."

"Those things you named are important, but they're not everything."

"Don't pacify me now, Alecia. I've got to face the truth. Even if it's almost too late. In fear I held on tight to her because she was all I had left in life. But even as I clung desperately to her, I could feel her slipping away."

Alecia slipped her hand into her pocket and clutched the Bible. "Even if you should lose Joanna this very night, still she's known all her life that her daddy loves her. Never, never has she had reason to doubt your love."

He shook his head. "I never even told her how wonderful her play part was. She was the best one there. When I saw her made up like that. . .looking so much like her mother. . . ." He was pacing now, his voice sharp with frustration. "Not little girl-like anymore, but womanlike, I was filled with a new fear. A fear that she really would become like Darlene. That's why I turned her interests to the work at the ranch. In my own clumsy way, I tried to keep her the way I wanted her.

"My wife Darlene was devastatingly beautiful. I loved her with such a passion." He slapped his fist into his palm. "Then I hated her with an even greater passion. She destroyed all that she touched."

"She gave you Joanna," Alecia said simply.

Rayne turned and folded his tall frame, kneeling at her feet. "I don't want to hate her. It's eating me alive. It's destroying me. Because of hate, I couldn't bear to call Joanna by her right name, or to let her become the little lady she deserves to be."

"Forgive her," Alecia urged him. "Forgive Darlene."

He shook his head. The muted light from the brass lamp reflected a tear streak on his cheek. "It's too late. Too much damage has been done. You can't forgive a dead person. I'm locked in."

She touched the tear to dry it away. He caught her hand and pressed it to his face. "Help me, Alecia."

"You can pray and ask the Lord to forgive your hatred of her. For Him to take it away."

"He can do that?" The question held a note of wonder.

"And whatsoever ye shall ask in my name, that will I do," she quoted John 14:13. She brought out the Bible to show him the passage.

"But it's so hard to ask."

"When you want something so desperately, it's never too hard."

Rayne's gentle eyes searched hers for a moment. Then he lay his head on her shoulder and surrendered over to the great ripping sobs that tore into the layers of pent-up bitterness and hate. His prayers, smothered in sobs, were heard by the One who could touch the deep inner wounds that no man's hand could heal.

Gently she stroked the dark, fine-textured hair and at long last gave vent also to her own reservoir of awaiting tears.

Later they would pray for Joanna Darlene. Together.

Chapter Ten

There was yet another day of endless vigil before Joanna's brown eyes fluttered open. From the moment she awoke, she never stopped talking. And her father was overjoyed, joking that she would probably never be that still ever again. But Alecia knew he was ecstatic to have her back.

The doctors' reports were optimistic that full recovery was on the way. Joanna was taken off the IVs and was allowed to walk a short way—on her crutches— that very day.

Alecia wearily excused herself late that night to return to Nancy's and attempt to get one good night's sleep before leaving for Minneapolis the next morning. When she left the room, Rayne and Joanna were deep in conversation, pinpointing why Joanna was thrown and what could have been done to prevent it. Alecia smiled inwardly, as her heart sang praises to God.

Following Galen's call, Alecia had located an isolated pay phone and called Mr. Harwood personally. She was pleased and thankful that he was willing to postpone the meeting. She took the opportunity to tell him about the work she had done while she was away.

"That's what I like about you, Miss Winland," he commented in his gravelly voice, "you never miss a chance to further your skills."

Although she realized she could not take all the glory, she decided to leave it at that. She could fill him in on the details later.

It was easy for Alecia to see why Galen's patience with her faltered. Still, it left her with a hollow feeling that he had not been more understanding of her position. At the same moment, she chided herself—had their roles been reversed, would she have been as cooperative? She wasn't sure.

She slept like a baby in her room at Nancy's that night. Every bone in her body thanked her for the comfort of a real bed once again. The next morning Nancy outdid herself preparing a delectable cheese and sausage omelette.

Loading the car took only a few minutes, during which time Nancy went on and on about how wonderful it was that Alecia had come to help. How she appreciated the company, the work, and the moral support. "I'm at a loss," she said as she swung the little overnight case into its nesting place in the full trunk, "to fully express my thanks to you. I can only pray that your time here will prove to benefit you for the rest of your life."

Alecia remembered what Mother had said. That if she gave of her time and energies, it would open the door for God to work His perfect will. She was certain Rayne's breakthrough was part of that perfect will and she was grateful she played a small part in it.

"I believe that our prayers are going to be answered to the fullest," Alecia assured her as they hugged good-bye.

As she drove slowly out of the drive of the Whitlow Ranch, she and Nancy frantically waved to one another like two teenagers parting at summer camp. There were moments when Alecia wondered how Nancy would fare alone, but her sister had regained much of her strength the past few weeks and was now back in the saddle, out keeping watch over her acres of pasturelands.

The glen at the twists in the road was cool and shady and curtained in an early morning mist. Alecia pulled her loaded car to a stop, hopped out, and stepped through the spongy grass to Jake's front door. "I stopped to tell you good-bye, Jake," she said as he opened the door.

"Jest like I told you," he answered with a wide grin. "I train me a good hand, then she ups and leaves." He stepped down out of the mobile home and extended to her his weathered hand. Shaking his head, he added, "I thought maybe you was getting sweet on the good-looking Lassiter boy, and then we'd get to keep you."

Alecia succumbed to an unaccustomed blush. "Rayne and I? How silly," she scoffed. "We're worlds apart."

"Yeah, well, I've heard that's what makes marriage interesting," he drawled. "Anyway, that's what old Roland Lassiter used to say about his little gal from Philadelphia."

"Philadelphia? Rayne's mother? You're kidding."

"Naw." Jake scratched at a place on his shoulder where his shirt was threadbare. "Mrs. Lassiter was a high-bred gal who fell for an old rawhide rancher. Purty rough on her at first, but she finally got used to us." Pausing for a gaping yawn he said, "Now you be sure to come back and see us sometime. Y'hear?"

"I will. And meanwhile, look out after Nancy for me. Y'hear?"

He gave a dry laugh. "Sure will, Miss Winland. That old bottle don't have such a tight hold on me now. I'm doing better and I'll look after her. Don't worry."

As she drove away from his little home among the trees, Alecia thought about how Nancy trusted Jake when no one else would. Now he was her friend for life.

Word had it that Josie was planning a big coming home party for Joanna, even though they were not certain when she would be released from the hospital.

A part of Alecia wished she could be there for the gala celebration. If only she could have known Josie better. . .and Sammy too, for that matter. And Roland. All of them suddenly seemed dear to her. They had each one been so patient with her. She couldn't wait to tell Delia about each and every one of them.

When she arrived at the hospital to give her last good-bye, Rayne met her outside room 226. His eyes were dancing. "Can't go in yet," he cautioned. "Just a little surprise." Then realizing how silly he sounded, he added almost apologetically, "You know how it is with kids."

"I ought to," she countered with a grin.

"Is she out there?" came a call from inside the room.

"Yeah, she's here," Rayne called back, part and parcel to the game in progress.

"Make her wait a minute. I'm not ready."

"I'm holding her back with all my might, but she's struggling," Rayne answered, attracting the attention of passers-by.

"What is this? A conspiracy?" she accused, loving every minute of it. Rayne's countenance was aglow with joy.

"Okay," Joanna called, "let her in. I'm ready."

"This took a lot of hurrying and conniving," Rayne said aside to her as they went in. "I hope you realize what a privileged character you are."

Rayne opened the door upon Joanna decked out in the yellow dress from Archer's. Her massive head bandage had been replaced by a smaller one and the nurse had taped a yellow ribbon to it. Other than appearing a trifle pale, Joanna was lovely!

Alecia didn't have to pretend her pleasure and surprise at the unique sight of a little girl sitting in a hospital bed, dressed in a frilly frock. One foot sported a yellow sock, the other was still partially covered in a cast. "Joanna Darlene. How lovely you look."

"Daddy bought it for me. Can you believe it? Isn't he simply wonderful?" she said, giving a big wink.

Alecia joined in the joke. "Wonderful? Wonderful just isn't the word." She walked over and rubbed the silken cloth between her fingers. "Hasn't the man simply marvelous taste in ladies' fashion and fabric?"

Joanna giggled. "I say, he really does. It's a rare thing these days, wouldn't you agree?"

"Quite rare, quite rare," Alecia agreed, nodding vigorously.

"Hey, you two. Knock it off," Rayne protested. "You sure make it tough on a guy who's trying to apologize and say he's been wrong."

"I think he's crying uncle, Joanna. We'd better give him mercy," Alecia cautioned.

"Oh," Joanna cooed. "Come here, Daddy. I'm sorry. We were just kidding." She motioned for him to sit on the side of her bed, then put her arms around his neck. "I love the dress more than ever. Now I feel like it's from both of you."

She motioned for Alecia to come sit on the other side of her. "Besides, the nurses said I could only wear it for a few minutes, then I'll have to put my pajamas back on. This was a special surprise for your going away."

"Thanks, Joanna. Seeing you like this is the best present you could ever give me. You have my address. I expect to receive a letter from you."

"Will you write me back?" Joanna wanted to know.

"I sure will."

"Will you write Daddy too?"

Alecia looked at Rayne. Looking into those deep eyes was difficult. She wondered what was really going on in there. "I don't know about that. We haven't had time to discuss it."

"He'll probably want to, now that you're pretty good friends," Joanna pronounced matter-of-factly, embarrassing the both of them.

"I must go now," Alecia said, shaking off the discomfort. "It's a long drive to Minneapolis. Good-bye, Joanna. I'm so thankful you're going to be totally well soon."

"Miss Winland, I love you." Joanna couldn't hold back the easy tears of youth. "You're the most wonderful teacher I've ever had. Please promise to come back and see me someday."

Alecia received the bear hug from the thin arms. "I promise. I will." She swallowed past the tightness rising in her throat.

"I'll walk you down," Rayne told her. To Joanna, he said, "You be back in those pajamas when I get back. You hear? Josie wants the dress fresh and clean for your coming home party."

"Do I have to take it off now?"

"Now," he answered, settling the matter.

Rayne walked quietly beside Alecia all the way to her car. The day was balmy and cotton puff clouds hung low in the baby-blanket blue sky. Alecia turned her face to the breeze to smell of its spring freshness. Already there had been hot days, warning of the humid Oklahoma summer to come.

"Alecia," Rayne said as they reached the car, "thank you for being a good friend to Joanna. I can see now how badly she needed someone like you. And I'm sorry for all the harsh things I said to you. I'm hoping you'll forgive me for being so ungrateful." He put his hand to the car door as though to open it, but let his hand rest there.

"It's done. I've already forgiven you. I said some harsh things to you too. And what I didn't say openly, I was thinking to myself. Actually I wasn't very fair with you. So the forgiving goes both ways."

"Most of what you said, I needed to hear," admitted Rayne. "You've helped me so much. The awful weight that I carried around for so long is gone. Really gone." His eyes were soft with wonder. "For the first time in years, I actually feel peaceful. I never thought it could be possible. You helped me to see that God's mercy could include me. I'm grateful."

"I didn't go about things very graciously at first. I suffered from a bad case of self-righteousness. It's not the best vehicle for displaying God's mercy. I wanted so much to see Joanna set free that I ignorantly rubbed salt in your wounds."

"But," he insisted, "if you hadn't come at me with all that sass and spitfire, I may not have heard."

"You mean you did hear?"

"I heard all right. And it hurt like blazes. That's why I got so mad." He gave a wry smile.

"We came through a lot in a few short weeks, didn't we?" Her thoughts flew to the rainy day in the stable. . .to the night they floated together on the dance floor. . .the special time in the chapel. In a flash she recalled every word, every fragrance, every tender emotion.

"An awful lot," he agreed. He gazed out over the parking lot. He had forgotten to pick up his hat and it seemed strange to see him bareheaded outdoors. The dark hair was riffled slightly by the breeze. She remembered how silky it felt as his head lay on her shoulder and his tears streamed into the fabric of her dress.

He returned his gaze to her face. "I wish you could stay a while longer."

A while? What did he mean by a while? A while was such a vague term. It could mean an afternoon, a summer, a lifetime.

"It would be nice," she replied. "But I have a job waiting. . .and a lot of work as well."

"And Galen?" he asked.

The question surprised her. He had not mentioned Galen even after that awful phone call in Joanna's room that night.

"Yes, Galen," she admitted, squinting against the morning sun streaming through the puffy clouds. She rummaged in her shoulder bag for her sunglasses. "Galen Rustin is my working partner."

"Is that all?"

Why should he want to know this now? Such a silly time to talk of Galen. "Well, no, not exactly. He's a confidant, a close friend, and a Christian brother."

"I see." He took a quick breath.

"And before I left, we were seeing one another regularly on a social level."

She wished if he had something to say, he would say it. His hedging was difficult to handle.

"Well, teacher lady, you might drop us a line now and then. Let us know how you are."

"Us," he had said, not "me." "I will, Rayne. Remember now, if a teacher brings Joanna home from school, and if her car dies in your drive—beware!"

Her levity broke the tension and his warm deep laugh sounded forth.

"Thanks for the warning ma'am, but you're too late." He placed his arm about her shoulder and for a moment she feared that he might kiss her again. She knew she couldn't bear that at this moment. Instead, he tilted her chin and placed an endearing peck on her nose. For a split second her heart cried out to hear him say, "Stay with me, Alecia. Stay with me forever!"

But of course, he didn't. Of course, he didn't. And the next moment, she didn't even want him to. That was insane thinking. She had helped him see truth. He was grateful for her help. That's all there was to it.

He opened her car door and she settled herself in, perching the sunglasses on her nose. "Good-bye, teacher lady," he said softly. "Don't forget us."

"I never could. Good-bye, Oklahoma rancher."

≈

The two-day drive, broken by an overnight stay in a quiet motel, gave ample time for idle pondering. Alecia assumed that as she stacked up the miles between her and Denlin County, the memories would diminish. On the contrary, they were growing larger in her mind.

Time, she reasoned. *Time and activities will erase them.* And once again, she turned her thoughts to the work that awaited her.

It was late when she parked in the underground parking garage beneath her high-rise apartment building. She grabbed her few pieces of luggage and locked the car. She and Delia could lug the rest of it up the next day.

She rang the bell first. She didn't want to frighten Delia who had lived alone for four months now.

"Who is it?" Delia sang out.

"Me, silly. Your long lost roomie." Quickly she was let in and there was as much hugging in coming home as there had been in leaving Oklahoma.

The two of them sat up and chatted until the wee hours of the morning. Delia had much to tell of new friends, a new promotion, and change of job position. Then she wanted to know all about Denlin County. Alecia complied with her request, omitting a few of the more harrowing and touchy details.

When Alecia finally crashed into bed, she was determined to call Galen first thing the next morning. He would probably take the day off to spend with her.

"Good morning," she said brightly to him when he answered her ring just after the sun had risen. "I'm home. Arrived late last night."

"I thought you might call me first thing when you arrived," he said in a guarded voice, not like Galen at all. "We could have had a midnight supper for old times sake."

She shook her head as though he could see her. "I would have been no kind of company last night. I was cross-eyed with weariness. Will you be coming over?"

"I thought we could catch the outdoor concert tonight. Sound good?"

"Sounds great. I missed the concerts more than anything." She hesitated. She had understood from Mr. Harwood that Galen would have a day off when she arrived. Their relationship was no secret at the office. "Will you be here this afternoon?"

"It doesn't look like I can," came his reply. "In fact you'd better drop by the office today, if you can. A briefing would be beneficial to you before the upcoming staff meeting."

With as much time as she spent on the phone and reading all the correspondence he had sent her way, she felt she was well briefed now. Could it be that Galen's feelings were more hurt than she had realized? She had made the mistake of riding slipshod over Rayne; it wouldn't do to make the same mistake twice. Tact and courtesy, that's the ticket!

"Fine, Galen," she agreed. "Whatever you say. You know better than I what's going on over there. I'll get unpacked and be there by one-thirty. Okay?"

She sensed his tension easing somewhat. "Good. I'll see you then. And, welcome home."

It was with sheer delight that Alecia hung her clothes in her own closet once again. There in the back of her closet was her rose-colored suit—one of Galen's favorites. She had almost forgotten about it.

That afternoon she donned the suit and took special pains with her appearance before leaving for the office. She would be especially kind to Galen and try to help him understand why she was detained in Oklahoma and why she was unable to call him.

He was alone in his office when she arrived. His secretary greeted Alecia with an expression of disbelief. "You finally came back," she said. "It's so good to see you again. He's in there. Want me to hold calls?"

Alecia smiled and nodded before knocking at his door and letting herself in.

All the stiffness that Galen put forth over the phone disappeared as he looked up and saw her standing there. His boyish expression seemed older somehow, more intense.

"Alecia." He breathed out the word. "I've missed you." He lay down the pen in his hand, quietly rolled the chair back, and rose to step around the desk and take her in his arms.

After struggling and fighting her emotions with Rayne, it was a relief to relax in Galen's arms and return his embrace and his warm kisses.

The following weeks were filled with hard work as she strove to put together the details and finishing touches on their project. She needed to contact artists, performers, and business people to solicit the services of those who cared enough to become involved.

She and Galen worked closely together and his initial coldness faded as he became more enthusiastic than ever about their relationship. In their work each day, he went out of his way to be kind and understanding to her. Socially, they went out several evenings a week and to church together each Sunday. But it seemed to Alecia like a surface relationship. Galen was as gracious to her as she could ever hope a man to be. Why then was she floundering so? Why was she so unsettled in her feelings?

The evening of the Fourth of July they attended a glorious fireworks display in the park near her apartment. Later, hand-in-hand, they walked through the fragrant flower beds, when Galen pulled her to a stop and invited her to sit with him on one of the benches. A hint of breeze gave a whisper in the leaves of the sprawling shade trees above them.

"Alecia," he began, taking her hand in his. "I want to talk with you about our future. Mr. Harwood has offered me a position in his immediate office. He says he likes the way I've been handling what we've been doing. It looks like I have a great future there." He pulled a small box from his pocket. "But no matter what the future holds, I want all of our tomorrows to be shared together. Will you marry me? I love you desperately."

Alecia was astonished at the size of the ring in the box. As a girl she had often dreamed of having a man present her with a ring like this. But storybook dreams have a way of being distorted in real life. Later, she wondered if he had expected her to come alive with a positive reaction. If so, it must have been awkward and painful for him when she sat there, quietly staring at the sparkling diamond, having no idea what to say.

Of course, she could marry Galen and possibly be happy the rest of her life. They had talked much about their mutual enjoyment of the arts, of children, of sports, and scores of other things.

"It's gorgeous," she said finally. "I'm flattered that it's being offered to me. But marriage is such an enormous step in life." Once again—for the umpteenth time—she asked herself if her appreciation of Galen constituted real love that would last a lifetime.

"I know what a big step it is. That's why I've waited until I was sure before asking you."

"I had no idea you'd purchased the ring. I'm tempted to receive it simply because it's so lovely. Please, though, be patient with me. Let me think it over."

Silently he closed the lid of the velvet-lined box. The taciturn manner she had sensed when she had returned home in May was surfacing again. "All right, Alecia. You think about it and let me know. I'm going to my brother's home in Duluth for a few days. I'm taking off work until next Wednesday. I'd thought about asking you to go since you love Jenny and the kids. But perhaps this would be a good time to spend apart, thinking and praying about our decision."

Sweet Galen. Always so methodical and proper about everything. "That sounds like a good idea. When you come back, I'll have an answer for you." Strange, she thought, that he should want to take a few days off now, but not when she came home. Such a piddling matter. Why should it annoy her so? She must be growing paranoid.

She received his gentle kiss at her door and they said good-bye. As she let herself in, she almost wished he would get really angry. At least she would know what he was feeling.

On Saturday morning she was up early. To her way of thinking, the Minneapolis summer was too magnificent to waste sleeping it away. The gardens around the lake were breathtaking and she hit the jogging trail early each morning, before the sun became too warm.

She pulled on her sweats and went to the kitchen to pour a glass of juice. Sounds of movement came from Delia's room. Luckily, both of them were early risers. However, whereas Alecia was anxious to get outdoors, Delia was anxious to get to her easel.

As almost a second thought, Alecia decided to quickly shampoo her hair and let it dry as she jogged. Later when the doorbell rang, she knew from experience that Delia would not answer it—the weekend artist never wanted to stop once she was started. "Don't disturb me unless it's a life or death matter," she would order firmly.

Piling a thick towel upon her wet head, Alecia was tempted to take difference with her roommate at this point. Delia may be busy creatively, but at least she was presentable.

There was no one of Alecia's acquaintance who would be up this early on Saturday. Unless Delia had a new boyfriend she had been keeping under wraps. Maybe it was a package, or a telegram. Her heart quickened. She hoped it had nothing to do with her parents—or Nancy!

Approaching the door, she could hear muffled voices on the other side.

As she opened it, a little voice called out, "Surprise!"

Chapter Eleven

Rayne was leaning against the wall with his hat tipped cockily forward and wearing a grin that rivaled the Cheshire cat's. Beside him, dressed in typical tourist fashion of pink shorts, shirt, and even pink Nikes with tennis socks, was Joanna—sans cast!

Alecia couldn't help but laugh at their expressions. No doubt they were laughing at hers. "I don't suppose you thought of calling ahead," she scolded, covering her shock.

Rayne shrugged. "You know how it is with kids and surprises."

"I ought to." They laughed again at their ridiculous hallway conversation. "Joanna, welcome to Minneapolis." She reached down to hug the girl. How she had missed her. "Come on in here," she ordered, ushering the two of them in. "How's the old head?" she wanted to know. "And the cast is off." Joanna's hair was a scant bit longer now. Quite attractive.

"My head's fine and the cast came off last week." She kicked the leg. "Feels so good to have it off." Her large eyes darted about the apartment, taking it all in. "Daddy and I are here on a business trip," she announced with aplomb.

"Oh, really?" Alecia looked at Rayne.

"The livestock show at the Convention Hall." His eyebrows went up. "Don't tell me you haven't heard?"

"You know how it is," she retorted. "Been so swamped around here, I clean forgot to catch the farm and market report each morning."

He pressed his lips together and shook his head. "Unforgivable. Wait till Nancy hears how you've fallen away in the short time you've been gone."

Joanna looked up at them. "Why do you two always talk so silly?" she asked. And they laughed again over the nothingness of it all.

"Miss Winland," Joanna said, "we want you to come to the livestock show with us. We're showing some of our livestock. It's going to be fun. Can you come?"

Looking at Joanna's face, waves of memories rushed over Alecia of the hours the child lay so deathly still. Now, here she was, not only recovered, but free from the shackles of her father's former fears. It was like beholding a miracle.

"Do we have to decide now?" she asked. "Why don't you sit down for a moment and let me get you something to drink and we'll talk about it."

Agreeing, Joanna bounded into the living room and sat down on the couch. Rayne's presence seemed to shrink the apartment. He maneuvered his long legs between the couch and the coffee table.

Joanna might blend into the throngs of summer tourists but Rayne never would. His tall form dressed in the pale green western suit commanded attention. The hat in his hands he placed on the table before him.

"I want you to meet my roommate," Alecia told them, hoping she could get Delia out long enough so she could slip away and dry her hair. "Delia!" she called out, knowing in advance what the answer would be.

"In a minute. Just a few more strokes on this scene."

"It's hard to interrupt genius," Alecia explained.

Joanna was studying her surroundings. "Is this where you live all the time?"

"All the time," Alecia confirmed.

"Is this all there is to it?"

"Well, no." Alecia realized how small it must look to her, although it was large compared to most city apartments. "Come up here and see the kitchen." She led her up the few steps to the small kitchen, which she felt was just the right size not to waste a step as she and Delia fixed their meals, both large and small.

"Oh." Joanna was not too impressed.

"The bedrooms are in the back. Delia's is down that hall, and mine is down that hall."

Her brown eyes were still questioning. "Where's your yard and how do you get to it?"

"Come here," Alecia said, attempting to conceal her amusement. "I'll show you my yard." This little rancher was bewildered by life in a high-rise.

Alecia took her to the bedroom window that overlooked the lake and the expanse of gardens surrounding it. In the early morning sun the entire park looked like a garden from a fairyland.

"Wow!" At last Joanna began to show a spark of interest. "All that is yours?"

"Actually, it belongs to the city, but they let me use it every day. See that path down there? I was about to go jogging among the roses this morning before you arrived."

"It's so pretty." Her nose was flattened against the window. "I'd like to see the water up close."

Alecia led the way back to the kitchen and put on the coffee maker, wondering how this day was going to work out. Should she go with them? She had no interest in a livestock show for heaven's sake, but they had come all this way.

Delia finally emerged from her room, having washed most of the paint smudges from her hands and face. "Sorry I took so long, folks, but when an artist...hey! Don't tell me. This must be the little lady who lost the battle with the cow."

"Steer," Joanna corrected.

"Excuse me. Steer," Delia agreed with a chuckle. "And this must be her father, Rayne. I've heard about you two. Greetings and welcome to the Minnie-apple. The great metropolitan snowball. Good thing you came after the thaw. You'll love it here. . .now."

Rayne was openly amused at her fast talking and her nasal twang. He shook her hand and drawled his greeting back to her.

Quickly Alecia set her roomie to pouring the coffee and fixing Joanna chocolate milk, while she excused herself to dry her hair. "Delia, tell them about the city and what to see. You've lived here longer than I have."

Before the droning of the hair dryer drowned out Delia's voice, Alecia heard her saying, "Livestock show? Sounds like fun! I bet Alecia would love to go."

Fun, my foot. Alecia fluffed furiously at her hair with her fingers. The only reason Delia would consider going to a livestock show would be to search for subjects for her paintings.

Her chestnut curls flew about her face, much too full for her liking. She preferred to dry it running in the sunshine, rather than using the blow dryer. And it seemed to have a mind of its own today. She applied a touch of quick makeup, then fastened her hair back with a silk ribbon.

When she returned to the living room, Delia was deep in detail with Joanna about the Children's Theatre Company and what was playing there presently. Joanna was enthralled—especially now that she had made her own debut on stage!

Rayne glanced up at Alecia. "That really was you under there, wasn't it?" he quipped. Then he stood. "Alecia, we've got to run. There are endless details to be taken care of at Convention Hall. We just wanted to come by and invite you to join us this afternoon. Can we pick you up at one o'clock?"

Her mind was made up. If they wanted her with them, then she wanted to go. "That's fine, Rayne, but let's do one better than that. Let Joanna stay with us. You take care of your business, then come back for both of us."

Joanna bubbled over at the suggestion. "Can I, Daddy? Please? Then I can go jogging in Miss Winland's backyard down there by the flowers and the water."

Rayne thought a minute, then gave a guilty smile. "It's still hard to let go. Sure, she can stay. I'll be back here at one o'clock, sharp. You two had better be ready," he warned with a broad smile.

After Rayne left and Joanna finished her chocolate milk, the two of them took the elevator to the street and crossed the busy thoroughfare to the park. "Is that ankle strong enough for jogging?" Alecia asked as they reached the path.

"Doctor said to exercise it as much as I could," she answered.

"Good." But Alecia slowed her pace anyway. "I didn't know ranchers took vacations," she commented as they progressed through the first leg of the jogging trail. "What made your daddy decide to bring exhibits to the livestock show?"

"It's not a real vacation," Joanna explained.

"But you are away from the ranching operations."

"Daddy's different now," she said simply. "One day he said, 'Joanna, we're going to travel more. You need to see something other than Oklahoma.' " Joanna had stopped to watch two swans glide delicately across the lake, leaving a silent riffle behind them. Alecia stood beside her.

"He's happy more of the time now too," the girl continued. "He never gets real mad like he used to." She dug the toe of her Nike into the grass. "If it took being thrown and gored by a longhorn to change him, Miss Winland, then I'm glad I got hurt," she concluded with childlike sincerity.

"Those are strong words. But I think I know what you mean. It shouldn't take calamities to wake us adults up, but sometimes it does. We can be pretty hard-headed, you know."

Joanna laughed. "Yeah, I know. Like Uncle Lavren."

Alecia involuntarily shivered at sound of the name. "What about him?"

"He's gone to Hawaii."

"Hawaii? What in the world is he doing in Hawaii?"

"Aunt Corrine went too. She says it's like their second honeymoon. She's says he's nicer now."

"Is that right?"

Joanna nodded. "Know what Daddy says?"

"Tell me quick. What does Daddy say?"

"Daddy says there's been more than one miracle in Denlin County since you came there."

Alecia felt herself blushing and hoped the redness from exertion disguised it. But as usual Joanna was unaffected.

Looking around her as they jogged on, she said, "This is an awful pretty place. I can see why you wanted to come back, but I'm homesick already. I miss my horse."

Now it was Alecia's turn to laugh. "Well, ignore those feelings and come on. When we finish the course, I'll show you a cute dress shop in the mall down the street."

"Miss Winland, I've been thinking." Joanna changed her jogging to happy little skips. "Since you're not my teacher now, can I call you Alecia? Like a friend?"

Alecia thought about it briefly. "I guess that would be permissible."

"Oh, goody, goody." The skips changed to little rabbit hops as they wound around to the end of the trail.

They were ready at one o'clock sharp just as Rayne instructed. Alecia changed into a comfortable skirt and blouse and sturdy walking shoes. She knew the size of the Convention Hall.

Delia waited until Rayne arrived before revealing her little tidbit of news. Alecia thought surely her roommate was above conniving little schemes. But she was wrong. With a sly smile, Delia asked Joanna, "How would you like to go with me to the Children's Theatre tonight? I just found out where I can get two tickets for great seats."

The brown eyes came alive. "The theatre like you were telling me about? Wow! Would I? But I don't know if I can. Can I, Daddy?" She looked up at Rayne.

"That's real nice of you, Delia," Rayne began, "but you didn't have to go to the trouble."

"Trouble? Ask Alecia here. I'm always looking for excuses to go to Children's Theatre. Looks kind of silly for a grown woman to go all by herself. You know?"

Alecia nodded with a little chuckle. It was so true. Her kooky friend loved that theatre more than all the others.

"Well," he intoned thoughtfully. "If you're sure."

"I'm sure. I'm sure. Meanwhile Alecia can show you how downtown Minneapolis glows at night. I bet she's been dying to get you into a Greek or French restaurant."

Alecia loved her companion's complete lack of subtlety. "I would at that," she agreed. So within minutes the day was planned and it looked great.

⁂

Several of Rayne's men had driven up earlier in the week, bringing not only the cattle, but a few of the horses as well. Sammy, of course, stayed behind to run the ranch.

The livestock show was unlike anything Alecia had ever seen. A spectacular showing of the prime of America's cattle, horses, hogs, and sheep. She was amazed at the magnitude of it all. Together they strolled through endless rows of stalls filled with every type and breed of livestock. At one point Joanna gave an excited shout. "There's our stall. That's our cattle."

Over the stalls hung bright royal blue banners with "El Crosse" emblazoned in white. Rayne explained to Alecia that he hadn't bothered with shows for the past few years, even though he was confident he had prize-winning stock and was well aware that winning shows helped to advertise breeding stock. But up until now, he said, it had seemed to be too much trouble.

Alecia knew this reluctance was due to his desire to withdraw from any outside activities that attracted attention to himself or to Joanna.

They continued viewing exhibits and Alecia found her interest growing as Rayne outlined the details of competition to her. The animal aromas, mixed with that of hay and leather, brought back memories of her work for Nancy and the thought of the quiet tranquility that was ever-present there.

The equine exhibits were the grandest of all, and Alecia hoped she could attend a day of judging next week. The competition would be exciting to watch.

"Now you get to see Midnight Melody," Joanna told her. "I've always wanted you to see her."

"Midnight Melody? Who is she?" Alecia was being pulled along quickly by Joanna's tugging at her arm.

"Daddy's best horse. She's beautiful. She'll take home the prizes. Wait and see."

They led her to yet another stall proudly displaying the El Crosse banner on the cross bar. And there she was! A horse every bit as beautiful as Corrine's, and more so. Midnight's coat was a deep sorrel that shaded into an ebony mane, tail, and legs. She was simply magnificent.

Alecia gasped. "She's so lovely." How thrilling it would be to work with a horse like this. Secretly Alecia had decided to locate a stable in the city and enroll in riding lessons. She had so much to learn. Aloud she mused, "Twilight Song and Midnight Melody. . .similar names. Any connection?"

"From the same dam," Rayne told her. "Both winners, but I haven't pressed to show. I don't want to step on Corrine's toes. I'll try showing where she isn't in competition."

Alecia laughed at that. "Quite considerate of you, but I'm sure Corrine can handle herself—win or lose."

"She can at that," he replied with a slight smile.

He moved into the stall to check to see that all was as it should be, talking easily to the filly as he worked.

"My horse Kaney-Kins is a winner too," Joanna was saying. "Daddy's given me permission to start practicing my barrel racing. Next fall I might be ready for the Denlin County Rodeo."

"Kaney-Kins?" Alecia repeated. "Don't tell me. Related to Nancy's horses?" Nancy had never told her.

"Raisin Kane is the sire of Joanna's filly," Rayne said from inside the stall as he bent to check Midnight's feet. "By the way, Nancy said to tell you Kane Brake will foal in the fall."

"How delightful." Alecia's head swam with all these fascinating names and wonderful mounts. Of course she knew it wasn't all fame and glory, for she had tasted of the hard work involved. She knew the price that was paid.

Rayne's ranch hands, Josh and Brock, came by and Alecia was introduced to them. They remembered her as the schoolteacher who couldn't get her car started at the ranch one day. She strove not to blush and Rayne grinned at her.

When it was time to go, Alecia found she wasn't ready to leave the grandeur of it all. But they needed time to get ready for their evening out.

ta.

In front of her high-rise Alecia stepped to the curb from the taxi, and Rayne stepped out with her. "I'll see you in a couple of hours." He paused as though there was something else on his mind. He stammered a moment then said, "Are you sure this is all right. . .this thing with Delia and Joanna?"

Alecia gave him a patient smile. Remnants of the overprotective, widowed father. "It's more than all right," she assured him. "They'll have the time of their lives. Delia's a nut and she loves kids." In a teasing tone she added, "Uh, are you sure it's all right. . .this thing with Rayne and Alecia?"

He shot her a sheepish grin and pushed back his hat. "Touché, my friend. I'll see you later." He folded himself back into the cab and father and daughter waved as they drove away.

If she had been apprehensive before, she was more so when she learned Galen had called while she was out. "What did you tell him?" she quizzed Delia.

"I told him you had unexpected guests from Oklahoma drop in."

"Is that all?"

Delia snickered. "I didn't tell him the most handsome rancher ever to stomp a boot stepped into our apartment this morning. But I could have. . .and not exaggerated."

"Delia, have mercy. Am I supposed to call him back?"

"Yes ma'am. As soon as possible."

Hurriedly she dialed Galen's brother's number in Duluth.

Galen's voice was as pleasant as ever as he greeted her. "Alecia. So good to hear your voice. I feel I've been gone a week rather than just a day. I want you to know that although you caused me a little confusion, I'm not angry with you. Please understand that."

"I understand, Galen. Likewise, you'll have to understand my position and my feelings."

"I love you, Alecia, and I want you to be my wife, but I'll be as patient as I can. I guess it's just that I hoped it wouldn't have to be something you'd have to think over."

"Marriage is sacred to me. It'll have to be 'till death do us part' in my life."

"You know we agree on that."

She did know. They agreed on so many things. What then was her holdup? Why was she torturing him like this? But that inexplicable, nameless restlessness could not be ignored.

"I'm glad you have company," he went on. "Friends of your sister's?"

Alecia forced herself to be honest. "It's the little girl who was in the hospital. She and her father are here."

"I see." Galen changed the subject then and began describing the delightful antics of his charming nieces who were ages two and four. They laughed together, although to Alecia the laughter seemed stiff and empty.

When she hung up and came into the kitchen for a cup of coffee, Delia took a look at her and gave a low whistle. "You two have a fight?"

"No. Why?"

"The long face."

"Actually, I haven't told you this, but Galen offered me a ring the night of the Fourth."

"Oooh, honey. What did you say? Obviously you turned him down."

"I told him I needed time to think and pray about it."

"Are you praying?"

Alecia nodded, sipping at the hot coffee, not really wanting to drink it. She poured it to occupy her hands while her mind was spinning. "I am. But I'm still so confused. He's a wonderful guy. So diligent in his work, and kind and considerate."

Delia's eyes twinkled. "Rayne's a wonderful guy!"

"Delia! Be serious. Rayne has nothing to do with this."

Delia plopped down on the couch and put her feet up. "Oh really? If a good-looking guy like that came all the way from Oklahoma to see me, I wouldn't be taking it as lightly as you are."

"Hey, you're supposed to be the level-headed one in this group. Is this why you've manipulated this evening so Rayne and I could be alone tonight? Rayne came up here for a livestock show. A place to show his livestock." She enunciated the words like a grammar teacher.

"Sure, sure. Now you're going to tell me this show—taking place in the city where you just happen to live—was the only one available in the nation. Right? Wow, are you dense."

Delia was speaking forth things she had been frightened to say even silently to herself. She shook her head. "I don't know. I think he's just overly grateful. Plus Joanna's crazy about me. That's all."

"Okay, have it your way." Delia hopped up to go get ready. "But if I were you, I'd wake up and be sure."

In the quiet of her room, Alecia changed into her white eyelet sundress with the delicate pink ribbon-and-lace trim. In her mind she fought against the things about which Delia hinted. Was there a chance that Rayne might actually love her?

She remembered the evening of the party at Corrine's. Had he sought her out because he truly cared for her, in spite of their harsh differences at the time? And was that why he had picked this show to attend. . .to once again seek her out? To be with her?

The thoughts bewildered her. Whatever would she say if he expressed his love to her? Did she love him in return? Or was it simply infatuation?

She vigorously brushed back her hair and fastened each side with pink satin ribbons, then fluffed the bangs across her forehead.

She was sure there could never be a life for her with Rayne. Even the very notion was ridiculous. Her a rancher's wife? Impossible. And besides, she told herself once again, his attachment to her was merely one of gratification. Her mother always told her once you showed someone God's mercy, that person would be forever indebted to you. And that was enough, really. To know that Rayne now trusted God and was taking Joanna to church regularly.

In times past she had recklessly let her emotions fly out of hand. She was determined not to allow that to happen again. Granted, she was flattered Rayne wanted to spend time with her, but she would remain level-headed about the entire situation.

From her bedside table she took her soft, worn Bible and turned again to Philippians 4:11, the verse she continually prayed would be fulfilled in her life. "For I have learned, in whatsoever state I am, therewith to be content," she softly murmured.

"Well, I'm learning," she told herself. She could be content that Rayne wanted to be friends. That was good enough. Plus she was thrilled to once again see Joanna. At least there was one area where she had no confusion. She deeply loved that little girl.

Showing Rayne the city was great fun. They meandered through Nicollet Mall and ate fresh fruit in a skyway café. They took in a play that turned out to be uproariously funny and they enjoyed much-needed hearty laughs together.

Later they viewed the city from the observation deck atop the IDS building. As Rayne beheld the metroplex with its relentless, steady streams of moving traffic and wildly flashing lights, he pushed back his hat with his thumb and shook his head slowly. "Don't you ever feel bunched up and hemmed in with all these people? It's enough to strangle a guy."

Alecia looked at the same scene with eyes that perceived the excitement and promise that it held. "Well," she admitted, "at one time, I was unaware of the peace and tranquility of the wide open spaces. I'd never experienced the feeling of being at one with God while looking out across an open plain and watching Him paint a new, fresh sunset each evening."

"And now?"

"Now that I've tasted of that. . .being very close to nature. . .yes, I must confess, since I've come back, I do feel a trifle hemmed in at times."

He nodded.

She hastened to add, "Actually, it's like taking a vacation to the Bahamas and enjoying the beauty and climate. Naturally a person misses that when he returns to his own work-a-day world, but it doesn't override the love for home. I also see the beauty and excitement here."

Still, she could tell by his face that he thought it incredible that anyone could live in such a hectic, crowded place.

Leaving the tower, he said, "We were going to eat sometime tonight, weren't we? Where are those foreign places Delia talked about? I'm so hungry I could eat a bobcat."

Alecia laughed. "No place that I know carries that item on the menu. Is it some sort of local native delicacy in the lowlands of Oklahoma?"

They caught a cab to a dimly lit French place at Saint Anthony Main. Rayne wasn't deterred by the strange cuisine nor the menu, but continued to pelt the patient waiter with questions until he was clear on every item.

Alecia was well-acquainted with the menu, but remained silent and let him fare for himself. He did remarkably well. Secretly she thought he would be like a fish out of water, but instead she was admiring him for adjusting so smoothly.

They lingered over their meal in the restful surroundings, engaged in relaxed conversation that seemed to flow easily. Lapses in their talk didn't scream out for forced remarks. If ever Alecia longed for a moment of time to be endless, this was surely that moment. Although she had been here dozens of times, she had never been so intoxicated with the atmosphere. Had Rayne made that much difference in her life?

Rayne's broad hand covered her smaller one. His infectious smile was brighter than ever. Leaning forward, he asked, "Has anyone ever told you that you're very beautiful?"

"Yes," she replied, surprised she could remain so casual, so relaxed. "Several have."

"Well then. . . ," the smile widened. "Has anyone ever told you your hair has a glossy sheen as lovely as a sorrel filly's?"

Her soft laughter spilled out into the golden glow between them. "I can honestly tell you, Mr. Lassiter, that no one ever has."

"Good," he said, lifting her hand and planting kisses on each fingertip. "I selfishly wanted to be the first one."

With a warm inner knowing, Alecia realized if she never saw Rayne again the rest of her life, this delightful portion of merriment and close companionship shared this special evening could never be taken from her.

Rayne's muscular arm held her close on the way to her apartment. Just before the cab came to a stop, he touched her cheek to turn her face to his to kiss her. "Thank you for a marvelous evening," he whispered.

The restrained, gentle kiss held none of the abandoned release of emotions as that rainy day in the stable. Yet the same thundering explosions were going off inside Alecia.

Desperately she clutched her emotions to her heart and held them there in silence.

They found Delia and Joanna having a giggling good time over popcorn and a game of Scrabble. Rayne's pleased expression told Alecia it was yet another new step for him to see Joanna getting on so famously with a virtual stranger.

Sunday held special moments as they worshipped together at Alecia's church. Waves of joy swept over her as they stood to sing the melodious hymns—she and Rayne with Joanna between them. At odd moments they caught glances and smiled at one another. Rayne's sonorous baritone voice was full and rich. At the closing prayer Joanna surprised them by taking each of their hands and placing them together on her lap.

After lunch in the mall Rayne asked Alecia, "Do you remember that long ago you promised to play me a game of tennis?"

She felt herself go crimson as she recalled where they were when he commented on the strength in her arms. "I vaguely remember it being mentioned."

"Good. Then let's use this sunny afternoon for you to show your stuff on the courts."

"Tell me," she retorted, "did you bring your tennis boots?"

It turned out to be another time of carefree hilarity. Never had she laughed so much, nor been challenged so strongly in her game. She got the last one over on him, but he had already won two.

"Oh well," she sighed and rubbed the back of her neck with her towel. "It was worth it just to see the Oklahoma rancher in tennis togs."

He snapped her on the leg with the tip of his towel.

Never had she known such joy in being with a person. But she was confident it was because she had made the decision not to become emotionally involved, but to simply enjoy Rayne as a friend.

There was more business for Rayne to attend to Sunday evening at Convention Hall. They parted after their tennis match with the promise that she would be at the Convention Hall Tuesday evening as soon as she got off work. She found herself counting the minutes.

She took her jump suit to work with her Tuesday to change into, and was more than anxious to get over to the Convention Hall that evening to see what was going on. As agreed, they met at Midnight's stall, then ate supper together at one of the snack bars.

"A far cry from the little French café," Rayne said as they quickly downed the tasteless hamburgers. But he had much to do to get ready.

Before judging time Joanna and Alecia went to the stands and Joanna filled her in on what the judges were looking for. The competition was a long drawn-out, but exciting, affair. Had it not been for Joanna's explanations, the judging would have made little sense to Alecia.

The arena was filled with well-groomed horses in their best form, performing flawlessly for their trainers. Rayne had changed into a golden tan suit with matching hat, and Midnight Melody wore a stunning silver saddle and bridle.

It wasn't until Midnight Melody's name came blaring over the loudspeaker as the grand champion winner, that Alecia realized how tense she had been. Suddenly she and Joanna were hugging one another and cheering and laughing.

There was a time of congratulating, photo taking, and awarding of the trophies that accompanied being a winner. Alecia watched, entranced, from the sidelines.

When Rayne was finally free, he hugged her openly. "We did it!" he exclaimed. "We won it!" He released Alecia and swept Joanna giggling off her feet and swung her around. "Let's celebrate. Where would you like to go?"

"You look a little tired," Alecia told him. "Let's just call Delia to have something ready at my apartment."

He rubbed at his mustache and grinned. "You're right, smart teacher lady. I'm bushed. I'll take care of Midnight and we'll go."

By the time they arrived, Delia had ordered two large pizzas and had soft drinks chilled. They couldn't have had a grander celebration at the most exquisite eating place in town. With Rayne, a person could have fun anywhere.

They were laughing when the doorbell rang and Delia went to answer it.

Alecia looked up from where she and Rayne were standing near the kitchen to see Galen enter the living room.

Chapter Twelve

"Galen." Alecia stepped toward him.

"I came back early," he said flatly, his face expressionless. "Thought I would drop by and meet your guests."

Distressed, Alecia made the introductions between Rayne and Joanna and Galen.

Rayne was kind. "I've heard lots of good things about you from Alecia," he remarked, although she had hardly mentioned Galen's name.

"Won't you have something, Galen?" Delia waved her hand toward the last of the pizza. "We were celebrating the Lassiters' win at the livestock show."

"Really? No, I've got to be going, thank you. I didn't mean to intrude." His attitude was saddening and exasperating.

Alecia wished she knew what to say. How could she ever explain? She knew how Rayne must look to him. She would have to try to clear it up later.

In a moment he had excused himself and was gone. It seemed to put a damper on the gaiety.

"I hope I didn't cause any problems," Rayne told her later when Joanna was in Delia's studio looking at the paintings.

"No, no. Don't be silly. Things aren't that serious between us."

"He looked crushed."

"Yes, he did. But that's not your fault."

"I didn't intend to come here and mess up your life."

She looked at his gentle face. "You could never do that."

"Alecia." He sat down beside her on the couch. "We'll be flying out of here in the morning. I want to thank you for a wonderful time. I don't know when I've ever had so much plain old fun."

"It has been fun, Rayne. It's a treat to be friends with someone like you."

She thought he was going to say something further, but at that moment Joanna came bounding out, insisting he come and see Delia's great paintings.

The evening was over too soon and a strange quiet settled into Alecia's heart and mind.

The next morning, before Rayne and Joanna caught their plane, they called Alecia at the office and said their last good-byes over the phone. "I wish you great success in your work," Rayne told her. She had explained to him that Galen was being moved up and she was soon to move into his office. It was a real step up for her. One she had been waiting for.

"Thank you, Rayne. I wish you the same."

"I'll miss you, Alecia," Joanna was saying with tears in her voice. "I wish we didn't live so far away from each other."

"Me, too, honey. Me too."

And then they were gone. It had been difficult to get over being away from Joanna last May. Now she found it doubly hard—for she knew she missed Rayne as well.

She tried, however feebly, to break the news to Galen that she could not marry him. She was certain of it now. When she married, it would be to someone like Rayne Lassiter. Of that she was certain.

Poor Galen could not separate in his mind the fact that she said no and the fact that he saw her having fun with Rayne in the apartment that evening. She assured him that Rayne had nothing to do with her decision. But in a way he did. Oh, it was all so impossible to sort out in her mind. How could she ever help him to see, when she didn't understand it herself?

After that, Galen seldom called, and later his promotion put him in another area of the office building. Her days grew somewhat lonely. In the evenings she spent her spare time at a riding stable. She drove out once a week for her lessons, and other times simply to ride. She had fallen hopelessly in love with horses.

She and the stable owner often discussed just which horse would be right for her to own. Her deepest desire was to purchase a colt and train it. But what did she know about training horses?

She dated a few men from her office, but none were the type of person she enjoyed being with, so that halted.

Notes arrived from Joanna. They were attending more shows and still winning. Her neat little handwriting said she had entered her first rodeo and won third place in her age division in barrel racing. Rayne never wrote, but Joanna always ended her letter, "Daddy says 'hi'." Likewise, Alecia ended hers to Joanna, "Tell your daddy 'hi' for me."

There were activities at church in which she and Delia were involved that were both entertaining and fun. But her inner restlessness clung like a cocklebur in Peppy's mane.

She assumed that when school began and she could see her project put into operation, the annoying sensation would be quenched. So when September rolled around and her jogging times were chilly from a distinct fall nip in the air, she was disturbed that the hollow nameless thing was still attached to her.

"What, Lord?" she would ask Him as she trotted around the paths and surveyed the crimson and gold trees. "What are You trying to tell me? What am I not hearing? I'm doing everything within my power to serve You and live for You. What is this awful void in me?"

She was almost jealous of her parents as she read their letters from South

America. Walt and Mattie were having such a gratifying time serving the Lord together. One Sunday at church Alecia lingered behind after the service to talk to her pastor about filling out applications for missions. After all, she was a trained educator. Surely she would be needed.

But that evening as she looked them over, Delia gave her a knowing grin and said, "Mmm. Most missionaries I know apply because God calls them, not because they are at loose ends."

Alecia wadded up the forms and hook-shot them into the waste basket.

The call that settled the issue came in the wee hours of the morning. She nearly knocked the phone off the bedside table as she grabbed for it and struggled to awaken herself.

"Miss Winland, please."

"Speaking."

"Ma'am, this is Dr. Islip, Denlin County Hospital. Your sister had a light stroke and was brought in by a neighbor, Mr. Shanks, earlier in the evening."

Alecia sat straight up in her bed, swinging her feet to the floor. "Nancy? Oh, no!" Her heart pressed into her throat like a cold, hard stone. "How is she now?" *Please, Lord, let me think clearly.*

"She's holding steady at present. Thankfully she was discovered by her neighbor who then called the ambulance."

Good old Jake, she thought warmly. *He had watched out for Nancy after all.*

"You stayed with Mrs. Whitlow after her surgery last winter didn't you? I believe I remember you."

"Yes, I was there."

"Do any members of your family live closer to Oklahoma?"

"No," she said, "I'm the nearest one."

"Then I suggest you come as soon as you can."

Alecia shivered in the early morning chill, tucked the phone under her chin, and grabbed for her robe. "I'll catch the first flight out, Dr. Islip. Please tell Jake to meet me at the airport."

"Certainly."

Immediately she roused Delia and together they prayed for the day that lay ahead for Alecia. By nine that morning she was gazing down at the clouds beneath her plane, wondering how her new assistant could possibly handle the details of the project while she was gone.

Her initial fright had waned and she was sure that Nancy, the fighter, would come through like a winner. A stroke was more serious than major surgery, but Nancy would make it.

And this would be a short stay this time, she reasoned. She couldn't get tangled into staying indefinitely as she had last spring. She would have to hire someone to stay with Nancy—perhaps a trained nurse. Or possibly their parents could come home for a furlough. Surely the people of South America weren't more important than their own daughter.

Abruptly Alecia stopped and shook her head as if to shake away the cobwebs of selfish reasoning. "Forgive me, Lord," she breathed as she viewed the glowing floor of clouds beneath them. "I want to learn to do Your will in this. Show me what to do."

A very somber Jake met her plane. As he drove her to the ranch in his ancient pickup, he described the frightening moment when he had returned to the house for no other reason but that he felt he should check on her one more time. He found her on the floor, struggling to crawl to the phone. "If I'd been plastered like I used to be all the time, I never would have found her," he said in a quavery voice.

"We're so grateful to you, Jake," she said gently. "So very grateful."

Nancy was no better, but only slightly coherent. There was great difficulty in understanding her. Her movements were stilted. Alecia was distressed to see her precious, loving sister suffering like this. Why had this happened to her? Someone so kind and good. . .always loving. . .always giving.

Rayne and Joanna were in Phoenix for a horse show, but when they returned and learned what had happened they were at the ranch to help.

Nancy resorted to writing out little notes of instructions with her left hand. Much work was yet to be done to get the place ready for winter.

The familiarity of the ranch was comforting. Dependable Peppy; excitable, hard-working Sparkie; proud Raisin Kane; and the very pregnant Kane Brake with her bulging sides—they all helped to make Alecia feel welcome.

It was difficult to explain later how it happened, but every evening Rayne was there—sometimes Jake, sometimes Joanna, but always Rayne. There wasn't time to talk about it, think about it, or ask questions. Only work to do between hospital visitations each day.

On the note pad Nancy feebly scratched out, "Watch Kane Brake."

Alecia complied gladly. She was terribly excited about the prospect of the new foal.

The days were Indian summer—warm, fragrant, and golden. The hints and whiffs of lingering summer played teasingly with the signs of fall. The leaves on the oaks in Nancy's back yard began to fall ever so slowly onto the lawn that was still green. To crunch them underfoot was to release their pungent odors of autumn. Fall in Minneapolis was sometimes depressing to her, but here at the ranch, it felt pregnant with promise. She was so sure everything was going to be all right.

Together she and Rayne rode the pastures and brought in the calves that Nancy wanted readied for the sale. The ones she didn't want to winter over.

They checked fences and worked to be sure each feeder station was in good condition for the cold days to come. Alecia was more than thankful for her riding lessons. She was able to be of more help than before. Rayne commented on her improvement, which pleased her.

She wasn't as good a cook as Nancy, but with a freezer full of steaks, roasts, and ground beef, it wasn't too difficult to turn something out when Rayne and Jake were there late. There was still a gold mine of tomatoes, squash, and carrots in the waning garden. These Alecia reaped and added to the meals.

In the evenings she and Rayne sat on the back patio with cups of coffee, taking in each golden splendorous sunset, breathing deeply of the clean, tangy fall air. Sometimes talking about the work, sometimes sitting in comfortable silence just thinking.

Each night Alecia fell into bed with a tiredness that was far removed from frustration. It was a genuine physical exhaustion that was erased with the dawn. Sleep was deep and restful.

Nancy improved slowly, steadily. Each afternoon Alecia drove to the hospital to spend time by her sister's bedside—praying, talking, encouraging, reading Bible passages that Nancy requested to hear.

Calls to Minneapolis revealed that her assistant was doing well in her sink-or-swim position. Mr. Harwood told Alecia it was because of the excellent groundwork that she and Galen had laid out during the previous year that others were able to step in and carry on.

One evening after Jake left, Rayne went out to the stable for one more check on Kane Brake before leaving for home.

Alecia was finishing up in the kitchen. She had swept her hair up off her neck in a casual do. It was an unusually warm October day. Presently Rayne was calling to her from the back door. "Come quick! Kane Brake's about to foal!"

She dropped the things in her hands and rushed to his side, as full of excitement as a small child at Christmas.

Anxiously, the mare paced in her stall. At intervals she lay down for a few minutes, then arose and began pacing once again. Alecia watched as Rayne worked with her. He had that special touch with animals. He spoke repeatedly to her in gentle tones to calm her. When she lay down again, and nickered and quivered in her frustration, Rayne was there at her head, talking. . .comforting.

A few hours passed slowly as they kept their vigil. Periodically the mare would lie down and bear down with all her might, but the foal did not emerge.

"Looks like she may have a difficult time." His voice was tinged with worry.

"Oh, no. I hope not." Alecia bit her lip. "Nancy would be so disappointed if anything happened to this foal. She asks about him every day. She's counting on this little fellow."

Kane Brake nickered again plaintively and nipped at her flanks. She emitted pitiful moans to express the pains that the pressure of birthing were causing within her huge midsection.

Reluctantly, Alecia went inside to bring out coffee. As she busied herself, she began to pray for the safe birth of the colt. Somehow it seemed to stand for something. For hope. . .for a new beginning.

When she returned, Rayne had donned rubber gloves from the vet bag in Nancy's tack room. "I was able to turn the foal," he explained. "One leg was twisted all out of position." He sighed, giving a weak smile as he removed the gloves. "I think it's okay now."

She left the stable door open. The night was clear and still. . .warm as summer. Carefully she set down the tray with the coffee.

"Come quick, Alecia," Rayne called.

Just as she stepped to the stall, the foal began to emerge. In a fraction of a second the miracle of birth was complete and the tiny creature was lying in a wet heap on the dropcloth that Rayne had carefully spread out.

"She's a filly," Rayne said excitedly.

Alecia was breathless with wonder and awe. She moved behind where he was kneeling and placed her hands on his shoulders to get a closer look. "A miracle of new life," she whispered.

Rayne lay his cheek over against her hand. "She's a miracle all right. She just about didn't make it."

The filly was sleek and wet with fluid, but immediately lifted her little head to sniff the air and greet the world. Kane Brake was busy cleaning her.

"Nancy told me I could name her," Alecia told him. "What do you think of Kandy Kane?"

He looked up at her. "That's a happy name. Sounds like something you would think of."

By now Kandy was struggling to steady her forelegs and pull her hindquarters up under her body to stand. She was beautiful. Every part of her was perfect. In a matter of minutes the quiet of the stable was filled with greedy, sucking sounds.

"Let's call Nancy," Alecia suggested.

"You go on in," Rayne told her. "I'll clean up around here and wash up. Then I'll be in."

Later, when Rayne stepped into Nancy's den, Alecia was sitting motionless in the wing-backed chair.

"Alecia." His voice was husky. "What's the matter?"

She forced her eyes to focus on his face. . .his kind, wonderful, concerned face. But the tears were hot and fiery in her eyes, blurring everything. . .blinding her.

"She's gone, Rayne. Nancy's gone. They called me just now...before I could call her. Peacefully, in her sleep, only moments ago. On her note pad was one last note: 'The foal is Alecia's.'"

Rayne reached out to lift her to him and quietly gathered her into his broad chest. The tears flowed freely and the sobs shook her body.

"Oh, Rayne," she said, "I never got to tell her. Now she'll never know."

"What, Alecia? Tell me."

"It was so important for me to tell her." She drew away from his arms to stand by the glass-fronted stove that had no need yet of a warming fire. "I've been so confused lately. Restless and empty. But tonight as the foal was born, there came a new revelation sweeping over me. I knew in my heart this is where I belong." Another sob sent a shudder through her. "As I watched the exquisite miracle of birth, I felt like I'd come home. I...I can hardly express it. I just knew."

"Alecia, my precious darling," Rayne said to her. "How I've hoped and prayed to hear you say those words. That you would come to know beyond the shadow of a doubt that this is the life you've chosen. Because I love you and I want you to share your life with me as my wife. The mistress of El Crosse, Joanna's mother, my friend, my lover."

Alecia dabbed at her tears with the handkerchief he pressed into her palm. Hearing him profess his love to her was like a dream come true. "Rayne, I love you, too. More than I ever hoped to love any man. But why didn't you tell me? I never dared to hope. . . ."

"I was unsure at first, and scared. It was all so crazy how I wanted to be with you to hold you and keep you, and yet hating everything you were saying. Then when I did know for sure, I thought perhaps you couldn't be happy being a rancher's wife." Gently he kissed the top of her head as he held her shoulders.

"I talked to Nancy about it," he went on. "She told me to be patient and to keep praying. So I did. And here you are by my side."

She rested her face against his chest. "Nancy said she prayed that my experiences here would benefit me for a lifetime. Her prayers were full of effective power. I believe it's because of her prayers that we're here together right now."

Rayne lifted her face to gaze at her. "She knows, Alecia. I'm convinced, she knows." As he kissed her with the full unrestrained emotions of a man excited for his beloved to be his own, Alecia's head swam with the bittersweet emotions of losing Nancy, yet at the same moment finding her kind, gentle Rayne. He emitted to her his tender strength, and she was gladly strengthened by it.

"We'll check on little Kandy Kane," he whispered, "then I'll drive you to the hospital."

Arm-in-arm they stepped out across the lawn to the stable. In the milky white light of a fat, swollen harvest moon, the fields lay peaceful and sleeping. They were her fields now. She had learned to be content. She had found her fields of sweet content.

From the Heart

Sara Mitchell

Chapter One

Soft music, appropriately funereal, floated around the almost deserted room. At the front, in solemn splendor, rested a closed casket draped by a single pall of white carnations. There were no other flowers. Only three seats of the large chapel in the funeral home were occupied.

Sitting in one of the padded chairs was Olivia Sinclair, spine rigid, head bowed. At her side, her mother sat with compressed lips and grim fortitude, biding her time until a polite interval had passed and she, Olivia, and Larry, brother of the deceased, could leave. At the moment Uncle Larry was looking at the casket, irritation the only emotion registering on his face.

There were no other family members, distant relatives, or friends present to acknowledge the departure of Alton Xavier Sinclair.

Reverend Tucker, the family minister, had spoken a few words some ten minutes earlier, his speech uncharacteristically awkward. In fact he had agreed to preside over the funeral only because Olivia had gently coerced him, her voice quiet but firm. Apparently not even Reverend Tucker entertained a remote hope that Olivia's father would now be in the presence of the Lord.

Olivia slid a brief look to her mother, whose only words these past interminable hours had been: "Well, I imagine he's finally where everyone wanted him, God forgive me. But if any man deserves to burn forever, it was your father, Olivia. The only reason we'll attend this farce of a funeral is because your uncle and I need the absolute reassurance that Alton is really dead and can't hurt anybody anymore."

If only that were true, Olivia thought now, staring at the coffin. He'd hoodwinked all of them over the years, her father had, with his deceptively charming smile and boyish good looks. First her grandparents, then Uncle Larry. . . then her mother and the three children she'd given him—Olivia, her sister Jennifer, and brother Tom. They were not the only victims, but every person at the bank, too, from the lowliest teller to the wealthiest depositor. Like tares among the wheat, Daddy's bankrupt soul had leeched the life out of everyone around him, leaving a bitter legacy of hatred and revenge. It was somehow fitting that he had died in January, the bleakest, most barren month of the year.

Olivia closed her eyes and tried to pray. The motion was wasted. She could not talk to God with all these feelings seething inside, choking her breath off and making her skin crawl with nameless dread.

The piped-in music ceased as the funeral director appeared from a side door. With undisguised relief they all stood.

"Let's get out of here," Uncle Larry muttered, practically dragging Alton Sinclair's widow down the aisle. "I need some fresh air, and God knows it will be the first time in over thirty years I'll be able to breathe it easily."

Olivia's last memory of her father was the silent mortician and his assistant wheeling his casket out of the parlor.

After the funeral, struggling with a multitude of tormenting thoughts, she found herself strangely reluctant to return to her store in Barley, a good hour's drive away.

Like thousands of other small southern towns, Barley, North Carolina, enjoyed a serene, slow-moving lifestyle, comfortably located ten miles off the interstate. Main Street boasted just enough businesses to stay mildly prosperous. There was even a mall on the town's eastern outskirts. Whatever couldn't be had in Barley "twern't worth having," according to the old-timers who daily gathered at the back of Mr. Clarke's seventy-year-old hardware store.

Through her wedding consultant service, The Bridal Bower, Olivia was doing her bit to ensure the town's diversity. She was also enjoying her second full year of operating in the black—for the bittersweet reason that nobody in Barley knew who her father had been. That was about to change, no doubt. The next hours, Olivia suspected, would signal the greatest changes of her life. She had said goodbye to her father, but she was shouldering all the burden of the family name.

❧

". . .and I still can't believe you're actually going through with this," Maria concluded her monologue.

Engrossed in her own thoughts, Olivia had waited patiently throughout the lecture, mouth curved in a half smile, watching her partner and best friend, Maria Santinas, who was still trying to decide if Olivia were teasing or serious. Maria loved to joke about the spaniel-solemn eyes that should have been brown instead of blue-gray, allowing Olivia to tell the funniest joke in the world without cracking a smile.

As a professional wedding consultant, the solemn look had proved useful, and the dry sense of humor had defused many an emotion-laden crisis. Right now, however, Olivia was as serious as she'd been in her entire twenty-six years.

"I'm going to try and atone for Father's cruelty and injustice all these years," she repeated. "One person can make a difference, remember?"

"There's one little fact you keep overlooking, kiddo," Maria drawled, pointing a well-chewed pencil at Olivia. "It was your father everyone wanted to tar and feather. . .not you."

Olivia didn't so much as wince. She'd spent the better part of her life coping with the shame. "I'm still a Sinclair—sins of the fathers and all that. Besides, I'm the only one left. Mom. . .Mom quit caring before I was even born. Tom's in California. And Jennifer married an engineer and moved to Alaska to start a new life—" She paused, furrowing her brow in concentration. "Remember the time Mrs. Duckworth read that Scripture in Sunday school, then pointed to me—'There's sin in Sinclair,' she said. . . ." Olivia stopped, fighting memories that still rankled years later.

In a reflexive action, she reached for the open daily calendar at the corner of her desk. "Now, I've been planning this for months, ever since Daddy was diagnosed with inoperable cancer last fall." She glanced up. "Don't worry. I'll still manage everything here. At least this is our slowest season."

Maria rolled her eyes. "Knowing your fanaticism for organization, if he'd kicked off in June, I'm sure you could have convinced every last bride in the tri-county area to reschedule for fall." She leaned over Olivia's shoulder, peering at the calendar. "Okay. . .there are no weddings for the next two weeks, and Rollie and I can cover the rest. So what's your plan—a blue-light special on mea culpas, passed along to all parties who've suffered the calculated cruelties of a twentieth-century Ebenezer Scrooge, otherwise known as Alton Sinclair?"

Olivia flushed but met Maria's skepticism without wavering. "Over the past seven years or so, I've compiled a list of sorts, listening to Daddy at the dinner table, reading newspapers, hearing other people talk. . . So far, I've got about half a dozen people I plan to see. I know I can't. . .atone. . .for everything, but I've got to ask their forgiveness at least, see if there's anything I *can* do—" Her voice trailed away. She was suddenly overwhelmed, not only by the impossible nature of the cross she'd chosen to bear, but by the look of sympathy Maria wasn't bothering to conceal. "And I don't need your pity," Olivia mumbled.

Straightening, she picked up her shoulder bag and headed for the back door of the shop. "I have to try, Maria, even if you and Rollie don't like it. I'll touch base with you every Monday morning and Friday afternoon, just as we discussed. Other than that. . .see you in three weeks."

"I think," Maria mused aloud, her voice following Olivia out, "that you just might be back here sooner than you planned."

Olivia paused at the back door of the shop, glancing around automatically to make sure everything was in order. She felt inside her purse for the pocket version of the daily calendar on her desk. It was there, in place, and she marched outside without a backward glance.

≥◆

Jake Donovan paused for a moment, resting against the ropes while he caught his breath, and enjoyed the freedom of dangling two thousand feet up the face of a sheer granite cliff. Far below, the valley floor shimmered and sparkled from the newly fallen snow, while above him a sky blue as an alpine lake stretched toward infinity. The air was so clear and cold it burned his lungs, the only sounds a whistling wind and the single triumphant shriek of a hawk diving toward its kill.

Alone up here, without the stultifying routine found in the rat race most people made of their lives, a man could really find himself. Jake lifted his face, feeling the invigorating bite of the wind. . .and the memory of last night's phone call from his sister intruded as subtly but as dangerously as pending hypothermia. "Ah—" he expressed his frustrations out loud, then finished his ascent. So much for a relaxing week bumming around the Rockies before his next job!

Four hours later he was back on the ground, swiftly and efficiently breaking camp. In four more hours he was at Stapleton Airport, Denver, boarding a plane for the first leg of his flight to Charlotte, North Carolina. Beth would be waiting at the airport, her drawn, care-worn face looking far older than its thirty years, brown eyes dulled by permanent fatigue.

What was wrong now?

She'd sounded so strange over the phone, almost—Jake searched his mind for a word, waving aside the hovering flight attendant who couldn't understand why he wouldn't eat the plastic meal she was offering—incredulous. That was the word he was looking for! Like his sister had just taken a fist in her stomach. No. . .that wasn't it, either. Beth hadn't sounded like she was upset or in pain, and she had promised Jake that nothing had changed for the worse with Davy. She just needed to talk something over with her big brother. No matter that she was the stable nine-to-fiver and Jake the proverbial rolling stone.

He leaned back in the seat, forcing his body to relax. All his life he'd taken care of his sister. She was the only responsibility he'd ever accepted without question, no strings attached. Whether he was tramping through a jungle in South America or biking through the Alps, all Beth had to do was call.

Ignoring the droning voices, the constant noise, the irritation of being confined, Jake closed his eyes and switched off. He had a feeling he was going to need all the rest he could manage. At least, for the next few hours, he didn't have to worry about insects or frostbite.

੨੪

Beth hugged him tightly, but avoided his gaze.

"I'll drive, you talk. . .but wait until we're out of the airport," he ordered, tossing his bag in back and gently bullying her into the passenger seat of the beat-up Ford she'd been driving for the last eight years. Jake hated the car, but sometimes Beth could dig in her heels more firmly than he. The last time he'd bought her a car, Beth had signed it over to some penniless widow down the street.

Night was approaching rapidly. Jake turned on the lights and fiddled with the heater. After Colorado, forty degrees seemed like summertime, but Beth was shivering. He maneuvered the vehicle out of the airport and headed southwest, toward the little North Carolina town where Beth and Davy lived. Now, of course, only Beth lived there.

Jake glowered at the bleak countryside, thinking his sister looked as gray and lifeless as the waning February day. "You said Davy's the same, right?"

Beth nodded. "I wouldn't lie to you about that."

She had married Davy when both kids were fresh out of the vocational tech school. Scrupulously saving, working sixteen-hour days, within three years they'd accumulated enough money to take out a loan for Davy to open his own small engine repair shop. Then—

"Talk," Jake said tersely, giving the road part of his attention while honing in on every nuance of Beth's subdued recital.

"Three days ago this. . .young woman came to see me," she began. Jake felt her staring at him, hesitating. He forced himself to wait, knowing Beth would clam up if he pushed too hard. "Her name was Olivia. . .Sinclair."

At that, Jake almost swerved off the road. "*What?*"

In the dim interior of the car, her faint smile was barely discernible. "I had the same reaction."

"You don't have to say another word," Jake said from between clenched teeth. "I'll handle this now, sis. You just tell me where the little—"

"Wait a minute, big brother, before you go all aggressive and protective on me—" Beth patted his shoulder. "Not, of course, that I don't need that, with Davy—" Her voice wobbled, but she rallied like she always did. "She looks so nice, Jake, it completely threw me for a loop. I was on my lunch hour, and she asked if she could join me. You wouldn't believe how hesitant, almost afraid she sounded."

Jake mumbled something to himself and Beth apologized. "Sorry. I know I'm rambling and you hate that. I'm trying to explain, but I still have so much trouble—"

"Just tell me what she demanded. Obviously, she's dear old Dad's new hatchet-man. Sorry. . .*person*. . .and—"

"I'm going to tape your mouth shut, Jake Donovan."

Jake rotated his shoulders and took a deep breath. For a few moments neither of them spoke. As always, he appreciated his sister's ability to bring him up short, then back off without harping on his regrettable temper. "I'm okay now," he promised, reaching one arm across in a brief hug. "No more interruptions or promises as to how I plan to wipe my boots on Ms. Sinclair and her jerk of a father."

"Her father's dead."

This time he managed to keep the car firmly on the road. "Good riddance."

Beth actually chuckled. "Yeah, well, that's what this is apparently all about. His daughter wants—in her words—'try and atone for some of my father's injustices.' She's been looking up some of us pathetic hard-luck stories and is begging for a chance to help."

"And pigs fly!" Jake shot back. "I'll have to hand it to her. . .the lady's got a unique approach, a lot more subtle than her old man's. I'm glad you called, mouse. You're much too soft and sweet to take on a female Attila the Hun." He grinned into the night, his thoughts churning. "But as well you know, I'm *not*."

Chapter Two

I don't know how much more of this I can take, Olivia thought, hands clutched tightly together in her lap. Yet she continued to sit quietly in her discreet suit, hair carefully arranged, face a serene mask. She had no choice. Quitting was not an option.

Head high, she allowed the contempt and vitriolic spate of words to wash over her, through her, each word a stinging verbal blow.

". . .and, young lady, I hope you're as humiliated and hurt as I was six years ago," Samuel MacKenzie concluded, leaning back in his massive desk chair and studying Olivia with satisfaction. "Yep, I trust you're squirming like I squirmed when your excuse for a father refused to extend my loan two lousy weeks, smiling like a shark and looking at me as if I were dockyard scum."

"I'm aware—very painfully aware—that I can't undo the past, Mr. MacKenzie." Olivia knew she sounded too mechanical, but then the powerful businessman was the sixth such encounter. At least she *could* finally make it through what she'd dubbed her "abasement spiel" without sounding like a cowed puppy. "As I told you when you agreed to see me, I only wanted to. . .to say I'm sorry and. . .and. . ." This was the hardest part, especially since thus far she'd encountered nothing but disbelief and flat rejection. Her voice hoarsened to a near whisper. "I wanted to ask, as a Sinclair, if you could possibly forgive what my father did to you."

Samuel MacKenzie snorted. "Give me a break. You one of those religious fanatics or something?" He shook his head. "You got grit, I'll give you that. Don't know another soul with the brass-bound gall to sit across from me and spout off that kind of drivel." He leaned forward, removing his glasses, and peered intently into Olivia's face. "Tell me, Ms. Sinclair, just how far would you go to secure forgiveness, as you say? Can you make financial reparations? Spend the next seven years or so in bondage to the various folks your father ground under his boot?"

The hot color crept relentlessly up her cheeks. "If I could, I would. Even though that's not possible, I just wanted. . .needed. . .to see if there was any way I could clear the Sinclair name. What my father did. . ." She stopped, biting her lip.

". . .you can't undo. Yes, Ms. Sinclair, you've already acknowledged that regrettable fact." Mr. MacKenzie stood and walked around his desk. The hard, booming voice softened a little, sounding so kind now that Olivia's eyes began to water. "But like I told you—you got grit, and I admire that. So I'll give you some free advice, which we both know is more than your old man would have done—"

He paused, then snagged a tissue from the box on his desk and matter-of-factly handed it to Olivia. As if in a dream, she accepted it and dabbed her eyes.

"You can see," Mr. MacKenzie continued, making a sweeping gesture around the plush office, "that I'm fairly successful in spite of your father. He might have controlled a lot of money and owned the largest bank in the area, but he didn't own the entire state of North Carolina. I got another loan elsewhere and paid him off. Then I moved here to Statesville and haven't looked back. My point is this: There are lots of ways to fight the battles in your life, including knowing when it's time to withdraw. Believe me, Ms. Sinclair, you can't win this one!"

Olivia wadded the tissue into a tight little ball. "Maybe not," she conceded, her voice shorn of emotion. "But I have to try. . . . I just can't live with the name any longer if I don't make an effort. If I find even one person who'll forgive what my father did, this whole thing will have been worth it."

The busy executive, whose secretary had warned Olivia he had the manners of a pit bull when annoyed, reached out and gently captured Olivia's small fist inside his big hand. "I don't hold much truck with do-gooder Christians gushing over God's love and forgiveness. They preach a good sermon on Sundays, then doublecross with the best con artists in the land on Monday. Of course, never in my fifty-nine years have I met a Christian quite like you." He dropped her hand and walked back around his desk.

"Since it means so much to you. . .okay. I'll forgive your old man. As it turns out, he probably did me a favor in the long run anyway. Now get out of here and let me get back to work. You've wasted enough of my valuable time—not to mention your own."

≥⋅

Olivia plodded down the sidewalk in a daze, clutching her coat against a raw February wind. She still couldn't believe what had happened, couldn't absorb the fact that, after two endless weeks of rejection and ridicule, someone had actually granted her wish.

Strangely enough, she didn't feel one whit better.

Shoulders slumped, muscles aching from the strain of projecting an attitude of calm determination, Olivia waited at the corner. When the light flashed to green, she stepped off the curb without looking.

"Watch it, lady!"

Hands yanked her backward as a small car careened by, missing Olivia by barely a yard.

"Wow, that was close! You all right, ma'am?"

She looked up into the concerned face of a gangling teenage boy. "Thanks. I guess I should have been looking."

He grinned. "And they say *teenagers* are dangerous drivers! The lady driving that car looked old enough to be my grandmother."

Olivia managed to smile back. "Well, thanks again. I'll be more careful in the future, and I'll tell all my friends with teenage sons to cut them some slack."

❧

Statesville was less than an hour's drive from Barley. Since it was only a little past four, Olivia decided to stop by The Bower. Maria and their tireless assistant, Rollie Jones, had thus far kept things going without a hitch, largely because Olivia had everything so meticulously organized that even a twelve year old could have managed.

Bone-deep weariness engulfed her, though she knew it was more exhaustion of spirit than body. She needed to do something, prove she wasn't an ugly worm in need of burial in the back garden. She needed. . .affirmation.

The Bridal Bower occupied the former site of a seconds fabric store, two blocks off Main. Olivia parked out front, then just sat there for a few minutes, basking in the tangible evidence of her success in at least one area of her life.

A hand-painted tangle of vines and flowers twined over the front door. Coordinating displays in the bay windows on either side advertised the various services offered by The Bower, from engraved invitations to catered receptions. A triangular sticker below the store's logo announced Olivia's membership in the Association of Bridal Consultants. Next to that was a fish-shaped sticker quietly proclaiming the store's Christian viewpoint.

Everyone—including and especially her father—had predicted her venture would go belly-up like the fabric store. At the thought, fresh tears stung Olivia's eyes. She grabbed her purse and went inside.

Maria, looking frazzled, was talking with two women, probably mother and daughter. They were sitting in the store's get-acquainted alcove, which meant this was an initial visit. Comfortably padded chairs were clustered around a large table holding brochures describing all the services available.

When Maria caught sight of Olivia, her chocolate-brown eyes widened in relief. "Ah, here's Ms. Sinclair now. Maybe she can better explain Bridal Bower's policies. . . ." Gracefully vacating her chair, Maria made way for Olivia and shot her an apologetic smile. Olivia suppressed a sigh. Even after five years and a reputation rapidly encompassing the entire state, their maverick policies still sometimes generated consternation.

"This is Janine Careyton and her mother, Vanessa," Maria said. "They haven't quite agreed on—"

"—on much of anything," finished Janine, her voice a shade away from outright anger.

"I won't have people accusing me of scrimping on my daughter's wedding. I have already explained that money is *not* an issue." Dripping with jewelry, hair fresh from a salon, Mrs. Careyton eyed both Olivia and Maria as if they were indentured servants.

Olivia was not unfamiliar with the look. She glanced at the younger woman, sensing immediately that her mother's words had pushed Janine over the edge.

"Mother, you *know* how Father feels, especially after the two of you went into debt when Belinda got married. If you recall, you almost divorced over it. Which—" she added nastily—"is exactly what Belinda and Mike did less than two years after you dumped twenty thousand dollars into their grand society wedding!"

Her mother's lips clamped shut and she darted her daughter a frigid look of displeasure.

Olivia decided it was time to intervene. "May I say something?" She kept her voice deferential but firm enough to command attention. Sitting with arms relaxed at her sides, leaning back in a nonaggressive pose, she waited until both women nodded.

Then she leaned forward slightly. "I have a feeling, Mrs. Careyton, that you still might not understand some of the basic philosophies we hold to here at The Bridal Bower."

"Oh, I did, and that's why—"

"Your assistant has shared that information," Vanessa Careyton's imperious voice overrode her daughter's.

Olivia inclined her head. "Including our promise to defer primarily to the *bride's* wishes, unless she specifies otherwise in writing?"

Two spots of color appeared on the older woman's thin, aristocratic face. "Madam, if I choose to hire you as my daughter's consultant, I will be paying the fees—and you will do as I suggest, or we'll find another consultant."

Olivia stood. "I understand. In that case, I don't think The Bridal Bower will be able to provide the quality of service you desire." She kept her face expressionless while mother and daughter swept out, the daughter with one last anguished backward look.

Maria came to stand beside Olivia, shaking her head. "Whew! Am I glad you stopped by. That woman could intimidate a dragon. I was sweating and stuttering like some blithering idiot." She grinned. "*You* sit there, calm and collected as a nun, then manage to get rid of them in less than five minutes. Which is why you're the boss, right?"

"Well. . .we learn the hard way."

"Ain't it the truth? Remember—" She stopped, then tilted her head to observe Olivia. "You look whacked. No luck today either?"

"I don't know." Olivia restacked the skewed piles of brochures on the table, aligned pads and pencils. She didn't look at Maria. "The last person I talked to was a Samuel MacKenzie. He's this huge grizzly of a man, a contractor, and, like everyone else, he spent the first ten minutes heaping abuse upon my head."

"Olivia—"

"But then he—he actually patted my hand. . .and agreed to forgive my father." She still couldn't believe it. "That's the first time it's happened, but Maria. . .I just feel empty." She swallowed the lump crowding her throat. "I don't under-stand. . .when this means so much to me."

Maria hugged her. "You can't force the issue, honey. You're sweet and com-passionate and determined, but unfortunately your papa was heartless and cruel. Most people aren't going to forget—much less forgive—no matter how nice you are. We've tried to tell you that, but you just refuse to listen. Stubborn as gar-lic breath you are."

"Thanks a lot." Olivia rubbed her temples. "I knew I could depend on my best friend and partner to give me a boost, salve my tattered self-esteem." When Maria looked stricken, Olivia managed to summon up a flicker of a smile. "I'm teasing, sort of, okay? Just ignore me. I'm going to work a few hours here and go home. So. . .didn't you tell me Barbara Drake finally settled on her colors? What about her gown?"

Looking relieved, Maria nodded. "No gown yet. Blue and cream for the col-ors. Rollie's out canvassing now—oh!" She smacked her head. "I forgot! Some guy stopped by, wanting to see you about some business matter, not a wedding, 'cause he said he wasn't engaged. He's a friend of Noel Chambers. . .you know, we did that wedding last August? Anyway, you should have seen this dude! If Rick and I weren't tying the knot, I'd have flirted like the dickens. His eyes—"

"What did he want, Maria?"

"—were this piercing gray and the way he looked at me made my knees weak. And his voice—"

"Maria!"

"Oh, all right. It was worth a try, anyway." She slanted Olivia a look of exas-peration. "You're such a contradiction, friend—running a business to ensure hap-pily-ever-afters to everyone else, but never making any effort to ensure your own."

Olivia gave a menacing gesture. "One more word and I'll stuff a sample book down your throat."

Maria laughed. "Sure you will! You're about as tough as a day-old kitten. That man now—okay, okay." She held up her hands, fending off Olivia's. Abruptly the playfulness ended. "I—um—hope you don't mind. . .I gave him your home address and phone number since he asked for you by name and knows the Chambers family. There. Now you have a good reason to choke me."

Stunned, Olivia licked suddenly dry lips. "I don't believe it. You *know* our policy, and the reason. . .and you gave the info anyway?"

"Well. . .I didn't mean to." Maria gave her a hangdog look. "I do know bet-ter, but he had a way about him, and before I realized it. . . . Anyway, I'm sure he's not a serial killer or something, but I did want to warn you. Forgive me?"

Olivia winced. "Don't be a goose. Of course I forgive you. But I sure hope this doesn't turn out to be more trouble."

Chapter Three

Drumming his fingers on the steering wheel, Jake scanned the quiet tree-lined street, blurred now with evening shadows. Just his luck Ms. Sinclair was working late, probably gouging some gullible, starry-eyed bride-to-be. A professional wedding consultant. Now *there* was a racket. Obviously Alton Sinclair had been only too happy to loan—or *donate*—a bundle to his daughter so she could have her own profitable business.

Jake shifted irritably in the seat, unable to erase the contrast from his mind— Beth in her worn, unfashionable skirt and blouse, juggling two jobs and living in a run-down duplex, and this chic boutique with the well-dressed assistant he'd met earlier. If Olivia Sinclair treated him in the same sophisticated, smarmy manner, well. . .he just hoped he could refrain from throttling the conniving female when he laid eyes on her.

The rules of whatever game Ms. Sinclair was playing were about to change, Jake thought, his gaze moving to the tiny house across the street. A boxy, one-story oddity sandwiched between two Victorian relics, the drab little house made Jake positively claustrophobic. It also made him uneasy, since that was where Olivia Sinclair was supposed to live. He wondered—not for the first time—if Olivia's friendly assistant had pulled a fast one on him.

More likely she lived in one of those pretentious Victorian houses, and he owed the charming Maria a return visit. The thought that two women might be stringing him along as if he were some gullible yahoo made Jake's blood boil.

A car turned into the driveway and he sat up, watching the woman driver alight. Mentally he ticked off her description—average height and shape, straight darkish hair just brushing her shoulders, wearing a snappy suit that shouted money and style. Yep, that must be the barracuda herself. And she was headed for the shabby cottage, pulling keys from her purse. Something didn't add up here, but Jake didn't waste more time in speculation.

He loped across the street, catching her halfway up the weed-infested path leading to her front door. "Olivia Sinclair?" She jerked around, looking both startled and resigned.

"Sorry," Jake apologized, not meaning it. "I thought your assistant would have told you I'd be waiting. My name's Jake Donovan."

"I—she did mention you, but I'm afraid I'll have to ask you to come to the store during office hours, Mr. Donovan. I don't conduct business from my home."

His gaze slid to the house, then back to Olivia's face. "Not surprising," he murmured. Even though it was almost dark, he could see a fiery blush sweep up her cheeks. Interesting. He wouldn't have thought a female like her still knew how to blush.

"Excuse me." She was trying to brush him off, turning her back to march on up the path.

Jake ground his teeth. "I'm not interested in being suckered into your fancy wedding consultant set-up," he called, pitching his voice just loud enough to reach her ears. "But we do have some business to discuss, Ms. Sinclair, and since I have plans tomorrow, right now's the best time for *me*." He joined her at the door and deftly lifted the keys from her hand. "Shall we go inside. . .or do you want this stuffy, southern-wealth neighborhood to hear what I think of the contemptible Alton Sinclair and his equally contemptible daughter?"

A quiver rippled through her, but other than that, Ms. Sinclair didn't respond a lick to his deliberate goading. Then, "Are you sure this can't wait until tomorrow?"

A cool customer, Jake surmised, doubtless accustomed to hearing a lot worse, if her reaction was anything to go by. Well, he'd be only too happy to oblige. "Not a chance." He unlocked the door, then gestured for her to enter.

"Come in," Olivia offered, her voice so dry Jake shot her a speculative look.

"Thank you," he returned, mimicking her tone.

She led the way through a dark entry hall, turning on lights. "Would you like something to drink—tea, cola—or would you prefer to start attacking my character immediately?"

The back of Jake's neck tingled, a bad sign. He eyed the contained, eerily calm woman standing in a pool of lamplight, looking for all the world as if she'd just asked his opinion of the weather. Ms. Sinclair wasn't showing a shred of emotion. Being a shrewd observer of human nature, Jake knew such behavior was unnatural—and thereby must be a calculated pose. What was her game? "I could use some coffee," he said, watching her closely. Olivia Sinclair wasn't what he'd expected, and Jake didn't like it.

"Have a seat. I'll be right back."

After she disappeared through a doorway, Jake prowled the tiny living room, searching for clues, for signs of vulnerability. His uneasiness grew. While Ms. Sinclair definitely had a flair for color and decoration, there was little evidence of the same prosperity he'd seen at her store. In fact, her furniture looked almost as shabby as Beth's.

Sitting down on a sagging, faded green couch, Jake tossed a tapestry throw pillow back and forth while he chewed over what to make of the woman in the kitchen.

She returned several moments later bearing a tray complete with cream, sugar, and two steaming mugs. Blue-gray eyes, large and uncertain, regarded Jake without blinking. He was beginning to feel like a complete jerk, but he suppressed the guilt.

"What did my father do to you?" she asked tonelessly, correctly assessing the reason for his visit.

This subdued woman was really Sinclair's daughter? Jake took a mug, ignoring the milk and sugar, then sprawled back against the couch. "My sister, Beth Carmichael, happens to be married to one of your father's many victims." He paused, waiting.

Comprehension lit the pale, carefully expressionless face. "I visited your sister a week ago and heard about her husband." Olivia stared across at Jake. "I know you won't believe me, but I hadn't known until then what had happened to him." She wrapped both hands about her own mug, as if to warm them. "I guess she called you after my visit?"

"Yeah. I'm all she's got, now that Davy's a permanent mental case and ward of the state—all courtesy of your charming father. Now you waltz in three years after the fact, thinking that a simple apology can wipe the slate clean?" Raw anger, still too near the surface, licked through his words. *Not smart, Donovan.* Jake took a couple of deep breaths, reluctantly admiring Olivia Sinclair's tremendous control. Or was it indifference?

"I know it doesn't sound like much—"

"You're mighty right about that!"

"—but I have to try." Abruptly, she set the mug down and leaned back in her chair, closing her eyes. The calm, competent professional metamorphosed to a haggard young woman who looked totally exhausted. "Can you possibly understand how it feels, knowing what my father was, having to live with his reputation. . .always wondering what everyone is saying behind my back?" She opened her eyes, gazing blindly over his shoulder. "I'd give anything to make it all right, fix the wrongs. But at least I can tell people I'm sorry. I need—" She clamped her mouth shut, so tight her lips turned white.

Irrationally, he found this first evidence of vulnerability angering him more than her seeming indifference. "You're sort of pathetic, lady, you know that?" Jake sat up, leaning his elbows on his knees, ruthlessly imposing Beth's drawn face over Olivia Sinclair's. "And your martyr act doesn't impress me, though I'll give you high marks for your creative dissembling. Now, suppose you come clean and tell me what you really want with my sister. The loan's paid off, I made sure of that two years ago. There's not a chance you can talk her into even setting foot inside Fidelity Bank. And since she's already married, she sure doesn't need the services of some dipsy-doodle wedding consultant. . .never mind that her husband's a drooling idiot who decided he liked being three rather than thirty!"

"I see no reason to discuss my motives further with you, Mr. Donovan," Olivia said. "It's your sister and her husband who were—" she swallowed hard—"victimized."

"Having trouble with the truth?" Jake jeered.

Olivia stood. "I've always accepted the truth. . .that's my problem. If you don't believe me, that's your problem. Your sister wanted *your* opinion, and I can respect that. As for the rest, I'm tired, so—"

Jake stood as well, drained his mug, then set it down on the tray. "I'll leave, lady, but I'll be back." He raked a cynical, unforgiving eye over the slender woman standing so straight in front of him. "And if you're really after some sort of absolution for your father, it's going to take a lot more than a few humble apologies."

Not trusting his temper any longer, Jake headed for the door. "You better hope your store can manage without you a while, Ms. Sinclair. It might be squeezing blood from a turnip, but I intend to come up with a way to make you pay for what your old man did to my sister and brother-in-law."

In the hall on the way out was a desk with a daily-planner notebook on top. Jake stopped, flicked contemptuously through several pages, then slammed it shut and opened the front door. "Program me into your busy life, Ms. Sinclair. And you can tell your sweet little assistant she'll have to con brides on her own for a while. *You're* going to be doing some real work for a change."

᪐

Olivia sat motionless after Jake Donovan left, too numb to do anything else. Earning forgiveness, she was learning, consisted of endless, exhausting lessons in humility. And after the brutal confrontation with Jake Donovan, she couldn't help wondering if she were about to reap a whirlwind of emotional destruction far more devastating than her father's lifelong cruelty.

Late that night, as on most nights, she fell asleep asking the Lord for help with the intolerable burden. . .and waiting in vain for comfort.

Chapter Four

"Morning!" Rollie opened the back door with her ample hip, sending cold air and rain blowing across the room. Balanced in her arms were several thumbed-through issues of the latest bridal magazines, which she promptly dumped onto her own desk. "Didn't expect to find you here today, especially this early."

Olivia finished rescuing several blown papers. After a restless night, she'd escaped to the shop practically at daybreak to work on the account books. Shrugging her shoulders to rid them of kinks, Olivia wondered if there was any use in asking her blunt, worldly-wise assistant about yesterday's encounter with Jake Donovan.

Rollie Jones looked like a plump, cherubic grandmother who loved to knit sweaters and rock on the front porch. In reality she possessed the energy of a four-year-old boy and could also inveigle the stripes off a tiger if she chose. After pouring a cup of coffee, she returned to prop a hefty hip on the corner of Olivia's desk. "What is it, honey? We both know there's nothing wrong with The Bower's financial solvency."

Olivia smiled briefly, toying with her pencil. In four years Rollie had come to know her too well. "Did Maria tell you about the man who stopped by here yesterday, asking for me?"

"The 'good-looking macho dude' who charmed her into giving out your address and phone number?" Eyebrows raised, Rollie surveyed Olivia over the rim of her mug. "Maria needs to watch that mouth of hers. I gather the gentleman did pay you a visit."

"You might say that," Olivia said, remembering the silky promise woven through Jake Donovan's parting words. "And. . .it is because of Daddy—not anything concerning The Bower."

The cherubic features hardened with censure. "Maria and I warned you that this notion of yours was asking for trouble. I still can't believe your mother let you—"

"I'm almost twenty-seven, Rollie, not seventeen. Besides, Mom doesn't know. I haven't spoken to her since the funeral. Right afterward, she flew off to the Virgin Islands for a month." Staring at the neat columns of figures on the desk in front of her, Olivia couldn't help wondering if her mother's brand of therapy was, in the long run, far more effective than her own.

"Mmph." Rollie came around and wrapped a comforting arm about Olivia, giving her a hard hug. "I'm thinking a long vacation might not be such a bad idea for you too. Now. . .before Maria blows in, and I have to go pick up the Bibles from the bookstore—eight this time, right?—tell me about this man."

Tell her about Jake Donovan. Olivia studied the middle-aged woman who had been widowed over half her life. Her unsentimental doctrine—"You made the bed, honey, so don't fuss about the dirty sheets—" consisted more of judgment than mercy.

She and Jake Donovan would make a good team, Olivia thought, even if Rollie was a charter member of Barley Presbyterian, and Jake. . .well, Olivia suspected the man would as soon swallow a snake as darken the doors of a church—any church.

"I'm waiting—"

Olivia walked over to the waist-high table where silk flowers, fabric samples of bridesmaids' gowns, and dozens of pictures littered the surface. Maria's enthusiasm for work never had included a sense of order. Olivia began tidying things up while she talked, not looking at Rollie. "Last week I visited a couple who took out a loan at Daddy's bank almost four years ago. The terms were—" she had to take a catch-breath—"outrageous. They couldn't make the payments, of course, and the bank foreclosed."

"Sounds typical," Rollie observed, voice matter-of-fact, as she helped Olivia straighten the table.

Olivia smiled mirthlessly. "Don't remind me. Only this time, the man couldn't cope with his failure. Dave Carmichael just gave up on life, his wife told me. I gathered he was always sensitive and introverted. Eventually he got so bad he wouldn't even eat, and she finally had to have him committed to a mental hospital. She's been told he might never come out of it."

"Olivia—"

"They'd only been married four years." Even now the shame and horror was overwhelming. She gripped the edge of the table, struggling to keep her voice even. "Now his wife works two jobs and eighteen-hour days to pay for his care."

"God have mercy," Rollie muttered reverently. "Poor soul." Then she crossed her arms over her chest. "But don't do this to yourself, Olivia. What happened to him—to all these people—it's not your fault. You've got to accept that. Just give the past, and your father, over to God."

"I can't." She shook her head, and the words spilled out in a torrent. "I've tried for years, and I can't. I used to beg Mom to do something. . .then my brother and sister. Even Uncle Larry. But they'd all given up and just didn't care anymore. Nothing was going to change Daddy, they said." She dashed an angry hand across her eyes. "So, I have to do *something*, anything, and when Jake Donovan comes around again, looking for me, I plan to do whatever he demands, see if *that* will make a difference. It didn't help when Mr. MacKenzie forgave Daddy—did I tell you? I still feel guilty and so full of this horrible *shame* that sometimes I think I'll go insane."

Neatly stacked behind them were the gift Bibles already engraved with the newlyweds' names. Olivia grabbed one and thrust it in Rollie's face. "*This* is why I have to do something. It's too late for Daddy, okay, I accept that. But I need the forgiveness. I need to—to try and somehow erase the sins of my father, like Jesus erases our sins." She lifted a hand to forestall Rollie's response. "So don't lecture me anymore about my 'scheme,' okay? I've made up my mind. For two weeks I've been begging people's forgiveness and, you're right, it hasn't worked. So I'll try Jake Donovan's plan. . .whatever it is."

૨૦

He strolled into the store two hours later, while Maria was helping six chattering bridesmaids in one alcove, and Olivia sat in another with an engaged couple, helping them decide on wedding invitations. "Finish looking through this book," she suggested to Janet and Mark, "and if you'll excuse me just a minute—"

Mouth dry, heart skittering like a pair of frightened mice, Olivia slowly made her way over to Jake Donovan.

He watched her approach through metallic pewter eyes as if contemplating where to make the first strike. Or, Olivia thought half-hysterically, maybe it was more like speculating how he planned to carve her up and use her for fish bait. He looked big and tough, dark hair tousled, his gray eyes cold as the February day. Olivia wanted to crawl under the nearest table.

"Busy morning," he greeted her blandly enough, his gaze raking the shop and its clients.

"Yes. Are—are you going to make a scene?" She knew the potential existed. Tension radiated from every pore of the tightly coiled, powerful body.

His penetrating eyes zeroed in on her. He frowned. "What would you do if I did. . .um. . .'make a scene?' "

Breath wedged in her throat, Olivia clasped her hands behind her back so he couldn't see her anxiety. "If I couldn't persuade you to leave, Maria would phone the police."

"I could do you—and this place—a lot of damage before the police could arrive, and be miles away without a trace." He paused, adding roughly, "Quit looking like that. Regardless of what you think, I'm not a wanton criminal or a heartless rogue like your old man. Besides, the idea here is to allow you the opportunity to grovel, isn't it? Work out some manner of penance to absolve you from responsibility for what happened to my sister and brother-in-law?" He smiled suddenly over her head at Maria and waved, looking so friendly and approachable that Olivia almost gasped. "Your assistant is palpitating with curiosity, Ms. Sinclair. Shall we join them, and you can explain the situation—" He arched one slashing brow. "Or can I interest you in a cup of coffee somewhere more private?"

"Nobody else here deserves having their joy, their dreams crushed, Mr.

Donovan. If you'll give me another thirty minutes, I'd be more than willing to hear what you have to say." She glanced back toward an oblivious Janet and Mark, happily poring over the style sample catalogs. "Right now I'm trying to help a young couple save as much money as possible so they don't start out married life head over heels in debt."

She tilted her head, watching him. "I know. Not in character for a Sinclair, is it? Don't worry, I'm sure you'll discover all my other flaws soon enough." In spite of her discipline, Olivia's voice shook on the last words, the sting of shame heating her cheeks.

Incredibly, Jake Donovan's hand lifted, the fingers skimming Olivia's hot cheek almost like a caress. "Every single one," he agreed softly. For a paralyzing second their gazes held. "Thirty minutes," he repeated. "I'll be waiting outside."

He left, the melodic door chimes ringing out its "Here Comes the Bride" melody in his wake. The absurdity would have made Olivia smile, except that her cheek was still burning from the light brush of the man's fingers. And for the next twenty minutes, she found her own hand creeping up to touch the spot.

Janet and Mark finally left, relieved to have found almost exactly what they wanted for a fraction of the price they'd been prepared to pay. "Remember," Olivia counseled as she walked them to the door, "marriage is supposed to be forever, so you need to commit yourself to a life of joy—not debt."

"Thanks, Olivia." Janet embraced her impulsively. "You're the greatest! I'm so glad we found The Bridal Bower. Thanks to you, our wedding is going to be the most wonderful event of my entire life!"

Olivia watched them walk down the street, arms entwined, heads close together, talking and laughing. The rain had ended an hour earlier, with a weak but welcome sun breaking through the clouds, warming the day. *I'll never have what they have, will I, Lord?*

Lifting her head, Olivia slowly turned toward Jake Donovan. Leaning against a lamppost, arms crossed and wearing a worn leather jacket and aviator sunglasses, he looked about as approachable as a Doberman.

Shouldering himself away from the post, he sauntered toward Olivia. "Touching," he observed, eyebrow lifted in another ironic arc toward the departing couple. "And to think I'm about to deprive you of more opportunities to arrange wonderful events for gullible young men and naive little girls with stars in their eyes."

"I'm not what you think I am," Olivia began, then shook her head. "Never mind—it doesn't matter. I am a Sinclair, which makes people like you blind to everything else. Let me fetch my coat, and I'll be back."

Maria slipped through the crowd of young women and hurried over. "Are you sure you know what you're doing?" she whispered, brown eyes filled with worry.

"He was so nice yesterday. . . .I still can't believe any of this. Are you sure?"

"No." Olivia tugged on her raincoat. "I just know I have to see what he wants, and agree if at all possible. I can't live like this anymore, Maria. I can't."

Maria lifted her hands. "Then be careful. I know you, Olivia. Don't let him chew you up and spit you out, hoping you'll feel better. Life doesn't work that way."

"He can't chew me up and spit me out—" Olivia tied the belt of her raincoat, checked her purse for her daily planner, and headed for the door. "Living with my father already did that."

Chapter Five

At eleven-thirty Barley's favorite downtown café was already crowded, but Jake and Olivia found a booth at the back. That suited Jake, who had spent the last hour prowling the town while he reassessed the enigmatic, disturbing Olivia Sinclair.

She wasn't turning out to be a female version of her father. In fact, she reminded Jake more of a fragile, wild bird about to be shot down by a hunter. And Jake was the hunter.

They slid into the sagging vinyl booth. Jake eyed the soiled, mostly hand-written menus propped between the condiments. "You'll have to recommend something," he said. "It's been years since I was in a place like this."

"What *do* you do, Mr. Donovan, other than act as your sister's avenging angel?"

If her words had been sarcastic and challenging, Jake would have verbally carved her into pieces. But the question was voiced softly, with an undercurrent of restrained humor. Her demeanor—even when Jake continued to sit there without responding—remained one of self-effacement. Like she was some whipping boy, waiting for him to wield the whip. Or a wounded bird poised for flight.

"I do anything I please," he bit out, more angrily than he intended, since this woman was destroying all his preconceptions of her, and making him feel about like the Marquis de Sade in the process. Irritably plowing a hand through his hair, he growled an apology that stopped short of a totally honest explanation. "Sorry. I've never been fond of crowds."

Olivia glanced around, smiling a little. "If this bothers you, may I suggest you bypass the mall on Saturdays."

The overworked waitress came to take their order, her manner brisk but not unfriendly. She knew Olivia and suggested the daily special. "It's extra-good today," she said.

They ordered two plates of cubed steak, mashed potatoes, and butter beans.

"At least you're not one of those vegetarian nuts who pretend a bowl of lettuce is the most fulfilling meal in the world," Jake commented.

"No, that's Maria. We argue about it all the time, but so far neither of us has convinced the other to recant." She studied him a second, looking indecisive. "Um. . .could you expand a little on your 'do-what-you-please' lifestyle?"

There was a moment of awkward silence. Olivia studied the table and Jake studied her, then shrugged, bowing to the inevitable. "I'm a sometime professional mountain guide, ex-pro football wide receiver, occasional adventure writer, and a few assorted other things I won't go into now," he reluctantly offered. He hated explaining himself, especially to this woman. But considering what he was going to propose, he figured he owed her at least that much.

"That explains it," Olivia said, surprising Jake even more. He had steeled himself for the usual feminine gushing or the equally feminine censorial commentary on his "selfish" lifestyle—not that short, cryptic response.

"Explains what?" he ended up having to ask when Olivia refused to elaborate.

Her sidelong glance brimmed with apology and wariness. "You seem. . . untamed, and very aware of your power. Last night—" She hesitated, then shrugged and admitted, "Last night you frankly scared me."

Jake leaned forward. "Well, Ms. Sinclair, you're frankly surprising *me*. And I don't like surprises."

"Why?"

Again, that disconcerting, almost ingenuous aura so contrary to what he'd expected. Jake found himself responding just as honestly. "In my experience, surprises can cost you your life." He sat up as the waitress returned with two steaming plates overflowing with the kind of hearty meal he'd forgotten existed on the planet.

And then—even as Jake looked on in consternation—Olivia bowed her head and closed her eyes.

"What are you doing?" he growled under his breath. "This is a restaurant, not a church, for crying out loud."

She ignored him, finished the brief silent prayer, and began to eat.

Jake followed suit, then laid down his fork. "You know, this is going to be incredibly difficult if we don't set things straight right up front."

Olivia put her fork down as well. "I agree." Leaning forward, she asked forthrightly, "Exactly what is it you're going to require of me, Mr. Donovan? I've already decided to go along with it, as long as it's not illegal or—" She colored slightly—"immoral."

"Call me Jake, and you forgot 'fattening.' " His mouth twitched at her look of incomprehension. " 'Illegal, immoral, or fattening,' " he quoted, smile broadening when she stared across at him as if he had two heads.

"You're teasing me," she accused incredulously.

"Yeah, Ms. Sinclair, I guess maybe I am." He toasted her with his iced tea. "So—now that you can see I'm not a rampaging madman, and I've discovered your eyes turn completely blue when *you're* teasing and rain-washed gray when you're nervous, I suppose we'd better hammer out the details of your. . .penance, did you call it?"

"Here?" She glanced around, still looking flustered.

"You don't seem to have a problem praying in public, so why worry about some old prunes overhearing the terms of your sentence, so to speak?"

"I hardly call blessing the food before I eat 'public praying.' As for—"

"Do you do that all the time?"

"Do what?"

She was really getting rattled now, Jake realized, a little taken aback by the spurt of intense satisfaction zinging through him. On the other hand, a disconcerted, uncertain Olivia was infinitely easier to manipulate than the controlled robot of last night.

"Pray," he said. "Do you do that a lot?"

"Um. . .before meals, yes. At night always. When I'm lonely, scared, don't know which way to go. Why, Mr. Donovan?"

"Jake."

Pressing her lips together, Olivia began folding her napkin, the movements crisp and deliberate. Jake watched, silently laughing, the savage need to humiliate changing rapidly to an exhilarating game of oneupsmanship. It was a game he thought he'd lost all interest in playing years ago.

The waitress paused at their table. "Everything all right here? Y'all want dessert?"

"It's delicious as usual, Maggie, but I'm afraid Mr. Donovan and I have to be going." Before Jake quite knew what she was about, Olivia had pulled out her wallet and handed some money to the waitress. "Thanks again. Keep the change, okay?"

"You're mighty welcome." She gathered the dirty dishes and left.

Without a word, Olivia rose and headed for the door.

Jake waited until they were out on the sidewalk. "Thanks for the lunch, Ms. Sinclair, but the—"

"Olivia," she interrupted, flicking him the small purring smile of a kitten who didn't know any better than to tease the tiger's tail. "If I call you Jake, you have to call me by my first name."

"Olivia," Jake growled, teeth clenched. "Don't patronize me again, lady, or you'll think my behavior last night was pretty tame." He held up a hand, cutting her off. "And lest you misunderstand, I don't have a problem with a woman paying for my meal. . .unless she's paying for the sole purpose of scoring points."

Olivia turned pale and silent. They walked down the sidewalk, past her shop, to the parked rental car. He opened the door, but Olivia didn't get in.

"I'm sorry," she all but whispered. "You're right, I shouldn't have paid for your lunch without asking you first. I—I don't know what came over me." She cleared her throat, spoke a little more firmly, though she avoided meeting Jake's narrowed gaze. "I'd like to know what you have in mind, so I can tell Maria where I'll be and when I'll be back."

"What's the matter, Olivia? Don't you trust me?"

"No—o. But I called your sister this morning, and I'll just have to take her word that you're basically a decent man who'd never dream of hurting someone weaker and smaller. She did warn me that your temper's as hot as a jalapeño pepper, but no matter what my father did to her and Davy, you wouldn't harm me. . .uh. . .physically."

Jake eyed her with grudging respect. "I hope she also warned you that with Davy pretty much out of the picture, I'll do whatever I deem necessary to take care of my sister—" He paused, then added with a provocative grin— "legally, of course."

"Of course," Olivia echoed. "Well. . .she asked me to pass along a message to you whenever I thought the time was right." She halted.

The little minx was leaving him dangling again, just as she had in the café. Propping his elbow on the car door, Jake determined to wait until they rolled up Barley's sidewalks if necessary.

A cloud crossed over the sun, and Olivia tugged her raincoat close, looking cold but collected. "I've decided," she finally announced to the lamppost Jake had leaned on earlier, "that her message can wait a little longer."

So. . .you do have a backbone, Jake thought, finding that the realization pleased instead of angered him. Soon he'd find out whether that backbone was made of straw or steel.

"We're driving to the outskirts of Charlotte," he told her. "And today I'll have you back by five. Now, you've got two minutes to tell someone before I come to fetch you."

She was back well within the time limit and slid into the passenger seat with an uncertain smile.

Jake leaned over, close enough to cause her to press back against the seat. "Listen to me," he ordered, very quietly. "I've played a lot more vicious hardball than you—than your 'ax man' of a father, even. I know how to read people, know what they're thinking, what they're going to do even before they themselves know." He smiled coldly. "So if you choose to play games with me, Olivia Sinclair, be prepared to lose. Because believe me, you will."

Olivia gazed straight up into Jake's face with haunted eyes. "I know." She stopped, her throat working. "I know all about the games people play," she finished in the most poignant voice Jake had ever heard.

"I doubt it." He straightened and came around and slid in beside her. "I seriously doubt it, lady, but it doesn't matter, since the only game you'll need to be worrying about for a while is the game of survival."

He started the engine and backed out without another word.

Chapter Six

After driving forty-five minutes toward Charlotte, Jake turned off the freeway onto a winding state road. Sitting beside him, Olivia finally broke a long uncomfortable silence, torn between amusement and anxiety. "So. . .where are we going?"

Jake chuckled deep in his throat. "I wondered how long it would take." He glanced down at his watch. "Twenty-seven minutes. I have to admit that's the longest a woman has ever sat beside me with her mouth shut."

He was baiting her deliberately, of course, but Olivia learned fast. She wasn't going to touch *that* comment with a twenty-foot pole. "My father hated distractions when he drove, and idle chitchat headed his list of distractions." She didn't add that Jake's caustic tongue rivaled her father's. If she possessed any survival instincts at all, Olivia knew she should end this whole business right now, before Jake Donovan cut his way past all her defenses.

❧

Before lunch—a lifetime ago—she'd promised Maria that Jake couldn't chew her up. Well, Olivia was wrong.

Glancing across at his hard, unforgiving profile, she had to repress a sudden shiver. Even if she were to insist, she had a feeling Jake wouldn't let her go now. He needed to see her pay for her father's misdeeds as much as Olivia needed to atone for them. There was no alternative. Whether she liked it or not, Jake Donovan was her ticket to freedom, her best and final bargaining chip.

Nothing else over the past humiliating weeks had turned out as she'd planned. God had to have sent this man her way, and that meant Olivia had to endure whatever Jake dished out. *I'll do whatever I have to, Lord. I promise.*

They entered the outskirts of Charlotte, and now Jake turned into an almost deserted parking lot. Across the cracked, weed-infested pavement, Olivia spotted several ramshackle buildings, one of which looked like an old house. She bit her lip, anxiety intensifying when a filthy, ragged old man shuffled into view, ambling toward the door of one of the buildings.

"Yep," Jake answered the unspoken question, "we're here." He slid out and came around and opened Olivia's door. "Come on, Olivia Sinclair. It's time for you to see for yourself what happens to people who've been stripped of all their pride, their ability to produce. People who become nothing but helpless pawns in the hands of powerbrokers like your old man."

As if she didn't already know. Clutching her purse tightly, Olivia meekly followed Jake across the parking lot, down a sidewalk that turned into a muddy path, and through a door sadly in need of paint and new hardware.

"Yo, Sherm!" Jake called out. "We're here."

Olivia took inventory. The large room had once been some kind of warehouse, she guessed, now transformed into a shelter. Tables and chairs of every size and description riddled half the floor space, with another area for sleeping, where a dozen or so cots were neatly lined up. On closer inspection, she could see that several were occupied. Men, and a few women, of all ages—disheveled and beaten-down—sprawled in the chairs, on the floor, or wandered aimlessly about.

Smells assaulted Olivia's nose. Always sensitive to odor, the nauseating scents of unwashed bodies, musk, and mildew—and the repugnant aroma of steamed brussels sprouts—almost sent her scrambling back out the door. Then she caught Jake's eye.

Smug, malicious satisfaction swam in the arctic gray, and a frankly wicked grin twisted his mouth. Swallowing hard, Olivia turned her back, watching the approach of a huge potbellied man with a balding head and full salt-and-pepper beard. As he came up to her, Olivia noticed with a jolt that he also had a graying ponytail streaming halfway down his back.

"Hiya, J.D. Glad you made it," he rumbled in a gravelly baritone, extending a hand the size of a cast-iron skillet. "Put 'er here, my man. It's been a while since I've seen you—two years, you ornery cuss. Now introduce me to the little gal here who stirred up your carcass enough to drag me outta my bed two nights ago with some harebrained notion."

Jake shook hands, pummeled the man's back. "Olivia Sinclair, meet Sherman Piretti, owner, director, chief cook, and bottlewasher of Sherm's Shelter." He winked. "Sherm and I spent our pro football years with the same team. He was a 'Sherman tank' of a linebacker."

Speechless, Olivia felt her hand grasped and gently squeezed. "We just go by first names here," Sherm informed her, eyes twinkling. "And I'll tell you right now, 'Olivia' is too much of a mouthful for me. Whaddya think, J.D.? You've known her longer than I have. What do you call her?"

Jake's gaze moved over Olivia in a leisurely study. "We-l-l," he drawled, "she doesn't really strike me as a 'Livvie' or even 'Liv'—" The wicked grin deepened.

Sherm eyed Olivia thoughtfully. "She's a little bit of a thing, J.D. You sure she's up to this? Most of these characters around here have seen more of the inside of a cell than they have a church."

Olivia decided enough was enough. "I can handle anything I have to," she announced. Hopefully the calm pronouncement disguised the quaking uncertainty weakening her knees. "And my name is Olivia. O-LIV-i-a."

Jake shook his head. "Stubborn, isn't she, even though she's the perfect candidate for martyrdom. But I trust you to take care of her for me."

The two men traded significant glances.

Oh, boy, Olivia thought, her own glance sliding over the motley assortment of pathetic souls scattered about the room.

"You know I'd walk on hot coals for you, J.D. 'Course you might not know most of these do-good church women give up after a trip or two out here."

Olivia stiffened in outrage that turned to astonishment at Jake's next words. "She won't give up," he promised. "She might break, Sherm, but I have a feeling she won't give up. And I'd better warn you—she's a born time manager, so be careful, or you'll find yourself as regimented as we used to be the week before the play-offs."

Sherm shuddered playfully, looking like a benign, balding Santa Claus. "Right. So. . .every other evening and one weekend a month, starting next week, right?" The two men shook hands, then Sherm was patting her shoulder. "Don't look so worried, O-LIV-ia. Who knows? Maybe you'll end up as this year's Mother Teresa—"

"You could have discussed the schedule with me, at least," Olivia observed on the way back to Barley. "I do have a career, you know, and other people are depending on me."

"You promised to do whatever I demanded, as long as it wasn't immoral or illegal. Since you set the terms yourself, I figured you'd already arranged all your fancy planner books accordingly."

Olivia sighed. There was no rebuttal to that. Leaning back, she closed her eyes, unable to shake the vivid memories, the appalling smell of Sherm's Shelter. *Lord, what have I done?*

She'd read the papers, seen the news, listened to her father gloat. She knew the homeless and disenfranchised were out there, knew their numbers were growing—some, yes, because of her father. The knowledge had tormented her for years, long before Jake Donovan showed up.

Out of genuine concern—and guilt—she'd contributed love offerings through her church and prayed with the rest of the congregation. But until today it had never occurred to her to offer her services.

She'd built a demanding career, and her time—like Jake had pointed out so bitingly—was organized right down to the minute. *Months* of careful planning had been required to ensure that The Bridal Bower could operate without her supervision for just three weeks.

Yet she had promised Jake. More than that, she had promised herself. . .and she had promised the Lord. She had no choice but to follow through on Jake's plan. Of course penance which ultimately led to absolution required great sacrifice. The last month had hammered home that bitter lesson.

Olivia prayed this time the payment would finally unlock the choking slave collar that had tormented her for so many years.

Night had fallen by the time Jake dropped her at The Bower to pick up her car. "Don't bother," he warned as Olivia automatically stepped toward the door of the shop. "We need to talk, so I'll follow you home. Whatever you planned to do here will have to wait a little longer."

You brought this on yourself, Olivia reminded her grumbling conscience as she turned onto her street some ten minutes later. Maria had warned her, Rollie had warned her. . .but then, Maria and Rollie hadn't spent the past almost twenty-seven years ashamed of their last names.

She turned into the driveway, and the headlights of her car flashed onto the house, illuminating the porch and windows. Olivia slammed on the brakes, gaping in horrified disbelief.

Streaks of scarlet paint and dozens of shattered eggs marred the entire front of her humble little cottage—smeared, oozing down the clapboard and windowpanes. Spatters and slimy drops clung to the bushes below the windows. The last of the bucket of paint had been poured over her welcome mat.

Olivia flung herself out of the car, dashing forward with an incoherent cry. She stopped short of the door, and stood frozen on the walk—stunned into immobility—wondering helplessly who could possibly hate her this much.

Unnoticed, Jake came up and took her arm. "Go back and sit in your car," he ordered, voice hard, commanding. "Whoever did this might be hiding somewhere close, waiting to see your reaction."

"My house—"

"I know. I'll help." Olivia stared up at him, uncomprehending. He sounded. . .concerned? "Come on, Olivia. Stay here in the car. Don't move. I'll be back in a minute."

Moving soundlessly, Jake slipped around the side of Olivia's house, alert for any movement or noise. The first rush of adrenalin had eased, but every nerve ending from the back of his neck to the tips of his fingers prickled. He cursed silently, fluently. Obviously the little martyr had stirred up a hornet's nest with her idiotic plan to seek forgiveness in behalf of Sinclair. That was the only plausible explanation for the sickening mess out front—and the one he intended to bully Olivia into explaining to the police.

Nobody was hiding around the house.

Jake tested the back door, found it still locked. After making a complete circuit of the yard, he returned to Olivia's car, which was empty. Alarm poured over him in a scalding rush until he caught sight of her stooped figure, fumbling with a wad of useless tissues at the front porch. Stubborn, stupid woman! Jake stalked across the lawn, preparing to scorch her ears.

Then he heard the sound of soft, strangled sobs. Anger evaporated as a flood of compassion caught him totally off guard. Reaching down, he lifted her resisting body completely up and away from the disgusting mess.

"You have to leave it until the police have seen it," he reminded her gently, tugging out his own handkerchief.

"Maria warned me," she choked out, the words husky, her voice thick with tears. "She told me I shouldn't go around reminding people of what my father had done to them. Rollie agreed. They both said I was asking for trouble—"

Jake wiped her hands, listening, trying to ignore the welling pity—and the fresh anger against the person or persons who had hurt Olivia. He didn't want to deal with those kinds of feelings, not now. Not with this woman.

"They were right." He gave up trying to clean her hands. "Come on, we'll go through your back door. They apparently left everything else intact. You can clean up while I call the police."

She jerked away. "I don't want to call the police. They'll find out who my father was. . .I'll lose all my customers, have to move to another town. I'll—I'll—"

"Stop it." He took hold of her upper arms and administered a light shake. The yellow glare of the front porch light cruelly illuminated her wild eyes and tear-streaked face. Beneath his hands her bones felt fragile as a bird's. Slumped and helpless, Olivia looked utterly humiliated. *That's what you wanted, pal, remember?*

"Come on, Olivia, get hold of yourself. Where's the calm, controlled woman I first met? The one who stared me straight in the eye and threatened to call the police?"

"I—you're right." From somewhere, Olivia dredged up the will to pull herself together, and Jake watched the return to sanity with reluctant respect. "I'll . . .just get my purse." She stepped away, took a shuddering breath.

Inside, Jake made coffee while Olivia washed her hands and face. Then he made her sit and sip while they waited for the police. Because she was just staring into space like a zombie, he found himself talking to her, chattering like a magpie to fill the aching silence. He couldn't stand the uncomprehending pain darkening her eyes.

". . .and after I left the pro sports zoo, I was so sick of people and their power games, I spent two years prowling wildernesses all over the globe. Hey, did Beth tell you we grew up in the mountains west of here? Maybe that's why I love wild areas so much. Not so many people there trying to get in your face." He paused to check Olivia's color. "Drink all your coffee, that's it. I know, it's stronger than yours, so make all the nasty faces you like, but drink it down."

The Barley police arrived—a grizzled sergeant with a paternal streak and his younger sidekick. They took photographs, wrote down Jake's and Olivia's statements. The younger cop, a homely young man with milk-pitcher ears, spent a lot of time consoling Olivia, pointing out how sick some folks could be and how she shouldn't take it personally.

Olivia stared at him with her big eyes gray as a raincloud and finally smiled a heartwrenching smile. "I *have* to take it personally," she said. "Whoever did this knows I'm a Sinclair."

The two policemen had never heard of Alton Sinclair, so Jake filled them in. When they were finished, he walked them to the back door, thanking them for coming, for promising to keep an eye on the area.

"You her boyfriend?" the young cop asked.

"I'm working on it," Jake responded, deadpan, then wondered why he had said that.

Revealing the present nature of their relationship would probably put his name at the top of their list of suspects. Besides, they'd never believe Olivia's warped sense of Christian ethics. Jake himself was having a hard enough time dealing with it, since he couldn't even remember the last time he'd set foot in a church.

When he returned to the living room, Olivia was reading through the daily planner she kept on the hall table. "It must be one of the people I went to see," she murmured, still looking like a gray-eyed ghost. "I suppose I should be grateful for *your* restraint, shouldn't I?"

Jake mentally replayed a few old calls from his football days until he had his temper under control. "Yes, you should," he agreed, voice deceptively mild. Reaching down, he cupped her chin in his hand, stroking the incredibly soft skin. "I told the police I was working my way around to being your 'boyfriend.' Be careful, or I just might be tempted to act the part."

Chapter Seven

Armed with ladders, old cloths, buckets, and the garden hose, Maria, Rollie, and Olivia canceled all appointments and spent the entire next day cleaning the front of Olivia's house. Fortunately the capricious February weather cooperated, providing a cool, clear morning and sun-warmed afternoon.

"I suppose I should be grateful they left the inside intact," Olivia observed at one point, glowering at the still pink porch. They'd tossed the welcome mat in the garbage. The police had confiscated the empty paint can.

"Are you sure you don't want to stay with me for a week or so?" Rollie asked. Again. Olivia had spent the previous night in the spare bedroom of her assistant's apartment. Roaring about in chenille bathrobe and fuzzy slippers, Rollie had berated Olivia, Jake, the vandals, and the dissolute condition of the entire world, punctuating each diatribe with offers for Olivia to move in with her for a while.

"You did tell Mr. Troublemaker Donovan you wouldn't be going to that—that place for the time being, didn't you?" Rollie asked now, plump face glistening with perspiration even though the temperature by late afternoon had dropped to the forties. "It's bad enough you're at the shop during the daytime, but leaving your house alone at night is asking for trouble." She wagged a red-tinged finger at Olivia, adding significantly, "And not just the house."

Olivia wrung out a rag and flopped back on one of the lawn chairs they'd dragged out front. "Rollie, you and Maria are worse than a baker's dozen of mothers."

"Speaking of mothers, have you told her yet? When does she come back from her cruise anyway?"

A dilapidated little car pulled into the driveway and stopped, sparing Olivia the necessity of a reply. The door opened, revealing a thin, youngish woman who hesitantly made her way up the path. Her face registered consternation and dawning dismay.

Olivia stood, walking slowly over to greet Beth Carmichael, Jake's sister.

"Oh, dear. Jake said it was bad, and I can see that it was, even though you've cleaned up a lot." She smiled at Olivia, the expression in her brown eyes so like Jake's that Olivia's heart jerked painfully. "I'm really sorry."

"Thanks. Um. . .what are you doing here?" Olivia waved a self-deprecatory hand. "I don't mean that the way it sounds—I'm just surprised." Maria came up beside them, her look questioning. "This is Maria Santinas, my friend and partner at The Bridal Bower. Beth Carmichael, Jake's sister."

Beth seemed awkward and nervous. "I wanted to talk to you, but this obviously isn't a good time." She shifted, tugging on a strand of straight brown hair hanging limply in unstyled layers about her care-worn face. "The trouble is, I've only got this afternoon. . .I have to be at work by six."

Maria glanced from Beth to Olivia. "Take her inside and we'll pack it up out here. It's getting too cold and dark to work anyway," she said, overriding Olivia's protests.

Faced with both hers and Rollie's mule-headed insistence and Beth's fidgeting, Olivia led the way inside.

"I'm sorry," Beth apologized again, sitting down on the edge of the chair and looking even more uncomfortable.

"Don't be ridiculous." Olivia collapsed onto the couch and heaved a sigh. "Actually, I'm beat, so you gave me a wonderful excuse to leave the pair of them to clean up. Now they can complain about me to their hearts' content."

Beth relaxed, finally. "Well. . .in that case. . .I wanted to talk to you about Jake. About what he's trying to do to you."

Massaging the back of her neck, Olivia sent Beth a dry look. "He doesn't have to try. He can intimidate and scare the heebie-jeebies out of me with a single look."

Beth leaned forward. "He hasn't a clue you feel that way, Olivia. I knew I needed to come talk to you. Jake's never behaved like this before—rock-dumb about a woman, I mean. You don't need to be intimidated by him. The only reason I haven't interfered before now was because Jake promised me you were doing this because you wanted to, not because he forced you."

"Do you do that a lot? Interfere in your brother's life?"

Beth looked appalled. "Goodness, no! Nobody tells Jake what to do. Probably the last person who tried is six feet under." She clapped her hand over her mouth, looking, if possible, even more horrified. "I didn't mean. . .he would never—"

"Don't worry. I know you're joking." This time Olivia was careful to let Beth know she was serious; Jake's sister needed reassurance.

Once again the memory of Olivia's behavior the previous night intruded. She'd been so shocked by the assault on her house she'd actually lost control and cried all over Jake like the worst sort of hysterical female. The kind her father had belittled the most. Alton Sinclair had known how to turn on his infamous charm, coaxing the victims to bare their souls, encouraging them to sign anything he put in front of them. Then he'd reduced them to tears—and laughed in their faces.

But Jake hadn't laughed at all. Olivia also remembered—vividly—the feel of warm, incredibly gentle fingers stroking her chin. Jake possessed mind-melting charm as well, but it wasn't anything like her father's.

Olivia straightened her shoulders. "Beth, I don't pretend to understand your brother, but trust me, I'm not naive or stupid. I spent a lifetime living in the same house with a man who derived great pleasure from making people squirm, watching their pain—" She broke off abruptly, staring straight up at the ceiling until an unexpected rush of tears subsided. "I do know Jake isn't like that. The trouble is, I don't think he can understand that I'm not like that either."

Beth shook her head violently. "He does know. It's just that for so many years he—we've both hated your father—" She shrugged helplessly— "which unfortunately translates to all things Sinclair—"

"That's why I'm willing to do anything to get people to forgive him," Olivia pointed out, weariness dragging at her words.

"Olivia—" Beth's face scrunched up. She pondered her wringing hands a minute, muttering half beneath her breath, "I have to do this. He's acting so strange, and I just know—" Her voice trailed away. She looked up, apparently determined to say what she had on her mind. "Jake's always gone his own way, but he's also always protected me, ever since I can remember. Our parents died when I was three, you see. My aunt and uncle raised us, mostly my aunt. She wasn't. . .very nice."

"I don't think—" Olivia began, uneasy with such stark revelations.

But Beth shook her head again. "Hear me out. I've thought about this for days, and I think you should know that I admire what you're trying to do, even though I disagree. I also love my brother, and you need to understand where he's coming from, so you don't—won't compare him to your father."

Olivia smiled a bittersweet smile. "Jake might share some similar traits here and there, but I'm convinced the resemblance is strictly superficial. I know inside he's nothing like my father." *God help me, please don't let him be like my father. . . .*

Beth looked brighter, but far from convinced. "Oh. Well, anyway, I want you to understand him. Maybe it's because I was younger, such a wimp. I was always shy, not real assertive, you see. Jake took care of me, protected me. A kid at school stole my lunch once, when I was in fourth grade. Jake got hold of the bully and dragged him two miles—all uphill—to our house, forced him to apologize. And Jake was only twelve himself. He's been that way about me all our lives, like I told you. But what you may not realize is that he's like that with anyone—anything—weaker and smaller and helpless."

I don't want to hear this, Olivia thought. Her defenses against Jake, flimsy from the beginning, were in danger of crumbling with every passionate word pouring out of Beth's mouth.

"That's why he was almost ready to kill your father after what happened with me and Davy. Why, when he found out about you, he hot-footed it back here and hunted you down, breathing fire. Then. . .when he realized what you're really like—" She glanced at Olivia, hesitating, looking irresolute.

"You might as well finish it," Olivia prompted. "Go ahead, I can handle it.

What does Jake really think of me?"

Hot color seeped under Beth's skin. "I know. I'm an interfering busybody."

"But you love your brother. I wasn't making fun of you, Beth. Maria, the girl you met outside, keeps reminding me how nobody knows when I'm teasing or serious. Well—I was teasing you, okay?"

Beth nodded, looking relieved. "Okay. Jake did mention how your eyes turn blue when you're teasing, and I can see they are, except now they're turning darker because of what I just blabbed, right?"

The anniversary clock on the end table chimed the half hour, and Beth's hands flew to her cheeks. "Oh, my! I have to hurry. Olivia, no matter how aggressive Jake might come across, he'd cut off his hand before he'd really hurt someone. That's one of the reasons he quit playing football. But he's also as stubborn as the granite in Grandfather Mountain, and he isn't going to drop this ridiculous notion to teach you a lesson." She stood. "That's why you have to convince him to drop it. Your father's dead and gone, Olivia, so why don't you get on with your life instead of—of trying to make up for what he did to Davy and me?"

"Do you go ever go to church?"

Nonplussed, Beth shook her head. "No, except maybe at Christmas, every so often. I took Davy last year, but he started crying so we left early. Why? What on earth does church have to do with all this?"

Olivia winced. "I learned something at church once that really struck me hard, as the daughter of Alton Sinclair—" She paused. "There's this verse in the Bible that warns us about the sins of the fathers and how they'll be passed on to their children. Well, it's true. All my life I've been an outsider and a scapegoat—a pariah. Nobody wanted to be my friend. And in high school, the guys rarely asked me for dates, no matter how nice I tried to be. I don't know why I always took it more personally than my brother and sister. Mom says it's because I'm the youngest, and my father got worse in the last ten years of his life—"

She rose, running her hand over tense neck muscles. "Anyway, I can't live like this anymore. That's what I tried to explain to you when I visited you that day. The Bible also talks a lot about paying for our sins, about how the Israelites had to make all these sacrifices. Well, I'm going to pay for what my father did—as much as possible, that is. That's why I don't care what your brother has in mind, as long as we work around my business commitments."

"Olivia, you don't know—" Beth began urgently.

But Olivia shook her head. "I do know. I'm insane, crazy, stupid, and stubborn like your brother." Olivia angrily swiped at a tear. "But I'm also desperate. I want to walk down the street and not be afraid of people. I want to live where I don't have to worry about coming home to—" She waved her arm toward the front window—"to this. Why do you think I invest every penny I make in my business, instead of my home? I want to sleep at night and feel good about who I am. And if dishing up nauseating food to dirty, downtrodden bums a few months results in Jake—and you—forgiving my father, I'll do it. Then I'll be free."

Beth searched Olivia's face. Suddenly she reached out a reddened, chapped hand and took hold of Olivia's clenched fist. "Somehow, I think it's you who need to forgive your father. Not Jake. Or me. Or anybody else you may have approached. Maybe if you can just let the past go, you'd be able to sleep at night, instead of torturing yourself. Or letting my brother manipulate you like you were one of the radio-controlled planes he used to play with."

"Model planes?" Olivia grabbed a tissue from a box beside the anniversary clock. She mopped up, feeling ashamed and ridiculous. And thoroughly defensive. She needed to forgive her father?

"You know, those remote control toy planes people fly? They do all sorts of loops and dives and crazy stunts, and the person on the ground just stands there and enjoys the process, risk-free."

"I—see." Olivia managed a watery smile. "Well, I suppose I'd rather be a toy airplane than a puppet."

Beth giggled. "Okay. I quit. Besides, I have to go."

They walked through the kitchen to the back door before Beth spoke again, humor gone, the urgency back in her voice. "Olivia, the other reason—the main reason—I had to come see you was to because Jake wants more from you than a couple of nights a week at Sherm's Shelter. Even though I talked with him until my voice was hoarse, he won't back down. Olivia, he's going to make you visit Davy at the sanitarium, spend a day there every weekend. And that's too much to ask, no matter whose daughter you are."

Chapter Eight

Wet and rank from two days without a bath, muscles pleasantly aching, Jake rappelled down the last twenty feet of rock to a ledge eight feet above the ground. In a burst of joy over his unfettered freedom, he unclipped the lines, then free-jumped the remaining feet. Stupid, of course, and as unprofessional as a tenderfoot, especially on a slushy February day when the winter earth was still hard and unforgiving.

Right now Jake didn't care. For the past week he'd mother-henned an endless succession of clumsy, jabbering parties on half-day hikes around the winter wonderland of the Shenandoah Mountains in Virginia. As a free-lance guide for Adventures Unlimited, he normally enjoyed the chance to introduce novices to the wilderness. This time, after sending off the last group, he'd disappeared up Hawksbill Mountain, trying to recover his inner balance. Trying—also unsuccessfully—to wipe all thoughts of Olivia Sinclair out of his mind.

No matter whether he was sweating up the park's highest peak or stretched out in his sleeping bag, Olivia's face intruded. And in his ear, Beth's voice called him every name from "stubborn goat" to "the reincarnation of Alton Sinclair!"

That last accusation was the one Jake couldn't shake. He'd thoroughly lost it with Beth, stormed out of her apartment ten days ago and hadn't returned. Yeah, okay. He'd behaved like a boor—the quintessential surly male. Now, freed from his climbing equipment, Jake flopped down with his back against a boulder, and proceeded—once again—to justify his actions.

First and foremost, independently of any pressure from Jake, Olivia had virtually given him carte blanche to "work out her penance."

Second, Beth had initiated everything in the first place by requesting his help, hauling him home from the best vacation he'd enjoyed in years. She had no call to criticize his game plan.

Finally, his idea for Olivia to help at Sherm's Shelter had been designed to benefit both parties—a lesson for Olivia and assistance for Sherm. What was so evil and manipulative about that?

Jake tossed back a slug of water from his water bottle, then dug out a pack of M&Ms. Munching thoughtfully, he recalled his last conversation with Sherm. His old football buddy had warned him that Olivia was acting like a cross between an unseasoned rookie and the coach.

"She works hard, never complains. But she's been sick twice. . . though she don't know I know. She's also taken a couple of the regulars under her wing, so to speak. Trying to reason with them." Sherm laughed. "She just don't understand the mentality, J.D., old buddy. Seems to think the only thing most of these bums need is encouragement and a chance, and they'll be transformed into pillars of society. A few of them do just need a helping hand, but most have chosen to drop out permanently. I tried to warn her, but you're mighty right about her take-charge mentality."

Shaking his head, Jake had to grin. That was Olivia, all right.

But Sherm's final words gave Jake a headache. "She's got this book-thing in her purse, sweet-talked real names out of half a dozen of our folks, and wrote every one down in that book. Promised she'd try to help. Last night she spent more time trying to instill the Puritan work ethic than she did dishing out vegetable soup."

Recalling the conversation now, Jake pinched the bridge of his nose, knowing he was going to have to straighten out Ms. Sinclair himself. She was supposed to weep over the condition of those poor slobs, not wade in and draft improvements.

As soon as Jake returned, he'd be taking her for her first visit with Davy. Trying to make sense out of his pathetic, drooling brother-in-law would teach her a needed lesson. *Yeah, that would bring her to her knees, but good. So why don't you feel vindicated, Donovan?*

Breathing deep soothing lungfuls of tangy mountain air, Jake finally conceded what had probably been inevitable almost from the very beginning, when he'd watched Olivia defending her shop. She'd stood there so poised and professional, calmly threatening to call the police because she actually believed Jake might start trashing the place. And she hadn't backed down an inch, even though Jake could snap her in two with one wrist.

Then—less than twenty-four hours later—he'd seen Olivia with all the barriers down, shell-shocked and bewildered as a child, tears streaming down her face while she tried to comprehend the ugliness of hate-fed violence. That this Olivia was so diametrically opposite the Olivia in her store was a paradox that left him feeling sandbagged. Sandbagged—yet exultant.

For the first time in over a decade—maybe his entire life—Jake was consumed with need for a woman that surpassed the physical. Persistent, inevitable as the tides, the depth of his feelings washed over him, sweeping him to an inescapable conclusion. He wanted Olivia Sinclair, all right. . .but he also wanted to protect her, understand her, shield her from the slimeballs who'd vandalized the front of her house.

Above all, he wanted to force from her mind forever all thoughts of atoning for her rattlesnake-mean father, so she would see Jake as a man—not just the means to an end. She couldn't erase the past, and she'd certainly never be able to whitewash Alton Sinclair. Why couldn't the woman just accept that fact, for crying out loud? But no, not Olivia. Nope, Ms. Sinclair had to trail around the countryside, babbling religious tripe about "earning God's forgiveness in her father's behalf."

All she'd earned so far had been a far more human form of vengeance, first from Jake. . .and now from some lunatic fruitcake.

"What kind of God shackles His people like that?" Jake found himself asking aloud. "She's nothing but a walking, talking bundle of shame and guilt. I don't need a God like that—and neither do you, Olivia Sinclair." Starting now, he determined to persuade her to break out of all those religious chains and focus on more important things—like Jake.

Decision made, he popped the last piece of candy in his mouth and rose, eager to fetch Olivia. Moving automatically, he broke camp, his mind sifting through possibilities, probabilities—and certainties. The lady didn't know it yet, but she washis.

Singing golden oldies at the top of his lungs along with the car stereo, Jake headed down the mountain, toward Barley.

 за

Unfortunately, Olivia had already left for the shelter, a distinctly unfriendly Maria informed him just before closing time the next afternoon.

"I hope you're satisfied with yourself," she berated Jake, gesturing with a handful of silk flowers. "Olivia's always been quiet, reserved. . .but she used to laugh too. Now she looks like a scarecrow, and all she talks about is how she's 'earning forgiveness' by helping those pathetic people at the shelter. She has a wedding next weekend. . .and I actually had to remind her of the date. She's never been absentminded like that."

Jake casually snagged the silk flowers out of Maria's hand and dropped them on a nearby table. "You look like an expensive vase," he observed, mouth twitching when Maria appeared ready to ignite into flames. "In the first place, Olivia agreed to the arrangements, as I'm sure she told you. In the second—not that it's any of your business—it's her father who's to blame for any and all of her compulsions. Not me."

Plonking her hands on her hips and tossing her curling black mane of hair, Ms. Santinas thrust her face right up next to Jake's and hissed, "You better not hurt her, Jake Donovan! She's too good for the likes of you, and don't you think I don't know it. Why I let you charm me into telling you where she lived—" She stopped abruptly. Her jaw sagged. "Her house—"

"Don't even think it," Jake snarled. "I was with her that night, you recall. And no, I didn't 'arrange' for someone to do it for me. If I were you, Ms. Santinas, I'd be trying to convince Olivia to watch her back, her house, and this place a little more closely for a while. The police can't monitor the place twenty-four hours a day, and unless I'm mistaken, whoever's trip wire Olivia stumbled over is just warming up."

Olivia's assistant stared round-eyed at Jake, momentarily silenced. He plucked one silk rose from the table and headed for the door. "Have a good one," he tossed over his shoulder.

❧

An hour later he surveyed the large room where he'd brought Olivia two weeks earlier, noting the changes. Curtains adorned the windows. Bouquets of artificial flowers, like the rose he was holding, were artlessly arranged in empty bottles and jars. A makeshift bookcase had been constructed out of boards and concrete blocks and now sported a ragged collection of used books. All Olivia's doing, Sherm had informed Jake when he arrived. Apparently she brought something every time she came. Right now she was outside, in the back.

"Some old geezer showed up the other day with an injured Canada goose in tow," Sherm related. "Threatened all manner of bodily harm to me and anyone else who called the humane society, or tried to hurt the bird." He tugged his beard, looking disgusted.

"So what's that got to do with Olivia? And why did you let her go outside—alone in the dark, for Pete's sake—with an unknown transient?"

Sherm wiped his hands on his apron, favoring Jake with the kind of knowing look that always made him very uneasy. "Well. . .it appears your little bird's charmed the socks off that old man, and the two of 'em treat that goose like it lays golden eggs. Never saw the like. And if you think I have any better luck than you telling that gal what to do, you're a whole lot dumber than you used to be. J.D., old buddy, my instinct's fairly screaming 'bout this one. Best get out while you can."

He left to return to the kitchen, and Jake leaned on the doorjamb, wondering if he should confront Olivia now, or wait until she came inside. When she still hadn't appeared in three minutes, he tossed the rose on a folding chair and headed out the end door.

Moving quietly, he maneuvered his way along a muddy path, which was easily visible even in the dark because of the security lights Sherm had installed the previous year. At the corner of the building he stopped, peered around the corner—and froze.

Sitting cross-legged in the dirt with the goose in her lap, Olivia was quietly stroking the graceful bird, one of whose wings inclined at an ominous angle. Across from her sprawled a little old man. In the bright artificial light, the three figures presented a surrealistic, almost macabre tableau. Especially since—on top of layers of shabby rags—the wheezing old boozer wore a lovely, and very feminine, lavender knit sweater.

Incensed both by Olivia's careless generosity and her reckless disregard for potential danger, Jake stalked across the yard. The goose sensed his presence first and started to struggle. Olivia turned her head, eyes widening even as she soothed the agitated bird. "Jake! You startled us." Firmly but gently she secured the bird's head. "Shh—it's okay. He won't hurt you."

"Just let him try," rasped the little old man, who staggered to his feet, weaving slightly. One hand searched beneath the layers of clothing.

Jake tensed, readying his body. "Hello, Olivia. Nice goose," he offered, not taking his gaze from the old man.

"You can't have my bird!" The old man took a step toward Olivia. "This goose is mine!"

"Don't worry, Eddie. Jake's a—a friend. He won't hurt your beautiful goose any more than I will. Did you know he's climbed mountains all over the world? He loves wildlife too—"

"Olivia," Jake interrupted, keeping his voice low with an effort, "I think maybe you'd better give Eddie his goose, and we'll go inside."

She started to say something, met his gaze, and closed her mouth. Eddie had finally succeeded in pulling a knife free, and now he brandished it at Jake with menacing intent.

Consternation flitted across Olivia's face. "Eddie, you know the rules," she remonstrated before Jake had a chance to speak. "If Sherm catches sight of that, you'll have to leave. He might even call the police."

"Olivia—"

"You stay outta her face, man!" He took a wavering step toward Jake, who feinted easily aside.

Olivia surged to her feet, goose and all. "Eddie, stop! You shouldn't do that." The goose began wildly flapping, honking, and Olivia was forced to let the creature go free. Unable to fly, it beat a noisy, awkward retreat toward the darkest corner of the lot.

"Now look what you've gone and done!" the old man yelled, words ending in a squeak as Jake's hand clamped down on his wrist and twisted. The knife dropped. Jake shoved the man aside and retrieved the weapon, straightening to face two pairs of accusing eyes.

"For crying out loud!" he snapped at Olivia. "I didn't hurt him."

The old man didn't say anything for a second. He just stood, looking shriveled and old and defeated. Behind Jake echoed the wrenching honks of the frightened goose. Abruptly, the old man turned and ran, disappearing into the darkness.

"Eddie, wait!" Olivia started after him, but Jake grabbed her arm.

"No—you'd only humiliate him more."

"But he's leaving his goose." She pulled away, straining to see around him. "Jake, we have to find him. . .we have to help the goose."

"Okay. Quiet, honey. . . . We'll find the bird. I love wildlife, too, remember?" She quit struggling, her expression almost stunned.

Jake sighed, mentally kicking himself. "Don't look at me like that," he muttered. "Come on, let's go find the bird. She can't be too far."

"How do you know it's a 'she?'" Olivia asked, totally irrelevantly, Jake thought.

"I don't. But the squawking and flapping are definitely female."

Olivia wisely resisted a retort, and they crept together toward the sound of the goose's diminishing cries. "Over there," Olivia whispered. "By the fence, in those weeds. Jake. . .she's frightened. Please be careful."

In the darkness, Jake could barely make out Olivia's silhouette, but he didn't need to see her to know that the huge eyes would be smoke-gray with pleading. Did she really think he was such a monster? "Try to talk to her, distract her, and I'll sneak up on the other side—"

An hour later an amazingly tame Gretel (so dubbed by Olivia) was nesting comfortably at the back of a small enclosed pantry. Olivia hand-fed the bird, crooning nonsensical phrases as if it were a baby and insisting that Gretel would be much happier inside.

Sherm called a woman licensed to rehabilitate wild game who promised to come for Gretel as soon as possible. In the interim, the goose could stay here where she'd be safe, warm, and well fed.

Olivia orchestrated the whole procedure with heartfelt earnestness and such unarguable logic that everyone ended up falling beneath her spell as tamely as the goose. With every third breath she also counseled Sherm to take pains not to let anyone hurt or frighten Eddie's bird.

"I think she's pretty much yours now," Sherm pronounced, scratching his beard thoughtfully, "though I can't promise she won't turn into somebody's supper before that wildlife gal comes to fetch her."

Roaring with laughter, he watched Jake trying to convince an irate Olivia all the way out the door that Sherm had been only joking.

Jake had almost succeeded in reassuring Olivia that Gretel was safe from harm when they reached the parking lot—to find all four of Olivia's tires slashed.

Chapter Nine

The senseless destruction hit Olivia in the face like a bucket of raw sewage. "I don't believe this," she whispered, shivering in the dampening night air. She walked around the car twice, Jake, seething with rage, beside her.

"Jake, could you control yourself?" she eventually suggested in a normal voice, so calmly Jake broke off midsentence to peer down into her face.

"Olivia? Are you all right?"

This time she'd show him she wasn't such a blithering idiot. "Of course." She cleared her throat, offering brightly, "Though I don't mind confessing to a certain queasiness. I've had to be cautious all my life, you see, since I'm Alton Sinclair's daughter. But I never—" Her voice trailed away as they moved into a patch of light and she glimpsed Jake's face. The intent, predatory expression would have terrified her two weeks earlier, but Olivia knew better now.

She wondered—hating herself—if he would comfort her with the same tenderness he'd shown the other time, when she had cried like a baby. *Olivia, your brain has turned to mush.*

"We'd better alert the police to put out an APB on your friend Eddie," Jake announced. "And after we call, I think I'll rip a strip off Sherm's hide for letting you out of his sight in the first place. When I think of you, outside in the dark alone with a knife-wielding derelict—"

"I don't think it was Eddie," Olivia returned, hugging herself, trying not to think about her favorite lavender sweater or the grain of truth in Jake's analysis. "He's not that kind of person."

"And just how do you know that?" Jake demanded. "There's no telling how many other assorted weapons he might have hidden under his clothes."

She didn't want to dwell on that possibility. Exhaustion sucked her toward a dark pit full of questions which Olivia wasn't prepared to handle right now. "He wouldn't," she repeated, struggling to summon words to make Jake understand. "I've gotten to know him. He. . .trusts me because I like Gretel, because I was nice to him."

Jake snorted. "Sweetheart, you need a crash course in reality. You think just because you're 'nice,' these poor slobs won't take advantage any way they can? They're desperate and devoid of self-esteem, remember." He growled something beneath his breath. "I must have been out of my mind to start this. Look—your car's a textbook example. We're dealing with the dregs of humanity here—society's victims. The 'have-nots.' Most of them aren't overly fond of the 'haves'—especially guys like your father."

"You're forgetting something," Olivia pointed out, leaning wearily against the side of the car. "Eddie wouldn't have known which car was mine." She lifted her chin. "It wasn't Eddie."

A light bulb clicked on in her brain then, triggering chills that feathered down her spine as Olivia faced a far more alarming possibility.

Jake started to say something, but checked himself. He stepped closer, staring down at Olivia. "Hey," he finally murmured, and it was the melted-chocolate voice he'd used once before. "C'mere." He gently tugged her into his arms, holding her head against his shoulder. "It'll be all right, Olivia. I promise. Trust me."

Trust the man whose uppermost goal was to humiliate her, make her crawl? Yet Olivia's hands crept up and burrowed into the folds of Jake's leather jacket. She was cold and shaken. And now she was also afraid. "Jake," she whispered, feeling the steady, reassuring beat of his heart beneath her ear. "Jake, what if it's the same person who threw the eggs and paint against my house?"

ↄ⸱

Ensconced in Sherm's private quarters, which turned out to be the small house Olivia had wondered about the first time she'd come here, they met with two patrolmen assigned to the case.

Nobody listened to Olivia's protests, not after Jake gave the officers Eddie's knife and recounted what happened out in the yard. Or rather, nobody listened until Olivia—equilibrium partially restored after choking down half a mug of Sherm's bitter coffee—calmly insisted on the possible connection to the vandalization of her house.

"My father was Alton Sinclair," she finished, watching as awareness dawned on one of the policemen. Her father's reputation unfortunately had spread as far as Charlotte.

"I remember. . .he died back in January, didn't he? Sorry, ma'am, though from the little I heard, he wasn't likely to be mourned too much." He cleared his throat, shifting uncomfortably.

"It's okay." Olivia dredged up a smile. "But I think we have to face the possibility that some recent actions I've taken might have incurred the—the vengeance of one of my father's many victims."

"That tears it," Jake muttered.

Olivia fumbled in her purse for the daily calendar. Explaining her visits to various people over the last month—and her motivation—she carefully withdrew the list of names and handed it to the now riveted policemen. "I'm not trying to cause any trouble, or make any accusations," she promised, praying she was doing the right thing. "But if there's a chance someone is—" She stiffened her shoulders, stood straight—"is taking out their anger on me because my father's dead and beyond reach, you need to know the circumstances."

"Yes, ma'am. We'll contact the county boys as well as—" he checked his notes— "Sergeant MacClary in Barley. In the meantime, ma'am, may I suggest you keep your eyes open. And limit the time you're alone."

Jake drove her home, face grim, manner forbidding, almost as if he were angry with her. He didn't say much, stuffing Olivia into his leather jacket, fastening her seat belt himself, then punching in a cassette of sixties oldies.

So much for my foolish dreams of a little tenderness and a few gentle words from Jake, Olivia scolded herself. If she weren't so distracted and admittedly unnerved, she would have pursued the matter. Instead she tried to focus on the music instead of Jake's stone-wall silence, and the policeman's parting words: *This might turn out to be a stalker. Been a rash of them the last couple of years. You be careful now, Ms. Sinclair.*

Unfortunately, unless the stalker was caught committing a crime, there was little the police could do.

"Olivia."

She turned her head, unconsciously inhaling the comforting smell of leather and Jake's clean, uniquely masculine scent. "Yes?"

"Have you ever been. . .involved. . .with anyone?"

Why on earth would Jake want to know? "What exactly do you mean by 'involved?'" Olivia countered, suddenly uneasy.

"You're not married, or even seriously dating, from what I can tell. And over these last weeks, there's been no mention of a man in your life. Seems a little strange, considering your vocation."

Well, at least he was finally talking, and he didn't sound cold or sarcastic. Probably he was just trying to divert her, keep her from dwelling on what had happened. "No, there's nobody like that in my life. Never has been, to be honest." She shrugged. "A lot of it's probably my fault. By the time I was old enough to date, I already carried enough shame to sink an ocean liner." *There's 'sin' in 'Sinclair',* she recalled bitterly. "Besides, who'd want to risk messing around with Alton Sinclair's daughter?"

She was glad it was dark so Jake couldn't see her face. Huddling deeper in his jacket, Olivia marveled at her flapping tongue. "My junior year in high school, there was this new boy. He didn't know about my father, and we used to talk, eat lunch together. It was wonderful. Then a group of kids decided to enlighten him about the 'Typhoid Mary' he was hanging around with. The next day at school when he tried to avoid me, I figured out real quick what had happened."

"And then?" Jake prompted.

Olivia shook her head. Here she was, spilling long-buried hurts to the man determined to crush her spirit. She must be an idiot, a masochist.

Then she smiled a twisted smile. Who was she fooling? Neither Jake's motives nor her own crusade mattered. She didn't understand how it had happened, but she wanted—needed—Jake to treat her as if she were a person of worth. Talk to her in that deep smooth voice of his, soothing raw spots on her soul that she hadn't realized until now were still hurting. Okay, so what if she was behaving more like a starry-eyed high-schooler rather than a grown woman almost twenty-seven years old? Right now she was too tired to care.

"I assured him my father only hired hit men to rough up guys over the age of eighteen. Then I turned my back and walked away before he could walk away from me. And I promised myself that someday I'd persuade everyone that my father wasn't really that bad."

"Except he was," Jake growled, half under his breath. His hand reached out and ejected the tape. Silence filled the car.

Olivia's tired mind focused abruptly, leaving her unsure, on edge. She wondered if Jake's conversational forays were deliberate instead of random, since he behaved more like a man pursuing a goal than a man trying to soothe a beleaguered woman. His next statement confirmed her uneasy suspicions.

"Why don't you just change your name legally, go by your mother's maiden name or something? Disown your father and the past like the rest of your family did and get on with your life?"

The words mimicked Beth's almost exactly. They must have decided to join forces. "I can't. You know that."

Without warning Jake pulled the car over and stopped, turning toward Olivia. "You know what? You're twisting me into knots. Nothing I've planned concerning you has turned out like I intended. Nothing." He shook his head. "When Beth called me last month, all I could think about was how I planned to inflict maximum pain and humiliation upon the person I figured had to be a carbon copy of Alton Sinclair."

"The realization hasn't escaped me—" Olivia muttered, feeling the intensity of Jake's emotion battering her with increasing force. Straining to see his face in the dark interior, all she could make out was a brief, unpleasant smile.

"Yeah. . .then I finally met you, and ran smack into your corkscrewed Christian notion of crawling around prostrating yourself on behalf of a man who patently doesn't deserve it. Between that—and some kook out for revenge—I don't know whether I'm calling the shots here or ducking out of their way." His fingers drummed an angry tattoo on the steering wheel. "I used to wonder about religious people, with their interfering noses and sour expressions, spouting off do's and don'ts and acting miserable. After meeting you, I don't wonder why anymore."

Lifting his arms behind his head, Jake stretched, rotating his neck and shrugging—a lean, formidable man who played to win. Who used words like weapons when he was thwarted. He'd even warned her.

Hot and cold prickles raced over Olivia's skin, leaving her slightly nauseated. "I'm not like that," she denied, but her words—unlike Jake's—lacked conviction.

Suddenly his arm dropped down on the seat behind Olivia, his fingers tucking her hair behind her ear, then tracing a path around its contours and down her jaw. "I thought a lot about you the last couple of weeks, up in the mountains. About what kind of God you feel compelled to placate in such a degrading manner. And you know what I concluded?"

Mute, Olivia shook her head, feeling the brush of his fingers against her neck before he finally moved his hand away. "I'm glad I don't have to deal with your God," Jake purred. "Sounds to me like He and your father would have made a great team."

Olivia flinched. "That's not true! You don't understand. My father was cruel and sadistic. . .he—he manipulated people. That's not what God does. Jake, listen to me. I'm trying to make everything right—like Jesus did when He was willing to die in our place. If I can pay for some of what my father did, then I won't feel this horrible, unbearable shame anymore. I won't have to hide out in a town where nobody knows the name of Sinclair. I'll be free." Faint tremors rippled through her body as she willed Jake with all her might to understand. "That's why I know God sent you to me. I believe you're His instrument. Helping at the shelter, visiting your brother-in-law. . .I'll do it all! I'll do anything, like I told you. And then—" Her voice caught— "then I'll be free."

"So. Now I'm elevated to the status of God's emissary instead of a hair shirt," Jake intoned, the low vibrations lifting the hairs on Olivia's scalp. He shifted again, moving closer, forcing her back against the car door. Now his fingers pressed against her lips, stilling her words. His head was suddenly a hair's breadth away.

Olivia went rigid. She was trapped, helpless, and all by her own hand. Once, Jake had tenderly held and comforted her. More often he'd goaded, mocked her. But until now she had never really been afraid of him. All the warnings, all the precautions over the years had flown out the window because she'd refused to heed the signals. Now she'd played right into Jake Donovan's hands, and there wasn't a thing she could do about it.

In a whisper of movement he was kissing her, a kiss that promised to grow more demanding. Olivia froze, still as a cornered mouse. Keeping her lips tightly pressed together, squeezing her eyes shut, she withdrew deep into herself and waited for the onslaught, like she used to do when Daddy was in one of his gloating moods. She was stupid. Stupid, naive, and foolish. Beth had been all wrong about her brother. Rollie and Maria had been right.

"Olivia, open your eyes. Honey, open your eyes. I promise I'm not going to hurt you."

He was stroking her arms gently. The voice—the one like warm melted chocolate—poured over her spirit. "Shh. . .it's all right. Don't pull away from me, okay? I'm not going to hurt you, Olivia."

She opened her eyes and gazed unblinkingly up into his face, wondering how he could look so hard, so unnervingly savage, yet talk to her so gently. "Are you finished?" she asked, distantly ashamed of the weakness in her voice.

"Boy, lady, you just scared me—" He paused, and took a deep breath, his expression softening. "Thank God. You're back with me."

Olivia realized all of a sudden that he was still holding her, his hands moving slowly from shoulders to wrists, warming her, calming her. And it was working. She felt her muscles unclenching, one by one, though a querulous voice inside denounced her continued weakness and stupidity. "I didn't think you believed in God."

"Right now I'll take all the help I can get," Jake returned. He studied her for a moment. "I'm sorry. I had no idea. I was angry and frustrated but—I never meant to scare you like that. Never in my life have I hurt a woman, no matter how flaming mad." A corner of his mouth lifted. "But then, I've never met anyone quite like you either. I'll try harder in the future to avoid lambasting you full force." He finished and said, very gently, "Okay, now?"

Somewhat to her surprise, Olivia nodded. "I guess so. Beth was right. You do have some kind of a temper. But you didn't. . .insist. . .uh, you didn't force—" She floundered, relief and shame causing her to stutter. "It was one of those games you told me you play all the time, right? And I—I messed everything up?"

His hands slid down to cover hers, rubbing his thumbs over the backs. Olivia tried to ignore the strange warmth creeping up her veins, melting the ice and causing shivers of an entirely different kind.

"Olivia Sinclair," Jake eventually murmured, dropping a feathery kiss on each palm, "I don't know what I'm going to do with you. And since nothing has been working like I planned. . .I have a feeling it's going to be totally different from what either of us expected."

Chapter Ten

The next day Jake called the editor of an outdoor magazine. The guy had been bugging him for months. By the following night, he was on his way to the southern Chilcotin Mountains in British Columbia to research a horsepacking photo safari outfit.

"What changed your mind?" the editor wanted to know. "When we talked last, you told me you'd be unavailable until May at the earliest."

"My plans changed," Jake snapped. "Fax me the info at this number." He read it out. "I'm booked on a flight to Seattle Friday."

Over the next days—most of which were spent snowbound in the main lodge—Jake nonetheless learned a good bit about Big Game Trails. He definitely approved of the outfit's commitment to shooting big game with cameras instead of guns. Garrick, his host, a wiry former rodeo rider from Wyoming who played a mean harmonica, placed safety for the client at the head of his list. And while not cordon bleu, the hearty meals available would satisfy most appetites. The magazine article Jake had agreed to write would be a definite thumbs-up.

He also learned one other inescapable fact: Olivia Sinclair was driving him nuts.

"I don't think she's an iceberg, exactly," Jake shared with Garrick late one night. "I just don't think she knows how she feels."

The two men had spent all day tromping through the snow, following tracks and having a whale of a time. Buoyed by the easy camaraderie that had sprung up between them, Jake had relinquished most of his usual tight-lipped reticence. Beyond that, Garrick projected a rare inner peace that invited a very confused Jake into his confidence.

"A couple of times I caught her watching me with this yearning expression on her face," he continued. "I'm familiar enough with that kind of look, I suppose, to recognize what it means." He acknowledged Garrick's snort by toasting him with his mug. "Except Olivia added a dimension I haven't confronted. She sends out the kind of nonverbals that tell me she wants me even if she wouldn't quite know what to do if she got me. Then, when she did, she was terrified out of her skull—" Jake paused. "My mood wasn't the best, of course. I had all these grand plans how I was going to initiate certain. . .changes. . .in our relationship, only Olivia snarled the lines—first with her naive faith in the inherent goodness of all humankind, then with this stalker business. I'll admit my timing was lousy, but I never expected her to freak out."

Garrick roused himself from his favorite spot by the fire to throw on another log. The rest of the staff had long since gone to bed. He and Jake might have been the only two men alive for a thousand miles. "Got no use for teasing women," Garrick drawled. "Baiting you with come-on eyes and smiles, then trotting out a saddlebag full of no's just to watch a man squirm."

"Olivia's not like that," Jake mused. Reeling with exhaustion, some subliminal portion of his mind cringed at this whole conversation. "I told you about her father?"

"The four-flushing three-piece-suit slimeball?" Garrick chuckled. "Yeah, you told me. No wonder she's messed up four ways to Sunday. Beats me why you don't dump her, 'specially after what happened in your car that last night."

A battering wind whistled down the mountains behind Garrick's timberframe lodge, rattling windows. In the fireplace a burning log crumbled, sending a shower of sparks up the chimney. Sitting across from Garrick in a comfortably deep chair, hands wrapped around the mug of hot apple cider, Jake should have been contented. Instead he was restless, uneasy as a mustang at mating time.

"She probably thinks I've dumped her," he finally admitted, staring into the flames. "But I had to get out of there. I told you how it all started—how I'd planned this perfect revenge for what happened to my sister and her husband—" Suddenly his line of reasoning took an unexpected turn. "Garrick, tell me. . .you ever think about God?"

Garrick scratched the plaid flannel shirt over his stomach and pondered the ceiling. "Well, I guess you might say the two of us share more than a nodding acquaintance. Sort of hard up here, y'see, not to accept the existence of Someone more powerful—and a whole lot smarter—than us poor mucked-up humans." His gaze dropped back to Jake. "You've been all over the world, man. I've read most of the articles you've written over the years. How can you see what you've seen, do the things you've done, and not think about God?"

Jake sipped cider and watched the fire. "Don't know," he eventually offered. "My sister and I lost our folks when I was nine and Beth was six. My mother's older sister raised us. She was a hardbitten mountain woman, and my uncle spent most of the time staying on the job to avoid her. He worked for the forestry service. The only time I remember hearing God mentioned was when Aunt Sophy threatened us with His wrath when we acted up."

Garrick grunted. "Know what you mean. Met a few religious harpies like that myself."

"The years I played pro football," Jake went on, "there were a few guys who called themselves born-again Christians. They used to spout off high-sounding phrases about Jesus, especially when we won. But most of them didn't act much different from the rest of us, and I more or less ignored what they said.

"And when I'm climbing a mountain or kayaking down a river, I just enjoy the incredible freedom. No ties. Nobody telling me what to do and how to do it. Wondering what's around the bend, on the other side—"

"You're still missing something, Jake. I can hear it in your voice, and don't try to tell me I'm wrong. Sometimes a man lays down tracks as easy to read as a herd of big horns, for anybody smart enough to read 'em." Garrick pondered the ceiling some more. "It's not just that messed-up woman you're pining for as hard as you're running from." He left off studying the exposed timber beams and scooped up his harmonica. "Might be you're missing out on getting to know God. Think about it, fella." He put the harmonica to his lips and closed his eyes, ending the conversation.

Much later, Jake lay in bed listening to the wind, while Garrick's words played over in his mind like the haunting melodies of his harmonica. On many levels Garrick reminded Jake a lot of himself—confident, assured of who he was, living the life he'd chosen to the fullest. But Garrick wasn't uneasy and restless, like Jake.

If Garrick did have some sort of "relationship" with God, it was a lot more comfortable one than the relationship Olivia struggled with every day. Her perception of God reminded Jake uncomfortably of the wrathful, punishment-minded Being Aunt Sophy used to threaten would fill Jake's britches with fire and brimstone if he didn't straighten out.

Jake hadn't wanted anything to do with that kind of God then, and—like he'd told Olivia—he didn't want anything to do with Him now. There was no freedom in living out a life full of fear, waiting for God to strike if you so much as made one wrong move.

If Jake ever decided to look into the matter, he'd go for Garrick's God, no doubt about it.

As for Olivia, well, Jake had chewed that one over more than he cared to admit for almost two months now, but he couldn't wriggle out of a couple of certainties. First and foremost, he'd blown it royally with the woman, treating her like he had, then running like a scalded cat. He owed her an apology.

The other certainty made him squirm even more uncomfortably: he was still attracted to Olivia Sinclair more than any other woman he'd ever known.

Yep, he'd learned a lot up here in the wilds of Canada, and that last lesson was by far the scariest.

❧

On a warm and sunny March day Jake returned to North Carolina. For the first time in his life he paid scant attention to the frothy pink and white dogwoods, the hot pink azaleas, and butter yellow forsythias splashing the surroundings in joyous bursts of color.

Dumping his gear on Beth's threadbare but immaculate living room rug, he hurriedly showered and changed, intent on making it to Olivia's shop before closing time. Fortunately Beth was at work and couldn't yell at him about the mess.

On the way to The Bridal Bower, Jake decided it was time to buy himself a car, instead of paying the usual outrageous rental fees he put out every time he stayed with his sister. Money was no problem; he had money to burn in investments, mutual funds, and banks all over the world. That in itself was a joke, though Beth's categorical refusal to accept more than token financial aid never ceased to rankle. Money had never been one of life's consuming passions for Jake, even though fate had capriciously blessed him with some semblance of a Midas touch. That is, he didn't care as long as he had enough to support his nomadic lifestyle.

Of course, buying his first car in eight years confirmed the radical shift in a few of those priorities. If he bought himself wheels, would a regular job with regular hours follow? A house with a white picket fence and a couple of dogs on the doorstep, for crying out loud?

Turning onto Main Street, Jake fought another terrific inner battle not to pull up at the nearest pay phone. In two hours or less he could be on a plane, headed anywhere he pleased—if he chose to keep running.

Olivia's storefront loomed through the windshield. The Bridal Bower. If that name didn't send a man high-tailing it out of town, he had to be as crazy as Davy, his poor slob of a brother-in-law. Davy had checked out of reality because he hadn't been able to cope with failure, or with all his responsibilities.

The skin at the back of Jake's neck crawled, big-time, but he didn't look for a pay phone.

He lifted his foot off the accelerator just as a couple emerged through the store entrance. Faces glowing, they were talking with Olivia, and Jake couldn't tear his eyes away from her graceful elegance, even dressed as she was in a simple short-sleeved blouse and tailored slacks.

Several more young women spilled in a noisy, laughing tide past Olivia, who was holding the door while she talked. Jake couldn't hear the words but, knowing Olivia, it was probably a litany of last-minute advice to somebody's bridesmaids.

He drove on past and turned down the alley behind the row of shops, parking next to the vehicles he recognized as those belonging to Olivia's two assistants. There was no sign of Olivia's car.

He slipped in the staff entrance without a qualm, startling a plump older woman into dropping the phone. Jake picked it up and handed it back. "Don't mind me," he reassured her with a grin. "I'm just here to see your boss."

The woman slammed the receiver back into the cradle. "I don't think so!" she pronounced in ringing tones, rising to block the door into the main part of the boutique with her considerable bulk. "You're Jake Donovan, aren't you?"

"Pleased to meet you." Jake waited, hands casually stuffed in the waistband of his jeans in a seemingly nonthreatening stance. He wondered how Olivia's self-appointed bodyguard would react if he picked her up and dumped her back in the chair. She might weigh close to two hundred pounds, but he could manage it. On the other hand—

"You might as well let me through." He spoke congenially, confidentially. "It's nice that she has such caring friends, even when they are way off base."

Ms. Amazon folded her hefty arms across her chest. "Your butter-melting mouth and wolfish charms don't faze me, Mr. Donovan. Do you have any notion what Olivia's been through since you skedaddled to parts unknown?"

"No. What?"

The woman swelled as if preparing for battle. "She let you chew her up and spit her out like a piece of bad meat, regardless of what we tried to tell her. Even though you left, proving you obviously couldn't care less, Olivia still goes to that shelter every other night. Or at least she did until night before last, when she came out from church and found all the windows in her car smashed." She nodded once, double chins quivering. "Mighty suspicious how you were conveniently gone, if you ask me."

The good-natured teasing pose vanished. Jake took a step forward, tightly throttling back on his temper. *Be cool now, Donovan.* "What's been done?"

Lips pursed in satisfaction, her censorious glare reminded him uncomfortably of Aunt Sophy. But her next accusation almost sent him through the roof in spite of his determination not to lose his temper. "I'm surprised the police haven't already taken you into custody."

"Rollie, the Edgerton gang left so we can finally close up shop," called a familiar voice from an inner office. "Did Maria remind you that they want us to go ahead with the reservations at—" Entering the room, Olivia caught sight of Jake and stopped dead. "Jake," she said, voice breathless, wary.

"Can we go somewhere and talk, or are the police already on the way?" *Not good, fella. You're supposed to keep a lid on it, remember?*

Olivia blinked, obviously recognizing the raw anger seething in the words. But she didn't retreat. Instead she whirled to face Rollie, who was hovering near Jake as if preparing to either tackle him or dive under the desk out of harm's way. "What have you been saying to him, Rollie? You told him about the car, didn't you? What else? Davy? Even when you promised you wouldn't?"

Jake felt as if his rope had broken, dropping him into a bottomless void. "Davy? What are you talking about?" Ignoring an abruptly silent Rollie, he stepped right up to Olivia, muscles aching with the need to take her in his arms. "She told me about your car. She more or less accused me of untold crimes. But nobody mentioned Davy."

Olivia dropped her gaze, but Jake had seen the flare of alarm. "Olivia?" he repeated, softly, dangerously. For two weeks all he'd thought about was how he planned to make up, soften her with apologies and explanations so that, when he took her in his arms again, she'd welcome his kisses.

Once again, their reunion wasn't turning out like he'd planned.

"Rollie's overreacting," Olivia finally confessed. Drawing on that deep reservoir of control Jake admired, once again she managed to pull herself together. She glanced toward the older woman with a cool gray gaze promising retribution, then back to Jake. He wanted to kiss her, badly. "The police verified—through Beth—your whereabouts at the time of this last incident. I vouched for your presence the other two times and assured them I was solely responsible for triggering the stalker's actions. You're neither under suspicion nor in danger of arrest. Rollie, don't you have some phone calls to make? You can use the phone at the front register. While you do that, Maria can clean up out front."

"Olivia, I never meant—he deserved—"

"I appreciate your efforts, but I need to talk to Jake. Alone."

Grumbling but vanquished, Rollie gathered up a notebook bulging with protruding papers and left. Olivia gently closed the door behind her. Silence, throbbing and intense, filled the room.

"I'm glad you're back, Jake," she finally said, once again avoiding his gaze, "even though this is incredibly awkward. It would help tremendously if you'd quit glowering at me. We both know losing your temper's only going to make things worse."

Was his little manager taking him to task? Very carefully, Jake snagged a nearby stool, dragged it over, and lowered himself to the seat. His gaze never left Olivia. She was thinner and purple circles marred the delicate skin beneath her eyes. But the steel spine was firmly in place, and though she was blushing now, she finally met his frank perusal without wavering.

Incredibly, Jake felt his anger subsiding. "All right," he promised amicably, hitching one foot on the second rung and propping his elbow on his knee. "The tiger's back in the cage. Satisfied?"

A corner of her mouth lifted. "How long will the tiger stay there?"

"Frankly, I'm not too sure. Probably not very long. . .if I don't get some answers." His voice hardened. "Tell me about Davy."

Olivia laced her fingers together. "I've spent the day with him the last two Sundays." The pulse hammered away in her throat. "I know that's where you'd planned to take me, before you left. Beth told me. She didn't want me to go, either, if it's any consolation, but gave in when I told her I'd go with or without her."

"A martyr mentality with a management obsession," Jake observed. "Deadly combination." He toyed with the stitching on his hiking boot. "So. . .what did you think?"

"I don't know how Beth stands it," she confessed. Moving restlessly, she wandered over to a counter behind Jake. "There's something else I need to say, something far more difficult than going to see Davy."

"Yeah? What could be worse than that?" He quit fiddling with his shoe and studied the graceful curve of her back, even though it was as stiff as a new pair of boots.

"I wanted to apologize for my behavior the last time we were together. I hadn't realized, until then, that I might have some major problems to work through on a number of levels."

He stood, hardly able to believe his ears. Olivia, apologizing to him? "Wait a minute. Back up. I shouldn't have come on to you when you were already upset over your car. It wasn't your fault. I was the one who was way out of line."

She still wouldn't turn around, seemingly wasn't paying any attention. "I told you I hadn't really dated a lot, and the relationships I have been involved in never went much beyond the surface—" There was a tense pause. "That's why it never occurred to me that my father's destructive personality might have bled over into my ability to—to—well, that's my problem."

"Olivia—"

"—and you need to understand that I don't expect you to change your behavior just because I have a few problems," she rushed on. "It's just that I didn't think you really meant what you said. . .about wanting me, I mean, and—"

"Olivia. . .turn around and look at me." The words might have been harsh, but he made his voice sound as if he were crooning a lullaby. When Olivia whirled around, Jake crooked a beckoning finger. "Good," he smiled, a slow beguiling smile that usually performed magical tricks on feminine willpower. "Now. . .come here."

Chatper Eleven

Even though Olivia knew Jake was charming her deliberately, she responded anyway. She knew that Jake knew that she knew what he was doing, and her mouth itched with the need to grin a just-as-teasing response.

Only she was also afraid and unsure.

For weeks her emotions had swung wildly, from humiliation to anger to hope and then to despair. Because whatever either of them felt for each other, Jake wasn't a Christian.

Olivia had learned, both from her parents' experience and through her vocation, that unequal yoking almost always gives birth to unhappiness. *Lord, he's not one of Yours. I know that. Help me. I have to stop this. Now.*

"I don't know what will happen if you try to kiss me again," she confessed to Jake instead, and wondered if she had finally lost control of all her faculties.

Jake's smile deepened. "Neither do I," he returned. "That's why—since you have the protection of two spear-hurling Amazons in the next room—we're going to conduct a little experiment—" The slashing eyebrow arched—"with your permission, of course."

"Of course," Olivia echoed, as if that's what she had in mind all the time. She stopped three feet away—mouth dry, palms damp, knowing she should run, yet wishing with every rebellious ounce of blood in her body that Jake would just hurry up and do it.

"Give me your hands."

"My. . .hands? Why?"

Jake chuckled. "I'll show you." He held his out, palms up, but made no move to force her compliance.

Olivia stared first at the hands, then up into his face. All her breath escaped in a whoosh. "They're—they're damp. I'm sorry," Olivia stammered, lifting her hands and lightly resting them in Jake's.

"That's because you're nervous," he explained kindly. His fingers closed around hers, and he lifted them to his mouth. Kissing her fingertips, he captured her wrist, counting the pulse. He laughed softly. "You're not the only one. Maybe it's time you learned a few things about me—" Quickly he placed her hand over his heart—"before we *both* suffer cardiac arrest."

Olivia's jaw dropped. Beneath her hand his heart pounded in a hard drum-roll as runaway as her own. She darted a quick look at him. "I'm not sure. . . you'll laugh at me—"

"Never. I'd never treat you like that. Look at me." His voice was so urgent Olivia obeyed instantly, meeting head-on his compelling, mesmerizing gaze. "I know I've bullied you, frightened you, treated you rotten, Olivia. And we both know about my lousy temper. But I promise you, I'll never ridicule you or put you down. We'll disagree—a lot!—and I'll probably continue to lose my temper every now and then, but I won't be trying to destroy your spirit, Olivia, ever again. You're one classy lady, even when you're fighting battles you can't win."

Gathering her close, he searched her face, the blazing desire softening into tenderness. "So. . .kiss me, sweetheart. . .please." His knuckles gently grazed her cheek. "And trust me. We can work it out, I promise."

They were standing so close Olivia could count the pulse beating strongly in Jake's throat, the same pounding rhythm as his heart. His warmth and strength enveloped her, but this time—instead of panic—she felt only a growing need to show him how she felt.

Tension pulsed between them. Resting both hands on his chest, her eyes drowning in his, Olivia leaned forward, lifting her face to his. She waited, but the horrible suffocating panic she dreaded still hadn't returned.

Dizzy, trembling with excitement and relief, she touched her lips to Jake's. . . and behind her the door flew open.

"We couldn't hear anything and Rollie was about to. . .oops!" Maria's voice intruded like a passel of uninvited relatives. "Sorry and all that, but. . .Olivia, are you sure you know what you're doing?"

Jake gently shifted Olivia to the side. "The door's behind you. Use it," he ordered in a pleasant voice that belied the look on his face. "If Olivia needs your help or advice, she'll call."

"That might be sort of hard for her to do the way things seem to be headed," Maria shot back tartly, unfazed.

Olivia squelched her roaring embarrassment and turned to face her colleague. "I'm fine, Maria. Truly. And I'll continue to stay that way if you leave us alone until I find out for sure—" She bit her lip, rattled and frustrated.

Maria's head tilted, though she did edge backward. "Find out what for sure?"

"Find out if I can kiss her 'til her toes curl,' " Jake supplied, smiling a knife-edged smile. "Scram, Ms. Santinas. Three's a crowd and all that."

"All right, already. I'm going! But I have a nice pair of very sharp scissors and a special length of florist's wire set aside just for you, Jake Donovan. . .if you catch my drift?" She pulled the door shut, then reopened it and poked her head back through. "We have to be at First Street Methodist tomorrow at ten, remember." Accompanied by a healthy bang, this time the door stayed shut.

"Like I said, Amazons," Jake murmured. He shook his head, stretched, then cast a rueful smile toward Olivia. "Care to take up where you left off, or did friend Maria effectively douse all the flames?"

Olivia shook her head, then nodded, relieved by his easy acceptance of the situation. An upsurge of shyness choked her, but didn't constrain the seed of elation springing forth. "I didn't freeze," she said, and smiled. "I didn't panic at all!"

"Just the opposite, I'd say." Jake tapped the end of her nose. "Next time, Ms. Sinclair, I'll put out the 'Do Not Disturb' sign."

"Does this mean you're not going to escape back into the wilds of Canada, or someplace equally as remote, Mr. Donovan?"

A muscle twitched in his cheek. Then the corner of his mouth curled, and all of a sudden—to Olivia's surprise—he laughed. "It's a temptation," Jake admitted. "Except now that I've had a nibble or two, I'm afraid I won't be satisfied until I've made the catch." His finger followed the contour of her cheek, stopping to tilt her chin upward. "Tomorrow, Main Street Methodist at ten, right? See you then, sweetheart."

And he was gone.

≥≈

That night Olivia called her mother. "I need to talk. Do you have a few moments?"

"Of course, honey. I was just sitting here in the den, watching TV and relaxing." Abruptly her voice sharpened with anxiety. "Has something else happened? To you? The shop?"

"No—no. Everything's fine on that front. Or at least, nothing new since my car windows were smashed." Stinging nettles of guilt pricked Olivia's conscience. Her mother had returned from the month-long sabbatical cheerful and more peaceful than Olivia could ever remember.

Then Olivia had had to confess how her attempts to clear Daddy's name had resulted in the unpleasant attentions of "a probable stalker," as the police termed it. Now every time Olivia talked to her mother, she could hear a painfully familiar thread of anxiety weaving through all her words. Mama could understand neither Olivia's motivation nor her stubborn refusal to at least move in with Rollie. From then on, Olivia had carefully edited the events of the past two months, including Jake.

Unfortunately, now she was drowning—and her mother unknowingly held the only life ring that might allow Olivia to stay afloat. Taking a deep breath, she plunged in. "Mama, I've met this man, and—and I think I've fallen in love with him. Only. . .he's not a Christian and I'm petrified he might turn out to be like Daddy. So I—I have to know what Daddy was like when you first met him." She stared at her inexpensive framed print of Monet's "Wild Poppies" on the wall opposite the bed, where she lay propped against the headboard.

Until this afternoon Olivia hadn't verbalized the issue, hadn't even wanted to face it. She wasn't the most obedient Christian in the world, but she really did try hard to do the right thing, live a life that would be pleasing to God. She thought again of the Bible admonition about unequal yoking. Well, falling in love with an untamed, risk-loving, non-Christian adventurer was about as unequally yoked as two people could get! Still, she couldn't take the words back now, nor could she deny their truth any longer.

"Heavens, child, what a thing to spring on me at half past nine o'clock at night! Olivia, I don't know what to say—"

Olivia closed her eyes, picturing her mother—her thin hair prematurely gray from constant stress, the permanent wrinkle between hazel eyes which were always veiled, always uncertain. Her mother never looked at anybody directly, not even her children. Was that what Olivia would become if she committed her life to Jake Donovan?

"Mama, I'm sorry. I didn't want to upset you, but I need to know." Adopting the same calm, persuasive voice she used with recalcitrant clients, Olivia set about soothing her mother, gently coaxing her back to a calmer state, injecting humor at the end. "Don't worry. I'm still your cautious, controlled, fanatically organized daughter who's always on top of things."

Weak laughter floated over the line. "I declare, when you talk like that, you sound just like he used to, pulling our legs so sober and serious like, with a twinkle way in the back of his eye. You do the same thing, you know."

"So I'm told," Olivia agreed. Memories wrapped around her heart. "Mama, tell me about Daddy. Please."

The silence lasted so long she feared her mother would refuse, after all, even though Olivia had just bared her soul more openly than she had since she was thirteen years old. She clenched the receiver tightly, praying hard. *I have to know, Lord. Please, I have to know. Let her tell me, help me—*

"Your father," Mama spoke slowly, reluctantly, "possessed the looks and charm of Lucifer. And like the devil, he showed a body only what he knew they wanted to see. I was young. Headstrong, too, and a little wild, so it was so easy for your father. Olivia, honey, if this man is anything like that, you'd better run as hard as you can in the other direction."

Olivia kept her voice steady with an effort. "Did you have any idea, any clue at all what kind of person Daddy was before you married him?"

Another long moment of silence passed. Then, "Yes," her mother whispered, her voice shamed, full of sorrow. "And to my dying day, I'll have to live with the awful weight of it."

Olivia sat up, hardly breathing. "How did you know, Mama? What did he do?"

"He was subtle, oh, so subtle—and the time or two I actually questioned him, he always managed to talk me 'round. . .he was a master at twisting words even then." The voice grew hoarse, the words even more halting. "You remember that he never lost his temper? I used to think that made him so strong, so mature when, if I'd listened to my conscience, I would have known it was because he—he just didn't care. But at the time, I didn't want to see all the warning signs—"

"What signs?" Olivia nudged, holding her breath. "What signs, Mama?"

Her mother's voice dropped once more to a near whisper. "His eyes were always. . .empty, if you really looked right at him. Empty behind the charm, I mean. And he—he teased animals. Nothing outrageously cruel, just tormenting. Making my pet dog beg for a treat, then throwing it in the trash instead of giving it to him. . .that kind of thing. And once—" This time the pause was so prolonged that Olivia was sure her mother had changed her mind about telling her story—"once we were out driving around. . .and a squirrel darted out into the road. Olivia, your father swerved. . .not to avoid hitting the poor little thing . . .but so he could deliberately *run over it.*" She finished on a whimper. "I'm sorry, baby, but it's true!"

"Oh, Mama—"

"He tried to brush it aside, convince me he'd never hurt anything so small and helpless, but I knew." Tears thickened the soft drawling syllables at last. "Deep inside, Olivia, I knew what kind of man your father was. But I told myself he'd change after marriage—I'd *make* him change. Just like you, baby. Just like you . . .trying so hard to see something good in your father. The difference is, I finally accepted the truth—"

There was another long pause. Olivia didn't know whether her mother was still there, or if she'd put down the receiver, too overcome with emotion to go on. Finally she spoke, her voice whispery-thin. "Olivia, if the man you're talking about is anything like that, I beg you. . .run away, honey. Run away before it's too late for you too."

Chapter Twelve

Saturday morning. Judy Wells's and Barry Seymour's wedding. Part of The Bower's service for this particular couple included Olivia's presence at the church in her directorial capacity—professional but warm, authoritative but not dictatorial. Everyone and everything were depending on Olivia's seasoned, skillful handling to orchestrate a joyous, unforgettable day.

A little past six-thirty, just after dawn, Olivia rolled out of bed. Staggering like one of Sherm's drunken derelicts—and looking the part—she showered, dragged on a windsuit, then sat at the kitchen table and stared at a congealing bowl of cold cereal.

Perhaps a walk would clear her head. Rollie wasn't picking her up until nine-thirty. Olivia could make it all the way to the mall and back in that time. Maybe exercise and fresh air would accomplish what a sleepless night had failed to achieve—finding the words, the strength to tell Jake good-bye.

Letting herself out the back door and carefully locking it with the new dead-bolt recommended by Sergeant MacClary, Olivia paused to inhale the fragrant aroma of dew on the honeysuckles and morning glories, and absorb the opalescent peace of early morning. With a sweeping scan, she also quickly confirmed that the stalker wasn't lurking about in the bushes between her cottage and the neighbors' houses.

An hour later Olivia trudged wearily back down the sidewalk, two blocks from the cottage. No words illuminated her soul, but at least a strange resignation had settled in her mind, allowing her to focus on the day's events instead of her own personal Gethsemane. She would somehow convince Jake that she couldn't see him anymore—but not because of any superficial resemblance to her father. How had her mother survived at all?

Over the years Olivia had attained a fair amount of insight into people and had dealt with every emotion from euphoric adoration to irrational temper tantrums. She was good with people. . .and she was cautious. After hearing about her father, Olivia was convinced Jake no more resembled Alton Sinclair than an ice cube resembled a glacier, except for one inescapable fact—neither man wanted anything to do with a personal God. Daddy had paid lip service on Sunday mornings to polish his image. A more honest Jake denounced religion openly—and so Olivia had to end it.

She might love him, be convinced he'd never hurt or abuse her, but Jake was not a Christian man. *I don't know why You're doing this to me, Lord, but I could really use Your help. . .*

Turning the corner onto her block, she waved to Mr. Potts, out watering his flowers. Birds darted about, chirping in the early morning sunlight. At least it was going to be another beautiful day, perfect for a wedding.

Olivia turned into her driveway, idly noting the sputtering engine of an approaching car. She half-turned, catching the blurred glimpse of a small blue Toyota. . .and something hard slammed into the side of her head.

The searing pain exploded in her skull. A dark roaring tunnel sucked at her consciousness while swirling lights blinded her. Staggering, fighting waves of nausea, Olivia tried to catch a last glimpse of the car. It was gone, the street empty except for the birds. She was too far away to summon Mr. Potts. She could never make him hear her.

Got to make it to the house, Lord. I have to make it to the house. . .phone—

Endless minutes later, her foot scraped the first step of the stoop at the back. She'd kept her wits about her long enough to make it to the back door, easier to unlock than the double set of locks on the front door. The swirling lights intensified. Then, mercifully, she blacked out.

≈

Jake knew it was too early, but he also knew that if he didn't convince Olivia to leave with him before Maria or Rollie arrived to pick her up, he'd be up to his ears in antagonism. Flexing his hands on the steering wheel, he wondered why now—when his entire life had turned upside down—every female with whom he came in contact seemed bent on either ripping a strip off him or delivering a sermon.

The previous night, after blistering his ears over his slovenliness, Beth had delivered what could only be termed a harangue on his disgraceful lack of consideration for the feelings of others. Grimacing at the memory, Jake turned down Olivia's street.

When Beth put her mind to it, she could carve up a hog with her tongue. The grimace transformed to an anticipatory grin. Olivia, no doubt, would have something equally as astringent to say when he arrived without warning on her doorstep, practically at the crack of dawn.

He parked in the driveway, thinking as he loped up the walk that maybe after finishing up at the church, the two of them could spend the rest of the day in Charlotte, looking for a new car for him.

When she didn't respond either to repeated ringing of the doorbell or his pounding fist, a very unpleasant sensation slithered down his backbone. Senses heightened and alert, Jake checked out the front windows, all of which were completely covered by drawn shades. He sprinted around back.

Olivia was leaning against the door, eyes closed as if she were enjoying the morning sunshine.

Jake reached her in four long angry strides. "Didn't you hear the doorbell—" He caught sight of an ugly swelling bruise covering her right forehead all the way down to her cheek. "Olivia, what happened to you!"

Her eyes fluttered open and focused vaguely. Jake started to swear, caught himself, and clamped his teeth together while he dropped to his knees beside her.

Years of on-site first aid training took over. Running his hands over her limbs, he noted the rapid pulse, clammy skin, and shallow respiration. Early shock, perhaps. . .but at least there were no broken bones, no sign of blood, and she didn't seem to be injured anywhere except her head. He glanced around, searching for clues to what might have happened.

"Hello—" His gaze whipped back to her face. Vague recognition flickered in the blue-gray eyes. "I needed to be rescued by you. . .but then. . .I need to be rescued *from* you—" She began to slump sideways.

Jake caught her arm, shifted her body so he was sitting beside her on the stoop. Carefully he slid her into a protective embrace. "Olivia," he repeated her name gently, though his insides felt like an erupting volcano. "Can you talk to me?"

"I thought I was." Her voice was blurred, so laced with droll humor Jake wanted to shake her—or lay his head against hers and cry. What was the matter with him? And what did she mean, she "needed to be rescued from him"?

"Can you tell me now what happened to you? Did you fall, hit your head?"

Groggily she made an effort to sit up, slapping at Jake's restraining hands. "I'm fine. You don't have to hold me. . .and I have to be at the church—" She started struggling in earnest. "Have to get dressed. Have to be ready. . .let me go."

"Not on your life." Jake stood, swinging Olivia up into his arms, easily ignoring her feeble struggles. "Easy, honey. We need to get you to a doctor before we engage in a wrestling match. Shh, now—it's okay. We can still make it to the church in plenty of time."

She calmed, rested the uninjured side of her head against Jake's shoulder, a boneless, weightless bundle. A quivering sigh shuddered through the delicate frame. Jake remembered that weeks earlier he'd compared her to a wild and fragile bird. Wincing, he closed his mind to the poignant memory and started walking.

"I never realized. . .how strong you were."

He slanted her an incredulous look, using every ounce of his massive willpower to keep her from seeing he was scared right out of his own thick skull. "It has its uses. You're strong too, sweetheart, where it really counts."

Her eyes drifted closed and a tear trickled down her cheek. "No, I'm not. I'm trying, I really am. But I'm not strong."

They reached the car. Carefully he lifted her in, then cupped her wan face in both hands. "I'll take care of you," he promised, his voice a rough growl. Olivia didn't seem to mind. A glimmer of blue washed into the turbulent gray sea of her eyes. "I know," she whispered.

He made her lie down with her good cheek resting on his leg. "Hold on, little one."

The doctor tried. The nurses tried. Sergeant McClary, interrupted at his breakfast by Jake's call, tried to convince Olivia to arrange for Maria to direct the wedding. Grimly amused, Jake watched from his unmovable stance against a wall in the county hospital emergency room while Olivia wielded her own version of Sinclair power.

"I don't have a concussion," she reminded the disgruntled physician. "I can manage the headache, especially if these pills work like you promised."

Outflanked, the doctor stuffed his stethoscope in the pocket of his white lab coat. "Everybody's different, of course, so I can't say for sure."

"But if they do work, you promised they wouldn't make me drowsy."

"Not supposed to." He shook his head. "You're doing the Judith Wells wedding, aren't you? I've known her since she was knee-high to a grasshopper. The wife and I planned to attend, so I reckon if you have a problem, at least I'll be handy."

That was the doctor.

Then the police officer started in. "Now, Ms. Sinclair, you know the more you expose yourself out in public, the better target you are. What if it's a bullet next time, instead of a brick? You have a capable assistant, so if I was you, I'd stay somewhere else for a day or two, 'til the boys and I have a little time to trace the car. You're sure about the driver?"

"Female, with short gray hair," Olivia repeated patiently. "It's not much, I know, but I had enough time between regaining consciousness and Mr. Donovan's arrival to sift it through my memory. I'm pretty good with details like that." She smiled. "I have to be."

"But you will at least move in with someone for a while? They've gotten personal now, ma'am. This is assault, a little more serious than malicious mischief."

Jake shouldered himself away from the wall. He'd had enough. "I'll take care of her," he announced in the tone of voice that never failed to produce the desired result.

It worked this time, too—with everyone except Olivia. Within five seconds the small emergency room of the county hospital had emptied, with polite farewells, advice, and shaking heads disappearing out the door.

Olivia, looking mulish, gingerly slid off the examining table. "You had no right to do that. It embarrassed me, and now they all think we're—" she stumbled, then finished defiantly—"involved."

"We are," Jake stated without cracking a smile, though he knew from Olivia's uneasy squirming that he'd successfully communicated his intent. He glanced down at his watch. "We can talk about it on the way to church. It's almost ten, and you're going to have enough trouble calming your two guardian angels as it is."

"If you're referring to Rollie and Maria, I prefer 'guardian angels' to 'spear-hurling Amazon bodyguards,' " Olivia grumbled, though she didn't resist the hand Jake slipped beneath her elbow. She fretted and muttered all the way to the car. "You called Maria to bring me some clothes, didn't you? I hope they fit okay. . .I have an image to maintain. . .we're the same size, I think—"

The county hospital was twenty miles away. Jake had to suppress the urgent desire to keep on driving, forcefully abducting Olivia like a marauding Viking and stashing her in the lodge in British Columbia with Garrick. Since he knew Olivia would never consent to that maneuver, he headed the car back toward Barley.

He thought she'd finally quieted down—until they turned onto the interstate. "Jake," she began, "I need to thank you before I say anything else."

"You already have. Don't you remember? At least every third sentence all the way over here." He grinned across at her. "It was my pleasure, ma'am. I'm just grateful the damage wasn't any worse than a huge bruise and a headache."

"I'll survive."

She didn't comment on the outcome of any future attacks, and, for the time being, Jake decided to play along. Timing, he knew, was everything, and right now, Olivia needed to pull herself together so she could marry off two kids with her professional persona intact. Deciding that teasing would put both of them in a lighter mood, Jake was mentally sifting through approaches when Olivia shoved him headfirst off a cliff.

"Jake. . .I don't know how to say this, and the circumstances aren't what I'd choose, but I need to say it and get it over with. Now. We—we can't be involved. Ever. On any level." He heard her swallow before continuing in a rapid, desperate monotone. "I just had to tell you now, especially after that little incident back at the hospital. It's impossible—all of it. I know I'm not a very good example, but I *am* a Christian, and I just can't handle a relationship with a man who only mentions God's name as a swear word."

Jake continued to drive without speaking until he knew his response wouldn't send Olivia scrambling for cover or tumbling into another panic-driven trance. "Is that your only excuse?" he finally asked. "You sure you're not comparing me to your father?"

"Your resemblance to my father is and was only superficial," Olivia promised, sounding sincere but unutterably weary. "I at least settled that in my mind last night. You wield tremendous power, and you're the most exciting, disturbing man I've ever known." Out of the corner of his eye, Jake saw her lift her hand to her head, then drop it limply back in her lap. "But, as you pointed out almost from the first, you certainly play a lot more vicious hardball than I can in the game of life. That includes a deeply held dislike and mistrust of the Christian faith, and I just can't risk that—"

"I promised you last night I'd never hurt you like that again." He knew he sounded harsh, cutting, but he felt as if he were at the bottom of a pile of three-hundred-pound linebackers.

"I know." Her voice trembled for the first time. "I believe you. . .now. But, Jake, when all is said and done, you still hold all my beliefs, my faith, in contempt. I struggle enough as it is, trying to be a good Christian. I just can't—" her voice broke, and her head drooped, "can't risk it. I know you wouldn't mean to, but you'd end up destroying me."

"I've never understood why people set such store by a God who does nothing but promote fear and guilt and shame. There's no freedom in a miserable life of constant penance, endless rules and regulations, always waiting for God to drop the other shoe." He glared straight ahead at the concrete ribbon of road. "I grew up in an emotional jail like that. . .and hell couldn't be any worse. Olivia. . .help me understand. I need you in my life. If God is part of the price, then at least figure out a way to make the Christian life more palatable."

For a long time Olivia didn't respond, but Jake was struggling with ego-bruising battles of his own, so he didn't force the issue. A second swift glance assured him that, at least physically, Olivia seemed to be recovering. She sat straighter and some of her normal color had returned. He couldn't see the injured side of her face, which was just as well. Confronted with such graphic evidence of her vulnerability, he might have given up the battle then and there.

And lost the war.

Two miles from Barley, Olivia spoke again. "I didn't know my Christian faith came across like that."

"Like what?" he asked evenly.

"Like God is nothing but a God of wrath, or a harsh, small-minded jailer, gloating over the helplessness of all His inmates."

Jake shrugged and narrowed his eyes in thought. "Ever since I met you, your whole purpose in life has revolved around earning forgiveness for your father. You claim that's what Jesus did to pay for the sins of man, and you're only trying to follow His example." They entered the Barley city limits and Jake slowed the car practically to a crawl. He had maybe five more minutes.

"Well, I confess I've never had any use for Christianity," he went on, "because I've known many more miserable Christians than contented ones. It strikes me as a little contradictory that you're still trying to do for your father what Jesus is supposed to have already done. He died for everyone, if I understand it right, and that would have to include your father, no matter how despicable he might have been—" In the silence that followed, Olivia could hear her heart pounding. But Jake wasn't through. "It would have been up to *him* to make his peace with God, not you."

"Turn right at the next street," Olivia directed in a barely audible voice.

Two minutes later the church appeared. Frustration curdling his insides, Jake turned into the parking lot and pulled up beside Rollie's van. He switched off the ignition and turned to Olivia. She gazed back at him with the stricken self-awareness of a child caught stealing cookies.

Jake set his jaw. "If my teammates were right years ago about the role Jesus played, I'd have to say it's not God who's put you behind bars, Olivia. You've done it to yourself."

Chapter Thirteen

Olivia is one classy lady, Jake thought to himself, *and I'm one messed-up guy.*

He watched her tolerate the ranting and raving of her friends long enough to calm them down, reassure them she would be fine, just fine. Then, looking unbelievably refreshed and confident in a borrowed dress, she quietly set Rollie to work and sent Maria off to the store.

With steadfast serenity, she ignored Rollie's questions as well as the gaping stares of the florist, photographer, and various other folk madly milling about. Over the next few hours—in spite of the fact that one side of her face looked like the aftermath of a barroom brawl—Olivia superintended the transformation of the quiet sanctuary into a lovely setting for the upcoming nuptials.

As a noticed but largely ignored bystander, Jake hovered in the background, so proud of this woman he wanted to stake a very public claim. . .yet so hurt, angry, and confused, he wanted to head for the mountains alone to lick his wounds. He still couldn't believe she'd given him the bum's rush because he didn't share her twisted, torturous views on God.

"Hello. I'm Michael Carmody, the minister here at First Street Methodist." Jake turned to face a comfortable-looking man wearing a gray suit and surprisingly fashionable tie. Calm assessing eyes behind a pair of wire-rimmed glasses waited for Jake to respond. Slowly he lifted a hand. "Jake Donovan."

"Are you part of the wedding party?"

"No way. I came with Olivia Sinclair, the busy little conductor over there talking to the organist."

"Ah, yes. Olivia. A lovely young woman who seems to be suffering greatly."

Struck both by the comment as well as the note of deep concern, Jake studied the older man a moment, frowning. "The doctor promised it's not a concussion, and he gave her some pills to help the headache," he offered neutrally.

"I wasn't referring to her physical discomfort," the pastor returned. Head canted slightly to one side, fingers idly stroking the underside of his chin, his gaze moved from Jake to Olivia. "A time or two, when you're not watching her, I've seen her look your way with the kind of soul-sick pain that would make the angels weep." To Jake's astonishment, one of Carmody's hands warmly gripped his shoulder. "They don't need me until two o'clock, so right now I'm sort of in the way no matter where I stroll. I think you're in the same boat, so. . .my office is just down the hall, away from the teeming hordes. Care to join me?"

The last thing, the very *last* thing Jake needed was a meddling, Bible-thumping preacher spouting off pious phrases. On the other hand—

"Sure, why not?" He shrugged, following Carmody and wondering if he'd finally gone round the bend for good.

A quiet oasis, the wood-paneled office was lined on two walls with floor-to-ceiling bookcases, the shelves full to overflowing. Sunlight streamed through a window onto the restful burgundy carpet. Off to one side a loveseat and two matching chairs surrounded a low table centered with a vase of cheerful yellow daffodils.

The preacher took one of the chairs, gesturing Jake toward the other. Ignoring the invitation, Jake prowled the room, reading some of the book titles, his skin crawling.

"Care for some coffee? Wedding punch?" Behind the glasses, brown eyes twinkled. "They're setting up the reception in our fellowship hall, and I reckon I could sneak us a couple of cups."

"No, thanks." Jake's eye fell on a worn Bible lying open on the table, next to the daffodils. With a sense of deep foreboding, he sat down. "Have you known Olivia very long?"

"She's done two weddings here, but I don't know her well. She's not a member of this church. And you?"

Okay, so he'd known when he came in here the guy would try to pick his brain, then start delivering sermons. If Jake objected. . .well, all he had to do was tell the preacher to take a hike. On the other hand, his best hope of understanding Olivia might be found with this man, who sat there watching Jake with the kindest pair of eyes he'd ever seen in his life.

"I've known her a couple of months now," Jake finally answered. Abruptly, he decided to see just what it took to rattle the Reverend Michael Carmody's cage. "I want her," he stated baldly, investing as much crudeness in the phrase as he could manage.

"I know," the preacher replied with a smile, almost knocking Jake out of the chair. "Don't look so surprised. You make it very obvious, you know—at least to me. Tell me—," he leaned forward—"does Olivia return your feelings?"

Jake couldn't remember the last time he'd blushed, but he could feel the heat burning all the way to the back of his skull. Maybe he ought to blister the man's ears, but good, with some of the choice phrases he'd learned over the years. . . but, no. He was a grown man, not a squirming adolescent boy who needed his mouth washed out with Aunt Sophy's lye soap.

Clenching his jaw, hands flexing on the chair arms, Jake met Carmody's gaze. "I think so, but she told me just before we arrived here that she doesn't want to see me anymore because I'm not a Christian." Rage and frustration and hostility boiled up and over, propelling him to his feet. He stood over the preacher and all but snarled. "So here's your chance. Don't you want to 'share the Good News?' 'Take me down the Roman road?' Convince me I need to be 'washed in the blood so I'll be saved?' "

"Sounds to me as if you've heard those words enough. From Olivia?"

Did nothing spook this man? "She knows better. Besides, she's so caught up being a martyr for her father, she hasn't had time to try her luck reforming me yet."

"A martyr for her father? Can you clarify that for me?" He held up a hand. "And no, I'm not asking you to divulge confidences or feel any more awkward than you already do." He watched Jake with a steady, unflappable compassion that all of a sudden reminded Jake of Garrick, except two more dissimilar men he'd never met. "Something's eating at you, son, isn't it? If you need to talk, why not give me a try? I promise not to back you into corners or preach any sermons."

Jake collapsed into the chair, propping elbows on knees, and resting his head in his hands. "I've never had much use for religion or people who call themselves Christians," he confessed. Then he lifted his head. "But I've never met anyone like you. Or Olivia. And I guess you might say I'm about to go crazy. Listen, Reverend or Doctor or—"

"Mike'll do just fine, son."

"Mike, then. You know a lot about this stuff, right?" He waved his hand toward the Bible.

"Some. Most days I learn how little I really do know."

Jake ignored the dry note of humor. It reminded him too much of Olivia. "Tell me why God would take a beautiful woman of poise and charm and compassion, and ruin her life by making her atone for the cruelty of her father?"

For the first time surprise flashed across the preacher's face. "God *wouldn't*," he responded instantly, firmly. "He doesn't work like that."

Jake's hands lifted and fell. "Not according to Olivia. She claims she has to go around making people forgive her father, so that she can be free. 'Right with God,' she put it once." He snorted. "Doesn't make sense to me. I don't think I've ever met a woman less 'free' than Olivia. And yet she's so committed to Christ she'll throw away any chance we might have, just because I'm not willing to shackle myself in those kinds of chains."

Lines of concern deepened in Mike's face, and the twinkle in his eyes was replaced by a small but intense flame. "I think," he began carefully, "that what we have here is a gigantic misinterpretation of God's Word. . .on both your parts. Let me make sure I understand—Olivia is trying to pay for something her father did? Yet she claims to be a Christian?"

"You got it. I know all about how Jesus died for mankind's sins. Could probably quote a few verses if I wanted to take the time to remember them. But when I try to point that out to Olivia, she just trots out this garbage about all the shame and guilt she feels because of who her father was." Mike looked blank so Jake obliged, too deeply involved now to care about Olivia's sensibilities. "Alton Sinclair. Chief loan officer and vice president of Fidelity Bank in Logan County. A twentieth-century Scrooge with a healthy dollop of Rasputin tossed in. Real charmer. He died in January. According to Olivia, she, her mother, and Sinclair's brother were the only three who attended his funeral. Not even the other two kids bothered to come. Olivia's the youngest and, for whatever reason, has taken on the burden of convincing people to forgive her old man's heinous deeds."

"Sounds to me as if Olivia is the one who needs to forgive her father."

"You're welcome to try to convince her."

Mike shook his head. "Forgiveness has to come from the heart, and only God can change hearts, son. That's a lesson every pastor learns, some of us the hard way. Now. . .take yourself."

Jake sat up, all of a sudden feeling very uneasy. "What about me?"

"Don't look so nervous. I just wanted to ask you a question." After a moment Jake gave a curt nod, and Mike leaned forward, his gaze unswerving, full of that disconcerting compassion. "Who is it *you* need to forgive for so poisoning your mind against God that all you see—like Olivia—is judgment, and none of His love?"

ॐ

Olivia signaled the organist, then slipped back into the small side room at the back of the church, where a nervous bride and three bridesmaids waited. Seconds later Rollie appeared with the father of the bride—Rollie bustling, efficient, and Mr. Wells, more nervous than his daughter and all three bridesmaids put together.

"Everything's ready," Rollie whispered to Olivia. Her gaze settled on Olivia's swollen, hideously discolored forehead and cheek. "I do hope none of the other guests catches sight of you. That's why *I'm* here helping, remember?"

Judy, radiant in spite of bridal jitters, slipped a careful arm about Olivia and hugged her, engulfing Olivia in rustling taffeta and the heady spice of gardenia blossoms. "I can't thank you enough for being here, when we all know how dreadful you feel."

"And *look*," Olivia added, touching her cheek and wincing. At least the doctor's pills had eased the headache. "Now, remember. . .smile! You're giving yourself to the wonderful, loving man God picked out just for you. Not only that, but your wedding has been skillfully organized by the best consultant service in three states! Now how on earth could you keep from smiling?"

A gust of light laughter rippled through the room, and everyone relaxed. As the last of the guests were seated, Olivia quietly positioned herself in back, by the last pew. "Here we go," she whispered moments later, sending the first bridesmaid down the aisle to the stirring strains of the processional.

And none of them—not even Rollie—suspected that, deep inside, Olivia's heart was slowly breaking into a million pieces.

Chapter Fourteen

When Olivia finally dragged herself outside the church a little past four-thirty, Jake was sitting on the hood of his car, waiting. She hesitated, and he slid down, walking toward her with lazy, catlike grace. In the golden afternoon sunlight his hair gleamed like the satin sheen of a black tuxedo lapel.

Suddenly nervous, Olivia darted a swift glance about the almost deserted lot. "Where's Rollie, or should I ask?"

Jake paused a few feet away, watching Olivia with the unswerving concentration of a falcon hovering over a rabbit hole. "With some—persuasion, shall we say?—I sent her on her way. You and I have some unfinished business."

For hours Olivia had been dictating the movements of excited, malleable girls and awkward men who looked sheepish and uncomfortable in the rental tuxedos. Standing before her now in faded jeans and chambray shirt, Jake bore about as much resemblance to that crowd as a bubbling brook to Niagara Falls.

But Olivia knew she might as well try to contain Niagara with a teaspoon as to try and tell Jake Donovan anything. She tried anyway. "There's no need," she told him, starting down the steps. "I'm exhausted, and my face feels like a block of concrete. Jake, please, can't you just accept what I told you this morning?"

"You really are tired, to ask a ridiculous question like that." Humor danced across his face. "Want me to carry you to the car?"

A flowing warmth swooped through Olivia in a groundswell, turning her stomach in a flip-flop. Her traitorous body easily conjured up the heady sensation of relaxing into Jake's strong, protective arms. *No way,* she opened her mouth to say, but "Yes," floated out instead.

Something flickered behind the gray eyes watching her so closely, and a deep chuckle wrapped around her heart as Jake's arms encircled her aching body. "You're always surprising me, sweetheart." He picked her up carefully, holding her close. "Here I am, geared for a battle royal, and you surrender without even lifting your sword."

"I'm too tired for fancy word games." She relaxed against him and closed her eyes, and tried not to think at all. "Jake, this is all wrong, and you're only going to make things worse."

"You'll feel better after we eat, and you take a nap." He placed her in the passenger seat, fastened her seat belt, then dropped a warm kiss on Olivia's drooping mouth. "Smile for me. It's not the end of the world."

"I wish you'd revert to your former intimidating self. I can fight that better." *Olivia, what are you saying?* She might as well send him an engraved announcement of her feelings.

"I don't want us to fight. I want us to communicate." He slid in beside her and started the car. "And, Olivia, I'll tell you right up front I had an extremely interesting conversation with Mike Carmody while you were playing Madame Wedding Director earlier today." His voice was soft, friendly—and implacable.

"Oh?" Headache and fatigue forgotten, Olivia sat up in the seat. She stared out the window, wondering where Jake was taking her, since they were heading back toward the interstate. "What about?"

"Lots of things. Like you, and me, and you and me. Like you and your father. Like—," he hesitated as if searching for words, and Olivia's head swiveled around. Jake, looking tentative? "Like a view of God so radically different from yours, from the one rammed down my throat when I was growing up, that I'm having trouble grasping it. I'd like to talk about it, if you're willing," he finished, very quietly.

If he'd slapped her face, Olivia couldn't have been more dumbfounded. Never, ever in all these last weeks had it occurred to her that Jake would be willing to openly discuss such a volatile subject. And after the way they'd parted this morning, when she'd pretty much closed all the doors. . .it was too much. "I don't understand." Her voice wobbled, sounding as weak and befuddled as her brain.

"I know. Rest now, and we'll talk about it after we get there and you have food and a nap." He reached across the seat to massage the taut muscles at the nape of her neck. "Close your eyes. Relax. We're going to work it out, I promise."

"But where—"

"Shh. You've been in charge all day, now it's my turn. Lean your head back and close your eyes. That's it. Ah—ah. No more questions. Rest, sweetheart—"

And because she was so tired, and so flummoxed, she gave up and did as she was told.

❧

She woke when they stopped and Jake turned off the engine. Dazed and groggy, face painfully stiff, Olivia blinked until her eyes focused on a small clapboard house. It looked somehow familiar. "Where are we?"

Jake came around and opened her door, leaning over. "Beth's. She'll be home in a couple of hours. I couldn't take you to your place because it wouldn't be safe, and I sure wasn't going to come any closer to your two—ah—guardian angels than I had to."

Olivia's spine stiffened. "I really am tired of repeating myself, but I refuse to allow the actions of a coward and a criminal to frighten me out of my own home."

Jake leaned over until his face was only inches away. "You misunderstand," he breathed, gray eyes holding her in a warm, intimate cocoon that paralyzed her breathing. "It's not the stalker I'm thinking about right now, little goose. It's what will happen if I'm alone with you. . .with no chance of interruption."

Olivia gasped. In an outraged flurry of motion, she yanked open the car door and practically fell out, face flaming. Jake—laughing deep in his throat—had to catch her by the waist to keep her from sprawling headlong into the grass. "Be careful you don't hurt your head any worse," he counseled, hauling her up by his side and setting her gently on her feet.

"Why did you say that to me?" she demanded, torn by the equally strong desires to kick him in the shin as hard as she could. . .and melt in a puddle at his feet. "I could never. . .I wouldn't!"

"You think so now, but remember what I told you in your shop? I have an idea that even *Christians* are human—"

This had gone quite far enough. Olivia's head snapped back and, hands on hips, she leveled a look at him that dried up his laughter quicker than snow melts in the hot sun. "Jake Donovan, I can only imagine what kind of women you've associated with in your life. I can further imagine what your response will be to what I'm about to say, but right now I—I just don't care!"

Olivia didn't have much of a temper, but the time or two in her life when something finally provoked her to wrath, she could rival a tornado while the fury lasted. And right now she was tired, hurting, and confused—totally incapable of maintaining any semblance of serenity. Jake's outrageous statement, uttered so confidently, sent the mercury straight over the top of the bulb.

"I will not let you do this to me! You can mock and make snide remarks about God and Christianity all you want, trot out all the clichés men and women in today's society use to justify their behavior. And don't think for one minute that, just because I haven't been around the block like you, means I don't know most of them." Olivia advanced, poking her finger against his chest, forcing him to retreat until he backed smack into the car. " 'Everybody's doing it,' " she mimicked in scathing sarcasm. " 'Who's it going to hurt if we both agree?' 'Hardly anybody waits until marriage anymore—' Does that cover most of it?"

"Olivia, I wasn't trying—"

"*Let me finish!*" Olivia roared, oblivious to her stiff face and the anvil pounding away in her skull. "I don't care *how* much I love you, Jake Donovan, I will *not* make love to any man except the man I marry. I may be the world's most messed-up Christian, but I do know the difference between right and wrong. Now leave me alone! Do you hear me?"

"I imagine the whole block can hear," Jake drawled, a strange light kindling the gray eyes, turning them to molten silver.

Breathing hard, Olivia glared around, ready to blister any unfortunate soul careless enough to have wandered within earshot. Then she realized what she'd said, and her verbal tornado evaporated with an abrupt little poof. Her gaze met Jake's, and she closed her eyes. "What have I done?" she whispered. "Dear Lord, what have I done?"

She felt Jake's hands on her arms, tugging her toward him. "No!" She wrenched free, heart pounding. She wanted to run, hide, disappear for at least a hundred years.

"Don't do this, Olivia." He made no move to reach out again.

Rigid, eyes monitoring every muscle twitch, every breath he took, Olivia frantically willed herself to be calm, in control. Lift her chin and face him down. She wasn't the first woman in the world to make a fool of herself over a man, and she wouldn't be the last.

Jake leaned back against the car and forced himself to relax. Very slowly, very casually he stuffed one hand in the front pocket of his jeans, the other on the car door. He had to be very careful. "Listen to me," he ordered, keeping his voice low, calm. "Olivia? Are you listening?"

Jerkily, she nodded once.

So far, so good. He tried a coaxing smile. "I didn't know you had such a fierce temper. I'll have to be more careful in the future not to provoke it."

Olivia's expression didn't change by so much as the flicker of an eyelash.

Hmm, Jake thought. He studied her flushed face, feeling pretty breathless himself. Over the years he'd enjoyed the attentions of a lot of forgettable women, some of whom had whispered honeyed words of love to his face, while mentally counting his money. And if they didn't care about his financial assets, all they wanted was a good time. To them, he was nothing but a challenge, untamable, like the big game he'd tracked a few times in the wilderness.

In all this time Jake had never really trusted the love of any other person outside of his sister Beth. And that included the first and last woman he had ever asked to be his wife.

"Did you know I was married once?" Ah. That little revelation elicited a response. Olivia blinked owlishly, throat muscles working. But at least she was listening now. "I was only nineteen. My wife died giving birth to our child." He'd never confessed the deeply buried secret to another person other than Sherm, who Jake knew would carry the information to the grave.

Now, desperate as he'd never been, even all those years ago, Jake unlocked his soul to Olivia. He owed her some indication of reciprocal trust, even though right now he realized her temper-induced declaration had been unintentional. The trouble was, he couldn't look into Olivia's eyes and share the disgusting story. He turned, staring over the top of the car, and began to talk.

"Maribel was seventeen, and both of us were wild as weasels. I was on my way to the pros, and one weekend we drove up to West Virginia and got hitched. Then I left for spring training. And Maribel realized she didn't want to leave home, after all." Why wouldn't Olivia say something? *Please, God, don't let her shut me out.* He found himself praying for the first time in his life—and meaning it.

"I'd come back when I could, try to convince her. The 'convincing' usually turned into a full-blown argument. Then she got pregnant—" Jake rested his arms on the roof of the car and closed his eyes. "By that time she hated me. And she hated the idea of having the baby. She refused to see a doctor, take care of herself. The town where we lived was two hours from the nearest hospital. She went into labor one night while I was playing a game in New York. By the time I made it home, she was dead. . .along with our son. They told me she died. . .screaming how much she hated us both—"

Behind him came the sound of a muffled sob. Jake spun, and Olivia hurled herself into his arms. "I'm sorry," she choked, tears streaming down her cheeks. "Jake, I'm so sorry. That must have been terrible. . .no wonder you—" She buried her head in his shoulder.

Stunned, Jake struggled to cope with Olivia's abrupt turnabout. Holding her close, automatically rubbing her shoulders and back, fractured thoughts and half-formed sentences crashed drunkenly around his brain. She was crying. . . for him? "Please stop, baby. You're killing me—and probably your head. It's okay, I promise." He kissed her hair, inhaling the piquant aroma of Olivia's perfume—and a lingering antiseptic scent from the medicine daubed on her face at the hospital.

"I'm sorry I told you," he soothed. "I just wanted you to understand, wanted you to know you can trust me not to take advantage of you just because—" *Shut up, Donovan, before you blow it even worse.* He gently tugged the hair at the back of her neck, forcing Olivia to lift her head. Carefully, carefully his hand cupped the uninjured cheek, thumb rubbing the tears away.

Then, helpless against the waterfall of feelings, he began to kiss her, soft, urgent kisses covering her eyes, her forehead, her mouth. In between kisses, he whispered nonsensical phrases, broken endearments, desperate to absorb her pain—and drown out his own.

With an inarticulate moan, Olivia's hands slid around the back of his neck and she clung to him so desperately that something deep inside Jake shifted, then melted away. And he knew that—no matter what she said—Olivia Sinclair loved him. Not just from her head, or her wildly swinging emotions, but from the heart.

Dear God, Jake prayed, *if You're anything like Mike Carmody said, I need help. Really bad, really quick.*

Chapter Fifteen

March blew into April, and Olivia's face healed. There were no further attacks on either her person or her possessions. The police continued to patrol her neighborhood regularly, and every few days one would check in at The Bower.

Rollie left for a week-long trip to Raleigh, Richmond, and Atlanta to check on new suppliers. Maria insisted that Olivia phone her every evening at bedtime and in the morning before she left for work. Tired of protesting, Olivia complied.

Days were checked off with clockwork efficiency. She continued to volunteer at Sherm's Shelter, and one rainy Saturday afternoon, she again accompanied Beth on her weekend visit to Davy.

Neither of them had heard from Jake for close to two weeks.

"What do you think Jake wants out of life?"

Beth stopped right in the middle of the corridor leading to Davy's room, staring up at Olivia in astonishment. "Why on earth would you ask me that now? Here? You don't speak ten words the whole drive over, and now that we're on Davy's doorstep, you ask a mind-boggling question like what I think my brother wants out of life?"

Always too thin, too pale, and too tired, Beth nonetheless manifested a bedrock kind of upbeat endurance Olivia envied. She was also never too tired to broadcast whatever was on her mind.

Olivia ducked her head to hide a flicker of amusement. "I haven't had the courage to bring it up before now," she replied. "And I also decided if I gave you time to think, you'd just manufacture a plausible answer you figured would be more palatable to my ears than the truth."

Both women stepped aside for a wheelchair-bound elderly man being pushed by an orderly. The orderly, a whippy-looking young man with one earring, flashed them a cheeky grin. To Olivia's surprise, Beth blushed.

"What was *that* about?"

Nervously fingering her purse, Beth shrugged. "Oh. . .that's Ray. He's tried to flirt with me a time or two, once in front of Davy. Nothing serious, but the last time I was here, Davy tried to imitate Ray. . .and put his arm around my waist too." She smiled sadly. "That's the first and last gesture of affection I've had from my husband in three years."

"I'm sorry." Olivia hugged her briefly. "I have a nerve, don't I, picking your brain about Jake. You're in an impossible situation, Beth. I think I admire you about as much as anybody I know."

They reached the door to Davy's room, and Beth flashed her a grateful look. "Thanks, Olivia. For whatever it's worth, what you're doing—coming here with me, I mean—means a lot to me. Jake thinks you have a lot of class, and I'd have to agree." She opened the door. "Hi, Davy Crockett! Look who's back for a visit today."

Davy had been sitting on the floor beneath the window, playing with some plastic cowboys and Indians Olivia had brought on her last visit. At Beth's cheerful greeting, he looked up, two tiny figures clutched in each hand. A tall gangling man with tousled strawberry blond hair and a wide grin, the look of vapid ingenuousness never failed to chill Olivia's blood. *How in the world does Beth stand it?*

She followed Davy's wife—wife!—across the floor and knelt with her beside Davy. "Hi, Davy." She forced herself to take his hand and pump it up and down.

Davy's pale green eyes smiled vacantly up at her. "Hi." He seldom spoke beyond simple greetings and an occasional giggle. The young man who had once dreamed of running his own small-engine repair shop. . .now played on the floor with plastic baby toys. Olivia never knew whether to cry—or rage—at both her father and Davy.

Watching Beth sitting cross-legged on the floor, quietly sharing the events of her day as if Davy understood every word, Olivia had to quell an uprush of tears. Ever since Jake left almost a month ago, her emotions had seesawed violently. She hadn't felt like crying like this since she was a lonely teenager.

"Ah, love!" Maria would wave her hands and look superior. "Crying comes with the territory, kiddo."

With determined cheerfulness, Olivia dug into the huge floral totebag she'd brought along. Dragging out a coloring book and box of crayons, she knelt on the floor, holding them out. "Look, Davy, I've brought you a present." She and Beth spent the next few minutes coloring with Davy, and when he lost interest, Olivia laid everything aside. "I'll wait in the lobby," she told Beth.

She always left Beth alone for the last thirty minutes or so of their visit. It was in these moments that she knew Beth tried to talk to Davy as if he were still a responsible man—husband, provider, protector, friend. Olivia might feel she herself needed to earn forgiveness, help pay for her father's sins, but she could not bear to witness this—this travesty of a relationship.

What would I do if Jake turned into a living mockery of a man? The very idea was a torture. Would she still accept and love him as Beth did Davy. . .or was she her father's daughter, after all, with shallow, selfish emotions that could be turned on and off like a water faucet?

Deep in thought, Olivia wandered back down the bright, sterile corridor to the lobby. In the long run, the depth of her love for Jake might be totally irrelevant. They had made no permanent commitment to each other, nor had Jake voiced aloud any passionate avowals of love for her.

In fact, when he told her good-bye last time, he'd been almost offhand, pre-occupied. "I think we both have some serious thinking to do, and being apart might make it easier right now." Olivia wasn't sure what kind of serious thinking a man indulged in while white water rafting, but with Jake, one never knew.

"I looked up one of the guys on my team who claimed he was a Christian," Jake had said in that same farewell conversation. "It's pretty humbling, I have to admit. I used to ridicule Tony, claim he was no better than the rest of us. He always agreed, said he *wasn't* better. . .just saved. When we talked the other day, I saw how wrong I was years ago. He might not be better, but he is different." Then Jake had cupped her chin. "He doesn't wallow in shame, Olivia. In fact, he reminded me a bit of this guy I met in Canada. And I think. . .I think I want to know more. And I think you need to take a look at a few things too."

Then he'd kissed her. "Throw out the old rule book, little one. We both might be surprised."

Right, Olivia thought now. If she believed that, she might as well move to New York and open a shop on Fifth Avenue.

Beth joined her forty minutes later.

"Any luck?" Olivia asked, and as always Beth shook her head.

After each visit with Davy, Olivia had noticed that it took Beth quite a while to return to her own reality. On the drive back to her home in Granite Falls, Beth would sit motionless in her seat, head back and eyes closed, drained and limp as week-old cut flowers. Then, stretching, shrugging her shoulders as if to slip off the unbearable emotional weight, she returned to her normal gregarious, artless self.

Today she surprised Olivia. "I talked to Davy about your question. Remember. . .you were wondering what Jake wants out of life? Davy was a big help." She grinned across at Olivia. "He let me talk without interrupting until I sorted out some thoughts."

"Beth, I didn't mean—"

"If you apologize again for what you perceive as your guilt over the way *my* life turned out, I'll open the door and jump out while you're driving sixty. Now . . .about my big brother." She rolled the window down a little, took a deep breath. "We both know one of the things he wants is you."

Olivia shifted uneasily, and Beth laughed. "Don't worry, I won't embarrass you like I did the day you'd been walloped by a brick, when I came home from work early and surprised the two of you right there in the driveway—"

Olivia scowled with mock ferocity. "Maybe it *would* be a good idea for you to jump out of the car."

"Okay, okay." Beth fiddled with the buttons on her blouse a moment, then threw up her hands in a gesture of surrender. "You and your Christian principles have tied Jake up in knots, and you know it. It's tying me in knots too. It blows me away that Jake's starting to talk like that himself. This is the man who used to run off to another continent if someone even suggested he might benefit from poking his head through a church door once a year or so." She gave a wry grin.

"And it was the kiss of death for any woman to even hint at the possibility of a long-term 'commitment.' Now. . .now my brother not only goes around talking like a preacher, he's making weird noises about settling down. I know he doesn't plan to kiss you off like he has all the other women who've made fools of themselves over him the last ten years or so. No offense."

"None taken." Olivia sighed. Sometimes Beth's ruthless candor could be as hard-hitting as Jake's.

"Nope," Beth continued, "Jake's not ready to write you off. But as to how that fits in with what he plans to do in the long run, your guess is as good as mine, Olivia. Jake's been a rolling stone and a rootless wanderer all his life—even before Maribel." She shook her head. "I still can't believe he told you about that. Between that—and catching him reading the Bible that last week before he left —about the only thing I know for sure is that he's changing."

There went her heart again, cartwheeling like her stomach. Olivia passed her tongue over suddenly dry lips. "You really do think he's changing?"

Beth nodded. "Yep. He keeps mumbling about this different view of God, and how maybe Jesus was more than just a reason for Christians to feel guilty all the time. You know, it's hard enough trying to understand your crackpot desire to pay for everything your father did. But now Jake's spouting off all these weird ideas about how Jesus was really God's plan to make everybody feel *free*, not guilty. I don't know what on earth is going on between the two of you, Olivia, but it's not like any relationship with a woman he's ever had before. Like I said, he's changing."

Looking unsettled and uncomfortable, Beth abruptly leaned forward and flipped on the radio. "Used to be all Jake wanted out of life was another mountain to climb. Now I don't have a clue as to what he *really* wants."

≈

Rollie, Maria—and Sergeant MacClary—were waiting in Olivia's driveway when she pulled up a few hours later. So many horrific possibilities stormed through Olivia's brain, the car almost plowed into the back of the police cruiser.

She threw open the door. "What is it? What's happened? The Bower?"

"Now, don't go pitching a hissy fit," Rollie interjected as Olivia skidded to a halt in front of them. "Everything's fine, except we're about to perish from boredom and thirst, waiting for you to stroll along home."

Rolling her eyes at the older woman, Maria took pity on Olivia. "Jake called," she announced baldly, grinning at Olivia's flabbergasted silence. "That's not the end of it. Next he called Sergeant MacClary." She nodded to the policeman. "This, now, is the kicker—Olivia, he wants you to join him."

"In Georgia," Rollie added. "But not tempting death in some little rubber boat going down the Chattooga. He wants you to join him at the home of some friends of his."

Sergeant MacClary, looking resigned but relieved, finally added his two cents. "Since you continue to refuse to move in with someone else a while, this would at least provide a mite more safety while me and the boys close in on our suspect."

Olivia caught her breath. "You found the woman driving the car?" she asked, ignoring for the moment Jake's high-handed machinations. "Why haven't you told me?"

"We-ell. . .I'm telling you now. But don't go getting too excited. We're hopeful, but we still have to check on a few things." To Olivia's growing frustration, he wouldn't add anything further except to say, "It would make my supper settle easier if you took a nice little trip for a week."

Tapping her foot, Olivia's gaze raked all three of them. "I appreciate the concern, but Jake had no right to go behind my back like this. Besides, this is our busiest season. I couldn't possibly go traipsing off in the woods somewhere right now." *Even though I'd love to just toss it all to the wind to be with Jake, no matter how it was arranged. . . .*

Hands on hips, Maria thrust out a stubborn chin. "Oh, yes, you can. Rollie and I have talked it over, and we've figured out a way to manage everything for one week without you to oversee, remind, plan, and otherwise check off blocks in your planner. So you're going and that's that."

"Olivia, you could use a vacation and you know it," Rollie chimed in. "You haven't taken any time off in at least four years."

Olivia wanted to pull her hair in exasperation and sheer disbelief. "What is this? You're all practically throwing me at the same man you threatened to boil in oil only weeks ago—"

At least Rollie had the good grace to look uncomfortable. Maria merely continued to smile like a gleeful matchmaker.

"Ah. . .can we talk about this inside, ladies?" Sergeant MacClary suggested, removing his cap and mopping his brow. "It's been a tad warm, waiting out here."

"Certainly." Olivia stalked up the path. "But I'm not going. I don't have time. . .it's simply out of the question."

Chapter Sixteen

Jake met her at Hartsfield International Airport in Atlanta. They hadn't seen each other in over a month, and so much had happened Jake couldn't decide if the time had flown in microseconds or dragged in decades. In those weeks he'd found himself waking in the predawn hours, listening a while in the dark reverent hush of night—and almost feeling God's affirming, sustaining Presence. It was so real, so life-transforming, that now it was Jake's former restless, wandering spirit that seemed alien and distant.

He still had a lot to learn, of course.

And he had some explaining to Olivia to get out of the way first, before he shared anything else. Waiting for her plane, surrounded by the crush of seething humanity, Jake was sweating bullets.

Okay, so maybe he should have called her to make the arrangements, instead of ambushing her through Maria and Rollie. Originally, he had called Olivia's friends to enlist their aid on how best to approach Olivia, and to convince them that his intentions—to quote the time-honored chestnut—were entirely honorable this time.

Maria persuaded him to circumvent Olivia entirely. "Trust me," she urged. "She needs someone to dictate her life for a while. And though I never dreamed I'd be saying this, in spite of first appearances, I think you just might be the man for the job here. Oh. . .while you're at it, see if you can charm her into throwing away her daily planner. She's giving me and Rollie flying duck fits, organizing us to the point when she schedules what time we can blow our noses."

The intercom crackled to life, announcing the arrival of Olivia's flight. Jake jerked upright, pulse wild as the Chattooga River rapids. *You there, God? I hope so, since Olivia's just as likely to deck me as she is to kiss me.*

Beyond that, he wondered what Olivia's reaction would be when he did have the chance to share the unbelievable odyssey that had led him from the white water of his former life to the quiet streams King David talked about in his book of Psalms. From a man who eschewed all ties to a man who was now committed to a lifelong relationship. A bonafide, one-to-one personal relationship with a Person whose reality Jake had spent a lifetime denying. As he'd done for days now, Jake searched his feelings, testing them. He still found mostly warmth and acceptance, while the residue of denial and panic continued to diminish.

Passengers from Olivia's flight began straggling through the door. Jake breathed deeply, forcing himself to be calm, watching from a spot off to the side where he could see Olivia before she saw him. When she finally appeared, clutching a huge floral tote in one hand and her briefcase-sized purse in the other, Jake's insides clenched in a sharp, exultant stab of sheer possessiveness.

Whether Olivia was ready to admit it or not, she was his.

Then Jake looked into her face. *Okay, Donovan, put a lid on it, fella.* Her mouth was set, face chalky, her pupils so distended her eyes looked like two black pits. Jake shouldered his way through the crowd in a silent rush. "Olivia." Then he stood there, just drinking in the reality of her presence.

His silence met head-on Olivia's indomitable control. "Well. . .I'm here." He saw her fingers move convulsively, but her step didn't falter as she walked straight up to Jake—looking steadfastly over his right shoulder the whole time.

"I see that," Jake replied, suddenly feeling as tongue-tied and dull as a twelve-year-old schoolboy. "Now. . .let's get out of here. I hate airports."

"I need to make a phone call first."

Her brittle, too-calm facade was driving him mad, but Jake at least had found his temper easier to control lately. "You can find a phone in the main terminal. I'll show you," he managed just as politely.

He waited—torn between incredulity and impatience—while she called Maria at The Bower and spent twenty minutes delivering three pages of instructions she'd apparently written on the flight down. Jake began to see what Maria meant about that daily planner.

Finally, after receiving Maria's promise to call Olivia's mother, and to check in with Sergeant MacClary at least twice a week, Olivia hung up. She smoothed her hands over her jacket, then brushed her hair back and turned to Jake, still looking like a professional female on a business trip.

Jake wanted to ruffle her hair and to shuck her from the jacket like an ear of corn. "Do you need anything to eat?" he inquired instead, wincing inside at the barbed civility of his own voice. Olivia coolly shook her head; maybe instead of hair-ruffling and coat-shucking, he should toss her over his shoulder—or dump her right here in the middle of the airport and let her find her own way back home. As always, his and Olivia's reunions never went the way Jake planned.

"Give me your baggage claim." Slowly, Olivia retrieved it from her purse and held it out. Jake plucked it from her fingers—and felt as if he'd plunged his hand into a bucket of ice cubes.

Their eyes met, and Jake watched as before his eyes the prickly professional pose crumbled, then dissolved like a sack of wet sugar. He tucked the ticket in his pocket, gently relieved Olivia of the cumbersome tote, then enclosed her cold, trembling hands in his own. "You're afraid, aren't you? So much so you've turned into a block of ice, inside and out."

Lifting her hands, he gently blew his warm breath across the chilled fingers, seeing for the first time the lines of strain around her mouth, her eyes. "What is it, sweetheart? I know they couldn't have bullied you into coming if you were really that scared of facing me away from your own turf, so to speak."

She ducked her head, faint color seeping under her skin. "It's not just that," she finally muttered.

"Then what?" Jake prodded, hefting the ridiculous tote over one shoulder while his fingers continued to stroke her trembling hand and the inside of her wrist where the pulse fluttered like a trapped animal's.

"I've. . .never flown before."

He couldn't have heard right. Letting the tote slide with a heavy thud to the ground, Jake took her by the shoulders and turned her toward him. "You've never flown? Not once in your entire life?"

"It's not a crime," she snapped, sounding cranky and belligerent and sheepish all at the same time.

Jake couldn't help it. He laughed, pulled her close and kissed her soundly, oblivious to the grinning passersby swarming past in an endless tide. "And here I was terrified your feelings toward me might have changed—" He kissed her again, bottling the protests. "Shh. . .lying's a sin, remember?"

That laughing aside earned him five minutes of stunned silence which carried them all the way down to the baggage claim area. Then, during the next irritating minutes of retrieving her single suitcase, the long walk to the Rover, and waiting to leave the car park, Olivia searched his features, would start to speak, then clamp her mouth shut again.

Not until they were headed north on the freeway did she finally manage to phrase a question, only it wasn't the one Jake had hoped for. "Is this yours?" she queried, gesturing to the Toyota Range Rover he drove. Apparently she still needed to reassess her faltering defensive line a while longer.

"Nope. Belongs to a friend of mine, Luke Farringer. That's where we're headed, by the way. He and his wife run an injured wildlife preserve a little over two hours north of here. You'll like them."

"You mean I'm not going to be screaming down a river in a little rubber raft or dangling off the side of a mountain on a rope the width of a clothesline?"

Now that was vintage Olivia. Jake felt his muscles relaxing, and a headache he hadn't even been aware of receded. "Well. . .I suppose I could arrange something, but I don't think you're quite ready to tackle 'Screaming Left Turn Rapids' or the 'Corkscrew' quite yet. As for climbing, maybe the hills behind the Farringers' place." He flicked her a challenging grin. "I know lots of hidden, private spots to show you."

"A day or two ago, your sister threatened to jump out of my car while I was driving along at about sixty miles an hour," Olivia mused, finally relaxing her spine enough to rest against the seat. "That kind of talk makes me want to jump too. . .and you're doing a little better than sixty."

I love you. He almost said the words aloud, but checked himself just in time. Jake had spent the last two weeks planning his moves carefully, as carefully as he planned his trips—methodically, down to the last detail, leaving nothing to chance. In that way, he and Olivia were very much alike. Jake smiled to himself. Soon, very soon, his lady-love would be discovering they had more in common than she could possibly have dreamed.

૪ઢ

Luke and Cattleya Farringer lived on three hundred acres of some of the most beautiful land on God's earth. Jake loved to visit them in the spring, when the wooded hills were all decked out in every shade of green on the palette, and redbuds and rhododendron were bursting open in a riot of color. The melodious gurgle of the stream could be heard at the bottom of the meadow behind their house. Delicate yellow trillium magically sprouted between dew-wet tree trunks. Graceful deer visited in the meadow at dusk.

If Jake ever decided to settle down, it would be somewhere in the southern Appalachians in a place like this. If he settled down. . . .

The Rover bounced its way up the winding dirt two-track road leading to the Farringers', and Jake waited to feel the old knee-jerk compulsion to head for the hills.

Out of the corner of his eye, he watched Olivia absorbing the peace and incredible beauty. Rolling the window down, she filled her lungs with the crisp, biting air of late afternoon. To his surprise, the only emotion registering with Jake was the consuming desire to have this woman with him—in a place like this.

So. . .You really do make new creatures out of us.

He tooted the horn as they rounded the last curve leading into the lush valley where Hope Hill sprawled under the shadow of the southern Appalachians. The track led right to the magnificent rambling old Victorian house Luke and Leya had spent the last seven years renovating.

At the sound of the horn, Joey Farringer and his usual assortment of animals spilled from the doors, off the wraparound porches, from under the porches. Across the yard Josh, Joey's twin brother, shimmied down a tree and scampered across the field like a chipmunk.

Olivia turned to Jake. "I've never seen anything more beautiful or. . .welcoming."

"I know exactly what you mean," Jake replied, his gaze resting on Olivia's wondering face. "Now, the two whirling dervishes approaching are Josh and Joey Farringer, five-year-old twins and occasional unholy terrors. Luke and Leya also take in foster kids. They've only got two at the moment because. . . Hi, Josh! How's it going, man?"

"You took forever to get here, Jake!" the child scolded. "I was the lookout, but I fell asleep." The blue-eyed urchin clambered up the side of the Rover and Jake ruffled the silky brown hair. His brother Joey dashed up to join Joshua, the only distinguishing mark setting the twins apart, the scar on Josh's forehead from falling out of the tree last year. Jake knew the boy was proud of that scar because it matched one on his mother's cheek.

"Okay, guys, back off so I can introduce you to my friend Olivia." Leya appeared in the front door of the house, then started across with Marsha, the fifteen-year-old girl who'd only been here a couple of months. Jake reached for Olivia's hand. "You look like a missionary about to be sacrificed to the cannibals. . .which is a good metaphor, since Leya used to be a missionary."

Olivia took another deep breath of the fresh country air. Her fleeting smile disappeared, along with the faint wash of blue in her uncertain eyes.

Jake winked at the twins, then slid across the front seat to wrap an arm around Olivia and hug her close. He wanted badly to kiss her, but knew that would only embarrass her, so he nobly resisted temptation. Just. "Knowing you, within two days you'll have the whole place marching to your tune—including the twins. Maybe I'd better warn everyone while I have a chance."

This time her smile lingered.

Jake leaned over and opened her door as Leya and Marsha drew abreast. "Well, here she is at last, gals. Olivia Sinclair, meet Cattleya Farringer and Marsha."

"Welcome to Hope Hill, Olivia." Leya held out a slim brown hand. "Luke and I are delighted you're here. Luke should be along for dinner. He's down at the corral with Nails. Nails is our. . .foreman, I suppose you might say," she explained to Olivia. "He accompanied some mustangs from New Mexico six years ago and refused to leave. He's been here ever since."

Jake followed Olivia out her side of the vehicle, then swept Leya up in a careful embrace. She was seven months pregnant and Jake—like Luke—tended to treat her like one of the fragile orchids for which she'd been named. Her long red-gold hair was coiled in its usual neat coronet on top of her head, the smiling eyes deep pools of serenity. Luke Farringer is one lucky guy, Jake thought. Or rather, he checked himself, he's been greatly blessed by God.

To the world, the result might be the same. Jake, however, had learned that therein lay a world of difference.

Chapter Seventeen

A storm swept over the mountains that evening, deluging Hope Hill with torrential rain and sending booming thunder rolling down over the hills. Olivia helped Leya prepare a late supper for the adults, while Marsha and Ben, their other foster child, supervised the twins' bedtime preparations. Jake and Luke braved the weather to double-check all the animals.

"We have livestock in two barns and wild animals in a third barn a mile or so away," Leya explained while she and Olivia puttered about the kitchen. "We'll show you tomorrow. It's over a foothill, so the sounds of their calls won't upset the domesticated animals. Our latest pride and joy, though, is the enclosed bird sanctuary Luke finally finished last summer—about half a mile from here."

Lightning lit up the night sky seconds before a teeth-jarring thunderclap rattled the pots and pans hanging above the stove. Leya peered out the window, a tiny frown puckering her smooth brow. "That's probably where he and Jake are now. A ranger over on Springer Mountain brought us a golden eagle who'd been shot last month. It's so frustrating. . .They're an endangered species, and the few left east of the Mississippi are only migratory." She gestured apologetically. "Sorry. I tend to jump right up on the soapbox." She handed Olivia a stack of mismatched plates from the cupboard, all of them unbreakable plastic. "Luke's been spending most of his days there. And a lot of evenings, as you see."

Remembering the depth of worry in Luke Farringer's vivid blue eyes, Olivia nodded. "Your husband is—" she hesitated, uncertain of Leya's response if Olivia voiced her compliment—

Leya turned, her tranquil smile banishing all traces of concern. "I know. Don't worry, Olivia. I won't accuse you of making eyes at my husband if you want to tell me how divinely wonderful he is."

Laughing, Olivia colored. "That's not exactly how I was going to put it, but yes—he is wonderful. Especially with you. He's so loving, and—and gentle." *Like Jake has been on a few memorable occasions with me.* Hope and despair battled in her heart, and she turned away so Leya wouldn't notice.

Unfortunately, Leya was as perceptive as she was friendly. "Jake has shared a little of your past," she volunteered casually. "It's a wonder you let any man within a hundred miles."

Mortified, Olivia didn't say a word, and after a moment Leya pursued the topic with gentle determination. "My father and I didn't get along very well for a long time, but from what Jake shared about yours, my father is a saint by comparison. Please forgive Jake for talking about you, Olivia. It's just that he's needed a sounding board as well as a spiritual counselor these last couple of weeks and. . .well. . .he and Luke have a lot in common." She came and sat down in one of the kitchen chairs, massaging the small of her back. "Whew. Don't you dare let anyone know that sometimes it does feel good to put my feet up a few minutes."

Olivia barely heard her last words. "What did you mean about Jake needing a 'spiritual counselor?' " she asked, dropping down into a chair across from Leya, feeling dazed.

Leya pursed her lips, studying Olivia. "I think," she mused carefully, "maybe it would be better if you heard it from Jake."

At that moment Marsha sidled through the kitchen doorway. "The boys are in bed," she announced in her timid, whispering voice, "but I don't know how long they'll stay, with this storm. Ben let them each take one of Sauce's kittens if they promised not to get up. Was that okay?" She looked, Olivia thought sadly, as if she were waiting to be struck.

"If they can keep the kittens in bed without getting out themselves," Leya returned serenely. "Otherwise, Ben will have to take them to their mama in the cellar. You might also tell him that if he'll read to the twins a while, I'll reward him with some molasses crinkles tomorrow."

"Can I have some, too, Leya?"

"Of course you can, Marsha. Now come here and give me a hug. I'm feeling droopy and need a pick-me-up." Marsha's embrace barely lasted a half second before she scooted back out the kitchen door. She hadn't once looked at Olivia.

"Just a week ago she wouldn't have touched me at all," Leya observed with satisfaction. "Thank You, Lord, for Your healing hands."

And yours and Luke's, Olivia added to herself. She looked down at her own hands, clenched so tightly on the table that the skin was mottling. She wanted to heal people, too, but thus far had met with nothing but failure.

"Before Ben came to live with us, he thought the only kind of books in the world had pictures of naked women in them. . .and the child only eleven years old," Leya continued musing in her lovely soft voice. "It just makes my heart feel all 'squishy,' as the boys would say, when we can see the Lord healing these poor unhappy souls."

"I don't understand how you do it," Olivia suddenly exclaimed, words spewing forth as if she'd sliced open a festering boil. "The children, the animals. . . even this house. . .everything you and Luke touch seems to bloom. And you're always so—so full of joy. . .and peace. I'm a Christian, too, but compared to you, I feel like a Pharisee or something equally despicable!   And no matter how hard I try, I end up making a mess of things!" *If you start crying, Olivia Sinclair, I will never forgive you.*

Suddenly, bright and violent as the lightning bolts outside, a shaft of inner illumination blazed across Olivia's mind. "Oh, dear God—" She stuffed a fist over her mouth. "That's my whole problem isn't it? I hate myself, I hate my father, and that means God can't forgive me, either. I don't know what I'm going to do—"

Cattleya inched her chair around until she could wrap an arm about Olivia's rigid shoulders. "The first thing you're going to do is to stop comparing yourself," she chastised, giving Olivia slight shake, "to me, or to anyone else. If the Lord wanted all of us to be the same, He'd have formed us with a cookie cutter!"

"Well, I know using Jesus as my example makes me look even worse," Olivia joked feebly, but the stinging pressure behind her eyes only intensified. Blinking hard and staring fixedly at her knotted hands, she would have run from the room except she had no place to run to except straight into a storm that mirrored the one raging in her soul.

"Olivia, did you know that—before this baby—I suffered two miscarriages? I almost died after the last one—"

Olivia froze, jerking her head up to face the steady compassion blazing out of Leya's eyes. "The doctor told us I'd probably never carry another child full term . . .yet here I am—," she rubbed her rounded abdomen lovingly— "evidence of another small miracle. God answers prayer in different ways, Olivia. But whatever the answer, it's always given in love. No judgment, not vindictiveness. . .but love. And forgiveness."

Olivia shook her head violently. "I know that! I just don't know how to accept it, internalize it. . .live it. All my life I tried to love my father, to understand him and try to forgive what he did. But *nothing* has worked. *Nothing.* How do you do it? How do you know?"

For a few moments Leya sat in thoughtful silence, absently stroking the jagged white scar on her cheek. Then she pulled one of the pins out of the simple coil holding her incredibly long hair on top of her head and held it out. "One pin at a time," she said, a look of profound sweetness flooding her face. "Life is lived one day at a time. . .just like I put this mass of hair up, one pin at a time, until it's anchored."

Seeing Olivia's gaze on her scar, she lifted her hand and lightly pressed it. "Pretty bad, isn't it? Yet it doesn't bother me at all, because for me it's a battle scar to be proud of. I received it when I was delivering a baby, many years ago, when I was only seventeen. It was also the day I met Luke." Her gaze softened into reminiscence. "He's the one who told me never to be ashamed of my less-than-perfect face, because it would remind me how I'd helped bring a new life into the world."

Olivia didn't understand, and the look of incomprehension must have been obvious.

Smiling, Cattleya tucked the pin back in place. "Luke and I had a hard time, coping with losing two babies," she explained. "Especially when one of the long-term consequences resulted in the death of a cherished dream as well. You see, Hope Hill was planned as more than just a sanctuary for abandoned or injured animals. We also wanted to turn our home into a refuge for disabled or abandoned children." Her smile was now tinged with regret. "Only my health didn't permit it."

Olivia felt the other woman's deep pain as if she had crawled inside her skin. And yet Cattleya Farringer wasn't bitter or guilt-ridden or desperate. Instead, she radiated the love of God all the way to her fingertips. "You must be helping some—Marsha, Ben—"

"We've only been able to accept foster children since last year. And when I became pregnant—and miraculously have kept this one—Luke and I engaged in several epoch-making battles. I see you find that hard to believe. Believe it, Olivia. We're blessed, and love each other very much, but we're certainly no better—or worse—than you and Jake."

"That's impossible," Olivia muttered.

"You just haven't learned to trust God like you need to," Leya finished, lumbering to her feet and moving to put on a pot of coffee. "You're a lot like Jake, you know. Both of you haven't fully grasped the truth of that wonderful chapter in Romans, where Paul writes so magnificently of the nature of God's love. Remember—it's not the past that counts. It's your attitude toward the future. And since *nothing* can separate you from God's love—including and especially the past—well. . .I know that's how I. . .'do it.' Tell you what—why don't you go check it out for yourself while I finish in here? There's a Bible in the den. The answers you find there are a lot more eloquent than mine."

"If Jake and Luke come in and find me lounging around reading while you slave in the kitchen, you'll be feeding my body parts to the birds tomorrow."

A glint appeared in Leya's dove-soft eyes. "You leave the men to me," she promised. "And, Olivia? God wants you to feel His love, His forgiveness, far more than you want to find it."

Forty minutes later the back door banged open and Jake burst through in a wind-and-rain-driven blast. Alerted by the sudden noise, Olivia jumped up from the couch and dashed into the kitchen. Drowsing in a chair, Leya followed more slowly.

Dripping water, Jake was hurriedly rummaging through cabinets and drawers. He looked up when they appeared, face hard, grim. "The eagle's gotten loose. We're going after it. Leya, I need flashlights, a couple of sheets, and a thermos of coffee."

Distressed, Leya didn't waste time with words. Swiftly, efficiently, she produced everything Jake required.

Olivia, standing off to the side feeling unnecessary, suddenly stepped forward. "I'll come too. The more people you have looking, the better chance of finding him."

"No," Jake returned flatly. "It's really bad out there, Olivia. We've got half a dozen people already, and someone needs to—"

"I said I'm coming too."

Jake raised his head and focused on Olivia for the first time. "Olivia—"

"Leya, do you have a coat I can. . .thanks." Olivia thrust her arms in the sleeves of the full-length vinyl slicker Leya grabbed from the back porch. "I'll see to the coffee while you finish finding anything else Jake wants." She shot him a brief stringent look. "Did you drive up in the Rover? Fine—I'll be waiting." And she ran out the door before he could argue with her.

"If you start whining about the weather, I'll truss you up like a goose," he threatened through clenched teeth as they jostled down the road at a bone-rattling speed. "And you'd better do exactly as you're told, or you can stay right here in this vehicle."

"Jake Donovan, you have no right to speak to me that way. I'm not some timid, hysterical little girl afraid of her own shadow. Besides, I'm good with birds. Remember Gretel?"

Lightning streaked across the sky, illuminating the harsh planes of Jake's face, the intimidating hardness of his body. He handled the Rover with ruthless skill, but the road was slick and once, when he turned sharply, Olivia fell against him with a hastily bitten off exclamation.

Incredibly, Jake chuckled. One hand left the wheel long enough to set her right. "Whatever happened to old Gretel the goose?" he asked.

"The lady licensed to take care of wild fowl came three days after Eddie ran off. I helped put Gretel in a cage, and Evie said I had an instinctive rapport that was rare and a relief for her to see."

"So there. All right, Ms. Sinclair—you've made your point."

The Rover skidded to a stop, catching in the rain-drenched yellow glow of the headlights the silhouettes of a half-dozen or so men. Jake killed the engine, then whipped one strong arm out and hauled Olivia close. "Stay with me, and don't get lost." He lowered his head and his mouth came down on hers.

Taken off guard, Olivia stiffened. But when the bruising demand softened into warm beguiling kisses, Olivia melted in spite of herself. She forgot the storm, the eagle, the milling clutch of impatient men. Closing her eyes, she relaxed in the embrace of the man she could not stop loving any more than she could calm the storm.

Someone yanked Jake's door open. "Can't you wait until we've found the bird, Jake?" Luke growled testily. "And what'd you bring her for, anyway? Where's the stuff you were *supposed* to gather?"

Olivia jerked free, wiping her face with shaking hands. "I came to help," she offered in a pitiful attempt at dignity.

"She's got an 'instinctive rapport' with birds," Jake drawled. "Besides which, trying to stop Olivia when she's made up her mind is an exercise in futility." He tugged the hood of Olivia's slicker up and over her head, tied the strings, and dropped a last kiss on her nose. "Remember—stay with me."

Olivia clambered down from the Rover while Jake handed out the supplies. Without asking, she grabbed the coffee and styrofoam cups, filled and passed them out to the men huddled together in the entrance of the barn.

Luke appeared at her side and gratefully downed a cup of coffee in three gulps. "Sorry for what I said. I know Leya would have been here if she could— so, thanks." In the wet, wind-blown darkness his teeth glinted briefly. "I take it you've had some experience with wild birds?"

"One Canada goose, for three days," Jake supplied as he joined Luke, and Olivia almost yielded to the childish urge to sock his jaw. He finished handing out flashlights, then grinned at her. "But I have to admit, she did have that goose eating out of the palm of her hand."

Luke shook his head, then turned to the impatient group. "Okay, everyone. Let's get this done. He can't have gone very far but he's panicked, injured, and, therefore, dangerous. Stay with your group, and remember what I told you about working the bow net. If you find him, do not—I repeat—do *not* shout. Speak calmly, move slowly, and send someone to let me know. Now, let's go."

They split up into three groups, Olivia tagging along with Jake and two men whose size and shape were impossible to determine. Within seconds, Olivia was soaking wet in spite of the protective covering, her face streaming water, vision blurred. She must have been insane to think she could help.

"He can't fly," Jake spoke right next to her ear, "except in short six or seven-foot hops. So look in the underbrush and in lower limbs." He thrust a pencil-thin Swiss Army flashlight into her hand. "Here. Try not to shine that in your face or anyone else's. It will take a while for your night vision to kick in, but do the best you can."

"I will."

Shivering and drenched, half-blind, Olivia tried to creep through the sodden undergrowth quietly, though the stinging sheets of rain and rumbling thunder masked the noise of everyone's movement. Wiping her eyes constantly, she moved the light in a steady back-and-forth motion, straining to see. Praying they would find the bird in time.

Scant feet away, she sensed Jake's presence, occasionally caught the rustling sound of his clothing. She obediently avoided the sweeping light of his high-beam flashlight, and she refused to dwell on either her sodden misery or the anguished look she'd glimpsed on Luke Farringer's face. Back and forth swept her little circle of light as she stumbled along, branches smacking her face and clawing at Leya's slicker. The light passed over a dark mass low in the swaying branches of some kind of hardwood tree.

Olivia took two more steps, then froze. "Jake," she hissed urgently. Turning, she carefully trained her light on the dark mass. It moved! Olivia dropped the beam and sidestepped through a spongy patch of underbrush, hand flailing out to snag a wet fold of Jake's heavy waterproof leather parka.

He stopped. "What is it?"

"Over there, in that tree. . .a little up and to the right of my beam." Her voice trembled with excitement, and she felt Jake's hand briefly press her shoulder.

"I see it. Way to go, sweetheart. That's our bird!" He melted away to alert the other two men.

Seconds later, heart pounding, Olivia followed the trio at a distance, clutching several flashlights so the men could better work their bow net. Six feet from their quarry, they paused. The eagle roused and tried to flee. Only one wing unfurled, causing the majestic bird to tumble gracelessly toward the ground, huge yellow feet clawing wildly at the earth.

Moving with blinding speed, Jake darted around the other side of the tree while the two men approached from the front. Lifting the net high, spreading it wide, they swooped down upon the struggling creature and dropped the mesh over its head. Jake pulled the cord—and it was over.

Olivia didn't realize that the wetness on her face was not only rain, but tears, until her nose plugged up. Moving as calmly as she could, she joined Jake by the bird's side while one of the men took off to alert Luke.

"Don't come too close," Jake warned. "Luke has the rufter and jesses, and until he gets here, keep your distance. One of the bird's talons is pretty weak, but it's still lethal."

"It's awful, having to restrain him like this." Oblivious to prickly clinging leaves and soggy earth, Olivia sank to her knees, eyes never leaving the bound and helpless bird. "It's okay," she began to murmur, as if she were talking to Gretel. " Don't worry—we aren't going to hurt you. We want to help you—so you're free again. Free to soar high, be the majestic bird God designed you to be—" Tears crowded her throat, but she kept talking, kept crooning a hoarse meaningless torrent of words.

And the eagle watched her, its dark eyes unblinking, gray beak quiescent.

Ten minutes later Luke arrived with the leather thongs and hood. Working with incredible speed and gentleness, in a short while he freed the now blind and snaffled bird from the confining net. With almost magical skill, he coaxed the eagle onto his forearm, over the heavy gauntlet, and began the long careful walk back through the woods.

Standing back out of the way, Olivia watched, heart overflowing. When Jake came to tell her it was time to go, all she could do was stare mutely up through the pouring rain into his blurred face. She couldn't see his expression, but all of a sudden his hands were cupping her face. Cold and wet, his touch was warm, and Olivia closed her eyes. He kissed her eyelids, her forehead.

"It's okay," he soothed as Olivia had tried to calm the eagle, his words low, laced with tenderness. "He'll be all right now. And you were great. . .wouldn't be surprised if Luke offered you a job. Shh, now. . .don't cry." He wiped clinging strands of hair away.

Giggling wetly, Olivia rested her cheek against the clammy front of Jake's parka. "I don't know what's the matter with me." She sighed. "Here we are in the woods, in a crash-bang thunderstorm in the middle of the night, and all I can do is weep. It's just. . .the eagle. To be so helpless and humiliated like that, and we were just trying to help—" Her voice broke again.

"Jake—"

He hugged her, wet slicker and all, then grabbed her hand. "Come on, let's get back to warmth and light, and then we'll talk." His hand tightened, then relaxed. "And this time," Olivia thought she heard him say, "this time, we're going to settle things once and for all."

Chapter Eighteen

As if to atone for the fury of the storm, the sun rose from behind the hills the next morning, draping the land in a warm shimmering veil of rosy light. Leaves dripped prism-colored droplets, and steam rose in a pearly mist among the gleaming wet tree trunks. By eight, the sky burned an enamel-bright blue, as clear and clean as the twins' innocent eyes.

Jake watched, trying to hide his amusement, while Luke corralled his sons and herded them into the Rover. Since Leya had her weekly check-up with the obstetrician today, Luke planned to drop all the kids off at the county school on the way down. On the way home after lunch, they'd pick Josh and Joey up at kindergarten.

"This is your chance, my friend," Luke told Jake. "For several hours there should be peace and quiet around here, so you and Olivia can sort out your respective snarls...spiritual and physical." He hesitated, a quizzical gleam shading the blue eyes. "If you'd like a little well-intended advice—try to keep your hands to yourself. I almost blew it once upon a time, because the flesh is particularly weak when you're dealing with the woman you love."

Leya came up then, slipping her arm about her husband's waist and lifting her face for his kiss. "We both know how easy it is, when you're young," she added, watching Jake out of those serene, dovelike eyes of hers.

Just then Joshua came flying off the front steps to land with a satisfying splash in a puddle, propelling muddy water all over his brother's clean shirt and slacks.

"That's it," snarled Luke, hauling both boys up and tucking one under each arm. "Cattleya!" he roared. "Let's get going before I have to tie these little rug rats to the bumper!" He winked at Jake. "They love it when I talk tough."

Leya strolled out on the porch, behind Marsha and Ben. She was listening to Olivia, who was promising to make sure the kitchen was cleaned, the beds made...and would Leya hush her fretting. Olivia could handle things just fine. Then her gaze met Jake's, and she turned as fiery pink as the row of azaleas blazing on either side of the porch steps.

Leya waved, then turned to hug Olivia. "Don't forget," she told her.

Moments later, with a last farewell toot of the horn, the Rover disappeared around the curve, and silence descended with a thud.

Jake began walking toward Olivia. "Don't forget what?" he asked, watching her step back, looking as shy and skittish as one of Luke's mustang fillies. He stopped, propping his hip on the porch rail and stuffing his hands in his waistband.

"I'd rather...not say just yet," Olivia replied. "I—um—I need to go clean the kitchen. I promised Leya and—"

"Come here, sweetheart." He didn't move, though inside he was melting with laughter and love. Olivia's hesitancy was almost comical. Never in his life had he met a woman of such contrasts—one moment radiating the calm authority of a general; the next, the entrancing uncertainty of a school girl, oblivious to her own charms. *Dear God, I love this woman. Help me here, okay? And oh, yes—give me the strength to resist the very powerful temptation. . . .*

She paused three feet away, hovering, blue-gray eyes wide, unblinking as a fawn's. "Why are you looking at me like that?"

"Like what?"

Olivia shrugged, her nose wrinkling. "Like you're trying to decide where to bite first."

He straightened and took a step, forcing her with the power of his will not to retreat, his gaze burning steadily, watching her pupils expand until they all but drowned out the irises. "Olivia. . .I've got something to tell you. You know that, don't you?"

She was shaking her head, hands coming up to fend him off. "I—I don't want to hear it," she stammered. "Jake—it's impossible, whatever it is."

"Don't you know, my darling, that with God, *all* things are possible? Even you and me?" He lifted his hand, wiping away a single tear with the pad of his thumb. "*Especially* you and me. Olivia, I love you. . .and I know you love me." Taking her hands between his, he kissed her, a brief but tender caress. "And—because I feel your fear all the way to the soles of my feet—I want you to know I also accepted Jesus as my Lord and Savior. Weeks ago, in point of fact. Not just because I love you and knew that would be the only way I could have you. . .but because *He loves me.*"

Olivia still didn't speak, just stood there looking at him in drowning misery. Jake was suddenly very uneasy. He'd bared his heart, leaving himself wide open and totally vulnerable. If she turned away from him now, he'd never recover. "Remember last night," he questioned desperately, urgently, "when we trapped the eagle? Remember how you felt?"

Slowly she nodded.

"You wanted that bird to understand that we weren't going to hurt it, or keep it caged. That we just wanted to help, so it would be free to soar like God intended?"

Throat muscles working, Olivia nodded again. "I remember," she whispered.

"That's what God does for us." Jake crammed his hands back in his jeans. "It's taken me weeks—years!—but I understand now who God really is. He wants to do for us what Luke will do for that eagle. He wants to free us to soar, carried by His love. *Love*. . .not judgment, Olivia. That's what being a Christian means. It's not all the thou-shalt-nots and the thou-musts. It's not the angry God with the big stick Aunt Sophy used to threaten me with. It's

Jesus, dying on a cross because He loved us.

"Luke showed me a verse last week, where Jesus Himself says He came not to judge, but to save. Olivia, judgment is reserved only for those who reject Him, *not* for those of us struggling to follow Him. That's the miracle of it all. He gives us love and forgiveness, not seven times or seventy times. . .*every time.*" He paused to watch her carefully, his voice very soft, very gentle. "Olivia. . .you have to believe it. You have to believe *me*. I love you. . .God loves you."

Unable to control himself any longer, he hauled her into his arms and held her close, pressing her head against his heart, the words spewing forth uncontrollably. "Let the past go—let your father go. You have to forgive, Olivia. That's all. You don't have to work for it, you can't earn it. . .and the burden is not yours to carry. Give it to God."

"I tried. I *can't*." She wrenched free, facing him with the angry passion of total desperation. "I don't know *how* to forgive—and because I can't, God won't forgive *me*. The Bible says that too. Jesus even told a story about it—the one with the servant who ends up in jail because he wouldn't forgive his fellow servant's debt? That's me. I'm in jail, and I know it. And I can't get out." White-faced and pleading, she searched Jake's face. "Jake. . ."

Frustrated, Jake gripped the back of a wooden rocking chair. She wasn't listening, and he couldn't *make* her understand. "You're a Christian," he grated, fear driving his words like the crack of a whip. "That means at some point in the last twenty years or so, you had to accept—in your heart—that Jesus Christ paid for every sin you ever committed, past, present, and future, right? You accepted it, didn't you? You didn't earn it, or work for it, or beg for it!" Olivia jerked under the lash of his tongue, but Jake was too angry now to care.

Control rapidly eroded as all the old instincts crowded back. "If you can accept the fact that God forgives you for all those unnamed sins, why in the name of common sense, can't you also give Him the burden of your father? If you really loved me, Olivia, you'd at least make the effort!"

The moment the words left his mouth he regretted them, but it was too late. Olivia's face turned the color of dirty laundry, and her dilated eyes began to lose focus. Moving stiffly, she crept toward the railing, leaning against it as if she'd fall down without its support.

"I didn't mean that, Olivia. I—" Jake clamped his mouth shut. His feelings were boiling, his newfound faith in tatters. Thanks to his temper, he'd just sent the woman he loved spiraling into another catatonic trance to escape his vicious tongue. *I'm no better than her old man, Lord.*

Filled with self-hatred, his eyes swept over a frozen Olivia. "Don't worry," he bit out, "I'm hanging it up. When the Farringers get back, tell them I'd appreciate it if they'd see about your return to North Carolina. I'll be in touch." He stalked past Olivia into the house, slamming the door.

Two hours later, loaded down with his gear, he left. Tromping across the meadow with the sun shining on his head and the soft spring wind filling the air, Jake was conscious only of Olivia as he'd left her—eyes glazed in a face drained of all color and expression. The way he'd botched things, he'd probably killed her love as well.

As the shadows lengthened, Jake faced some of the most painful realizations of his new life as a Christian—old habits die hard, and every love story doesn't end happily ever after.

Chapter Nineteen

Olivia drove to Sherm's Shelter the evening after her return to North Carolina. At home, silence screamed at her; at work, Maria and Rollie fretted and petted and worried her to death. She couldn't call her mother because it would only upset her, and the last person she wanted to talk to was Beth.

So she drove to Sherm's. There she could be with people whose needs were far more fundamental than Olivia's fractured heart. And, to her great relief, Sherm stayed too busy to pick her brain about Jake.

Even the thought of him made her hands cold and clammy, and sickness still swam in her veins when she remembered their parting. He hadn't even said good-bye.

She parked under the brightest light in the parking lot. Sergeant MacClary's lead had proven to be another dead end, so Olivia continued to be extra careful. Sometimes, though, she was tempted to stake herself out like a tethered goat and get it over with.

"Evening, O-LIV-i-a," Sherm called from across the room, where he was sweeping the floor. "Missed you last week, gal."

"I missed being here too." Olivia did her best to inject some life into her voice. She smiled at the greetings of various regulars as she walked over. "What needs doing this evening?"

"Well. . .seeing as how you've been gone a spell, I guess for starters, maybe you'd better apologize to everyone. We've missed your smiling—hey!" he broke off. "What's this?" Sherm quit sweeping and peered down into Olivia's hastily averted face. "Don't tell me you're crying."

He sounded so appalled that a tiny spark of laughter helped to stave off the aching tears. When she recovered from all this—if she ever did—Olivia vowed she would never cry again as long as she lived. It was a debasing, useless, humiliating emotion, just like her father used to say.

"Sorry," she eventually managed, with a fair amount of control. "Something must have flown into my eye—probably a speck of dust." She shook off his concern. "Looks like you're through with dinner. How 'bout if I fetch my box of goodies from the trunk of my car. We did a wedding over the weekend, and they had so much food left from the reception, they practically begged me to take it off their hands. I thought of you, and—here we are."

Sherm shook his balding, pony-tailed head. "If that don't beat the berries. You're all right, Ms. O-LIV-i-a Sinclair. Need any help?"

"I can handle it. Go on with your sweeping."

She unloaded one box and returned for the last one. As she passed the end of the building just before reaching the parking lot, she glimpsed a sudden movement from the corner of her eye. Alarm kicked through Olivia. She took one step backward, preparing to run, or scream. . .or both.

"Psst. 'Livia! It's me—Eddie!"

Mouth cotton-dry, Olivia hesitated, still poised to flee. "Eddie?"

A shuffling, hesitant shadow separated itself from the wall, and Eddie sidled into the corner of the security lights. "Been waitin' here every evenin' for you." He cleared his throat and spat, scuffing a battered loafer in the dirt. "Wanted to say I was sorry. You was nice to me and Nan. . .Nan, that's what I named her, y'know. I found out what happened, how she went to a place where they'll take care of her wing so's she can fly."

"Thank you for coming back." Light-headed with relief, Olivia was nonetheless touched and humbled by this poor wretched man's honesty. She had to make him understand that it was okay. "I know you didn't mean anything. You were just scared, just wanted to protect. . .Nan."

"Nan's my wife's name. She died four years, seven months, twenty-one days ago." He blinked at Olivia, the sad, sunken old eyes almost childlike. "I miss her. Don't see much use in livin' without her, so I just sort of amble around, waitin' to die. It felt real good to help that old bird, though."

"I know," Olivia said softly. "Eddie, why don't you come inside with me now? I've got a lot of delicious food, and—"

"No. Don't want no more trouble. Just had to wait until I could tell you thanks." He shifted uneasily, looking furtively around. "And—and it weren't me that slashed your tires, 'Livia—"

"Oh, Eddie, I knew that."

"—but I did see who done it, and that's the other reason I been watchin' here, waitin' every night." He cleared his throat, spat again. "She's here, 'Livia. . .and I had to tell you, so's you can be careful."

Olivia felt as if she were seeing Eddie through the wrong end of a telescope. "She's *here?*" She forced the words past constricted throat muscles. "The. . . woman. . .who slashed my tires?" Dazed, blood roaring in her ears, she wondered, with some remnant of lucidity, what Eddie would do if she nose-dived right at his feet. *If it's the same woman, then it must be the stalker. The one who vandalized the house. Threw a brick at me.*

" 'Livia? I had to tell you, didn't I? But I don't want no trouble, so I gotta go." He reached beneath the same filthy jacket he'd been wearing weeks ago and pulled out a newspaper-wrapped bundle, thrusting it toward Olivia. "And—and I wanted to give this back. I—it's too fine for me. It would be a . . .I mean, it would do my heart good if you'd take it back." The paper unfurled and a fold of lavender knit spilled out.

As if in a dream, Olivia accepted her sweater.

"I'm gonna take off now—you be careful, y'hear? That old woman. . .she's been here every night, just like me. It's like she's waitin' too."

Olivia closed her eyes. "I. . .see. Thank you, Eddie. You've been a big help. And—I'll always think of you when I wear this sweater."

He ducked his head, then turned. "Eddie!" She darted after him, touching the bony shoulder. "Eddie, that woman? Where is she?"

Hunching down, he peeked around Olivia, lifting his arm and pointing a trembling finger. "Right yonder, 'cross the street by them dumpsters. She parks there, outta sight. She don't even notice me—" He shifted nervously. "You'll be careful?"

Olivia patted his shoulder. "I'll be very careful, Eddie. Are you sure you won't come inside?"

But Eddie had already melted back into the night, a lonely, forgotten old man who quite possibly had just saved Olivia's life. Moving stiffly on legs which had no feeling, she headed back toward the common room.

Sherm called the police, explained the situation, and stashed Olivia in a corner of the kitchen. There she sat, fidgeting and anxious, while Sherm peeled potatoes and rattled off old football stories to distract her while she waited.

But it was a good thirty minutes before a wiry patrolman sauntered into the room and Sherm went to meet him, motioning for Olivia to stay put. Ignoring him, she rose and followed.

"Olivia Sinclair?"

"Yes. Did you—*was* there a woman behind the dumpster?"

"Yes, ma'am. Ma'am?" the police officer asked abruptly. "Do you need to sit down?"

And the next thing Olivia knew, Sherm had snagged a chair and shoved her into it as if she were a sack of meal.

"I'm fine," she insisted, shaking her head to clear the ringing. Smiling a little, she amended, "Well, almost. May I see her please, Officer?" Looking stern, the policeman was about to refuse. But Olivia insisted. "I'd really like to see this woman. I don't plan to make a scene or do anything foolish. . .but I need to see her. She's outside?"

Without waiting for a response, she headed across the room, having found long ago that sometimes more was accomplished by charging full steam ahead while asking permission to do so. The disgruntled cop caught up with her at the door and escorted her to a squad car, where a female detective was trying in vain to stem the vituperative flow of words gushing from the mouth of a dainty little old woman, barely five feet tall.

When she caught sight of Olivia, the woman screeched and would have lunged at her, except for the restraining handcuffs joining her to the long-suffering detective. "You deserved it! All of it! You have no right to walk around free when my daughter's life is ruined! Ruined!"

"That's enough," snapped the detective, but Olivia calmly faced the infuriated woman.

"It was my father, wasn't it, who ruined your daughter?" she clarified.

"Yes!" shouted the woman, shaking her free fist. "Yes, your father, Alton almighty Sinclair, may he burn forever!"

With a warning look, the patrolman moved to stand at her side. "This is not a good idea, Ms. Sinclair," the detective said. "We've read her her rights, and she claims to understand. Nevertheless, this is highly irregular, especially since your presence is only inciting her further."

"I don't care," the woman hissed, practically vibrating with the force of her emotion. "All these years, watching my Alice, knowing what that no-good, sorry—" She stopped, slanting a sly look to either side before shooting Olivia a triumphant, malevolent glare. "I couldn't do anything to your father, but I waited. And then you came, begging my daughter to forgive. *Forgive!*" She spat the word as if it were an obscenity. "She spent three years in therapy and lost her job, her husband—everything! And nobody knew what your father did except me. Sometimes I thought Alice would take her own life. Do you know what that does to a mother? Do you have any idea what I've been through?" All of a sudden the seething anger dissipated. With a dry, heaving sob, the woman began to cry.

Reeling with shocked recognition, Olivia heard the familiar words as though she herself were speaking. She understood that kind of pain, even understood why she was the target of the woman's venom. This hurting mother had simply attacked the only available substitute for Alton Sinclair himself.

"What's her name?" Olivia asked the detective.

"Sylvia Blecker, Hickory address. You ever see this woman before?"

An errant memory flickered, then crystallized. "In Statesville," Olivia said slowly, staring hard at the defeated old woman with her gray hair fashioned in tight permed ringlets. "It was you that day, wasn't it. . .You ran the light on purpose, tried to run me down?"

"If that boy hadn't pulled you back, it all would have been over," Mrs. Blecker muttered dully. "It would have been over, and I'd be free. You'd have paid for what your father did to my daughter."

You'd have paid. . . This is my body, broken for you. He who did not spare His own Son, but gave Him for us all. . . .

Olivia felt as if the sun had just hurtled from the sky into her chest, exploding in a blinding, burning fireball of spiritual illumination. As if she were walking along the road to Damascus instead of Paul, Olivia felt her entire life change in one revelatory instant. *Felt* the change in her head, in her heart.

Lifting wondering eyes to the suddenly silent trio of faces watching her,

Olivia finally knew with absolute clarity what she had to do. And along with that knowledge flowed a single rivulet of peace, calm and serenely blue as a summer sky at twilight.

Olivia stepped right up to Mrs. Blecker, so close she could see the sweat beading her upper lip. Looked into the tearful, bloodshot eyes and saw the bottomless pit of vengeance slowly destroying Sylvia Blecker's soul. "Mrs. Blecker, we both must accept the fact that nothing I say or do can change what my father did to your daughter. Can you do that?" she asked, very gently.

Mouth working, blinking rapidly, the older woman stared down at her feet for what seemed like an eternity. Then she nodded, once, not looking at Olivia.

Olivia felt as if she were floating in a cloud high above the misery and drama of the ravaged earth. "And would you be willing to accept, here and now, that there is nothing *you* can do—including hurting me—that will *undo* what my father did to your daughter?"

The two policemen stirred restlessly, but Olivia reassured them with eloquent eyes, so confident of her decision that the certainty pulsed from her heart all the way to her fingertips. Shrugging, the female detective nodded in agreement.

With great effort Sylvia Blecker lifted her head to search Olivia's face. "I—it hasn't helped," the syllables dragged out. "I thought if I could watch you suffer, do something to you that would make you hurt like my daughter was hurt, that I'd feel better."

"Why haven't you done something to my store? You've been following me, you know where it is. Why?"

Looking old and shrunken, gaze dropping to the hard metal handcuff enclosing her wrist, Mrs. Blecker mumbled, half-sheepishly, "I wanted to hurt you, not anyone else. I saw all those young people coming and going, all of them leaving with smiles on their faces. So glowing, so full of life like my Alice used to be." Her mouth trembled as tears oozed from the corner of her eyelids again. "I didn't want to hurt anybody else." She slumped back against the patrol car. "And. . .and I guess I sort of realized, deep down, that you weren't anything like your father. Only by then I just couldn't let it go. All that anger. . .like a hard knot deep inside, and all I could do was just keep on."

Olivia inhaled slowly. "Mrs. Blecker," she said, each word falling into a silence so intense it seemed even the crickets were holding their breath, "would it help that knot to go away if I promised you that I truly understand why you did all those things, and that I—that I forgive you?"

Mrs. Blecker's chin quivered, and the tears ran faster. "I was wrong, I'll have to pay. . .I'll have to go to prison. . . ."

There was a long pause before Olivia spoke again. "Not if I refuse to press charges."

The woman gasped, and one of the officers stepped forward to protest. "Ms.

Sinclair, this discussion needs to take place in the presence of a lawyer. You can't make that kind of decision based on the emotion of the moment."

Olivia picked up Mrs. Blecker's thin hand and gave it a gentle squeeze. "It's not a fleeting emotion," she promised quietly. "Mrs. Blecker, you have to let go of what my father did. It's in the past. Don't let his wickedness destroy your life too. Trust me. . .I understand."

"But how can you possibly forgive what I did to you—your house—your car?" She jerked her hand free and covered her eyes, weeping.

The tranquil blue stream flooding Olivia's heart widened into an ocean of love. "How can I?" she repeated in a voice bubbling with light, effervescent joy. "Actually. . .it's incredibly easy, easier than I could have ever imagined." She shook her head, as if not quite believing it herself. "Mrs. Blecker," she began again, "from the bottom of my heart, I do forgive you. Now, how about coming back inside with me? We'll share some leftover wedding goodies, and you can tell me about your daughter."

Looking disgusted and disillusioned, the detective unlocked the handcuffs. "I think you're making a big mistake," she informed Olivia with rigid formality.

"Thank you for coming so promptly, Officers." Smiling, Olivia put her arm around the stunned, unresisting Mrs. Blecker. "You won't believe this, I know, but everything really *is* going to be fine."

Shaking their heads, the two climbed into their car and sped off, while Olivia led a trembling, hopeful Sylvia Blecker toward the warmth and welcoming light of Sherm's Shelter. She couldn't wait to tell Maria and Rollie that the stalker had been caught, and that she'd invited her in for tea.

And someday—*soon, Lord?*—she'd be able to tell Jake she was out of her own prison, on permanent parole.

Chapter Twenty

Wandering around the Chattahoochee National Forest like John the Baptist in the wilderness didn't help.

Another exhilarating, challenging run down the Chattooga rapids fell flat.

Landing back on the Farringers' doorstep hungry, dirty, and exhausted earned him food, bed, and a bath—and some comforting words. But no peace.

More unsure of himself than he'd ever been in his entire life, Jake at last flew back to North Carolina, where his only hope for reconciliation and joy rested in the fragile heart of the woman whose spirit his temper had crushed. Maybe permanently. A Christian woman who'd never learned how to forgive.

He delayed long enough in Charlotte to buy the only Range Rover sitting on the lot—a black one that suited his present mood. Ignoring the salesman's flabbergasted sputterings, Jake signed papers, slapped down a personal check that left everyone gasping at the ease with which it cleared, and took himself and his new vehicle off.

Driving with grim determination up I-77 toward Barley, Jake spared scant seconds to enjoy the first automobile he'd owned in almost a decade. Instead, he spent the entire journey playing and replaying in his mind all the potential scenarios with Olivia which could unfold. At the far end of the spectrum, he nursed a growing fear that she would end up in the room next to Davy, her mind forever imprisoned in mental as well as spiritual chains.

When he almost missed his exit onto the state road, Jake punched in a cassette tape of Christian music Tony, his old teammate, had given him. Jake still preferred his golden oldies. But right now he needed spiritual nurturing more than entertainment.

Naturally, it was a gray, dingy afternoon, the air muggy and rife with noxious odors produced by civilization. *Well, Donovan,* he thought with wry humor, *the mood you're in, she's sure to jump right into your arms and welcome you home.*

His chest felt like a hot poker was probing around. And when a sign indicating a roadside picnic area flashed by, Jake hit the brakes. Pulling up under a stand of loblolly pines, he switched off the engine, leaned back against the new-smelling leather seat, and closed his eyes.

This is it, God. Luke claims You really do know when we're at the end of our rope, and all You require is that we let go and fall into Your waiting arms. Well . . . I gave up last week, and if You don't catch me, I'm afraid the fall this time might be fatal. I don't deserve Your forgiveness, much less Olivia's. . .but I guess I either accept those words I hurled at her in anger—or choke on them.

Jake opened his eyes, feeling a totally foreign stinging sensation at the corners. Lifting a wondering hand, he swiped at the salty drops; for the first time in over thirty years, he was actually crying. *Father, forgive me. Then help us both.* He restarted the engine, then paused, a sheepish grin hovering at the corners of his mouth. Aloud, he finished the heartfelt prayer, "And, God. . . thanks."

❧

Only one car was parked in front of The Bridal Bower. As Jake pulled in two spots down, the door opened and two women emerged, heading for the car. *So far, so good*, he thought, waiting until the women headed off down the street. Then he climbed out, took a deep breath, and entered the lion's den.

Of course, when a man has primed himself for battle, but the bugler plays "Here Comes the Bride," most of the drama is reduced to farce. A lopsided grin, unwanted but relentless, spread across Jake's face when Maria glanced up to see who had come through the door.

Her brown eyes opened wide, then narrowed, and she rushed over to meet him. But instead of the tongue-lashing Jake expected and deserved, Maria grabbed his arm and hauled him toward the back room.

"It's about time," she hissed out of the corner of her mouth. "We've been on pins and needles and thumbtacks, waiting for you to finally stick your gorgeous body but stubborn head through the door." She whipped her head around to make sure the room was empty. "This is great! We don't have any appointments scheduled until three-thirty." She surveyed Jake archly. "You *are* here as the handsome prince instead of the wicked villain, aren't you?"

Jake finally found his wits. He felt light-headed, as if he'd inhaled a tankful of nitrous oxide. "Olivia?" For some reason he couldn't manage anything more, but every hope, every longing, and every bit of love he had for her was invested in that one word.

Maria reached up and kissed his cheek. "She's here, and she's fine. And she needs you as much as you need her, Jake. Go on. . .it's all right." She gave him a push, then flashed a saucy grin. "Trust me."

Moving like a sleepwalker, Jake made his way down the aisle, around a dressmaker's form clad in a wedding gown, and to the door of Olivia's office. When he put out his hand to open it, he saw that his fingers were actually shaking.

Olivia and Rollie were at Rollie's desk, talking. They both looked up when Jake came into the room, but Jake hadn't a clue as to Rollie's response. He was looking at the woman he loved. . .and he couldn't tear his gaze away.

She didn't look like the same Olivia. Blue sparkles of joy crowded out the gray of her eyes. And when she spoke, she sounded as if she'd inhaled a thousand sunbeams.

"Jake—" She mouthed his name, then shouted it joyously, "Jake!" Slowly straightening, she moved out from behind the desk and took one dreamlike step toward him.

Suddenly the words bubbled forth, as swift and free as the Farringers' creek after a rain. "Olivia, I'm sorry. I'm an insensitive, selfish, hot-headed louse and I don't deserve anything after the way I treated you. But I love you and I want to marry you. . .mmph!"

Olivia hurled herself into his arms, hugging him so tight he couldn't have pried her loose with a crowbar. "I love you, and I'm sorry, too, and—and you were right and I was wrong!"

This time Jake interrupted Olivia, but only with his mouth, kissing her with all the pent-up longing of the past week of self-reproach and fear. He kissed her soft, trembling lips, her eyes, her cheeks, the pulse throbbing in her temple, all the while trying to whisper his love, his shame, his need for her to understand. To forgive.

Olivia somehow managed to wriggle her hand between them and gently lay it over his mouth. "I have so much to tell you," she said, her eyes shining with love and peace.

"As long as it's yes, I don't care what else you have to say," he murmured. But even so, Jake held his breath.

"Later." She laughed. "I have a few things that have to come first. . .like, I forgive you—from deep down in my heart—so you can stop hating yourself for what happened at the Farringers'."

His hands gripped her shoulders urgently. Then, with exquisite tenderness, he tilted her chin up with his thumbs. "What's happened, sweetheart?"

"Just like I said. . .you were right and I was wrong," Olivia repeated, gazing up at him with her heart in her eyes. "Jake, I've learned more about being a Christian in the past week than I have since I accepted Jesus as my Savior twenty years ago."

"And what's that?" He lovingly caressed the blush heating her cheeks. "And what was it I was so 'right' about?"

"Forgiveness. You can't earn it, or work for it." She closed her eyes briefly, and when the translucent lids lifted, a sheen of tears shimmered like sunlight off the surface of a lake. "It's your attitude—and you can't *force* your attitude to change. You can only accept God's promise to *help* you change. And. . .and it just happens. In your head, in your heart. Like a beautiful sunrise. Like Easter morning. It's *real*, Jake."

He brought his forehead down to rest against hers, so weak with relief, with gratitude he didn't know how he was still standing. "I love you."

From behind them Rollie finally spoke up, her voice testy but indulgent. "Not that my presence has put a damper on your latest, and hopefully *last*, reunion. . . but if you can break it up long enough for Olivia to tell you the news about the stalker, I'll give you some privacy."

Jake turned to face her, still holding Olivia. "What about the stalker?"

Looking like a plump broody hen, rocking back in her desk chair and watching unabashedly, Rollie heaved herself to her feet and chuckled. "I'm dying to see your face when she explains. Go on, Olivia—tell the man."

Flushed and laughing, Olivia tugged at Jake's hands, and he reluctantly released her. "You're incorrigible," Olivia informed her partner, "and I think maybe I should fire you."

"Fire away," Rollie retorted.

Throwing up her hands, Olivia took a couple of steps back and clasped her hands. "I don't know what you're going to think of this, Jake," she confessed a little bit nervously.

Jake's eyebrow lifted. "Right now I'm thinking if you don't get on with it, Rollie's going to be very disappointed, because in two seconds I plan to show her the door myself." Then, when Olivia continued to stand there chewing her lip, he pressed, more gently, "Just tell me. What's happened with the stalker? Has she finally been apprehended, I hope?"

"Yes. . .in a manner of speaking."

Maria slipped through the door to add her two cents. "What Olivia is hesitant to share is that, after catching the woman in the act, hearing her confess to everything—*and* with the police standing there holding the woman in handcuffs—Olivia refused to press charges."

High as the heavens within the security of their restored relationship, Jake merely cast Olivia a questioning look. "And why would she do that?" he drawled, drawing his finger down the cheek that a month ago had been an ugly, swollen mess.

"I had to, Jake. You see—that's when I finally understood about forgiveness. Her name's Sylvia Blecker, and six years ago her daughter was one of my father's victims. . .one of the people who slammed the door in my face when I tried to talk with her. Her mother—Mrs. Blecker—happened to be there that day, and when I left, she followed me."

"And set out to get revenge." He winced, thinking of his own unholy agenda.

"Jake, she was hurting just like me, and if I hadn't dropped the charges, she could have gone to jail for aggravated assault. The only way out. . .for *both* of us was for me to forgive her—" A single tear slid down her cheek. "So, you see, I had to do it. I—I—"

"It's okay, sweetheart. I understand." He tugged her back into his arms. "Only moments ago I felt like I was behind bars myself. . .and until you forgave me, there was no way out for me either."

Relief sagged her shoulders. "You *do* understand, don't you?" she breathed. "Now we're free."

"As an eagle." Jake winked.

"As a forgiven child of God," Olivia amended. "Remember that parable? The one that always bothered me because the servant was thrown in jail until he paid his debt?"

"I remember."

"I understand what Jesus was trying to teach now. The master wasn't worried about the money owed—he just wanted the servant's attitude, his *heart* to change. You know what else? I'll bet that jail wasn't even locked, because the servant had put himself there and slammed the cell door shut. Just like I did . . .like Mrs. Blecker—"

Jake hugged her close. "And then you got smart, didn't you, and finally heard what God had been trying to tell you all the time? That He sent Jesus to cancel your debt, mark your account 'Paid in Full,' and set you free once and for all. And that it's a pretty heartless businesswoman who wouldn't pass that kind of deal along to the next person."

"Enough sermonizing already," Maria piped up. "When's the wedding?"

Jake and Olivia gaped open-mouthed at Maria, then at each other. Then he watched the blue-gray eyes transform back to teasing blue.

"Statistically speaking," Olivia began, "couples who have known each other less than a year should have longer engagements."

"Oh, no you don't, Ms. Sinclair! No more delays." Jake planted a lusty kiss right on her lips. "Say yes, or I'll have to resort to more drastic forms of persuasion."

"Yes!" Olivia cried. "But, Jake," she whispered, sobering, "I can't promise that longstanding behavior patterns will disappear instantly. I have to be honest— you've seen what I allowed my father's warped character to do to me."

Jake held her at arm's length. "You've seen that I still have a lousy temper," he intoned solemnly.

"And *I* still have a daily planner."

"This is getting serious. I might even have to give in to the urge to take off for the wilderness every now and then."

"*I* might give in to the urge to come along. I could organize the trips, coordinate times—" She twisted out of his arms, laughing.

Jake charged. Squealing, Olivia darted behind a table. Rollie and Maria prudently edged toward the door, while Jake stalked his quarry. She feinted left.

Jake followed suit, catching her easily, and wagging his finger. "Never try to outmaneuver an ex-pro wide receiver."

In a quick economy of motion that left Olivia breathless, he whisked her off her feet and carried her over to Rollie and Maria. "The three of you can plan the wedding," he announced, "but *I'll* take care of the honeymoon." Lowering his head, he captured the lips of his bride-to-be in another long, thoroughly satisfying kiss. *On the other hand, I think I'll leave the happy ending to You, Lord. . . .*

Unnoticed, Rollie and Maria slipped out, closing the door behind them. "Well," Maria said, sighing, "at least they've come to the best place in three counties to plan a wedding. Come on, Rollie. Let's get busy."

Llama Lady

VeraLee Wiggins

Chapter One

The savage attack on the front door caused Teddy Marland to do more than drop a stitch—the entire sweater flew from her grasp. She checked the clock; it was only half past six in the morning. Gram had just put breakfast on the table and she had just picked up her knitting after having finished feeding and watering the livestock.

"Lord, grant me patience with the fool who's on the other side of this door," she prayed, heading for the door that seemed about to crumble under yet another brutal attack. Jerking open the door she discovered a huge blond man with his right arm raised and ready to administer still another round of battery. His face looked like one of the thunderstorms common to Bend, Oregon—one of the bad ones.

Teddy stood tall in the doorway. "What do you think you're doing?" she asked.

The stranger, with his large hand still suspended in air, looked at Teddy, and looked some more. His craggy face began to relax, then his mouth tightened again. "Get the owner of this zoo!"

Teddy started to yell for Gram, but the tiny woman had already scurried in from the kitchen and was now wiping her hands on the sides of her pants. Rushing to Teddy's side, Gram snaked her skinny arm around Teddy's slim waist which was about even with the old woman's shoulder. "All right, buster," she announced in a gravelly voice that was bigger than she, "we've had it up to here with your tantrum. If you want something, ask like a gentleman. Otherwise get on down the road."

The man's mouth slackened; his eyes darted from Teddy down to Gram and back up to Teddy again. Then the corners of his mouth began jerking, and a low belly laugh rumbled from somewhere deep within.

"Well, can we help you, or did you just have the urge to destroy our house?" Gram's guttural voice demanded.

"Did anyone ever tell you two that you make a crazy looking pair?" he finally asked.

"Is that a fact?" Gram replied, peering up at the man from her four-foot, eleven-inch frame. "Well, you have one up on us. It doesn't take two of you to look crazy."

The man stood silent, his shoulders still shaking.

Teddy looked at Gram who was her mother, father, and entire family rolled into one tiny dynamo. Why would they look crazy together? True, the top of Gram's yellow-gray head was several inches short of reaching Teddy's shoulder, and Gram looked so thin she might not cast a shadow. But she still appeared beautiful to

Teddy, even in her size ten, boys' bib overalls and red-plaid flannel shirt. Then Teddy looked down at her own worn jeans and faded tee shirt and realized she did not look too gorgeous either. But crazy?

The tall man returned to life, possibly remembering why he came. His lips tightened again; red streaks brightened his already sunburned skin and his eyes blazed. "I asked for the owner of this spread," he told Gram, tersely.

Gram straightened her shoulders and stood tall. She tightened her grip on Teddy's waist. "You're looking at 'em." Her voice sounded like a gravel crusher.

He pulled out a scrap of paper, checked it, wadded it in his hand and shoved it back into his jeans pocket. "The mailbox says Theodore Marland."

Gram jabbed a bony thumb toward Teddy. "That's Theodore Marland. You got a problem with that?"

The man considered a moment. "No," he said firmly, "I don't have a problem with, uh, her. But I want to talk to a man."

"Well, you won't find one of those around this place." Gram leaned back, looking up into his face. Then she smiled, and her faded blue eyes crinkled. "Come on, sonny, you got a problem, tell me. Maybe I can fix it."

After a moment of indecision, he spoke. "How many times a week are you supposed to get water?"

Gram jerked her old head up at him. "Who, may I ask, are you?"

"I'm Brandon Sinclair. I bought the ranch just west of here, and I was told that this is my water day."

Gram turned her back and headed for the kitchen. "I don't have time to spoon-feed every greenhorn who comes along," she grated over her shoulder. "If you'll help the fool figure out his water problems, Teddy, I'll hold breakfast for fifteen minutes."

Teddy sighed and stepped onto the rickety porch. "Come on out and I'll show you how it works." She closed the door and stepped gingerly down the rotting steps. "I don't understand how you could mess up your water. You're the last one on the line."

"I may be a greenhorn," he bellowed, "and I may also be a fool, but even I can see that you're taking my water!"

Teddy did not not respond as he followed her across her overgrown yard through the gate and into the pasture. Llamas appeared from several directions and followed the two across the pasture, their heads resting on Teddy's or Mr. Sinclair's shoulders. Other llamas, in their eagerness to be with her, bumped into Teddy.

"And why are you raising these, uh, goats?" he shouted.

"I'm not deaf," she said quietly, striding beside him. "And I'm sure you know they're llamas. We raise them because we make several times the money with them that we did raising cattle. And we have a lot more fun doing it."

In a few minutes they reached a bubbling stream about three feet wide and two feet deep. As they continued to walk across the pasture, Teddy explained how the Deschutes County ranchers shared the water. "The water comes from the Deschutes River and is divided into many lines so each rancher gets enough to survive but not a lot more than that. A line is simply a wide ditch with lots of water flowing through it. There is one ranch before mine on this particular line, and you are the last. We each get water twice a week. None comes through on Sunday. The first ranch gets water on Monday and Thursday, I get it Tuesday and Friday, and you get it Wednesday and Saturday."

"I know all that. Is this Wednesday?" he asked, obviously struggling for civility.

"This is Wednesday and you're getting the water." She glanced at the rushing water again. "You can see there's plenty in the ditch."

They approached the gates and Teddy could not believe her eyes. Water gushed through her open gate, into her nearly filled pond! She pushed the lever that closed her gate and sent the water coursing through his ditch into his nearly dry pond.

Her bright blue eyes looked into his, laughing at him. "I don't know how you bumbled the gate open, but I closed it this morning. I always do it at exactly six o'clock, the shut-off time."

"How could I bumble?" he shouted. "I don't even have a gate; I get water when no one else wants it."

Even though Brandon Sinclair stood there accusing her of stealing his water, Teddy's kind heart went out to the frenzied man. "No one's stealing your water, Mr. Sinclair," she said softly. "Ranchers work together. We not only share water, but anything else the other person needs. You go on back to your own place now, and things will be all right."

As Teddy watched her new neighbor trot to the old log fence and jump over, she wished she could have met him under more favorable circumstances. She had never seen such an attractive man. His shoulders were wide and his legs went on forever. And his sun-streaked blond hair and bright brown eyes could really do something to a girl. Wait a minute! What was she thinking about, anyway? She was not shopping for a man.

When Teddy crossed her unstable porch floor again, she wondered for the hundredth time how soon they would be able to repair the old house. They had mortgaged the ranch to buy the llamas and all repairs had been put on hold until the loan could be paid off. She opened the door, removed her shoes, ran through the completely empty living room to the bathroom to wash up, then slipped into her chair at the kitchen table.

Gram asked the blessing then poured coffee into fat brown mugs. "Well, did you get him calmed down?"

Teddy shook her head. "I don't know, he's pretty upset." She took a sip of the delicious liquid. "I tried to explain about the water. But our gate was open. I told him he must have done it. I remember closing it after I finished the chores."

Gram nodded. "Wonder what he's doing on a ranch. Looks as if he wouldn't know which end of a cow to feed."

Teddy and Gram finished breakfast and stacked the dishes in the sink. Then they hurried across the pasture to set up the irrigation system in the alfalfa. They would use up what water they had left from yesterday then start all over again on Friday. The fifty-acre alfalfa field provided enough hay to keep their llamas through the winter.

They barely had four of their eight monstrous water gun sprinklers set up when a horse and rider pounded up to them. He jumped from the saddle, marched up to Teddy, and leaned over her, his face contorted. "Do you really want the water or are you just trying to make me crazy?" Brandon Sinclair yelled.

"Are you sure the gate's open again? If it is, it must be faulty," Teddy said trying to keep her voice calm.

Sinclair put his hands around Teddy's waist, hoisted her onto his horse, then hopped up into the saddle. "We'll see what's faulty," he informed her.

When they reached the water gate, Brandon Sinclair rolled off his horse and jerked Teddy down beside him. The curious llamas surrounded them as they walked toward the wide open irrigation gate.

Almost before he could point at the unobstructed water gushing toward her pond, Teddy pushed the lever and the gate instantly swung shut. "It seems to work just fine," she said, determined to keep calm.

"You bet it works! And if this happens again, I'm reporting you to the water master!"

Teddy felt her patience growing taut. "Mr. Sinclair," she said, a little louder than necessary, "no one around here steals water or anything else for that matter. I'd be much more likely to share my water with you than to steal yours."

"Glad to hear it. Just the same, you'd better remember I'm watching my water as if it were diamonds rolling through that gate." He jumped on his horse.

At that moment, a beautiful cream and dark brown llama named Iris walked up, took the lever in her mouth and pulled back. The gate opened and the water once again rushed into the Marland line.

"Iris! What did you do?" Teddy pushed the lever, even as she yelled at the llama. "Did you see that?" she said, looking up, wide-eyed, at the man astride the horse.

Brandon Sinclair dismounted. "I wouldn't have believed it if I hadn't seen it. How long have you had her trained to do that?"

"Don't be ridiculous. I suppose she did it because she sees me doing it all the time."

The tall man remained silent a moment, then laughed out loud and climbed back onto his horse. "Sorry I accused you of stealing my water," he called, starting back toward his own ranch. A moment later he stopped short. "The problem is located, but not corrected," he yelled across the distance.

"I'll think of something," she mumbled as she watched him gallop back to his own ranch. She walked away slowly with her arm around the animal's neck. "Come on, Iris, you have to stay in the small corral until we get this figured out."

❧

The next afternoon Teddy hauled fence posts and wire out to the irrigation line to build a fence and gate to keep Iris away from the water gate. Working in the warm June sunshine, she dug four post holes, buried the posts, and started unrolling the wire fencing.

"Think that'll do it?"

Teddy turned at the sound of the warm deep voice to find Brandon Sinclair standing, feet apart, watching her work. "I hope so," she replied. "Iris is so mad at me for penning her up that she won't even look at me."

Sinclair took the wire from her hands. "Here, let me help. I'm probably a little stronger than you." They worked together until the fence protected the water gate from the llamas.

"I understand what a cattle ranch is all about," Brandon said, "but how do these things make you money? You don't eat them, do you?"

Teddy reached her arm around a long woolly neck. "Never. Don't talk like that in front of my girls. How do llamas make money? Well, the wool is worth two dollars an ounce, as compared to one dollar a pound for sheep wool. Llama wool is much stronger, warmer, and comes in many beautiful natural colors. A llama produces around five pounds of wool a year. Our herd numbers around 500 right now. Are you doing your arithmetic?"

Brandon's eyes grew round. "If you're telling me you take in $80,000 a year on llama wool, then I'm getting rid of my cattle tonight."

Teddy laughed. "I'm telling you we could. And some people do. But we don't shear our llamas. We sell the young. We get $10,000 to $15,000 and sometimes more, for females, and $1,000 or more for males. People buy them before they're born and take them when they're weaned, at about six months. We sell about 200 young each year, and so far we've been having slightly more females than males. Now, Mr. Sinclair, it's my turn to ask some questions."

"Brand. My friends call me Brand." He looked down at her, a soft friendly look replacing the anger. The sun sent gold flecks skittering around in his eyes.

"All right, Brand. How long have you been ranching beside us?" Teddy looked west to the shining white fences, the monstrous white barns, and metal loafing sheds. The three-story, white colonial house stood on a small knoll, overlooking the ultra-modern ranch. She knew it had been empty for the last six months since the old rancher had died.

"Arrived on the scene early this week. I'm still getting it set up."

"Where are you from?" The llamas jostled the two as they walked along, often distracting them from their discussion.

Brand shoved a large black llama away. "I'm from Alvadore, near Eugene. Western Oregon, you know? My folks had a large ranch there but they retired and moved into Eugene. I'd helped them from the time I was a child so ranching is in my blood." He held his arm out and up and shoved the llamas away again.

"Why Bend? Why did you buy in our area?"

He smiled. "I've always liked Bend. It's such a nice clean little town." He shoved two woolly heads away, then grinned, almost embarrassed. "And I suppose the fact that you can buy a lot more ranch here, for the same money, may have influenced me some."

One extra large red and white llama insisted on hanging its head over Brand's shoulder, so Brand gave it a mighty shove. The llama stepped back a few feet from Brand, raised its head as high as it could, laid back its ears, and began chewing vigorously. "No, Casanova, no!" Teddy yelled, but she hardly had the words out of her mouth when the llama let loose a great green missile which found its mark, splattering all over Brand's face.

Chapter Two

Brand's hands flew to his face, his fingers clawing the horrible stuff away. As the stench filled her nostrils, Teddy's stomach threatened to turn. When Brand was able to see he ran to the irrigation ditch, dropped to his stomach and splashed innumerable handfuls of water on his face. Then he sat down in the grassy pasture and looked up at Teddy. "What was that?" he implored.

"I guess I forgot to tell you that llamas spit when they get really upset. You shoved Casanova one too many times."

"Oh." Brand turned his hands over, looking at them as though they might fall off at any moment. "I'm not sure I want to know, but what do they spit?"

"It's half-digested food."

"I'm keeping my cattle, after all. I knew there had to be a catch."

❧

That night Teddy told Gram about Brand helping her fix the fence and also about Casanova spitting on the poor man. "Teddy, when you talk about Brand, you have a new sparkle in your eyes," Gram said after they had finished laughing.

"No way," Teddy replied.

Gram nodded her wise old head. "All right. Just take my advice and don't mention Brandon Sinclair to Lynden."

A quiet tap on the door ended the discussion about Teddy's new sparkle. Lynden Greeley, Teddy's boyfriend since high school, stepped into the large bare room. The thin, brown-haired young man left his shoes at the front door, moved through the bare living room to the bathroom to wash his hands, then went to the cozily furnished country kitchen. Settling into the worn but comfortable couch, he glanced at Teddy. "Why the sparkle in those big blue eyes tonight?" he asked, absent-mindedly stroking Thor, the old yellow cat, who had climbed onto his lap.

When Lynden said "sparkle," Teddy's bright eyes flew to Gram's faded ones. She made up her mind never to think about Brandon Sinclair again in her entire life. "Anything exciting happen today?" she asked. Lynden worked at the *Bulletin*, Bend's daily newspaper, and Teddy thought he learned something new and stimulating every day.

Lynden shrugged and reached into the candy dish for some jellybeans. "No, we can hardly find anything to fill the local pages." He grinned at Teddy. "What do you expect from our nice quiet little town?"

"Young man," Gram said, interrupting the conversation, "you know I don't mind your eating that candy and I don't mind your petting the cat, either. But not at the same time in my house. Don't you dare stick your hand back into the candy dish until you go wash it with soap and water."

Lynden pushed the cat onto the couch, obediently went to the kitchen sink to wash his hands, then returned and sat down.

"What do you want to do tonight?" Teddy asked.

"I'm awfully comfortable. How about watching TV?"

"Sure." She flipped the switch. "Mind if I knit then?"

He nodded. "Whatever makes you happy."

૨૦

Sunday morning Lynden Greeley called for Teddy and Gram at exactly quarter past nine, as he always did, to take them to church. "You look lovely," he told Teddy, as he helped her into the back seat of his compact car. "I especially like the light green suit you're wearing. You knitted that last year, didn't you?" Then he turned his attention to Gram and helped her into the front seat.

When they walked into the small white community church, Teddy gulped. Brand Sinclair sat on the far end of the last row of pews. After a moment of staring, she followed Gram and Lynden to their usual seat on the aisle, half way down. Teddy barely heard the sermon; she was so aware of the big man sitting in the back of the church. To make matters worse, she felt he was staring at her during the entire service.

After church the members of the small congregation lingered in the warm sunshine, visiting. Eventually Brand greeted Teddy and she introduced him to Lynden.

"Anyone invite you home for lunch?" Gram asked in her usual brusque style.

Brand shook his sunshiny hair and his brown eyes danced. "Not yet, Mrs. Marland, but I'm still hoping."

"Nelle," Gram said. "Call me Nelle. Why don't you come on over to our place? You already know where it is, and you won't have far to go home."

"Well, Nellie—"

"Nelle, sonny, not Nellie. All right, we'll see you in a little while. Don't be too long, because our meal is all ready. You know the commandments, I suppose."

When they got home, Teddy changed her clothes in a hurry so she could help Gram with the food. They had it steaming on the table when Brand joined them.

"Leave your shoes at the door and wash your hands in the bathroom," Gram barked when Brand stepped inside. "Shoes are filthy things."

One golden eyebrow rose, but he said not a word as he stepped out of his boots and strode through the empty living room to the bathroom to comply. When he returned, he hesitated, looking the table over.

"Well, sit down there by Teddy," Gram commanded but Lynden dropped into the chair. Gram waggled a finger at Brand. "You can sit by me, then. I'm almost as good company as Teddy, don't you think?"

Brand sat down beside the tiny shriveled woman and took her hand. "Sure, Gram, you're all right."

"Nelle, sonny." Her old eyes spun over the young faces around her. "Everybody's hands still clean?"

Lynden and Teddy nodded. Brand looked at his, front and back. He nodded too.

"All right, I guess you're the guest, Brand, so you just go ahead and ask the blessing."

"Look, Gram," Brand said, "I don't know any blessings except 'God is Great.' You don't want that, do you?"

Lynden cleared his throat and prayed a prayer so long that Teddy knew for sure the chicken would be cold. She peeked to see if he was about to wind down, and met Brand's golden gaze. He winked at her, then closed both eyes tight. Teddy closed hers too.

After the meal everyone sat down on the couch, love seat, and rocking chair to visit. "What did you do before coming here, Sinclair?" Lynden wanted to know.

"Helped my folks on their ranch," Brand answered willingly and then he invited them all to see his ranch. "It doesn't have anything exotic, like Teddy's goats," he joked, "but I'd like to show you anyway."

"I've been wanting to get a good look at that fancy place," Teddy said.

"You two run along," Gram said. "Lynden and I'll stay here and see if we can eat all the candy."

Brand and Teddy jumped to their feet and Lynden raised himself half off the couch, then settled back down. "Don't be gone too long," he said, unwrapping a small candy bar.

In their eagerness to be off, Brand and Teddy literally ran off the porch but, when they stepped through the yard gate, the llamas surrounded them and forced them to slow down.

"Are we in danger?" Brand asked.

"No. Casanova is the only one that spits and you're the third person he's spit on. But I'll call the dogs." She stuck two fingers into her mouth and let out a whistle that almost knocked her own ears out of her head. A moment later, two gray and white dogs appeared. Teddy made a sweeping motion with her arm. "Take them back there," she said softly.

The dogs quietly went to work and, in a few minutes, they had herded the llamas to the back side of the pasture.

"Wow!" Brand said. "Those dogs are worth more than the llamas."

Teddy shook her head. "No, but they're worth a lot."

"Who's that jerk who ate lunch with us?" Brand asked as they walked across the pasture toward his place.

Teddy smiled. "That *jerk* is my boyfriend. We've been going together for a long time."

Brand shook his head but said nothing more about Lynden. "How come your grandmother wears boys' jeans to church?" he asked.

Teddy laughed out loud. "She wears boys' clothes everywhere, hadn't you noticed? She's pretty tiny and they seem to fit."

"Yes, but to church?"

Teddy's blue eyes flashed mischievously. "She does dress up for church. She wears jeans to church rather than bib overalls, and tee shirts rather than flannel. And besides that she wears newer sneakers."

"Okay, I can handle that. How come you live with her?"

"Who else would I live with? I'm not married or anything, and we work the ranch together."

They came to the border fence—a rotted, falling-down, log fence. Brand looked the fence over as he helped Teddy across, but said nothing. "What about your folks?" he asked when they were on their way again.

Teddy's cheeks burned. He had asked the one question she could not handle. "I don't have any folks except Gram," she snapped in a voice that brooked no further discussion. "Gramp died just before I was born."

"Okay, one more question. Whose ranch is it?" His eyes asked Teddy if that question was okay, and she smiled.

"Legally, it's mine," she answered. "Gram insisted on putting it in my name when I turned twenty-one. But really, it belongs to both of us."

Brand stopped walking and turned to face Teddy. "How old are you?"

"Twenty-one on my last birthday. Why does that surprise you?"

"Well, I thought you were a kid, maybe sixteen."

They started walking across his pasture toward the neat, modern buildings scattered over the huge place.

"My turn," Teddy said, laughing. "I have to know why you said Gram and I made a crazy-looking pair."

Brand turned amused eyes on her. "It looked like a mouse defending an elephant."

"Cute! Really cute. Of course, there's no question who the elephant was, is there?"

Brand moved to Teddy's side and dropped a long, sun-tanned arm across her shoulders. "You're a graceful willowy girl, Teddy, and I'm sure you're well aware of just how beautiful you are. I've never seen such soft, shiny hair, and the gold highlighting the dark color is nothing less than spectacular. And your shockingly blue eyes are entrancing. But. . .Have you ever seen anyone as tiny as your grandmother in your entire life?"

Teddy laughed and moved away from Brand, causing his hand to crash to his side. "I guess I'm used to her," she said. "She's just right to me."

When he was finished showing Teddy around the ranch, Brand suggested they look at the inside of the house.

"I better not go inside," she said hesitantly.

"Twenty-one's old enough to go into a neighbor's house," Brand said. "Anyway, we won't be alone." He took her arm and led her through the yard, which Teddy noticed was immaculately weeded and trimmed, unlike her own jungle.

"Hannah, Rolf," Brand called when the front door closed behind them. The house must have been about 150 years newer than hers. Thick, cream-colored carpets covered the wide expanse of floor and modern paintings hung in exactly the right places on sparkling white walls.

She followed him through a large dining room, into a kitchen, the likes of which Teddy had never seen.

"We're here, Brand," a voice called from somewhere, and a middle-aged couple appeared through a door.

Brand smiled. "Rolf, Hannah, this is our next-ranch neighbor, Teddy Marland. Teddy, these are the people who take care of the place and me. Especially me. The Perrys, Rolf and Hannah."

Hannah, probably in her early fifties, red-headed, freckled, and large, shook Teddy's hand, then dropped it and hugged her. "We're glad to know you at last," she said.

Rolf, a little older and with gray hair, took Teddy's hand and pumped it vigorously. "Yes, at last."

After a few minutes of visiting, Brand invited Teddy to see the stables.

"What was that 'we're meeting you at last,' stuff?" Teddy asked as they walked through the equally well kept back yard. "Have they been here a long time?"

Brand grinned foolishly and shook his head. "No, they came from Alvadore with me. I may have mentioned your name a couple of times," he confessed at Teddy's raised eyebrows. Then he opened the stable door, motioning Teddy in. "Let me introduce you to our horses. This is Misty. She's a real lady. Spicy, but sweet." Teddy took in the sleek palomino mare.

"And this is Thunder. You probably recognize him from my crazy ride to your place. Thunder is my special stallion. He can always give me more than I bargain for." Teddy looked up at the huge black stallion. She had no doubt he would be more than she could handle.

Brand showed her the two other horses, a large chestnut gelding, Pharaoh, and Powder, a fat dark mare.

Teddy turned glowing blue eyes to Brand. "I love them. We don't have any horses and I've always wanted some."

"Want to take a ride?"

"I'd love to. . .if you'll be patient with a greenhorn and a fool besides."

Brand saddled Thunder and Misty and helped Teddy onto Misty, who pranced daintily in one spot, eager to be off.

They walked around the pasture for a little while, then Brand trotted Thunder and Misty followed. "Want to ride over to your place and show Gram the horses?"

"Yes! Let's do. But she wants you to call her Nelle."

As they approached the house, Teddy mentally compared her home to Brand's. Half as large and all on one floor, its sides were made of weathered logs. The wooden windows looked old and worn. And the inside! She would rather not even think about that right now. Her eyes lifted to the bright blue tile roof. Such a fancy roof looked silly on the decrepit old house, but Gram said if they always repaired it with good material, one day the house would look great. Teddy was not so sure about that.

Teddy nimbly slid off the friendly little palomino's back and sprinted toward the old house. He followed her up the rickety steps. Both carefully skirted the most severely rotted area. They laughed together at the sheer delight of the afternoon. Suddenly the door burst open and Lynden stood in the opening. He was not laughing.

Chapter Three

The laughter slowly died to a stiff silence. "Do you realize you've been gone over two hours, Teddy?" Lynden asked in a stern voice.

"No!" Teddy said with a little gasp. "I completely lost track of the time."

"Time passes quickly when you're having fun," Brand quipped.

"Butt out, cowboy," Lynden snapped. Returning his attention to Teddy, he spoke roughly, scolding. "We planned to go to a concert in Pioneer Park this afternoon."

"I forgot all about it. Is it too late?" Teddy felt breathless for some strange reason. . .and guilty.

"Of course it's too late. It's nearly over."

Brand took Teddy's upper arm in his fingers. "Good, let's get a drink of water and ride some more."

Lynden knocked Brand's hand from Teddy's arm and jerked her away. "Not so fast, big shot, she's staying with me."

Brand's golden brown eyes burned into Teddy's. "Teddy?"

"Oh, I don't know," she said. "I should stay with Lynden. But I should take Misty back too."

"Don't give it another thought," Brand said. He turned to go, then faced Teddy again. "Where's Gram?" he asked.

"Out making sure the llamas have plenty of food and water," Lynden replied.

"And you didn't go help?" Brand asked. "Will you tell Gram thanks for the fantastic meal?" he said to Teddy. "See you later."

"Where does he get off, calling Nelle, Gram?" Lynden asked.

Teddy shook her weary head. "I don't know. I just don't know." She felt as though the sun had disappeared behind a black cloud. Stepping into the living room, she listlessly pulled off her boots. Lynden followed.

Just then Gram came in, singing a hymn at the top of her voice. "Everyone out there's fat and happy," she announced at the end of the lively chorus.

"I'm sorry, Gram," Teddy said, "I didn't realize how late it is."

Gram made a silent "Pooh." Teddy thought her grandmother's old eyes had a special glint in them. "Who keeps track of time on Sunday?" Gram added. "I was glad for the exercise and it didn't take a minute. Brand came out to help, but I was finished. I noticed he led the palomino back home. I hope you didn't get hurt."

"No, I decided to stay here with Lynden."

"Oh? He decide to do something? The candy must be gone."

Teddy glanced at the empty candy dish. "What would you like to do, Lynden, go for a ride?"

"What's to see? Another mile out and there's nothing but sagebrush."

"Should we go to Pioneer Park? It's shady and pleasant."

"What's the matter with here? It's shady and pleasant here, too, isn't it?"

Lynden stayed for supper but never quite recovered from Teddy's neglect through the rest of the afternoon.

≈

After Teddy went to bed that night a big, windblown figure galloped around in her head, astride an enormous black stallion. "This is ridiculous," she told herself and asked the Lord to help her empty her mind and fall asleep. He did.

"You look as if you need another two hours' sleep," Gram announced cheerfully the next morning when Teddy slid into her chair.

"I'm all right, Gram, I just need my coffee."

Gram filled a fat brown mug with the steaming liquid and slapped it down beside Teddy's plate. "What're we doing today, kitten?"

"Moving the herd to the north pasture. After that, we could go through and knock out the big weeds. As scarce as water is, I can't stand feeding and watering weeds."

"Sounds good. I'll be out before you finish moving the llamas."

Teddy's eyes gazed toward the west as she opened the gate between the two pastures, then she walked out to the llamas. She hoped she would run into Brand today. He had not seemed bothered when she decided to stay with Lynden, but why should he? They were barely friends and she had told him right off that Lynden was her boyfriend.

Teddy looked around at the llamas, all walking or running toward her, the babies keeping near their mothers. She stuck her fingers into her mouth and whistled. The dogs appeared, trotting casually to her. "Hi, Brutus, Caesar," she greeted them. "Okay, guys, take us to the north pasture, but real easy."

Teddy began walking north with llamas surrounding her. Casanova and Iris crowded so close they bumped against her as they walked. The dogs separated, one to the east, one to the west, and trotted casually back and forth, keeping the llamas in a fairly tight group. "Great going, guys," Teddy called to the dogs.

Then Casanova stiffened and his ears flapped back against his head. Teddy turned to find Brand about fifty feet behind her. "Don't come any closer," she called softly. "We'll have these guys put away in a few minutes, then I'll join you."

She locked the gate that connected the south and north pastures and returned to Brand. "Now, what can I do for you?" she asked with a welcoming smile.

"I didn't want anything, especially. I saw the dogs working the little camels and thought I'd watch. Why did you stop me? Afraid I'd stampede the buffalo?"

She grinned. "I did it for your own protection. You seem to have made an enemy among my flock."

He looked surprised. "I didn't see Lynden anywhere."

Teddy chuckled. "Maybe you made more than one enemy, come to think of it. I meant Casanova. You remember him?"

He nodded and grinned. "Oh yes. The dirty bird that spit on me! Believe me, I'll give him plenty of clearance from now on."

"Want to sit down a minute?" Teddy asked.

"Here?" He looked around the grassy pasture. "Sure as I sit down, I'll find a llama pie."

Teddy shook her head. "No way. Llamas all go to one corner. Not only does it keep the pasture clean, but it makes fertilizing the garden awfully easy. Now, back to your problem with my friend, Casanova," she said mischievously. "He remembers you and evidently the memory isn't pleasant. Before llamas spit, they tense up, their ears flatten and they start chewing. He saw you before I did and alerted me. I noticed his head go up. He would have spit if you'd kept coming."

Brand grinned. "He's just jealous. So's your other friend for that matter."

Teddy pulled up her knees and put her arms around them. "I don't think Lynden's jealous. I haven't given him any reason to be."

"He has reason to be jealous of anyone who lives and breathes and moves. Now, to change the subject, why don't you tell me about yourself," Brand suggested. "Where did you go to college?"

College? Teddy had been so busy with the ranch she had not even thought about college. Now she felt embarrassed to admit it. "Nowhere," she finally said, softly. "I suppose you went to some fancy school?"

He shook his head. "Nope. I went to Oregon State University. Majored in business administration and animal husbandry. Ranching, I guess you'd call it."

"So. . .we're going to watch a rancher who does it by the book," she replied.

Hearing a buzzing noise like a million extra-loud bees, they looked up to see Gram pile off her motorcycle. "Hey, is this the way you're getting the work done?" the old lady called in her guttural voice. But, as she trotted nearer, Teddy noticed a definite gleam in her faded eyes. Either the old lady was kidding or she had a crush on Brand.

"Sit down a minute and catch your breath," Brand said, patting a spot beside him.

"Brand's just telling me about his college education," Teddy said.

"And Teddy's telling me she hasn't had hers yet," Brand added.

"Oh, she's educated," Gram said. "She graduated from the college of hard knocks with a master's degree in Good Judgment from Bad Experience. She's also taken many classes in gaining good experience from bad judgment." Then she said, "I have to get busy. You two can waste this gorgeous day if you want to." She kicked the motorcycle to life and tore off toward the house. A few minutes later she started across the pasture on foot, whacking away at the weeds with her sharp hoe.

"I have one more question," Brand said. "Is your name really Theodore?"

Teddy's eyes smiled, though her mouth remained still. "That's my name."

"Why?"

Teddy shrugged. "I guess Gram liked it. Maybe she didn't know it was a boy's name."

"Gram. Always Gram. Is she really your mother?"

This time Teddy did smile. "I'm twenty-one, she's seventy-eight. Does that tell you anything?"

He looked into Teddy's blue eyes with curiosity. "Grandmothers usually don't name their grandchildren," he said softly.

Ugh. If she could just learn to keep her mouth shut every discussion might not turn to her origins. Why did everyone have to be so nosy, anyway? Thank goodness Lynden had never been curious about her relationship with Gram.

"I'm not supposed to ask that?" His voice remained soft and caring.

Teddy wondered if she could even answer. "Right," she murmured. To her surprise he took her hand and touched her fingers to his lips, then to hers, and walked off the way he had come. Teddy could not have been more shocked if he had really kissed her. Nobody had ever done such a sweet thing to her before. But then she had never known anyone like Brandon Sinclair before. Nobody.

❧

The next morning Teddy stepped back to see how much area the big gun sprinkler was covering. She looked up and noticed the black stallion, with Brand astride, leaning low over the heavily muscled neck, galloping straight for the dividing fence. A moment later, Brand dismounted. He stood at the stallion's head, patting him while he yelled at the top of his voice. "Call the dogs. Your pesky goats are all over my place."

"How did they get over there?"

"Walked over the rotten logs you call a fence."

Gram, hearing the ruckus, dropped the wrenches she had been using to set up the irrigation system and ran to Teddy. "Just keep your shirt on, buster. Those llamas won't hurt a thing and we'll have them back in a flash."

"Oh, really? You should have seen my cattle scatter. They won't go near those long-necked camels."

Teddy began laughing. "You don't have to defend me, Gram. Brand has a big mouth, but he won't hurt me. He thinks you're a little mouse defending an elephant. . .me."

"Oh he does, does he? Maybe we should let him figure out how to get the llamas off his dumb cattle ranch."

Brand simmered down and grinned. "That mouse and elephant business does sound pretty harsh when you play it back. I'm sorry." He winked. "Now, will you please call your goats home, Gram?"

"I'm not your gram!" she shouted in a voice that would have frightened a tornado cloud. "And they aren't goats. Come on, Teddy, let's go have lunch."

Teddy snatched the old woman's hand and hauled her back beside her. Then she stuck two fingers into her mouth and whistled for the dogs, which appeared almost immediately.

"We better check the fence before you set the dogs on the llamas," Brand said, leading Thunder northward. "I don't know much about llamas, but cattle can get out of a hole they can't possibly return through."

When they got there, they saw that ten feet of the rotten log fence lay flat on the ground. Teddy instructed the dogs to bring the llamas back, and in a few minutes, the llamas started returning to their own pasture. The dogs did not stop until they had every llama on its own side of the broken-down fence.

"I'll bet those two dogs take the place of a hired man," Brand said. "How would you like to sell them?"

"No way, sonny," Gram said. "We couldn't operate without those dogs." She grinned. "Besides, they don't know what a cow is."

"Okay, I'll have to find my own dogs. How would you girls like to share the expense of putting up wire fencing between our ranches?"

Gram shook her white head. "Not yet. We'll just fix the log fence, even though I'd bet your cattle knocked it down."

Brand's face started to redden. "Wait just a minute, Gram! Were my cattle on your place?"

"No, your cattle are too dumb to walk through the fence they smashed down. And don't you call me Gram!" She turned and walked off. "I'll bring some logs, Teddy," she called.

Brand went home. Teddy finished setting up the irrigation, then joined Gram at the broken-down fence. They spent the afternoon repairing it and went into the house, tired but satisfied with their day's work.

Later in the evening there was a tap on the front door. "That'll be Lynden," Gram said. They were watching summer reruns on TV; Teddy was working on her red sweater and Gram was cutting out pink butterflies for her quilt.

Lynden settled onto the couch beside Teddy, sprawling until he sat almost on his back. He watched the TV for a few minutes, then looked from Gram to Teddy. "Since you girls aren't watching much, would you mind if I switched to another station?" Without waiting for an answer, he flipped to a program he wanted to watch. The women's eyes met and Gram barely raised a bushy, white eyebrow. Teddy's lips turned into a tiny smile. Then she shrugged. "Anything new at work today?" she asked brightly. She always asked because a newspaper should be an exciting place to work.

Lynden shook his head no, held a restraining hand toward her, and leaned closer to the TV.

Gram grinned and Teddy gave her a little push. The big yellow cat climbed into Lynden's lap but he saw nothing except the television.

A few minutes later Gram laid her scissors down. "Anyone want some pie and ice cream?" she asked.

Teddy pushed her knitting to the back of the needles and dumped it onto the coffee table. "Sure, I'll help."

"Sure nice to have your boyfriend visit a couple of times a week," Gram said with a wicked grin.

"Well, he feels at home," Teddy said. "And I enjoy having him over."

Lynden rushed to wash his hands, accepted the dessert and gulped it, all the while with his eyes glued to the television. "Could just as well have fed him oatmeal," Gram said.

Teddy ate the last bite of her dessert and stood to take the dishes back to the counter when a frenzied attack on the door nearly made her drop the dishes. It actually caused Lynden to look away from the TV.

Teddy threw the door open and Brand strode into the room. Suddenly it felt as though the sun had come from behind a cloud and warmed the entire house.

"Just thought I should check to make sure you girls are all right before I hit the sheets," he said, wearing a wide smile. "I see you aren't."

Gram pointed to Brand's feet. "Take off those boots before you come into my clean house," she yelled.

Brand backed to the front door. "Sorry." He flipped off his boots.

"Now go wash your hands. Those boots are dirty."

Brand complied. "Now, do I get some of whatever you had in those dishes?"

Teddy cut a wide slice of the warm apple pie, piled ice cream beside it, and handed it to him.

"Thanks," he said after he cleaned up the dish. "Hannah's a good cook, but she hasn't produced anything like this." He looked from one to another, then back to Teddy. "Looks as though I interrupted a lively evening."

"What should we have been doing?" Teddy asked.

"Anything. At least you could look more lively."

Gram slapped a long reddish box on the table almost before he finished talking. "Here's a game that'll bring you to life."

"How many are going to play, Gram?" Teddy asked recognizing the box. Gram always hauled it out when they had company because it required four to play.

Everyone looked at Lynden who, eyes on the TV, seemed unaware of anyone's presence. "Looks like it'll be three," Brand said. "What's the game, Gram?"

The little old woman wagged a finger at him. "Nelle," she said, as softly as her gravelly voice could speak. "Pictionary," she said. "Think you could keep up with Teddy and me?"

He raised his golden eyebrows at Gram. "A drawing game?" He smiled at Gram. "If you can do it, so can I. Bring it on."

"We really need four to play this right," Teddy said. "But I just figured out how we can do it with three." She explained that one would draw and the other two guess. The one who drew and the one who correctly guessed would advance their tokens on the board. Brand decided to draw first while Teddy and Gram raced to see who could guess what it was.

"A sailboat?" Teddy yelled.

"No, it's a horse," Gram announced in her gruff voice.

"No!" Teddy bellowed, "it's a table. Those are table legs, Gram."

As the game went on the players grew louder, laughing hysterically as they tried to draw recognizable objects before the sand disappeared from the hourglass.

Finally, Lynden roused himself from the TV and leaned over the papers. "I don't see anything so funny," he said. "Looks stupid to me."

Brand sobered up enough to speak. "Why don't you give it a try, city boy? It may be stupid but it's not easy. And it definitely is funny."

"You three are making major fools of yourselves," Lynden said, dropping into the empty chair. "I'll join you if you play something sensible."

Gram shook her head. "Anybody who is anybody is playing this game," she said. "Join us in this one, or go back to your TV."

He watched a little longer, then assuring them he could do much better, agreed to play. He and Teddy became partners and Gram and Brand played together.

When Lynden played, Teddy could not guess what he drew for anything. "It's a marshmallow," she said. "A piece of popcorn. A cotton ball." Lynden soon grew impatient with her. When the time ran out and he told her it was a cloud, she told him clouds are mostly flat on the bottom.

When Gram and Brand crossed the finish line before Teddy and he reached the halfway mark, Lynden jumped up, knocking the playing pieces off the board and onto the table. "I need to go home," he muttered. "I guess I'm the only one here who has to get up at a certain time. I mean with a real job."

Brand bounced to his feet. "What time do you get up, city boy?"

"Seven o'clock. . .no matter what time I get to bed."

Brand shook his head in disbelief. "Is that a fact? Well, I have my cattle all fed by six o'clock. Every morning."

"That's hard for me to believe," Lynden said. "After all, you don't have a boss checking on you. Come on, Teddy, kiss me good night. I have to go." He pulled Teddy to him and covered her mouth with his. She tried to pull back but he held her tightly. Finally, he let her go, put on his shoes, and stepped outside.

Teddy wanted more than anything in the world to go brush her teeth, but Brand stood in the kitchen doorway watching, his eyes mocking her. Unable to control herself, she swiped the back of her hand across her lips. That helped a little, but she knew for sure Brand saw her do it. And that he knew why.

Chapter Four

"I guess it's time for us all to get to bed," Brand said. "Gram, you're some artist. You just whistle anytime you get the urge to draw again." He laughed softly. "Just be sure we play on the same team again."

"You got that right, sonny. I'm not about to play with that lump of dough that just left."

After Brand had left, Gram turned to Teddy, her faded blue eyes dancing. "You've never been kissed like that before, have you, kitten?"

"No, and I hated it." Teddy shuddered, remembering. "I felt his yucky teeth and. . . . Gram, is something wrong with me?"

"Nope. It's the toad that kissed you. Maybe now you can wake up to find the handsome prince."

"Like who?"

Gram shrugged. "How would I know?"

Teddy took a shower and brushed her teeth. Then she went to bed, wondering what Gram had been babbling about. She had been referring to Brand, of course. After asking God to bless and guide her, she fell asleep.

❧

The next afternoon Teddy noticed that one of Brand's water gun sprinklers was not rotating. He would have a flood in almost no time if the huge sprinkler was not fixed—it threw out fifty gallons a minute. She dropped the hammer and spit out the nails she had been using to repair a weak spot in the fence between the north and south pastures. Then she dashed to the shed for her wrench and took off toward Brand's place. Thirty minutes later she gave the sprinkler a final testing; she smiled at the smooth and steady way it turned.

Waiting until the hundred-foot stream of water passed the spot where she would climb the fence, she zipped out behind its path and scrambled onto her own property, pleased that she had discovered the problem and helped a neighbor.

She shook her head. She could not be disappointed that Brand had not come out to help. She did not need him. *Why does Brand invade my mind all the time?* Teddy wondered as she continued working on the fence. *I've never spent time dreaming about a man, not even Lynden, and this tall, bronzed giant walks into my life and knocks me completely out of whack.* "Father," she whispered, "I've always been a sensible down-to-earth person. Please help me to stay that way. Thank You." She gathered up her hammer and nails and started working on her fence again.

"I'll bet I can guess whom you aren't thinking about."

Teddy dropped the hammer and nearly swallowed two nails. Brand must be a mind reader. She pressed her hand to her chest. "Okay, whom am I not thinking about?"

"The blob. The one with absolutely no personality."

Teddy stared into his brown eyes. . .the ones where the sunbeams learned how to dance. She said nothing.

"Oh, come on, Teddy, surely you remember the blob. He's the guy who kissed you last night."

"Oh."

"Did you enjoy that kiss?"

Teddy felt her face redden. "What I enjoy and what I don't enjoy couldn't possibly be of interest to you."

"Oh, but it is." He leaned back on his heels and watched her embarrassment. "When are you going to send him down the road?"

"I have no intentions of sending him down the road. And what makes you think I didn't enjoy the kiss?"

"Because he forced you, kicking and screaming all the way. I was just ready to rearrange his face when he let you go."

He knew. Evidently he stood there with Gram, watching the show they put on. "He's not that bad," she mumbled. "I'm just not into rough kissing, and I thought he wasn't, either. I can't figure out what got into him last night."

"I can. You've heard of animals marking out their territory? Well, that's what that turkey was doing. And I'm still mad about it."

Gram arrived on the scene and heard his remark. "What are you mad about, sonny? Because she's his territory, or that he marked her as his?"

"I don't know, Gram, all of the above? I guess I'm just mad." He pulled his hands from his pockets. "I'd better be getting back. It's about time for evening feeding. See you later." He took off in an easy run and a moment later Teddy and Gram watched him scramble over the old log fence.

"You let him call you 'Gram,' and didn't even yell about it," Teddy said, her bright eyes sparkling.

The leathery old face creased into a wide smile. "I believe I did, at that."

≈

The next Sunday Lynden took Gram and Teddy to church as usual, and Lynden followed Teddy down the aisle, into the pew. After they sat down, Teddy kept wondering if Brand was in the little church, but she refused to turn around to check. She was in deep thought, enjoying the quiet organ music, when a rustling to her left caused her to meet two laughing brown eyes. Brand scooted through the pew from the other side and sat down beside her.

When the opening hymn was announced, Teddy's hand collided with Brand's as they reached for a hymnal. She pulled back as though his touch was distasteful, but she did not feel that way. . .not even a little bit that way. What was the matter with her, anyway? Then she felt Lynden tense up beside her.

When they rose to sing, Brand motioned for Lynden to share his hymnal with Gram and he held his out for Teddy. Lynden could hardly ignore the sensible-sounding request—there being only two hymnals in each pew—so

Teddy shared Brand's book and learned he had a strong clear baritone voice.

The minister chose for his sermon the verses that said, "Inasmuch as you have done it for the least, you have done it for me." For some reason that made Teddy think of Lynden. She decided she must treat him better. After all he had been coming over for several years and had been faithful and kind all that time. Brand's arrival had upset Lynden as well as her—and she wondered if maybe he had even knocked Gram off her always-even keel.

Afterward, outside in the warm sunlight, Brand held his big brown hand out to Lynden and shook hard. "Great sermon, wasn't it, brother?" Then he turned to Gram. "Hannah has prepared lunch for six, Gram, so could I persuade you folks to help us eat it?"

"Hey, that sounds fantastic," replied Gram. "What do you think, kitten?"

Teddy thought it sounded interesting but she had just told herself to be more considerate to Lynden. She turned to him. "How about you? Would you rather eat at our place?"

"Frankly, I would, but it looks as if I don't have any choice." His bottom lip puffed out as though a bee had stung it, making him look for all the world like a pouty child. "Are you going to ride with me?" he asked crossly.

"Of course, I'm riding with you," Teddy said. "But you do have a choice, Lynden. I can fix a meal that will fill you up. Really I can. I'd like to go home and change my clothes first anyway. No telling what we'll be doing before the day ends."

After lunch, everyone settled into luxurious white leather chairs and sofas in Brand's comfortable living room and visited for a while.

"Well, my lunch has settled," Brand announced about midafternoon, "how about everyone else's?"

"Yeah," Lynden agreed. "You have a comfortable place here."

"Thanks. Anyone want to go riding?"

Gram was on her feet before he finished talking. "You know, sonny, I thought you'd never ask."

"Me too. May I ride Misty?" Teddy asked.

"I think I'd better head for home," Lynden said. "Why don't you come on into Bend with me, Teddy? We have plans for later, you know."

She bounced over and captured his hand. "No, you don't. You're going to ride with us. Our plans are for much later."

Brand saddled Powder, a dark fat mare, for Gram. "Just what she needs, Gram, a tiny little lady. She's going to be a mama in about five months."

Then he saddled Misty for Teddy and Pharaoh, the big chestnut gelding for Lynden. "Here's your steed, Greeley, think he'll be fast enough for you?" Brand asked, mischief jumping in his brown eyes.

Lynden looked the gelding up and down, and from one end to the other. "That thing looks pretty big," he mumbled. "And I'm not real used to riding. Maybe you should take him and let me ride yours."

"Okay," Brand agreed. He stepped to the next stall and brought out Thunder. "Here he is. He's the largest stallion in these parts and his name is Thunder for a reason. Do you want to saddle him?"

Lynden looked doubtful as he watched the monstrous horse prance and rear in its eagerness to go. "No, I really think I should be getting back to town."

Gram stepped up to Brand and indicated Lynden with her thumb. "He's pretty skinny. Think he's too heavy for Powder?"

"I suppose not, if he treats her carefully. Did you decide not to ride?"

"No way. I'm riding Pharaoh."

Finally, everyone rode down the long driveway toward the highway. "I know this neat riding trail, about a mile west," Brand said. "Rolf and I've been riding it."

Everyone walked their horses until they hit the trail, then Gram urged Pharaoh into an easy canter. Brand and Teddy followed and Lynden's pregnant mare, Powder, who was not about to be left behind, stepped up to a fast trot. "Hey, Sinclair," Lynden yelled after a few minutes. "How do I stop this thing? It's shaking my teeth out."

"Pull back on the reins, gently," Brand called, but Lynden only heard the first part of the instructions and jerked the reins as hard as he could. At the same time, his heels dug into Powder's tender flanks. The mare stopped short and stood on her hind legs, then put her head down and kicked her back legs straight above her head. Lynden flew several feet into the air, landing on his back on a bed of pine needles.

Teddy sucked in her breath, wondering if Lynden was all right. But Brand instantly flew off his stallion, caught Powder's reins, and examined her mouth. "There, there, girl, we won't let him do it again." He hugged her dark neck and patted her. "I'm sorry, baby, he's just a mean man, but you're all right, now."

Then he turned to Lynden with fury written all over his face. "What were you trying to do?" he bellowed, "Tear her mouth off? Don't you know horses have feelings? Guys like you ruin perfectly good horses."

Lynden struggled to his feet. "If you think I'm climbing back on that horse, you're crazy. You just gave her to me because you knew she'd do something like that."

Brand said something under his breath then stood quietly for a few moments. "If you think I'd let you on any of my horses after that performance," he finally said, "you're the crazy one. Now you just high-tail it back to the ranch. I think there's some candy on the kitchen counter. That ought to keep you busy for a while."

"Gladly. Come with me, Teddy."

Teddy looked at Gram.

"Don't ask me," Gram said. "You already kissed the toad. I don't know what the next act is, but you're going to find out, one way or another."

Chapter Five

"Please, Teddy," Lynden said quietly. A butterfly's song could have been heard in the ensuing silence. Teddy had been looking so forward to the afternoon ride, but she really should go with Lynden. After all, he had been her boyfriend forever. He wanted her company, and he had a right to ask.

She smiled at the super-thin young man. "Sure, I'll come. What shall I do with Misty, Brand?"

"Uh, take her to the house and get Rolf. He'll take care of her."

Teddy turned Misty to walk beside Lynden, who now wore a satisfied smile. They had walked a few steps when Brand called to her. "Teddy, would you lead Powder back? You might tell Rolf that Misty feels cheated and needs a nice run. Suggest he come ride with us." He handed Powder's reins to her, mounted Thunder, and turned to Gram. "Okay, Gram, are you ready for some serious riding?"

"Never been more ready in my life. Let's go." Thunder and Pharaoh gracefully galloped away, and Teddy felt morose.

Lynden walked swiftly back toward the highway, with Teddy, riding Misty, beside him, and leading Powder. "Thanks, Teddy, I really wanted a little time alone with you."

"It's all right, I can ride another time. I really do like horses, you know."

"No, I didn't know. Why don't you get some of your own?"

"You know we mortgaged the ranch to the limit when we changed from cattle to llamas. Well, Gram's been putting every spare dime on the mortgage. She took a notion it had to be paid off in five years, and we're right on schedule. Then we can get some horses. And fix up the place. And whatever else—"

"How about I hop up behind you?" Lynden asked, as they turned into Brand's long, long driveway.

Teddy shook her head and slid out of the golden horse's saddle. "I can't, Lynden, but I'll walk with you." Both horses plodded along behind the pair.

"Are you getting hooked on that guy?" Lynden asked.

Teddy shook her head. "He's nice, though," she said quietly.

They talked about inconsequential things until they reached the house, and Lynden went inside for Rolf. He returned a few minutes later with a handful of candy. Teddy laughed out loud. "I see you remembered the candy."

A half-hour later they reached Teddy's house and, after having removed their shoes, they went through the bare living room and flopped onto the kitchen couch. "Well, I guess we got our exercise, even though it didn't turn out quite as I'd planned," Teddy said with a quiet sigh.

Lynden rested a moment, then scrambled to his feet. "I'll make some sandwiches." He opened the refrigerator and pulled out roast beef, mayonnaise, lettuce, and white bread. A short while later, he set the small plate on the coffee table, put two tall glasses of milk beside it, and sat down next to Teddy.

"Aren't you going to ask me if I know anything exciting?" he asked. He took a huge bite of his sandwich, and washed it down with some milk.

"Okay. Hey, Lynden, I was just wondering, have you learned anything exciting lately?"

He nodded, and wiped his chin with a paper napkin. Then, he pushed himself back on the couch and sat up straight. "It's about your fancy neighbor. Do you still want to hear?"

Suddenly Teddy did not feel hungry anymore. She laid her sandwich down. "Of course I do. Tell me." She waited a moment, then realized she was holding her breath.

"What do you know about the guy anyway?"

Teddy thought a moment. "Not much." She felt stifled as though the air were too hot to breathe. "Get on with it, Lynden, I'm curious."

"Well, it was this bank robbery in Eugene. Isn't that where he came from? It happened just a few weeks before he showed up here. We got a short item and picture concerning the robbery and it's Sinclair, Teddy. I'd swear it is. Not only the picture and description match, but that truck he drives is the getaway rig."

Teddy shook her head. "No way, not Brand. You have the wrong guy."

"Maybe. Maybe not." He looked so smug that, for a second, she almost did not like him. "How much did that ranch cost, Teddy?"

"I don't know. A bundle, I guess."

He leaned closer to her, his eyes boring into hers. "Where did he get the money? Not too many guys his age have that kind of money and almost as few have the credit to borrow it."

"Where did you see it, Lynden? Show me." Teddy felt breathless, but she would not let Lynden know.

"Well, it hasn't been published in our paper yet. Since it's old news anyway they'll wait until we have a little space to fill. Who'd ever expect him to be hiding out over here?"

"Could you bring me a copy of the picture? And also the item? I might even show it to Brand."

Lynden shook his head vigorously. "I'll bring you a copy but you better not show it to Brand. He may be dangerous."

⁊⁊

Teddy went to bed that night with Gram's praises of Brand ringing in her ears . . .and his golden good looks floating in her mind as he rode like the wind on his beautiful black stallion. *I wish Gram would keep quiet about him,* she told herself, turning over for the ninth time. *He's only a friend. I want to spend my time thinking of Lynden.* But Lynden's face refused to take form in her mind. *What's happening to me? Brand has given me no reason to think about him like this. Besides, he may be a dangerous bank robber.* She laughed out loud at the ludicrousness of that, turned over, and whispered, "Lynden's been my special friend for so long I keep thinking You've given him to me. Is that Your plan for me, Lord? And if Brand's a criminal, won't you help me find out for sure?" Finally, she fell asleep.

Teddy did not see Brand for several days, but her thoughts were constantly on what Lynden had told her. Come to think of it, she did not even know how old Brand was. But he certainly did not look or act like someone hiding from the law. Finally, she could not stand it any longer and asked Gram what she thought.

"Why don't you ask him?" Gram said. "Nothing works as well as communication, I always find."

"I'm not sure why I haven't asked, but Lynden told me not to as he might be dangerous."

"Pish posh," Gram bellowed. "Brand's about as dangerous as Cocoa." Cocoa was one of their best llamas and also one of the gentlest.

Lynden asked Teddy to go to a play the following week and she eagerly looked forward to it. She was eager not only to see the play, which she always enjoyed, but also to ask him again about that newspaper article he had mentioned. . .about the Eugene bank robbery. She did not get the chance until they came back at ten-thirty that night after the play.

"Want to come in for a minute?" she asked.

"Sure. For a little while." He sprawled on the couch and pulled the candy dish onto his lap.

She had to ask him now, or she would drive herself crazy wondering. "Anything interesting at the paper these days?"

"No, not in this quiet little town." He unwrapped another mint.

"What about that bank robbery thing? Did it ever get printed?"

He popped the mint between his teeth and reached for another. "I don't think so. I guess the editor thinks there isn't much chance of the guy's being around here. Think I should turn him in?"

"No! I mean, you don't even know if it's him."

He looked sharply at Teddy. "You do have something going with him, don't you?"

"Of course not. You've been with us every time we've tried to do anything. And wrecked it, too, I might add."

Lynden lumbered to his feet. "Well, I'm glad I wrecked your fun with him. I don't approve of his coming around here. Now I have to go home or I'll never get up in the morning."

Teddy walked to the door and waited while he put his shoes on. Then he gave her a peck on the lips, his usual good-bye. "See you Sunday."

≈

The next afternoon Teddy worked on the north pasture fence again, with the llamas crowding so close she could hardly work. Finally, she threw down her hammer and spent thirty minutes loving her woolly friends.

"Looks like the real thing to me."

Teddy pulled her arm from Romeo's neck and smiled. "What's the real thing?" she asked.

"Love. It looks as if you and your llamas really love each other."

"Oh. Well, we do."

"I suppose you're going to tell me that you know all your llamas by name."

"Of course I do." She started pointing at individual llamas. "That's Lily, there's Cocoa, one of our best young llamas, and there's Angel, Rose is over here, that black one is Belle, Duska is beside Belle. . .and the baby llamas are Peanut, that's the brown one, and—"

Brand cut her off with a deep laugh. "Whoa! We could be at this all day. But one thing I've been wondering about. Have you ever looked across my cattle? All red, wide, and exactly alike?"

Teddy nodded. "Exactly alike."

"Well," Brand continued, "that makes me feel as though my cattle are all the same breed."

"I know. Hereford. That's the kind we raised."

Brand flashed her a friendly smile. "Right. But when I look at your multicolored herd of goats," he shrugged, "I think you have a bunch of mutts."

"You're wrong, Brand. Llamas come in every color from white through reds and browns to blacks, and all mixes. The color doesn't matter and you never know what a female will throw. It's the conformation that counts." She grinned. As Teddy talked, the llamas crowded and bumped them until they could not stand still. "Let's get out of here so we can talk."

In a few minutes they sat in the lush grass of the empty south pasture about ten feet from the disappointed llamas. As they visited, Teddy could think only about Lynden's terrible news concerning Brand. She just had to find out if it was true. "Uh. . .how old are you?" she asked when a lull developed in the conversation.

"Okay, nosy, I'm almost thirty." He tweaked a dark brown curl. "Old enough to be your father."

"Have you ever been married? Had any kids?"

Teddy thought Brand's eyes opened a bit wider, but he took the question in stride. "I thought I was just getting old enough for those things. Are you applying for the job?"

As Teddy tried to think of a clever answer, something wet and green plopped against his forehead and bounced onto her lap. Brand wiped it off his face while Teddy scraped the horrible stuff from her lap and threw it as far as she could. But that awful odor remained. He took her hand and they ran to the line of old bath tubs that supplied water for the llamas. He washed his face and she literally poured water over her pants. They both washed their hands. . .and washed their hands. . .and washed their hands. When she met Brand's eyes, she realized he was more than unhappy, he was furious!

"I'm sorry," she began, "I didn't see Casanova around this morning. He must have come up after we left the llamas."

He started off toward his own ranch, muttering under his breath. The rest of the day seemed colder and darker to Teddy. In fact, she barely noticed when the sun dropped behind the trees. When she could not see to drive nails anymore, she quit and trudged to the house.

Gram offered no sympathy when told about the incident. "Don't worry, kitten, he'll get over it."

But Teddy did worry. She had a hard time getting to sleep, thinking about Brand. He might not come back anymore, after two run-ins with Casanova. Then her mind wandered to the news that Lynden had so eagerly pressed into her ear. If Brand had any criminal tendencies he was the best actor she had ever met. Well, what was it to her, anyway?

≥●

The next morning Teddy filled the watering tubs and checked through the llamas, especially the young ones, making sure everybody was happy and well. As she worked, she thought of Brand. She had to admit she hoped he did get over being mad. He really did brighten her days. After she finished feeding, she remembered she had not noticed Casanova. She walked back through all the milling llamas and still did not see him.

Chapter Six

Oh well, how could she expect to see each of 500 llamas every time? Still, it bothered her and she mentioned it to Gram at breakfast.

"Let's go have another look," Gram said.

They wandered through the herd for an hour and a half but did not spot the large red and white llama. "We can look again after lunch, Gram. He's probably lying down somewhere in the shade."

But several more checks convinced Teddy that Casanova had disappeared. Where could he have gone? No llama had ever disappeared before. Not only was Casanova a good friend, but they had paid $14,000 for him. And for Romeo too. They were top breeding stock. A ranch the size of Teddy's—one of the largest in the United States—must breed good stock.

That night Gram busily cut out pieces for her quilt and Teddy worked on her red sweater. She hoped to finish it that evening and start on the matching skirt. "Just how mad was your neighbor when he left the other day?" Gram asked.

Teddy laughed. "Pretty mad, and I don't blame him. You can't believe how awful that stuff is."

"Mad enough to do something to Casanova?"

Teddy's throat constricted and a fat lump formed too far down to swallow. No. Brand would not do something to any animal. He was too kind. But where could the big llama have gone? After asking her Heavenly Father to care for the llama, Teddy felt better and went to bed.

≈

The next morning Gram went with Teddy to do the morning chores, and they both searched behind every tree and in all the sheds, as well as among the many sizes and colors of llamas. He simply was not on the place.

"I think we owe our neighbor a visit," Gram said, after they finished washing the breakfast dishes.

"Maybe just one of us should go, Gram. He might think we're being unfriendly if we both go."

"He might be right too," Gram said, nodding her head.

They both took off across the uninhabited south pasture. After climbing the old log fence, they trotted across Brand's pasture, through his yard, and up to the house. Gram banged on the front door; Teddy wished she were small enough to hide behind the tiny old lady.

Brand's middle-aged helper, Hannah, opened the door. "Well, our neighbors. I've been wishin' you'd come see me." She opened the door wide. "Come right in. I'll fix something to munch on."

Teddy stepped forward and ran into Gram's steel arm. "We didn't come for socializing," Gram said in a stern voice. "We'd like to see Mr. Sinclair."

"He ain't here, Mrs. Marland. He and Rolf had a business engagement in Sisters this morning. Think they hauled an animal over there. I don't know when they'll be back."

"Humph! You tell Mr. Sinclair we have urgent business with him the minute he gets back. Understand?"

Hannah nodded. "I understand, Mrs. Marland. I hope everything's all right."

"Just tell him." Gram turned Teddy around and marched her down the steps.

Neither said a word until they jumped the fence into their own property. Then Teddy stopped Gram and looked into her faded blue eyes. "You don't think they hauled Casanova to the Patterson Ranch do you?" The Patterson Llama Ranch was the largest in the country and located in the tiny town of Sisters.

"I'd rather think that than that he killed the animal."

"It could have been someone else, Gram."

"Sure, and Brand wasn't mad at Casanova."

"Someone could have taken him for the money."

"Come on, kitten, your brain's turning to mush," Gram puffed as they trotted across their pasture. "Anyone who knows how much Casanova's worth would know Cocoa and several other females are worth twice that much or more. Don't you think they'd be likely to rustle the females—or both?"

Teddy's mind felt like mush all right. She had had enough worries, fearing some of the llamas might get sick and die after mortgaging the ranch to pay for them, now she had to start worrying about rustling.

An hour later Brand drove his black truck down the driveway amid a cloud of dust, turned into the yard and skidded thirty feet to a stop. He ran to the front porch, where Gram and Teddy sat, taking a breather from their work.

"Hannah said you girls are all upset about something," he said. Breathing hard, he plopped down on the front steps. "How can I help?"

"What did you go to Sisters for?" Gram asked in a voice resembling a moose's call.

Brand's eyebrows shot up in surprise. "We sold an unneeded animal," he answered a moment later. Another long silence followed. "Have I done something wrong?" he finally asked. He looked from Gram to Teddy and back to Gram.

Teddy could not answer. In fact, she could not bear to be making this rift. But Gram did not seem to mind. "Any idea how much a good breeding llama's worth?" she asked.

After a short silence that seemed an eternity, Brand answered. "No, Gram, I don't. I hadn't considered it vital information to my operation."

"Well, it's vital to our operation, young man. We paid $14,000 for that llama that spits."

Brand whistled. But his eyes never left Gram's face. Then he shook his golden head. "Seems like an animal worth that much money could learn who his friends are, doesn't it?"

Gram jumped from her chair and towered over Brand, who still sat on the top step. "I've had enough game playing, Brand. Why don't you just tell us what you've done with Casanova."

Brand sprang up beside Gram, reversing positions, and peered down at her, the benign expression gone from his face. "What do you think I've done with that cheap camel? I haven't been near him—and believe me that's the way it's going to stay." His stormy gaze met Gram's thunderous one. "I hate that animal!" he finished, with feeling.

Gram nodded. "So you hate him. I'll ask you once more. What did you do with him?"

In the moment that followed, Brand's eyes lighted with understanding. "Oh, you mean you want to know what I did to him, do you? Well, I shot him and fed him to my cattle." He cast one furious look at Teddy and stomped down the steps.

"Well, what do you think?" Gram asked, as they watched the truck disappear in a cloud of angry dust.

"I think he's innocent."

"I don't know. He got pretty riled."

"Wouldn't you? If someone accused you of purposely doing someone out of $14,000?"

As Teddy went about her work that afternoon she thought about Brand. If he did do something to Casanova, then he probably robbed the bank too. She did not exactly know why one would have anything to do with the other, but that is how she felt.

෴

The next Sunday Brand did not sit beside Teddy at church, and she felt very lonely. Even though she felt she had lost a personal friend in Casanova, and that they could hardly handle a financial loss of that magnitude, the fact that Brand would do such a thing was the most painful thought to Teddy. She had been so sure that he would not even step on an ant. Later at home, Lynden seemed unusually happy. "I wonder why the big cowboy didn't push himself on us today."

"Because one of our llamas spit on him," Gram said in a hard voice.

Lynden burst into one of his rare fits of laughter. He slapped his knee. "Fantastic! How did you get her to do it?"

"It was Casanova," Teddy explained. "And this was the second time he did it. Somehow he took a dislike to Brand."

"Wise animal."

A lot you know, Teddy thought. *You have never shown the slightest interest in our llama herd.*

"Lunch is ready. Have you washed your hands?" Gram asked, looking sharply at Lynden.

He held out his hands. "As soon as I came in, Nelle," he answered with a good-natured laugh. "You have me trained."

Teddy put the roast on the table and slipped into her chair. Lynden speared a piece of meat almost before Gram finished asking the blessing. "The thing is," Gram said, "Casanova has disappeared now. Completely gone." She helped herself to a large roasted potato and drowned it with brown gravy.

Lynden took two more bites of roast beef, then his eyes snapped to Gram's. "Did you say Sinclair did something violent to your llama?"

Gram's eyes never left her plate, but she nodded slowly. "I think I'd say that."

Lynden dropped his fork onto his plate, forgetting his food for the moment. "This just might be the story that'll get me the advancement I deserve. After we finish eating, I'll write it up."

"No you won't." Teddy laid her own fork on the edge of her plate. "We have no idea what happened to Casanova, other than he's gone."

Lynden laid an assuring hand on Teddy's arm. "I'll just write a story about the disappearance of a valuable animal. Then I'll casually mention that it spit on Sinclair the day before it disappeared." He burst into laughter again. "I'll bet he was really mad."

Teddy nodded. "I don't blame him a bit. I got it, too, and it's awful stuff."

After lunch the three sat around visiting. About an hour later, Gram became restless. "Did you notice I mowed the lawn?" she asked.

"I did, Gram. It looks beautiful and smells heavenly." She grinned at her wiry grandmother. "We really should mow more than three times a year. I mean I should, not you."

"Right. Well, I mowed it so we could play croquet this afternoon. If we don't watch out, summer will be gone with no croquet games."

In a little while the wickets all stood in their proper spots and the players had each chosen a mallet. Gram made each play count, but Teddy and Lynden could not seem to get going. They were still headed toward the far post when a black pickup truck drove slowly up the driveway. It stopped near the house and a short balding man jumped out.

"Would you happen to be missing a llama?" he called.

Everyone dropped their mallets, the game forgotten. "We sure are," Teddy said. "It's a red and white male. A really huge one."

The man nodded. "That's him. You pay for the damage he's done and he's yours. Personally, I wouldn't have the filthy thing. He crawled over the fence and bred my two females. Then he spat on me when I tried to catch him." The man looked at each of them to determine the effect his story had. "And I wanted my females bred to something really good," he finished sadly.

"Well, don't shed too many tears about that, junior," Gram said to the middle-aged man. "You got a lot more than you bargained for. That llama's worth a mint, and his breeding services go for $3000, but since he called on you, uninvited, I guess you just received a $6,000 gift."

The man's face brightened. "Are you sure? He's really worth all that much?"

Lynden nodded emphatically, as though he knew all about llamas.

"I'll follow you home and collect him right now," Teddy said.

When Casanova saw Teddy he ran toward her as though he would smash her into the ground. But Teddy held out her arms to the big llama, who skidded to a stop beside her. Then he nuzzled her face, obviously happy to see her. "Come on, you big turkey, let's go," she said, walking toward the open gate with her arm over Casanova's back. She steered him to the horse trailer and he walked in.

❧

"Well, Brand didn't do Casanova in," Teddy said to Gram that evening. "I guess we owe him another visit."

"Yep. Fair is fair," said Gram. "Let's get going."

Brand's eyes opened with surprise when he answered his doorbell. He did not smile, but looked at Gram warily. "Good evening," he said, without expression.

Gram put her tiny wrinkled hand on Brand's arm. "May we come in, sonny?" she asked kindly. "We have something to say."

Brand backed up. "I thought you said it all the last time." He hesitated a moment, then swung the door wide open. "Sure. Come in."

"We wanted you to know that Casanova's safe and sound," Gram began.

"Oh, so I'm exonerated. I'm sure glad he turned up. Otherwise I'd have been guilty forever, wouldn't I?"

"Teddy knew you didn't do it, Brand."

Brand offered Teddy a small smile. "Thanks."

"Well, young man, would you like to know what happened to Casanova?"

"I'm sure you're going to tell me."

"He heard the song of romance and deserted his many wives for a new love," Gram said, obviously trying to make Brand laugh.

Brand nodded. "I figured as much. You really need to get a fence together that will keep your camels inside."

After a little while of forced conversation, Gram told Teddy they should go home.

Teddy got up then turned to Brand. "We came to say we're very sorry we accused you of doing something to him. I know you're much too kind to do something like that."

Brand almost smiled. "Oh, I'm not so sure about that. But I'm way too scared of that spitting fool to try anything with him. As far as I'm concerned, his weapon is deadly."

Back home, Teddy and Gram started work on their respective projects. "What did you think, Gram?" Teddy asked.

"I think he's a nice boy. Why do you ask?"

"Do you think he'll be able to forgive us?"

"Of course he will. Just give him a little time."

"Do you think this means he's not the guy that robbed the bank?"

Gram threw back her head and laughed. "I don't see what one has to do with the other, but didn't you ask him?"

"Not exactly. I asked him some personal questions and somehow never got around to that one. He ended up thinking I was proposing to him."

Gram thought that one over for a minute. "He's not the kind of person who'd do something dishonest. I doubt he'd even cheat on his income tax and that's borderline." Teddy did not laugh. The sound of Gram's scissors carefully cutting out several butterfly parts snipped a duet with Teddy's clicking needles for a few minutes. Then Gram laid the scissors down. "I was kidding about income tax, you know. Cheating's never borderline. To God, cheating's stealing. And we know the commandments." They worked in silence for a while. "Now, maybe I'll get to ride Pharaoh again," Gram said. "I'd been worrying about that."

Teddy laughed. "Shame, Gram. I never thought you'd be so small."

"Oh, pshaw. You've always known I wasn't very big."

Teddy hugged Gram and trudged off to bed. Tomorrow would be another busy day, just like all the rest. She asked God to watch over her, keep her on the right track, and fell asleep in the middle of the *Amen*.

❧

All the next day Teddy watched over her shoulder, hoping to see a big golden man striding toward her, but Brand did not show up. Nor the next day or the next.

When Teddy walked into church beside Lynden the following Sunday, her mind was not on the man she came with. Would Brand come and sit beside her? Just having his big frame beside her on the pew would make her happiness complete for that one day. Her heart beat loudly as she peeked fearfully back toward the door.

Chapter Seven

Teddy quickly determined the big man was not in the church. She was not brave enough to turn around again, but her senses stayed tuned to the back. "*Forgive me, God,*" she silently prayed when she discovered she had missed the entire service waiting for Brand.

After the benediction, Gram led her little group outside into the sunshine where the members greeted each other and visited briefly. Then Teddy saw Brand getting into his sports car, and he was not alone! A tall, dark-haired girl sat in the passenger seat, looking very happy.

"Do I detect a grump in you today?" Lynden asked after Teddy had cleared the lunch dishes away and joined him on the couch. "It couldn't have anything to do with that fox Sinclair had with him, could it?"

"Why should I care who he has with him?" Teddy asked testily.

"Well, I care who Brand had with him," Gram said. "I was hoping to go riding this afternoon. That Pharaoh's some animal. I can't handle an afternoon of doing nothing. Maybe I'll ride a llama."

A big laugh burst from Teddy and she felt better. "Maybe we'll all ride llamas," she said, joining Gram's foolishness.

ॐ

Teddy and Gram spent the following days fertilizing and watering the alfalfa field. They also kept busy with their other duties, such as irrigating the pastures and caring for the llamas. They always had fencing that needed repairing, but it had to wait its turn. Teddy kept an eye out for Brand all week, but he seemed to be busy elsewhere.

Friday night Lynden took Teddy to a movie in Bend starring Kurt Russell. "I suppose you think that Russell guy is some kind of sex symbol," Lynden kidded while they drank milk shakes later.

Teddy nodded. "As a matter of fact, he's gorgeous. Admit it, Lynden."

Lynden laughed. "He isn't to me. You are, though." Looking a little surprised at his own words, he took the straw back into his mouth and noisily sucked his half-melted drink.

Teddy felt her face redden. She had been thinking she was just another friend to him and here he gives her a compliment. The very first one! Ever!

"Thanks, Lynden." She pushed the large, frost-covered glass to one side and leaned on her elbows. "That was a sweet thing to say. You're so nice to keep taking me around and I truly appreciate it. You're a good friend, and I enjoy being with you. But is that enough? Shouldn't you be looking for someone who will fall gloriously, crazily in love with you?"

Lynden snapped to attention. His eyes narrowed and his lips straightened into a hard line. "Is that how you feel about Sinclair?"

"Of course not. I'm not ready for a serious relationship. That's why I wanted to talk with you."

"Are you sure?"

"Of course I'm sure. I've barely seen Brand when you weren't with us."

Lynden released an audible sigh. "I'll take your word for it then. I guess we may as well carry on as we have been. I enjoy your company, too, and I'm also not ready to get serious with anyone." He chuckled. "Not rich enough, anyway. But our friendship means everything to me. I vote we carry on." He reached his right hand across the restaurant table and shook hers firmly.

A wide smile lighted Teddy's face. "Okay. Great. But I have one addition to our relationship. We'll take turns paying from now on, okay?"

He shook his head. "We both know what a bum I am, hanging around your place all the time, eating off you. You're lucky if it equals out. And I do enjoy both you and your grandmother."

Teddy went to bed that night wondering exactly what had happened in that restaurant. She had intended to cool things with Lynden a little, and now she liked him better than she ever had. He had shown insight and sensitivity she had not known he possessed. But she still liked him only as a good friend.

&a

Brand smiled and greeted Teddy and Gram at church that Sunday but did not introduce them to the dark-haired girl who was very much with him.

Back home, Teddy tried desperately to hide the depression she felt. Surely Brand's girlfriend had nothing to do with her feelings, even though she could still see the girl laughing into Brand's eyes while he looked as though he would like to kiss her. The girl's black hair and eyes looked at least part Spanish. With her olive skin and highly-colored cheeks and lips, Teddy had never seen a more beautiful woman in her entire life. Not that she minded Brand having a beautiful woman—he deserved it as much as anyone else. And their contrasting looks, his bright hair and her dark, complemented each other. She was glad for him . . .well, she was.

&a

Tuesday morning Teddy opened her water gate at six o'clock and started getting the irrigation set up so she could use every drop of water that ran into her pond that day.

"What're you going to do when you finish that?"

Teddy's heart doubled in size instantly and she could barely breathe. She had not talked to Brand for two weeks and here he was, right beside her, in gorgeous living color.

"This will take a while. Did you need something?" Teddy hoped he could not detect her breathlessness. Or, if he did, maybe he would think it was from moving the long pipe.

"I don't need anything, but you do. I'm pretty well caught up right now and I wondered if you'd like some help. We could try to make those rickety fences last another year or two."

"Thanks, Brand. Gram and I will be working on fences as soon as I finish here, but I can't think of any reason you should help."

His wide lips parted in a smile. "To protect the neighborhood? And my good name? How about to keep a nice old lady off the streets—I mean pastures?"

Teddy nodded. An afternoon off would not hurt Gram a bit. She probably took the old woman too much for granted. "Sure, that would be nice. I'll be ready to start early this afternoon."

He took the big wrench from her hands. "I'll help you with this job, which incidentally is much too heavy for a woman, and we'll get on the fence in a couple of hours."

They hooked up several water gun sprinklers and tested them. They all worked fine, except a new one that refused to turn. Teddy worked on the sprinkler head while Brand walked on down the line to check a connection. After she forced a few drops of oil into the right place, the sprinkler began its slow circular motion, shooting a large stream of water more than a hundred feet. She watched it move smoothly in its circle a moment, then, acting on an impulse, spun the head until it drenched Brand.

"Hey!" He lowered his head and charged toward Teddy, but not until the water had soaked him through. Teddy laughed wildly when he reached her dry spot.

Brand shook his head, sending droplets over Teddy. "You did that on purpose, didn't you?" he yelled. Grasping her by her arm, he took off running—right into the heavy deluge.

Teddy gasped. That water was colder than she had expected. She tried to jerk free, but Brand held tightly, laughing down at her, his dripping hair hanging in points over his forehead. In less than a minute she was as wet as he. They laughed and shouted like two children, pushing each other into the spray as it came around, and playfully trying to escape from the other's grasp. Finally, they ran from the water into the warm sunlight and stood looking at each other for a long moment.

Brand broke the spell. "Recess is over, kid. Hit the trail." They worked as energetically together as they had played, neither saying much.

By mid-morning they finished the irrigation and started on the much easier fence repairing. Brand lifted the heavy logs and Teddy drove the huge nails.

"Did you know you have a pretty cute grandmother?" Brand asked sometime later.

Teddy nodded and pulled a nail from her mouth. "Only the greatest. And she can work as long and hard as I." She shoved the nail back between her teeth and swung the four-pound hammer with all her strength.

They worked a couple of hours without talking, then Brand took the hammer from her and pulled her to the ground beside him. "Break time," he said.

Teddy gladly relaxed, allowing the warm sun to continue drying her soaked clothing and hair. "Gram and I don't know the meaning of breaks," she said, searching for something to say. "We work until we finish and quit."

Brand studied Teddy as though he wanted to say something, but remained quiet.

Gram seemed to be a good subject, Teddy decided. "Gram sure enjoyed riding Pharaoh."

Brand nodded. "I know. She should ride again. And you too. You haven't ever had one good ride, yet. That, uh, blob that hangs around won't let you finish."

Teddy decided to ignore the slur Brand had aimed at Lynden. "Gram really wanted to ride Sunday, but I wouldn't let her interrupt you with your new friend."

"You mean Celia? You tell Gram she can come over and ride anytime she wants. Celia would be glad to have her join us."

So. . .Celia did ride with Brand. Teddy felt like crying but she took a deep breath and swallowed. "Does Celia ride Misty?" she murmured without looking up.

"No, she rides her own horse. That's where we met, on that trail I tried to take you on." Brand put his finger under Teddy's chin and lifted it until her eyes met his. "Don't you want her riding Misty?" he asked softly.

Teddy's eyes dropped to her lap. She swallowed again. For some reason it really hurt her to imagine anyone else on Misty, especially Celia. Or could it be that she did not want anyone else with Brand? "She's your horse," she replied. "I don't care who rides her."

Brand hopped lightly to his feet and held his hand to help Teddy. "Break's over," he said, handing Teddy her large hammer.

They had not worked long when Gram roared up on her motor bike. "I fixed lunch for you two," she yelled over the motor. "Figured it was the least I could do since I'm having the day off." She gave it the gas and roared away across the pasture.

Teddy dropped her hammer and followed Brand toward the old ranch house.

≈

Several hours, much friendly conversation, and many feet of repaired fence later, Brand and Teddy rested on the pasture floor again. He looked as though he wanted to say something, just as he had earlier in the day.

"Say it," Teddy said, laughing. "You're bursting with something, so spit it out before we both shatter into fragments."

Brand hesitated, then shook his head. "No, I better not." Then he smiled. "Maybe I'll ask this instead. How are things going between you and the boy reporter?"

"Just fine. He's trying hard to get a promotion."

A scowl drew Brand's golden eyebrows almost together. A moment later he got to his feet. "I think I'd better call it a day," he said. "I still have several things to do before Celia comes over to ride."

Teddy scrambled to her feet too. "Okay, thanks a lot for the help. We repaired as much fence in one day as Gram and I would have in three."

They separated, Teddy walking toward her house and Brand heading for the fence that divided their two places. "I notice I didn't get an invite to ride with the beautiful Celia and Brand," she muttered to herself as she crossed the pasture.

Teddy did not eat much supper that night; she was not hungry. After supper Gram kept looking at her as they watched TV and worked on their projects. "Are you sick, kitten?" she asked.

Teddy grinned. "Almost. Gram, do you think I could be in love with Brand Sinclair?"

Gram's blue eyes glistened. "I don't see you how you could _not_ be in love with him. I know I am."

"Come on, Gram. I mean really."

"So do I. Now, what are you going to do about it?"

"I don't know. Once upon a time he acted as if he knew I was a woman. But he never notices anymore."

Chapter Eight

Brand arrived early the next morning to put in another day repairing fences, so Teddy chased Gram inside again. "Just to the house, Gram, not to a home," she said, patting Gram on her curly top.

"What was that all about?" Brand asked after Gram left.

"She's feeling somewhat useless. But a little rest won't hurt her a bit."

They worked well together and the fence began to look as though it would hold for several more years. After a long comfortable silence, Teddy began to search for a topic of conversation. "How was your ride yesterday afternoon?" she asked, then wished she had not brought up the subject.

He leaned back on his heels. "Great," he said. "We had a long, relaxing ride."

Teddy held a nail to the log and smashed it into the old wood with a vengeance. She just bet they had had a long, relaxing ride. But she had to ask. . .and she really did not want to know one thing about those two. Well, what she really wanted was for there to be nothing between them for her to know.

"Did city boy come over and eat all your candy last night?" Brand asked.

Teddy straightened up and returned Brand's wicked grin. "No, he comes only on Tuesdays and Fridays. . .just like my water."

"And just as welcome I suppose."

Teddy made a big deal out of hesitating before answering. "Uh, well, maybe just a teeny bit more so, I guess."

Gram made lunch for Brand and Teddy again and they worked until five o'clock. He laid the last log over and held it for Teddy to nail, then wiped his hands on his jeans. "Guess that about does it for today," he said.

"Why, do you have to go riding again?" Now why did she do that? The last thing she wanted to know was what those two did every night.

He scowled, as though trying to figure her out. "I hadn't planned to, but would you and Gram like to go after supper? According to the schedule, your paper boy wouldn't interfere tonight."

Teddy felt as tired as she ever had in her entire life, and her arm ached from swinging that hammer. Keeping up with Brand took everything she had and a little more. *Father, help me get rested up really quickly tonight, okay? Thanks.* "I wasn't fishing for an invitation, but I'll check with Gram. I didn't realize how much she likes to ride."

His smile outshone the sun. "Great. I'll be waiting to hear."

Gram could not wait to ride, so Teddy called Brand and accepted his invitation while Gram put supper on the table. Both women wolfed down the food in anticipation of the planned activities. Then Teddy noticed that she felt a lot better. Almost no aches or pains from swinging the heavy hammer and well rested. _Thanks, God,_ she tossed silently into the sky.

Brand had the three horses saddled and ready to go when Gram and Teddy arrived. Powder, the dark mare, reached her head over the fence to Teddy, who petted her and talked to her a few minutes.

"I'll say thanks for Powder," Brand said. "She doesn't get as much attention as she'd like, now that we seldom ride her."

Gram rode Pharaoh, Teddy the dainty palomino Misty, and Brand climbed on Thunder, the huge black stallion. They rode on the trail for two hours and returned well exercised and feeling better, including the horses. But Brand treated Teddy as a good friend. Period.

He helped repair fences all week, except when he handled his own irrigation, but did not cast a look or say a word to indicate he thought any more of her than a neighbor who needed a hand.

Lynden took Teddy and Gram to church again, and Brand took Celia. Although Brand's greeting could not have been more cordial, he did not stop to visit and therefore did not introduce Celia.

After eating the delicious meal Teddy and Gram had prepared and emptying the candy bowl, Lyndon invited Teddy to sit with him on the couch. "I brought that article," he said, "as well as another that just arrived in the office." He pulled an envelope from his jacket pocket.

Teddy, sitting beside him, instructed herself to breathe calmly as he pulled the bits of paper from the envelope and placed them in her hand. She unfolded the picture first that turned out to be from the hidden camera in the bank. The picture of the man holding the gun was so fuzzy no one could identify anyone from it, but it showed he had blond hair, wide shoulders, lean hips, and long, long legs. She drew in a long breath and handed it back to Lynden. "I see the resemblance, but lots of men look like that. You could never, ever use that picture to identify Brand."

She unfolded the two articles and read them, learning little. "I don't think you could identify Brand from these articles either," she said. "All I see that could help is that the man has a guttural voice—and Brand's voice is anything but guttural."

Lynden put the articles and picture back into the envelope. "Well, people do strange things with their voices, you know. And it gives a pretty good physical description of the man, Teddy. Did you read it? It matches Sinclair closer than you could describe me."

Teddy had to agree but managed to get the subject changed for the entire afternoon.

Gram and Teddy had a talk that evening after Lynden finally left. "I'm afraid I must give you that advice I spoke of," Gram said. "You're going to have to get rid of Lynden." Gram sat at the table, tracing the butterfly pattern onto pink broadcloth. "That is if you want Brand to notice you. He's an honorable man and right now he sees you as Lynden's girlfriend."

Teddy had been thinking along the same lines. "I don't know if I can, Gram. Lynden's really nice. And he hasn't done anything to deserve being dumped. I guess I feel sorry for him."

"Feeling sorry for someone in a situation like this is like taking a week to drill a root canal. Believe me, it'll be less painful if you do it quickly and get it over with."

Teddy remembered Lynden's articles about someone like Brand being sought for that dumb bank robbery. "I have another reason to stay in touch with Lynden, Gram. Remember him saying that Brand robbed a bank just before he came here?"

Gram shoved out a hand, as though pushing the thought away. "Posh. Don't believe everything you hear. Brand didn't do anything of the sort."

"I know he didn't do it, but I still want to learn everything I can about it. I'll have a talk with Lynden, Gram, that I'd like to remain friends with him if he'll do that."

Gram nodded wisely. "All right. Then you and Lynden will understand how it is, but how's Brand going to know?"

Teddy thought about that after she went to bed that night. As far as Brand would know, she and Lynden would still be romantically involved. But she could not walk up to the man and explain that she was now available, could she? And did she have any slight fears that Brand might be the bank robber? No, he could never do something like that. Even so, she doubted she could be cruel enough to completely follow Gram's suggestion of totally dumping Lynden.

❧

A couple of days later, in the afternoon, Gram and Teddy started clipping the llamas' toenails, a job they dreaded but did anyway every three months. Llamas have split hooves like cattle, but a small nail that grows out over the hoof has to be clipped, somewhat like a human toenail. By evening they had finished about sixty llamas, and, after the usual feeding and watering, both women were more than ready to quit for the day.

They started again the next morning right after six o'clock and were going fine when Thunder, with Brand aboard, galloped up the driveway and back to the barn where they worked.

Brand dismounted and approached the women. "Looks as though you two are keeping out of mischief today." He watched a moment. "Hey, I never have to clip my cattle's hooves. Are you sure you wouldn't like to go back to raising cattle?"

Gram's blue eyes flashed. "Not on your life, sonny. Llamas are more human to handle, if you get my drift. You can have the cattle."

Brand pulled off his Stetson and shoved his hair back. "That's sort of what I'm here for. I'm loading 200 head of cattle today. We have the near ones in the corral, but over 100 have escaped to the back of the pasture. We're having a terrible time. I was wondering, do you think your dogs would run cattle?"

Gram jerked her head toward Teddy. "You go help. I'll carry on here."

Teddy finished her llama, released it, then stood up and stretched. "These dogs have never even seen cattle, as far as I know, let alone worked them, but we'll see what happens."

Brand put Teddy on the horse with him and the dogs ran alongside. Thunder took them out to the pasture where the ill-mannered cattle milled around, bawling nervously. Teddy called the dogs and told them to take the cattle in. They cocked their heads and she motioned at the cattle. When they understood what she wanted, they went to work, quietly but effectively. Soon the cattle bunched together, moving slowly toward the gleaming white corrals, where several huge trucks awaited their turns at the loading chutes.

"Well, looks as if everything's under control," Teddy said, her nostrils filled with the stench of many cattle.

"Yeah," Brand answered, never taking his eyes off the two dogs working together. "Those dogs are worth their weight in gold. Didn't we say they took the place of a man? Well that bunch of steers ran through six men, and the two dogs are handling them just fine."

Teddy nodded, satisfied. "I'm glad. I didn't know whether they'd work cattle, but they're great dogs." She had one more comment she wanted desperately to make but hardly dared. She drew in a deep breath. "I hated to be a party to what you're doing to those cattle," she said. "Can you blame them for running off? They were only trying to save their lives."

Brand nodded. "I thought of that. I feel sorry for them, and no, I don't blame them. This earth isn't perfect, is it? Did you know the Bible tells us that after Jesus returns to claim His own nothing will be hurt or destroyed anymore?"

The dogs driving the cattle into the corrals where they would be loaded into the trucks interrupted the conversation. Brand sent several quick glances Teddy's way as they walked slowly along.

Sensing him watching her, Teddy began to feel embarrassed. Then she stumbled and nearly stepped in a fresh pile of manure. "Your pasture's a mess," she told Brand, laughing. "I'd forgotten how filthy cows are. Sure you don't want to change to llamas?"

"Don't tempt me. Seriously, I couldn't afford to right now, no matter how badly I wished. I invested all my ready money in the cattle."

All the money you got in the bank heist? No! She knew better than that. How could she even let a thought like that pass through her head?

Another silence fell between them. Teddy felt Brand struggling with himself again. "I owe you one," he finally said. "How can I repay you?"

"How about a steak dinner for the dogs?"

He shook his head. "How about a steak dinner for you?"

"You don't owe me; I didn't do a thing."

He reached for her hand and held it until they stepped up to the corral. Then, after slipping the board that locked in the recalcitrant animals, he turned back to Teddy. "I'm afraid I'd feel embarrassed, taking two dogs out to dinner. Won't you go? Please?"

What about Celia, Teddy wondered. But she could think of nothing in the whole world she would like better than to go with Brand. . .anywhere, anytime. So why not?

"If you'd be more comfortable, and your cub reporter would feel better, Gram could come too," Brand offered just as Teddy opened her mouth to accept his invitation.

"All right, we accept. She'll do justice to any steak you can buy."

Brand's eyes shone as though the sun lived in his head rather than in the cloudless, blue sky above. "Great. How about Saturday night? Let's dress up, okay?"

Thunder, Misty, and Brand took Teddy back home. Brand delivered Teddy to her door, saluted smartly and trotted off down the driveway leading Misty. She hurried inside to tell Gram about Brand's taking them out to dinner. Finding an empty house, she hurried out to the barn where Gram still trimmed toenails.

"It worked, Gram. Brutus and Caesar did just great. And Brand's taking us out to dinner Saturday night. For a sort of reward, I guess. I tried to get him to take the dogs, but he thought he'd be embarrassed."

Gram sat on a small wooden box, working on a quiet llama's toenail. Her furrowed face wrinkled into a big smile. "That's fine. Just fine, but I'm not going." Her rough voice sounded happy. "Stand still, Daisy, I'm not hurting you. Dating's for young people, not an old, worn-out woman. Besides, I heard somewhere that three's a crowd."

Teddy picked up her trimmers and started on Maybe, a gray and white llama with an all-gray, female baby llama by her side. "But you have to go this time, Gram. He expressly invited you. If he wants to take me out alone, he'll ask."

≈

By Saturday night Teddy and Gram finished trimming the llamas' nails and felt like celebrating the finishing of the big job. "Brand said we were supposed to dress up," Teddy said as Gram came from the bathroom, her curls even tighter than usual, and smelling of powder and cologne.

"Oh, he did, did he? Okay, it doesn't matter to me." The old lady flashed a toothy smile and disappeared into her bedroom. Teddy gratefully took her turn in the shower, hoping to wash her internal butterflies down the drain.

After she dried her dark hair with a blow dryer, she used a curling brush to make it perfect for the evening. She chose a long dress of huckleberry-colored satin and taffeta. The double-puffed sleeves accentuated the simple waist and the double ruffle at the bottom of the outer skirt turned up in the back and narrowed to a V at the waist, creating a bustle effect. After arranging the dress to her satisfaction, Teddy deftly applied makeup, something she hardly ever bothered with. Tonight she wanted Brand to notice her.

She stepped into the living room to find Gram already there, her head twisted around, checking her jeans for something. "Do you see something on the back of my pants?" she asked. "Cat hair, maybe?"

Teddy brushed the back of the already clean jeans. "They're fine, Gram."

Gram looked Teddy over, from shining hair to matching huckleberry sandals. "You really like the guy, don't you, kitten? Think he'll notice you?"

"Did I overdo it, Gram?"

"No way. You look just right. Trust me."

When Gram opened the door for Brand, his eyes darted from her to Teddy, back to Gram, then back to Teddy. Teddy drew in a ragged breath. She had never seen a man look so splendid. His black tuxedo and bow tie made his streaked blond hair look lighter and his tan darker. His shoulders seemed wider and straighter, and his legs seemed to have grown an inch longer.

While Teddy had been looking Brand over he had been doing the same to her. Finally his face turned from puzzlement to a happy laugh. "You look so beautiful you take my breath away," he said to Teddy. He still had a strange look on his face, though. Turning to Gram, he leaned way over and kissed her apricot cheek. "You look. . .happy tonight," he whispered in her ear.

She turned on him in mock indignation. "So I don't take your breath away! I have a mind to stay home, just for that."

Teddy and Gram stood in the middle of the bare room, ready to leave, but Brand hesitated. Teddy wondered what she was supposed to do, but decided to wait and see what he wanted. Finally he seemed to make a decision. "May I use your telephone?" he asked.

He went into the kitchen, where Teddy heard him cancelling a reservation. "All set," he said a few minutes later. "Let's be off."

They stopped a few minutes later at Denny's, where Teddy felt terribly overdressed, but the light and friendly atmosphere soon made her forget anything but the good food and company.

An hour later they climbed back into Brand's car and headed down the highway to their ranches. "I never had better steak, sonny," Gram growled from the back seat. "Thanks a lot. Been several years since I went out to eat."

Brand reached back and caught the tiny hand in his. "Glad you came, Gram. You have a way of brightening the corner where you are, if I can steal a line from a song."

Brand went in when they arrived home and Gram took off to her bedroom. "Want to play a little gin?" Teddy asked.

Brand thought a moment. "We could. Or we could just talk, whichever you'd rather."

Teddy brought coffee and settled beside him on the couch. "Okay, talk," she instructed.

"I hope you weren't disappointed tonight when we went to Denny's."

Teddy smiled, remembering how she felt when she first went in. "Well, I did feel a little overdressed at first, but I soon forgot all about it. It was really nice. And the steaks were great."

He took her hand in his and patted it with his other one. "Do you know why we went there?"

"No, did we need a reason?"

He nodded. "I had reservations at Cyrano's, but I'd completely forgotten how Gram dresses up. I was afraid you'd be embarrassed at Denny's, but they wouldn't have let the little upstart in at Cyrano's. So I guess you'd say I was between a rock and a hard place."

Understanding flooded over Teddy, and a warm tender feeling for Brand came with it. How sweet and thoughtful!

"Anyway, your beautiful dress and even more beautiful you hasn't been wasted. I can't tell you how much pleasure I've had just looking at you tonight."

Teddy's eyes dropped and her face felt warm. "Thank you, Brand. I had a fantastic time too. Really I did. And I noticed how gorgeous you look too." She rolled her eyes. "What a shame, wasting all this gorgeousness on Denny's."

He leaned toward her and her heart nearly stopped. He was going to kiss her and she had never wanted anything more. She turned her face up and closed her eyes. And waited. And waited. Teddy's blood boiled through her veins in anticipation. Finally, she peeped one eye open a bit.

Brand's face was about a foot from hers and he wore an expression of wonder. Then he lowered his lips to hers and they touched, as gently as a cloud drifting past. Her arms flew around his neck and pulled him closer. As his arms tightened around her, her reasoning left. What she wanted was for him to hold her close, and he did. Her hands did what they had been wanting to for as long as she could remember—they combed through the softest, blondest hair she had ever seen. . .or felt.

Then he pushed her away and she dropped to earth with no parachute. "I'm sorry. We shouldn't have done that."

"Why?" She thought for a moment, then she knew. Celia!

He smiled tenderly into her eyes and love shone from his brown eyes, reaching straight into her heart. "Have you forgotten, my little Teddy Bear?"

She nodded her head, feeling like a pushy child. "I remember. Celia."

"Celia?" A deep laugh rumbled from his broad chest. "Celia? No, Teddy, not Celia. . .Lynden. Your boyfriend, remember?"

Chapter Nine

The next morning Gram studied Teddy's face. "You look as if you'd won the lottery, kitten," she said, dropping into her chair across the table.

"That's exactly how I feel, Gram. Brand kissed me last night. Oh, Gram, I *am* in love with him."

"Is he in love with you?"

Was he? He had not said so. "I don't know, Gram, but he kissed me."

Gram bowed her head and asked the blessing, filled both plates with eggs, bacon, and hash browns, then continued the conversation. "I couldn't be happier for you. As I told you before, I'm in love with Brand myself, but I want you to be careful. Men are strange creatures."

"But he only kissed me, Gram. A tender, gentle, beautiful kiss."

Gram spread apple butter on her toast and munched it as she drank her coffee. "All right. Just one more thing. You're absolutely certain he's not the one who robbed the bank on the other side of the Cascades?"

Ugh! Teddy had forgotten all about that. But she knew it was not Brand. There was not any hard evidence and it had been only a figment of Lynden's imagination. Brand would never do a thing like that. Never. "I'm sure, Gram, but I'll ask him right out one of these days. Like you said, nothing replaces good old communication."

૨ઢ

As always, Lynden arrived to take them to church on Sunday. "You look positively radiant this morning," he told Teddy. "That yellow dress matches the stars in your eyes."

Just then Gram came tearing out in her high-water jeans. She looked extra fancy too, in the crisp white shirt she had tucked into the pants. She motioned to Teddy and Lynden. "Come on, you slow pokes. We don't want to be late."

Brand came into the church soon after with Celia and a short, handsome, Mexican man with a wide smile and white, even teeth. Brand led them down the aisle to Teddy's pew and they all settled down. Brand reached for Teddy's hand and gave it one quick squeeze before gently replacing it in her lap. Nothing had ever felt so right to Teddy.

After church, Lynden went to the restroom and Brand brought the two strangers to Teddy. "I want you to meet Celia and Jesse Guitterres," he said. "And this is my love, Theodore Marland."

Lynden arrived on the scene just then.

"Glad to meet you folks," Teddy said. "I'm sure we'll see you again." She grabbed Lynden's hand and headed for his car with him in tow. Gram followed.

He turned the car around and threw gravel twenty feet as he tore out of the church yard. "I saw that turkey holding your hand, Teddy. I'd expect it of him but what's wrong with you?"

"We'll talk after we eat lunch," Teddy said calmly. "That is, if you're still eating with us?"

"What kind of question is that? Are you trying to get rid of me? If you are, just say so."

Teddy reached over the seat and put her hand on Lynden's arm. "I'm not trying to get rid of you. Let's just go home and eat, then we'll all have a good talk, all right?"

The roast tasted like cardboard to Teddy, and the potatoes could have been balls of yarn, but eventually they finished eating and Gram left them alone.

"We've always agreed to be honest with each other, right?" she asked Lynden.

"Yeah. Is that what you called that performance in church?"

"Well, I really want you to be my good friend, but Brand and I have discovered we're more than that."

Lynden rewrapped his chocolate caramel and shoved the candy dish back onto the coffee table with a clatter. "So. . .you're more than friends. What are you?"

"We're. . .uh. . .I don't know what we are. We like each other a lot."

He sprang up from the couch. "I'm not going to sit still while that cowboy messes up your head. Just tell him to waddle on down the road."

Teddy grinned impulsively. "Too late, Lynden, my head's already messed up. My heart too. The question now is whether you'll still be my friend."

He marched out of the kitchen, through the living room to the front door, with Teddy following. He opened the door, then turned back to her. "One thing you may have forgotten, he still has a price on his head. If you insist on this foolish behavior I may have to report his whereabouts to the authorities."

"Please don't do that," Teddy began, but the door slammed and Lynden was gone.

Ten seconds later he quietly opened the door and reached inside for his shoes. "Sorry," he said sheepishly, "I forgot these." This time he closed the door quietly.

Teddy dumped herself on the couch and reached for the last remaining peanut butter kiss, feeling as though someone had kicked her in the stomach.

"Don't you worry about him," Gram said, when Teddy told her about Lynden's reaction. "But as I see it, you'd better learn for yourself what Brand has or hasn't done before Lynden blows the whistle."

"That could be easier said than done, Gram," Teddy said. She reached for a tissue and blew her nose.

≈≈

The next morning Teddy finished her breakfast and stepped outside when Brand rode up on Thunder. He dismounted, looped Thunder's reins around a small bush and opened his arms. Teddy ran into them and turned her lips up to receive his kiss. His wonderful kiss that turned her inside out and upside down and her knees into peppermint jelly.

"Well, didn't you get enough of that Saturday night?" a gravelly voice asked.

Teddy jerked away and faced her grandmother. "Hi, Gram. We were just saying hello."

"Some hello. What are we doing today, kitten?" She waved a gnarled old hand in their direction. "Besides that, I mean."

"We're fixing fences, Gram," Brand answered. "Could you possibly find something else to do? I mean, we both love you, but we have some private talking to do."

The tiny shoulders reared back and Gram wheeled around. "I can always find something to do when I'm not wanted." Teddy detected a twinkle in Gram's caustic words.

"Okay, my little Teddy Bear, let's get busy." He collected the box of spike nails and the four-pound hammer and headed for the south pasture. They worked together, reassembling the fence and replacing logs that were too far gone.

"How am I ever going to repay you for all this work?" Teddy asked after a while.

Brand flashed a joyful smile. "What a short memory you have. You already repaid me, or should I say, Brutus and Caesar paid your debt?"

"That wasn't anything. It took only a couple of hours. I plan to pay hour for hour. Not that my hours are worth as much as yours, since you're so much stronger."

"Well, I have an idea. Why don't we have an instant replay of our dinner out the other night?" He hesitated. "Minus Gram?"

"Sure, I'd like that. And Gram wouldn't mind a bit. Although she told me several weeks ago that she's in love with you."

"She didn't mean it."

"Well, not like me." Teddy gasped. What had she just said? Maybe Brand would not notice.

But Brand did notice. He jerked upright and the log he was holding dropped to the ground. His brown eyes shot stars. "So, Teddy Bear, you're in love with me, huh?"

Teddy's face burned. Never had it felt so hot. "I meant like I would. . .you know. . .she's older."

Brand took her in his arms and held her tenderly. His lips brushed hers. "I know she's older, but that wasn't what you said." He pulled away and looked into her eyes, laughing. "Teddy Bear, I was going to ask you to marry me the night we went to Cyrano's." He lowered his head and proceeded to kiss her thoroughly. When he released her they both breathed in ragged gasps. "But I don't see how I can wait that long. I want to marry you, and soon, my little love."

They sat down on the ground to talk. Somehow she had to make sure he was exactly what he appeared. "You're way ahead of yourself," Teddy said. "We don't even know each other. I may have some deep dark secret in my past and for all I know, you may have a whole closet full of skeletons."

Brand quieted and became serious. "I already have yours figured out, and I don't have any, so what's to learn?"

"Mine? What do you have figured out about me?"

"Your mother died when you were born? That's why Gram named you. I didn't push because I know it makes you sad. Your blue blue eyes are so beautiful when you're happy. They're pretty with tears in them, too, but I'd rather make them laugh."

Oh. Her mother. In a way that was a deep dark secret she did not want him to know about. But she would worry about that another time. Right now, she must not be diverted. She had to learn where he got the money to buy his ranch. "What I was trying to do, was find out if you had some secret in your past that we should talk about."

He nodded. "Okay. No, I don't have any secrets you should know. Satisfied?"

"What about any that I shouldn't know?"

He studied her face a moment. "Are you asking about the women in my life?"

"If there were any you want to tell me about."

He shook his head. His sun-streaked hair fluffed back and forth, looking so soft and bouncy that Teddy wanted to run her fingers through it and forget all about skeletons.

"One thing I've wondered about—where did you dig up enough money to buy your ranch? That's a lot of wampum for a guy your age."

For a fraction of a second he looked stricken, then recovered. "Well," he drawled, "I've been digging a good long time. Sure enough, after I kept at it long enough, I found the money."

"But where, Brand?"

He looked mysterious. "In a secret place where no one else on God's green earth could look."

Teddy watched Brand's face. . .and waited. But he did not say anymore. "Okay, buster," she said, mimicking Gram's gravelly voice, "get to work if you expect a paycheck on Friday."

They laughed and went back to work. But Teddy did not feel quite satisfied. One thing was certain. If he had done something so terrible as robbing a bank he would tell her at this point in their relationship. Wait! What was she thinking? Of course, he would. . .not. Anyone who would rob a bank would not hesitate to lie about it. She would have to ask him point blank and watch his face. But what a horrible thing to ask a man who had just proposed marriage.

She decided to forget the whole thing and just enjoy the new relationship for a while. Her first love. They continued repairing fences together for the next three days and enjoyed it as much as though they were on wild and romantic excursions together.

Then one evening, Lynden called sounding a lot less than friendly. "You'd better read the paper tonight."

"I always read the paper, Lynden. Is there something you want me to see?"

"Yeah. On the inside of the front page. It's coming into the open, Teddy." A loud crash, then a dial tone told Teddy he had finished the conversation.

"What a rude pig," Teddy said aloud, reaching for the evening paper. She opened it to the second page and folded it over so she would be sure to find the article. She already knew what it was and it did not take long to find, nor to read. Just a small item about the not-so-recent bank robbery, stating the date, the details of the robbery, a description of the man, the rig he escaped in—a black 1984 truck with a winch in front—and that the Eugene police department had reason to believe the man had settled down in the Bend area.

Teddy dropped the paper on the floor and collapsed on the couch, trembling. The description matched Brand right down to the Stetson he always wore. And the description of the truck sounded exactly like the one Brand drove around the ranch. She lay there, trying not to think, until Gram came in and found her. Then she gathered up the paper and showed it to the old lady.

After reading the article through, Gram sat down on the couch and gathered the top half of Teddy's five-foot, eight-inch frame into her arms as though she were still a baby. "I'm sorry, kitten," she crooned, rocking back and forth. "It isn't a nice situation, but you're going to have to find out. Why don't you show him the paper and tell him about Lynden's insinuations?"

Teddy nodded. "I'll have to do that. I'll just have to." She rounded up the scissors and cut out the notice. Twenty minutes later, the now familiar attack on the door jolted both women.

"Hey, do I have a great idea!" Brand said, pulling off his boots and hurrying to the bathroom to wash his hands. Then he took Teddy into his arms for a gentle, but thorough, kiss. He draped an arm over her shoulder and steered her back to the kitchen where Gram still sat. He leaned over and kissed the old woman on her wrinkled cheek. "How's my favorite Gram this evening?" he whispered into her ear.

She reached up a small hand and imprisoned his larger one on her shoulder. "Flattery will get you everywhere," she said.

Brand dropped to the couch and patted the place beside him. When Teddy complied, he continued. "I have to go visit my folks this weekend and I want you to go along." His eyes never left hers. "What do you think?" he finally asked.

What did she think? It sounded exactly like the opportunity she had been waiting for. Surely she could not spend a weekend with Brand's family without finding out something about his history, good or bad. And she would be able to postpone confronting him with her clipping until after the trip.

Chapter Ten

"Well, what do you think?" he repeated.

"It sounds like fun," Teddy said, "but why would you want me to go to your folks' place?"

He seemed so excited he could barely sit still. "I want to show you off to them. And I want you to meet them too."

Gram had been sitting quietly. "Go on, kitten," she finally said, "it'll be good for you."

Gram! Teddy could not leave her alone to care for the llamas. "I'd like to, really I would," she began. "I almost said yes, but I forgot you, Gram. I can't go off and leave you with all the work."

"Pish posh. We have it all caught up. I'll just feed and water. That'll leave me most of the day to get into trouble."

"I can send Rolf over to help," Brand suggested. "He isn't always busy, either."

"You send Rolf over with Pharaoh, if you're so intent on helping," the little woman said, laughing.

"I'll do that. With instructions to ride with you. Now, Teddy Bear, there's nothing to stop us."

But Gram was not finished. "Don't you dare tell him to ride with me, sonny. My death wish isn't to be shot by a jealous wife."

But Brand had Teddy in his arms and they did not hear Gram's old joke.

ॐ

When the sun awakened Saturday morning, it found Brand and Teddy crossing the Cascade Mountains, excited to be together. Teddy had a doubt or two about the integrity of her spy trip, but she told herself she would just enjoy herself, meeting his family and getting to know Brand better. After all, he had asked her to marry him. She had not given him an answer but the offer was still good as far as she knew.

They talked nonstop as they drove through the beautiful forests and paused at several waterfalls on the Clear Lake Highway. Then they drove out of the trees, through Springfield, and into Eugene. "My folks live about a mile out on River Road," Brand explained as he expertly threaded through the dense traffic of the large city.

Ten minutes later they drove up to a neat, white, two-story house surrounded by tall firs and pines. The front door opened and Brand's parents ran down the steps to engulf him in their arms. As they all talked at once, asking how each had been, Teddy could not help but notice the close relationship, and how happy Brand and his parents were to be together again.

Then Brand remembered Teddy and hauled her to his side. "I almost forgot to tell you I brought someone along." Brand introduced them, and assured them he had a nice little Teddy Bear.

Brand's mother, Donna, had lunch ready and they gathered around the little table on the north porch. "Tell us about Teddy, and how you met her," Brand's father, Frank, suggested.

Brand winked at Teddy. "I met her when she tried to steal my water. Water's semiprecious over there."

"He tried to smash the door out of our house, he was so mad," Teddy added, laughing.

"Then she tried to lay the blame on an innocent animal," Brand continued, his eyes taking on a dreamy look as he remembered.

Teddy pounded him on the shoulder. "You saw her do it."

"All right, you two," Frank said, laughing, "there won't be any dessert until you get this all straightened out."

Brand stopped short. "Dessert? Well, I guess Iris was the water thief, but we fixed her wagon. But then those crazy llamas broke down the fence and invaded my ranch."

"Llamas?" Brand's parents yelled together.

Brand laughed. "Yes, llamas. She raises llamas next door to my cattle ranch." He shrugged. "There goes the neighborhood, but what can a guy do?" His eyes twinkled at Teddy. "But she's making so much money she chooses not to shear their wool, whereby she could make another $80,000 a year."

"Gram's with you, Brand. She thinks we should shear them but I just can't do it," Teddy said.

The little group visited through the rest of lunch, Frank and Donna learning something about the two ranches and also about Teddy and her grandmother.

"Well, what would you like to do while you're here?" Frank asked when they had finished eating.

"See the ocean?" Teddy piped up before Brand had a chance.

A happy smile spread over Brand's tanned face. "I'll bet you haven't been to the coast too many times."

Teddy willed her face to stay nice and white. "Well, I'm embarrassed to tell you, but I've never seen the ocean. Gram and I just stay home and work."

Brand nodded his head. "Hmmm. So that's why you came, is it?" he asked in mock seriousness.

Frank laughed loudly. "Can't think of a better reason if the girl hasn't seen the Pacific yet. Let's do that in the morning. But what about today?"

Brand turned to Teddy and nodded, then raised his hands several times in front of him, as though pulling information from her. "Come on, out with it. Surely you have our itinerary all planned."

"Okay." She turned to face Donna. "I want to learn all about Brand. All the good things he's ever done, and also the bad. I want to leave here knowing the total man."

"Unfair!" Brand protested. "I've never done anything good, and I don't want you knowing the bad, so let's not get into that. I'll just have to keep you so busy you forget all about that idea. I was thinking we might go out for dinner tonight. Maybe The North Bank?"

"Great, and I'll bet you want to take Teddy out to the ranch this afternoon," Frank said. "We've been helping the new owners a lot, so we're sure of being welcome."

Donna showed Teddy to her room at the head of the stairs. "You have your own matching bath through this door," Donna said, opening a narrow door into a sunshiny, yellow bathroom. Then she pulled back the gold-specked white drapes in the bedroom, revealing a sliding glass door opening onto a private balcony facing the backyard.

"What a gorgeous home," Teddy said.

"Thank you. We had it redone before we moved in." She left Teddy alone to put her things away. Teddy had not brought an evening dress, but she had a nice short one. It was a light green chiffon, which she hung up so the wrinkles could hang out while they ran to the ranch.

The ranch looked a lot like Brand's. Hereford cattle dotted the green pastures as far as the eye could see, and the buildings showed excellent maintenance. Teddy looked into Brand's shining eyes. "It's as nice as your ranch," she said softly.

He swallowed and reached for her hand. "At least." She knew at that moment how much he had loved this beautiful place, and how many memories it had given him. And instinctively she knew that his Central Oregon ranch was an attempt at a replay. How she would love to help him make a million memories of their own.

After they left the ranch in Alvadore they drove past Fern Ridge Lake where Brand swam and canoed as a boy. Then they hurried home to prepare for the evening.

Later, Brand's eyes lit up with joy when Teddy came down the stairs in her mint chiffon dress. She had pulled her dark hair all to one side, letting it fall in a cascade of curls.

"Don't you think we make a fantastic pair?" Brand asked his mother as they drove downtown to the restaurant.

"You look beautiful together, yes, but are you a pair?" Donna answered, her eyebrows raised questioningly.

Brand looked at Teddy. She returned his gaze, saying nothing and feeling everything. Finally, he looked back at his mother, grinned foolishly and shrugged. "I don't know, Mom, I'm working on it."

Back home, after a wonderfully impressive dinner, everyone changed and Donna served coffee. "Well," Teddy said, "this must be the time for my education. Tell me all about Brand."

Donna sipped her coffee, slipping off into some other time and place. After a moment she returned. "Brand was the best kid anyone ever had. He may have told you that we were almost middle-aged when we married, so he was an only child. He's been a wonderful son. Sometimes during the years, we'd forget who was the child and who were the parents. We've all taken care of each other."

"You mean he never got into trouble?" Teddy asked, trying to bring anything she should know into the open.

"No, but he should have, a couple of times," Frank volunteered. "Remember the time you lambasted that guy with potatoes, Brand?"

Brand slapped his hand against his forehead. "He never forgets. He's like an elephant. I swear he is. I'd forgotten all about it. Dad had sent me to the dump to get rid of several sacks of rotting potatoes. It was dark and I started heaving them down into the dump. Then I saw this flashlight down there, where someone was evidently gleaning—strictly against the rules. I just happened to start throwing in that direction, and you never saw a flashlight come out of a hole so fast."

Everyone laughed at the memory. "Tell me more." Teddy said when everyone quieted down.

"How about the times he skipped the Boy Scouts to go see a girl?" Frank asked, and roared with laughter.

Now! This sounded interesting. She might as well learn about the girls in his life.

"That was nothing," Brand said, laughing. "I was only fifteen at the time and after about the third time, the leader discovered me missing. He went next door to the girl's house after me and raised such a stink the girl never spoke to me again."

"And the blind date that you couldn't handle at first sight? Remember what you told her?" Frank threw back his gray head and laughed heartily again.

"Dad! How many more of these incidents do you have ready to zap at me?"

"Go on, son, tell Teddy how you got out of that date," Donna said. She laughed too, remembering days gone by. Obviously very precious days. Teddy could see they both felt intense pride in their only child.

"Well. . .I'm not going to do it. You don't have to testify against yourself even in a court of law." Brand winked at Teddy, got up and took her arm. "We're going to check on the moon. We'll talk to you when you've found a new subject." He took Teddy to the sliding glass door and they stepped out into a silver fairyland.

"Oh Brand, it's nice out here," Teddy said, taking in the small waterfalls and stream that occupied center stage in a perfectly groomed backyard.

"Yeah, and even the moon is trying. It's getting toward full. Come over here and sit with me."

They sat on a stone and wrought iron bench beside the waterfalls. The sound of the falls and bubbling creek, together with the fragrance of roses, petunias, and alyssum, and the moon spilling silver beams over everything in sight, made an even more romantic ambiance than the restaurant had. When Brand pulled Teddy to him, she lay her head on his shoulder, drinking in the beauty and peacefulness of the night. His spicy aftershave blended with the other smells, a few crickets added their music to the evening, and Teddy decided she could stay just like this forever.

"I love you, Teddy," he whispered. "You look and smell like my own special heaven." He put his hand under her chin and turned it up. The moment his lips touched hers, Teddy heard her own heavenly music and felt a bright pink cloud settling down over them, protecting them from any harshness of reality.

She knew she loved him. And she also knew he could never have done anything immoral, unethical, or illegal, let alone rob a bank. As he repeated the kiss, she lay in his arms, enjoying it to the fullest.

"Anyone out here?" Frank's piercing voice broke the magic and Teddy sat up with a guilty jerk, looking toward the sound.

Brand said something unintelligible under his breath before he answered. "We're out here by the waterfalls."

Donna and Frank stepped out of the trees into the moonlight, then settled onto the other bench beside the water. They sat outside for an hour getting acquainted and watching the moon flitting in and out of small white clouds. Finally Brand put his arms around Teddy again. "You're cold," he said against her cheek. "I'm taking you inside."

Frank and Donna followed and Teddy gave up all hopes of being alone with Brand. She visited a while longer and went to bed.

Before sleep came, Teddy lay in the comfortable bed and went over the afternoon and evening. Frank and Donna were certainly ready to welcome her into the family. And Brand seemed to have been the ideal child. If he had ever done anything wrong his parents did not know about it. The family was far too frank and open to be concealing anything major. They had put every doubt to rest—not that she had ever had any.

&.

She jerked away when she heard a voice, but fell right back to sleep. Then she heard it again and opened her eyes. Sunlight streamed through the sheer curtain at the window and Brand's voice and gentle knock drew her to consciousness.

"Good morning, my fairy princess," Brand said in his endearing way. "I'm waking you for breakfast. We need to get with it if we're going to the coast this morning." He seemed to pause outside her door and then turned and walked down the hallway.

Teddy showered quickly and climbed into white pants and a red sweater. She would rather have worn jeans, but Brand saw her in those every day of his life. She would like to look somewhat special today. She put her hair in a ponytail, each with a red ribbon, added a touch of red lipstick, and ran down the stairs.

The family sat at the table drinking coffee while waiting for her. "Wow," Frank said, when he saw her, "this girl isn't old enough to be so far from her mother."

Brand got up and put his arms around Teddy and kissed her tenderly, then seated her at the table beside him. He grinned at his father. "You're almost right, Dad. She's twenty-one."

Donna served waffles with strawberries and ice cream for breakfast. "They'll stay with you until we get around to eating lunch," she said.

Then they all jumped into Brand's car and took off for the coast. Teddy barely heard the conversation, so eager was she to see the ocean.

Brand laughed at her preoccupation. "You won't see the ocean for nearly an hour, so you may as well enjoy the trip." Even though it was only the last part of August, lots of trees showed golden, orange, and red colors.

Finally they left the mountains and, in a little while, drove through Florence, a busy little coastal town situated almost in the exact middle of Oregon's coastline. Teddy watched for the ocean, but did not see it until they almost drove into it. Bright blue, as far as she could see, with glittering silver stars where the sunbeams kissed the waves. The waves rolled in perfect symmetry until they neared the shore, where they burst into wildly foaming water and crashed onto the sandy beach. Brand jumped out, ran around, pulled Teddy from the car, and hugged her to him.

The wind snatched at Teddy's hair and stung her eyes. And she could not tell whether the enormous roar she heard was the wind or the ocean, or both. Then Frank and Donna got out of the back, allowing the door to slam against the car with a force that made Teddy jump.

"Wow, I've never felt wind this strong," she said, closing her eyes against the sand that blew into her face with tremendous force.

Brand opened the car and retrieved their sweaters. All of them took off their shoes and put them into the car.

"The sand feels wonderful on my feet," Teddy said, "but stings my face. Do you think we can walk in this hurricane?"

Brand took her hand and started toward the roaring ocean. "Sure, we can walk. It always blows this way down here." When they neared the ocean they turned and walked along the beach, watching the waves creep ever farther onto the sand. When a super big wave burst a few feet from them, Brand shoved Teddy into it.

Teddy had not expected that. She screamed and jumped into Brand's arms, pulling her feet up from the now-receding water. "That stuff's cold," she yelled above the roar. "It should have icebergs in it."

Brand laughed and carried her back from the water a little way and set her on her feet. "Roll up your pants," he commanded, doing the same with his own.

"We're going wading. You'll be surprised how soon the water loses its cool."

They continued walking south, following the curve of the beach. Sometimes they walked in the shallow, foaming waves and sometimes they plodded along in the wet sand. Teddy did not care, as long as Brand held her hand.

"Are we going any place special, or just walking?" Teddy asked after about a mile.

He nodded. "We're going to the jetty. It's fun to walk on, and we can check out the fishermen."

In a little while they walked the length of the jetty, watching the waves crash into the rocks and send twenty-foot walls of water flying into the china-blue sky. "Where are your folks?" Teddy asked when they climbed down from the mammoth structure.

Brand grinned and shrugged. "Who knows? Want to hide from them?"

"Of course not. They love you and want to spend this time with you." They both had to shout, for the wind tried to snatch away every sound while the ocean joined in, roaring out its mighty strength.

"Okay, let's go back," Brand yelled into her ear. They walked hand in hand as they retraced their steps over the two-mile distance.

Brand drove to Devil's Elbow for lunch. Mountains on three sides protected the much smaller beach from the wind. They took off their sweaters to enjoy the meal while watching the ever-changing ocean.

"Are you ready to go home?" Frank asked after they tossed the remnants of the food to the sea gulls and put the other things back into the car.

"I guess," Brand answered. "I really wanted Teddy to see the sun set over the ocean, but we still have to drive home."

Brand packed their things into the car as soon as they got back to his folks' place. It would be midnight when they reached their farms.

Frank and Donna walked out to the car to tell the young people good-bye. "How'd you like the ocean, Teddy?" Donna asked.

"I loved it. I can't wait to see it again," Teddy bubbled.

A wide smile split Frank's face. "Of course you liked it," he grinned impishly. "That's why Brand takes all his women there."

Chapter Eleven

Donna smacked Frank on the arm. "His ex-girlfriends, you idiot," she said, laughing. "And I don't remember him ever taking anyone else to the coast. You're just trying to make the poor girl jealous."

"I'm trying to help her see that Brand's a good catch," he said.

"I give the girl credit for having good sense," Donna said. "Why don't we let her discover how nice he is all by herself? That's part of the thrill of finding each other, remember?"

Brand sat comfortably in his bucket seat grinning at both of his parents, neither embarrassed nor upset in the least. He started the car and stuck his head out the window for a last kiss from first his mother, then his father. He pushed the gearshift down and eased away. "You guys come see us real soon," he called as they glided into the street.

Teddy leaned back and closed her eyes. She had learned all she would from this trip. A lot—and all good.

Brand slipped his hand over hers. "What do you think of my family?"

"I like them a lot. It sort of made me think about. . . ." She had been thinking about her mother and father. No, not her own mother and father, but how her life might have been if she had had a mother and father around for her. Now, how could she have even thought that? Gram had done her very best for her all the time. "They sure like you a lot," she finished.

"Not any more than Gram likes you." He stroked her hand with his thumb. "You were about to say it made you think about your mom and dad, weren't you? Wouldn't you like to talk about your folks, little Teddy Bear?"

She did not answer, but shook her head. She knew Brand wanted to comfort her, but her parentage was one subject that would always stay buried, as far as she was concerned. She searched for a subject strong enough to drive the other one out of his mind. "Do you really take all your women to the coast?"

Brand signaled, then turned off the freeway onto the McKenzie Highway, laid his head back on his headrest and laughed. His laugh sounded almost like Frank's, only more refined. "You're the first one ever, and I'm glad. It was special to me, introducing you to the ocean."

"Me too. I want to go back, Brand."

"On our honeymoon?"

She burst out laughing, feeling a great relief. He really wanted to marry her. "So you didn't take your women to the coast. Where did you take them?"

He hesitated a moment, then glanced her way. His lips twitched and his brown eyes sparkled pure gold. "Oh, I usually took them to dark, quiet places."

Teddy knew he was kidding but could not respond.

"Hey, why the silence," he asked a moment later. "Do you love me so much you can't stand the idea of me ever having had another girlfriend?"

She nodded.

He reached for her hand again. "To tell the truth I haven't had that many girl-friends, and no serious ones. I was always too busy studying or helping Mom and Dad on the ranch. As I got older, so did they, and at the last I worked from dawn to dusk." He chuckled. "You know, like we both do now."

"Do you care about my other boyfriends?" she asked mischievously.

He slowed for a bird eating something from the roadside snow, then resumed his speed. "Not a bit."

She tossed his hand back into his own lap. "What a thing to say! You could at least act a little jealous, couldn't you?"

His hand slid into hers once more. "You can't even imagine how jealous I'd be if I had a reason. I'd tear any man apart who touched you now, and maybe any that ever had." He retrieved his hand to negotiate a sharp upward curve, as they drove into the mountains. Teddy's eyes met his, and saw love in them that made her stomach flutter.

They talked about everything and laughed about anything as they drove through the mountains, then over the open country to their ranches. Much too soon, Brand carried Teddy's suitcases into the old run-down ranch house. He set them down in the empty living room, kissed her good-bye, and disappeared through the front door.

"Well, get those shoes off and tell me about your trip," said Gram.

"He isn't the one, Gram. They're really great people. And I love him, and—" Then it hit her like a spiked volleyball. Gram might not feel quite so happy about her new love. What would they do with Gram?

"That's what I needed to know," Gram said. "Of course, we both knew he was all right, but now we're sure." She glanced at the clock on the stove. "Do you see what time it is? Those fool llamas will be ready for breakfast at five o'clock no matter what time we want to go to bed."

The clock read twelve-thirty when Teddy crawled into her bed, tired, but exhilarated as she had never been. She set her alarm for quarter of five in the morning. But she could not seem to fall asleep. *Father,* she prayed silently, *won't You please help me know for sure if You want me to marry Brand. If for any reason You don't, could You please make me feel uneasy about it when I wake up? Thank you, Father. I love You. Good night.*

❧

Teddy turned off the alarm at the first chirp and jumped out of bed, feeling as high as a cloud and just as fluffy. Brand loved her and they would be married! And best and most important of all, God wanted her to marry him!

She left the house quietly so she would not awaken Gram, but Teddy found her in the barn, loading feed onto the pickup. "Gram, did you forget I'm back?" Teddy asked, laughing from pure happiness.

Gram's yellow-gray curls shook. "Naw, but I thought you might be tired."

"I'm too happy to be tired." Teddy told Gram more about her trip as they fed the llamas together.

Brand did not show up all day and Teddy thought she would go wild if she did not see him soon. She could not bring herself to leave Gram to go to his place, and she felt a little shy, anyway. He would come as soon as possible.

As Teddy and Gram sat down to supper, he arrived in his sports car and they invited him to eat with them.

"I hear you're in love with my girl." Gram's granite voice made it sound as if he had stolen the crown jewels.

He buttered a hot biscuit and spread honey over it, then nodded soberly. "I'm in love with both of you, Gram. Right now, I'm trying to figure out how to get us all into the same family. Teddy hasn't said yes yet. Would I have better luck with you?"

Gram swallowed a big bite of corn she had just chewed off the cob. Then she waved the cob at Brand. "No, you have to deal with her, but I'll push while you pull."

Brand flew off his chair as though catapulted. Forgetting all about his uneaten supper, he grabbed Teddy from her chair, wrapped his arms around her and danced wildly around the room. Finally, he fell to the couch with her still in his arms. "That's it, baby, there's nothing to stop us." He kissed her quickly, then looked into her eyes. "Say it, Teddy Bear, say you'll marry me."

Teddy got to her feet, then cast an impish glance at Brand. "Sorry about that tornado that just blew through. Shall we finish eating now?"

Brand jerked her back down beside him and crushed her in his arms. "This is going to get tighter until you say the word." He pecked her on the cheek, then tightened his grip.

"This is nice," she said. He tightened his arms again and she struggled for breath. "How come you've never hugged me like this before?" she wheezed.

He squeezed her again, then released her and tweaked a curl gently. "I can't hurt you, even though you're a brat," he said. "I give up." He started toward the door. "I'll just go find someone else."

Teddy followed Brand to the door and told him good-bye. As he climbed into his car she called to him. "If you can't find anyone else who'll marry you, I guess I could. You know what they say, it's a dirty job but someone has to do it."

He piled out of the car and raced to the house with the speed of sound, hitting the steps like a bolt of lightning. He went through the third one with the crack of thunder—sprawling all the way to the top. Teddy dropped to her knees on the porch so she could look into his face. "Are you all right?"

He winked at her. "I don't know. If I could get my busted leg out of the step I might be able to tell."

After resting a few minutes, he managed to haul the leg out and, leaning on Teddy's shoulder, he managed to hop back into the kitchen. Before leaving the porch, he looked back at the mangled steps. "I suppose you're going to sue me for wrecking your steps."

When Teddy had Brand seated comfortably on the couch, he pulled a small package from his shirt pocket and laid it on the coffee table. "So you're going to do it, huh?"

"Marry you? Was there ever any doubt?"

He pointed to the small box. "Well, that's for you, but not until you feed me the rest of my supper."

Teddy reached for the box but Brand grabbed her hand and held it firmly. "Not until I've had my supper," he repeated.

"I just wanted to look at it, and see how heavy it is," she said.

"After my supper."

Gram jumped up, refilled Brand's plate with warm food, fixed two more biscuits and filled his coffee cup with steaming brew. Then she put the plate into his eager hands. But he took his time eating.

"Does your leg hurt much?" Teddy asked fifteen minutes later. Food still covered half his plate.

"Only when you get too near that little package on the coffee table."

Teddy helped Gram with the dishes. At least it kept her busy and away from the package. Her hands flew. Maybe she could get all through before Brand finished his food.

"Could I have some more biscuits, please?"

Teddy buttered and honeyed two more of Gram's fluffy golden biscuits, carried them over and dropped them onto Brand's plate, then turned and tried to snatch the box. But Brand's uninjured foot flashed over the package, covering it neatly and so strongly she could not dislodge it. Teddy gave up and continued with the dishes.

"I need another ear of corn, please?"

What was this? Teddy had never seen Brand eat like this. And with an injured foot? He was probably getting even for her own mischief. Well, she could outfox a fox, any day of the week.

"Could you fix Brand's corn, Gram?" she asked. "I have to go feed the llamas. I'll be back in about an hour and a half."

"No, don't go." Brand jumped to his feet—and fell over again. Teddy ran and helped him back onto the couch.

"You did hurt yourself," she said trying to make him comfortable.

His face had paled somewhat under his dark tan, but his mouth spread in a wide laugh. "No, just trying to get attention. Now, are you ready to open this little box?" Teddy leaned over and kissed him as he put the long-awaited box into her hand.

Sitting on the couch beside him, she unwrapped the blue foil from a lightweight cardboard box. Hmm, not exactly what she had expected, but there must be another box inside this one. She carefully opened the lid and pulled out—a feathery fish hook? Disappointment flooded over her like ocean waves, breaking and spilling until she felt about as tall as a grain of sand.

Chapter Twelve

Then wild laughter caught her attention. "I must have given you the wrong box," he said laughing some more.

When she looked into his love-filled eyes, he pulled her to him and kissed her softly, then again, not quite so softly. Her heart started beating again and she found she could not breathe. He pulled out another box, this one covered with red foil, and laid it in her hand.

She looked into his eyes. He nodded silently and smiled. When she pulled the foil away, she held a royal blue, felt-covered jeweler's box in her hand. This was it! If she could just hold her hands steady enough to open the box! She fumbled a moment before a strong hand took it, opened it, and put it back into her hand.

There it was, winking at her! The most beautiful diamond she had ever seen, nestled in soft, red velvet. She felt hypnotized, unable to take her eyes from it. Then, a single tear formed in her left eye. Why would she cry now? At the happiest moment of her life. She blinked it away and started laughing. "Oh, Brand, thank you, thank you. Gram! Come see it."

"I've already seen it, kitten."

"How could that be? I've only seen it just now."

Brand took the box from her and lifted the ring from its velvet nest. "Let's see if it fits, Teddy Bear." He took her left hand and slipped the ring onto her third finger—a perfect fit.

Teddy looked at the ring sparkling on her finger then threw her arms around his neck and kissed him. "It fits perfectly," she said a little later while they all ate the cake and ice cream Hannah and Rolf had brought in response to Brand's call. The decorated cake had *Congratulations Brand and Teddy* written on it in pink letters.

"Somehow everyone knew about this little party but me," Teddy said laughing. "But how did you know my ring size? As if I didn't know. You traitor, Gram."

"He got your ring some time ago," Gram said, "so of course I had to see it. I sent the first one back. It was too small." Gram's faded old eyes twinkled. "The diamond, I mean," she finished, cackling over her joke.

"What am I getting myself into?" Brand asked no one in particular. "Two women, and they're both determined to give me a bad time."

After a while, Teddy looked out the window and noticed darkness settling around them. "We're through opening presents, we're all stuffed on ice cream and cake, I wonder what we're supposed to be doing now," she mused aloud.

"Dreaming, I guess, my little Teddy Bear. Dreaming about tomorrow and the rest of our tomorrows."

Hannah and Rolf stayed until it was bedtime for everyone so Brand kissed Teddy good-bye while they all watched, and then went home.

Gram and Teddy returned to the kitchen to relax a few minutes and rehash the evening. Teddy's blue eyes radiated happiness. "Oh, Gram, I never thought I could be so happy," she said, almost purring.

"I'm glad. You've missed enough in your life. You deserve somebody special, and for my money you got him."

Teddy dropped a kiss on the withered old cheek. "Don't say that, Gram. You've been everything to me."

Gram smiled and her old eyes twinkled with merriment. "Until the handsome prince kissed you. I thought he never would, after that toad messed you up." Then she became serious. "Have you decided which ranch you'll live on? I'm sure his is a lot nicer."

"We haven't talked about that at all, Gram. Now we'd better get to bed, and you sleep in a little late in the morning. I'll do the early chores."

❧

Teddy had barely finished her chores the next morning and sat down to Gram's good breakfast, when Brand limped into the house with a newspaper in his hand. "I took off my shoes, Gram," he said walking to the sink to wash his hands.

"Sit down and have some breakfast," Gram said, putting on another plate.

Brand waited until after Gram asked the blessing to tell them what he had found in the paper. "It's a little announcement about the county fair, coming up next week. We could go if you want. Let's go over to Redmond today and buy tickets for it."

"Sounds like fun," Teddy said.

After they bought the tickets in Redmond, they stopped at an ice cream store for a peanut butter parfait before going home. "Have you thought about Gram?" Teddy asked while they ate their cool treats.

"Lots of times. Why?"

"I mean what am I going to do with her when we get married?"

Brand laid his spoon down and swallowed. "What kind of question is that? What did you plan to do with her?" He almost sounded indignant.

Teddy shrugged, embarrassed. "I don't know exactly. That's why I'm trying to talk to you about it."

Brand picked up his spoon and shoved in a huge bite of the ice cream confection, chewed and swallowed, before he spoke. "I don't even know where we're going to live yet, do you?"

Teddy shook her head.

He continued as though he had not stopped. "But wherever we live, she'll live with us." His eyes softened. "I asked you both, remember?"

A fantastic peace flooded throughout Teddy's being. She should have known. "Brand, have I told you how terribly much I love you? You've just made me love you a tiny bit more, and I didn't think that was possible."

They finished their treats and drove home. "Do you think Gram's worrying about what we'll do with her?" Brand asked as they let themselves into the house and took off their shoes.

"I don't know. Let's talk to her right away, just in case."

In a few minutes Gram came in the back door. She had already shed her shoes and washed up in the utility room.

Brand took Gram's small hand in his. "Gram, we've been thinking. Where would you like to live after we're married?"

A small cloud passed over her face, but the sun broke through and her happy smile showed only the slightest hesitation. "I guess it's up to you two. The ranch is Teddy's, you know. If you're going to live on your place, maybe I could just stay here. Otherwise, I can get an apartment in Bend."

"No way," Brand said, stroking the frail hand he still held. "Where we go, you go. I was just wondering where you think that ought to be."

Gram shook her head. "I wouldn't feel right about that. Young people should be alone."

"Don't you give it a thought," Brand said. "And wherever we end up, I promise I'll check my boots at the door—and wash my hands quickly. Actually, I think it's a good idea."

ஒ

A couple of days later Brand arrived with a small trailer behind his pickup. Teddy dropped her hoe and went to meet him. After his usual hug and warm kiss he stepped over to the trailer. "I'll bet you can't guess what I have inside."

Gram threw her hoe down and joined Teddy at the high-sided trailer. "Open this thing before we rip it apart," Gram instructed as Brand stepped to the back of the truck and unfastened the tailgate.

"It isn't alive," he informed the two women as he lifted the wood section out and placed it on the ground.

"Oooh," they said in unison when they saw a bright blue bicycle inside. A tandem bicycle.

Brand put a strong arm around Gram and pulled her close. "Sorry, Gram, I couldn't find a bicycle built for three."

"It's okay. We can take turns."

Brand unloaded the long bicycle and motioned for Teddy to climb onto the rear seat. He straddled the front. "Let's take it for a spin, Teddy Bear."

Teddy threw back her shoulders. "Aren't you being the least tiny bit chauvinistic? Maybe I want to ride in front."

Brand laughed. "I wasn't being a pig, at least not purposely. Okay, we'll do it right. How much do you weigh?"

"That's a sneaky way to learn my weight."

"The people at the bike shop said the heavier has to ride in front." Brand raised his chin a couple of inches. "And I might add that he's the captain."

Teddy laughed and gave his shoulder a small shove. "You made that all up. So . . .what is the other person called?"

"I didn't make it up, Teddy, really. The back person is called the stoker, and they said this is a neat place because this person can eat lunch or most anything he wants to. But the captain absolutely must tell the stoker when they're coming to a bump or corner or stop sign." He raised his right hand to his forehead and executed a smart salute. "Got it, stoker baby?"

"Got it." She climbed onto the bike.

"Ready?" the captain yelled. "One, two, three, blastoff." He gave a hard push with his foot and they were riding down the driveway. Wobbly, but riding.

"Wow, this is different!" Teddy yelled. By the time they reached the highway, they were moving so fast it frightened Teddy. "I'm scared," she yelled.

"I'm braking," he returned. "We're slowing for the corner." After they negotiated the corner, they picked up speed again.

In a little while Teddy felt comfortable and sat back, releasing the handlebars. "If only I had my knitting," she yelled.

"You won't have to knit your own clothes, anymore," he said. "I plan to buy you the most beautiful wardrobe in the world—to match you."

"Idiot!" she screamed into the wind. "I don't have to knit my clothes. I love to. It has something to do with pride—and satisfaction."

They rode on for a while and the farther they went, the more Teddy enjoyed the ride. It was different from a single rider bike. She felt a loss of control, but was able to relax so much more. Well, she would not want to ride this way all the time, but sometimes it was fantastic.

"Ready to go back?" the captain yelled, and suited the action to the suggestion. In a moment they were headed back toward the ranches, rolling along at a fast clip.

It seemed to take much less time to return than it had to go, probably because they had learned how to handle the bike better. They stopped and got off the bike beside Brand's pickup.

"Thanks a lot," Teddy said. "That was really fun. Maybe we can do it again someday. May I ride with you to take it back?"

"Back?" Brand look at Teddy questioningly. "Oh, you thought I rented it? Teddy, this bike is ours—for romantic riding anytime, anywhere. Could we keep it in your garage?"

"Aren't you forgetting something?" The gravelly voice came from behind an overgrown shrub. Then Gram stepped out. "I'm ready for my try now. Who's riding with me?"

Brand smiled at the old lady. "Since I'm used to riding in front, and since you'll be in back no matter who goes, I think it'll be safer for you if I take you this first time. Okay?"

"Cut the talk and let's go." She climbed on the back seat and lacked six inches of reaching the pedals. Brand dropped the seat as low as it would go, and the two took off down the driveway.

Teddy watched with a dreamy smile on her face. She watched them all the way down the driveway and noticed they had turned in the same direction she and Brand had. She knew he would be extra careful with Gram, realizing how fragile her old bones had become. As she stood there thinking about Gram and Brand and what a lovely life she had before her, an old car turned into the driveway and lumbered slowly toward her. She waited.

Finally, the car wheezed to a stop, amid a cloud of black smoke from the exhaust system, and a woman in her late forties stepped out. "Is this the Marland ranch?"

Teddy glanced at the woman. She stood a little shorter than Teddy, and was somewhat heavier. Her dark blonde hair, straggling to her shoulders, looked as though it had never been washed. Too much dark blue makeup surrounded pale blue eyes, and oversized glasses hid much of her face.

Her bright red lips opened to reveal darkly stained teeth. "Well, don't you know who owns this dump?" The woman practically spat the harsh words at Teddy.

Teddy nodded. "It's the Marland ranch."

The woman's pale eyes swept the yard and nearby area. "Well, where's the old lady?"

Teddy began to feel uneasy. This could be anyone. "She's not here right now. May I help you?"

The woman looked Teddy up and down. "Of course you can't help me. Get the old lady."

Teddy did not know whether to tell her that Gram would be back soon, or to get rid of her. She looked at the woman again, feeling as if she should know her. Maybe she had seen her somewhere before, but could not think where.

"If I can't help you, you may as well leave. I don't know exactly when she'll be back." Teddy tried to sound kind but businesslike.

"You ain't going to get rid of me that easy, you smart-mouthed kid. I'll wait." She turned to her old car, pulled the back door open, and a huge mutt jumped to the ground. It took one look at Teddy and then ran off.

"The dog can't be loose here," she said. "Call it quickly." The woman just glared at her. "Please! We have valuable animals." Still the woman did not move. Teddy turned and ran in the direction the dog had gone but could not find it.

She looked for ten minutes. The dog was nowhere to be seen.

She returned to the woman, who sat on the rickety porch, smoking a cigarette. "Aren't you afraid the dog will get lost?" she asked. "This is a strange place for it, you know."

"I certainly do know this is a strange place. No doubt better than you. But as for the dog, I wish it would get lost, but that thing would come home if you dumped it in the middle of the ocean." She exhaled a breath of dark smoke, then watched it disperse, as though it were the most interesting thing she had ever seen.

A noise caught Teddy's attention and she saw Brand and Gram pedaling up the driveway. The woman saw them too, and stood up to watch. They stopped and Gram hopped off and walked toward the porch and the women on it. Brand followed. Teddy could not believe how happy she was to see them.

Gram walked up the broken steps carefully, with Brand right behind. The woman stepped forward as Gram reached the top of the steps. They looked at each other, like two wary cats meeting for the first time. Teddy felt a horrible fear clutch her by the throat. Somehow, she knew this woman was bad news.

"Good afternoon," Brand said pleasantly. "May we help you with something?"

"Butt out, big boy. You don't belong here," the woman snarled. Her watery blue eyes never left Gram's face.

Brand tried again. "Pardon me, ma'am, but I do belong here. Could we do something for you?"

After a long, uncomfortable silence, Gram's lips moved. "Fritzi?" she whispered, almost inaudibly. A terrible choke came from Gram's throat as she tried to repeat her question. "Fritzi, is that you?"

Chapter Thirteen

"Of course it's me, you old fool. Have your eyes gone bad like the rest of you? You look about a hundred and ten years old."

Brand stepped up and dropped a well-muscled arm over Gram's shoulders. "Look here, young lady, if you won't be civil you can leave right now. No one comes around here and insults Gram."

Gram put a hand on Brand's arm. "It's all right, sonny." She turned to the woman, Fritzi. "You don't look like any spring chicken, either, in case you haven't been near a mirror lately. Must have been living in the fast lane."

"Where's the kid, old woman?"

"Don't you dare ask me about the kid. Don't you ever ask me about the kid again. Do you understand?"

Immediately Teddy knew who the woman was! The rickety porch floor seemed to move under her feet and she felt her knees give way—then nothing.

&

"Come on, baby, you're all right." The gravelly voice was one of the sweetest sounds Teddy had ever heard, even though it seemed far away. Teddy opened her eyes to find herself on the porch floor with Gram kneeling beside her, holding a cool cloth on her forehead. She raised her eyes to meet Brand's concerned look.

"I don't faint," she said trying to sit up. The porch began moving again, and she settled back down. "Never," she insisted as she lay quietly. Then she saw the woman, standing on the edge of the top step, looking around at the ranch, a cigarette hanging loosely from her mouth. Teddy raised a hand and pointed to the woman, but no words came from her throat.

Gram nodded. "I'm sorry, kitten. I hoped this would never happen, but we'll be all right."

The woman wheeled around. "You hoped I'd never come back? Never see my own kid? So what did you do, give it away?"

Teddy sat up and clutched her throat. She tried to speak but could not get it out. "I'm your kid," she finally squawked in a strange voice. "I'm the kid you didn't even name."

Fritzi whirled around to face Teddy. "What? A big horse like you?" Her questioning eyes went to Gram. "My kid must be about twelve, isn't it? And I can't remember if it was a boy or girl. You'd better not have given it away and you'd better get it out here, old woman, or I'll have the law on you."

Struggling to her feet, Teddy moved to the love seat at the end of the porch.

Her face felt wet and she discovered she was crying.

Gram's eyes looked steel hard as they met Fritzi's. She pointed to Teddy. "She was your kid, but only until she got outside your body. Then you couldn't shed both of us fast enough, could you? Walked out the hospital door, when you were so weak you could barely stand on your two feet. How do you think that made me feel, Fritzi? But you wouldn't understand a mother's love, would you? You wouldn't have any idea how it feels to be terrified for your child, week in, week out."

Fritzi grabbed Gram by the shoulders and started shaking her, but Brand snatched the offending hands and threw them against their owner. "I want you to get into the car and take off," he growled. "And don't come back."

"I'll bet you'd like that, wouldn't you, cave man? Well, I'm not going anywhere." She pointed at Gram. "That old woman is about to die and I'm here to take over the ranch."

Brand sucked in a big breath and so did Teddy, but Gram laid her head back and cackled with laughter.

Fritzi looked alarmed as Gram continued laughing. "What's the old woman laughing about? Is she senile?" she asked.

"You came home because you loved us so much you couldn't handle it anymore. Is that how it is, Fritzi? But you can't even bring yourself to call me anything more personal than 'old woman'. Well, not-so-young woman, I have news for you. This ranch is now worth well over a million dollars, including the livestock. What do you think of that?"

Fritzi's eyes grew round, and they swept over the pastures, the alfalfa fields, even the yard. "I'm going to sell it the minute you die. Hopefully that won't be too many days from now."

"What about your little girl?" Gram asked, a crafty look in her eye.

Fritzi's eye flicked past Teddy. _She still has not asked my name or how I have been all these years,_ Teddy thought. _And worse than that, she does not care one thing about Gram. How could anyone grow up with Gram and not love her?_

"What about her?" Fritzi repeated.

"Wouldn't you want her to have at least part of it?" Gram's lips stretched in an imitation of a smile.

Fritzi looked at Teddy again, then back to her mother. "Old woman, you don't know anything, do you? Here's the way it works. When you die, I get it. When I die. . ." she groped for a name, then settled for, "she gets it. If there's anything left. But I plan to spend it all." She dropped her cigarette butt on the old porch floor and lit another.

Gram laughed heartily, almost as though she were enjoying herself now. "Well, not-so-young woman, don't spend it too fast. I told you the truth when I said this ranch is worth more than a million, but I forgot to mention that I don't own it anymore. I'm just fortunate enough to live here."

Fritzi sprang at Gram, her face twisted into a horrible sight. Once again Brand stopped her, stepping between. "You aren't going to hurt Gram," he said softly. "We love her very much and plan to keep her a long time. Now, why don't you leave?"

Fritzi turned on Brand and attacked him with insane rage. Before he could stop the woman, her long fingernails raked his face several times, leaving tiny rivulets of blood oozing down his cheeks. Then long red streaks appeared on his bare arms. Brand pinned her arms to her sides, rendering her helpless before she could do any more damage. The more she struggled, the tighter he held her, until her face grew so red it looked as though it might explode.

"You...you...you!" she screamed. "You bought the ranch, didn't you? Where's the money? I want the money, and I want it now!" She jerked wildly for another minute, then relaxed, coughing and totally exhausted.

Brand turned to the older woman with a quiet smile. "Gram," he said pleasantly, "could you get some fingernail clippers, please?"

A moment later Gram reappeared with the requested item. Brand pulled Fritzi against him, her back to his chest. His arms held her so tightly his blood smeared over her dress. "Gram's going to trim those fingernails," he murmured, almost in a whisper. "If you want the ends of your fingers left intact, I suggest you hold still." He held one of Fritzi's hands to Gram. "Cut them close," he instructed.

Fritzi held her hands still and said nothing during the ten-minute procedure, but whimpered quietly the entire time. When Gram finished, everyone, including Fritzi, knew the fingernails would not scratch anyone for quite some time. "Will you behave if I turn you lose now?" Brand asked.

Fritzi nodded. He released her and she examined her hands. "They'll be so sore I won't be able to use them," she wailed.

Just then, llama cries, the sound of several dogs yapping, barking, and finally screaming, interrupted the confrontation on the porch. Brand tore past the hole in the steps with Teddy close behind. Gram came as fast as she could. They all temporarily forgot Fritzi, but she followed Gram as they all ran to the north pasture where the horrible sounds emanated from.

When Teddy arrived she found Brutus and Caesar standing over Fritzi's badly chewed-up mutt. A three-year-old brown llama stood to one side, her head hanging and blood running down her chest. Teddy pointed at the dog on the ground. "Keep it there!" she screamed to Brutus and Caesar, then turned to Brand. "Help," she whispered.

Brand moved to the llama's head and Teddy began searching for the source of the blood. She found a slash on each side of the llama's throat and shoved her hands against the wounds. But the blood flowed between her fingers. Almost immediately the llama dropped to her knees, then turned on her side and lay flat on the ground. Blood still flowed from the wounds, but slower. A moment later, the blood stopped and the llama's eyes opened with a glazed, unseeing appearance. Brand took Teddy into his arms and softly held her.

"I'm sorry, Teddy Bear. I'm so sorry." He bent his face against hers and said nothing more, just continued holding her tight. Teddy cried for several minutes, then took some deep breaths. There were things to do here and she must get hold of herself. The dog! Her dogs would still be watching it but they must be relieved.

She lifted her bloody, tear-streaked face. "Thank you, Brand. I'm all right, now." She turned to see Brutus and Caesar, their fangs bared, standing over the other dog. Fritzi stood watching, but Gram had disappeared. Teddy turned back to Brand. "Where is she?" she asked.

He shook his head. Then Teddy followed Fritzi's eyes toward the old log house. Gram hurried toward them, holding a small rifle in her hands! The old lady looked at no one and said nothing, but walked up to the dogs. She made a sweeping motion with her right arm and spoke to the dogs. Brutus and Caesar jumped to their feet and disappeared into the herd of llamas that were standing around. Then Gram shot the dog in the head from a distance of about six inches.

"I'll call someone to take care of the carcasses," she said calmly, then walked away toward the house.

Brand put his arm around Teddy again. "Are you ready to go, love?"

Teddy walked to the llama, knelt beside it and petted its back with both hands. She buried her face in the soft wool. Then she stood to her feet, and held out her hand to Brand. "I'm ready."

They walked slowly to the house, arm in arm. Fritzi followed, several feet behind. When they reached the house, Brand looked at the blood covering his arms and clothes, his own, from Fritzi's attack, and the dead llama's. "I better go shower and change. I can be back in twenty minutes."

Teddy nodded. "Yes, I'll do the same." Brand barely touched her lips with his and then carefully ran down the steps. Teddy stepped inside and took off her shoes. She had nearly reached the hall door when she heard Fritzi clattering across the floor, and Gram appeared from the kitchen.

"Get those shoes off before you come into my house," Gram yelled, pointing at the front door.

Fritzi looked shocked, but backed up and stepped out of her scruffy pumps. Then Gram pointed to the utility room. "Now go wash the filth off you." Fritzi moved in the direction Gram indicated and Teddy ran for the shower.

Brand reappeared in less than thirty minutes looking clean and shampooed. The deep red lacerations in his face looked even angrier than before he left. He moved straight to Teddy. "Are you all right?" he asked tenderly.

Fritzi, rocking in the old wooden rocker, stopped suddenly. "What's this 'poor little Teddy' stuff? She only lost a silly looking animal, and she has a million others just like it. That old woman shot my dog right in front of my face. My pet that went everywhere with me. And don't think she's going to get away with it. What's more, I'm positive those two white-eyed dogs of yours killed that. . . thing. When two dogs get together anything can happen. I read that in the paper. I'm going to call the Humane Society right away." She headed toward the telephone.

Gram stepped between Fritzi and the phone. "Shut up and sit down!" she growled. "Let me tell you something. If it hadn't been for those two white-eyed dogs of ours, we'd have lost many llamas, rather than just one. Let me tell you something else. Each and every llama is a personal pet of Teddy's. You saw how much she loved Cocoa, didn't you? Now, let me tell you this. That llama your dog killed was worth $20,000, maybe more, and she was due to have a baby in four months, which would have been worth a considerable amount too. One last thing. Ranchers around here take a very dim view of stock-killing dogs. No way, no way in this world could your dog have lived after what it did."

"Maybe you'd like to make some monetary restitution for the llama," Brand added quietly.

Fritzi did not answer, but pulled out a cigarette. "Don't light it!" Gram's harsh voice instructed. "No one has ever smoked in this house and you aren't going to be the one to start."

Fritzi shoved the cigarette back into her purse and stood up, facing the group. "So, it's going to be three against one, is it? I didn't expect to be welcome here. Well, don't think I came back because I wanted to. I hated this place when I left, and it hasn't improved a bit. I only came back as a last resort, and I mean I tried everything else. I have a bad knee and can't stand on it to cook anymore. So I guess I'm stuck with you."

"That may well be," Gram said, "but I'm not sure we're stuck with you. You have absolutely no claims to our home, our food, our devotions, or our care. You forfeited that years ago, as well as all rights to Teddy."

"Tough, old woman. I don't have two dimes to rub together, and owe several thousand on charge cards, so what are you going to do, pitch me out in the street?"

She cast a quick glance at Brand. "I suppose you're the guy who bought the ranch, so you must have enough money to put up with me."

Gram shook her old head, but her eyes had a gleam. "I didn't sell the ranch, not-so-young woman. I gave it away several months ago. In fact, you're just six months too late."

Fritzi shook her head. "I'll admit you're dumb, old woman, but you aren't that dumb. You didn't give it away."

"Want to see the papers?" Gram got up and disappeared into her bedroom, returning a moment later with some stapled papers and tossed them to Fritzi.

After reading the papers a moment, Fritzi's face whitened. Her eyes met Teddy's. "She gave it to you? She gave this whole stinking place to you? For nothing?" She turned back to her mother. "How could you do this? She's only a granddaughter. I'll break this like a piece of cracked glass. I've heard about breaking wills before."

Gram smiled gently. "Isn't a will. I gave it to her. Well, technically, I sold it to her for one dollar. Just to be legal." Her eyes, filled with love, turned to Teddy. "Now, kitten, see why I insisted? It's all yours, safe and sound."

After Brand had left, Teddy made up a bed in the spare room for Fritzi and they all went to bed, feeling much exhausted from the highly charged emotions of the day, and with nothing settled as far as Fritzi was concerned. As Teddy tried to have her evening talk with her Lord she kept hearing bumps and thumps from Fritzi's room. How mad was she, anyway? Finally Teddy told God goodnight and fell asleep.

≥≥

The next morning, when Teddy went to feed the llamas, she found Brand already starting. "I thought I'd like to be with you this morning. I knew it would be hard, this first time after Cocoa . . .you know." She walked into his arms and he held her for a little while. The llamas watched and nudged them, eager for their breakfast. Suddenly he pulled away and looked around. "Where is he?" he asked, as though frightened.

"Who? Oh, you mean Casanova. He's around somewhere. Maybe he's getting used to you."

Brand started breaking apart bales of alfalfa hay and dropping them behind the pickup. "He might be, but I don't feel like taking any chances." He worked a little while, then began chuckling.

"What could be so funny at half past five in the morning?"

"I just got to thinking. Wouldn't it be funny if Casanova spit on Fritzi?"

"I don't know. Brand, I'm sorry I never told you about my mother. Would you like to talk about it now?"

Chapter Fourteen

He reached inside and shut off the motor, and they climbed onto the hay in the back of the pickup. "I want to know everything about you, my love." The baled hay jiggled when he pulled her close, but they managed to stay put.

"I never had a father. None at all. If Fritzi knew who he was she never told Gram. I've cried a lot of tears over being. . .illegitimate."

Brand kissed her soft brown hair. "Baby, why should you be so upset? You didn't do it."

Teddy snuggled close and continued talking as though she had not stopped. "Fritzi wanted an abortion in the worst way, but they weren't legal yet, and Gram hated the idea. So she had me, but when I was one day old, she ran away from the hospital, cleared out her and Gram's $3,000 checking account, stole Gram's almost-new car, and that's it. We never saw her again. I should say Gram didn't. Fritzi never saw me, even before she left. She refused." Teddy gulped. "And she didn't even remember whether I was a boy or girl. Or how old I was."

Brand rained kisses over her face. "How old was she when you were born, Teddy Bear?"

"Seventeen."

Brand nodded. "Pretty young. That isn't any excuse for what she did, though, to either you or Gram. Let's see, she's about thirty-eight now, then. I can't believe it. She looks fifty-eight."

Teddy nodded, holding Brand tightly. Then her head flipped around. "Let's get out of here. Casanova's coming."

They jumped off the hay and started feeding the llamas. Casanova remained calm.

After they finished feeding, Teddy asked Brand if they could talk about him for a little while. They settled onto the tail gate of the pickup. "Okay," he said. "Am I in trouble?"

"No. But I've wondered about Celia. What really happened between you two. I thought I saw sparks."

He laughed. "So it worked! We thought it a dismal failure. Well, I met her on the riding trail as I said. But that's about where the story should have stopped. She's married and her husband was out of town. She asked me to take her to church so I told her about you and how I couldn't get to first base. So. . .we hatched up our little scheme to make you jealous." He held up his hand. "And don't get jealous now. The only thing we ever did was laugh and talk to each other when we knew you were watching. Otherwise, we're just friends."

Teddy heaved a sigh of relief. Now she could relax. For a fraction of a second the other problem—the one about the bank robbery in Eugene—tickled her mind, but she thrust it aside. She knew for sure that story did not have any more substance than the Brand and Celia one. She hurried in to breakfast with Brand, feeling clean and free. "How's the sore knee this morning?" she asked Fritzi.

"Well! I thought no one even heard that I had one. It's sore. It's always sore. I can walk but not much."

Brand wiped the last bite of his pancake in syrup and forked it into his mouth. "Gram, I hope you never forget how to make these fantastic pancakes," he said, then turned back to Fritzi. "I'm taking you to a doctor this morning."

"No, you aren't! I've been to plenty of doctors and they can't find the problem."

He nodded pleasantly. "We'll try one more." So, a little later, Brand took off toward Bend with Fritzi sitting unhappily beside him.

"What are we going to do with her, Gram?" Teddy asked after the car drove out of sight.

The old woman shook her head and Teddy thought she looked tired. "I don't know, kitten. We'd be within our rights to pitch her clothes out and lock the door, but I couldn't do that to anyone."

"What do you feel for her, Gram? Or would you rather not talk about it?"

Gram's eyes shot across the room to where Teddy sat. "How do I feel about my long lost daughter? I'm not sure. I may not feel anything. Then again, I may hate her a little for what she did to you. . .and me. And maybe, behind all these feelings, I still love her. I really don't know. Sometimes emotions are like that, you know. It takes a while to figure them out. Let's wait and see what the doctor says."

Brand and Fritzi came home an hour later with no news. "I paid the doctor and made Fritzi agree to ask him to talk to me," Brand said. "The X-rays showed nothing, there is no swelling or discoloration, but the doctor said there could be tenderness. He said knee problems are impossible to verify or disprove."

Fritzi looked triumphant. "So, old woman, are you going to throw me out?"

Gram looked grim. "Are you able to pull your own weight around here?"

"If I were, I wouldn't be here."

Gram looked at Teddy. "What do you say, Teddy?"

"I can't imagine turning out my own mother," Teddy said, smiling ruefully. "But then again, I can't imagine this person being my mother. It's up to you, Gram, she's a complete stranger to me."

"May I interrupt this family discussion?" Brand asked. "Why don't you not make any decision at all, but just take it one day at a time?"

"See here, you conceited jerk, you keep your big mouth out of family discussions." Fritzi reached in her pocket for a cigarette, then pulled it back empty.

"Wait a minute," Gram said. "Brand is very much a part of this family. Much more so than you, so don't expect him to be barred from anything that goes on around here."

"How does he get the privilege of calling himself a family member? What great thing did he do?"

"I'm marrying Teddy," Brand informed her. "And Gram, too, for that matter."

Fritzi pointed at Brand. "He's marrying her for the million," she yelled at Gram. "He couldn't want her. She's nothing but a kid. Don't you people have a brain in your head?"

Ignoring Fritzie's rude comments, Gram scrambled to her feet and stood over her. "Brand had a great idea. You can stay for now, but only if you get that rotten tongue under control. You gave up your place in our home and hearts many long years ago. If you stay now, you're nothing but a charity case, so sweeten up, or take off. Which will it be?"

"I have no choice. But neither do you. I'll stay and take whatever you barbarians dish out. I don't even have a dog to be on my side."

"Don't you ever mention that dog again!" Brand shouted. "You'll answer to me if you do!"

Fritzi got up and rushed to her room, closing the door with a crash.

"Let's hope she stays there," Gram said, smiling wryly.

Brand got to his feet. "I have work to do, but may I come over tonight?"

"Of course," Gram answered. "Plan to eat with us."

After Brand left, Teddy and Gram went outside and did their necessary work. When they stopped for lunch they did not see Fritzi. "Let's just keep real quiet," Gram whispered as they ate.

She appeared while Gram and Teddy cooked supper that night; she did not offer to help. Brand arrived for supper, and the meal was relatively pleasant. Fritzi kept quiet.

Brand helped do the dishes then took Gram aside. "Teddy and I'd like to go into Bend for a movie," he said quietly, "but we're wondering if you'll be all right alone with Fritzi."

"Sure. She won't bother me. You two go on and have a nice evening."

After the movie, Brand took Teddy to Pioneer Park, beside the Deschutes River. They walked hand in hand to the sparkling water, which was bubbling enthusiastically against the stone wall. The half moon dropped its silver beams on the quiet park, turning the lush, green grass to silver and the trees into large, dark shadows, moving gently in the small breeze. They sat at a picnic table beside the water and watched the moon playing hide and seek with fluffy white clouds.

"Are you warm enough?" Brand asked.

"Yes, but the nights are really getting cold. Pretty soon it will be freezing every night," Teddy said.

"I guess we'd better bring quilts next time we come. Well, my little Teddy

Bear, have you thought any more about getting married? I'm not in favor of long engagements—especially ours."

She leaned her head on his shoulder. "I did for a while, but Fritzi sort of blew everything else from my mind. Oh, Brand, what will we do with Fritzi when we get married?"

Brand turned Teddy in his arms. "You look like an angel with the moonlight bathing your face," he murmured. His lips dipped to hers and her arms found their way around his neck. She felt his hair and dug her fingers through it, as his lips fluttered against hers. He gave her one more quick hug and pulled away from her. "She isn't going to live in the same house with us, that's for sure."

"Who isn't going to do what?" Teddy asked, plummeting back to earth.

"Fritzi isn't going to live with us."

"What about Gram?"

"She's going to live with us."

"What if Gram has to take care of Fritzi?"

"No way, love. Fritzi isn't an invalid. She's going to have to figure something out. Something besides Gram's charity. Gram's quite a woman, but a little too old to start caring for a miscreant."

When Teddy walked into the old ranch house, Gram was busily sewing pink butterfly quilt pieces together and Fritzi was nowhere to be seen.

Gram motioned toward the bedrooms. "Watched a couple of programs and took off. Didn't say a word all night." Gram's eyes twinkled merrily. "She was a lot better company than I expected."

&.

The next morning, as the three women ate breakfast, strange screeching noises brought them to the front porch. Brand had brought a small load of lumber on his pickup and, with a crowbar, he stood busily ripping the porch off the house.

"I do believe Superman has come to the rescue," Fritzi said.

Brand looked up and smiled, then got to his feet and kissed Teddy. "Good morning, Teddy Bear. I decided to repair my damage."

"We didn't fix your leg; you don't have to fix our house," Gram said.

"Oh, but I do. I'll probably be the guy who falls through the hole. This is your water day, Teddy, so I know you and Gram don't have time to help, but Fritzi, you're going to help me."

The frowzy woman looked down at her old polyester dress. "And what would I look like after I handled that mess?"

"We have a shower for that purpose," Gram answered. "And, while you're at it, please wash your hair. I have a hard time eating with that mess sitting at the table. Come on, Teddy." They walked a few feet, then Gram turned back to Brand. "How long's that job going to take, son?"

"Most of the day, I think." he answered. Then he grinned. "Not quite so long with Fritzi helping."

The gravelly voice answered immediately. "She'll help. Lunch will be served at noon. . .to everyone who spends the morning working. And supper at six o'clock likewise."

Teddy and Gram took off and spent the morning handling the irrigation. At noon they found the old steps gone and the new ones coming along. Fritzi had disappeared.

Brand shook his head when Gram asked if she had been helping. Fritzi did not put in an appearance at the lunch table. "How are we going to keep her out of the food while we're working?" Teddy asked.

"Easy. We're going to lock her out," Gram said.

Teddy gasped. "You wouldn't dare!"

"Oh yes she would. And I'll be the bouncer," Brand said, laughing out loud.

Gram knocked on Fritzi's door. "Come out of there and help Brand finish the steps."

No response.

"Go get her, Brand. I don't feel like begging."

"I'm coming in," he called, then opened the door, walked in, lifted Fritzi off the bed, and carried her to the front porch, despite her kicking and screaming.

Gram locked the door and handed the key to Brand. "You may need to go in."

Later, when Gram and Teddy came, tired and dusty, to prepare supper, Brand was sitting on the top step. He stood and touched Teddy's lips with his, then he made a sweeping motion over the steps as his eyes met Gram's. "What do you think?"

"Better than when they were new," the grating old voice answered. "I especially like that rough stuff you put over the top. A person would have to work at slipping on them now."

Teddy looked around for Fritzi. "Where's your helper?"

Brand shook his head. "I haven't had a helper. As for that woman, I have no idea where she went."

Fritzi did not appear for supper but came in later, left her shoes at the door, and went to her room.

"Shampoo your hair and shower," Gram said as she passed by. But they did not hear the water run.

Teddy read her new llama magazine while Gram worked on her quilt. Brand had gone home to shower. "Hey, Gram, here's something that sounds interesting. An exotic animal sale, including llamas, in Macon, Missouri."

"Too far away."

"I know. I was just telling you about it."

"How much are the llamas?"

"It's an auction, Gram."

Brand walked in, removed his boots, washed his hands, and settled down beside Teddy. After kissing her hello, he removed one of her hands from the magazine and held it. "What's this about an auction?"

"Oh, I just saw it in this magazine. An exotic animal auction in Missouri. They're going to sell llamas."

He came to life in a hurry. "Hey, that would be fun. Do you want to buy more llamas?"

"No," Gram said. "We have our full herd."

"I wasn't thinking about buying," Teddy said. "I was wondering how much one of ours would bring at a national auction. We have some fantastic animals."

No one said anything, and Teddy started searching her mind for her best llama. One that had been born on the place. Her prettiest young female popped into her mind. Cocoa. She sat a moment, then ran to the bathroom and dropped to a sitting position on the edge of the bathtub. Putting her head in her hands, she let the tears run. After a while she got herself under control and washed her face in cold water.

Gram walked through the open door while Teddy dried her swollen face. "It's Cocoa, isn't it?" she whispered.

Teddy nodded, keeping her face covered with the towel.

"She's the first one that came to my mind, too, but we have lots of beautiful llamas."

"Yeah," Brand added, from the bathroom doorway, "we can find plenty of good animals, and I'll go along and help you."

"Wait a minute," Gram said, as they walked back to the kitchen. "Who said we're taking anything to that auction?"

Brand shrugged. "Sorry. It sounded to me as though you were."

Teddy felt sorry she had ever mentioned the silly sale. "Of course we can't, but I was thinking of taking only one. We might lose our shirts at a place like that."

Brand turned on the TV and captured Teddy's hand. Gram worked on her quilt and Teddy half-watched the program, leaning on Brand's shoulder, while she read her magazine.

"If the sale were only a few hours' drive away, it would be different," Gram muttered, forty-five minutes later.

Teddy looked up and smiled. "I know, Gram. It's way too far."

After a while Brand flipped off the TV. "I don't mean to be a trouble maker, Gram," he said, "but Fritzi hasn't eaten since breakfast. Do you still feel that she should do some work around here?"

"I sure do."

"Well, I think you fell on the only way to make her work. But how can we keep her out of the kitchen while you sleep?"

Gram's eyes flashed around the roomy old kitchen. "I doubt we could lock the refrigerator. And if we could, there's food in a lot of cabinets. I don't know." Her eyes turned to Teddy. "I'm a little too tired to take turns watching. What do you think, kitten?"

Teddy looked around. The only hope would be to lock Fritzi out of the house, which they could not do at night. Or could they lock the kitchen? She looked at the doorway into the living room. It was not very wide. Maybe they could block it. Then her eyes fell on the old door pushed against the wall. She had looked at it all her life until she did not even see it anymore. She jumped up, moved the chair away from the door, and closed it. "Voilà!" she cried triumphantly.

"Hey!" Gram said. "I'd forgotten all about that door. But how could we lock it?"

Brand examined the door and how it fit against the frame. As he looked it over, his eyes danced. "I'll bet I could rig up a lock on there."

In a little while he had it locked from the kitchen side. "But how are we going to get through?" Teddy asked.

"I'll lock it and go out the back door for tonight," Brand said. "In the morning you'll have to go out the front way and in the back door. Be sure not to lock the key in the kitchen. Tomorrow I'll get a hasp and padlock."

Chapter Fifteen

When Teddy returned from her morning chores, she found Gram busy in the kitchen and Fritzi sitting on the front porch. "She's plenty mad," Gram said, stirring the oatmeal.

"I notice she isn't in here helping you, though."

"Nope. She hasn't come to that yet. Are we really going to let her wait to eat until she works?"

"I don't know, Gram. You have to be the judge. Do you know if she tried to get into the kitchen last night?"

"She sure did. Cussed me out royal for locking it."

"That wasn't very nice. What could she do today that wouldn't be too strenuous?" Teddy laughed.

Gram thought a moment. "How about the laundry? Surely loading three loads of clothes into the washer and dryer wouldn't be too much."

"Right. And let her fold the stuff too."

Gram snapped her fingers. "Rats. If we let her into the utility room, she won't do the laundry, she'll get into the food."

Teddy shook her head. "You can stay inside and watch her. There isn't much to do outside right now. You can work on your quilt or make some applesauce."

"All right. Let's eat, then you can go tell her."

A little later, Teddy sat on the love seat beside Fritzi. She gave Fritzi a friendly smile. "Gram wondered if you'd do the laundry this morning? It's only three loads, plus whatever you have." It was the first time she was alone with Fritzi, and she felt a little nervous.

"What's with you, kid? Do you have a mind of your own? Or are you some kind of robot of the old woman's?"

"I think I have a mind of my own. Why do you doubt that?"

"I never heard of anyone starving their own mother to death."

"You aren't a mother to me, Fritzi. Gram's my mother. A fantastic one too. She's been everything to me. Mother, father, grandmother. I couldn't have asked for more. But that's beside the point, isn't it? No one's trying to starve you. But don't you know, even the Bible says if you don't work you don't eat? We aren't asking you to work like Gram or me. Just a little to show some family spirit." She reached for Fritzi's hand, but the older woman jerked it away. Teddy stood up and smiled again. "Come on, what do you say, are you ready to join the family?"

"What can I say? I suppose I'll have to try, even if it puts me in the hospital."

"Great. And I promise we won't ask you to do too much. I'll see you at lunchtime."

As Teddy moved the llamas from the north pasture to the south that morning, she looked them over carefully. Which would she take if she did happen to go to that sale? She had a lot of fine animals, and it really would be exciting to see how they compared to other herds. When Teddy came in for lunch she found Fritzi lying on the couch in the kitchen, worn out, but the laundry had been done and put away.

Gram announced lunch and Fritzi staggered to her feet. "Where's lover boy?" she asked in a petulant voice. "Doesn't he eat all his meals here?"

"Not yet," Gram grated, "but soon."

Fritzi barely waited for Gram's "Amen" to snatch a sandwich, which she stuffed into her mouth before she tasted her soup. "Yeah, when is this big wedding coming off?" She drank her milk in one long gulp, then broke a handful of crackers into her soup.

"We haven't set a date," Teddy said.

"You messed up their plans," Gram added.

Everyone ate quietly for a few minutes, until Fritzi dropped her soup spoon onto the table with a clatter. "I'm ready for dessert, old woman," she announced.

"Is that right? Well, just get yourself an apple from the refrigerator," Gram said.

"Forget the apple," Fritzi snarled, walking out of the room.

Gram looked at Teddy, the corners of her mouth jerking up and down. "I'm not sure she has the family spirit down pat yet."

Teddy laughed, walked around the table, and hugged Gram. "I hope you aren't letting her get to you. Just remember, you're the best."

Gram's eyes misted. "Thanks, kitten. I needed that. Now, what are we going to find for our fine guest to do this afternoon?"

"More? Today?"

"Of course, more. Are you quitting for the day? Am I?"

"No, but—"

"Do you trust her to iron your clothes?"

"Sure. I don't have anything that great."

But when Teddy came in after the evening feeding, she found Gram alone in the kitchen. "Her royal highness refused to work," she told Teddy. "I'm predicting she won't work unless she's on the brink of starvation."

Teddy and Gram ate alone before Brand called to say he would be over, but it would be late.

Teddy hauled out her knitting and turned on the television, disappointed that Brand was not with her. She could not believe how much she missed him.

Fritzi joined them in the kitchen and watched the programs, too. "Is TV the most exciting thing you ever do around here?" she asked Teddy.

"We do lots of exciting things," Teddy said. "Remember the day you came?

Brand had just brought a tandem bike over and we all learned to ride it."

"Yahoo," Fritzi said in a monotone. "I hope I never have to do anything that exciting. It might cause a heart attack."

"Well, it was fun to us," Teddy insisted.

A light tap on the front door interrupted the conversation. Sighing, Teddy went to the door. She had recognized the tap and threw open the door, less than eager to face Lynden. He stood on the porch, all smiles, looking even thinner and paler than she remembered.

She forced a smile to her lips. "Well, Lynden, what a nice surprise. I'm glad to see you've forgiven us for. . .whatever we did." She opened the door and he stepped in, dropped his shoes, and made for the bathroom to wash his hands. When he returned, she led him into the kitchen.

"Fritzi," she said, hesitantly, "I'd like for you to meet our good friend, Lynden Greeley." She held her hand toward Fritzi. "Lynden, Fritzi."

Lynden greeted Gram and sat down beside Teddy on the couch.

"Who is she?" he quietly asked Teddy.

"Oh, didn't we tell you?" Fritzi gushed. "I'm Teddy's mother. Yes, she's my little girl."

Lynden sat still a moment, attempting to watch television, then turned to Fritzi. "Her mother? I didn't know she had a mother. Where have you been all these years?"

Fritzi bowed her head sadly. "We've been separated." She raised her head and smiled victoriously. "But we found each other again several days ago, and we're all so happy we just don't know what to do."

"Wow, a reunion! I know what to do. I'm going to write a story about it for the paper!" He rose off the couch in his excitement.

"You aren't writing anything," Gram snapped.

He settled back down like a balloon going flat. "Come on, Nelle, don't say that. This sounds like my big chance."

"It may sound like it, but believe me, it isn't. Forget it." Gram's coarse voice sounded as though she meant business.

If Gram had slapped his face, he would not have looked more injured. Fritzi moved from the rocker to the couch and hooked an arm through his. "Come out to the porch and I'll tell you all about it, Lynny. The old woman's just too shy, but she really wants you to know."

She tugged on his arm and he stood up, looking considerably happier. They started out the kitchen door into the living room.

"Freeze!"

They both stopped in their tracks. "Lynden," Gram said, "I know you're upset with Teddy, but I also think you care for her and wouldn't hurt her. Well, take my word for it, if you put one word about this in the paper you'll hurt her so badly she'll never recover."

Lynden's gray eyes searched out Teddy's. "Is that right?"

Teddy nodded. "It has no place in the paper. I don't know what Fritzi would tell you, but it's a sad, rotten story. Please don't."

He hesitated. "Maybe I'll just listen to it."

"Let her tell it in here then," Gram said.

Lynden nodded and settled onto the couch beside Teddy. "Great with me."

Fritzi did not return, but headed for the hall. "Let them tell you then, turkey," she spat at Lynden before she disappeared.

Lynden turned expectantly to Teddy. "Okay, I'm all ears."

Gram sighed and leaned back in her chair. "I'll tell him. It's an ugly story, Lynden, and you agree this is off the record, right? It's also a short story. Fritzi ran off right after Teddy was born and we didn't see or hear from her again until she appeared on the place a few days ago."

Lynden's face turned a shade whiter. He sat quietly a few moments, thinking about what he had heard. Then he turned to Teddy. "How awful! Somehow I supposed your mother was dead. What about your father?"

Teddy shook her head.

"Oh. I'm sorry, Teddy. I really am sorry, and I wouldn't think of printing that." He reached for her hand and brought it into his lap. A moment later, he lifted it into his view. "What do I feel on—" He stopped when he saw the dainty ring with the large diamond reflecting the kitchen lights. "When did all this happen?"

"About a week ago," Teddy said. She could not keep the happy smile away from her face.

"I told you not to do this," Lynden said. "You know the guy's nothing but trouble waiting to happen, don't you?"

"She found out he's not the man," Gram volunteered. She had her quilt piece in her lap again, sewing the butterfly to the bright background.

"What did she do, ask him?" he asked sarcastically.

"Don't worry how she did it," Gram advised, quietly. "Just be thankful she's not marrying trouble."

"Teddy," Lynden cried, "you've been misinformed. I know he's the man. Positively. More news has come into the office and it all points to Brandon Sinclair. It leaves no doubt in my mind that he's the bank robber. None at all. He'll have a nice long prison sentence to face when he's caught. And I'm going to make sure he's caught." He got up and marched straight to the front door, stiff as an overstarched shirt.

Teddy heaved a sigh, but followed him. "Why do I feel like I'm living through a rerun, Lynden?"

He pulled on his second shoe and turned the doorknob. "I'd like to wish you happiness, Teddy, but wishes don't come true when you purposely go against what you know to be right." He shut the door and Teddy threw the dead bolt.

"Gram, isn't it time we had a little tranquility in our lives?" she asked, picking up her knitting.

Gram put her work down and got up. "I was just thinking that. Want some coffee?"

The front door nearly crumbled beneath the next attack and Teddy jumped to her feet. "Make some for Brand too, Gram. I'm ashamed to say I forgot all about him for a few minutes."

Gram waved Teddy toward the front door. "Go get him. I want to talk to you both."

"Sorry to be so late," he said, kissing her. Then he clasped her to him. "Just hold me a minute, love."

Teddy looked at his ashen face. "What's happened, Brand?"

"Is it that visible? Well, I don't want you to get upset, and it really isn't all that terrible. I'm just not very tough. We just lost a calf. The mother's going to be fine with a few days' good care, and the calf wasn't worth a whole lot of money. I just feel bad about the loss of life." He shook his head. "It tried so hard to live." He gave Teddy another squeeze and she felt him swallow hard. "And we tried really hard to help it live. The vet said it just wasn't meant to be."

"Sit down and have a cup of coffee," Gram said. "I want to talk to you two. Maybe it'll help for you to think about something else."

Brand and Teddy settled onto the couch, she in the circle of his arm. "You don't know how good you feel, Teddy Bear," he said, kissing her cheek.

Gram set the coffees on the low table and put a plate of oatmeal cookies between them. "How would you two like to take a couple of llamas to the sale in Missouri?" she asked.

"I'd love it!" Brand said without hesitation. "Teddy, get your magazine."

"Just a minute," Gram held up a hand and Teddy settled back down beside Brand. Then Gram spoke to Brand as though Teddy were not there. "You've seen what came home to roost, haven't you, son?"

He nodded.

"Well, you understand that things like that could make an old woman a little crazy, but I have to say this, crazy or no. I'll be happy for you two to make the trip, but only after you promise me that my girl will come home as innocent as she leaves. I love her far more than my own life and I couldn't bear for anything to hurt her."

"I love her more than my own life too," he said. "I'd never hurt her, Gram, even her reputation, so why don't we all go? Let Fritzi take care of the place." He stood and kissed the wrinkled cheek. "Let's make it a vacation. I'll bet it's been a while since you've had one."

Teddy laughed, pulled Brand to the couch, and handed him his coffee. "I agree with Brand, Gram. Please won't you go with us? You'd get so excited at the auction I'd have to hold you down."

Gram shook her head. "Somebody has to mind the store, you know."

"I'll send Rolf over," Brand said. "Our work is slowing down a lot, now."

"What about Fritzi?" Gram asked.

"Let her take care of herself," Brand said. "We know for sure she's able to do that much."

Gram's eyes beamed with joy. "Well, I'll think about it. I'm just not sure we can both leave. But you can't believe how happy I am that you asked. Now, I'm going to bed and leave you two alone."

Brand pulled a hasp and padlock from his pocket. "No need, Gram, we aren't going to sit and spoon. I'm going to fix this door."

She went to bed anyway and Brand had the lock all screwed on in ten minutes. "Let's go sit on the porch and see if we can see the moon," Brand suggested.

They settled onto the love seat. "I don't see the moon," Teddy said, "but I see a fantastic trip in our near future. I'm already getting excited. I wonder, what llamas I should take?"

Chapter Sixteen

Pandemonium broke loose in the form of cheering, foot stomping, whistling, and laughing. The crowd rejoiced with Teddy and she felt so weak she could not even move. Brand leaned down to her, his eyes laughing. "You don't believe it, do you, Teddy Bear? Do you still want to watch the camels, ostriches, and other stuff sold? Or do you want to leave?"

Suddenly Teddy felt adrenalin pumping through her and she wanted to jump up and down. "I want to watch the others being sold, but I can't sit still."

"Let's get out of here for a while then. Maybe we'll come back later."

As they walked out, the loudspeaker crackled. "There they go, folks, the proud owners of the Marland llamas. We'll break for lunch now and, at half-past one, we'll start with the llama's large relative, the camel. See you in an hour and a half."

Teddy, Gram, and Brand were mobbed before they got to the pickup. Many in the crowd just wanted to congratulate them, but several inquired about buying llamas. Teddy gave them each her card with her address and phone number.

Finally they sat in the truck and looked at each other in shock. "Duska just made you famous," Brand said. "Your llamas will always bring good money now." He rubbed his forehead with the heel of his hand. "And I hardly believed you when you said you could sell a female for $10,000."

Someone tapped on the window so Brand rolled it down. A big burly man thrust his hand in and shook hands with all three of them. "Fantastic," he said. "I'm really pleased with what this did for the llama industry, but your llama would have probably brought more at the Hart sale. They sell only llamas and all the llama breeders go there."

"We're just happy with the price we got," Brand said, unable to stop smiling.

"Right. I don't blame you, and the llama people will be more serious about this auction from now on too."

The man walked away and Brand wasted no time getting the pickup on the highway. "Hungry?" he asked.

"No. Yes. I'm too excited to know. But we'll have to go back and tell the llamas good-bye pretty soon."

Brand turned to Gram. "You haven't said a word, young lady. What do you think? Are you too surprised to speak? Are you disappointed?"

Gram smiled then laughed out loud. "I'm just pretending I'm not here. That way I can enjoy the two of you a lot." She quieted for moment. "Yes, I guess I'm too surprised to talk. Wait until Fritzi hears."

They stopped at a restaurant to eat, but Teddy could not push the food down.

She knew what had happened, but just could not believe it.

"Want to call Fritzi, Gram?" Brand asked as they walked out and past a telephone.

Gram shook her yellow-white hair wildly. "I want to see her face when I tell her. I don't think she believed we could ever get $20,000."

They went back to the auction and told Duska and Playboy good-bye, but Teddy could not sit down to watch the other sales. "I know I'll be sorry. How many times in my life am I going to see zebras and cougars auctioned off? But I can't help it, I want to go home."

Brand nodded understandingly. "I don't blame you, love."

They collected their bank-guaranteed check for the price of the two llamas, plus the thousand dollars from Lolli's auction market, minus ten percent for the auction fees. They walked away from Lolli's with a check for $75,150 tucked into the corner of Teddy's purse. When they reached the truck, she handed the check to Gram. "I'd feel a lot better if you held onto this," she said. "You know how I keep losing things."

"Let's head for home," Brand said after Gram had deposited the check into the most secret pocket in her purse.

They left in the early afternoon and hashed and rehashed the sale, laughing like happy children. After a tiny silence, Teddy uttered a long sigh.

"Are you okay, Teddy Bear?"

"Yes, but it just hit me that I'll never see Playboy or Duska again. But don't you agree they got good homes?"

"You bet! If I paid a fraction of that for an animal, I'd keep it in the house on a pillow. Teddy Bear. . .$65,000 for one animal?" And that launched yet another rehash of the sale, as they told each other how much prettier their llamas were than the others.

Finally, the sun crept low in the western sky, then disappeared, pulling the daylight behind it. "I think I'm hungry," Teddy announced sometime later.

"Shall we stop for the night?" Brand asked. "Or should we eat and drive on? I could easily drive a few more hours."

After eating and then driving on for a few more hours, they finally stopped at a motel after midnight. "We're making good time," Brand said. "It's late and we're all exhausted, but we'll be home sooner than we expected." He kissed both Teddy and Gram good night and went to his own room. Teddy dropped into bed and fell asleep thanking God for answering the prayer she did not pray. . . and answering it more abundantly than she could have ever dreamed.

ða

The next morning Brand awakened them before six o'clock and they drove three hours before stopping for breakfast. Then, on again. That night, as the sun disappeared from view, Teddy asked to stop for the night. "Let's go out for a nice supper."

Gram decided to rest in the room and order some food from room service. Teddy had not come down from her cloud since the sale so she and Brand walked into the restaurant giggling together. They both enjoyed the perfectly prepared steak, salad, and french fries, followed by an out-of-this-world chocolate mousse. Then they walked around under a moon that looked round and orange.

A three-wheeled bike pulling a small carriage pulled up beside them on the quiet street. "You guys like a ride in the park?" the driver asked.

Brand looked down at Teddy, who nodded eagerly. He helped her in and they snuggled together as the man pedaled slowly along.

"Our life together reads like a storybook," Brand said, holding her close.

"Yes, rich, famous, and happy," Teddy giggled. "With fourteen children."

Brand jerked as though shocked. "What's the matter?" Teddy murmured. "Did I say the wrong thing?"

Then he laughed. "How many children? How about four or six? But fourteen?"

Teddy pulled him close and forgot all about children. In fact she forgot everything in the world except Brand and her. Then, "This is the end of the line. Hey, buddy, we're back where we started."

Brand helped Teddy down. He silently paid the man, who rode away on his contraption muttering, ". . .didn't even see the park."

They both burst out laughing and raced back to the motel. "The poor guy was right," Brand said, "we saw only each other."

Teddy pulled his head down for a quick kiss. "What else is there?" she asked quietly.

❧

They pulled into the old ranch at midnight the next night. Gram ran up the new steps and unlocked the door. They all tumbled inside, each as glad to be home as the others. They went into the kitchen where Fritzi sat on the couch. Brand winked at Teddy. "Yeah, Playboy really shocked us. He brought $17,500."

"Wow!" Fritzi said. "That sounds pretty good if you're telling the truth. But you took a female, too, didn't you? Didn't she sell?"

Gram looked at Teddy who looked at Brand. He put on a sad look. "Yeah, she sold, but she only brought. . ." He looked mournfully at Teddy, as though he couldn't say it.

"$65,000!" Teddy screamed.

Fritzi jumped out of her chair. Then she dropped back down. "No way. You're just saying that to make me feel bad about Cocoa. I know what you're doing."

Gram did not say a word nor change expression. Teddy laughed happily. "She did, Fritzi. That Duska is one fine lady. But we have lots more like her."

"Know what we're going to do as soon as possible?" Brand asked.

"Get married, I suppose," Fritzi said, sarcastically.

Brand turned sincere eyes on Fritzi. "We were almost too busy to think about a wedding but once in a while the subject cropped up. We remembered we love each other though. Do you remember how it feels to be in love?"

Teddy walked out with Brand and left the two women snarling at each other like stray cats. "It almost seems as though we shouldn't be parted anymore, after the last week," she told Brand.

He kissed her gently and climbed into the pickup. "Thanksgiving can't get here quickly enough for me," he said. He tweaked her fingers that lay on the pickup door and drove away in the dark.

≈

In the days that followed, Teddy and Brand worked hard and played hard. Every day of work and play brought them closer together, leaving not an inch of room for doubt of the rightness of their love.

Fritzi not only shampooed her hair but began fixing herself pretty and acting pleasantly. She cooked gourmet meals several times a week and always invited Brand to share them. One evening at supper, Fritzi turned her prettiest smile on Brand. "When are you going to teach me to ride?" she asked.

Brand's golden eyebrows shot into his forehead. "I wasn't aware that you wanted to learn."

"Of course I do. I'm only human and you always take the old woman. Why can't I go?"

"I'm not sure you could ride Pharaoh," he said thoughtfully. "He's pretty spirited."

"Ha! Surely you don't think the old woman can ride something I can't."

"That's exactly what I think."

"Let me ride Misty. The kid doesn't have to go all the time."

"It's all right," Teddy said, "she can ride Misty."

"Misty's your horse, Teddy Bear, and no one except you is going to ever ride her again. Got it?" He snatched Teddy's hand, pulled it to his lips, kissed it, then returned it gently to her lap.

The next evening Brand rode over on Thunder, leading three horses. "Who's that?" Teddy asked, pointing to a beautiful gray mare with dark spots on her back quarters. Her mane, tail, and feet were dark too.

Brand shrugged, grinning as though embarrassed. "I picked her up today. Been looking at her for a while, but couldn't justify buying her. What do you think?"

Teddy took the kind head in her arms. "She's a gorgeous animal, Brand. What's her name?"

"Dove. She's an Appaloosa. I don't know whether she's gray like a dove or harmless as a dove. Either fits. She's a nice animal. But no race horse."

Teddy continued to pet Dove. "Hey. You bought Dove for Fritzi, didn't you?"

"For Fritzi to ride sometimes." He raised his eyebrows. "Great for a kid too. She's a beginner's horse."

They rode after supper and Fritzi managed to stay on Dove's back. "You really should ride beside me, Brand," she whined. "I might need you if the horse bolts."

Brand grinned and stayed with Teddy. "She's not going anywhere. You can just be thankful if she keeps up with the rest."

"Pharaoh isn't happy with this stroll," Gram said. "We're going for a little ride." She gave the large horse his head and disappeared around a bend in the path.

"The old woman's going to kill herself," Fritzi mused. "But then I guess you'd like that. All those llamas would really be yours then."

"You be quiet!" Teddy yelled. "The llamas are already mine, as well as the ranch. You saw the papers, so just be quiet. I love Gram and can't imagine living without her."

Fritzi shook her head and flitted a silvery laugh toward Brand. "Tsk, tsk. Quite a little fireball, isn't she? Doesn't take much to set her off."

Chapter Seventeen

One evening after supper, Fritzi went into her bedroom and returned freshly made up and combed. She had even put on a fresh dress. "I was just wondering, Brand, honey, I need to run into Bend this evening for a minute. Could you do the honors?"

Gram sighed, dumped her quilt on the coffee table, and got up. "I'll take you. Let's go."

Fritzi cast an angry glance at Gram. "Sit down and work on your quilt, old woman. You're too old to be running around at night." She put the frown away and brought out a pretty smile. "How about it, Brand?"

Brand looked at Teddy. "I don't see why not. We haven't anything planned for the evening. What do you say, Teddy Bear?"

"Sure, we can find something to do while Fritzi does her business."

Fritzi's smile disappeared and the scowl covered her face again. "You may as well stay and check the llamas or something," she said.

Brand reached for Teddy. "Where I go, Teddy goes."

The smile came back. "I don't want her to come, Brand. Don't make me tell you why."

"You'd better, because if she doesn't go, I don't." Brand's placid look was gradually tensing up.

"All right, if I have to." Fritzi pulled Brand away from Teddy and stood on her tiptoes to whisper something into his ear. When he heard what she said, Brand relaxed and his eyes brightened. "Oh. Okay, Fritzi, I understand, but couldn't Gram take you tomorrow?"

Fritzi made another pretty face. "I ask you, how much help would the old woman be?"

Finally, with a little more begging, Brand and Fritzi drove off toward Bend. "I wonder what she said to soften him," Teddy mused aloud.

"I don't know, but I don't like it. That woman is not good news. We'll have to watch her." Gram bit off a thread and spit it halfway across the room.

The two returned a few hours later, Fritzi in a fantastic mood, and Brand snapping at everyone.

"Was your trip successful?" Gram asked.

"Well, not exactly," Fritzi giggled. "But we sure had fun. We ran all over the malls until Brand was thirsty, so we stopped for some ice cream treats." She turned to Teddy and actually smiled at her. "Gotta admit, kid, you got good taste in men."

❧

Brand had long since replaced Lynden as Gram and Teddy's escort to church.

The first week, Fritzi had almost agreed to go, but backed out when she saw Gram's Sunday clothes. "Why should I go and be embarrassed by an old woman who's too senile to know she's in church?" was her excuse for staying at home.

But one Sunday morning she came from her bedroom with a yellow and black dress, deep blue eyelids, and a red mouth. She pranced out and danced toward Brand. "I decided I was being a bad girl, staying away from church just because of the old woman. Everyone knows she's crazy, so I guess it won't hurt me to go."

Gram jumped off the couch where she had been waiting for Teddy. "Well, I'm embarrassed to go with a clown. You can count me out." She took off her straw hat and headed for her bedroom.

Teddy and Brand shook their heads and laughed. "They don't get along any better than they did when she was seventeen," Teddy said.

"And now you can see why, can't you?" Fritzi asked, giggling. "The old woman never could stand me. Jealous, I suppose. You know she was forty years old when I was born. That's older than I am now." She made an exaggerated shudder. "I just can't imagine having a baby now."

"You couldn't imagine having a child when you were younger either, the way I hear it," Brand said in a gentle voice.

"Hear, hear!" Teddy said, happy to hear him standing up to Fritzi. Teddy, also embarrassed by Fritzi's outlandish makeup, felt like following Gram's lead, but did not because of Brand. It was not his fault he got into this mess.

In church Brand sat between Teddy and Fritzi and Teddy noticed that Fritzi crowded him more than she did. So she moved a little farther away; she did not want to do anything like Fritzi.

≈

On the fourth day of November it dumped fifteen inches of snow in six hours. Teddy and Brand helped each other fix the loafing sheds to make the livestock comfortable, with hay and water handy.

That night Brand called and said he would be over later and for Teddy to be ready for some fun. She could not wait. She barely ate any supper and the clock hands crept around slowly. At half past seven, the familiar attack on the front door brought Teddy to her feet. Fritzi beat her to the door, though barely.

Brand stepped inside, covered with snow. "Get some warm clothes on, Teddy," he instructed, after lifting her to his frosty kiss. "We're going for a ride."

"How about poor wittow me?" Fritzi asked, talking baby talk directly into Brand's face. "I never get to do anything fun. Don't I get to go with you?"

"Sorry. The rig is only a two-seater. Hurry, Teddy, I'm getting too hot in here," he called.

"I bet that's because of little old me, don't you think?" She winked at him as Teddy arrived, dressed in a warm snowsuit with the hood pulled over her head and tied securely.

"I'm ready, Brand, and I feel like a snowman." She put on the boots she had carried to the door and they stepped out into the wintry world.

"Gram! Look what we're going to ride in." Thunder, Brand's huge stallion, wearing a dark blanket, stood hitched to a small red sleigh. Fit for a snow queen, the sleigh was, low in front, the sides rising toward the back, with lots of fancy squiggles and curls all around. Thunder wore a gala red harness edged with small bells. When the large horse moved, the bells filled the night with their music.

Brand helped Teddy inside and tucked the heavy woolen blanket around them. "This is fantastic, Brand. I've never ridden in a sleigh."

Brand gave her a toothy smile and began singing "Jingle Bells." His clear baritone voice rang out through the first verse and chorus. Then he stopped and looked at Teddy. "Do you know the second verse?"

"Yes, shall we sing it together?" And they did, harmonizing through the second verse and chorus, the harness bells accenting the song.

After they finished, Teddy relaxed in the curve of his arm. "I love you for this," she said. "You couldn't have done anything more romantic."

Brand leaned across all their blankets and heavy clothing to kiss her. "I love you," he whispered.

They talked about the future as Thunder pulled them through the still night. Whether they should run both cattle and llamas or change entirely to llamas, whether they should live in Gram's house and run her farm and get someone to help Rolf with the other.

"I can't believe how still the night is," Teddy said. "Only Thunder's bells. Thank you, Brand, I love it. And I love you. . .so very much."

"In that case, it was worth all the trouble, my love."

"Was it a lot of trouble?"

"Sure was." His twinkling eyes contradicted his statement. "I had to take Thunder out behind that back shed and hook it up." He held her close and rearranged the wool blanket over them. "You see, I bought the sleigh several weeks ago, and I've been waiting impatiently for the snow."

"You mean the sleigh is yours?"

"Ours."

"Then we can go again?"

"Anytime you want. Are you ready to go home yet, Teddy Bear?"

"Yes, and it's been the greatest night of my life. Thanks again, my love."

Thunder realized he was on his way home and broke into a smooth canter several times.

When Brand walked Teddy to the house, they discovered Fritzi sitting outside in the love seat waiting for them. "My turn," she sang out.

"No way," Brand growled. "It's too late."

"Come on, you know you want one more little spin." She put both hands around his upper arm. "Please? I'd really like it."

Brand moved away from Fritzi. Her hands dropped to her side. "I'm tired and Thunder's getting cold," Brand said. "Maybe Teddy can take you for a ride tomorrow."

Fritzi threw her head prettily. "But it won't be the same." She swept her hand over the snow-covered vista. "If that isn't a story book scene I've never seen one. Please take me tonight."

Teddy stood on her toes and kissed his lips. "Why don't you take her for a little ride?" she whispered. "Just down to your driveway? I'm afraid her life has been pretty bleak."

"No!"

"Just for me?" she whispered again, their lips still touching.

He spun away, angrily. "Come on, Fritzi, but it's going to be short." Nevertheless, he helped Fritzi into the sleigh and carefully tucked the robes around her.

Teddy went into the house and removed her snowsuit and sweater. Gram sat in the rocker, sewing finished quilt blocks together. "Where are the others?" she asked.

"Brand took Fritzi for a sleigh ride. Gram, he's so wonderful. He really didn't want to but after I badgered him into it, I noticed he covered her up so very gently and carefully."

"Hmph."

Teddy laughed. "What in the world does that mean, Gram?"

"It means she didn't need a sleigh ride."

"Oh, Gram, that's not like you. It's not like Brand either, but she sounded so pitiful I felt sorry for her."

"You should have left him alone," Gram finally grumbled.

"Gram," Teddy said, "that's not the way you taught me. You've always said it never hurts to go the extra mile for anyone—no matter whom."

"Humph! Well, I'm not saying it right now. I meant someone who needed help, not someone who wanted to tear up other people's lives." Gram's fingers slowed for exactly the amount of time it took her to say the ugly words, then began pushing the needle in and out again, with the speed of a bird picking up seeds.

Teddy picked up her knitting. She probably would not get anything done, but she hated to waste time. She worked fast and finished three rows, then held it up. "See, Gram, isn't it pretty?" She held a red piece of fuzzy rib knitting, the beginnings of a skirt to match the sweater she had just finished.

"Why don't you go on to bed, Gram?" Teddy asked fifteen minutes later. "I'll wait up to let Fritzi in."

"I'll wait with you."

After nearly a half hour, Teddy began to feel uneasy. "They couldn't have had an accident, could they, Gram? After all, what can happen in a sleigh?"

Finally, Gram grinned. "They could have gotten into a snow drift and got caught."

Then Teddy remembered her own sleigh ride. "Gram, Brand sang 'Jingle Bells' to me while Thunder's harness bells jingled in the still night. It was so beautiful. And romantic." Her knitting needles stopped as she remembered how glorious it was. "Gram, did you ever go sleigh riding?"

Gram's needle did not stop. A bright pink border began to appear around the butterfly. "Sure did, kitten."

"With Gramp?"

Gram's throaty laugh filled the room. "Don't ask. No, it was before I met your grandfather." They talked a while and somehow got around to the subject of Fritzi's leaving right after Teddy was born.

"Poor Gram. I've thought about how awful you must have felt to be saddled with a baby after you had raised your own and I've thought about how you must have worried about Fritzi. Was it awful? What did you tell people?"

Gram's eyes, looking all soft, turned to Teddy. "You've been the second biggest blessing, close behind your grandfather, of a large assortment of blessings that God's seen fit to shower on me, Teddy. Don't worry about that for a minute. What did I tell people? For a while I hedged, trying to protect Fritzi because I was certain she'd come back. But after a while I simply told people I didn't know where she was and that you were legally mine. That was the truth, you know. After a certain time, I forget now how long you have to wait, I got legal custody of you."

The front door slamming interrupted their talk and they both ran to the living room.

Fritzi stood by the door, looking as though she had been on a ten-mile hike. Her hair and even her eyelashes had turned white. Her shoulders also had more than a snowy cape over them. Teddy also noticed packed snow on both sides of her mittens. As her eyes took in the entire picture, she saw a lot of packed snow on Fritzi's knees. Knees that had only nylons between them and the snow.

"Well," Gram said almost jovially, "looks like you crawled home on your hands and knees." She laughed as though pleased about the whole thing.

"Why are you laughing, old woman?" Fritzi asked. "That Dr. Jekyll and Mr. Hyde that Teddy wants to marry is crazy. First he sang 'Jingle Bells' to me right in time with Thunder's harness bells. When he finished the song, he just picked me up, laughing like a maniac, and dumped me overboard—several miles from here. Then he told that big horse to run home fast. I heard him. And the horse took off as though the devil himself was chasing him. He probably knows how daft the man is."

Chapter Eighteen

Teddy was shocked at what she had just heard. Never had she seen any trace of emotional instability in Brand. But she felt almost worse about something else—Brand had sung to Fritzi! Part of the thrill of the night had been that he had sung that song for her. . .just for her. And then he had sung it for Fritzi! Well, she had forced him into taking Fritzi for a ride.

Then she heard a big gravelly snort. "Bosh! Who do you think you're kidding?"

Of course it was not true. Fritzi just made it up. Teddy's eyes lifted to the older woman. She had to believe that Fritzi had just walked in the snow. Teddy's heart beat fast and hard. "Where's Brand now?" she whispered. Fritzi did not hear so Teddy swallowed hard and repeated the question.

"I don't know," Fritzi answered in a hard voice. "Probably whipping his horse into a lather somewhere trying to make it go faster."

Gram stood straight as a poplar tree. "Be quiet!" she demanded. "Teddy!" Teddy jumped to the harsh sound and looked down at Gram, who still stood stiff as old bread. "Don't you dare believe her. Don't you dare!"

"I want to hear her story once more," she told Gram. "Tell us again, Fritzi."

"Well, things started out real nice. He sang several songs to me. And—"

"Which songs?" Teddy interrupted to ask.

"Well, 'Jingle Bells' was one. Then you'd never believe the change that came over him. He acted so strangely I almost expected to see him growing fangs."

"You're exactly right," Gram snorted. "I don't believe it. In fact, I don't believe anything you've said." She stomped from the room.

Fritzi's eyes met Teddy's. "She can deny it forever," she said softly, "but you're the one who's going to be saddled with him. Better watch it, kid. He's not normal."

"I'm going to bed," Teddy replied, her voice as raspy as Gram's. "We can talk tomorrow." She turned and ran through the door.

When Teddy passed Gram's open door she stopped and plopped down beside Gram on the edge of the bed. "What do you make of that?" she asked her dearest friend in the world.

"Bah! I don't make anything of it and you'd better not either. Fritzi probably jumped out of the sleigh at the end of our driveway and ran home so she could ruin your relationship with Brand. I've seen how cute she is around him. Haven't you?"

Teddy nodded. "But I didn't think anything of it. I figured that's how she treats men. . .all men."

Gram looked at her bedside clock. "We'd better hit the hay, kitten. Those fool llamas will think they're starving in a few hours. We can talk about this in the morning—if it's worth talking about. Good night." She gave Teddy a little push toward the door.

Don't we live a crazy life around here, Lord? Teddy asked silently as she lay on her bed in the dark. *Bless us and guide every move we make and even our thoughts so we'll be just what You want us to be and help us find out what happened tonight. Could You even help me forgive Brand for singing to Fritzi? Thank You, God. I love You.* She prayed longer, not asking for anything, just to be close to Him and savor His love and nearness.

≥●

The next morning she hopped out on the first peep of the alarm. She finished the morning chores, taking special care to check the young llamas, and headed for the house, feeling strong in the Lord. With Him she could handle anything.

Gram had breakfast on the table as usual but Fritzi had not put in an appearance yet. "Did you sleep?" Gram asked, looking very tired.

Teddy nodded. "Not too badly. Where's Fritzi?"

"Leave her alone," Gram grumbled. "Maybe she'll have a change of heart and tell us the truth."

Before they sat down to breakfast, the phone rang. Brand? "I'll get it," Gram said, rushing to the shrilling instrument.

"Tell him to come over," Teddy said just as Gram put the phone to her ear. After listening a moment Gram nodded at Teddy. "Teddy wants you to come over. Could you do that? Thanks, sonny." She jammed the receiver back on the phone. "He's coming."

Teddy ate a large bowl of oatmeal and a slice of toast. Then she started washing the few dishes in the sink wishing Brand would hurry and tell them what really happened the night before.

Brand did not execute his usual energetic attack on the front door, but opened it quietly and slipped inside. "I'm here, Gram," he called quietly. "I'm dumping my boots."

Then he strode into the kitchen, looking fresh, well rested, and happy. After washing his hands, he rubbed them together. He looked from Teddy to Gram. "I thought one of you were gone. Where's your little truck?"

Gram's bushy white eyebrows shot up. "Right where it always is. I guess it's covered with snow. Are your eyes giving you trouble, Brand?"

He moved to the window. "I see tracks, Gram, but no red truck."

Teddy and Gram both dashed to the window and, sure enough, tracks led right past the house and down the driveway.

"Fritzi!" they yelled at the same time stampeding for her bedroom. They did not find Fritzi in her bedroom. Neither did they find any of her clothes nor the blankets, sheets, and pillows that had been on the bed.

"She's gone," Teddy said. "Why would she do that?"

"She decided the ranch was out of her reach," Brand said, "so she moved on, I guess."

The three looked in every corner and crevice of Fritzi's room but the woman had been thorough—nothing of value remained.

"Do you have a cup of coffee?" Brand finally asked, smiling at Teddy. "Personally, I'll feel more comfortable in the kitchen than in this room."

In the kitchen, Gram turned on the coffee. Brand dropped to the couch and motioned for Teddy to sit beside him. Somehow, having him there reassured Teddy. Soon, all sat around sipping the welcome, steaming brew. "Fritzi's leaving is for the best, you know," Brand said to Gram. "She'd never have been satisfied to fit in here."

"Oh, I know that, but we have to ask you a couple of questions, sonny. All right?"

"Of course. Just don't get on that tack Teddy was on for a while, wanting to know all the commandments I broke while growing up."

"Nope. This is now. Last night to be exact. Fritzi told us you turned from Dr. Jekyll to Mr. Hyde—went stark raving mad—and threw her out of the sleigh into the snow, then whipped Thunder into a wild run getting away from her. That's what she said. What do you say?"

Brand set down his coffee, leaned his head back on the couch, and laughed. "Neither of you believed that, did you?"

Teddy shook her head. "No, but we could tell she had walked in the snow and we need to know what really happened."

"I hadn't planned to come home tattling like a little kid. But if you're sure you want me to. I didn't want to take her in the first place as you know, Teddy. I wanted to go to bed with our ride fresh in my mind. I was so exhilarated that I started telling Fritzi all about it. I even told her about singing to you, Teddy." He shook his head. "She told me she's closer to my age than Teddy, and would be much better for me. I tried to turn her off gently but she kept coming on to me—like a steam roller. Said Teddy's just a dumb kid and I'd get bored with her in a little while. Finally, I told her, in no uncertain terms, that I'd never be interested in her if we were stranded together on a deserted island." He nodded again. "That did it."

"I guess that was a relief," Gram said with a smile.

"Well, not too much. She stopped trying to kiss me and started trying to kill me. That's when it got tough. A guy can't hit a woman, you know, so I tried to protect myself somewhat without hurting her. Finally, she got tired of the whole thing, jumped out of the sleigh, and took off walking. I followed her half way and she told me to get lost."

"I should have known," Gram said. "I'd noticed her buddying up to you for some time now. I should have—"

Suddenly, although snow fell quietly on a still world, the sun broke through and shone brightly in Teddy's heart. Brand had not sung to anyone but her! He had not sung to Fritzi!

Then a dreadful thought occurred to her. "Gram!" she yelled. "Do you have anything around that Fritzi could have stolen? I'll bet she knows exactly what's on the place."

Gram stopped short, rushed into her bedroom, and tore open the bottom drawer of her huge chest. They all saw the sagging door of the little fireproof box which had obviously been emptied. Gram turned to face the other two, her face pale. "Well, so much for all the cash we had around—close to $1,000, I think, and my only valuable jewel—my diamond wedding ring."

"Anything else?" Teddy asked.

"What about the deed to this place?" Brand asked.

"Oh yes, it was in there too." She wiped her forehead and sat down on the bed.

"Don't worry, Gram," Brand said. "That's why deeds are recorded at the court house. We'll just report it stolen."

Before the day ended they discovered Fritzi had taken Gram's heirloom silver flatware, three gold ingots, and several of Gram's handmade quilts.

"Are you going to report all this to the police?" Brand asked as he changed the outside door locks.

Gram laughed. "Naw," she boomed in her big voice. "Everyone's always telling me how much their kids beat them out of. Fritzi just takes hers in big bunches. Maybe she made me feel a little guilty, giving the ranch to Teddy. Not sorry, just guilty. Anyway, she cured my guilt."

Brand shook his head. "You're some lady, Gram."

That evening, Brand gathered Teddy into his arms. "I'm sorry our exquisite evening turned out so awful," he whispered into her ear. "We'll do it again and again, until we forget all about this."

Teddy pushed herself a little away from Brand so she could see him. "One more question. What did she whisper in your ear that convinced you to take her to Bend that night?"

"That? Oh, she said she wanted to buy you a wedding present. But she forgot all about it as soon as we left here. After that I knew she wasn't up to any good with me." He smiled ruefully.

"Let's try to forget we ever heard of her," Gram said.

❧

The days went by and Brand tried to make Gram and Teddy truly forget the past few weeks. They rode horses almost every day. "You know Pharaoh's yours, don't you, Gram?" Brand said one day while they put the horses back in the barn and rubbed them down.

"Dear me, no," Gram rasped. "I couldn't take him from you. I do love him, though."

"He's yours, just as Misty's Teddy's. I'm glad for you to have him, Gram, because I'm so proud of the way you handle him."

The gruff old voice laughed happily. "We do get along, don't we? Thanks, son."

The snow melted, but returned a few days later, though not as deep. One morning a fresh blanket of snow covered the roads, with light flakes still drifting down. Brand bundled Teddy into the warm sleigh blankets and took her out again.

"Where do you want to go?"

"I want to go into Bend." So they drove right through the center of town, Thunder's bells jingling all the way. People called out to them, laughing and throwing snowballs. Teddy waved, feeling happier than she ever had.

When they reached Teddy's driveway, Brand did not turn in, but directed Thunder on down the highway past his place. After a small effort to turn in, the horse seemed content to trot on into further isolation. Teddy and Brand sang together. They sang all the sleighing songs they both knew, then taught each other others.

Finally, Brand turned Thunder around and laid the reins at the edge of the sleigh. "Are you eager for Thanksgiving?" he asked. "And our wedding?" He cuddled her as close as possible with all their heavy winter clothes and warm blankets.

"Yes, it's only two weeks. Nearly everything is ready. The church people really took over the preparations. Gram is making the dress. Oh, Brand, it's so beautiful—and more so because she's doing it for me."

He reached a frosty mittened hand to her face and gently brushed a rosy cheek. "Did you know I love every little thing about you? Your bright blue eyes that reveal your whole being to the world. I love your innocence, I love your kindness. . .to Gram, to your animals, to me, and even to—that woman who wasn't very nice. I love your enthusiasm for your work and also for life. I love the way you love our Lord Jesus, and always talk to Him. Oh, Teddy Bear, our life is going to be heaven right here on this little earth."

Teddy lifted up a little and planted a kiss on his cold lips. "I love you so much I can't begin to tell you, Brand. I love you so much I touch your cup after you drink your coffee, and feel jealous because it touched your lips. Your golden hair and laughing brown eyes live in my every dream. Yes, I guess I'm eager for our wedding all right."

The harness bells had become still and Teddy came out of her cocoon, expecting to find herself at Brand's barn, but Thunder had brought them to her ranch house. "He's getting smarter every day," Brand said chuckling as he guided her down from the sleigh.

৯৯

Brand helped Teddy do her chores all the time now, leaving his to Rolf. Feeding, keeping plenty of fresh, unfrozen water available for the llamas, and making sure they were comfortable made up the bulk of the work now. "Aren't you glad we don't have to haul loads and loads of manure from the loafing sheds?" Teddy asked Brand with a wicked twinkle.

He shook his head. "Never quit, do you woman? Just don't tell Rolf that your llamas are housebroken; that's all I ask."

Brand took Teddy sleighing every time they had a fresh snow and she taught him to ice skate. They laughed over his clumsy first attempts to skate, but he learned quickly. Then she took him to Mount Bachelor where she taught him to ski. They went to several theater productions and an art show. And they entered Gram's new butterfly quilt in a quilt show.

Teddy and Brand spent nearly every waking hour together, doing something exciting, working, or doing nothing at all. Teddy's only desire was to be with him.

"Good thing you two are getting married next week," Gram said one evening. "It almost takes a stick of dynamite to get you apart these days. Not to mention the trouble I had finishing the wedding dress without you seeing it."

Brand agreed. "It's getting tough all right, Gram. One more week and we can be together all the time."

"Where?"

Two pairs of eyes watched Brand, waiting for an answer. "You know," he began, "I like your house a whole lot better than mine. Would you girls be terribly disappointed if we lived here? At least for a while?"

Happy smiles covered both faces. "I guess it's all right," he said. His brown eyes met Teddy's happy blue ones. "I'd live anywhere you want, you know."

"I know, and I feel the same way. You'll have to make the choice."

"Hey," he said, off on a new subject, "I read in the paper some dog sled races are starting from Bend tomorrow morning at six o'clock. Would you like to go watch them take off?"

Teddy wanted to go, so they got up extra early, finished the chores, ate Gram's buckwheat pancakes, and took off in Brand's pickup. In spite of the early hour, the large crowd provided a festive atmosphere. Vendors sold lots of hot coffee and sweet rolls; the harnessed dogs yapped their eagerness to hit the trail.

"What are they waiting for?" Teddy asked.

"I think they have a certain time to leave." He looked at his watch. "Didn't the paper say six o'clock? That's only five minutes away. Want some coffee?"

Teddy did not have time to answer for two men came up against Brand, turning him from the crowd. "Are you Brandon Sinclair?"

"Yes, I am. What can I do for you?"

"We'd like to ask you some questions, Mr. Sinclair. In fact, I have here a warrant for your arrest on suspicion of bank robbery."

Chapter Nineteen

Brand's face blanched. "Bank robbery? What are you talking about?"

The parka-enclosed man pulled a slip of paper from his pocket and read: "You have the right to remain silent, Mr. Sinclair. If you give up that right, anything you say can and will be used against you in a court of law. You have the right to have a lawyer present during questioning, and if you can't afford one, the court will appoint one for you."

Brand wrenched back from the officer. "Wait a minute. I haven't the foggiest idea what you're talking about, but you have the wrong man."

The officer looked at his warrant again. "Brandon J. Sinclair, 1234 Highway 20?"

Brand nodded, looking very puzzled. "That's my address, but I don't rob banks."

"Are you from Eugene?"

"Yes, but—"

"Come on, Mr. Sinclair, we can talk about it where it's a little warmer. Will you come willingly? Or do I need the cuffs?" He gave Brand a shove, but Brand put on his brakes and reached his right hand toward his pocket. The man knocked Brand's hand away from his pocket and handcuffed him so quickly Teddy almost missed seeing it happen. Then the man did a quick search of Brand but came up empty.

"You thought I was after a gun, didn't you?" Brand asked incredulously.

The man nodded. "The thought crossed my mind."

"Teddy," Brand said calmly, "would you get my keys out of my pocket and bring the pickup down to the station? We'll need it to drive home."

"Come on, Sinclair, we don't have all day. And you won't be going home for a while." Brand gave Teddy a small smile and walked away between the two police officers.

Teddy ran to the pickup and drove through the snowy streets to the police station. "I want to see Brand Sinclair," she said to the first uniform she saw inside the door.

The officer pointed toward the door. "You may as well go on back home, lady. Sinclair won't be receiving visitors today."

"But I have to help him."

He shook his head. "Somehow I don't think you're the right person to be helping him. You go home and come back tomorrow."

Suddenly Teddy simply had to talk to Gram. "May I use a phone?"

He nodded toward a pay phone by the door and Teddy hurried toward it, eager to hear Gram's beautiful gravelly voice.

"Why don't you do as the man says, kitten, and come home?" Gram suggested calmly when she had heard the news. "We can sort it out together."

Teddy drove as fast as she dared on the snowy highway. "What are we going to do, Gram?" she asked when she finally got home.

Gram settled Teddy onto the couch and put a mug of steaming coffee into her hands. Then she stirred her own and sat down in the rocker. "The officer was right, we can't help Brand. We can alert Rolf so he'll take over all the work over there. Otherwise. . . . Hey, I'll bet Lynden turned him in."

A frown creased Teddy's forehead. "Of course he did. I think I'll call him and tell him what I think of him."

"Better not. On the slight chance that he didn't, he's the last person we'd want to tell. I suppose it'll be in today's paper anyway, though."

The telephone rang and Teddy lifted the receiver. Brand's voice greeted her, and he sounded tired. "The Eugene police are coming for me in the morning," he said. "It's just as well. I'm as eager as they are to get to the bottom of this thing. Are you all right, Teddy Bear?"

"I'm all right. Brand, I'm going to Eugene, too."

"No! I want you to stay right where you are. Will you call Rolf and tell him he's in charge for a few days?"

"I already did. I'm going to Eugene Brand. I have to."

"We won't get to see each other. It'll be a wasted trip."

"So it'll be a wasted trip. I've wasted things before."

"If you must go, be sure to stay with my folks. And tell them what's happened. They'll help."

❧

Rolf readily agreed to care for the llamas while Teddy was away, so she left early the next morning. Driving over the treacherous winter roads in the icy mountains gave her little time to think about her wedding that was supposed to be less than a week away.

Could Brand be guilty of this crime? She had finally put it from her mind and now she must keep her faith. *But how could they have arrested him for something he did not do?* She knew Brand did not do it. Had she not asked God to give her peace if everything was all right? And uncertainty if it was not? She had never had one worry since that prayer. If she could not trust the Lord, whom could she trust?

Finally, about noon, she turned into Frank and Donna Sinclair's driveway and pounded on the door. Frank opened the door and, seeing Teddy's grim face, helped her into the house.

"What's happened to Brand?" the older man asked, closely watching Teddy's face.

Teddy sniffed and swallowed hard, then pulled a tissue from her purse and wiped her nose. "He's all right. He hasn't been hurt or anything. Could we sit down, please?" When they all found seats, Teddy continued. "Please don't get excited, but Brand is in jail."

Frank burst out laughing. "What did he do now, rustle somebody's post holes so he could put them together and use them for a well?"

"No, they arrested him on suspicion of bank robbery."

Frank laughed even louder.

"Bank robbery?" Donna repeated. "He wouldn't even shoplift a candy bar."

"If he robbed a bank, he'd give it all to the poor, like Robin Hood," Frank said, starting up his loud laugh again.

"This isn't funny, Frank," Donna said. "Let's go to the police station."

They arrived at the station at almost the same time Brand did. Teddy's heart beat wildly when she saw the tall blond man. He had never looked more beautiful to her, though his ordeal showed on his face. The police let him hug his folks and kiss Teddy. "I love you," he said wearily. "We'll laugh about this in years to come when we tell our grandchildren." He gave her an extra squeeze and released her. "Somehow, it isn't all that funny right now."

"We're with you, son," Frank told him. "Surely they can't keep up a farce like this for long."

"They say there was one witness, the bank teller," Brand explained. "They'll try to get her in this afternoon. When she sees I'm the wrong guy, that'll be the end of it. I took a polygraph in Bend. They wouldn't tell me how it came out but I've heard they're usually accurate. They also told me they've checked my pickup and it's exactly like the one used in the robbery, even the tires. Too bad they didn't get the license number." He looked at his folks. "If we could remember what we were doing the morning of May 2 it would help."

Brand and his parents hashed the date over for a while but none of them could come up with anything on that particular date. "Who's going to remember what he did at a certain time on a certain day seven months ago?" Frank asked.

"Can we be here when the woman comes in?" Teddy asked the officer.

"I'm not sure," the man said. "If you sit quietly over there by the wall they may not think about chasing you out."

Brand's parents and Teddy were allowed to wait with Brand until word came that the woman had arrived. The guard took Brand away, saying he would be back with a group of men. Teddy remained with Frank and Donna on a bench in the quiet corner.

After a half-hour wait, a woman walked in accompanied by a police officer. "You just sit here," he said to her, "and in a few minutes we'll have seven men come in and go to that center table. I'll be with them and make sure to talk to each of them. They know a witness is in the room but there are several other people too, so you watch and listen but don't say anything."

Teddy felt faint when the seven men, all tall, broad-shouldered, and blond, all dressed in dark slacks and light sweaters, came in. They walked around the room, close enough for Brand to give her the slightest wink. Then the police sergeant led them to the big round table in the center of the large room. They all sat down and talked for about fifteen minutes before the officer casually led the men out.

The man in blue returned almost immediately and pulled on his earlobe as he talked quietly to the woman. The little group, waiting so eagerly, could not hear the discussion.

After about half an hour, the woman left and the guards brought Brand back in. They all sat around the same table where the men had been. "The woman couldn't finger you," the man said. "She said she'd have thought any one of the seven did it if she'd seen only one. Your polygraph came out negative and we didn't find anything when we searched your place in Bend other than the pickup.

"We really don't have any reason to hold you longer. It appears to be simply a matter of coincidence, looking too much like the man who did it, and owning a matching rig. But I do wish you could come up with a solid alibi—just to close the case against you with 150 percent certainty."

Teddy looked into Brand's jumbo brown eyes and loved him more than she thought possible. How awful that he had been put through such an ordeal, and even worse that she had had moments of doubt.

Brand's wide smile reached almost to his ears, and his white teeth sparkled in the winter sun. "Let's get out of here." He held out his hand to the police officer. "No hard feelings," he said. "I want you to catch the guy as much as you do, but I sincerely hope I never have to go through something like this again."

Teddy and Brand stayed with his folks that night, so they could all travel back to Bend together for the wedding. After calling Gram, Teddy enjoyed staying up late with the family, talking about the ordeal they had just been through, then about the llama and cattle ranches and how Teddy and Brand planned to handle them both.

The next morning they all sat around relaxing and drinking coffee after a potato, ham, and egg breakfast, Teddy feeling secure in the crook of Brand's arm. "I know some people who'd be glad to stay in your house and help around the ranch for the rent," Frank said.

"Yeah? Who?"

Frank belched out a long jolly laugh. "Why Mother and I, of course. We're not only bored with city life, we're lonely for you."

Brand jumped up and cranked Frank's hand up and down. "Great, Dad. We'll be happy for you to stay as long as you like. The house will be taken care of, we'll all be together, and first thing you know, you'll have that grandchild you've been whining for."

The little caravan pulled into Gram's place at mid-afternoon and everyone stayed for supper. Before the evening meal, Brand managed to find Gram alone and suggested she call on him to ask the blessing for supper.

"You bet you can ask the blessing, son," Gram said. "Not only tonight but all the time. I'm glad to learn my boy's all grown up now."

Brand asked a special blessing on each member of the family gathered there that night—in a thoroughly adult way.

"Want to go for a ride?" he asked Teddy after they did the evening chores.

"Sure. Where are we going?"

"I want to give Lynden a bad time for turning me in. Not that it was his fault."

They parked the pickup and walked into the newspaper office where they found Lynden scribbling on a yellow pad. "I want a retraction put in the paper immediately," Brand ordered in a harsh voice.

Lynden looked up, surprise showing on his face, and scrambled to his feet. "Sure thing. You just tell me what this is about and I'll take care of it right away."

"You know what it's about!"

Lynden shook his head. "Sorry."

"My arrest for suspicion of bank robbery?"

Lynden's eyes opened wide. "You were arrested?"

"You bet, and spent two days and one night in the slammer."

Lynden tried to keep his mouth straight, but ended up unable to suppress a relieved smile. "I didn't report you, Sinclair, but I'm glad someone did. That's a serious crime."

"Who did report me then?"

Lynden shrugged. "I guess that's your problem." He picked up his black pen and started writing again.

Brand snatched Teddy's hand. "Let's go to the police station."

"I'd like to see the record of my arrest," he said, once they were inside the brick building. "I want to know who turned me in."

"Mr. Sinclair," the police officer began, "it was just rotten luck. Your description exactly fit the one given by the only witness and you also could easily be the guy in the bank picture." He shoved the pad to Brand and turned it around so he could see it.

Brand read a moment then turned to Teddy, pointing, "There it is, in black and white. *Fraedrick Marland*." He studied it another moment then raised his eyes to the man at the desk. "Can anyone turn anyone in for any old thing and get them into this much trouble?"

The man read a little farther. "Not just from a description, but this says the woman heard your girlfriend and her boyfriend talking about the crime, as if you had definitely done it." He looked up with a question in his eyes. "Your girlfriend has another boyfriend?"

Teddy almost stopped breathing.

Brand shook his head. "I'll be getting to the bottom of this." He turned Teddy toward the door and steered her outside into the snowy world.

"What was that all about?" he asked when they sat in the truck with the motor running and the heater going full blast. "I take it Greeley is the one Fritzi called your boyfriend. Did she make this up out of thin air or did she hear you two say something?" Then his eyes opened wide. "Teddy, did you know anything about this bank robbery?"

Teddy scrunched down in the seat and pulled her coat closer around her throat. "That's why I've been asking you personal questions," she mumbled. "Lynden brought me some items from the newspaper a few times and tried to tell me you did it. Then, when you refused to talk about it, I never felt quite sure."

Brand shoved it into reverse and backed out, then slammed on the brakes, killing the engine and sliding twenty feet across the icy snow. "I might be able to understand how you could believe something like that before you knew me, but how could you have the faintest doubt later?" He started the truck again and headed gingerly toward home.

"I believed in you after I knew you," she said. "The night Fritzi was talking about, I told Lynden to get lost. She hid around the corner to listen and turned the story all around." She stopped and watched him, but he seemed to be concentrating on negotiating the icy road. She had to say one more thing. "But you never would tell me where you got the money for your ranch." She spoke in a whisper, then drew several small breaths. "Not even yet."

He glanced down at her and stopped the truck in the middle of the snowy road to take her into his arms. "You know what? The cops knew I'd paid cash for my ranch and they wanted to know where I got the money too. They thought that was just too much coincidence. But I was able to prove I got the money legally. I should have told you long ago, love. The only excuse I have is that my folks believe strongly that it's in poor taste, even tacky, to reveal your financial prowess. I should have told you when we grew closer." His eyes grew misty. "But you should have told me about Fritzi too, you know."

He started the truck and explained to her as the pickup slowly found its way home. "My folks got nearly two million dollars for their ranch in Alvadore. They gave me about two-thirds of it. Said the ranch was more mine than theirs, as I'd worked so hard for so long." He drove a while then took her mittened hand. "It was sort of like Gram giving you her ranch, understand?"

She understood. Then she remembered the pickup. "How come you never drove the pickup anywhere? You drove it to my place and around on yours, but that's about it. A person could think you were hiding it."

He looked at her, a surprised look on his face, then burst into laughter. "Tell me, Teddy, would you drive that thing anywhere important? That rig's what I call a real bummer."

At last she understood it all. They hurried home to tell their folks what they had learned.

"Why should you be surprised?" Gram asked. "Fritzi merely paid you for rejecting her advances."

"Guess what else we remembered while you were gone?" Frank said when a lull in the conversation allowed. "You didn't even own that pickup at the time of the bank robbery. It came as part of the equipment from the ranch. Now, if we could just remember what you were doing on the morning on May 2."

Brand nodded. "You're right. I'd never have bought a pile of junk like that. I should have remembered and told the police. Anyway, let's forget the whole thing and get on with our lives."

"You know what this all reminds me of," Teddy said, snuggling close to Brand. "All the time I kept telling myself I believed in Brand, I still had doubts. We do the same thing with God, know that? Whenever things don't go exactly as we think they should, we begin to doubt. I'm going to use this as a reminder to keep my faith in God no matter what."

"Right," Brand said. "I made lots of mistakes that caused you to doubt me but He never makes any. I hereby pledge to keep my faith too."

ॐ

Three days later Teddy stood trembling in a small dressing room at the church. She pulled the lacy white creation over her head and watched breathlessly as it fell around her. Leaning over, she kissed the little gray head. "Thank you, Gram. It's the most beautiful wedding dress I've ever seen. And you're the most beautiful person in the world. I love you so much."

Gram, her mouth full of pins, kept adjusting the train. "Hold still, kitten. There, that looks right. I'm glad you like my work, Teddy, because I'm planning to make christening gowns for all of your babies."

Then Teddy found herself on Frank's arm, walking down the aisle. Brand stood at the center front of the church, dressed in a white tuxedo, white frilly shirt, white cummerbund, and white bow tie. His sunstreaked hair lay combed back but rebelling here and there to fall over his ears. His brown eyes filled with love when he saw Teddy. He stepped forward on his long, long legs to accept her from his father. Teddy's heart felt full to bursting as he took her arm in his and turned to ascend the rostrum—to be together forever.

As they climbed the three steps, Teddy's eyes met those of her matron of honor—Gram. The old woman smiled happily and gave Teddy the thumbs up sign with both hands.

Teddy's eyes turned to Brand, who tightened his hold on her arm, gave her an almost imperceptible wink, then smiled broadly. Together, they faced the minister.